WHEN CHEERS ARE NOT ENOUGH

Slavko Ray

SLAVKO RAY

FriesenPress

One Printers Way
Altona, MB R0G 0B0
Canada

www.friesenpress.com

Copyright © 2024 by Slavko Ray
First Edition — 2024

All rights reserved.

No part of this publication may be reproduced in any form, or by any means, electronic or mechanical, including photocopying, recording, or any information browsing, storage, or retrieval system, without permission in writing from FriesenPress.

ISBN
978-1-03-918173-1 (Hardcover)
978-1-03-918172-4 (Paperback)
978-1-03-918174-8 (eBook)

1. FICTION, OCCULT & SUPERNATURAL

Distributed to the trade by The Ingram Book Company

It is easy to celebrate a winner;
The true fan finds a reason to cheer even in the darkest of times.
—Anonymous

Music is the only form of magic in this world, except maybe for love.
—J. J. Knight

This town will have its Cup parade ... I guarantee it.
—Xander Galahad

CONTENTS

Preface	THE WISDOM OF SOLOMON	ix
Prologue	FOUR SPIRITS AND A SACRAMENT	xviii
Chapter One	ON THE BANKS OF THE MISTY RIVER	1
Chapter Two	A SIMPLE PLAN	11
Chapter Three	PERREAULT	22
Chapter Four	FIREWORKS	29
Chapter Five	GO GREEN!	39
Chapter Six	BAKERS' COVEN	49
Chapter Seven	WHO GETS THE C?	58
Chapter Eight	FIVE YEARS	73
Chapter Nine	A THANKSGIVING PROPOSITION	83
Chapter Ten	CUBBY	88
Chapter Eleven	H O X I X O H	105
Chapter Twelve	SKULL AND PUFFBALLS	117
Chapter Thirteen	MAKE US HAPPY	135

Chapter Fourteen	SAMHAIN	146
Chapter Fifteen	IT'S IN THE CARDS	157
Chapter Sixteen	BAD NEWS COMES IN THREES	169
Chapter Seventeen	MY KINGDOM FOR A HORSE	181
Chapter Eighteen	ANOTHER TIME	186
Chapter Nineteen	LE ROI EST MORT	195
Chapter Twenty	THE SEASON OF GIVING	207
Chapter Twenty-One	OPENING STATEMENTS	218
Chapter Twenty-Two	EMPTY GREETINGS	227
Chapter Twenty-Three	ON THE NICE LIST	238
Chapter Twenty-Four	MATCHMAKING	245
Chapter Twenty-Five	BUTTERFLIES, BATS, AND PARTY HATS	251
Chapter Twenty-Six	SIREN'S SONG	257
Chapter Twenty-Seven	HOUSTON, WE HAVE A PROBLEM	261
Chapter Twenty-Eight	MR. ONE-EIGHTY	265
Chapter Twenty-Nine	HALLELUJAH	276
Chapter Thirty	DIVINE INTERVENTION	285
Chapter Thirty-One	A MOST UNUSUAL DRAFT	293
Chapter Thirty-Two	88 LINES ABOUT 22 PINES	301

Chapter Thirty-Three	REVELATIONS	308
Chapter Thirty-Four	PRAYERS	318
Chapter Thirty-Five	THE PILGRIMAGE	326
Chapter Thirty-Six	A SIX-PACK OF LEGENDS	338
Chapter Thirty-Seven	A WALK IN THE SNOW	347
Chapter Thirty-Eight	MARY	355
Chapter Thirty-Nine	THE HORROR	359
Chapter Forty	PRAY THAT THEY HEAR	371
Chapter Forty-One	PINES WHISPERERS	383
Chapter Forty-Two	BREAKING THE LENTEN FAST	390
Chapter Forty-Three	THE BOY WITH HIS NAME ON THE CUP	394
Chapter Forty-Four	MAN PLANS; GOD LAUGHS	411
Chapter Forty-Five	THE END OF THE WORLD AS WE KNOW IT	424
Chapter Forty-Six	THE ZOOM MEETING	433
Chapter Forty-Seven	MASKS AND METAPHORS	443
Chapter Forty-Eight	A NATION OF CHARLIE BROWNS	451
Chapter Forty-Nine	WONDER ROAD	459
Acknowledgements		471
About the Author		473

PREFACE
THE WISDOM OF SOLOMON

Go, Pines, go . . . Go, Pines, go . . .

It is one of the most storied and iconic cheers in sport. As a rallying cry it is simple and to the point. The refrain of three words echoing through the ages; three syllables, three beats—one-two-three, tap-tap-tap, dot-dot-dot—a pure and powerful music to the ears, like the four notes that open Beethoven's Fifth. In fact, Luddy's great opus would serve quite nicely as musical accompaniment to a crowd chanting, "Go, Pines, go!" Or perhaps Aaron Copland's "Fanfare for the Common Man," or better yet, the dramatic opening to that Strauss piece used in the film *2001: A Space Odyssey*. The very thought of it produces spinal shivers and goosebumped flesh.

I should know, having voiced the words myself on more than a few occasions—because, you see, I am a hockey fan. The place I call home happens to be the highly-charged hotbed of hockey that is the Greater Toronto Area, home to the most fabled and seminal of professional hockey franchises, known throughout the sporting world—and beyond—as the Toronto Mighty Pines. It stands to reason that I support the men in green and white, and therefore by association belong to a brotherhood of fans called Coney Nation: a people whose very rhythms of life pulse in harmony with the vicissitudes of the team to whom we have pledged allegiance.

Presently, however, I am alone, engaged in chronicling an extraordinary series of events that occurred this past year to some friends of mine who also happen to be fans of the Mighty Pines. The task of putting my story to paper is something I have chosen to do the old-fashioned way, in longhand, with a candle at my elbow, like a postulant illuminating the gospels at his workstation in an abbey scriptorium. All that's missing is some vellum, a quill pen, and a scratchy woollen robe on my back.

Then, as if on cue, the candle flame flickers in a characteristic manner and I know they are here; the spirits have arrived. Although not visible, their presence is felt nonetheless, and while spectral visitations might sound ominous to the uninitiated, I have grown accustomed to them. Rest assured, the motivations of these invisible entities are not malevolent. On the contrary, I get the sense they are here on hockey business—*Mighty*

When Cheers Are Not Enough

Pines hockey business. I imagine they are players from years gone by who simply want to fraternize, like locals in the town pub, enjoying each other's company. And just as children are lured by the calliope call that heralds the arrival of an ice cream truck, the same can be said of hockey oldtimers—living *or* deceased, apparently—who eagerly gather whenever opportunities to share old "war" stories present themselves. (It has me wondering if I can draw some inspiration from these spirit callers, the same way Saint Matthew had the benefit of a shoulder angel to assist him in his task of storytelling?)

A noise causes me to look up from the page, and I realize the sound is coming from outside. A neighbour has fired up a gas-powered device, no doubt prepping the property for the coming winter. I should mention that it is late October 2020, midway between the autumnal equinox and the winter solstice. Mother Nature is in a transitional phase, manifested by dramatic changes in her colour palette: the brilliant, fiery hues gradually being doused by an increasingly persistent November grey. And while some may regard this part of the year as dreary, I have learned to look beyond it toward my season of preference: winter. A time of darkness and cold, to be sure, but also one of romance, mystery, and magic. The stuff of which stories are made. It wouldn't be a stretch to say that the central protagonist of the story being set down here is winter itself and, by extension, the great game of hockey.

These ruminations about winter and hockey have triggered a nostalgia for those precious days of my own childhood, when my greatest concern was wondering how soon the pond would freeze over so I could lace 'em up and work on my game, all alone, with just a stick and a puck for company. Not that I was unique as a kid in this respect. Bring up the topic of winter and a child's thoughts invariably turn to snowballs and snowmen, tobogganing down hills, skating on backyard rinks—and hockey. I challenge anyone to come up with two words that can produce a more robust response in a strapping Canadian kid than "winter" and "hockey."

It is only fitting, then, that Canada, a cold-weather country, lays claim to ice hockey, a cold-weather game, as its signature sport, its national pastime. There is a beautiful, elemental harmony in how the climate of this land melds perfectly with its sporting heritage. Anything else would be incongruous. (It would be hard to imagine a sport like, say, beach volleyball, inflaming the passions of this country's citizens from coast to coast to coast.)

Granted, Canada is not exclusive in this regard. Other nations in the northern hemisphere could make similar claims, but this story is not about them. No, the story that follows is set in the GTA and centres firmly on the Toronto Mighty Pines. Unfortunately, the venerable organization's days of wine and roses and dynasties have given way to a championship drought that has achieved legendary status. In fact, it could be said there was a growing concern with respect to the game of hockey and its place in the lives of the local citizenry, young and old alike. There was mounting evidence that the appeal—or better yet, the relevance—of hockey, and of winter for that matter, was being replaced by summer and cottages and barbecues. And for this the Toronto Mighty Pines had to share in the blame.

Perhaps now is a good time, dear reader, to pull up a chair and settle in with the hockey spirits as I endeavour to explain—

* * * * *

It was the summer of 2019, just a little over a year ago, and we were riding high following the Raptors' sensational run through the post-season on their way to being crowned NBA champions, with the sweet and satisfying taste of victory still lingering on our tongues. There was also a buoyancy that came with knowing a new decade was rapidly approaching. Indeed, Father Time was wielding the blade of his scythe on the remaining days of the year as deftly as big bad "Lumber" Jack McGee had brandished his stick on opponents' ankles back in the day. The last time we lived through a decade of the twenties, it was described as "roaring." The coming one was sure to be just as awesome, especially since we'd be launching it with nothing less than the "Year of Perfect Vision." (It looked even better in print! Its Roman numeral designation, MMXX, was cleaner than what we'd had to deal with in the past decade with all those additional I's and V's complicating things.)

Despite this promise, lurking just offstage and out of the spotlight of our championship bliss was a niggling sense of something not quite right, an odd phenomenon, felt more keenly by residents in and around the city of Toronto. Plainly put, something was peculiar about our summers.

Someone outside the scientific community recently pointed out how our summers of late seem longer than most typical seasonal forecasts might predict. It is a phenomenon, however, that goes beyond the meteorological effects of climate change. Residents of Southern Ontario don't need the Weather Channel to tell them that the season officially begins on the May long weekend (notwithstanding the annual solstice celebrations held around June 21 in recognition of the sun's position in the celestial sky). It then takes a final bow twelve weeks later when the annual Canadian National Exhibition comes to a close on Labour Day. Lately, however, a troubling trend has developed wherein the summer season is more likely to begin by the third week of April, such that Earth Day has replaced Victoria Day on the calendar as the landmark of its arrival.

The notion that millions of Canadians might take issue with the addition of another month to the front end of the summer seems counterintuitive, especially in a country where the snow flies six months of the year, but such is the case for fans of the Toronto

Mighty Pines, for whom truncated winters have become a source of some consternation. As a case in point, the summer of 2019 for the team and its loyal supporters began on April 23—following their first-round playoff elimination. In fact, it has been many years since Torontonians could cross Star Wars Day or Cinco de Mayo off their calendars before discussing the Pines' final loss of the season around the water cooler. Watching their heroes go on holiday in April year after year is frustrating for Pines fans, and doubly so when pre-season predictions increasingly have the team high on the list of Cup contenders. But to hockey enthusiasts with discriminating ears, the value of such prognostications ring hollow because, as a wise man once said, "Forecasting is the art of saying what will happen, and then explaining why it didn't."

Truth is, the Toronto Mighty Pines hockey franchise and all its faithful followers—the aforementioned Coney Nation—have been wandering the wilderness for decades, seeking explanations for why, yet again, a championship didn't happen.

The Old Testament Israelites, the great Hebrew nation, spent forty years roaming the desert searching for the Promised Land, and *did* ultimately arrive at their destination. The great Coney Nation, in comparison, has been lost in a wasteland of hockey mediocrity for more than half a century. A promise of Clarence Cup glory, handed down through the years from our heroes who had last held it high—legends like Cal Ubank, Frank "Sugar" Watson, and Jackson Schmeltz—has yet to be fulfilled. Generations of Mighty Pines who had succeeded them as prophets draped in green and white were unable to lead their people out of the bondage that losing creates. Though their eyes had ever been glued to the prize, ultimately, it had proved beyond their grasp.

This prize, this Clarence Cup, is for every hockey player and fan the preeminent reward, representing nothing less than the land of milk and honey. (Such present-day esteem contrasts with the inauspicious circumstances of its introduction in 1902, when it had been offered as a temporary replacement for the Dominion Cup, the original championship trophy donated nine years earlier by Lord Duncan of Chestershire before its tragic loss in the waters of the Pacific after tumbling overboard off the rail of the steamer ship carrying the Whitehorse Renegades back to the Yukon following their challenge series victory over Seattle.)

These days, the Clarence Cup is widely celebrated. Its yearly coming out party is held around mid-June, near the time when the sun hovers over the Tropic of Cancer, approaching the sabbat of Litha, a festival strongly associated with flame and heat—thereby producing a true commingling of fire and ice. Annually presented to one team in the Premier Hockey League that proves itself worthy of claiming it as their own, the Cup takes centre stage in the subsequent victory celebration. When the decisive game of the final series has ended, it is reverently carried out to centre ice on a red carpet by its keeper, whose attire includes jacket, tie, and white gloves. It is then presented by the league commissioner to the winning team's captain, who, by custom, is given the honour of being the first to lift it high overhead and take it for a short skate. In this fashion it is passed from player to player, the ritual repeated by every member of the team—including coaches, ownership, management, and support staff. It is fondly embraced, ceremonially kissed, and showered with champagne. (Were Titian alive today, it's a good bet the Venetian master would place the Cup prominently in his depiction of a mythic bacchanal.) In ordinary times, it can be viewed standing regal and proud, like a silver monolith, perched in its throne room in the Hockey Hall of Fame.

Alas, for Mighty Pines fans, the days of Cup glory in Toronto are so far in the past that they may soon fall under the category of ancient history. This dearth of hockey success cannot be understood in a vacuum. The reasons for failure are myriad and go back decades. Poor coaching, poor trades, poor draft choices; missed opportunities by management, and missed calls by officials; ownership motivated more by money than winning; the loss of key players to an upstart rival league; team mutinies, fan mutinies, and tanking to win the draft lottery; poor goaltending, poorly timed injuries, poor choice of captain to no choice of captain, repeated playoff suspensions to a key player—and, oh yes, if you believe in conspiracy theories, a curse so potent its influence can still be felt some sixty years after it was first placed.

On and on, circumstance after circumstance, season after season, year after year. It all sounds so biblical. In fact, the author of the Book of Ecclesiastes would no doubt feel right at home documenting how the seasons came and went for the Mighty Pines as the league carried on and continued to expand. Franchises moved, collapsed, and returned. Dynasties rose and fell, competitive parity among teams was achieved, seasons were interrupted by player strike action and owner-initiated lockouts, key rule changes produced fundamental changes to the way the game itself was played, and lest we forget, a hard salary cap was instituted. Oh, the salary cap. Like the world bearing down upon the shoulders of Atlas, the cap firmly limits teams from spending their way to the Clarence Cup, and, like Atlas, the Toronto Mighty Pines are buckling under its weight.

Thus, the $81.5 million question is this: when will the Pines ever again win the honour of holding high and drinking from the sacred chalice of hockey?

It boggles the mind: the last time anyone saw the Pines skate in a Clarence Cup final was fifty-eight years ago. The date deserves to be recognized, perhaps with a local holiday. It was Tuesday, May 2, when the league commissioner stood at centre ice in the old Mighty Pines Coliseum and uttered the following words: *"Ladies and gentlemen, it is now my great pleasure and responsibility to present the Clarence Cup to the Mighty Pines hockey club for the eleventh time. Now I ask the captain of the Toronto club to come forward and accept the trophy."*

Since that day in 1962 when George Daly stepped up to embrace the three-foot, thirty-five-pound prize, no less than twenty-five different captains from nineteen different teams across North America have accepted the Clarence Cup on behalf of the cities they represented. Alas, none of those proud cities was named Toronto. Adding to the shame for Coney Nation is that in all those years, its team has not even appeared in the final. Would it be asking too much for present-day Torontonians to experience the joy of cheering their team on during games in the month of May? Rare indeed have been the years when the team played meaningful games past Tax Deadline Day. And beyond that? Well, truth is, in all their history, the Toronto Mighty Pines have never played a game in June.

What is the answer, then? How can an organization like Toronto's fend off its challengers and once again ascend to the throne of hockey supremacy? And if the opinion that in the world of professional hockey Toronto is the most difficult place to play and operate is true, how can a team possibly excel and win in such an environment? Despite the efforts of hockey's brightest minds, the answers to those questions remain elusive. For the masses of grumbling and frustrated Pines fans, there is nothing left but to gaze upward to the heavens in order to seek favour in the form of some divine right to win and to ask "When, in the cosmological scheme of things, will it be our turn for victory?" They long for the day when the god of hockey goes to her almighty wardrobe and chooses a Pines jersey off the rack of thirty-one team colours, pulls the green and white overhead, and places an all-powerful thumb firmly on the opponent's end of the rink, effectively tilting the ice in Toronto's favour.

Unfortunately, passively hoping and praying for a benevolent hockey god to smile down upon you is no way to win in today's PHL. This was certainly the case for the Mighty Pines' troika of President Xander Galahad, General Manager Kyle Bulac, and Head Coach Kayden Koch. These men would be the first to admit that a winning hockey team is built not on the whims of the gods, but rather through shrewd moves based on wisdom borne of experience.

Ah, yes, the benefit of wisdom. As a gift from God, its value was revealed in the biblical Book of Kings when King Solomon was asked to pass judgment in the case of two mothers both laying claim to the same infant child. (You may remember how his solution was to slice the baby in two so that each woman could share in one half, only to have the real mother relent and give up her claim to it. Upon seeing this, the king, in his wisdom, awarded the unharmed boy to that woman, recognizing that only a true mother would be willing to give up her child to preserve its life.)

King Solomon certainly deserves credit for making his winning call under pressure, but let's be honest: the task of decision-making was easier back then. After all, where was the media circus in ancient Jerusalem? Just imagine if Solomon were the Pines' GM today and that his judgment regarding the two mothers was handed down within the context of a hockey season. He would be obligated to face a media scrum, with cameras running and microphones thrust forward, confronted by the game's cognoscenti with questions like, "What was your plan B if the women called your bluff on cutting the child in half, and the situation went into overtime?" followed by, "What about the false mother? Did you let her off the hook, or will team management dole out a fine or suspension?" and then perhaps, "Why didn't you at least secure future rights to the kid in the event he displayed some promise as a top-tier defenceman?"

In all seriousness, for Toronto fans who would free the genie from the bottle, two wishes might suffice to change their team's fortunes: 1) grant the Pines the divine right to win, and 2) bestow unerring wisdom upon team management. Would that be too tall an order? Well, from this perspective, one might have more success asking for peace on earth. Let's face it: the way forward for the Pines is so fraught with complexities that negotiating them might require a bit of help from the hockey gods. Would it be considered beyond the pale if Pines management admitted to making key personnel decisions based on spiritual guidance or divine intervention? Of course, such a strategy could amount to career suicide for some individuals—but then, that would depend, as always, on wins and losses.

Admittedly, this sounds like so much doom and gloom, yet hope still springs eternal, and despite nearly six decades of darkness there is presently talk of a rebirth; the dawning of a renaissance with the arrival of the next Michelangelo on skates, a genius who will guide the team back into the light of victory. Now the promise rests in the hands of a new generation of players, led by the likes of Mason Andrews, Ricky Randall, Ben Bellamy, and Gianni Valentino.

And so, as the team embarks on another season, with its attendant changes of fortune and the pressures of trying to win while at the centre of the hockey universe, I encourage the citizens of Coney Nation to keep the faith, and to show resilience and optimism when all around is cynicism and doubt. May we all continue to love the game and find joy in the journey. May we refrain from resentment of others who succeed, and may we cheer with open hearts, because when victory does come—*and it will*—it will be all the sweeter.

Finally (and with apologies to King Solomon and his Book of Ecclesiastes) I offer these words to consider:

> *Mighty Pines teams come and go, but it makes no difference. The puck is passed then shot and passed around some more to be shot again. The team travels south and north, east and west, home and away, through eighty-two games. Players*

When Cheers Are Not Enough

don the green and white, but the goal is never met, and the calendar flips to a new season and still the same result. Fans are unutterably weary and tired. No matter how much they watch, they are never satisfied. No matter how much they win in the regular season, they are never content. So, I saw that there is nothing better for Coney Nation than that their team should win the Cup, for that is what they are here for, and no one can ensure they will win in the future, so let them enjoy it now.

For real winning happens in the post-season, and the time for it is long past due:
    A time to win and a time to lose,
    A time to cheer and a time to boo,
    A time to score and a time to defend,
    A time to tank and a time to contend,
    A time to get hot and a time to stumble,
    A time to chirp and a time to be humble,
    A time to hit and a time to rise from the deck,
    A time to dump 'n' chase and a time to back check,
    A time to be undressed and a time to stack the pads,
    A time to draw a penalty and a time to take one for the lads,
    A time to fight and a time to embrace,
    A time on the bench and a time on the ice,
    A time for blocked shots and a time for one-timers,
    A time to play golf and a time to win in the Final.

While getting to the Final and winning it is the dream of all hockey lovers, the desire to see that dream fulfilled is particularly profound in Toronto. The following pages tell a tale of a small collective of kindred spirits within a great "Nation" of devotees and dreamers, and how they grew tired of standing by, helpless, watching their team flounder. It is a story of five souls who together set out to change the fortunes of a Canadian institution. In the process they endured misery, sadness, and heartache, but they also experienced joy, exhilaration, and love. In the end, they attained knowledge and, like King Solomon, gained an understanding that led to wisdom. And that is a treasure greater than any championship laurel, be it a cup, crown, or trophy. (How much greater is difficult to say, because we lack a point of comparison.)

There is no evidence that Israel's wise king ever thought to establish a championship trophy for the sporting heroes of his day; to bestow upon his people a prize called, say, the Solomon Cup. (More's the pity, as this world is sorely lacking in fabled artifacts.) Even so, while the Ark of the Covenant has been lost to humankind and the Holy Grail is but a myth, the Clarence Cup exists today as a real treasure among us and has served

THE WISDOM OF SOLOMON

to slake the thirst of ice hockey champions in North America since 1902. And though drinking from it may not endow one with eternal life, it does at least entitle one to don a mantle of hockey glory, which is something that can be worn for a lifetime—and even beyond, as the spirits in this room can attest, and as my story will reveal.

—B.B.

PROLOGUE
FOUR SPIRITS AND A SACRAMENT

There have been moments in history when the act of looking backwards, in and of itself, has been put into question. Take the case of Lot and his wife, escapees from Sodom and Gomorrah, both of whom discovered the hard way what happens when you stop to check out the scene in the rearview mirror. And then there was baseball's Satchel Paige, the ageless wonder of the Negro Leagues, who made famous his own opinion on the topic of looking back and why it was generally a bad idea. Despite these lessons, our story will periodically require us to gaze into the past, all the while safe in the knowledge that we are neither turning away from God's salvation nor glancing over a shoulder to check on our closest pursuers (real or imagined). So cue the wavy flashback effects as we briefly revisit some key events during the early years of the Toronto Mighty Pines hockey club.

The reason the franchise exists at all today is due to the efforts of one Nathaniel Sinclair, heir to the Sinclair family fortune—a legacy built on the success of his father's construction company, Northern Pines Industries. When the young Sinclair returned home from military service in the Great War, having attained the rank of Lieutenant-Colonel on the strength of his courage and leadership in the face of the enemy, he was unexpectedly thrust into the role of company CEO; the old man having succumbed to heart disease soon after Armistice Day.

As a war hero in charge of a thriving construction business in the country's second largest city, Nathaniel came to be fondly known as "Colonel" Sinclair. He proved to be a shrewd businessman who was not averse to taking calculated risks, a penchant that came in handy when the opportunity to own a franchise in the Premier Hockey League presented itself in 1932. Two years later, with the financial backing of a trusted circle of investors, he erected a shiny new palace to house his hockey team. Mighty Pines Coliseum was state-of-the-art and could seat nearly 15,000 patrons (provided they came attired in their Sunday best and agreed to abide by a strict code of fan conduct). The PHL's newest owner brashly promoted the potential of the Pines, vowing to deliver a championship before the end of the decade. He didn't disappoint. The team won its first Clarence Cup within four years, then won another for good measure, making it two Cups in a row to close out the 1930s.

On the ice, the men who played prominent roles in shaping that first dynasty would come to be legends in the eyes of today's fans; men like Beezer Sharpe, Jersey Joe Zedelko, and Cal Ubank. It may interest readers to learn that, despite having long since departed this world, these same men, along with a handful of others, still manage to support the team today—not just in spirit, but *as* spirits.

* * * * *

A Sunday in May, twelve years ago.

He felt thin—and vulnerable—hence the air of discomfit about him. Feeling thin was something he could handle, but vulnerability was a situation he preferred to avoid altogether. Especially when it came to playing hockey. One learned those lessons quickly, and sometimes brutally. Like skating across the blue line with one's head down or admiring a pass to a teammate in the neutral zone. He recalled the horrific incident in game one of the '42 finals, when linemate Sid Graham had been flattened at centre ice and rendered unconscious by Detroit's Marcel "Cinder" Blacque, a bruising defenseman who had certainly lived up to his moniker on that occasion.

Presently however, some instinct told him this sensation was no cause for alarm—that it was only short-term, and his apprehension was unfounded. All the same, the sense of peril was unsettling, as if the substance that had to sustain and support him was weak and tenuous. It felt like coming back too soon from an injury—a broken ankle, say—the offending bone not yet fully knitted and apt to refracture under the slightest stress.

There had been times when he had played hockey, years ago, that feeling this way—thin and wispy—was associated with positive attributes like speed, quickness, and stamina. Back then, a feeling of thinness had equated to a feeling of strength, his movements effortless and precise as he had negotiated that span of hard, frictionless whiteness broken by lines of red and blue.

He remembered skating at speed, the blur of objects in his periphery, the rush of cool air on his face. And the sound, oh, the sound, of his blades' bevelled metal edges carving the ice with the deftness of a woodworker honing his tools by passing steel over a whetstone. The sound had mattered; it had truly meant something. The fans in attendance had seemed to understand this because it was in them, watching from the stands, that the sound produced chills and palpitations—and awe. They would emit their own collective vocalization in response, built out of anticipation. It would crescendo into a jungle roar of amazement, echoing in the end with whispers of disbelief, an incomprehension that sometimes manifested itself as mirth, laughter, or simply joy. All these experiences crystallized before him as he hovered there in midair, gradually gaining strength, the memories almost nourishing him.

Then came another image from the past: an early recollection of being thin, frail, and uncertain. He had been a child, standing in his room in the middle of a pile of newly acquired hockey gear, clad only in his long underwear. The gear had been handed down from a cousin or a neighbour. He recalled the anticipation of donning real equipment for the first time. He recalled how it had turned to dismay with the discovery that his twelve-year-old thighs were too spindly to fill out the socks—resulting in the thick, knitted fabric pooling around the tops of his knee pads. The same thing had happened when he had pulled on the oversized hockey pants. With no bum to speak of, he'd been basically swimming in them. The boy had been undersized for his age and wouldn't be "fully formed" for another six seasons, when a late growth spurt had seen him metamorphose into a specimen of young manhood.

As the images from these memories came into focus, a nostalgic warmth overtook him. He considered the idea of being "not yet fully formed" and recognized his own present condition as fitting that description. He really needed to focus on the here and now, since materializing out of thin air required his full attention. This particular "filling out" process just needed an honest willingness—as straightforward as responding to his mother when, as a kid, he had been skating on the stretch of ice in the alley by his house, and she had called him in for dinner.

There was Ma, in overcoat and galoshes, standing ankle deep in the snow at the edge of the ice surface.

The boy had, instead, invited her to join him. *"Ma, come on over and stand between the pipes for a spell. I'll show you a new move that will deke you out of your stockings!"*

"I'm perfectly content to stay right here and keep my stockings on my legs, thank you very much," she'd said, but with a smile. *"I'm heading back to the house now, and you better be close behind. You've got to change out of those clothes—they're soaked through—and wash up before dinner. The stew is hot, and the rolls are going in the oven."*

"OK, Ma. I'm right behind you."

He'd be soaked through with sweat (Ma was right), extremities freezing, physically and mentally fatigued, but still fully engrossed in the reverie of the activity. Oh, what a magnificent feeling. What a thing of beauty. What a game it was that could take a young man to such heights of athletic sensation. Icarus be damned! Fashion him wings, and he would fly across the sea to one of those frozen Danish canals. There he could drive his legs and pump his arms and reach amazing speeds, never having to slow down to change direction. There he could skate forever.

But that had been a different time, a different era, a different life.

FOUR SPIRITS AND A SACRAMENT

Here, today, he was but a wisp of a man; actually, more the wisp than the man. Because, you see, he was a ghost. A spirit from a realm just beyond our own physical world. And he was entirely self-aware, fully cognizant of the fact he was a ghost (unlike, say, the Bruce Willis character in *The Sixth Sense*). The fact that he had materialized here, in answer to a summons, was normal. He had arrived from the spirit world for what was evidently a special occasion. It had to be, as it was only for such events that transformations into the physical world occurred.

In life this ghost had been an important man, some would even say a heroic man, who had spent the better part of his days—his youth, the years of his athletic peak, and finally, the early part of middle age—focused on playing the game of hockey. It could be argued that his talent was unparalleled. The evidence of his elevated standing was in his uniform. At the prime of his earthly existence, when he had plied his trade and fought in the trenches known as PHL arenas, his uniform had consisted of a green-and-white woollen jersey, the front of which was emblazoned with a stylized pine cone, representing his team and his town, while the back of the shirt displayed a large number ten. One other detail, probably the most significant, had been seen on this man's jersey alone, just above his heart, and that was a simple, crisp capital letter C. Like the stars on the sleeve of an army general, the C denoted this man's status among his peers. It could be said that he wore the uniform—that logo, that number, and that letter—as well as anyone else before or since.

Yes, he had been the captain of the Toronto Mighty Pines hockey team. In fact, he had been the captain of what many considered the greatest Toronto Mighty Pines team ever assembled. The 1948–1949 collection of players had gone on to claim the Clarence Cup that year and needed only nine playoff games to do it. It had been their second in a row, and sixth overall for the team whose jerseys were emblazoned with the cone of the magnificent eastern white pine.

"*This Toronto team is the best of them all,*" Cyril Quinn—the team's top goal scorer—had said.

"*The 1949 team compares with any club in history,*" had been the opinion of Coach Emmett Pepper.

"*This is the greatest team I ever had,*" owner Nathaniel Sinclair had declared.

On April 14, 1949, Toronto had just swept Boston in four straight games to be crowned PHL champions. Calvert Merlin Ubank had been captain of that legendary hockey team. For the third time in his ten years with the Mighty Pines, Cal Ubank (or Captain Cal, as he was fondly known) had been given the honour of being the first to embrace the Clarence Cup when it was presented after the game. That time, however, it had been in a different way, because this man's embrace of the Cup had been carried out with the knowledge that it would be his last. When the final horn had sounded to end that Cup-clinching game, it had also brought down the curtain on his professional hockey career. His face beaming on the heels of a decisive win over Boston, Ubank had held the glittering prize for all to see, as custom and courtesy dictated, and then passed it on—along with the team captaincy—to Beasley Sharpe, his second-in-command. And then he'd walked away from hockey for good.

In his present spirit form, Cal Ubank answered countless calls. Calls generated by family and friends, calls dispatched by members of government, and calls originating from leaders in communities who sought to christen the next public entity in his name—be it a park, a street, a school, or a community centre. And then there were the honours that reflected his personal history and accomplishments as a father, a public servant, and a hockey legend (the bulk of the hockey honours being initiated by the Toronto Mighty Pines' management). Yes, it was a fact of the afterlife that the spirit of Cal Ubank was regularly summoned.

On this occasion, he was being drawn to attend what appeared to be an intimate family gathering with just over a dozen members present. All were strangers to him, so the person among them who was responsible for the bidding, and its purpose, was not immediately clear. The family members were congregating in a church, complete with an altar, a large crucifix suspended on the facing wall, and a tabernacle off to the side. Central to the proceedings was a young couple and their infant child. They were stationed near a marble basin. The baby was dressed in white, which suggested that the assembled were there to witness the initiation of the child into the Church. The spirit of Cal Ubank understood this much: he had been summoned to be present at a baptism.

He observed the solemn event with interest. Such proceedings were not foreign to him, having attended several during his physical time on earth. Yet, any confusion at finding himself there, among strangers, was tempered by his curiosity to discover the full reason for his being summoned. A clue presented itself in due course, when the priest, dressed in his surplice, addressed the parents.

"What name do you give this child?"

The mother and father responded in unison: "Calub Merlin Elyk."

Ah, yes, the spirit thought. The reason was clear now: he was the child's namesake, for the most part. The middle name, "Merlin," made perfect sense. The child's first name, however, was close to but not quite "Calvert." But he had definitely been summoned, and so there had to be a connection. Perhaps the answer would be made clear as the proceedings continued.

"What do you ask of God's Church for Calub Merlin?" the priest said.

"Baptism."

The priest then called on a litany of saints, and the gathering of family and friends responded after each name.

"Saint Joseph."
"Pray for us."
"Saints Peter and Paul."
"Pray for us."
"Saint Joshua and Caleb."
"Pray for us . . ."

". . . I baptize you in the name of the Father, and of the Son, and of the Holy Spirit . . . God is the giver of all life. May he bless the parents of this child . . . they will be his first teachers . . . may they be the best of teachers . . ."

* * * * *

When the ceremony was done, the Sacrament of Baptism having been administered and young Calub Merlin initiated into the family and faith of the Catholic Church, the attendees slowly exited the building and gathered in groups outside, taking advantage of the glorious spring weather.

Aunt Zoey immediately broke the ice, remarking to the baby's father, David, about his son's name. "Calub is a beautiful name. I don't hear it much these days."

The proud dad gazed lovingly at sleeping baby Calub in his arms. "You make a good point. It comes from the time I spent teaching at the Cal Ubank Youth Centre."

"That was your first teaching gig, wasn't it?"

"That's right. A tough place to work, but it was an impactful experience. Funny thing though, in all the time I was there, we never much mentioned the man the place is named after. It's called the *Cal Ubank* Youth Centre, but it might well have been called the Cherry Blossom Youth Centre for all it mattered. It wasn't until I asked my students to do some research on Cal Ubank that I acquired a greater appreciation for him and his many achievements."

David's brother-in-law, Allen, jumped in. "Cal Ubank: The greatest captain in the history of the Mighty Pines franchise!"

"Daddy, didn't you always say Beezer Sharpe was the best captain Toronto ever had?" Marinelle Elyk asked. Marinelle was standing next to her father because, as baby Calub's older sister by eight years, she felt it her responsibility to be available to provide any assistance if necessary. Apparently, she was also somewhat of a hockey historian, and her uncle Allen had just said something inconsistent with what she'd been taught.

"That's my girl," her dad replied. "You've been paying attention. Yes, I did say Beezer was the greatest to wear the *C*."

"C'mon, Dave, what are you teaching your kid?" Allen smiled mischievously, looking to incite a debate.

"I guess I'd rank Beezer and Ubank as number one and one-A. But let me get back to that Cal Ubank assignment. It was an eye-opener for me. I was amazed at the things he'd accomplished while maintaining the highest level of class and integrity."

"Dave's a master at getting his students to do all the work for him," Allen teased, for the benefit of the others listening to the story. "Tell us, David, what did the kids discover about Cal Ubank?"

"Cal Ubank was a football star, a track star, an Olympian, and a PHL legend who led the Toronto Mighty Pines to three Cups. He was also a politician—an MPP who held the portfolio as minister of correctional services in the sixties. Plus, he served in the Canadian Army during World War Two. He was even voted Canada's Father of the Year, for Pete's sake. The guy was almost too good to be true!"

Listening to the conversation, the spirit of Cal Ubank had to smile in spite of himself. He also had to correct a few minor discrepancies. "Actually, *four* Clarence Cups, and it was for three years in the *seventies* that I held the portfolio as minister of correctional services—"

"And you won a gold medal in the javelin event at the British Empire Games, and you scored two hundred and one goals in your PHL career—"

Cal Ubank turned to see an old and dear friend positioned next to him. The spirit of Beezer Sharpe had materialized in response to the mention of his name during the family's conversation.

"Hello, Beasley. It's always a pleasure to find myself in your company. But as for my two hundred and one goals, let's not forget that you scored thirty more than me in your career." As gracious as ever, Captain Cal felt the need to recognize Beezer's achievements.

"Sure, but I played four more years than you, Cal. If you hadn't replaced your skates with army boots and traded your hockey stick in for a rifle going off to fight in the war . . . gosh, you lost two years of your prime. That's another forty goals, easy. Then if you had hung on for another couple years instead of retiring after our Cup win in '49, by Joe I'm guessing we'd be talking pert near three hundred goals for you."

"Right. And if my donkey had wheels, she'd be an automobile."

With David still expounding on the exploits of Cal Ubank, baby Calub's grandfather, Grandpa Merlin, happened to catch some of the conversation about great Pines captains and felt compelled to share his opinion on the matter.

"Sorry, David, but I always thought George Daly, the Chairman himself, was the greatest to wear the C."

"I'll admit there's a strong argument to be made for the Chairman, principally because of the two Cups he won as captain of the team," David conceded. "And let's not forget Jan Pieter and Wayne Brody, both great players and terrific captains in their own right—but, unfortunately, they didn't win. Winning a Clarence Cup has to be on your resume in this case. Either way, if not for the great captains of the past, the Toronto Mighty Pines wouldn't be such a venerated franchise today."

Recognizing that her father was becoming preoccupied with the debate, Marinelle interrupted him. "Daddy, can I hold Calub for a while?" She leaned on his elbow, looking up at him with her big, beautiful green eyes.

"Sure, honey. But try not to wake him. Here you go." He gently transferred the child to his daughter, who seemed remarkably comfortable and sure-handed with him.

Zoey had a question. "I always hear Joe Zedelko's name mentioned. Did Cal Ubank and Joe Zedelko ever cross paths? I mean, did they ever play together?"

"They did—for one year. Zedelko's rookie season was Ubank's last year in the league before he retired."

"How many Cups did he win?"

"Zedelko? Three, I think. In fact, he clinched the third by scoring that famous overtime goal in the final."

With her brother in her arms, Marinelle toned down her voice. "Isn't that Jersey Joe in the picture we have on the wall downstairs, Daddy?"

"You're right, honey. That's him."

"That was his last game." Marinelle turned to address the others in the group. "Jersey Joe Zedelko went missing that summer, when he was out fishing in his canoe or something. He wasn't found until Toronto won their next Clarence Cup, many years later."

Aunt Zoey was impressed. "You know that story Marinelle?"

"Yup. My dad has told me lots of hockey stories from the old days. I know about Joe Zedelko and Jackson Schmeltz and Beezer Sharpe and Cal Ubank..."

"Jackson Schmeltz. Now there's a name I'd forgotten," Uncle Nick said. "How many Cups did he win?"

Grandpa Elyk had the answer. "He won five, the same as Beezer Sharpe. You know, Jackson Schmeltz is another guy, like Cal Ubank, who took time off from pro hockey to serve in the war. He could've won *six* Cups."

While Marinelle held baby Calub, Aunt Zoey looked at the child in admiration, then brought the topic of conversation back around to his Christian names. "Dad's so honoured that you chose 'Merlin' for Calub's middle name," she said, giving her father a playful nudge. "I've never seen him standing taller; like he's been given the keys to the city."

"That choice was easy," David replied, "seeing as it basically fell into my lap. Not only is it granddad's name, it also happens to be Cal Ubank's middle name."

David's explanation confirmed for the spirit of Cal Ubank that there was a definite connection between his own name and the newly-christened baby's. His thoughts were then interrupted by the echo of a strong vibration, or a rumble, emanating from the trio of David, Marinelle, and baby Calub. It was immediately followed by the appearance of the spirits of Joe Zedelko and Jackson Schmeltz.

Sharpe was the first to greet them. "Well, look who it is, Jersey Joe and Jacko. When was the last time we got together like this? Now we've got a foursome for a hand of pinochle—or maybe some poker."

"Ha! I learned my lesson early, Beezer," Zedelko replied, still displaying the youthful energy he'd had in life. "I don't play cards with you. You're too good for me."

"Hello, fellows," Cal said. "What might Messers Zedelko and Schmeltz be doing here?"

"Your guess is as good as mine," Zedelko said, and turned to Schmeltz. "What about you, Jacko? You got any notion of our purpose here?"

"Beats me, but I figure the reason will present itself in due time." Schmeltz motioned to the child. "Looks like we're at a christening. Are they discussing the boy's name now?"

Sharpe was impressed. "That's quite observant of you, Jacko. Evidently, you offer a lot more than *just* five Cups and two 'Tenders."

Even in spirit form, Jackson Schmeltz could be made to blush. "Aw, Beezer, go on with ya. I just happened to overhear the conversation; my ears still serve me good as ever."

As the others chuckled, Zedelko joined in on the fun. "Speakin' of the 'Tender Trophy, I once heard that it was originally gonna be named after Jacko here."

"Truly?" Ubank's response carried a tone of amazement.

"I'm serious—on account of his proficiency in net." Joe's eyes twinkled, betraying the coming of a punchline. "But the suits in the league office couldn't bring themselves to name their goalie award 'The Schmeltz.'"

Once the laughter subsided, Beezer Sharpe addressed Schmeltz with a request. "Hey Jackson, be a pal and tell us how it was people got to calling you 'Jacko.'"

Before he could begin, however, Zedelko cut in to tell his version of the story first. "I'm pretty sure it goes back to when somebody noted the spaces between Jackson's teeth—on account of all the pucks he took tending goal—and compared them to the gap-toothed smile of a *Jack-o*-lantern." His laughter was contagious; he'd always been the life of the party.

Chortling along, Schmeltz nonetheless felt compelled to set the record straight. "Truth be told, the gaps in my teeth are just something I was born with. I'm proud to say I had the healthiest set of chompers a person could ask for—it was always easy to floss. But now it's Joe's turn," Schmeltz said, seeking to turn the tables on Zedelko. "Remind us how you got *your* nickname. I'm certain it's not because you were born and raised in the swamps of New Jersey."

"That would be correct. I'll have you know I hail from the tobacco town of Tillsonburg, Ontario," Zedelko answered, forthrightly. "The name 'Jersey Joe' goes back to the day I signed my first contract with Toronto. Somebody produced a Mighty Pines sweater for me to try on and, let me tell you, boys, it was the proudest moment of my life. I swear, there were tears in my eyes. For the next few weeks I wore that jersey everywhere, and that's when I acquired the nickname. My family, friends, and teammates—including you fellows—all picked up on it, and it stuck."

With his appetite for rehashing old stories fully whetted, Zedelko next turned to Ubank. "Cal, why don't you tell us about the time ol' Colonel Sinclair recruited you at the university football game?"

"Now, Joseph, you've heard that story so often, you likely remember it better than me."

Jersey Joe flashed his brilliant smile. "Nah, you tell it best."

"Well, alright then." Cal gathered himself, as if trying to remember the details. "It was my senior year at McMaster, and we were slated to play Toronto. Colonel Sinclair had made the trip into Hamilton that weekend to watch his U of T Blues play our Marauders. He was sitting in the stands behind the Blues' bench. Let me tell you, the man was nothing if not passionate about his team. By hum he had a set of lungs. And he never quit the entire game. 'C'mon boys!' he'd shout. 'Trounce those maids in maroon, those McMaster Maroons!' He would repeat it again and again, 'Maids in maroon! McMaster Maroons!' It shames me now to say it, but his insults were making me ornery. I was growing very annoyed with his ceaseless razzing. Truthfully, that was all the motivation I needed. I had one of my best games of the year. The more he yelled, the better we played. By the end of the game, the Colonel was so vexed by how we walloped his Blues, he was whistling through his nose."

Zedelko was caught up in the reminiscence. "Boy, old man Sinclair must have been ill-humoured after the game. Isn't that when he came and spoke to you, Cal?"

"That's right. He approached me after the game. By then, he had settled down enough to articulate his proposition in a civil fashion. It wasn't too complicated: he offered me a contract to play professional hockey with his Mighty Pines."

"Sounds like that was a humdinger of a day for you," Joe said, "what with the big win and then being offered the opportunity to play professional hockey."

"For the most part, yes. But you have to remember, back in those days there was a stigma attached to turning professional. It was more honourable to be an amateur athlete, for sure. So, for me the choice was simple: I had to decline his offer to maintain my amateur status, so I could compete in the 1936 Olympics in Berlin the next summer."

"You turned him down right then and there, huh?"

"Yes, I did."

"That must have put him over the edge."

"Not really. His response was pure Colonel Sinclair. He said, 'Good! Maybe if we beat them Krau...uh...Germans'—he used another word—'on the field of sport, they won't be so inclined to challenge us on the field of battle.' Of course, he had seen enough of German aggression in the Great War."

"The Colonel was a cracker, that's for sure," Jacko said.

Cal chuckled. "Yessir. That was my introduction to the man. But now I'd like to share an even better story, one I haven't told anyone before. It was the last time the Colonel and I spoke in person, and it happened to be shortly after he'd given up his stake in the franchise."

Jackson knew too well the circumstances to which Cal was referring. "Humph, the Stroud era," he grumbled. "Those were some grey days."

"It was a rough patch in the history of the organization to be sure," Sharpe added in agreement.

Zedelko, however, was nescient regarding the matter, so Cal provided a brief synopsis.

The grey days of the "Stroud era" had begun soon after Toronto's Cup win in 1962. Strother Stroud was a wily businessman, a shipbuilder whose company was based in Nova Scotia, producing a line of freighters called "Nova Tankers." Some financial chicanery by Stroud allowed him to buy up shares from the other stakeholders of the Mighty Pines franchise until the time came that he'd acquired enough to hold majority ownership. In the meantime, Colonel Sinclair had become disenchanted with the direction the organization was going, and had taken the extreme step of giving up his stake in the franchise and walking away. In what had amounted to one fell swoop, Strother Stroud had essentially supplanted the Sinclair name from the workings of the organization. His next move had been to drastically renovate old Mighty Pines Coliseum, squeezing in another 4,000 seats, hiking ticket prices, and (as a final insult) changing the name of the building to Nova Tank Arena.

It had been the source of no small amount of consternation for Sinclair, as evidenced by the following conversation he'd once had with Ubank...

* * * * *

"What kind of name is Nova Tank Arena?" Sinclair had asked, in his usual rhetorical fashion. *"And for that matter, what kind of name is Strother Stroud? Hell, he isn't even a true Canadian."* The Colonel had spit on the ground for emphasis. *"His business may be in Nova Scotia, but the man is a Yank. He lives on Nantucket Island, for Chrissake."*

FOUR SPIRITS AND A SACRAMENT

"He has effectively taken everything this franchise once stood for and reduced it to nothing more than a dollar sign. If it was up to me, I'd cast a spell and make it so the Toronto Mighty Pines have seen their last championship." His facial expression had changed, then, as though he'd just experienced a 'eureka' moment. "In fact, that's just what I'll do. I will place a curse upon the organization and its team—and you can be my witness, Cal."

Ubank had clearly been blindsided. "Witness? Me?"

"Sure, to make it official. Ready? Here we go." Without a moment's hesitation, Sinclair had raised his right hand and placed his left on an imaginary Bible. "May there never be another Clarence Cup parade on the streets of downtown Toronto." Sinclair's face had glowed, encompassed in a halo of pride as he'd looked to Ubank for an endorsement.

Cal had been less receptive, however. "Whoa! Isn't that a little harsh, sir?"

"Hell no. No harsher than the way Mr. Stroud finagled his way into majority ownership."

"But that's figuring to be a long-lasting curse. Heck, it's likely to out live us."

"Which doesn't really amount to much. Listen, if I live to be a hundred it still comes out to just a forty year curse. I would expect any hex of mine to do me proud, like, say, eighty or ninety years—heck, let's make it a century!"

"But what about the fans; all those loyal supporters who bleed green and white? Are you willing to make them suffer for so long?"

"Think of it as breaking some eggs to curse an omelette—or something like that."

Recognizing that the Colonel would not be dissuaded, Ubank had needed to think fast. "I don't know. Based on my limited knowledge of the way curses work, there should be some built-in condition, so that there's at least a chance of the curse being broken over time."

Sinclair had locked eyes with the man across from him. "OK Cal, I'll amend it for you. But it's only because you and I go back a ways, and I respect your sincerity. Now, how about this:" He'd straightened up and done the thing with his hands again. "The Toronto Mighty Pines will not win another Clarence Cup until the following two events transpire: First, the PHL holds its playoffs entirely in the summer season, say, anytime between July 1st and the end of September."

"And—?"

"And the Clarence Cup Final is played entirely in Canada."

Ubank had instantly grasped the implications. "That means the Final would have to be an all-Canadian affair."

"Damn right, that's exactly what it means—unless for some crazy reason it happens that every possible site in the US is unavailable or off limits."

"Boy, a summertime Clarence Cup playoffs with the Final held entirely in Canada," Ubank had summarized, allowing the weight of the words to settle upon him as Sinclair nodded.

"I dare say it's more likely that hell freezes over first."

When Cheers Are Not Enough

* * * * *

"That was forty years ago," Ubank said, wrapping up the story. "The Colonel died two years later."

"But Sinclair loved the Mighty Pines," Zedelko argued. "The team was his pride and joy. I can't believe he of all people would have cursed it in such a fashion."

"Well, I suppose there's a chance he rescinded the curse at some point in time afterward. But if he did, I wasn't a witness to it."

"You know, the rumour of a curse has been circulating for some time," Beezer Sharpe said, "but this is the first I've heard anything concrete."

"Consider the rumour true," Ubank assured him. Then he shifted gears along with his attention to the family members still gathered in the parking lot. "But I can't help wondering why you and Joseph and Jackson were called here today."

"Hmm, perhaps it's the infant," Sharpe suggested, pointing out the strength of the aura radiating around baby Calub. "It's not steady, but by golly, it's strong. Maybe the kid has some psychic attraction."

"Goodness, he's awfully young and small," Ubank said. "If you're right, he'll be a force when he grows up."

"He'll be a magnet for spirits; that's for certain."

"So, you're saying it's the little tyke who 'invited' us?" Zedelko asked. "But why? Usually I'm just called to give moral support and such. That or somebody's singin' 'Back Panel Vignette.'"

"Back Panel What?"

"Vignette. 'Back Panel Vignette.' You know, the hockey tune by O Wretched Bliss."

"Yes, of course, the song which includes a verse about you." Ubank said, appraising Zedelko anew. "So, somebody singing that song serves to summon you, does it?"

"Yeah, most times."

"Now I'm wondering if we're here merely as witnesses to this event, this gathering," Sharpe said.

"Like how three wise men attended the nativity of baby Jesus, except there's *four* of us?" Zedelko suggested.

Jackson Schmeltz could hardly believe what he'd just heard. "Ha, that's funny, Joe. Neither of us has a royal bloodline, and sorry, but I don't recall either of us having left behind a legacy of wisdom."

Ubank wasn't so quick to dismiss Zedelko's idea. "All kidding aside, Joseph might have a point there."

"How do you figure, Cal?"

"Well, none of us can detect a specific reason or purpose for our being here. And that would agree with our circumstances if the infant was, in fact, the source of the psychic energy. Newborns don't make conscious requests of us as spirits. Therefore, the suggestion that we are simply here to witness a special event, like the christening of this exceptional child—who happens to bear my name—seems to make the most sense."

The group of four spirits turned as one and gazed at the infant child in the arms of his sister.

Baby Calub was awake and growing restless, so David took him from his daughter and attempted to soothe the child. Marinelle went back to where her mother was starting to round everyone up so they could adjourn to Allen's house for the celebratory lunch. Allen's wife, Helen, came over to where her husband and David were looking intently at the boy, almost as if they were sharing a secret.

"Hey, you two, we should be going. Deb wants to be home before little Merlin gets beyond his feeding time."

"Merlin?" David said, with a raised eyebrow.

"Oh, um, yes. Don't take this the wrong way, Dave, but the little guy is such a Merlin to me. When he looks at you with those green eyes, it's like he knows your mind." Then she added with a wink, "If you've got questions, he's got answers."

David beamed at his sister's remarks as only a proud father could.

"Well, Helen," Allen said, "If he's Merlin to you, then he's 'Cubby' to me."

"Cubby?" Helen and David replied in unison, both wondering if Allen was serious.

"At least Merlin is his middle name," Helen remarked. "Where are you getting 'Cubby' from?"

"Simple. Take the 'Al' out of Calub and you get 'Cub'—or 'Cubby'. It's a perfect name for the little guy. I can see him growing up to be whip-smart, spunky, and determined—as a hockey player he'd be every coach's dream."

"OK, but right now Deb wants to get Calub Merlin 'Cubby' Elyk home."

Allen nodded. "Alright, we're coming."

As Helen walked back toward the cars, the two men lingered behind for a moment longer. "Look at him. He's got his sister's eyes," David said. Then he looked intently at his brother-in-law. "I'd feel blessed if he achieved half as much as his namesake, Captain Cal."

"I'm tellin' ya, Dave, he's got the athletic genes. Now it's just a matter of teaching him the game, so he'll acquire the smarts. That's where you can count on me, if you're willing." Allen was smiling, but he wasn't joking. After all, he had coached high school and university hockey for going on two decades. "I told you before, anything I can do to turn Calub into a forty-goal scorer, I will. Hell, everyone knows how the GOAT, Gabe Wozniak, had a lot of help from his dad. Maybe we can do the same with Cubby."

David smiled in appreciation of Allen's offer. "We've still got a few years to worry about that."

"Oh, sure. But time flies, and before you know it, he'll be four years old and in preschool. I'm putting my plan together now." Allen let himself dream. "Imagine, the little guy leading a PHL team to a Clarence Cup—maybe even the Pines. The way things are going, I wouldn't doubt it would take another twenty to twenty-five years for them to win one anyway. Cubby'll be in his prime by then."

David chuckled as they walked to the car, absorbed in the thought, while little Calub was wide awake now and beginning to squirm, on the verge of crying. David rocked him in his arms and spoke softly to him. "What do you think, little guy? Do you prefer Calub? Or maybe Merlin? Or how about Cubby—? Are you ready to grow into a mighty white pine? The future backbone of the franchise?"

The newly-christened child stopped fussing and appeared to be listening to his father intently, as if soberly weighing the options being presented to him.

Cal Ubank could sense the energy by which they had originally been summoned dissipating. "Well, boys, it feels like it's time to move on."

"Yeah, the spark sure fizzles out quickly, doesn't it?" Joe Zedelko observed.

"I don't think we've seen the last of baby Calub and his family—or of each other," Beezer Sharpe said. "I'll see you fellows at the next summons."

As his three spirit companions faded, Ubank was left hovering there alone, watching the cars exit the church parking lot. He sensed one last psychic pull coming from one of the vehicles, but before he could be sure of its source, he—and they—were gone.

CHAPTER ONE

ON THE BANKS OF THE MISTY RIVER

Mid-August, 2019

Conrad, Angus, and Baker sat crammed together in the back seat of the taxi driver's Toyota, from left to right, in precisely that order. It was Baker who looked out his window at the blur of trees and glimmers of sunlight on water and reflected on how the acronym made by their names spelled CAB, and that perhaps it was an omen of how the fates were in charge tonight.

He was desperate for a sign, some guidance. It was only five minutes ago that a flash of inspiration had him resolving not to put his grand scheme off any further. The plan had come to him a few weeks ago and would require the cooperation of his three friends. There were days that his idea seemed brilliant in its ingenuity and simplicity, but then other moments had him reconsidering the whole thing as a silly, childish notion. And now, in the middle of an uncomfortable fifteen-minute cab ride from Mas's cottage into town, he found himself waffling, thinking maybe it was best just to let events play out according to the whims of the gods. Let the game come to him, so to speak.

"Mas" was Masaccio Clementi, who at the moment was riding shotgun. He, along with his three companions in the backseat, made up a modest four-piece amateur alt-rock band, and it was for the band's benefit that he had generously donated the use of the Clementi family cottage. The cottage property on the water served as a lovely lakeside retreat for Mas and his wife, Salina, and their eight-year-old twin daughters, Hazel and Lily, through the summer and a few weekends in autumn. It was a stout little three-bedroom bungalow built on a protrusion of Canadian Shield in a sheltered inlet off Georgian Bay called Sandy Cove.

But while the cottage was built on solid footing, the same could not be said of his band, which was as yet nameless and came to be formed, about a year earlier, out of convenience and common interest. They were a group of dabblers, playing for pleasure, getting together whenever their respective schedules allowed. As such, it wouldn't take much for it to fall apart. Any little change in schedule, obligations to family, or a drop in any one member's level of interest or inclination would bring whatever they had built crashing down. The demands of being schoolteachers also often got in the way of the group achieving consistency where music-making was concerned.

You see, Angus, Baker, Conrad, and Masaccio were all members of the teaching staff at Holy Mother of Virtue Catholic Secondary School, about an hour southwest of Toronto. Anyone familiar with the institution simply referred to it as HMV, and it was a good bet that, if asked, the majority of its student body couldn't tell you the proper name of their school. (In fact, if forced to guess at what the initials stood for, they would likely answer with "His Master's Voice.") They just always knew it as HMV. It was short, easy to remember, and had a teen-friendly catchiness about it.

And so, this foursome of high school teachers was heading down a sunset-stained road in search of small-town Muskoka night life, to one of the local pubs for a few beers and maybe a chance to catch a live band. It being a Thursday in the middle of August, Masaccio hoped to avoid the large, annoying crowds that flocked to those parts on weekends during the height of the summer. He'd insisted on ordering the cab, thereby making moot the necessity for a designated driver.

It wasn't long before Baker, squished in the cab's backseat and looking to get his mind off feeling like a piece of stale laundry in an overstuffed hamper, decided to share some mindless trivia. He chose Angus as his target. Angus Fletcher was the band's drummer and the youngest of the four, having fallen in with the group after landing a fulltime job at HMV as an educational assistant the year before. As a drummer his musicianship was decidedly limited and his repertoire of songs extended not much further than the clutch of tunes on the band's set list. What he lacked in technique, however, he made up for in energy. Presently, he was seated between Conrad and Baker, his knees annoyingly set wide apart, encroaching on the personal space of the men to either side of him.

"Hey, Angus, what make of car is this?" Baker asked, pushing back with his leg and repositioning himself, ostensibly to face his friend.

Giving Baker some resistance with his own knee, Angus adopted a formal tone for his simple answer, "This, Mr. Brooks, is a Toyota Camry."

"Well, did you know that the words 'a Toyota' combine to form a palindrome?"

Masaccio was listening in from the front seat. "Do they really?" He worked it out under his breath. "Oh yeah, that's pretty cool."

From the other side of Angus, Conrad cut in with a trivia question of his own. "Hey, do any of you guys know what the longest palindrome in literature is?"

Conrad was the senior citizen of the group, approaching his late fifties, having retired from teaching two years ago, after which he had agreed to step into the newly vacated position as school chaplain. He was easily the most accomplished musician of the four, having played with several bands in his younger days. When he and his wife, Winnifred, had started a family, however, his days of spending weekends playing in random venues across Southern Ontario had ended. So, for going on twenty years now, his playing had been restricted to moments of personal enjoyment and general skill maintenance.

"No. But seeing as you're the school chaplain, you probably found it in the Bible," Angus jabbed.

"Nope."

The cab driver joined in at this point. "I'll bet it's something from Shakespeare."

"No, not Shakespeare."

"Hemingway?"

"Not quite. It's from a James Joyce novel."

The answer was met with an expectant and slightly awkward silence, everyone looking at Conrad. Even the driver was eyeing him via the rearview mirror.

"And that word would be—?"

"Oh, right. Um, the word is—" He took a moment to think. "The word is 'tattarrattat.'"

Conrad's answer brought on much "tattarrattat"ing from the others, who felt compelled to mimic it aloud. Angus and Baker argued that it wasn't a real word, but Conrad defended it. "Oh, it's a legitimate word, alright. It was an onomatopoeia used to describe a knock on the door."

"That's a word that makes the sound of what it describes, like 'buzz' and 'sniff,'" Masaccio explained from the front seat—mostly for the benefit of Angus, who in turn directed a hairy eyeball at the back of his head.

"So, Conrad," Baker said, changing the subject, "what've you and Winnie been up to?"

"Well, the kids are all home for the summer, so it's been a full house. But Winnie and I did manage to get out and do some day trips. I tell you, when school starts up again next month, she'll have a lot of time to herself."

"The house empties out, huh?"

"It does indeed. Two kids are away at university, one at Carleton in Ottawa, the other at U of T. Two are in high school, and the youngest—the most brilliant of the bunch, if you ask me—is heading into grade seven."

"And papa Conrad will soon be back at school every day, too," Angus said.

"Oh, I've already been into the building a couple of times," Conrad said. "Gerry wants me to come in again next week and meet some of the new staff, particularly those in the religion department."

"That's why, being the chaplain, you get paid the big bucks," Baker said, exhibiting no sympathy for him. "Me? I'm just the art teacher. The only time the principal needs me is when he wants to hang artwork in his office."

Angus, who was always fishing for talent among the new staff, pressed Conrad for information. "Tell us about these new teachers. Any pretty young things?"

"And what makes you think I could answer that?"

"What, you're too old to recognize good-looking women?" Angus asked.

"I haven't met them yet. Gerry sent me the information via email."

"And—?"

Taking a deep sigh and looking to the heavens for strength, Conrad volunteered what he knew. "There are four new teachers, two male, two female, if I'm not mistaken." He then directed his attention to the driver, if for no other purpose than to shift the topic. "I was meaning to ask you, what is that hanging from your rearview mirror? Some kind of a dream catcher?"

The driver smiled. "It *looks* like a dream catcher, but it's actually a representation of my spirit guide."

"You have a spirit guide?"

"We all have spirit guides. It's just that people don't much go in for them, or they don't think about them."

"What's with Saint Christopher then?" Conrad inquired, pointing to a small statue that was affixed to the car's dashboard.

"Simple: I like to hedge my bets."

Baker took the opening and dove right into a topic that was never far from his heart. "You want to know who needs a spirit guide—or spirit *guides*? The Mighty Pines, that's who."

"Damn right!" Angus concurred. "They need, like, a hundred of them, like guardian angels whispering in their ears and coming to them in their dreams with instructions on how to win."

"I guess the Raptors found *their* spirit guide," Masaccio said.

"Yeah, they had a good one," Conrad replied. "His name was Kawhi Leonard."

Just then the cab made an abrupt turn as it pulled into a parking lot. "Here we are, gentlemen," the driver announced. "The Blue Beacon."

"Thank God," Angus said. "I was learning way too much in here."

"Holy shit, the parking lot's packed," Baker observed.

"Look at the lineup to get in."

No sooner did the driver put the cab in park than Conrad and Baker were climbing out, relieved at being able to straighten up and stretch their legs. Angus followed, his eyes taking in the females in the crowd. Mas established the pickup time with the driver and then joined them. Heat was emanating off the asphalt, and the lack of a breeze off the bay combined to produce what would surely be a hot and thirsty crowd.

"Why is it so busy?" Baker wondered aloud as the cab pulled away. "On a Thursday night no less."

Mas pointed to an events sign. "It looks like Thursdays are 'Dance Till You Drop' night. It looks to be a younger crowd, you know, university kids and such."

"Well, what do you want to do? Are we going to get in line?"

Conrad shook his head, in the mood for something less hormone-charged. "This isn't exactly what I had in mind."

"Me neither," Baker said, then noted where the much younger Angus's attention was directed. "Sorry, Angus."

"We could walk back over the bridge and try the Misty River," Masaccio suggested. "We passed it on the drive here."

"How long a walk is it?"

"Not very. Five minutes back to the bridge and it's just down the road from there. Ten minutes, max."

"Let's do it then."

Conrad was hesitant. "I take it the Misty River isn't hosting a similar dance night?"

"Actually, it looked pretty quiet when we drove past."

As they walked, Masaccio regaled them with stories of his experiences in town during his younger days. "When I was growing up, we never knew that place as the Blue Beacon. To us it was always the Red Beacon. That's how the locals referred to it, because of the kind of business being openly transacted on the premises."

"Wait a minute," Angus cut in. "You're saying . . . that's where you could find the hookers?"

Masaccio laughed. "Yeah. Being just a kid at the time, you can imagine how it might have piqued my curiosity, wondering what kind of sins were being committed at the Red Beacon."

"OK, so now that we know why it was called the Red Beacon," Baker said, "what about its real name, the Blue Beacon?"

"The Blue Beacon refers to the lighthouse out on the point. It's nothing to write home about, not like Peggy's Cove or anything, but it serves its function. Anyway, it's painted a sky-blue colour. Has been for years. We'll be able to see it once we get to the other side of the bridge."

When they reached the far side of the bridge, Angus stopped to take a picture of the scene, with the blue lighthouse on the rocky shore and sailboats moored in the harbour, the sky over it all colouring up nicely. They lingered for a minute, then resumed walking toward the pub.

As they approached their destination, it was evident that, compared to the Blue Beacon, the Misty River Bar and Grill was older and rundown, showing its age, in keeping with the rest of the community on the south side of the river. With evening setting in, a marquee sign in the parking lot was lit, advertising the best wings in town and a live band. Masaccio and Conrad led the way to the front doors while Baker noticed Angus veered off slightly to the side of the building. "Angus, the entrance is this way, man."

"I'm just looking for evidence of the world's oldest profession." Angus flicked his head toward two women smoking beside a car at the far edge of the parking lot. "Speaking of which, what do you think those two are up to over there?"

"I think they're just having a chat over a cigarette. Let's go inside. Hell, I was already craving a beer in the car. Now I'm really thirsty."

They all settled in around a table and placed their order. A pitcher of beer came soon thereafter.

"Heads up, Conrad, the waitress is coming up behind you with our beer." Baker assessed the approaching server, who looked to be in her forties. She was wearing a tight-fitting black T-shirt with the words "Misty River" in bold script across the chest. A black stretch mini extended down almost to mid-thigh. The fabric of the T-shirt and the mini skirt were at the limit of their integrity, the former due to an ample bosom and the latter owing to a rather protrusive middle-age belly. For a moment Baker thought she might be with child, but she was too old for that. She wore a black cap with a ponytail extending out the back. The ball cap highlighted the image of a canoe paddle crossed with a hockey stick and the words "Joe Zee" stitched under it. The woman looked tired, so Baker gave her his warmest smile and joined the others in thanking her as she placed the pitcher on the table.

"I love your hat. It's first-rate. Jersey Joe Zedelko!" In Baker's mind, the blankness in the look she gave him couldn't have been colder if he'd asked her when she was due—which, to his horror, was exactly what Conrad inquired of her. Baker cringed inside, readying himself for a hostile response from the insulted waitress.

"It's going to be a Christmas baby," she said, extending Conrad a smile that revealed beautiful teeth and, in the process, took a good ten years off her face. "I'm hoping to work at least until Remembrance Day." She placed four menus on the table and sighed with a smile. "I get so tired being on my feet."

"Well, congratulations," Conrad said. "Don't work too hard." With a wink he closed with some advice. "Remember, next to love, a mother's health is the best thing for a baby."

"Oh my, that's so sweet. I'll remember that. My name's Dee Dee, by the way. You boys give me a shout if you need anything." Then she was gone, back to the bar to load up with beers for the next table of customers.

"Holy shit, Conrad," Baker said, lowering his voice. "How'd you know she had a pregnancy belly and not a beer belly?"

"Baker, I've got five kids, for Chrissake. I should be able to recognize a pregnant woman by now."

Mas filled everyone's glasses and then raised his in a toast. "Gentlemen, here's to finishing off the summer in style." They voiced their agreement, clinked glasses, and took long swallows to slake their thirst. Mas topped up everyone's glasses, then settled in to peruse the menu.

Angus began to fidget. He was turning in his chair, scanning every corner of the bar. "I'm just trying to get my bearings here. The blue lighthouse shines out onto Georgian Bay, right?"

"Uh-huh."

"And the river we crossed back there runs into Georgian Bay . . . what's it called?"

"What's what called?"

"The river."

Mas smirked. "Um, well, we are presently sitting in a restaurant that is built on the river's bank, and the name of the restaurant is the *Misty River* Bar and Grill, so the river is called—?"

The question hung in the air as Angus failed to make what to everyone else was the obvious connection. "How the hell should I know what it's called? That's why I'm asking the question."

No one spoke. Finally, Conrad had had enough. "Angus, it's called the Misty River."

"Kind of obvious, isn't it?" Mas added.

Angus's cheeks grew pink. "Hell no, it ain't obvious. It could be called the Sasquatch River for all I know. I thought 'Misty' was used as an adjective—you know—like there's lots of fog on the water—hence the lighthouse and all that."

"Jesus, Angus, don't overthink it. Misty is a proper noun in this case, not an adjective."

Angus could only join the others in laughing at himself. "Aw, you guys are all assholes," he said as he reached for the pitcher of beer. "Are we done with this yet? I'm gonna order another one." He topped up his glass, emptying the pitcher just as Dee Dee the waitress did a flyby, gesturing in a circle with her hand that the table was ordering another round. It was then that Baker stopped her with an inquiry.

"Excuse me, but I couldn't help noticing that there are instruments on the stage but no sign of a band. Are they not playing tonight?"

"They won't be playing tonight. The drummer apparently became ill." She pointed across the room. "The guitarist is still here though. He's the guy sitting alone over there in the booth by the windows."

Baker looked over at the man, who was sporting John Lennon glasses and absently picking at a plate of fries and nursing a beer. An idea began to incubate, causing him to weigh several options. He recalled his original plan to let the game come to him tonight, but he also knew that at some point . . . well, carpe diem and all that. He looked at his friends, then he looked at the man in the booth, and then he looked at the instruments on stage. *Fuck it,* he thought. *Let's seize this sucker.* He turned to his closest confidant.

"Mas, I have a proposition for you." He got up and motioned for his friend to join him at the bar. "Excuse us for a minute guys."

Mas obliged and followed Baker. "You've got something on your mind; I can tell. What is it?"

"You know when we were jamming on the dock this afternoon? We sounded pretty good, didn't we?"

"Actually, we did sound good," Mas smiled at the memory. "And it seemed the neighbours thought so too. I was worried we'd get told to quiet down, and then they went and asked us to turn it up!"

Baker drew his friend's attention to the raised platform occupied by some lonely looking musical instruments. "Look at that stage there. See what I see? A couple of guitars, a bass, and a drum set."

Mas sensed what was coming. "Oh, man, don't tell me . . . you're actually thinking—"

"I see some instruments that aren't going to be played tonight. What are the chances that that guy over there lets us perform a short set?"

"I'd say slim to none." Masaccio's flat response made Baker's face fall. "Hey, I like the idea, but I'm doubtful that he'd be inclined to let four strangers strap on his instruments and play, that's all."

The conspiratorial look on Baker's face indicated he wasn't about to be dissuaded. "C'mon, Mas. I'd hate myself if I didn't at least ask the guy. Let's go chat him up."

Baker got up and led Mas to the booth by the windows. The man looked up as they approached. "Excuse me," Baker said, "Sorry to bother you—"

"No bother, mate. How can I help you?" The man presented an Australian accent and seemed friendly.

"Well, I understand that you're part of the band that won't be playing tonight due to a medical emergency?"

"Crikey, word gets around fast. Stevie, our drummer, was suffering some abdominal pain, poor bloke. My other mates took him to the hospital as a precaution."

"I'm sorry to hear that. I hope it's nothing too serious." Baker hesitated, as if taking in the news about Stevie, then continued. "Um . . . we were just wondering if maybe, uh . . . we could, you know . . . use your instruments on stage to play a set . . . just a short one?"

"Just you two?"

"Uh, no. There's four of us. The other two are sitting back there." Baker turned and pointed to where Conrad and Angus were seated. They were looking over, wondering what the conversation was about.

"My name's Baker," he said, offering his hand. "I play guitar and sing lead vocals. This is Masaccio. He plays bass."

"Hiya, fellas. My name's Sid." The man shook their hands, then looked over at the other two. "Let me guess, the young fella plays drums, and the older one plays guitar."

"Yes, you're bang on. Angus is our drummer, and Conrad is quite accomplished on lead guitar."

It didn't take long for Sid to reach a decision. "Fellas, it sounds like a crackin' idea. The instruments are just sitting idle, after all." He looked around as if to take inventory of the crowd. "It's just too bad you don't have a bigger audience. Have at it, boys. You got my blessing."

Baker and Mas exchanged looks of disbelief and excitement. They thanked Sid and were about to head back to share the news with Conrad and Angus when Sid stopped them. "I've got one condition, though."

"Sure, anything."

"I reserve the right to pull the plug if I deem that your band sounds better than mine."

Baker eyed Sid to confirm that he was, in fact, joking. Mas just snorted. "Fat chance of that."

"I don't think you need to worry, mate," Baker said. "This will be our first time on stage—*any* stage."

"Well, good luck to you, then. Break some legs, boys."

Baker and Mas could barely keep themselves from skipping as they headed back to their table. "OK, you two, stop drinking and listen up. We just got the go-ahead to use the instruments on stage there and play a short set."

"You fuckin' serious?" Conrad had had a notion that Baker was up to something.

"Yeah. The band's guitar player is sitting over there. His name's Sid. Seeing as his band won't be performing tonight, I asked about the possibility of us borrowing their stuff to play. He likes the idea."

"Here, Mas, take this pen and start drawing up a set list of songs," Conrad said, clearly game for the chance to play. Then he looked over at his drummer. "Sounds like fun. Whadda ya say, Angus?"

Angus was looking pale. "Guys, I can't play on someone else's drum set. First of all, I might damage it. Second, they'd feel different. I wouldn't be able to do a good job—not that I'm very good as it is."

"Don't worry, man," Baker said, reassuringly. "We just need you to keep a basic beat. Hell, you were rockin' it pretty good today out on the dock."

"Oh, I don't know—" Angus couldn't have looked more panicky if Baker had announced that the waitress's water had just broke and they'd have to help with the emergency delivery. He looked at his beer glass. "I'm not that sober either."

"Stop making excuses. Besides, you know you'd hate yourself if you let this opportunity pass."

Angus didn't say anything more. He simply sat there, his eyes alternating between leery glances toward the drums on stage and gazing straight ahead, like a deer caught in the high beams of an oncoming tour bus.

CHAPTER TWO
A SIMPLE PLAN

Whenever he felt stressed, Angus found that air-drumming settled him down, which is precisely what he was doing at that moment, albeit under the table. As he tried to psyche himself up for their impromptu set, he looked at Baker seated next to him and confided one of his biggest fears. "Man, I just hope I don't lose my sticks."

"Same here. I fumbled a few picks today when we were playing out there on the dock." Baker was referring to a problem that he and Angus had yet to solve: the habit of losing the tools of their trade mid-song. During their dock session that afternoon, Baker had needed to put down his guitar and wade out into the water twice to fetch a plectrum that had fluttered out of his grasp mid-song. Meanwhile, Angus had lost his grip on a drumstick now and then. One had rattled off the dock, another had landed in the sandy beach, and twice a stick had splashed into the water.

Feeling the need to get up and move around, Angus left the table to take a walk around the parking lot. On his way to the door, he made a pit stop at the men's room. Once outside, he engaged in various stretches and other movement activities, to clear his head more than anything. He allowed himself two minutes before going back inside and then made a beeline for the stage. Angus approached the drum kit tentatively, walking around it as though it were a guard dog on a leash, forcing him to negotiate his way past. He made some adjustments to the seat to accommodate his reach, found the sticks, and proceeded to twirl one in his left hand, moving right into a practice run. He should have stopped there. Instead, Angus attempted a right-hand twirl, and nearly put his eye out. The stick flew out of his hand, cracking him on the bridge of the nose before clattering onto the floor. His nose was stinging, causing him to tear up, so although his eyes were spared, his vision was compromised nonetheless.

While Angus was acquainting himself with the drums, Baker, Conrad, and Masaccio finalized the playlist for their set. They settled on seven songs and then added two more, just in case they found themselves firing on all cylinders. After all, a couple more songs would be like an encore in a sense. Four handwritten lists were drawn up, one for each member to have as reference. They headed over to join Angus on stage, Baker delivering one of the lists to his drummer, who was blinking and red-eyed.

After a quick tuning and a bit of a warm-up, Baker approached the microphone and greeted the handful of patrons. "Good evening, everybody. We've been given permission to make a little noise and maybe liven things up a bit. Feel free to dance if you get the urge. We're called . . . uh . . . The Misty River Replacements."

Conrad winced at the name, and Baker shrugged, having just made it up. He backed away from the mic to make a visual check with the others when he saw Angus anxiously waving him over.

Baker manoeuvered his way to the front of the kick drum. "What's up? You ready?"

"I guess, but . . . um, the first song?"

"Yeah, 'Ring of Fire.' It's on your set list."

"I know, I've got my list right here. It's just that, uh . . . remind me, Baker . . . how does it go again?"

Baker would have been forgiven if he'd chosen to pull the plug and walk off the stage right then and there. Instead, his instinct told him that his friend just needed a slight push start, after which he'd be able to cope. He leaned toward Angus and, under his breath, sang the gist of the melody and beat.

Angus nodded in time with the rhythm, and then the light clicked. "Got it. Thanks, Baker."

Baker straightened up. Then he had a thought and leaned back in toward his drummer. "When we finish 'Ring of Fire,' we're going right into 'The Darkest One.' Are you good with that?"

"No problem, man. Let's do this."

Baker gave Conrad a nod, who, in turn, counted them in and confidently kicked off the opening song. It always amazed Baker how Conrad could transform himself from a mild-mannered academic into a guitar-wielding, face-melting old-time rocker. His entry into "Ring of Fire" proved it yet again, as without hesitation he led the group into Social Distortion's punky cover of the Johnny Cash hit by dragging his plectrum up the neck, scratching into the classic lead line. Baker did a passable job as the band's vocalist and generally managed not to mangle things on rhythm guitar. Overall, he considered it a good start to the set, and he was playing fast and loose with his strumming when, heading into the final repeat of the eponymous chorus, an aggressive down stroke produced an overly sour chord. He looked down to see a snapped and flapping guitar string.

Thankfully, Conrad was able to carry through to the song's end with minimal damage. And so, as the crowd offered its polite appreciation for the effort, Baker was forced to leave the stage and go back to Sid's booth, but not before he stepped back to the mic, regretting to inform the audience that the band had to deal with some technical difficulties, necessitating a short pause in the set.

Sid was ready for him. "Whatcha got there? Ahh, the E string tapped out, eh? Let me take care of that."

"Thanks, Sid." Baker sheepishly passed the guitar over to its owner. "Sorry. This is really embarrassing."

"Not at all, my man. For all we know, the string was ready to give up the ghost anyway. It won't take me long to replace it."

Baker watched as Sid reached into a small duffel bag next to him on the bench, retrieving a packet of guitar strings and a pair of needle-nose pliers. Meanwhile, up on stage, Masaccio started playing the bass line of Nirvana's "Come as You Are," joined in turn by Angus and Conrad, which was enough to fill the downtime and keep the folks tapping their toes.

Before long Baker was back at the microphone, guitar in hand, and introducing the band's second song, "The Darkest Hour," a no-risk proposition since it was practically a law of nature that Canadian audiences who came to hear live bands were suckers for a Tragically Hip tune. They managed to play with no further mishaps, and all too soon it was time for Baker to set the audience up for the end of the set. "We're going to finish up by playing two more songs for you now. We've had a blast—hopefully you've had some fun too. This is called 'Kids.'" The Current Joys quirky little tune was followed by a rousing rendition of "Fireworks" by, who else, The Tragically Hip—and, just like that, the maiden voyage of the Misty River Replacements was over.

The crowd was oddly appreciative, allowing the band members to take quick bows to sustained cheers. Once the applause died down, Baker and Mas made their way over to Sid to thank him once more for his generosity. Sid was ungrudging with his praise of their performance. "That was OK, fellas. You say that was your first time on stage? Very commendable." He graciously declined another drink, expressing how he was just happy to help them get their feet wet.

Baker and Mas rejoined their two ebullient friends at the table. Baker was particularly proud of their drummer, who was understandably the sweatiest of the four. "Congrats, Angus. You did it! You fucking did it."

Mas was shocked at how warmly the other patrons, despite being few in number, had received the performance. "Did you notice there were actually people on the dance floor?"

"I didn't see a thing," Angus said. "I was too busy concentrating. Man, the last time I focused that intensely I was making out with this hot chick during spring break, trying not to—"

"Yeah, we get it Angus," Mas said. "Hey, I'm starving. Let's order something."

"Conrad, call 'mama to be' over here," Baker said. "I need a drink. I'm parched."

"Her name's Dee Dee. But why don't we just go to the bar and get it ourselves?"

"Even better. Let's go."

They requested a pitcher of beer for the table and squeezed in a platter of nachos and wings just before the kitchen closed for the night. Later, with their whistles wet and their bellies attended to, the four of them rehashed the evening's experience, comparing notes, celebrating the high points, and laughing at their assorted miscues. Inevitably, the conversation veered toward school as they fell in to talking shop, focusing on the prospects for the upcoming year at HMV. That got Angus back on the topic of the new teachers on staff. He turned to Conrad, mining for more information, but despite his best efforts, all he came away with were sketchy, evasive answers.

"I told you, I didn't meet them in person," Conrad said. "I just sent emails welcoming them to HMV."

"You did say two of them were female, right?"

"I assumed as much, but come to think of it, I never really confirmed their genders."

"That's the most important detail, man." Angus couldn't let it go. "Do you remember their names at least?"

"Let's see, there was a Sam, a Carm, a Perreault, and a Terri, with an *i*. Don't even ask me about their last names."

"Let's review: we've got a Sam and a Carm. Hmm, we can't determine gender with those names. Then, what did you say? A Perreault? How do you spell Perreault? Is it like Ross Perot—P-e-r-o-t?"

"No, it's French—P-e-r-r-e-a-u-l-t." Conrad spelled it out, but Angus determined that the name was no help.

"At least we know that 'Terri with an *i*' is a female, right?"

"Christ, Angus, you need a girlfriend," Masaccio concluded.

"That's what I've been trying to tell you guys."

"Nah, you're still a young buck." Conrad remarked. "Hell, you're barely twenty."

"Twenty-two," Angus corrected, flashing two peace signs for emphasis.

Conrad simply waved him off. "Baker here, on the other hand . . . what are you now, thirty-five?"

"Easy there, big fella. I turned thirty-two on the nineteenth of June."

"Holy shit," Angus said. "That's my man Randall's birthday."

"You wouldn't happen to be referring to *Ricky* Randall, star winger for the Pines, who shines in the regular season and then disappears in the playoffs?"

"That's the one!"

"Well, you're off by ten days," Baker informed. "Ricky Randall was born on the ninth."

Conrad picked up on the reference to the Pines forward. "Boy, we sure could have used more playoff productivity from all of our big guns."

"Don't remind me," Baker said. "It makes me sick just thinking about it."

"Boy, you really took that first-round loss hard," Mas noted.

"I did. I can't deny it. I was in a bloody funk for weeks after that."

"C'mon, you must be used to early-round playoff losses by now," Conrad said, pragmatically.

"It's more than that. It's to the point where this team is ruining the most wonderful time of the year for me."

"What? The Pines are wrecking Christmas for you?" Angus wondered.

"No . . . not Christmas."

"But I thought you loved Christmas."

"No . . . I mean, yes . . . I mean, I do, but I'm not referring to Christmas. There's *another* most wonderful time of the year, especially for sports lovers in springtime. It's the time when the PHL playoffs, the NBA playoffs, and the new MLB season are all aligned."

"Aahh, yes," Conrad said, savvy to Baker's reference. "And don't forget March Madness basketball . . . and Masters Weekend."

"And the days are getting warmer," Mas added. "And the patios are opening up."

"Exactly." Baker replied, reassured by his friends' empathy. "So, yeah, that most wonderful time of the year is being soured by the Pines' annual playoff disappointments."

"I'm tellin' ya," Angus said, "That's where some female companionship will help you get over them."

"What would really help is the team just moving on to the second round." Baker shook his head at the thought. "Ughh! I can't let it die. The road was paved for a finals run last year. It was such a missed opportunity."

"Shit, it wouldn't surprise me if it happened to them again this year."

"Dear, God. How can you talk like that, Conrad?"

"Listen, I want them to win just as much as the next guy, but face it, they're not there yet. They're not mature enough, not experienced enough, and the team isn't built for four playoff rounds."

"I disagree. I contend that this team, when healthy, can stack up against any team in the league. They've got offensive firepower, they've got plenty of depth where the forwards are concerned, they've added to the defence, and they've got a top-five goaltender. Now they just need to name a captain and everything will be tied up with a nice neat bow."

"Hmm, someone's been drinking the Kool-Aid," Conrad observed. "You sound like the team's publicist."

When Cheers Are Not Enough

"I like how Galahad has put this team together," Baker said in his own defense.

"Wait . . . Galahad? What about the GM?" Mas wondered. "Isn't it Kyle Bulac's job to make personnel decisions?"

"On paper, maybe. But I suspect the guy pulling the strings is *Xir* Galahad. Bulac doesn't make a move without the president's blessing."

"I guess that only makes sense," Mas said with a smirk. "Galahad *is* the 'logo' after all."

"The 'logo'?" Angus wondered.

"Yeah, the silhouette hockey player on the PHL crest," Mas informed, "is Xander Galahad himself."

"No shit! That's news to me," Angus said, reaching for his phone to call up the image. "Now I gotta see it for myself."

"The 'logo'. . . phooey!" Conrad spat in derision. "I'm convinced he got the job more for his name value and stature he earned during his playing career than anything to do with his ability to build a winning team. The guy arrived full of big promises. Remember how he vowed to bring Toronto's Cup drought to an end?"

"Of course. It was during his very first media event as the Pines' new team president."

"One thing he wouldn't have said aloud to the media—although he probably thinks it often enough," Masaccio said, "is that the damn coach needs to show some imagination when it comes to the way he uses his players."

"I doubt Kayden Koch's gonna change," Conrad said. "And anyway, I'm not convinced he's the problem. They have bigger issues. Hell, Ricky Randall hasn't even signed a contract yet. Wasn't that supposed to have been done in July?"

"Yeah, that's a disappointment," Baker agreed. "These huge money contracts—all they do is make a few guys rich at the expense of the team's success. I ask you, where is the noble act of sacrifice for the greater good of the Toronto Mighty Pines? Is there no one who can impress upon these guys the profound legacy they're toying with here?"

"Someone needs to take a haircut for the team!" Angus exclaimed.

"Win a goddamn Cup, *then* make your millions is what I say," was Masaccio's opinion.

"How about just get to a final?" Baker said sarcastically.

"How about get out of the fuckin' first round?" Conrad was always good for a reality punch to the gut. "I'm telling you, don't be surprised if they flame out again this year."

Baker was so caught up in the swirl of Mighty Pines talk that he didn't pause to fully consider his rejoinder. "Not if I can help it," he said.

In the months that followed, whenever he recalled this moment, sitting at the table with his friends in the Misty River Bar and Grill, Baker would swear that his comment, a sentence of six words, caused all the activity in the pub to stop—as if a Most Wanted man had just entered through the saloon doors and every head had shifted in his direction. There was no going back; this was his moment of truth, his Rubicon.

Conrad was the first to respond. "What the hell does that mean?" he demanded.

"Yeah," Angus said. "What could you possibly do to help it?"

With great deliberation, Baker lifted his half-empty glass, bent his elbow, and drained it. He returned the glass to the table, slowly and dramatically selected a chicken wing, and held it up for all to see. Then he employed his best Robert De Niro impression in a scene from *The Deer Hunter*. "You see this? This is this. This ain't somethin' else. This is this."

The other three stared at Baker, then at each other, then back at Baker. "What the fuck?" Angus said, speaking for everyone.

Baker was disappointed to see his movie moment wasted on them. "Did that just go over all your heads? C'mon, man. None of you ever see The Deer Hunter?"

Conrad nodded and pointed at Baker. "Ah-haaa . . . I thought I recognized De Niro in there. But in the movie, he was brandishing a bullet, not a hot wing. What's a chicken wing got to do with Toronto's hockey team?"

"Actually, nothing I can think of. I just couldn't resist the chance to act out a great scene." Baker's face, which was a model of mirth, now grew a frown as he proceeded to explain. "Look, all summer long I was stewing over the Pines' playoff loss, actually searching for answers. That's how shitty I felt about last season." He shifted in his seat and leaned forward. "That's when I decided that I'm done with playing the loyal fan who sits on his hands, helplessly cheering from a seat at the bar . . . or the living room couch."

"Come now, Baker," Conrad said. "You know that's what it means to be a fan. It's what you sign up for."

"I disagree. I think we can do more," Baker declared. "I'm done with being a cheerleader," he said with a tone of finality. "Cheers are not enough."

Conrad leaned back in his chair. "So, if cheers are not enough, as you say, what do you have in mind?"

"Yeah, what's your plan?" Angus demanded.

"It's really quite simple." Baker moved closer but lowered his voice, forcing the others to lean in, like football players in a huddle. "I got to thinking about how a small group of guys—you know, serious fans, like us—might be able to influence the fortunes of a sports team."

"Hang on," Mas said. "Before you start, what time is it? I don't want us to be late for our cab."

"It's almost midnight."

"OK, so you've got about forty-five minutes."

"That should be plenty. Now keep this confidential, just between the four of us. Here's my plan. And like I said, it's simple."

Baker casually lifted a bum cheek as if to fart, but instead he reached into his back pocket and pulled out a small notepad. As he flipped through it, the others saw that it was filled with what looked like random scribbles in pencil and ink. He found his page and flattened the booklet on the table before him. Perhaps it was because he was high from the evening's events or simply because he had consumed too much beer, but Baker was quite loose lipped about the scheme he'd hatched over the summer. He spent the better part of the next twenty minutes pitching his plan, now and then referring to the notepad. It would require the participation of all four of them as a group over the next six to eight months.

He figured it was a testament to the strength of their friendship, their passion for seeing the Mighty Pines succeed, or both, that nobody laughed at him as he spoke. They listened, they interjected with pertinent questions, they listened some more, and they even offered suggestions that might increase the effectiveness of the endeavour that Baker was proposing.

"I'll admit I don't know too much about this stuff."

"What's there to know?" Conrad asked. "We're all Catholics, so we're well-versed with solemn ceremonies and sacred rituals. We can take cues from the rituals we engage in at Mass every week."

Baker shook his head. "Sorry, but the picture in my mind doesn't bear much resemblance to the rituals of a Catholic Mass. We'd just be playing a couple of songs dedicated to the Pines."

"Oh, I know it," Conrad replied. "But it's the strength of the idea that intrigues me. Remember what Jesus said? 'Where two or more are gathered in my name, there I will be.' The power of gathering as a group, strength in numbers and all that. And don't forget Saint Augustine: 'He who sings prays twice.' We shouldn't underestimate the power of music and voices united in song." Conrad's reference to music touched off a round of ideas and suggestions. Angus started things off.

"Hey, let's write our own songs!"

"What?"

"Better yet, let's recruit professionals to write the songs."

"What?"

"Who are the best songwriters?"

"Do they have to be Canadian?"

"I guess."

"Gord Downie?"

"Um, I think it would be helpful if they were alive."

"Damn. So, I guess Stompin' Tom Connors is out too?"

"Why, is he dead?"

"Neil Young?"

"I just told you, they should be alive."

"Idiot, Neil Young *is* alive."

"Kevin Drew?"

"Jesus, Baker. Now you're just showing off."

"Leonard Cohen?"

Baker saw the need to tap the brakes. "Wait, wait. Timeout. I see where this is going, so before we get there, let's set some limits: No Drake, no Justin Bieber, no Celine Dion... It's likely we'll have to do this ourselves."

"Baker is right," Mas said. "We'll need to write our own songs, sort of. They don't have to be epic ballads a la Gordon Lightfoot, but simple verse put to common tunes."

"That's it!" Baker said, energized by the spark of a thought. "We don't have to compose original music. We'll Yankovic this shit. We'll put our own words to established songs of our choice. That shouldn't be too hard."

The idea was well received and precipitated some more discussion. It was the last piece of the puzzle. Once the dust had settled, a few ground rules had been laid: They were informally sworn to secrecy, agreeing to keep their actions just between the four of them. Their meetings would be referred to as "band sessions," which was not far from the truth anyway. Everyone agreed that it would be most convenient if the sessions were held at Baker's house, since he was the only one of the four who lived alone. Finally, they would attempt to meet regularly, beginning sometime around early October, so as to coincide with the start of the PHL season.

Angus was touched by the fever of possibility. "We can hold ceremonies on game days prior to puck drop, then settle in and catch the game, you know, to see the fruits or our labours ripen before our very eyes—over beer, pizza, and wings, of course."

"Um, I don't want to dampen the mood, but while I admire your enthusiasm, I'm going to have to draw the line at watch parties," Baker said. "Truth is, I'm not inclined to watch games with friends—on the odd chance the Pines lose, you know?"

"But they're not gonna lose," Angus declared. "Not after we cast our victory spells on them."

"Listen, even first-place teams lose twenty to thirty times a year," Baker argued. "I get so bummed out during losses. So, while your sentiment comes from a good place, I must insist."

"Oh, alright then. No watch parties," Angus relented, then took solace in another chicken wing.

Conrad assessed Baker from across the table. "I'm OK with doing what you're proposing, but you should know that my parish priest would condemn the lot of us over this—me in particular."

Baker was wondering when the religion card would be played, surprised it hadn't been mentioned sooner. "I've been wrestling with the dilemma of defying church doctrine myself. I guess I was hoping the pagan angle wouldn't be an issue. It's a relief to know you're agreeable to my plan."

"Hey, it gives us an excuse to get together and play. I'll never pass up an opportunity to play."

Mas was idly watching Angus clean up the last of the wings and gathering up the crumbs from the nacho platter when he jumped up. "Hey, what time is it?"

Baker pulled back his sleeve. "Oops. It's 12:35."

"Ay caramba! We'd better pay up and get outside." Mas reached into his pocket and pulled out some bills. "Here's my contribution."

"Keep your money, Mas. The three of us will settle the bill. You go out to the parking lot and tell the driver that we're right behind you."

"Alright. Thanks, guys."

They split the bill three ways, leaving a generous tip for Dee Dee, then hurried toward the door. The place had emptied out considerably, and Baker thought of Sid sitting alone in his booth by the window. He looked back and saw that the table was vacant and tidied up, devoid of all evidence that anyone had ever been there. Then Baker scanned the stage, only to discover that sometime after their performance Sid must have quietly packed up the instruments and left for the night.

"Angus, did you happen to notice when Sid left?"

"You mean the guitar player? Uh, no, I didn't see a thing."

"Too bad. I would have liked to thank him again."

Once outside, they found Mas still waiting for the cab to arrive. Save for the ever-present mosquitoes, the night had turned quite pleasant, having cooled off since earlier in the evening. The group was feeling good, with lots to consider and look forward to on the heels of Baker's plan. It was Conrad who broke the spell.

"Hey, Mas, where did you tell the driver to pick us up—the Misty River or the Blue Beacon?"

Mas jerked his head around to read the marquee, as if to remind himself where they were. "Aw, shit! I forgot that we decided to come here *after* he dropped us off. He's probably waiting for us at the Beacon."

"Well, he's not gonna wait all night," Baker said, springing into action. "Let's get going, boys." He began to jog, with Angus close behind. Conrad, however, was resistant to such activity.

"Uh-uh. I'm not jogging anywhere right now."

Baker didn't flinch. "OK. You and Mas wait here. Angus and I will hustle over to the Beacon to meet the driver. We'll pick you up."

The two of them had barely arrived at the bridge when the cab met them on the road. The driver saw them first and touched his horn to get their attention.

"Hop in, guys."

They piled in, Baker taking the front seat and apologizing on behalf of the group as he explained the reason for the mix-up. "How did you know to drive in this direction?"

"Well, you gotta thank your buddy for that. He gave me a heads-up."

"Who?"

"A guy with an Australian accent and John Lennon glasses. I was waiting in the parking lot at the Beacon when this dude taps on my window and asks me if I'm there for a group of four guys. He's the one told me you'd be at the Misty River." The driver was about to pull the cab back onto the road when he remembered something. "Oh, and he asked me to give this to the guy named Baker. Is that you?" He held up two small objects.

At first Baker didn't fully comprehend what they were: a small packet containing a length of wound-up wire and a guitar pick with the words *Misty River* stamped on it.

"I take it he's a friend of yours?" the driver asked.

Baker looked at the guitar string and the plectrum in his hand, while St. Christopher stared at him from the dashboard and the not-a-dream-catcher hung from the rearview mirror. With his heart thumping and the words *spirit guide . . . spirit guide . . . spirit guide . . .* repeating in his brain, Baker turned to the driver.

"That was Sid. He's just someone we met at the Misty River tonight."

CHAPTER THREE
PERREAULT

Early September, 2019

"My grandfather—Papi Rene—turned ninety last week. He was born on August 29, 1929, two months to the day before the stock market crashed, leading to the Great Depression—a pretty ominous sign for any soul to begin life on this planet, wouldn't you think?"

Perreault Thoreau was seated at a table in the HMV staff room, sharing a birthday story with Conrad, Masaccio, and Angus. It was the first week of school, and the lunchtime crowd was noisy and energetic as teachers caught up with old friends and colleagues after the summer holidays and got acquainted with the new people on staff—Perreault being one of the latter.

"Yes, that could potentially suck," Conrad said.

Perreault continued with the story. "Yeah, so after living through almost a century of the greatest growth and fastest societal changes in history, do you know what he did to celebrate?"

"I'm gonna guess he did *not* take the family on some fabulous cruise," Conrad replied.

"You would be correct. We just settled for a nice intimate family get-together and went ten-pin bowling and wall climbing!"

"So, a ninety-year-old man chooses to go wall climbing?" Mas wondered aloud.

"In his younger days, Rene was a keen boulderer. He'd climb anything that posed a challenge: trees, fences, walls, rock cuts along roadsides—so he must have got it in his head to relive those glory days."

"Don't tell me he actually climbed the walls in the gym."

Perreault laughed at the thought. "Well, if hanging onto a ledge six inches off the ground fits the definition, then yeah, he was climbing the walls in the gym. They fitted him into a harness, and on the backside it had to be cinched up good and tight to support his little bum, but up front, boy, his junk was hanging pretty heavy. You had to be there to see it. Rene was having the time of his life, and we were in tears."

"Did he ever do any serious climbing," Conrad asked, "like scaling eight-thousand-metre peaks and such?"

"No, nothing like that. He was more into cycling, actually. He modelled himself after old-country Frenchmen who are born on the saddle and ride for hours every day. In fact, it was his idea for us to head out to the Maritimes for two weeks and ride around Nova Scotia and Cape Breton Island."

"That sounds like quite an adventure," Conrad observed. "Was that this year?"

"Yes. I'd just finished teachers college and was job hunting, applying at school boards and securing interviews. One day my grandfather suggested we get away and see a bit of the country. He planned for a trip out east, but not your average tour of the Maritimes. We were going to do our own 'Tour de Cape Breton,'" Perreault explained, putting the title in air quotes. "My mother would travel out there with us, serving as our support team from out of a van that Rene had purchased expressly for the trip. Everything was planned right down to the smallest detail. He didn't miss a beat. It was going to be my last great adventure before I 'turned pro.'"

"Your grandfather sounds like quite the character."

"You got that right. He likes to regale us with stories of the things he had witnessed firsthand in his lifetime. I guess the biggest one would've been his attendance at Toronto's Cup-clinching game six victory at Mighty Pines Coliseum in 1962."

"Holy shit," Mas blurted, impressed. "Your grandpa was there—in person—the last time the Pines won the Cup?"

"That's his claim. But then he's always been a huge Pines fan. Poor guy has lived through a lot of pain and heartbreak with that team. In fact, he has a favourite saying, a constant refrain: 'May the good Lord grant that I live long enough to witness another Pines' Clarence Cup.'"

"You've committed it to memory?"

"Yes. He's got it framed and hanging on the wall in his kitchen. A lady friend of his put it in needlepoint as a prayer." Perreault turned sentimental. "I tell you, if there's one overriding reason for me to want to see the Pines win the Cup, it's so Rene can live to experience it."

"I like that," Conrad said. "I'm going to write that down." He selected one of the many random pieces of paper strewn on the table and jotted down Papi Rene's saying, having Perreault repeat it back to him slowly and formally.

"I'll share this with Baker. What do you say, Mas? Maybe he can incorporate it into one of his song lyrics."

"Sure. Where is he anyway? Did he mention anything to anyone?"

"He said he had to scoot home to paint some exterior trim while the weather was good," Angus replied.

"Who's Baker?" Perreault asked.

"He's the fourth member of our band," Mas explained. "Lead vocalist who also plays rhythm guitar." Then he brought the subject back to Rene. "What else did your grandfather witness in person?"

"He's a big Blue Jays fan too. He was in attendance at Exhibition Stadium the night Dave Winfield killed the seagull. He was also at the ten-home-run game. And, of course, he was there a few years ago to see the greatest inning in baseball playoff history, the Bautista bat flip game . . . what else?" Perreault thought for a moment. "Oh, he saw Tiger Woods hit the greatest shot in Canadian Open history from the fairway bunker on eighteen at Glen Abbey."

"Man, he's like Forrest Gump," Mas observed.

"Hey, speaking of Forrest Gump," Conrad said, "did I ever tell you guys about my close encounter with Terry Fox?"

"Whoa," Angus blurted, "you met Terry Fox?"

"Meet him? No. I said a *close encounter*." Without skipping a beat, Conrad commenced to chronicling his story. "It was a gorgeous Saturday afternoon in July, and I was playing baseball with a group of friends. It was just my luck that one inning while I was behind the plate catching, I happened to get my face in the way of a wild swing. The end of the bat cracked me here, under my ear."

Perreault was first to make a diagnosis. "You were concussed?"

"To tell you the truth, a concussion never occurred to me. As I got up off the ground, I could feel that my bite was off, and my jaw hurt everytime I moved my head."

"Sounds painful."

"Not as painful as listening to my dad. My father was the master of 'I told you so.' You see, growing up he had no time for sports, being the product of a farming family in northeast Germany. So, when I took up baseball, football, hockey, track and field, wrestling, etcetera, etcetera, he unloaded on me about 'the needless risks involved when engaging in recreational sports.'"

"My dad was the same way!" Perrault laughed. "My parents wouldn't let me into contact sports until the high school football coach tried to recruit me to be the field goal kicker. But that's another story. Please, carry on with yours, Conrad."

"Not at all," Conrad objected. "You go ahead. Field goal kicker you say?"

"That's right. I was in grade nine, the first week of school. My friends and I were heading home at the end of the day, cutting across the practice field, when someone picked up a stray football and challenged me to kick a field goal."

As it happened, Perreault launched the ball, held on the hash mark at the thirty-five-yard line, on an arc that was high and true, to the back of the end zone. Watching from the sidelines was Mr. Dunn, the school's vice-principal, who coached the special teams. Mr. Dunn wasted no time in challenging Perreault to repeat the feat, moving back in five-yard increments. Three successful kicks later, when the ball cleared the uprights from midfield, he knew the team had its field goal kicker.

The problem was that Perreault's parents, Anna and Jean-Paul, had serious reservations about their kid's recruitment to the squad. Their apprehensions regarding the potential for injury were based on Jean-Paul's experience as a family doctor, having seen his share of contusions, sprains, and breaks in youngsters participating in sports. On top of it all, he was singularly proud of his kid's nose, calling it a gift to behold and especially striking when in profile. It was for that reason that Dr. Thoreau fairly forbid his child from engaging in any activity that could threaten the "health" of such a treasure, meaning that contact sports, hockey and football in particular, were out of the question. He would always suggest—in joking fashion, but serious all the same—that studying music and chess would provide excellent avenues to success, all the while helping to preserve, as Jean-Paul described it, "one's God-given handsomeness."

Both the head coach and the special teams coach made every effort to assure Mr. and Mrs. Thoreau that Perreault was, in fact, the best junior-age kicker in the school and, as such, would be essential to the team's success that year. The coaches admitted that it would be impossible for them to guarantee Perreault's safety, but in their experience, it was more likely that a student would suffer bumps and bruises negotiating the crowded hallways between classes than a kicker get injured during the relatively short junior football season. Jean-Paul was tempted to ask for the data on how many students had broken their noses negotiating the hazardous hallways between classes, but in the end it was Perreault's self-assurance and general determination to contribute to the football team that swayed Anna and Jean-Paul to give their consent. Good thing too, as it turned out, because by the end of the season, the junior boys' football team had its scoring leader—intact and unharmed—and what was originally expected to be a long, painful rebuilding year turned into one where the team posted a .500 record and squeaked into the playoffs—

"Hang on," Angus interrupted, confused. "Where's the part where you get hurt?"

"Oh, there's more to the story," Perreault assured him, then continued.

When the football season was over, a decent singing voice found Perreault in the school choir, which eventually led to a role as Joseph in the school's production of *Joseph and the Amazing Technicolor Dreamcoat*. During one of the rehearsals, the staging of a particular scene required that Pharaoh enter descending a staircase. The part of Pharaoh was played by Anthony Finocchio, the football team's quarterback, whose voice was strong on the field but comparatively weak on stage. He had won the role because of his physical stature more than anything else, being tall and dark, with a strikingly regal and pharaonic bearing. He also made a passable Elvis, a look perfect for the part. That day's rehearsal was the first time Anthony had come down the stairs in full Pharaoh regalia, so he was struggling to balance an Old Kingdom crown on his head and swish his feet under a heavy cloak. As he descended, the fabric of his cloak gathered underfoot. With four steps to go, he lost his balance, and instead of looking to land safely, he reached up to secure his crown. Poor Anthony would have crashed painfully onto the floor if not for Perreault who, standing nearby as Joseph, stepped forward to break his fall. In the process, Anthony's arms swung wildly, and the one holding the heavy crown came down and caught Perreault flush in the face. The snap was heard by everyone on stage. Unfortunately for Perreault, it was the crown that came away unscathed.

"So in the end, my prized schnozz became collateral damage in a musical theatre accident rather than a casualty of a collision on the football field," Perreault said with a smirk of irony, then dramatically turned sideways as if posing for an 8x10 glossy, to reveal an evident bump in an otherwise perfect Roman nose.

Mas made a show of assessing the new teacher's profile. "Well, in my opinion, you can rest assured: your God-given handsomeness still remains intact."

"Thanks, Masaccio. You are mighty kind," Perreault replied drolly.

"Hey, look at it this way:" Conrad offered. "At least you didn't have to suffer a bunch of 'I-told-you-so's' from your parents."

"That is true," Perreault conceded. "Now go on with your story—how much did you actually hurt yourself playing sports?"

"You mean other than my jaw? I broke my leg once in a hockey injury I sustained when my pea-brained linemate . . . um, well, you know, it's better if I tell the whole story." Not waiting for permission, Conrad ploughed ahead with his yarn. "The year I broke my leg I was scoring at will. I was on pace to exceed fifty goals."

"Wow, fifty goals? Get a load of Lightning Lambert here," Angus teased—comparing Conrad to the legendary Montreal forward who had been the first to tally fifty goals in a single PHL season.

"OK, so it was only house league hockey," Conrad admitted, "but fifty goals is fifty goals. And my left winger, Mr. Pea Brain, was matching me goal for goal; we were tearing up the league. Then, during a game late in the season, he and I were on an odd-man rush. He had the puck and skated toward me as he crossed the blue line. I was expecting him to do something creative, but no, he just wound up and took a slap shot, and slipped and fell—on me!—fracturing my tibia. That was the end of my season. I never did attain the fifty-goal plateau."

"*That* is a sad story," Angus concluded.

"I haven't told you the worst of it. To add insult to injury, a few weeks later I was checking the local paper for the house league standings, and I saw an article celebrating how that same pea brain was the league's only fifty-goal scorer!" This last detail was greeted by disbelief and laughter.

"That's a good one," Mas said. "But what about your close encounter with Terry Fox?"

"Alright . . . so, we go to emerg and the doctor says the X-rays show my jaw has been cracked in two places and would need to be wired shut."

"How complicated was the surgery?"

"More than I was expecting. I remember asking the doc if I'd be home by supper. Boy, the look he gave me; you'd think I had just told him I was screwing his wife. He said I'd be in hospital for *three days*.

"'You mean I'm sleeping here tonight?' I asked as my life passed before my eyes. So, they did the surgery—the date was Sunday, July 13, 1980. I wouldn't remember the date under normal circumstances. I'm not wired that way—no pun intended. I like to forget the embarrassing events in my life, and for me, breaking my jaw was one of them—especially since my father considered me a loser for it. But July 13 happened to be the day that Terry Fox ran through the city of Burlington on his way to Hamilton—it was day ninety-three of his Marathon of Hope. And what was I doing? I was out cold, having wires woven through my teeth. That's what I was doing when history was made; when a true Canadian hero passed through our lives."

Angus couldn't resist rubbing it in. "Wow, Conrad Widdershins is out cold while Terry Fox is making history across the street on his marathon tour. Now that *is* sad."

The mention of a "marathon tour" reminded Mas of something, so he turned to the rookie at the table. "Perreault, you didn't quite finish telling your cycling story. How did your 'Tour of Cape Breton' turn out?"

"Oh, right. Well, like I was saying, everything was planned, and we got in a good deal of training before we headed east . . ."

"I sense a 'but' coming," Conrad said.

"But . . . we were forced to cut it short. I needed to undergo a bit of treatment for a benign tumour that was discovered when we were midway through our cycling adventure."

"What? A tumour?" Angus was floored. "You mean, like, cancer?"

"Yes. I'd been experiencing some abdominal discomfort in the time leading up to our trip, but I brushed it off as something related to all the mileage I was doing. Then it got quite painful during the first week of the trip and absolutely unbearable during the second week. I checked into a hospital in Halifax to get a medical opinion. Next thing you know, we were packing up and driving straight back to Toronto to have the offending growth excised."

"What kind of cancer was it?"

"Oh, I had to have a fallopian tube removed," Perreault said matter-of-factly. There was a moment of uneasy silence, which she broke with a smile. "But they let me keep the other one! And not in a jar, either, for all the doctor and I joked about it."

CHAPTER FOUR

FIREWORKS

Tuesday, September 3 – Monday, September 9

While the first week of September witnessed the fresh faces of school-age children returning to classrooms across the land, it was the weekend that saw the pride of Canada reflected in the face of this country's newest tennis sensation as nineteen-year-old Mississauga native Bianca Andreescu defeated Serena Williams, the grande dame of the sport, to win the US Open Women's Tennis Championship. In the process Andreescu became Canada's first tennis Grand Slam singles title winner.

In Washington DC, Donald Trump was the self-professed "orange face" when his Energy Department rescinded the Obama-era regulation that would have phased out incandescent light bulbs. Trump declared that fluorescent lighting was bad and that it made him look orange. So said the man who had been mocked with names like "Orange Julius" and the "Angry Creamsicle."

The staff room door swung open with purpose, and Baker swept past the mailboxes, recycling bins, kitchenette counter, and copy machine, producing a vortex of energy that lifted loose paper products and even caused a few heads to turn in his wake. He was making a beeline for the table where his bandmates typically gathered to chat and discuss the previous night's sporting events, and sometimes other less pressing worldly matters. He whooshed past one of the new teachers on staff—who was standing at the photocopier—without even acknowledging her, but something pleasant lodged in his subconscious, and it was only later that he identified it as the whiff of apples and cinnamon.

"Emergency band session tonight!"

Because it was Monday morning of the second week of the school year, Baker's announcement was unexpected and was greeted with different reactions. Mas, initially caught off guard by the sudden directive, recognized an inconvenience when he heard one. Conrad's reaction was one of consternation. Angus simply grinned, as if it was a birthday surprise, or he had just woken up to an unexpected snow day.

"Really, Baker?" Mas replied. "The Pines' regular season doesn't start for another month. I don't think we need to panic yet."

Conrad's response was more to the point, "Damn you, Baker—you and your short notice."

Baker would not be put off so easily. "Yeah, sure. I know it's inconvenient, but Pines training camp starts this weekend, and we have to try and influence these negotiations with Ricky Randall. It's probably not a stretch to say this entire season is gonna turn out to be inconvenient for us. So, you guys remember how to get to my place?"

"Hang on a minute," Mas said. "Have we even agreed to this impromptu 'band session'?"

"What's the problem? We're barely two weeks into the semester. Your workloads can't be all that heavy."

"You might be right about that," Conrad admitted. "There's not much going on presently, but some of us have family obligations." He then saw the dismay in Baker's previously highly-charged face. "Look, I'm happy to jam with the band, but I would appreciate a bit of advance warning, that's all."

"Conrad's right, Baker," Mas said. "Can we hold off until maybe next week? I'm sure Kyle Bulac and Ricky Randall can settle things without our help."

Baker was almost pouting by that point. "Yeah, that's what we've been saying since July. That's what we said about Addy Brouwer last year, all the way up until December first."

"Well, if you insist on doing this tonight, it's going to have to be here at school," Conrad said in compromise.

"Ohh . . . I don't know," Baker said. "I was planning on heading home early today. I've been putting off painting my exterior doors for a year now."

"But that's what weekends are for," Angus noted.

Baker shook his head. "Nah, it's supposed to rain all weekend."

"So you're telling us you'll be busy at home after school?" Conrad said.

"Yes. That's why I can't meet here in the music room today," Baker replied.

"Then how the hell were you planning on hosting us at your place tonight if you're so gaw-dam busy?" Conrad replied, logically.

Baker was caught short. "I . . . I guess I didn't think it through . . . completely."

"Let's talk about it at lunch," Mas said. "We'll figure something out for next week." Seeing Baker's disappointment, he tried to reassure him. "Don't worry. Randall will get signed before training camp. You'll see."

FIREWORKS

The warning bell rang, and everyone made for the door and into the bustling hallway, heading to their respective assignments. Baker trailed behind, trying to figure out where he'd gone wrong in his plans. As he opened the staff room door, he felt the presence of another person behind him, so he politely held it open and glanced over his shoulder, coming face to face with a face he'd never really taken note of yet. It was the same person who had been at the photocopier when he first entered the room. She gave him an effervescent smile and leaned in close—at least that's what he thought, until he discovered she was only adjusting the shoulder strap of her work bag.

"I agree with Masaccio" she said. "Kyle Bulac won't repeat the mistake he made with Addy Brouwer last year." Then she leaned in close for real this time. "Randall will get signed."

She capped her statement with a smile of assurance as Baker caught a scent of cinnamon and spice, but not for long, because in a flash she was gone, heading down the hall in the other direction. She was quickly swept up in the rush of students on their way to their first-period class, leaving Baker to wonder who the hell she was and how she had so quickly dispelled his concerns regarding contracts and salary caps.

A few hours later, when classes dismissed for lunch, no sooner had the last student stepped out the door of Baker's art room than Angus stepped in. He looked hungry, which was not unexpected, but he also looked anxious, which was.

"Angus! To what do I owe this pleasure?"

"Your call for an emergency band session this morning got me thinking about our plans for this season."

"OK." Baker shouldered the strap of his lunch box. "Let's go to the staff room. We can walk and talk. Where's your lunch?"

"I just brought a couple of energy bars—ate 'em during first period. I was starving. What'd you bring?"

Baker made an effort to recall what he'd packed. "A tuna sandwich, a banana, an apple, some cheese curds, and crackers. Maybe a yogurt too."

"Sounds dee-lish," Angus said and left it at that. Any other day he would have inquired as to which of the lunch items Baker might care to dispense with, but presently he seemed too preoccupied.

As the two teachers negotiated the crowded hallways, they discussed the Toronto Mighty Pines, although there was no mention of the players or the management. No, this Pines talk dealt solely with magic, and the misgivings Angus had about the methods Baker was proposing they employ to influence the team's fortunes this season—as if casting musical spells was somehow underhanded, even unethical. Baker was caught off guard by his friend's concerns and chose to make light of them, even downplaying the significance of their planned enterprise.

"If you're expecting some weird, hardcore magic, you have nothing to fear. I anticipate us starting slow and taking things one day at a time. If anything, it'll be very amateurish at best." It hurt to have to describe it that way, but he didn't want to lose a member of the band before they had even met for their first session.

The staff room was already filling up when they entered. Masaccio was there, seated at a table close to the kitchen counter and the microwave, waiting for his turn on the appliance to nuke a frozen dinner. Because of the secretive nature of their conversation, Baker and Angus opted for a table further removed from the rest, at the far end of the room by the broken photocopier. Baker motioned for Mas to join them when he was done heating his food, which he did a few minutes later, gingerly carrying an overheated tray of butter chicken by the edges with the tips of his fingers. Conrad, who had just entered the staff room, was close behind, toting a foot-long sub and bottle of carbonated water.

Mas set the tray down to cool, allowing Angus to enjoy the aroma.

"Mmm, that smells good."

"I'm willing to share if you can find a utensil."

Angus took a quick look around. "Baker, you got a fork in your lunch box?"

Baker pulled out a plastic teaspoon. "Just this for my yogurt."

"That'll do." Angus took the spoon, scooped a hunk of saucy chicken from Masaccio's tray, and shovelled it into his mouth, then promptly let it drop onto the table.

"Ahh . . . That's hot!"

"Jesus, you're gross," Conrad said, passing Angus some napkins that were wrapped with his sub.

"Careful," Mas warned. "I think that microwave is set too high. It tends to overheat stuff."

Baker, meanwhile, got everyone up to speed on the topic of discussion. Then he addressed Angus directly, trying to assuage his fears. "You know, it's not like this sort of thing hasn't been done before. For example, back in the seventies, Whitey Kilpatrick used pyramid power during the Pines playoff run."

"And don't forget the Lucky Loonie," Conrad added, having unwrapped his sandwich too carelessly and was now tucking stray pieces of lettuce, tomato, and green olives back into the bun, "The one that was embedded at centre ice at the Olympics in Salt Lake City."

"Exactly. Let's not kid each other," Baker declared. "Athletes and coaches are always looking to benefit by tapping into the mystical forces of nature."

Reluctantly, Angus agreed. "I guess you're right."

"The difference here is that none of us have any direct access or connection to the team. We are simply arm's-length fans doing what we can to help the cause." Baker regarded the various lunch items on the table before him, then reached out and repositioned the slightly bruised banana on a diagonal toward Angus, as if moving a chess piece to another square on the board.

"You sure?" Angus said, his eyes brightening.

"Yeah. It's too ripe for me."

"Thanks." Angus hungrily peeled the fruit and bit off half, then spoke through the mush. "I know our cause is a good one, but all the same, I'd like to keep this kinda quiet, you know."

"Yes, of course," Baker assured him, wincing at the sight. "No one outside our group of four needs to know about our activities. In fact, I'm pretty certain that's what we agreed upon last month at the Misty River, didn't we?"

Conrad smirked in amusement at Angus's fears. "Oh, we'll be sure to keep this quiet, because if the Pines miraculously win the Cup, we could be implicated as the masterminds behind the scandal of the century."

Masaccio laughed. "We might be accused of being a cult of fans who resorted to black magic to influence games during the Clarence Cup playoffs."

"Just imagine, the PHL conducting an investigation," Conrad said, looking up as if at an imaginary headline. "Commissioner Stetson's Inquiry into the use of Occult Practices Intended to Influence Team Athletic Performance."

"Holy shit, that sounds kind of ominous," Angus observed, his apprehension renewed.

"Don't worry, Angus. They're just kidding," Baker assured him. "What we're doing is no different than bringing in a motivational speaker to pump up your boys' volleyball team before a big game. Or maybe you arrange with Conrad here to hold special prayer services before games."

"In fact, the football team actually does that," Conrad admitted. "Part of the pre-game routine is a fifteen-minute prayer service I hold for them in the chapel."

"But that's cheating!" Baker teased. "How dare you call on otherworldly forces to help guide the football team to victory?"

"There's your front-page story," Mas said. It was his turn to hold up both hands as if reading the headline. "Sports scandal hits HMV: Chaplain Wiederschoen banned from team sports."

"And football team forfeits every win that was the direct result of his prayer services," Baker added.

Mas laughed. "You'll be ostracized, like Ben Johnson at the Seoul Olympics."

"Don't you mean *unfairly* ostracized?" Conrad asked.

"There was nothing unfair about it," Mas replied. "Ben Johnson was rightfully disgraced. He got what he had coming to him." He noted the contrary expression on Conrad's face. "You don't agree?"

"Dear, dear Masaccio Clementi, I thought you knew me better than that."

Mas sat up straight and cupped both hands around his mouth. "Everybody, listen up! Conrad's gonna tell us why we Canadians should be proud of Ben Johnson."

"Before you start," Angus said, "please remind me . . . who's Ben Johnson?"

"What do you mean, 'Before I start'? What makes you think I'm going to start in on something?"

"Because Mas said so. He announced it just now."

"Well, the only thing I'll say is that Ben Johnson was at the centre of both the greatest and saddest of Olympic moments for Canada. And frankly, I'm tired of hearing people shit on the guy."

Baker was used to Conrad's alternative takes on history. "Conrad, you're the best. It's no wonder they call you Mr. One-Eighty. Next thing we know you're going to convince us Judas and Hitler have gotten a bum rap."

"Actually, I do have an argument in defence of Judas—but Hitler, not so much."

Angus laughed. "Leave it to our man, Conrad frickin' Widdershins, to defend Judas."

"Jesus, Angus, I wish you'd stop butchering my name," Conrad growled. "It's Wiederschoen—*Vee*-di-shen—not Widdershins."

Out of respect for his friend Angus relented. "OK, OK. Conrad frickin' *Vee*-der-shen. Happy? Now, tell me about Ben Johnson."

Conrad sighed. "It's a long story. Suffice to say, Ben Johnson won the gold medal in the one hundred metres at the 1988 Seoul Olympics, vanquishing the mighty Carl Lewis in the process."

"I remember that vividly," Mas said. "His achievement was awesome—for a couple days, anyway."

"Yes, I can attest that for forty-eight hours there was no prouder nation on earth. It was the greatest Olympic moment in Canadian history." Conrad looked at everyone in silence, savouring the memory. "Then two days later it was revealed Johnson had tested positive for steroids."

"Oh, yuck!" Angus said. "That sounds monumentally shitty."

"You don't know the half of it. It was like being told the moon landing was a hoax. Every Canadian felt deceived, duped, and angry. Everything and everyone came crashing down: Johnson, along with his coach Charlie Francis, and the entire Canadian system of developing world-class sprinters. And to this day, Ben Johnson is an outcast, a leper, and a joke."

"So, what's your point?" Mas asked. "They cheated and justice was served."

"My point is twofold," Conrad said. "Number one, the people in this country can be oh so holier-than-thou about some things. Get off your butt, they'll say, and climb that ladder to success, but for heaven's sake, don't let me see your knickers on the way up. Canadians demand the sausage, but they don't want to see how it's made."

"Don't talk about food," Angus complained. "All I've had to eat today is a couple of protein bars and Baker's bruised banana."

Mas looked up. "Baker's bruised banana? Um, you may want to keep that to yourself."

"Oh, yeah, heh, heh."

Baker moved another chess piece toward Angus; this time it was his apple.

"What's this?"

"Mutsu."

"Bless you."

Conrad slid the other half of his veggie sub across as well. "Eat this . . . and shut up about it."

Angus set the apple to one side and dug into the sandwich while Conrad continued with his argument. "The second reason Canadians were so quick to condemn Johnson and Francis is that they played the wrong sport."

"What do you mean?" Baker asked.

"Simple: Ben Johnson was a sprinter. If he played hockey, Canadians would have given him a pass."

"Oh, c'mon," Baker said. "You can't believe we'd accept our hockey players if they took PEDs."

"I'm not talking about drugs, per se. I am referring to cheating in general. You're telling me you didn't cheer when 'Cementhead' Selwyn took the lumber to the wrists of Boston's Vernon Paxon back in '93, effectively putting him out of the playoffs? Selwyn became nothing less than a fuckin' hero over that move."

Masaccio looked at Baker. "Oh, jeez, I guess he's right. Boston was up in that series until Paxon had to sit out the rest of it."

"Right." Conrad continued. "So I ask you now, what's worse: circumventing the rules by assaulting an opponent who is threatening to defeat you on the ice, or by taking an injection every three months that allows you to recover more effectively after workouts?"

"That's like comparing snowballs to hand grenades," Baker countered. "Slashing is something we accept as a part of the game. But taking steroids, well, that's stepping over the line."

"Maybe, but just hear me out. What if, despite years of training and competing, you have never quite attained the podium? Then one day you look in the mirror and see your prime years fading away. Someone you trust offers the poison pill as an option.

Feeling the pressure, you decide that making this personal sacrifice allows you to serve God and country the best way you can."

"I get it," Mas exclaimed. "What's to stop the family of an eighteen-year-old kid who hits a hundred on the radar gun from choosing to forestall inevitable elbow problems, sacrifice a year of his career and get the surgery done, knowing he'll come back stronger?"

"Thanks for making my point," Conrad said. "Maybe it's just a question of degree. Whether George Daly skates in the Clarence Cup finals on a broken ankle or soldiers are willing to die to defend their country, why is it so hard to believe that some super-patriotic athlete, a wannabe hero, wouldn't be willing to give up a limb in the name of national glory? What's to stop a track athlete, say, from having their legs amputated and then fitted with prosthetic blades, especially if they're convinced it offers a better chance of success?" Conrad leaned in and dropped his voice. "I don't want to sound like a conspiracy theorist, but what are the chances that certain countries are actually supporting and sponsoring such programmes?"

Mas shook his head, put off by the thought of it all. "Man, that all sounds so creepy. I prefer the good ol' days when our Canadian hockey heroes were scoring goals against the Soviets in the Summit Series."

"There you go again," Angus complained, "talking about stuff that happened before my time."

Baker nodded, feeling a kinship with him. "Yeah, me too, but at least we know the song, right?" He nudged Angus and then started in on the opening line of The Tragically Hip's "Fireworks" under his breath. Angus instantly recognized the musical reference and joined his friend, upping the volume in the process (the added flatness of his tone doing nothing to dampen their overall enthusiasm).

Singing about how few events in life can compete with the time when we first experience the spark of young love, not even the momentous occasion of witnessing a certain historic goal in 1972, they were joined on the next line by Masaccio and Conrad, perfectly timed. Then, like drunken sailors, all four combined to make a raucous noise of the second verse, after which much laughter and backslapping ensued—at least that was the plan, until they were halted in their intended revelry by a lone voice carrying on into the chorus. Effortless, sweet, simultaneously innocent and experienced, it displayed a fullness that suggested practice but with a raw upper edge.

It was one of the new teachers on staff, the same one who, just that morning, had assured Baker that the contract negotiations with Ricky Randall were nothing to worry about. She had been seated at the next table, intrigued by the conversation about Ben Johnson and cheating in sport, when she dovetailed her voice so seamlessly into the verses that none of them noticed until they stopped singing.

"Hey, why'd you stop? Don't know the words?"

Despite being left hanging, she wasn't the least bit fazed or put off. It seemed that to her it was completely normal to sing in public, and anyone who knew the words was naturally welcome to join in (at least, those were the rules where she came from).

Conrad had caught the unmistakeable glint of gold in the pan of water and riverbed gravel. He alone recognized that they were in the presence of a higher power, a considerable talent whose voice could possibly elevate their band to new levels of achievement. It was not operatic by any estimation, but nevertheless revealed its pre-eminence in twelve words, barely two lines of the chorus. He was not about to let this opportunity pass them by.

"Perreault, who knew you possessed such a brilliant singing voice? Come join us."

Conrad's comment caused Perreault Thoreau to suddenly turn coy. For Baker it was the first time he put a face to the name—so *that* was Perreault, and to think it only took him a week to make the connection. As he watched her response to Conrad's remark, it was as if a veil was lifted from his eyes. He wasn't sure whether her cheeks turned pink before she dropped her gaze, of if she looked down first, and then blushed. Either way, he was smitten; the girl had just turned his legs to jelly. Good thing he was sitting down. But not for long because, in a stroke of bad timing, the clock on the wall indicated he was late for an appointment with a student. Baker got up from the table and said his goodbyes, confirming with everyone that band practice had been rescheduled for next week. As he did, he made momentary but heavenly eye contact with Ms. Thoreau, who was standing between him and Conrad. There was that faint scent again, of cinnamon or potpourri or something. He reluctantly turned to leave, concentrating on his movements to ensure they were smooth and graceful.

Conrad repeated his invitation to Perreault, inviting her to sit down. He had a penchant for occasionally addressing people in a manner that evoked conversation heard in a Viennese café during its Golden Age. Dawdling in the vicinity of the mailboxes, Baker caught a bit of the dialogue.

"Young lady, I'm sure you are acquainted with the genius of Joni Mitchell, but have you ever experienced the aural splendour of B. B. Gabor?"

Then he heard Angus contribute something silly yet humorous, eliciting a burst of laughter from those around the table. He allowed himself to steal a look back at the group, his gaze lingering on Perreault a little too long, causing him to nearly collide with Jackie Klein coming into the staff room. Jackie, who taught grade nine and ten girls' healthy, active living, was all bubbles and vivacity and had a well-honed rapport with Baker.

"Eyes front, Mr. Brooks. Heaven forbid you get in an accident on the way to class. Then who's gonna show your kids how to mix primary colours?"

"Well, it sure as hell won't be you. You're too busy teaching girls how to speed walk to the mall."

"Ooh, feeling a little combative today, huh? I like that." Catching a glimpse of collarbone under Baker's open shirt, Jackie was reminded of something. "Hey, when are you planning to pose for your class? I want to make sure I have an excuse to drop in that day."

"That would be for the life drawing unit, which is not until next week, and you know you're always welcome to pop by my classroom; no excuse required. Right now, I'd better get a move on, though."

"Leaving so soon?"

"Afraid so. See you around, Jackie. Have a nice lunch."

"See ya, Baker."

He smiled at Jackie and continued through the door, but not before sneaking one last peek beyond her to where Perreault was now deep in conversation with Conrad. Newly inspired, Baker mentally mapped out his evening. Of one thing he was certain: tonight, he'd sit down and finally finish putting words to that song he was working on. Paul Simon? Move over. Ron Sexsmith? Step aside. Baker Brooks was in the house, and he was presently transforming something by the Proclaimers into a musical spell that just might serve to change the Pines' fortunes.

Moving through the hallway, Baker found his step to be significantly lighter, the few clouds of care that had been hovering over him just a minute ago suddenly vaporized. Life in general carried much more promise. He was Francois Toulour, the "Night Fox" in *Ocean's Twelve*, kicking up his heels after nimbly slipping through the museum's heavy security laser field on his way to stealing the Faberge egg. Baker negotiated the crowded corridor, and though it wasn't exactly a laser field, his steps were precise and efficient, like he was on one of those moving walkways in an airport terminal, allowing him to glide across a great expanse effortlessly. This particular sidewalk of destiny had unexpectedly brought him face to face with the muse, and her name was Perreault.

CHAPTER FIVE
GO GREEN!

Oh, green, go green, it helps to get lucky in June
Oh, green, go green, we hope Lady Luck smiles on you.

Friday, September 13 – Wednesday, September 25

Among the stories swirling around the Toronto Mighty Pines at this time of year, of great interest were the faces of those attending training camp—or more to the point, those who were not in attendance. Star winger Ricky Randall was notably absent, having yet to agree on a contract with the organization. Another question still unanswered was whether team management would name a captain, and if so, when?

Twenty-four hours later the announcement that Coney Nation had been waiting all summer to hear was made: the aforementioned Randall had settled on a deal amounting to eight figures over a six-year term. The Pines now boasted a foursome of Mason Andrews, Gianni Valentino, Ricky Randall, and Addy Brouwer, who, combined, would command nearly half of what was available to the team within the PHL's salary cap structure. If nothing else, it put the team's financial status on precarious footing, with little to no flexibility for additional roster moves.

In other news, TIME Magazine published a photo of Prime Minister Justin Trudeau, taken in 2001, cavorting in brownface at an Arabian Nights–themed dinner party. The news was shocking to those who saw him as someone who espoused inclusivity and tolerance. Trudeau responded to the news by making a public apology. In the meantime, federal party leaders continued on the campaign trail as the days counted down to the federal election on October 21.

Finally, red faces abounded within the Mighty Pines organization when breaking news out of Baton Rouge, Louisiana revealed that star centre Mason Andrews was facing a charge of disorderly conduct following an incident last May on the Louisiana State University campus. Andrews was alleged to have been involved in what was described as a prank staged on the main quadrangle serving the girls' dormitories.

When a number of young men in various states of undress were approached by campus police, they refused to cooperate, all the while making derogatory comments and directing lewd gestures toward the officers. For his part, Andrews admitted to an "error in judgment" by keeping the club in the dark about the charge. General Manager Kyle Bulac did not comment on whether the incident would impact the player's candidacy to be the Pines' next captain.

It had to be a personal best. Baker never left school for the day much earlier than 4:00 pm, but he was out the door with the kids at the 2:30 bell, and seeing that the dashboard clock read 2:38 as he was pulling out of the HMV parking lot, he reached over and gave himself a pat on the back—and got a honk for his hubris from a passing car in the next lane.

With a list of things to do before the others were scheduled to arrive (including a stop at his favourite "wheelhouse"—Babe's Pizza and Wings—followed by a Sugar Watson's stop for a box of coffee and a dozen doughnuts), Baker was glad to have beaten the end-of-school-day gridlock. Good thing, too, because both errands took longer than expected, so by the time he pulled into his driveway, the carpooling trio of Conrad, Masaccio, and Perreault had already arrived and were climbing out of Conrad's Subaru wagon.

Baker parked beside them. "You're early!" he exclaimed as he got out of his vehicle, armed with junk food.

"Well, ya gotta start on time, ya know," Mas replied, in a failed attempt at sounding like Kayden Koch.

"You should really work on that K.K. impersonation, Mas."

"Need a hand with anything?" Perreault asked as Baker balanced a stack of two pizzas and a box of doughnuts.

"Sure. You can grab the coffee in the front seat there. Thanks, Perreault."

Mas came over and took the doughnuts off the top of the heap while Conrad took the pizzas.

"Now I've got nothing to carry," Baker complained.

"Shut up and open the front door," Conrad instructed.

Baker led them into the house, cleared space on the kitchen counter for the food items, then got busy setting things up in the adjoining living room. "I'm just going to organize myself in here."

GO GREEN!

"You go ahead," Conrad said. "Mas and I will take Perreault outside for a tour of your property."

"Great idea. Go and enjoy what's left of the beautiful day."

It was late September, and a full two weeks had passed since the morning Baker had burst into the staff room calling for an emergency band practice. Now the day had finally arrived, and none too soon. Despite the relief he felt with the news that Ricky Randall and the Pines had come to an agreement over the terms of his contract, the fact remained that October 2 and the start of the season was just around the corner. His sense of unease was exacerbated by the shocking news of Mason Andrews' disorderly conduct charge. Whereas some considered the story humorous, Baker saw it as something that could potentially sabotage the club's season. And yet he was aware that such events were entirely out of his control, so if there was any consolation to be gleaned it would come from the knowledge that the band was finally meeting at his place to perform its first ceremonial "gig." Now *this* was a Pines-related event that he *did* have some control over, which is not to say that Baker knew anything about hosting a coven event—because he didn't. He'd simply resigned himself to the reality that he would probably have to wing it for their first gathering. At least the damn song was finished.

Ah, yes, the song. It turned out to be a bigger challenge than he'd anticipated. Baker had lost considerable sleep in trying to complete his modified version of the Proclaimers' "Oh Jean," which he retitled "Go Green!" But his responsibilities didn't end there because he also needed to make sure the other members of the band knew their parts as well. Of course, these considerations were in addition to his primary obligations as a high school teacher, which included the daily prep work of lesson planning and the ever-present ball and chain that was his marking of tests, quizzes and assignments.

In truth, there was one more reason he was glad to have completed his work on the song, and her name was Perreault Thoreau. The high that Baker had experienced after their introduction two weeks earlier hadn't faded much and was actually fortified by his anticipation of hosting that day's session. You see, more than anything at that moment in his personal life, Baker wanted to better acquaint himself with Ms. Thoreau. The problem was, he never saw her much during the usual workday, and when by some good fortune they did get the opportunity to exchange pleasantries, it was always in the company of others and, therefore, came across as merely a contribution to the general group dialogue—there was nothing personal or immediate about it. Another complication was Angus. Baker had become aware of a musical bond building between Conrad and Perreault, and it was evident that Angus had manoeuvred himself into the mix, ostensibly as the drummer for the songs Conrad was proposing that Perreault have a go at. And then there was the problem of Baker's inclination for taking a less aggressive approach when it came to his romantic pursuits—which is where the song came in.

Since Perreault was slated to sing backup for their performance of "Go Green!" Baker expected that she would inevitably need some input from him along the way, at which point they would, side by side, iron out the rhythm and tempo and harmonies and such. In that intimate setting, he hoped they might begin to get to know each other better. All things considered, it was the mere prospect of her being present and participating in the band's activities at his place which served to infuse a strange giddiness in him.

Baker's "place" was about twenty-five minutes north of HMV, in the next county, where the paved roads turned to gravel, and the mixture of aggregate from one of the many local quarries would, depending on the season, cause one's vehicle to perennially be either blanketed in gritty dust or splashed with slimy muck. For Baker the real value of the place was in the property—three gently rolling acres of parklike trees and grass and rocks, and all the privacy a person could ask for. The house itself was a modest two-bedroom bungalow, nothing to boast about, but a generous kitchen opened up to a living room with a vaulted ceiling, which (because Baker hadn't gotten around to fully furnishing it) was a convenient place for the band to set up and practise in. Angus's drum kit could stay put, along with an old electronic keyboard and stand that Janet Sax, HMV's music teacher, had generously donated to them last year. An IKEA "Kivik" loveseat was placed off to one side of the living room, leaving space for a round faux wood table that Baker had acquired when the school's librarian, Lawrence Wynn, needed to replace the old library furniture with new items that the school board had issued. The only plant life was a potted rubber tree—an old housewarming gift from his mom that had somehow thrived and was now dominating one corner of the room. Any other semblance of greenery came courtesy of the view through the windows, the property having no lack of mature maples, white pine, fir, and cedars. Some books and binders were piled neatly in one corner along with a stack of empty cardboard boxes, the kind that had previously contained bundles of letter-size paper used in bulk quantities by the staff at school. One of the walls displayed a collection of framed prints that Baker had picked up for cheap when his university bookstore had its annual print and poster sale. (Back then he had been partial to the works of the French Impressionists and so came away with a Seurat, a Degas, and a couple of Monets.)

Being a true neophyte where coven rituals were concerned, Baker nevertheless hoped to create an environment dedicated to the success of the Toronto Mighty Pines through an atmosphere of positive moral support. To that end he had draped a Mighty Pines flag across the library table, upon which were displayed two large coffee table books. One was an old favourite about the Clarence Cup. The other dealt with the history of the Pines franchise. By sheer luck, while rummaging through his supply room at school, he found stored away in a box four little wire-and-plaster sculptures of generic hockey players that a few of his grade nine students had made one year. He brought them home and propped them up around the table as well. In the centre of it all was the cutest little replica Clarence Cup, all shiny silver plastic and not more than six inches tall. Baker did the best he could to give it prominence, setting it on a small gift-box pedestal and surrounding it with four pillar candles, each positioned to coincide with the compass points. (Baker had heard somewhere that there was some significance to this, so in his ignorance he figured it wouldn't hurt to model that practice.)

"Nice table, Baker," Conrad observed. The group had come back inside from touring the yard, bringing Angus in with them, who had just arrived on his own. "Did you get this from Lawrence?"

"Yup. One of the best freebie acquisitions I've ever made—that and Janet's keyboard, of course. Hi, Angus, how was the drive?"

Angus had a cheek full of sunflower seeds and was spitting shells into a used coffee cup. He was more interested in the food on Baker's kitchen counter. "Pizza, doughnuts and beer! When you put on a spread, you don't hold back, do you?"

"Don't give me too much credit. I didn't get a bag of Spitz for you. Barbecue, right?"

"No worries, man, but if you must know, I'm doing dill pickle flavour today. Time for pizza, though." With that Angus spat a mouthful of seeds into his cup and set it down by the drum kit. Baker watched with Perreault, mesmerized by the grossness of it all, then shook himself out of it and made a general announcement to the group. "OK, everyone, don't be shy. Help yourselves to pizza, and I've stocked the fridge with beverages. Coffee's on the counter there. And, Mas, I put out a bottle of wine if you're interested."

"Thanks, Baker, don't mind if I do," Mas replied, then hesitated. "... It's not a merlot, is it?"

"No. But, remind me, why does merlot get such a bad rap?"

"Have you not seen *Sideways*?"

"I have, actually, but I didn't grasp why it was so intolerable to Paul Giamatti."

"It shouldn't have been," Conrad said. "Not the original French version of it, anyway. But after the grape came to California, it apparently became mass produced and mass consumed and in the process earned a reputation as a bland wine. The movie didn't help either."

"No shit. Would you know if the Niagara version has the same rep?" Baker asked.

"I wouldn't. You'd have to try some for yourself—or ask Gabe the GOAT," Conrad said, making reference to the fact that retired hockey great Gabe Wozniak had recently opened up a winery in Niagara-on-the-Lake.

"Sure, and then we'd know if the Great *Woz* makes great *wine*."

Conrad and Masaccio responded with simultaneous groans as Baker slipped away to chat with Perreault and Angus, doing the rounds to make sure his guests lacked for nothing. Angus had his head in the refrigerator, checking out the beer selection. He picked one out for himself and another for Baker.

"Here, have a beer with me."

Baker took the bottle from Angus and, despite it being a twist cap, took advantage of a vintage bottle opener he had mounted to the wall beside the fridge. There was the remnant of a hockey stick on display next to it, and Baker tapped the newly opened bottle on the stick before taking a drink.

"What's that?" Angus inquired.

"It's a Grady Sykes hockey stick—a broken one. It was gifted to me by somebody I used to teach with. He knew a Pines assistant trainer who salvaged one of Grady's discarded sticks after a game."

"Did you notice any blood on it? Because Sykes likely broke it over someone's head." Angus said, and got a look of disgust from Baker. "Never mind. Explain the business of tapping your beer on it."

"Oh, that. It's just something for luck, you know."

"OK, then. For luck!" Angus tapped his own bottle, already half empty, on the stick.

After everyone had eaten their fill of pizza, Conrad approached the unopened box of doughnuts with Mas and Angus in tow.

"You know, I believe a person's choice of doughnut reveals a lot about them," he said. "I'm sure Sigmund Freud would have had an opinion on it, what with his psychoanalysis of everything that moved."

"Well then, let's do some psychoanalyzing ourselves," Mas said with a wink. He removed the lid from the box and took inventory of its contents. "We have two honey crullers, a chocolate dipped, two sour cream glazed—"

"Mmm . . . I've got dibs on that chocolate dipped one," Angus declared, "If no one else minds."

"That's interesting," Conrad observed. "I kind of thought you'd go for the biggest of the bunch."

"No need. Considering that we're looking at a box of twelve, and there's only five of us, we will each get at least two doughnuts . . . and some of us three. Therefore I chose based on the tasty scale as opposed to sheer mass."

"Listen to you," Perreault laughed, "doing the doughnut math in your head like that. I'm impressed."

"Let's keep going here," Conrad said. "Who's next?"

Perreault took a sour cream glazed, while Baker indulged his inner child and opted for Mister Sprinkles. Mas settled for a cruller.

"And what about you, Conrad?" Baker said. "What does Herr Doktor Freud choose?"

"When it comes to doughnuts, I don't discriminate. I'm happy with almost any type—except maybe a dutchie."

"What the hell is a dutchie?" Angus asked.

"Let me see . . . how does one describe a dutchie?" Conrad scanned the area, then he eyed the cardboard boxes in the corner and pointed at them. "You see those boxes there? Take one, fill it with dough, add some raisins, and dip it in glaze. There's your signature dutchie."

"C'mon now, they aren't so bad," Mas objected.

"I think it's the raisins," Perreault said. "Raisins in baked stuff makes it seem too much like fruitcake, and you know how people feel about fruitcake."

"My mom makes great fruitcake," Angus said with pride as he picked out an apple fritter, plopped it on a saucer, and brought it over to Conrad. "Here, allow me to make the decision for you." He hovered over the library coffee table, taking a close look at how it was decorated. "Baker, your table is impressive. I'm actually excited about holding our first Mighty Pines, uh . . . what? Ritual? Ceremony? Service?"

"All of the above," Baker said.

"What is it properly called, though?"

"I guess it's a ceremony—or a ritual. They both work," Baker acknowledged. "By the way, did you all bring your copies of the song? If not, I have some extras."

He was heartened to see everyone had come prepared.

"Well, then, it looks like this band is ready to perform some magic," Mas declared.

Conrad rose to his feet and motioned for them to huddle up. "Gather 'round everybody. I propose we begin with a prayer."

"What did you have in mind?" Baker inquired.

"Oh, I don't know. What would you say to getting us started?"

Although he didn't have anything prepared, Baker nodded, feeling it was only appropriate he commence the ceremony with some words.

Conrad then turned to Perreault. "And how about you finish with that little ditty of your grandfather's?"

"Fine with me," she replied.

The group formed a circle around the table and instinctively clasped hands with their neighbour. (Baker was secretly thrilled to be standing next to Perreault as she took his right hand in her left.) Angus came around from the drum kit and closed the circle between Perreault and Conrad.

After taking a moment to collect his thoughts, Baker began. "We have gathered with sincere hearts and genuine hope that our efforts today may somehow be felt by our heroes in green and white. May they not lose sight of the potential they have for greatness in this city, and may they endeavour, with nobleness of heart and mind, to fulfill that potential." He gave Perreault's hand a gentle squeeze to signal it was her turn.

She responded with perfect timing. "And may the good Lord grant that I of death will not drop before I can witness another Pines Clarence Cup."

No one moved, each of them uncertain as to what should happen next. Baker looked across at Conrad for direction, but his eyes were closed, so he cleared his throat. "Um . . . Amen?"

Conrad opened his eyes and looked across the circle at Baker, then smiled. "Why not . . . Amen." Perreault, Mas, and Angus added their "Amens" and the circle broke as everyone quietly returned to their music-making stations. Then an unexpected shriek ruptured any sense of solemnity that had been established.

"Whoa! Hang on a sec, everybody. Baker, you got a fly swatter?"

Baker shut his eyes, summoning some patience. "Yes, Angus. There's one in the corner behind you."

Angus instead grabbed the closest thing he could find, which was one among several *Economist* magazines strewn on the cardboard boxes. He rolled it up tight and poised himself. "Look at the size of this thing. What is it?"

Baker came over for a look. "Oh, I call them wood bugs. Others call them stinkbugs, probably because they smell when you squish 'em. They're pretty gross but harmless."

Angus lifted the magazine high overhead, then swung it down upon the skin of the drum with concentrated malevolence, creating a commotion of resonating sound and spilled sunflower seed shells and saliva—effectively establishing a new definition for the word "overkill."

"Ugh, its guts are blue. Pass me that roll of paper towels."

Conrad ripped off a section of towel and reached across with it.

"Don't get cheap on me, now," Angus cautioned. "Just pass the entire roll."

"Jesus, Angus, it's a bug, not a snake."

"Don't be surprised if you see one of those too," Baker warned. "I find the odd baby milk snake in here."

"What?" Angus was appalled. "What the fuck, Baker? How can you live like this?"

"You get used to it."

"Me? Never!"

By the time Angus was done cleaning the wood bug's remains, half the roll of paper towels was spent.

"Are we ready now?" Conrad asked, his patience at its limit.

Requiring a moment to compose himself, Angus finally took his drumsticks in hand and nodded his readiness. Conrad made a final check with the others and then counted them in. He and Baker kicked the song off with the D-A-A-D chord pattern, accompanied by Perreault working a tambourine. Then it was time for Baker to put a voice to his words. He made every effort to deliver the message with as much conviction as the Reid twins themselves.

> *I've never had luck with the Pines, I confess*
> *They earned my disdain for their lack of success*
> *'Cause even though fans kept on fillin' the house*
> *Their team's inept play kept them quiet as a mouse*
> *But green, oh, green, you weren't good at hockey it's true*
> *Oh, green, go green, please play better hockey, won't you?*

Whew, Baker thought, *that first verse went well, and the chorus was even better, thanks to Perreault's backing vocals.*

> *In knee deep sludge the franchise was mired*
> *Then came the announcement that Zander is hired*
> *The Prez then recruited a head coach named Koch*
> *And Bulac got busy fixing what was broke.*
>
> *Oh, green, go green, we hope Lady Luck smiles on you*
> *Oh, green, go green, it helps to get lucky in June.*
>
> *Love them I love them I love them*
> *Love them I love them I love them*
> *Love them I love them I love them*
> *Love them I love them I love them*

Perreault handled the second voice remarkably well. She even threw in harmonies in a way that boosted the overall impact of the vocals. Baker looked over at Conrad to see if he was hearing it as well. Conrad's look confirmed that he was.

> *Pines fan that I am I will do something bold:*
> *Beseech the dead heroes and spirits of old*
> *So kneeling my body I pray I'm around*
> *To see a Cup win 'fore I'm laid in the ground.*
>
> *Oh, green, go green, it helps to get lucky in June*
> *Oh, green, go green, we hope Lady Luck smiles on you.*
>
> *Love them I love them I love them*
> *Love them I love them I love them*

Baker repeated the underlying verse until it basically amounted to a chant. Above that Perreault sang the two lines of chorus here and there while intermittently throwing in other expressive guttural sounds and such.

Love them, I love them, I love them, I love
Love them, I love them, I love them, I love

The Proclaimers certainly delivered their songs with gusto, and Baker was seeking some semblance of that same honesty and passion to elicit the requisite desire. As the song progressed, he found the effect quite primitive and tribal. He began to understand how such fervid chanting could stir a group into a frenzy, or how, say, indigenous warriors would psych themselves up for a fight by dancing, chanting, and singing. (Add to that a potent dose of stimulants, and it was no surprise they'd charge through hellfire during battle.)

I love them, I love them, I love them, I love them
I love them, I love them, I love them, I love them

If it was repetition Baker was looking for, he sure got it with this tune. In the end he repeated the words "I love them" a total of 208 times. The final line capped the song by repeating the team's primary colour seven times, putting an exclamation point on the ceremony.

Green, green, green,
Green, green, green,
Green, yeah!

While he was lost in the fervour of the song building to its climax, Baker also lost his pick on the final chord, and discovered later that he'd even broken a string. He was fired up, exhilarated. He was also exhausted and sweaty. Now *that* was his original intent in performing such a ceremony. He couldn't have been more delighted with how it had turned out. The others seemed inspired as well.

Now if only such inspiration could pass on to the Pines in time for their opener next Wednesday.

CHAPTER SIX
BAKERS' COVEN

"Wow, that was fun!" Angus exclaimed.

"I didn't know the Proclaimers could be so intense," Mas said.

"Perreault, you sure you're not related to the Reid brothers?" Baker asked. "Maybe their long-lost triplet sister?"

"How is it you are so comfortable with the song and the lyrics?" Conrad inquired.

"I grew up with the Proclaimers. Sunshine on Leith was a staple in my house. It was one of my mom's favourites." Perreault replied, capering over to the counter to retrieve her tea while the others fired off random comments in their excitement.

"Well, if that's what these rituals are gonna be like, count me in."

"You're already in, dummy."

"Oh . . . yeah."

"I don't know what effect that'll have on the Pines, but it sure inspired me."

"Me too. When can we do this again?"

"Damn straight. Let's do this again, and soon."

"OK. But we need a name."

The group fell silent, pondering what had just been said. The suggestion had come from someone, but who? Then he said it again.

"Did you guys hear me?" (It was Conrad.) "It's time we christened this baby."

"You mean, like, right now?"

"Sure. Everyone's here. There's energy in the room. It'd be a good opportunity to toss some ideas around."

"Um . . . everybody?" Baker was timidly holding a hand up at head height, as if he needed to apologize for so boldly taking the floor. "On the topic of names . . . I was thinking for a while now that we should start considering ourselves as, um . . . something more than a band?"

"Ha! That's ambitious," Conrad scoffed, "Considering we're not even much of a band."

"C'mon, man," Angus said. "We're improving, aren't we?"

"Sure, Angus, that we are," Conrad admitted, backing off a bit. "But right now, I'm curious as to what Baker wants to transform us into."

Perreault was also intrigued. "Tell us, Baker. What do you mean by 'something more than a band'?"

"I'm not sure. It's just that, maybe we should start to look at ourselves as . . . um, heh, heh . . . this isn't easy to say out loud . . ." He was clearly struggling to make his point.

"We promise not to mock you," Mas assured him. "Just spit it out . . . please."

Masaccio's pledge served to embolden Baker. "Alright. I've always had a level of respect for the power of names. So, here we are, friends gathered together through a common desire, a common need. And since the five of us are trying to perform a small bit of magic, maybe we should look at ourselves as, a sort of—" Baker swallowed hard. "A coven." As the word passed his lips, it provoked a flinch in him, almost a cringe. "I'd like to refer to our group as a coven."

There was a collective exhale. "Baker, there's no need to be so apprehensive," Conrad said. "We're not puritans from the sixteen hundreds here."

"Yeah, you've got our attention," Mas added. "You want to anoint us as a coven—so keep talking."

"I just thought that the notion of us being a musical coven could give us ideas as we attempt to come up with a name."

"Does that mean the name you introduced us as at the pub last August—"

"You mean the 'Misty River Replacements'?"

"Right. Is that name not an option?"

"I wouldn't think so," Baker confirmed. "That was just something that came to me in the moment. It's not really pertinent anymore. Besides, Perreault wasn't on board then."

Angus dropped his eyes to the can of beer he'd been turning in his hands, his gaze landing on the image of a playful Diablo beneath the brew descriptor. Then, like a shoot of vetch in pavement cracks after a summer rain, an idea sprouted: "What about 'The Craft Brewers?' They're all the rage these days."

"The Craft Brewers?" Baker repeated, making sure he had heard Angus correctly.

"Yeah. It would have a 'witchy' association—you know, with brewing and such. But it would be inconspicuous, like Batman's cave entrance behind shrubbery, or Superman's true identity behind Clark Kent's glasses. Something hidden in plain sight."

Neither Baker, Mas, nor Conrad seemed very impressed, but Perreault looked like she'd won the lottery and pointed her index finger at Angus as if to accuse him, or confer a blessing upon him. "Hang on, now. Baker has expressed how he'd like us to consider ourselves a coven, right?"

Everyone voiced assent.

"Let's say we start with that. You know, to maintain the 'witchy' connection Angus just mentioned. From there we combine it with Baker's name, so now you've got a Baker's Coven." Perreault looked at the others as if she were playing charades, urging them to understand her clues. "It would be a take on a baker's *oven*, only we're a coven, and his name's Baker . . . and Bob's your uncle!"

The idea was met with silence. Finally, Angus spoke. "Perreault, you are a fucking genius," he said.

She nearly coughed up her beverage. "I've never been called a genius before, let alone a fucking genius."

"Well, consider it a compliment."

"Anybody want my opinion?" Baker inquired.

"Sure."

"I hate it."

"Jeez, Baker, don't roll it in doughnut sprinkles," Mas said. "Tell us how you really feel."

"Think about it," Baker urged. "I don't want my name on the band name. I mean, it's not *my* band, per se. And besides, people would think it highly pretentious of me."

"Well, you're going to hate it even more when you hear my suggestion," Conrad said.

"What's that?"

"Drop the determiner."

"You mean get rid of the 'The'?"

"Right."

"So, it'll just be Baker's Coven?"

"You got it. Remember the scene in The Social Network? Sean Parker tells Zuckerberg to drop the 'the' on 'The Facebook,' saying 'It's cleaner.' Also, you might remember the band The The—their name was a comment on all the bands that had names starting with 'the,' so they made a point of showing how ridiculous it could get."

"Um, I don't really think that's why they chose that particular name," Baker said.

"Well, that's my take on it," Conrad concluded.

Perreault looked around at them as if taking attendance in class, then she addressed their host. "You know, Baker, if it's deeper meaning you're seeking, I can think of a few things, beginning with the fact there are five of us."

"Oh yeah?" Baker tried to keep his sarcasm in check.

"Uh, huh. Think of the magic associated with the five-pointed star—the pentagram. The number five itself is a symbol of harmony, justice, and love. And the Vitruvian Man, which is a symbol of perfect proportion. Then there's the *quint*essence, which means the core or heart of everything."

Angus looked down at his hands. "Five fingers, five toes . . ." They all turned toward him, watching as he worked through the possibilities. "Five senses . . . um, five oceans, five Olympic rings to represent the five continents . . . uh, five boroughs of New York . . . houseflies have five eyes, don't they?"

Conrad shook his head. "I don't think so, Angus, but we get the point."

"Baker's Coven—a magical group of five," Perreault said. Then she raised her glass. "To us, a new band with a new name . . . to Baker's Coven."

"Just a minute!" Baker demanded. "Is that the name we're going with then? Despite my objections?"

"It would appear so," Conrad replied. "Consider yourself lucky. You know what they say, 'Whatever you do in life, surround yourself with smart people who will argue with you.'"

Baker rolled his eyes. "I can't believe you're quoting John Wooden to me."

"That was Wooden, huh? Well, then, who are you to object?" Conrad raised his glass. "To Baker's Coven!"

"Wait, hold on," Baker said. "Before we make it official, I'd like one thing clarified: is the apostrophe *before* or *after* the s?"

Perreault knew where he was going with this. "I hear you. It would be less a reflection of *your* name if the apostrophe came *after* the s."

"Exactly!"

"No problem," she assured him. "Consider us all bakers, and it's *our* coven."

"Great. Now that we've established where the friggin' apostrophe goes—" Conrad raised his glass again. "To Bakers' Coven!"

Everyone reached for whatever drink they had and chimed in heartily "To Bakers' Coven!" They bent elbows and took generous swallows. Glasses, mugs, and cups were drained of beer, wine, coffee, tea, and water, respectively.

"Bakers' Coven," Angus repeated. "That's fuckin' awesome!"

"You know, it kind of feels like we are embarking on a bit of a journey," Baker said, allowing himself to get caught up in the moment." Like a quest—in pursuit of a cherished treasure."

Conrad had never seen this side of his friend. "I wasn't aware you were such a fan of medieval romances, Baker, with this talk of quests and treasures."

"Actually, I'm not so much a fan of Arthurian legends as a fan of great events in human history. And it's getting to the point where the chances of Toronto winning the Clarence Cup are fairly high. Therefore, I intend to be a part of history as it unfolds."

"Do you really believe the Pines winning the Cup would rate as a momentous and historic event?" Mas asked.

Baker stepped forward and leaned in for emphasis. "I believe a bomb—a fuckin' hydrogen bomb—will drop on the GTA, and it will consume Southern Ontario, and the ripples will be felt across this country. And I intend to ride that radioactive wave. Winning the Clarence Cup is an event that will impact us not just on a sporting scale but on a cultural one as well. I mean, we're talking a real 'fireworks-from-the-CN-Tower' moment. It'll be a story that will be retold for the next hundred years."

"Hoo boy, I'm getting goose bumps here," Angus said.

"Yes, it's an exciting thought," Baker agreed. "But it's not enough that it happens sometime soon, like in the next few years. No! I say, let it happen this year. The 2019–2020 PHL season should end with the Toronto Mighty Pines hoisting Gawain's Grail."

Conrad guffawed. "Now you just sound like a sucker for punishment."

"Maybe. But it'll be less painful than cheering *against* the Pines and watching them succeed."

"Who said anything about cheering against the Pines?"

"Sorry, I should explain. There was a time when I actually despised the Pines. You see, I haven't always been a full-bore, card-carrying fan. That only happened recently."

"Whoa, now the truth comes out!" Angus cried, feigning shock and awe at Baker's admission.

"I know, scandalous, huh? But seriously, I had such disdain for this team—this franchise—that the only reason I paid any attention to PHL hockey was to cheer *against* the Pines."

Angus cringed. "There's something slightly sick about that."

"I agree. It's not normal."

"What changed your attitude toward the Pines?" Perreault inquired.

"What changed? The Pines changed," Baker replied, now standing at his Pines-bedecked table with a lighter. He carefully set the four candles aflame. "It was actually a series of events that convinced me the time had come to board the wagon. I realized that if I continued to cheer against the Pines, soon I'd have to live through their daily successes, and my existence would be misery. I figured it's better to be on the happy side of such memories."

"What was this series of events?" Perreault pressed.

"It began six years ago. First event: Xander Galahad is hired to be the president of the organization. I think to myself, now here's a winner—three Cups, an Olympic gold, a Hall of Fame inductee—I mean, the guy's got an impressive resume."

Angus nodded. "Among the one hundred greatest players of all time," and winking at Masaccio he added, "And the logo to boot."

Baker continued. "All the talk of a 'Xanderplan' really got my attention. Then the second event has Kayden Koch signing on as the Pines' head coach. Now there's another guy with an eye-popping CV."

"Highest-paid coach in the history of the PHL," Angus added.

"Third and final event: Galahad brings Kyle Bulac into the fold as GM."

"Babyface Bulac!" Angus sang.

"Babyface Bulac, indeed," Baker said. "Suddenly, the three top management positions in the Mighty Pines organization represent a blend of Hall of Fame prestige, old-school leadership, and youthful perspective. And that's when I drank the green Kool-Aid and signed on with Coney Nation."

"You really think they can get it done this year?" Mas asked.

"My expectations are sky high." Baker raised both his hands as if hoisting the chalice overhead. "Clarence Cup high."

"You and the rest of Coney Nation," Perreault said as she set to boiling water for some tea. "For that reason it kind of makes what we're doing here a little more purposeful—transforming popular songs into abracadabra-like spells, all in the hopes that somehow we can help the Pines win the Cup."

Baker reached into the centrepiece display, skillfully avoiding the candle flames, and lifted the six-inch Clarence Cup replica by its neck, as if it were a clay wine goblet from a medieval pub. He placed it on his outstretched palm, gazing at it with a mixture of admiration and wanton lust. But before he could say anything, Angus cut in.

"Look at that thing. You know what they say about the size of a man's replica Clarence Cup, eh?"

Baker chuckled along with everyone else. "Sorry, folks, I have no clever comeback about how size doesn't matter. But I will ask you to look beyond the diminutive scale of this replica and name me any other championship trophy that garners as much awe and respect, carries as much history and colour, and occasions as much ceremony and tradition in the winning of it. You can scour the world's trophy room till the cows come home, but I contend you won't find anything to compare with the silver cup donated by Clarence Hughes back in . . . whenever." Baker paused, almost daring them to disagree. "And the tradition that has developed around winning it is second to none," he added with finality.

His audience of four considered the argument in silence, none apparently seeing any value in refuting Baker's claims. It was Angus who posed the next question.

"Why do people call it 'Gawain's Grail'?"

"Did you know it's also called 'Charlie's Chalice'?" Baker noted.

"Fascinating," Angus replied dryly, "—but *why*?"

"Dr. Charles Gawain apparently hated the name 'Clarence' Cup. He was the league commissioner back then and would have preferred it to be called the 'Laurel' Cup, a name befitting its status as a symbol of hockey supremacy—but that's another story altogether."

"But the donor's name was Clarence *Hughes*. Why didn't they call it the 'Hughes' Cup?" Angus wondered.

"Who knows? Maybe the 'Hughes' Cup sounded too much like 'Whose Cup?' or 'Hiccup.' Or perhaps they just liked the alliteration of Clarence Cup."

"All this talk about the Clarence Cup is overlooking the biggest question for the Mighty Pines:" Conrad noted. "Who's going to be the first player to hoist the Cup if they win it this year? They still haven't named a captain."

"Shit, that's right," Baker admitted.

"And what about the Mason Andrews business down in Louisiana?" Perreault added. "That must've been quite the unexpected curve for the team."

"Dear God, I just had a thought," Conrad announced, his eyes wide. "Can you imagine the shit show? Galahad, Bulac, and Koch, all holed up together in an office, debating who the next captain should be? And in the middle of the squabbling, the news about Andrews drops on Twitter."

"I can just picture them," Baker said, "going around and around, like Abbot and Costello plus one, wrangling over who's on first—or more like, who gets the C?"

"That sounds like it could be funny," Masaccio observed. "Which of them do you think does most of the talking?"

"That's easy," Baker answered. "Coach Koch."

"Hmm, I might have thought it'd be the boss."

"Galahad? No. I'll bet he's in the habit of excusing himself at regular intervals, under the guise of having to do vital errands, just to get out of the office, you know?"

"Yeah, then he gets himself a drink or a smoke," Angus joked. "Or better yet, a spliff."

When the laughter abated, Perreault voiced another suggestion.

"Listen, Baker, if you want a quick, hassle-free tutorial on holding coven gatherings, I've got just the person for you. Her name is Dorcas Blanchard. She's a practising Wiccan."

"You mean, like . . . a witch?"

"Sure. Who better to tell you how a coven should work than a witch? She lives near Fergus, if I'm not mistaken, not that far from here."

"How'd you meet her?"

"My family moved to this area when I was a kid. When my parents were shopping around for a house, Dorcas, who was a realtor back then, drove around with us on weekends, checking out properties."

Baker still had reservations. "OK, but I don't want to be recruited into a witch's coven or attend a séance or anything."

"No, that's not her style. She's pretty cool. Just tell her you want an introduction to the fundamentals of coven craft. But let me talk to her first and I'll tell you what she thinks."

Baker took a moment to consider the offer. "Alright, that sounds doable."

"In fact, why don't I give her a call right now?"

Baker was a little taken aback by how fast things were moving, but he couldn't think of a good reason to object, so he allowed himself to be swept up in the coven current. Perreault went into the other room to make the call. Meanwhile, the other four members of Bakers' Coven took the opportunity to refill their glasses and indulge in more doughnuts. Soon the talk turned to the band's prospects.

"So, what do you think will be our first gig?" Mas asked.

"I thought the set we played at the Misty River was our first gig," Angus said.

"As great a moment as that was, the fact is, Bakers' Coven wasn't born yet," Conrad noted. "We were just a bunch of dicks jammin' in front of a handful of locals."

"Yeah, well, that handful of locals might be the biggest crowd we ever play for."

"What's with the pessimism, Baker? You sound like fuckin' Eeyore."

"I might have a solution," Perreault said, having returned from her phone call. "I'll make sure we're signed up for events at school. I can think of three off the top of my head. There's the Battle of the Bands in November and the Christmas concert in December before the holidays. There's also the talent show in May."

"Oh yeah? You think the student council is going to just let us perform in their events?" Baker asked.

Conrad looked at Perreault. "What do you think, boss?"

There was a wrinkle of uncertainty on Perreault's brow, then it disappeared. "Sure they will. I mean, as far as I know, we're the only teachers' band in the school. The kids would love to see us up on stage making fools of ourselves. And now we've got a name."

"So, did you get a hold of her?" Baker asked.

"Yes, I certainly did," Perreault answered. "Dorcas said she'd be happy to meet with you."

"Great. Did she say when?"

"She said, and I quote, 'A fortnight and a half from tonight would be perfect.'"

"Perfect... I wish I knew what that meant, though."

"I didn't know either, so I asked her, and she explained that a fortnight is equivalent to two weeks. Therefore, a fortnight and a half equals two weeks plus one week. Basically, she'll be here three weeks from tonight, which is October sixteenth."

"Ah, how cryptic. And did she suggest a time for her visit?"

"Yes, and once again I will quote. She said: 'Three weeks from right this minute,' which was about four minutes ago."

The clock on the stove told Baker it was 6:40. "Hmm, 6:36. That's got a nice, fat, palindromic roundness to it, wouldn't you say, Conrad?"

"Whatever it may mean to your Wiccan friend, it tells me I'm late," Conrad replied. "I told Winnie I'd be home by seven. I'd better get a move on."

Mas, Angus, and Perreault followed Conrad's lead and migrated to the front door to take their leave. (For her part, Perreault was surprised to find herself tantalized by the prospect of singing vocals in a music/magic-making enterprise. Maybe, just maybe, this coven activity would result in some Pines success, and that would be a dream come true for her Papi Rene. She couldn't help but wonder what else might be in store for her rookie year of teaching.)

After seeing his guests off, Baker was left basking in the glow of the evening's success and feeling a strong sense of triumph combined with relief. He was able to quell them enough to settle in and attack some school work he'd been putting off.

By the time he finished, two hours had passed and he was ready for bed. Before turning in, he took one more look at his Pines shrine, the candles having long since been extinguished, but the little replica Clarence Cup was still resplendent on its central perch. He suddenly felt compelled to take one of the large books to bed with him. It was called *The Mighty Pines: An Illustrated History*. Once in bed, propped up by pillows, Baker perused the many black-and-white photos of past Pines dynasties. He reflected on the state of the current team and how, earlier that evening, he and his friends had joked about the idea of the present Pines' triumvirate debating the captaincy while the Mason Andrews controversy swirled. Now, however, alone in the solitude of his home, Baker thought it might have been imprudent to mock something so serious to true Pines fans. He could only hope that the prayers and the song offered earlier that evening would offset any harm they might have perpetrated.

Baker shifted onto one side and settled deeper under the covers, closing his eyes as he tried to imagine which player would best fit the mould as the Pines' captain. As he did so, the open book slid closer to the edge of the bed and, as the pages fanned out with the bending of the spine, flipped to a new page, revealing a photo of Cal Ubank and Beezer Sharpe, the legendary team captain and his eventual successor, both beaming with pride, holding the Clarence Cup between them.

CHAPTER SEVEN
WHO GETS THE C?

Scene: *The office of the head coach of the Toronto Mighty Pines in the executive suites of Nova Tank Arena is occupied by team president Xander Galahad and the coach himself, Kayden Koch. Both are seated in oversized stuffed leather chairs on opposite sides of a large walnut desk. They are awaiting the arrival of General Manager Kyle Bulac, who is running late for their meeting—a meeting that will resolve the question surrounding the identity of the Pines' next captain. The last player to wear the C was Dante Leclair, exactly 1,324 days ago.*

Koch: *(agitated, glances at his wristwatch.)* Kyle *does* know about this meeting, right?

Galahad: Of course he knows. He's on his way.

Koch: 'Cause it's important to start on time, you know. It's like puck drop. Ya gotta start on time.

Galahad: *(sighing, having heard it many times before.)* Yeah, let's save the life lessons for the players.

Koch: I'm just saying, we need to get this figured out, you know, 'cause I told the media we'd announce our decision by the time—

(Koch is cut off mid-sentence as Bulac arrives. Normally a whirlwind of youthfulness, today he looks tired. He is impeccably dressed but slightly dishevelled, his designer necktie and glasses fashionably askew, and sporting a red mark on his forehead, as if he'd been leaning on something for too long.)

Bulac: *(appearing winded, he takes a second to catch his breath.)* A thousand apologies, guys. Thanks for waiting. I can't believe it. I fell asleep, face down, at my desk. *(He places a sixpack of doughnuts on the desk and takes his seat.)* Here, I stopped at Sugar Watson's on the way to get us some treats. Help yourselves.

(The other two men move toward the box, but Galahad gets there first and opens the lid.)

WHO GETS THE C?

Koch: Thanks for the doughnuts, Kyle. Hey, Gally, I got dibs on a dutchie if there's one in there.

Galahad: *(looking into the open box like a hungry wolf peering into a nest of bunnies.)* Nope. Sorry, Kay. There's a cream-filled one, covered in pretty sprinkles, but I know that's not your style. There's also a chocolate cruller, a Boston cream, and the rest are the special-edition Mighty Pines doughnuts, slathered in green-and-white icing.

Koch: A Boston cream? *(Gives Bulac a look of disgust.)* Really, Kyle? Shame on you. I'll take the cruller.

(Galahad hands the doughnut to Koch, then dives back into the box and comes out with the Boston cream. Bulac reaches in and pulls out one of the Pines-themed doughnuts. He looks at Koch.)

Bulac: A dutchie, Kayden? Seriously? I didn't think they even made those anymore. I mean, why would they? Nobody eats them—except you.

Koch: Don't dismiss the classic dutchie, Kyle. It's still a favourite among homegrown Canadians. Why else would Sugar's still keep a place for it on the rack behind the glass? Hell, enjoying a dutchie takes me back to the glory days of the Pines in the sixties. A time when Sugar Watson himself was alive and well and patrolling the blue line—and baking doughnuts on the side.

Galahad: *(his mouth full, enjoying the Boston cream.)* Oh, man, he wuzh a tuff mudder-fugger, wuzhin' 'ee?

Koch: *(looking nostalgically at the honey cruller in his hand.)* Yeah, those were the days. Enemy forwards were sure to keep their heads up with guys like Watson defending the zone. *(He directs his gaze at Bulac.)* Unfortunately, it doesn't look like this team's in the market for players like that.

(The flesh tone of Bulac's face and neck is replaced by patches of lava red.)

Galahad: C'mon Kay, let's not go there now. That's not what this meeting's about.

Koch: *(addressing Bulac.)* You have to excuse me, Kyle. I can't help thinking back to the time when this team had players like George Daly, Max Moore, Wayne Brody, Sugar Watson . . . gosh, four Clarence Cups in six years. Wouldn't it be nice to get back to that kind of winning?

Bulac: Uh, can we get back to the point of this meeting? Right now it's hard to even conceive of that kind of success. *(He looks purposefully at both of his colleagues.)* So... who's got the C?

Koch: *(appears confused.)* Don't look at us; we didn't bring any. You know Dianne sets up the beverage counter, and she's left the office. I think the pot's still out though.

Bulac: *(looking around, doubly confused.)* You've lost me. Aren't we meeting to discuss the team captaincy?

Koch: Ohhh, I thought you were asking about the coffee. Dianne always takes care of that. She sure brews a good cup o' Joe.

Bulac: Uh, no. The C still refers to what it has always referred to in this game: the letter on the sweater.

Koch: Well, maybe if we'd started on time—

Galahad: Oh, Christ! Let's get back to the C.

Bulac: Actually, speaking of coffee, I could go for a cup. Do you guys mind if I step out to the counter in the hall and pour myself some of Dianne's famous flavoured brew? I'll still be able to hear the conversation.

Koch: Sure. Hurry it up, though.

Galahad: *(projecting his voice to Bulac in the hall.)* So, just before you got here, Kayden and I figured that it's down to one of three guys for the captaincy: Mason Andrews, Ben Bellamy, or Gianni Valentino.

Bulac: *(from out in the hall.)* Yeah, pretty much everyone in the hockey world knows that. But it's our call to determine who among those three it should be. Hey, do either of you know if Dianne's gonna do pumpkin spice this year? It's about that season, isn't it?

Galahad: Probably next week I should think. More toward Thanksgiving weekend.

Bulac: I can't wait. Mmm... and then around Christmas she splits between egg nog and ginger spice.

Galahad: Yeah, my personal favourite is Irish cream. *(Koch flinches at that.)* But I think she serves that around Saint Paddy's Day. But let's get back to our captain to be. Who should we go with? The "young superstar," the "team veteran," or the "savvy, seasoned statesman"?

WHO GETS THE C?

Koch: Boy, you make them each sound so enticing, kinda like your fancy coffees. Of course, I take my coffee black, so I don't really pay attention to the flavoured stuff. But I gotta give Dianne props. Her dark roast is brewed to perfection.

Bulac: *(re-enters the office with a full mug, two creams, two sugars.)* Listen to you with the "props." Adopting some of the young-generation speak, are we?

Koch: Sure. I figure I should pick it up—to reach the kids better, you know. I'm just now getting a hang of their names.

Galahad: What? You don't know everybody's name yet?

Koch: Nah! Of course I do. But it's crazy. It's like their given names aren't good enough. Now they need names like "J-Lo" and "A-Rod" and "Spicy P." Hell, just the other day I heard somebody referring to Addy Brouwer as "A-Bro."

Galahad: I guess it's just a matter of time before they have a name for you; maybe "Coach K.K."

Koch: That would be fine. I've heard all kinds of things over the years. Two I remember best are "Coach Crotch" and "Coach Cock."

Bulac: Gosh, those are pretty crude names.

Galahad: No doubt courtesty of some disgruntled players—guys who were in your doghouse at the time?

Koch: You're both wrong. I consider those names badges of honour. I got them when my players saw me come out of the shower after practice one day.

(This elicits a coughing fit from Galahad while Bulac smiles shyly and stares into his coffee as a blush spreads across his baby-soft cheeks.)

Galahad: *(When the coughing fit passes, he begins massaging his temples, groaning.)* Oh man, I feel a thumper coming on.

(Out of nowhere Koch emits a low, manly chuckle, causing the other two to exchange quizzical looks.)

Galahad: What's so funny, Kay?

Koch: What? Oh . . . uh, nothing. I just thought you were picking up on the "Coach Cock" thing, heh, heh.

When Cheers Are Not Enough

Galahad: Jesus, Kay, I was referring to my headache, not what's in my pants. *(Sighing, he gets up from his seat and buttons up his suit jacket.)* Listen, I'm gonna scoot down to the underground PATH and hit the drugstore for some pain relief. I've got a feeling I might need it. I won't be long. Anybody want anything?

Koch: Yeah, come to think of it, get me a bag of Spitz. In fact, make it two, if you don't mind. One barbecue flavour, the other all-dressed.

Galahad: You got it. What about you Kyle? D'you want anything?

Bulac: Some chewing gum would be great.

Galahad: Anything in particular?

Bulac: Oh, I dunno ... something green.

Galahad: Green?

Bulac: Yeah. And if not green, then something white.

Galahad: Kyle, chewing gum comes in flavours like "spearmint" and "peppermint," not "green" and "white."

Bulac: Sure it does. You just haven't been paying attention.

Galahad: OK. In the meantime, you two continue discussing the captaincy.

(Galahad leaves the office as Bulac takes a seat across from Koch. He regards the coach for a moment. A fly buzzes around above the desk, then lands on a corner of the open doughnut box. Koch shoos it away.)

Koch: Where's my goddam fly swatter? I know there's one around here somewhere.

Bulac: I think that's it behind you on the window ledge.

(Reaching back, Koch arms himself with the flyswatter, sees that his prey has disappeared for the moment, and places it on the floor by his chair, within arm's reach.)

Bulac: I didn't take you for a flavoured sunflower seeds guy, Kayden.

Koch: Actually, I'm not. Typically, I go with straight-up salted, but a couple times a year I'll indulge in a flavoured bag.

Bulac: No kidding. I like dill pickle myself.

WHO GETS THE C?

Koch: Dill pickle? *(Chuckles)* Maybe for you suits in the press box. Not for me though, no sir. Hell, I can't even say the words without having an attack of the giggles. It's like trying to say "skid marks" with a straight face. Try it. See if you can say it without laughing.

Bulac: *(dryly and with a straight face.)* Dill pickle.

Koch: *(He snorts and nearly snots on himself in the process.)* See what I mean?

Bulac: *(adjusting his glasses.)* Maybe we should get back to which of Andrews, Bellamy, or Valentino should get the C.

Koch: *(He wipes his eyes.)* OK, sorry. *(Takes a moment to regain his composure.)* Well, for me the choice is clear. When it's time to pick between two players, my motto has always been "the tie goes to the veteran." So for my money, the captain should be Valentino.

Bulac: The only problem with that logic is the last time I looked, they were all veterans.

Koch: Alright then, the tie goes to the *most* veteran. Anyway, you know what I mean. Valentino has been in the league for ten years while Ben's been playing, what, six? Mason's only got three years under his garter. Taking my argument to its logical conclusion, Gianni is the most veteran of the three so he gets the C. Besides, he best represents the team's identity.

Bulac: The team's identity? No offence, but I don't think we've established an on-ice identity yet.

Koch: None taken. After all, I can only work with what I've been provided.

Bulac: Yes, you've made that quite clear to everyone outside the organization.

Koch: You're referring to some of my media scrums?

Bulac: *(frustrated to see where the conversation is going.)* Forget it. Let's get back to your point about veteran leadership. Now, what if I argued that the most veteran *Mighty Pine* should get the C? Valentino may have played ten years in the PHL, but he's served only one year with the Pines, compared to Andrews and Bellamy. And since Ben is the longest-serving Pine, he would get my vote. By the way, did Gally tell you who his choice would be?

Koch: I haven't asked him directly, but all signals would indicate he'd agree with me and want Gianni to wear the C.

Bulac: Signals? What signals has he given you?

When Cheers Are Not Enough

Koch: I can read Gally pretty well. We speak the same language.

Bulac: Oh, OK, but why don't we just ask him when he gets back? In the meantime, I honestly think any one of Ben, Mason, or Gianni would serve as first-rate captains.

Koch: Then just put an *A* on each of their sweaters, and leave it at that.

Bulac: Naw—that would be weak. It'd look as if management can't make decisions.

Koch: Well, that's the truth, isn't it?

Bulac: *(ignoring the offhand shot.)* I just see Ben as having earned a level of respect and recognition both around the league and among his teammates. He's among the top players at his position, he works his butt off every day, and he's got a good head on his shoulders, and that's important when having to navigate the hot lights and hard questions that come with the Toronto sports media.

Koch: You could say the same of Gianni and Mason as well.

(Galahad reappears with goodies from the drugstore.)

Bulac: Wow, you're fast.

Galahad: Yeah, it's actually not that far when you know where you're going along the PATH. *(He tosses a packet of gum to Bulac and two bags of Spitz to Koch.)* Hey, Kayden, I was surprised to see the variety of flavours Spitz now carries. Did you know they had dill pickle?

(Koch snorts, and Bulac closes his eyes. Galahad's face is a question mark. Recovering from his titters, Koch sets the bags of sunflower seeds on his desk beside the box of doughnuts. Meanwhile, the housefly settles on the wall directly behind Koch, keeping all five eyes fixed on the open box of treats.)

Koch: Did you get your pain relief, Gally?

Galahad: Got it. Now, how far did you two get? Who gets the C?

Bulac: *(adjusting his glasses)* So far, Kay and I are stuck between Valentino and Bellamy. He likes Gianni's veteran chops, but I prefer Ben's Pine pedigree and leadership.

Galahad: Do I get an opinion on this matter?

Koch: Of course, Gally! Hell, you're the man. It's your team.

WHO GETS THE C?

Galahad: Alright then, I'd like the three of us to consider Mason for a moment.

Koch: *(with more suspicion than curiosity.)* OK, but just for a moment, heh-heh.

Galahad: C'mon, Kay, what's so objectionable about Andrews being this franchise's twenty-fifth captain? He's its most talented player, its most high-profile member, its highest-paid, and quite possibly its most important when it comes to this team's overall success.

Koch: All true. But he's young. There's enough on his shoulders as it is without the added burden of the C. I'd like to wrap this mantle of responsibility around a more mature, seasoned player like Valentino.

Galahad: There are other considerations, not least of which is the fact that Mason will be twenty-six when his present contract runs out.

Bulac: Boy, that's gonna be a tough contract negotiation.

Galahad: My point exactly. Lately, we've seen a trend by superstars to play closer to home at some point in their careers, like Valentino leaving Washington and coming here last year, and more recently Kawhi leaving the Raptors and signing with the Clippers. Mason might be inclined to do likewise in five years and opt to play closer to Louisiana. So, I gotta believe that wearing the C will almost certainly oblige the big guy to re-sign with us, wouldn't you think?

Bulac: It's always a gamble to bet on what someone's personal intentions might be.

Galahad: Maybe, but having Mason wear the C would be a titillating prospect for the fan base.

Koch: Titillating? *(Saying the word elicits a fit of giggles.)* That's one way to describe it.

Galahad: Well, you've heard my take on who should get the C. *(He glances at his watch.)* But you'll have to excuse me again, I gotta zip down to the liquor store and pick up a couple of items for tonight. Won't be long. *(He goes to leave but then turns back.)* You guys want anything?

Bulac: What are you getting?

Galahad: Some wine, a bottle of Baileys, that sort of thing.

Koch: *(winces, then recovers.)* Can you get me a bottle of "Gabe's" red? The GOAT Merlot? I tell ya, nothing like a good ol' vintage from Niagara-on-the-Lake.

When Cheers Are Not Enough

(Galahad exits, leaving Bulac and Koch alone with their thoughts.)

Bulac: You know, Kayden, I wasn't going to say anything or tell anyone, but now that Xander's gone, and it's just us two—

Koch: (cuts Bulac off with a question of his own.) Have you noticed some weird behaviour in Gally lately?

Bulac: Huh? Weird behaviour? Not really. Why?

Koch: Jeez, I don't know if he's testing us or having a bit of fun at our expense, but—how do I say this? He's been goin' all Boston on us.

Bulac: Boston? What's that mean?

Koch: I'm not sure, but twice during this meeting—well, take for example the doughnuts you brought. What did we all choose? I took a cruller, and you went for a Mighty Pines special. But what did Gally pick?

Bulac: I didn't notice.

Koch: He freakin' chose the Boston cream!

Bulac: Oh my gawd. Are you serious?

Koch: Pretty scary, right?

Bulac: No! I mean, are *you* serious? Do you really think Xander eating a Boston cream doughnut means anything? Maybe he just likes Boston cream doughnuts.

Koch: OK, but did you catch what he's buying at the liquor store? A bottle of Baileys! Christ, he's drinking Irish cream, and what city's more Irish around the league than Boston?

Bulac: *(adjusts his glasses, then mutters under his breath.)* God help us.

Koch: What's that?

Bulac: Nothing . . . never mind. Can I tell you my story now?

Koch: Of course. I'm listening.

Bulac: Remember how I said I fell asleep at my desk earlier this evening?

Koch: Yeah, you must be pretty beat, what with the contract negotiations and all.

WHO GETS THE C?

Bulac: Sure, sure. What I didn't mention, though, is that I had a crazy dream. Or, more like . . . a vision, or a visitation. I was visited by . . . spirits.

Koch: Spirits?

Bulac: Yes! And not just any spirits; hockey spirits, old-timer Mighty Pines from the past.

Koch: Seriously? What do you think it means?

Bulac: I don't know what it means, or even if it means anything at all.

Koch: Did you happen to get a good look at these old-timer Mighty Pines? Could you identify them? Were they the players or were they coaches and GMs—or owners?

Bulac: I'm pretty sure they were players, but I can't name any specific individuals.

Koch: OK. What about uniforms? Were they dressed in their hockey gear?

Bulac: I guess they were wearing hockey gear. Sweaters for sure.

Koch: What colour were the sweaters, white or green?

Bulac: Jeez, Kay, does it really matter?

Koch: Sure. A light sweater could indicate a friendly visitation; a dark one could mean they've come to cause some shit or something. Details, details.

Bulac: Listen to you, Sherlock. You sound like a murder mystery detective.

Koch: A murder? No. A mystery? Yes. Hey, could it be they looked like those metal statues on the Acropolis here in Elysian Square?

Bulac: No, they didn't look like bronze sculptures come to life. I remember them wearing dark clothing. But I don't think their presence was meant to be malevolent. *(He looks at Koch with a critical eye.)* You're not mocking me now, are you?

Koch: *(points an index finger at his chin.)* Look at this face. Do you see me laughing?— OK, well, maybe at first I found it funny and that you were overtired and just needed an excuse for being late to our meeting.

Bulac: C'mon, Kay, I wouldn't do that. I know how much you insist on starting on time.

Koch: Yup. We see eye to eye on that much, anyway. In truth, I'm OK with notions of invisible forces and otherworldly stuff, especially when you realize that our job here puts us in charge of a storied franchise that has all kinds of history.

Bulac: It's comforting to think we have friendly spirits watching over us.

Koch: But what was the point of their visit, d'ya think? Did they have opinions about our backup goaltending? Or maybe some suggestions for a right-shot defenceman?

Bulac: No, nothing was said—in words—exactly. However I came away with a strong image of the Pines teams of the sixties. You know, the Chairman, and Whitey Kilpatrick, and Sugar Watson—all that nostalgic stuff.

Koch: *(sits up in excitement.)* Holy shit! That can only mean one thing:—you're being visited by spirits of the glory years of the past. Multiple Cup wins and all that. Do you think they might be connecting their eras to this one?

Bulac: *(unconvinced.)* Uh . . . maybe, I guess?

Koch: Sure, it's clear as day to me. It means that what we're doing here, using the principles of old-time hockey, tried and tested, will lead to Cup success for this franchise. Now I'm pumped. Are you pumped?

Bulac: I'm not so sure. You know what happened after the '62 Cup. The hockey landscape was changing. Guys in the front office found themselves in a different world but couldn't adjust to it. You know the saying, "Failure is not fatal, but failure to change might be."

Koch: Aha. Now you're quoting John Wooden to me. You know I'm a big admirer of his, but you gotta be careful not to take his quotes out of context. Something Wooden said that I think is more pertinent to our team's present situation is, "The worst thing about new books is that they keep us from reading the old ones."

Bulac: Hmm . . . so you believe the spirits might be urging me not to forget the past?

Koch: The more I think about it, the more I'm convinced that's the message.

Bulac: Hard to say. But one thing's for sure, when I woke up from the "nap," instead of feeling groggy, I had a lot of energy. I was seized with a newfound sense of purpose and I wanted to share that revelation. It felt like . . . like Pentecost Sunday. I needed to share the "good news" with the team. To clear my head I went outside for a walk. And then I saw a Sugar Watson's shop and felt compelled to go in . . . Is that dumb?

WHO GETS THE C?

Koch: Maybe the doughnut part, yeah. But as for the rest, no, there's nothing dumb about what you're telling me. Hell, this team can use all the help it can get, even if it means petitioning the spirits of Pines past. I just wish these hockey spirits would do something fast and stop taking their time about it.

Bulac: Thanks again for the support, Kay. But speaking of time *(he glances at his watch)*, we better decide on who gets the C. Xander will be back soon.

Koch: Aw, what the hell. Maybe Gally's right. Why not make Mason the captain. He's a good kid. He's got swagger, skill, strength, and snipe-ability. You can even add stewardship to the mix. *(In his mind he has reached an accord.)* OK, Kyle, Mason gets the C. We'll make the boss a happy man when he gets back.

Bulac: And speak of the devil, here he is now.

(Galahad returns, loaded down with purchases from the liquor store, slightly out of breath. Placing a box on Koch's desk with a satisfied thunk, he reaches in and pulls out a bottle of wine.)

Galahad: Alright, Kay, here's your "Gabe's Merlot." Now, did you guys come to a decision? Who gets the C?

Koch: Yup, we've both agreed on the player who will be this club's twenty-fifth captain.

Galahad: Sounds great. Don't keep me in suspense.

Koch: *(hesitates, then motions to the bottle of wine.)* Maybe we should pour three glasses and make a toast to this momentous occasion. I'll just open this if it suits you. Kyle, if you don't mind, I think there's some glassware out in the hall at the coffee counter.

Galahad: *(appraises the bottle.)* Are you gonna need a corkscrew?

Koch: Nah, it's a twist cap.

(Bulac returns with three mugs, sets them on the desk, and Koch pours. The coach picks up his mug and motions to his colleagues to do likewise.)

Koch: Gentlemen, a toast to the team that's been without a captain for almost four years, and to the man who will wear the C and lift the Clarence Cup for the first time in this city since 1962. Here's to— *(notices Bulac is distracted by his device.)* Kyle, put the damn phone down!

Bulac: Hang on . . . sorry . . . my Twitter feed is heating up. (*He sets down his mug and fiddles with his phone, focusing on the message before him. As he reads, his face displays a range of emotional contortions never before seen by his colleagues.*)

Galahad: Kyle? Everything alright?

Koch: Yeah. You don't look so good.

Bulac: (*adjusting his glasses.*) Jeez, fuck!

Koch: Whoa! What's got your jockstrap in a knot?

Bulac: Aw, fuck!

Galahad: (*puts his glass down.*) Kyle, what's going on?

Bulac: It says here Mason's in trouble with the law in Baton Rouge because of some incident that happened back in May on the university campus.

(*Alarmed, Galahad and Koch get up from their seats and come around to either side of Bulac so as to get an angle on the offending text. All three read in astonishment.*)

Koch: Holy shit. It says he was involved in a nasty prank in the girls' dormitory!

Galahad: There were about two dozen guys . . .

Koch: And they were buck naked, streaking around the quad . . .

Bulac: Yeah, but some kept their underwear on—Mason included.

Koch: (*sarcastically.*) Oh, that makes it better.

Galahad: And all of it was caught on camera.

Bulac: Why the fuck didn't he tell us?

Galahad: We'd better call him and get all the details.

(*They stand silently, each struggling with his thoughts and considering the possible fallout of the news. How will they spin it to the media? What kind of a distraction will it be for the team? What discipline, if any, will be imposed by the PHL? And perhaps most importantly, how will Stanfield's, a major sponsor of the team, respond to the fact that clearly caught on the security camera was Mason Andrews wearing Fruit of the Loom briefs?*)

(*Then another thought dawns on the group. Koch is the first to speak.*)

WHO GETS THE C?

Koch: So, who gets the C?

Bulac: Damn! Just when we had this thing figured out too.

Galahad: What are you saying? Mason was your choice for captain?

Bulac: Yeah. *(Turns to Koch.)* I guess we should revisit our decision, eh, Kay?

(Galahad gets up and heads for the door, humming a tune to himself.)

Bulac: Where're you going?

Koch: Yeah, we're not done here yet.

Galahad: Huh? Oh, yeah . . . um, I'm just going out . . . not for long . . .

Bulac: Out? Where to now?

Galahad: *(Standing in the doorway, he shakes out of his fog and turns back around to face them.)* To the "Hunny Pot." You guys want anything? *(Waiting for an answer but getting no immediate response, Galahad, still in a zombie state, exits the room, now singing, in a scratchy falsetto, the lyrics to the tune he was humming.)* More than a feeling (more than a feeling), I see my Marianne walking away . . .

(Hearing Galahad, Koch looks up in alarm at Bulac, who remains sitting, limp and silent.)

Koch: Who wrote that?

Bulac: Who wrote what?

Koch: That song, "More than a Feeling." Gally was singing it just now on his way out.

Bulac: I'm guessing Journey . . . or maybe Aerosmith.

Koch: Nah, I don't think so. *(Koch stares at the top of Bulac's head a moment, then reaches for his phone.)* Jeez, I gotta Google that. *(He types in the title of the song and sags in dismay as he gets the answer he was dreading.)* Dear God . . . just what I was afraid of. He's obsessed with that city . . .

(Bulac looks up, confused, but before he can say anything, a slight movement on the desk catches his eye.)

Bulac: Uh, Kay . . . pass me that fly swatter, will you?

(Koch reaches for the item and tosses it to Bulac, who catches it in midair. He lets it hover for a moment over his prey, then in whip-like fashion, swings it downward . . .)

* * * * *

WHAM!

Like a judge's gavel bringing down the final verdict in a hushed court room, *The Pines: An Illustrated History* slid off the covers and hit the floor with a resounding thud. Baker was rudely awakened. It took a moment for the fog to clear before the realization came that he'd been dreaming. The bedroom was still lit. He'd fallen asleep with the table lamp on.

Checking the time on his clock radio, Baker couldn't believe it was only 12:15. He felt as if he'd slept eight hours. God, what a dream—it had felt so real. He'd never experienced such vivid dreams before. He leaned over the edge of the bed and reached down to the floor to close the book, but stopped when he saw it was open to an iconic photo of the Chairman, George Daly, smiling as he sat in an open top convertible next to the Clarence Cup during the victory parade in '62. The last one Toronto had seen.

Still leaning over the edge of the bed, Baker thought about the possibility that this was some kind of sign. Then feeling the blood rushing to his head, he closed the book, turned off the lamp and tucked himself in to resume his slumber. Sleep, however, didn't come for another hour. His mind was active with the images and conversations from his dream.

What would be the fallout from Mason Andrews' indiscretions? Who would ultimately be awarded the captaincy? Could the spirits of old exert any influence on the Pines' fortunes this year? And then, there was probably the most pressing question: what were the chances that Perreault Thoreau was awake right now and thinking about Baker Brooks?

CHAPTER EIGHT
FIVE YEARS

We've bought five years, with these four guys
Five years, what's your ring size?
We've got five years, it's going to get hot
Five years, better not be for naught

Wednesday, October 2

It had been 162 days since the final horn sounded on the season for the Toronto Mighty Pines last April, following a miserable 6-2 loss to Washington in game seven of the first round of the playoffs. And now, following a summer of rest and regeneration, growth and maturation, trades and salary negotiations and free-agent signings, the long wait was finally over. The team was ready to pop the cork and drop the puck on the franchise's eighty-eighth chapter of professional hockey, and since the opening night foe would be the Ottawa Federals, the game was naturally promoted as the Battle of Ontario (or, as some preferred to call it, the Clash of Capitals).

As things stood, this 2019–2020 Mighty Pines model was supposed to roll off the assembly line and capably navigate the waters of the regular season, sailing smoothly to a first-place finish in the division and quite possibly the Eastern Conference. And while such talk would normally be pretty intoxicating stuff for Pines fans heading into October, something reserved only for the wishful thinkers, the truth was that the dreams were more substantive than anyone could remember for many a year. The citizens of Coney Nation were living in rare air considering the height of their expectations. So stratospheric were they—one might describe them as "Everestian"—that unless someone was a biological descendant of Himalayan Sherpas, they would need the assistance of oxygen tanks to dwell in the same company. All of this hypoxic hope was owed to a roster that—on paper anyway—was as good as any seen around these parts in decades.

When Cheers Are Not Enough

Perhaps the greatest source of anticipation for fans and media alike, apart from the game itself, was the pending announcement of the team's new captain, a decision that was revealed during the player introductions prior to the start of the game. With the house lights turned down and the ice surface bathed in green, the Pines support staff and coaches were introduced first, followed by the players, one by one, name by name. The public address announcer capped off the player introductions with the call: "Ladies and gentlemen . . . please welcome . . . the twenty-fifth captain in franchise history . . . from Toronto, Ontario . . . number ninety-five . . . Gianni Val-en-tee-nooo!"

As for the game, it actually lived up to the hype, with the teams combining for eleven goals. There was even some drama in the final ten minutes as, with the Pines trailing 5-4, they converted on two late power plays and hung on for a 6-5 comeback win. Mason Andrews added to his reputation for getting off to hot starts by potting two goals (Coney Nation had taken to calling him Mr. October—with apologies to baseball great Reggie Jackson) while Ricky Randall registered a goal and two assists.

And so, with the opening game of the Mighty Pines' 2019–2020 season providing several feel-good moments for the team and its fans, it was completely understandable then that those same fans would be expecting many more such notable accomplishments in the coming months. Their team was undefeated, and all was right in Coney Nation.

"The Pines have top-end talent, but there are those among us who are not convinced and are of the opinion—ahem, Conrad—that this team is not ready to win yet, not this year anyway. However, we want them to win this year. We *need* them to win this year—" Baker stopped mid-sentence.

It was Thursday after school, and the five members of Bakers' Coven were assembled in the music room, having spent the last fifteen minutes rehashing the previous night's victorious home opener. Now they were listening to Baker explain his rationale behind the theme of the song for that day's coven session, but he'd allowed himself to get sidetracked with a movie reference.

"Wow, did I not sound just like Colonel Jessup there?" He adopted his best Jack Nicholson voice: "You *want* me on that wall. You *need* me on that wall!" Baker looked at them for approval. "*A Few Good Men*?" Getting none, he shook his head. "Aw, it's pointless with you guys. Now, where was I?"

Angus mimicked Baker. "We want them to win. We *need* them to win."

"Right." Baker took a moment to recover his train of thought, then continued with his point. "OK, correct me if I'm wrong, but as of Ricky Randall's signing, this team has five years of certainty where their top four skaters are concerned. I'm referring, of course, to Andrews, Brouwer, Randall, and Valentino. Now, I don't know about the rest of you, but I can't watch this team throw away one of those precious years. So, I thought we might embrace that sentiment, you know, to make it the theme of our next request."

"So, the essence of our request is that the team not waste this window of five years?" Mas asked.

"Exactly." Baker distributed copies of his lyrics. "I thought the song 'Five Years' by David Bowie would suit our needs."

"Great album, Ziggy Stardust," Perreault said. "And good choice with 'Five Years.' The title is perfect."

"I thought so too," Baker replied. "And listening to Bowie sing those words, I mean, it stirs feelings in me that match the way he sounds—the fervour in his voice, you know?"

"If it's that powerful, then who are we to argue?" Masaccio asked.

"And, Baker, you're good with singing the lead?" Perreault inquired.

"I think so, yeah. I'd like to give it a shot anyway."

Angus took his place at the drum kit and began warming up. Meanwhile, Masaccio was fussing with his bass and plugging in to his amplifier.

"Hang on there, Mas," Baker said. "I'm thinking we need you to play piano on this."

Up to that point the band had built a repertoire of nine tunes to play before a live audience, and of those nine, Masaccio's services were required on keys three times. It was then that he would pass his bass over to Baker. But with the addition of Perreault, the guys assumed she'd handle the task of pulling off a simple bass line.

Without missing a beat, Mas removed the bass strap from his shoulder and held the instrument out vertically by the neck for Perreault to take. Her initial response was to back away, palms up, shaking her head—as if he was presenting her with the carcass of some roadkill, held by the tail and stiff with rigour mortis. Perreault's poor reception forced Mas to adopt a less aggressive approach. He took the shoulder strap and offered it in a more inviting fashion, like holding an overcoat open for someone to slip into.

"C'mon, Perreault, it won't bite. We need you to fill in here."

Perreault finally relented and donned the bass while Mas adjusted the strap for her.

Conrad watched Baker painstakingly tuning his instrument. He turned to Perreault, "You said you dabbled with the guitar as a kid. Do you still know any chords?"

"A few. Most of the open chords. I remember a couple of barre chords as well, but those'll be rusty."

"Well, shit, that already makes you more proficient than Baker. Hey, Baker, switch instruments with Perreault and you play bass."

Baker never looked up from tuning his guitar. "Ha, ha, asshole."

Conrad wasn't finished, though. "No? Alright then, but one sour chord, and you'll be relegated to backup vocals and tambourine."

"Hey Baker, if tambourine's not your thing, I've got a cowbell you can whack to help me keep the beat," Angus said, unable to resist contributing to this spontaneous dismantling of Baker.

"'Keep the beat?' Is that what you call it? I was wondering what you were doing back there the whole time we were up front here, playing the goddamn songs."

"Oh, snap!" Mas laughed from behind the keyboard. "Need some help getting up off the floor, Angus?"

"Wait, did I really just hear Masaccio employ the word 'snap' in a sentence?" Conrad asked.

"Indeed, you did," Angus replied. "Sorry, Mas, but I don't think 'snap' is appropriate for men your age."

The banter was interrupted by a succession of bass notes booming across the room. Perreault was plucking open strings in a quick rhythmic pattern, working up the neck to hold down random notes and then progressing to simple combinations. When she was satisfied, she stopped and nodded. "Let's go, boys. I think I'm good here. But don't expect too much from me."

The next forty-five minutes were spent working out the song in its most basic form and ironing out the kinks to the point where it was passable. At one point they got through to the end of the song surprisingly unscathed, prompting everyone to look around at each other as if to confirm what they'd just heard.

"That last effort was almost tolerable," Conrad announced. "What do you say we give this thing a go? You ready to sing this time, Baker?"

"Sure, let's do this."

Angus began the song with the simple drum lead, repeating it twice before Conrad came in with his twelve-string acoustic guitar, replacing Bowie's xylophone by running his pick over the strings. Then Masaccio hammered the opening piano chords. That was the cue for Baker's vocal entry:

> Pushing through Elysian Square
> So many of the fans sighing
> Another season too soon over
> But not for lack of trying

The guys took turns stealing glances at Perreault, assuring themselves that she would come in on time. Her fingers were poised over the strings as she focused on the bass sheet that Mas had written up for her. To her credit, the notes were plucked cleanly and on time as Baker continued with the second verse.

> *Sports guy smiled and told us*
> *What Pines' money's buying*
> *Let the parent company take on debt*
> *A Cup win is what they're eyeing*

As they progressed through the first two verses, it became apparent to Baker that Bowie's range by the third verse would prove a challenge for him. He found it a strain when it came time to describe "all the people" four times over. Stepping away from the microphone, he waved his hands for everyone to stop playing. "I can see I'm going to have trouble with the vocal range here. Let's try Conrad's idea and have me play bass while Perreault sings." He knew this arrangement would result in improvements to two aspects of the song: he'd be able to handle the bass runs, and Perreault could be expected to handle Bowie's vocal range.

"That's sounds fine to me," Perreault replied, removing the instrument and handing it over to Baker. "At least now I'll be in my element. You must have noticed how I left out three quarters of the bass parts."

Baker, Mas, Conrad, and Angus all politely and simultaneously voiced dissenting viewpoints, offering up varying levels of positive feedback.

"Well, now I know you're all liars." She smirked, then took a copy of the words and headed out of the main classroom. "I'm going to lock myself up in the rehearsal room for five minutes, so I can get comfortable matching Baker's words to the song."

Baker nodded. "Perfect. It'll give me some time to work through these bass runs."

"Sure. But I may need to call you in there with me." Without another word, she gathered her laptop and was gone.

Baker mentally kicked himself for feeling like a twelve-year old in looking forward to the opportunity to spend a couple of minutes alone in a room with Perreault. He busied himself with the bass and asked the other three to play along with him through the early verses.

A short time later, Perreault did in fact request Baker's company to look at the possibility of tweaking some of his words.

"You've come up with some clever lines here," she said. "I'm just looking to alter the rhythm on some of your lyrics, to get them to more naturally follow the bouncing ball, if you know what I mean."

"That's fine. Got anything specific in mind?"

Perreault showed Baker where she'd stumbled while trying to match his lines with Bowie's original words, and together they came up with a few minor adjustments. She sang through the changes, and as she did, her face went through a beguiling range of expressions. To prevent himself from staring, Baker forced himself to look down at his page of lyrics. Even more incredible to him was the fact that this woman, this cinnamon dynamo, seemed completely oblivious to the effect she was having on him.

"I think that about covers it, Mr. Brooks," she said after going through the song twice. Perreault's cheery voice brought Baker back to the present. "I'm ready," she continued. "Let's go do this. It should be fun."

Everyone resumed their positions, this time with Perreault manning the centre stage microphone. The five of them exchanged looks of readiness, and then Angus counted himself in and began. Perreault grabbed the mic with one hand, her lyrics sheet semi-scrunched in the other, then shook her hair out and stood with her eyes closed, rocking gently to the beat.

With her first words, it was obvious to the others that, from that point forward, everyone's job was going to be a lot easier. As for Baker, leaving the vocal responsibilities to someone else allowed him to concentrate solely on playing his instrument.

The first two verses went off much the same as their first take when Baker sang lead, except this time the bass filled in more. But it was with the third verse that the change took effect. Perreault displayed a preternatural ability to precisely interpret the text and then express it in a way that left no doubt. She effectively encapsulated the degree of passion and yearning of the long-suffering Toronto Mighty Pines fans in her delivery.

> *They used cell phones, game film, scouted European teams*
> *Spoke with coaches, scouts, GMs, and VPs*
> *The brain trust drew a plan up, it had no time to spare*
> *Punched so many numbers to afford everything out there*
> *With all the highly skilled people, and all the hard hitting people*
> *And all the really fast people, and all the super smart people*
> *Most of the money went to these four people:*

Perreault delivered Baker's words with force. It was nothing less than a desperate plea to the Pines' front office and the team players, and even the gods of hockey, all rolled into one.

> *When Valentino became a UFA*
> *Pines brass needed to sign him*
> *Local boy agrees to seven years*
> *The yearly cost: eleven million*
>
> *In 2016 we win the lottery*
> *Andrews is picked; Pines fans are jacked*

> *Has wicked hands; a goal scoring prodigy*
> *Cashes in with a long-term contract*

With each new verse, Perreault was revealing a sort of integrity that went beyond just jamming and having fun—although it was obvious she was having a blast. Her ability to time the rhythm of Baker's words with Bowie's original lyrics was spot on, which was put on display with the Addy Brouwer verse, especially the second and third lines. Her nailing those lines elicited spontaneous smiles from everyone else, as if to say, "Damn! Who knew she could be so entertaining?"

> *The next hit was Addy Brouwer*
> *He held out for way too long*
> *His passing, stickhandling, and skating sublime*
> *Without him we can't complete this song*

The next verse was Baker's favourite. He liked what the words expressed and how they matched Bowie's unique inflections, leading nicely into the chorus.

> *Then the time came to sign Ricky Randall*
> *And we thought it'd be done by the start of the summer*
> *The cap hit: eight figures or else he would walk*
> *Pay him, he's beautiful, it's no time to balk*

It was at about the time when Perreault sang of the cap hit for Randall that Janet Sax quietly opened the door and eased into the classroom, trying not to disturb what to her sounded like a pretty good moment. Perreault was facing away from the door, so she never did see the music teacher enter the room. Baker saw Janet and gave her a knowing nod as they swung into the chorus, but that caused him to miss his cue to sing backup at "Five Years." Perreault didn't forget, though, half turning and vigorously waving for him to come forward and share the mic.

> *We've bought five years, with these four guys*
> *Five years, to claim the prize*
> *We've bought five years, it's going to get hot*
> *Five years, 'cause that's all we've got*
>
> *We've bought five years, what's your ring size?*
> *Five years, tell me no lies*
> *We've got five years, it's all that we've bought*
> *Five years, better not be for naught*
>
> *We've bought five years, time to get wise*
> *Five years, to win with these guys*

We've got five years, you can bet the whole lot
Five years, to go home with the pot

We've bought five years, ain't no disguise
Five years, gotta win with these guys
We've got five years, is this what you sought?
Five years, don't waste what you've bought

As Baker continued with the supporting vocals through the final four repeats of "Five Years," Perreault echoed his words, except she screamed hers in anguish.

Five years
Five years
Five years
Five years

With the vocals finished, Mas and Conrad, on keyboard and guitar, respectively, let their final chords fade out, leaving Angus to close the song alone with the drumbeat and then silence, which was broken by an emphatic burst of applause and a whoop and a whistle, startling Perreault. When she turned and saw it was Janet, she stepped away from the mic and gave a little bow.

Baker looked to Conrad as if to verify what he had just experienced. Conrad was smiling and nodding as if to say, "Yes, I heard it too." If they hadn't realized it before, it was certainly evident now: there was a distinct talent among them. They had a lead vocalist who was willing to leave it all on the floor.

"Wow, that was terrific, you guys," Janet cheered. "And Perreault, you *are* Ziggy Stardust. We just need to dye your hair red and paint a lightning bolt on your face."

"Good idea," Angus said. "What do you say, Perreault? Hell, if you don't do it, I will."

"Janet, stop putting ideas in his head," Perreault scolded.

"Sorry. But that was great, really terrific. What's the name of your band?"

"We, uh . . . well, we call ourselves Bakers' Coven," Baker replied. "But the name doesn't refer to me. It refers to . . . you know, to bakers in general."

"Really." Janet didn't seem to be buying what he was selling. "Well, I guess it's a catchy name. Still, it doesn't hurt that someone in the band is named Baker."

"What do you think we've been telling him?" Mas said, giving Baker an *"I told you so"* look.

"What kind of stuff do you play?" Janet inquired. "Like, does the name Bakers' *Coven* mean you sound sort of 'witchy' or 'Gothy'?"

"No," Perreault replied. "I can't say we sound anything like Ministry or Bauhaus."

"How about Mother Goose then?" Janet was having fun now. "Or the Pillsbury Doughboy?"

"If by 'Mother Goose' you mean like Raffi, then no," Conrad replied. "And I have no idea what kind of music would fall under the category of the Pillsbury Doughboy. We basically play whatever one of us suggests from time to time, like the Hip, REM, the Weakerthans—come to think of it, quite a bit of Canadian content."

"And David Bowie, of course," Janet said.

"Right," Conrad agreed. "And now with Perreault on board, I can see us expanding our range considerably—perhaps Rufus Wainwright, some classic Neil Young, or putting a female spin on Eddie Vedder and Pearl Jam."

"For sure," Janet said. "But tell me, with the song you just played, it sounded like you were singing different words in places."

"Yes, if you had stepped in earlier, it would have been more obvious how we changed the lyrics."

"Really? What's up with that?"

No one answered immediately. Instead they turned to Baker, waiting for him to do the honours of trying to explain what Janet had heard.

Finally, Conrad rescued the group. "It's just something we're having fun with for now, Janet. But I'd like to shift gears a bit and play something else, if it's OK with Perreault." He shuffled some pages on his music stand and pulled out a sheet of lyrics, passing them across to his new vocalist. "Big Yellow Taxi?"

Perreault was caught off guard, but just for a moment. "Sure...yeah. Angus, you OK if we try this now?"

Angus nodded and that left Perreault to explain to the others what they were about to hear. "Conrad, Angus and I got together a while back and put together this arrangement of Joni Mitchell's 'Big Yellow Taxi.' Have you ever heard of B. B. Gabor?"

Janet shrieked like a sixteen-year-old. "Oh my God! I love B. B. Gabor. You guys are gonna perform *his* version of 'Big Yellow Taxi'? Now I'm feeling privileged." She settled in, exhibiting a heightened anticipation. Baker and Mas followed suit, grabbing a couple of chairs and sitting next to her. The three of them were treated to a pared-down version of B. B. Gabor's take on Joni Mitchell's masterpiece. It turned the punchy, sparkly original version into a musical lamentation, a rock 'n' soul requiem, with a hint of psychedelia. Conrad started it off with the mournful bluesy guitar line, repeating it once more before Perreault's rich, unhurried vocals expressed pure regret.

Baker watched and listened, impressed with the chemistry his three bandmates displayed. He was convinced it was the power of Perreault's vocals that made everyone better, and in his mind, he credited their overall proficiency to her absolute command of the material. He mouthed the word *"wow"* to Masaccio, who mouthed something in return that Baker couldn't make out, so he just assumed it was in Italian.

It was around the part in the song where Perreault sang about DDT and spots on apples that a knot of students gathered just outside the door in the hallway, peering through the window to get a look at what they were hearing. Spellbound, the students didn't move a muscle until the song was over.

The song ended, of course, with the repeated refrain of eight words that described how paradise had been reduced to a parking lot; a line so brilliant it could be found on the short list of most memorable in the annals of popular music. Perreault held the last two words and let them fade as the accompanying music died out. Then following a pause, it returned in a blast of guitar that brought to mind 1970s Rush. With that, the song officially ended.

Baker, Mas, and Janet all stood and whooped it up, joined by the four or five students who were eavesdropping in the hall. Janet went and let them into the room, so they could mingle with the teachers. They all hovered around Perreault, Conrad, and Angus, after which Janet escorted them out and shut the door before returning to the group. "Thanks for doing honour to one man's interpretation that, in my opinion, doesn't get enough credit," she said. "I was almost in tears. You guys should commit to making yourselves available for music events here at school because I'm including you in every talent show and open mic night we hold this year." She held up her arms and stared over their heads across the room as if admiring a marquee. "'The teacher's band—Bakers' Coven.' The kids will go apeshit."

Before she left, Janet warned Perreault that she'd be recruiting her services as a vocal coach when rehearsals began for next spring's musical. Then, after reminding Baker to lock the instrument storage room on his way out, Janet wished them all good luck and a good evening and took her leave.

The band—that is to say, the four original male members—matured that day, each one recognizing that he now had an obligation to do his best to support this person they previously knew simply as *"Perreault with the nice voice."* They had broken through the envelope that separated an insignificant, part-time band from a group that now needed to overcome shyness, eliminate silliness, and make a commitment to acquiring instrumental proficiency.

Baker drove home that evening newly inspired, struck by a song idea for the Coven's next session. It was influenced by what he'd just witnessed in Perreault's performance; they could give way more space to her vocal range and dramatic moxy. The more he thought about it, the more he was convinced that Perreault's talents would best be served by the music of Sheryl Crow.

CHAPTER NINE
A THANKSGIVING PROPOSITION

Thursday, October 10

A week had passed since the Pines' opening night victory over Ottawa, and in the interval, the green and white had played three games and posted a record of 1–1–1; lukewarm for even the most optimistic of fans. Those same fans, therefore, were hoping that Thursday night's affair against Tampa Bay would produce something with substantially more heat. Granted, for most observers the Pines' fifth game of the season had no significance beyond the fact that it happened to follow the fourth and precede the sixth. But for Kayden Koch, that night's match was meaningful because it closed out the schedule's first segment of five games.

In navigating his teams through the slog of a PHL season, Koch divided the eighty-two-game schedule into five-game "segments." According to the coach's math, a realistic goal for each segment was to earn six points. With sixteen such segments in the season, an average of six points per segment would earn his team ninety-eight points in the standings, which was typically enough to ensure a berth in the playoffs. Thus, the Pines would need to earn at least a tie in that night's game for those six points.

Unfortunately, the Pines extended their losing streak to three games and closed out the first segment of five games in dispiriting fashion with a mediocre 2–2–1 record, collecting only five out of a possible ten points. Much of the pre-season hype and hope was negated by the team's flaws, which were wide-ranging. Any adjustments by the coaches and players would have to be made on the fly, however, as the hectic pace of the first month of the season proved a challenge for the team. The second segment would begin on Saturday with a game in Detroit.

On the brighter side, while the hockey gods were taking a dim view of the Pines in early October, the weather gods were looking upon the GTA with favour as a week of sunshine and balmy temperatures allowed people throughout Southern Ontario to bask in glorious autumn weather while taking in the brilliant fall colours.

When Cheers Are Not Enough

It was on the Friday of the Thanksgiving long weekend that Baker was relaxing alone in his classroom on his lunch break, enjoying the view from his third-floor window and finishing a sandwich, when he heard a knock at the door. Upon answering it, he was greeted by Paul Young's smiling face. Paul was among a number of HMV graduates who, each year without fail, when their hectic post-secondary lives allowed, would return to their "old" high school to catch up with their "old" high school teachers. Paul had made a habit of dropping in to say hi at least a couple times a year ever since he graduated two years ago. (He had taken visual art classes with Baker in three of his four years in high school.)

"Hey, Mr. Brooks."

"Hiya, Paul." The name came to Baker instantly, much to his relief.

"I hope I'm not interrupting. We have no classes today, so I came by to visit some of my teachers."

"Of course. C'mon in. I was just finishing my lunch." But before Paul could make it through the doorway, Baker blocked his entrance, looking him up and down. "Is it just my imagination, or have you grown? God, you're taller than me now. What have you been eating?" That was one way to break the ice with ex-students he hadn't seen in at least a few months. One could always count on them coming back looking different in some way, especially the guys. Paul proudly admitted to a growth spurt, food being a major factor in the equation, of course. The two of them proceeded to catch up on other aspects of their lives since the previous June. Paul was in his second year of film studies at a Toronto-based community college and was enjoying every minute of it. The conversation inevitably turned to the Raptors' and Pines' respective seasons, with Baker and Paul expressing like-minded opinions on the chemistry and plucky work ethic displayed by the Raptors thus far and a general dismay at the Pines' inconsistencies.

Before long, Paul got around to why he had really stopped by. "Sir, I've got this assignment requiring me to produce a music video. For some reason, I immediately thought of the teachers' band. Are you guys still getting together after school and playing?"

"As a matter of fact, we are."

"That's great. Is it all the same teachers—yourself, Fletcher, Clementi, and Widdershins?"

"Yup, the same gang. Except we've recruited another member this year. Miss Thoreau is our lead vocalist."

"Oh? You've got a female front person now? That sounds like it's got possibilities."

"Yes. She's totally committed, and she has a great voice, so we lucked out." Baker pulled a chair around to his desk and directed Paul to sit down. "Oh, and we even have a name for ourselves." He spent a few minutes rehashing the band's thought process in the genesis of the name and then moved on to further discuss Paul's assignment. As the conversation progressed, Baker found himself growing quite intrigued at the idea of a music video. He shared his own visions with Paul, much of which centred on his plans for a song based on Sheryl Crow's "If it Makes You Happy." It was then that Paul dropped the bomb:

"You should understand, sir, I have every intention of getting this video as much exposure as the law allows. I'll have to check the copyright on some of the images I'm planning to use, and as we're performing a derivative, as they say, of Sheryl Crow's music, I'll see if I have to obtain permission. Other than those considerations, I'd need everyone in Bakers' Coven—I love that name, by the way—to consent to having their images posted in a public forum. I'm going to leave that to you, if you don't mind."

It was a lucky coincidence that the Coven had planned to meet briefly that very afternoon. For Baker, pitching the idea of a music video to his bandmates wasn't much cause for concern. After all, if they were willing to go so far as to engage in coven rituals, what would be the big deal about creating a music video? Nevertheless, Baker prepared himself for some resistance all the same.

He began by distributing copies of his new song, having spent most of the past weekend working up Sheryl Crow's hit single into an alternative version that he titled "Make Us Happy." When he proposed the concept of the music video, he attempted to downplay the idea of the project, partly to temper his own enthusiasm, as well as to forestall any potential negative reactions that the others might have—but Baker was amazed at how badly he had misread his friends.

"Good God, where's your vision?" Angus replied. "I thought you were the big idea guy."

"What's your point?"

"Can't you see where this could go? Can't you see the potential?"

Baker grinned. "Hey, everybody, listen up. Angus has had an epiphany."

"Joke all you want, but what are we doing here? The original plan was to impact the fortunes of the Toronto Mighty Pines, right? Well, isn't this one way of doing that?"

"Not to be repetitive, but what's your point?"

"Isn't it possible that people will see this on YouTube? The people who matter, I mean. People affiliated with the Pines and such."

"Sure, I suppose anything's possible, but—"

"But nothing." Angus waved his copy of "Make Us Happy" in Baker's face. "You've come up with a catchy cover of Sheryl Crow's song, right?"

"Well, yeah, I guess so."

"Good. So, now the song gets picked up—except with your new lyrics—and played at Pines games. You know, like how they play 'Sweet Caroline' at Red Sox games."

"But they're already playing a goal song when the Pines score. You think they're suddenly going to change that?"

"I'm not talking about a goal song. I'm referring to something different. Picture this: it's the third period in a playoff game, and there's a TV timeout, and Pines management has adopted a policy of playing our song over the public address system. The words are flashed up on the giant video scoreboard, like a massive 'follow the bouncing ball,' and the fans start to actually look forward to this moment, to sing along with your words at the top of their lungs. Every home game they blow the roof off the place." The more Angus got revved up, the more alarmed Baker looked. Undaunted, Angus continued. "Then it gets to where the TV broadcast doesn't even cut away to commercial because they want the viewing audience to experience it. You know how people said they tuned in to catch five minutes of Coach's Corner? Well, now they'd be looking forward to five minutes of 'Make Us Happy.'"

"Oh, my gosh," Perreault cut in. "I just thought of something: imagine the crowd out in Elysian Square doing the same thing!"

"Jesus, Perreault, not you too?" Baker sounded horrified. "Listening to you guys, two words come to mind: keep dreaming."

"OK, let's say we are dreaming," Perreault replied. "Isn't it a wonderful dream? I mean, how hard-hearted must a team be to hear their fans in song, full-throated and jubilant, and not respond with some increase in their effort level? It would be like a shot of pure Adrenalin. Oh, and Baker, then we could honestly say our mission was accomplished."

Baker was refusing to let himself get caught up in the hype. It was Conrad's cooler head that actually got them all to find common ground.

"Lady and gentlemen, you can stop arguing because it's all a moot point anyway. Nobody in the Pines' promotions department is going to pick this up off YouTube, Coney Nation won't be singing it during home games, and it won't be adopted by our federal government as this country's new national anthem. Why? The video won't be posted on social media in the first place because this kid, Paul, ain't gonna get permission to use Sheryl Crow's tune." Angus and Perreault looked like whipped dogs. "But hey," Conrad continued, "isn't it enough that we're making a music video together? I'm excited just to have someone willing to spend time and energy doing this with us. I mean, this is still a damn good idea, Baker. Don't let a defence mechanism prevent you from recognizing the fact that we're all behind you."

"Alright," Mas said, "so Conrad has brought us back down to earth, but he's also reminded us that even if this project doesn't get widely distributed, there's value in the experience. And Baker, don't get cynical. Keep on dreaming. Keep being the guy we all know and love, the guy who approached Sid at the Misty River last summer to ask if we could play a set. The guy who's been gathering us as a coven to engage in some pretty outrageous stuff. And now, the guy who approached us to do this music video."

Baker graciously accepted the kind words of support. He didn't let it show, but deep down he felt a growing surge of exhilaration. Now if only his favourite hockey team could string together some wins.

CHAPTER TEN
CUBBY

Wednesday, October 16

In Canadian politics, on the heels of the previous week's English and French language debates, federal party leaders headed into the home stretch of the campaign leading up to the October 21st federal election.

South of the border, Daryl Morey, General Manager of the NBA's Houston Rockets, tweeted his support of protestors in Hong Kong who were demonstrating for basic human rights and democratic freedoms from their authoritative government. What followed was an eight-day firestorm of media attention when China responded by severing ties with various American professional basketball entities. Among the usual suspects who were asked to comment, Golden State's Steve Kerr was unusually tight-lipped about the Chinese government's reputation, citing a lack of information regarding a complex issue. Unable to resist, US president Donald Trump weighed in on Kerr's ambivalence, mocking the coach who he regarded as otherwise outspoken, especially when it came to criticizing the White House Administration. Kerr responded by describing himself as an easy target in this instance, because people of Trump's ilk looked for just such opportunities to pounce, as if he were a shiny object, or a piece of fresh meat.

Kerr's description of himself was most apropos for how Detroit's hockey team must have looked to other PHL clubs, including the Mighty Pines. The Dieseldogs were in the midst of a rebuild and were expected to be woeful this year. Toronto ultimately made easy work of Detroit, winning 6-2, and then followed it up two days later with a workmanlike 4-2 victory in Minnesota.

It had been a winning week for the Pines, and Toronto wins always put Baker in a good mood. Such was his disposition now, standing before his fourth-period grade nine art class, happily sharing one of his favourite stories.

Baker loved stories. He loved to *tell* stories, especially when they helped to make his lessons more impactful. Even better, he was *good* at telling stories. He also had an affinity for magic, but not the kind that involved magicians at birthday parties. Baker preferred magic that inspired wonder and awe at the mysteries of nature. And from his experience, performing magic for high school students was doable. It just required a bit of planning, a combination of energy and passion, and a keen working knowledge of the subject matter: all things Baker could supply on demand.

And yet, kids would be kids, and no matter how enthralling his tale might be, classroom distractions were ever-present and numerous—so as a remedy, Baker found that inserting select students' names directly into the story at random produced a noticeable adjustment in their posture and a refocusing of eye contact, which basically helped to keep them alert. So, with all the ingredients on hand and minutes to spare, Baker brought his present narrative about "The Mystery of Tom Thomson's Death" to its denouement.

"To this day, *Jessica,* no one can be sure where Tom's remains lie. The mystery has never been solved. And although the truth behind the circumstances of Tom's death may never be revealed, what we do know, *Richard,* is that he left us a wonderful collection of sketches and paintings through which we have the opportunity to see the beauty and power of our land in a fresh light. But people still love a good ghost story, and so, *Cassandra,* if you went up to Algonquin Park today, no doubt you'd hear folks claiming to have seen a man—quite possibly the ghost of Tom Thomson—alone in a canoe, noiselessly paddling across the surface of the lake at dusk, near the place where he died, in the park he loved best."

Baker ended the story and appraised his audience. The silence of twenty-six students could be powerful, with only the hint of a sigh or an intake of breath. Then the school bell sounded to break the spell, and the students gathered their things and rose to leave. On their way out the door, Katelyn and Sam, walking shoulder to shoulder, arms wrapped around binders and books across their chests, stopped by Baker's desk. "Sir, you asked us earlier to remind you to get the children's books we'll need for tomorrow's class?"

"Oh, yes. Thanks for the reminder, girls. In fact, I'll go down to the library and do that right now." He scanned the room to make sure everyone was gone and that nothing had been left behind. Katelyn and Sam stood watching him, so Baker felt he needed to continue the conversation. "Boy, this felt like a long week, didn't it? Oh well, one more day till the weekend. Thank goodness tomorrow is Friday." The girls giggled in agreement, poster children for teenage awkwardness. He escorted them out into the corridor, then turned to lock the door behind him. "You two stay out of trouble, OK?" he joked. "See you tomorrow."

"Bye, sir," they replied in unison, making a turn left and walking down the hall to their lockers.

Baker turned to the right, heading for the stairwell that would take him one floor down to the library. Upon arriving he proceeded through the scanner, whereupon Lawrence Wynn, sitting at his computer behind the checkout counter, greeted him with a welcoming smile. "Good afternoon, Mr. Brooks."

"Afternoon, Mr. Wynn. What's goin' on?"

"It's been pretty quiet around here today, to be honest, but it gave me the opportunity to get caught up on cataloguing that shipment of new books." He pointed to a stack of crisp new titles farther down the counter.

"It's hard for me to describe how happy I am for you, Larry. I just came by to take some items off your shelves. I need some of the children's books for tomorrow and into next week."

The books were, in fact, Baker's personal property, but rather than store them in the art room, where shelf space was always at a premium, he had asked Lawrence to set aside a special place for them—separate from the regular book stacks. Baker often employed the illustrations in the books as exemplars for his watercolour painting unit.

"Help yourself to a newspaper while you're at it," Lawrence said, getting out of his chair and coming around the counter. "Listen, I'm heading downstairs to the main office. Would you mind keeping an eye on the room for me for a few minutes?"

"Sure, but you're going to trust me not to burn the place down in your absence?"

Lawrence hesitated, thinking of better days. "Boy, it was nice when Helen was here. We could cover for each other. But until I get a new assistant, I guess I'm on my own. There's a fire extinguisher by the exit, though," he added dryly, "just in case."

As Lawrence left, Baker made his way to the shelves and was struck with a sense that he had done this before. The combination of circumstances—sharing stories with his students, the time of day, his visit to the library—it all precipitated a feeling of déjà vu, which gave way to a distinct recollection. He slowed down to let the memory play out in his mind, some instinct telling him it was important to think it through, to recall the entire series of events of that particular afternoon. He looked up to see he was standing by the table where Cubby was seated the first time they met—roughly one year ago.

* * * * *

It was midweek, early in November 2018. Baker was in the library to do a quick inventory of the children's books and was surprised to find one was missing from its usual place on the shelf. He checked again, this time more carefully. Then he became aware of a child's voice. The child was reciting sentences that sounded as if they were taken from the story of the very book Baker was searching for: "We all taped our sticks like Claude

Lambert." A giggle. "We all skated, hunched over, like Claude Lambert." The tiny voice grew in volume. "And when we scored, we even celebrated like Claude Lambert."

There was no mistaking it. Those were the classic lines from Felix Cote's *My Hockey Stick*. Although he could appreciate the kid's enthusiasm, Baker noticed how the poor soul was butchering the icon's name each time, pronouncing it "Clod Lamb-burt." Thus it was for two reasons that Baker decided to approach the boy. First, he thought he could use a gentle lesson in French pronunciation. Second, he simply wanted to get his hands on that book for the following day's class. The watercolour illustrations suited his needs perfectly.

He sat down at the table, thinking he might chat the kid up and find out where he was from—it was unusual to see elementary school kids in a high school library—and determine what his intentions were vis-a-vis the book in his hands.

"That happens to be one of my favourite hockey stories; it's a good one."

The boy looked up at Baker, then back down at the pages open before him. "I like the pictures."

"You know something? I like them too."

Baker watched the boy with fascination. He also noticed that the child had a green Toronto Mighty Pines cap, but rather than being perched on his head, it was on the table at his right elbow. (Like every other member of the teaching staff, Baker frowned upon the wearing of hats indoors, especially in a school where hats were not part of the uniform.) Seeing this as a refreshing departure from the habits of today's youth, he found himself developing a fondness for the kid.

"Do you play hockey yourself?"

"Yup. I play defence—and sometimes forward, whenever my coach needs me to." He looked back down at the illustration that displayed Claude Lambert's unique skating form. "Did the players really skate like that?"

"Not everybody. That style was unique to Claude Lambert." Baker pronounced the name using his strongest Quebecois accent, causing the kid to look blankly at him for a moment, not comprehending. Then he flipped to a previous page that featured a watercolour illustration of the legendary centreman.

"You mean this man? Clod Lamb-burt?"

"Yes, him. But he was French, so his name has a French sound. Clod Lamb-burt is really pronounced *Clode Laahm-bare*."

The boy looked at the name on the page, then mimicked Baker, "Clode Laahm-bare."

"That's right," Baker said. "By the way, my name is Mr. Brooks, what's yours?"

"Cubby. My dad calls me Cub, but my friends call me Cubby."

The child turned his attention back to the open book before him, idly flipping pages and repeating *"Clode Laahm-bare"* under his breath in time with each turn of a page.

As Baker watched, he wondered if Cubby had seen the movie *Elf*—specifically the scene in which Will Ferrell similarly flips the pages of a storybook, quietly savouring the name *"Fran-SIS-ko"* as it rolled off his tongue. Catching himself staring at the boy, Baker diverted his attention to the other items on the table, including a *Toronto Star* newspaper, back issues of *Sports Illustrated*, *Wired*, and *People* magazines, and a hardcover coffee table copy of *The Clarence Cup: A Tradition Like No Other*. Baker found the title curious and wondered how people associated with the Masters golf tournament would feel about it. He reached across the table and pulled the book toward him. Cubby looked up.

"That's Aunty Helen's . . . but you can look at it."

"Aunty Helen?"

"She's back there, behind the counter."

It was making sense now. For the past couple of years, Helen Nella had been assisting Lawrence in the library. Baker could now assume that Cubby was under her care and that she was probably babysitting her nephew for the afternoon.

The boy straightened up in his seat. "Aunty Helen is the librarian's technical assistant."

Noting the formality in Cubby's words when he announced his aunt's title, Baker wondered if he was mimicking Helen's voice.

* * * * *

The same oversized book was in his hands now. When did that happen? He must have found it in the stacks and, not thinking, removed it from the shelves. Baker sat down at a table and leafed through the book, which was heavy with classic photographs, starting with grainy black-and-white images of men sporting stylish moustaches and woollen jerseys emblazoned with thistles or winged feet on their fronts, not to mention lots of horizontal striping. For Baker, those were halcyon days, when hockey and the PHL had been like a medieval romance (maybe Conrad was right about his affinity for such stories) where splendidly armoured knights had wielded brilliant weapons on magnificent stallions, rearing up in the face of their foes on the field of battle. Those days had been long before he'd become a self-initiated member of Coney Nation.

Coney Nation. Ha! Such a prideful title. And what was it, really? A rabbit hole that chewed people up and swallowed them down into some muscular digestive sac, to be broken down with all the other loyal, suffering fools. Nothing more than a company of chyme—ugh, what a disgusting thought.

Baker shook himself out of this toxic thought process and instead flipped backwards through pages that recalled the Toronto teams of the 1940s. He flipped through images of Cal Ubank, Beasley Sharpe, and Coach Emmett Pepper celebrating multiple Cup victories. There was Jersey Joe Zedelko, with his Hollywood hair and boyish smile, always in the front row during Cup presentation ceremonies. Then back even further in time, when Colonel Nate Sinclair had gambled and hustled his way to majority ownership of the newly purchased and freshly outfitted and minted Toronto Mighty Pines. In the eyes of many at the time, Sinclair had also gambled—and won—with the construction of his grand hockey palace. He'd built Mighty Pines Coliseum, ultimately filling it with formally dressed capacity crowds and growing legions of diehard fans, the proto–Coney Nation. And then a Clarence Cup in 1937: the first of eleven Cups that the Toronto Mighty Pines would win. Eleven times the Holy Grail would reside in the house that Sinclair built, the man ruling like some twentieth-century King Arthur, presiding over his own fiefdom, his own Camelot, for king (then queen) and country.

Turning the glossy pages, Baker stopped at the section that explored the historic rivalry between the Montreal Nationales and the Toronto Mighty Pines. Through the decades of the 40s and 50s, the Montreal Nationales had won the Clarence Cup ten times while Toronto had been close behind, winning it seven times. The domination of Montreal and Toronto meant that back then it was always the Nats or the Pines, or both, in the finals. One of the stars on those multiple Cup–winning Nats teams had been Claude Lambert. More than a star, he had been a living legend, especially among the French-speaking population in Quebec. In 1945, in just his second year in the PHL, Lambert had accomplished something that was considered mythical and unattainable: he had scored fifty goals in one season. Since the regular season had consisted of fifty games at the time, the hockey world had referred to the feat with the catchy descriptor "fifty goals in fifty games."

Baker ruminated on how things hadn't changed much; how seventy-five years later, today's twenty-first-century game still marvelled at any player who could score fifty goals in a season, despite the fact the season had since been extended to eighty-two games.

Baker turned his attention back to the iconic picture of Lambert, suited up, skating toward the camera in attack mode, eyes ablaze. As one of the great Canadian sporting heroes not fighting in the war, Lambert had been mounting his attack on the fifty-goal plateau while the Allied forces had been sweeping in on Germany. He'd ultimately scored his fiftieth in the fiftieth (and final) game of the season. That, coincidentally, had been exactly fifty days before Germany's unconditional surrender to the Allied armies on May 7. (Unfortunately for Montreal fans, there was no such surrender to their heroes in the playoffs that spring, as Toronto eliminated the Nationales in the semi-finals before defeating Detroit in the final to claim the Cup.)

Baker would have continued reading, but his absorption was interrupted when a pair of students entered the library bearing two plates heaped with brownies, evidently from the cooking class. They hovered around the checkout counter, then saw Baker and approached him.

He could only focus on the two gaudy baseball caps coming his way. "Hats off please, boys."

"Sorry, sir." They both reached up and whipped off the offending headgear with such efficiency that it was obvious they had lots of practice. "Do you know where Mr. Wynn is?"

"I sure do. He went downstairs to the main office. He should be back soon."

"Hmm. Could you maybe tell him Calum and Jorge left this for him?"

"Calum and Jorge left their brownies. Got it. I'll tell him."

"Thanks, Mr. Brooks. Oh, and help yourself if you want."

"I'm good for now, but thanks for offering. See you, guys."

"Bye, sir." The boys left the plates on Lawrence's counter and exited the library, placing their caps back on their heads before they were through the door.

Baker shook his head as he watched them leave. Then he remembered that his conversation with Cubby had been cut off in a similar way about a year ago.

* * * * *

Helen Nella approached them, carrying a tray of juice boxes and oversized chocolate chip cookies.

"I thought you two might like a snack. The students in Food Services class brought some treats down here last period, and I have some of these juice boxes left over from one of our council meetings."

Cubby's eyes lit up. He carefully positioned what looked to Baker like an oversized, homemade bookmark between the pages of *My Hockey Stick*, set it aside, and laid out the napkin his aunt provided before him on the table. He looked hungrily at the cookies and then at Baker, and waited. Baker took note of the boy's hesitation. "You go ahead, Cubby. The kids in the cooking class sure do make some tasty treats."

While Cubby dug in, Helen turned to Baker. "I just brewed a fresh pot of dark roast if you're interested." She pointed to the windowed workspace behind the checkout counter and, taking one last look to make sure her nephew was comfortable, headed that way to return to her post.

A fresh cup of coffee sounded good to Baker, so he excused himself, leaving Cubby to munch away, and headed over to Helen's desk.

"Help yourself, Baker. Mugs are on the counter next to the carafe. Sugar's there too. Cream's in the fridge."

Baker noticed three mugs: one decorated with van Gogh irises, another stamped with the 1970s-style Toronto Mighty Pines logo, and the third an HMV school-issue coffee cup. He chose the van Gogh mug, more for its elegantly flared shape than anything else, then unscrewed the carafe lid a quarter turn and poured.

"Just tip and pour," Helen said as she attended to her computer screen. "Don't unscrew the lid or it will spill everywhere." Baker could have used that information two seconds earlier, as before he knew what had happened, coffee had sloshed onto the counter.

"Too late!"

Helen was there with paper towels, sopping up the spill. "I should have warned you earlier. Everybody makes that mistake. It's a good carafe, but it seems to catch people off guard. I'm just afraid someone's going to burn themselves with hot coffee one day."

Once order was restored, Baker and Helen settled into the two office chairs that were available.

"So Cubby's your nephew?"

"Yes. His father dropped him off after school today because he had an appointment. I could watch Calub any day of the week. He's a wonderful kid."

"Who? Calub? He told me his name was Cubby."

"Oh, yes, well, his family calls him Cubby, but his Christian name is Calub. I never got into the habit of calling him Cubby, so I stick with Calub or just Cal."

"Like the hockey player."

Helen nodded. "Like the hockey player."

"Cubby—er—Cal, tells me he plays hockey."

"Oh, yes. Cal has been playing for a couple of years now. Apparently, he's quite accomplished. He's undersized for his age, and he lacks some foot speed, but his hand-eye coordination is exceptional, and his hockey sense is off the charts. This is all just stuff I'm told, mind you."

"Stuff you're told? Who are the experts telling you this, if you don't mind my asking?"

"Two people, mostly: my husband, Allen, and Cal's dad, David. Allen and David both say he has an instinct for the game. They say he looks like Gabe Wozniak at that age, a small kid who has the puck on his stick a lot of the time, not because he's faster or stronger than the other boys but because of where he positions himself." The entire time she spoke about her nephew, Helen was looking across the room at him, almost in adoration. "But I'm not the one you should be asking. My husband could tell you so much more. He's the mastermind behind Cal's development as a hockey player . . . him and David."

"By the way, what name should I address him by?" Baker asked. "He told me he prefers Cubby."

"That's fine. Call him Cubby. I might be the only one who calls him Cal, and he's used to that."

"OK, Cubby it is then. I'm gonna go back now and see if he's done with my book."

"He's got a book of yours?" Helen sounded slightly alarmed.

"Oh, it's nothing. I was just hoping to take the book he's reading because I need it for a class tomorrow."

"He's not giving you a hard time, is he?"

Baker assured Helen that her nephew had been a perfect gentleman. Then he took his coffee with him back to Cubby's table.

"Did you get a chance to finish reading the story?" Baker asked.

Cubby seemed to waffle on a response, looking at Baker, then at the book, then back again. "Mostly."

"Mostly? I'll tell you what, Cubby. I need to use this book for my lesson tomorrow. I want my students to paint pictures like the ones in this story, so they're going to need to see them. If you let me take the book today, I'll read through it with you right now before it's time to leave. Would that be OK with you?"

Cubby smiled and accepted the offer. Opening the book, Baker saw the boy's bookmark slip out. It was clearly homemade: a laminated piece of card stock, oversized, roughly comparable to a page from a paperback novel. The front side consisted of a rendering—and a fairly good one at that—of the Clarence Cup. It was finished in pencil crayon. Rising out of the bowl was a green Toronto Mighty Pines pinecone. An unseen light source caused the Cup's shadow to fall to the right. Instead of the usual five main rings, this one only had three. The bottom ring had the name "Calub Elyk" added in impeccable print, complete with a curved aspect so as to follow the cylindrical shape of the ring itself.

The back of the card was more intriguing. Affixed to the centre of the card was what appeared to be the slip of paper that one finds in a fortune cookie. Its message consisted of three lines:

> *Your name in silver*
> *Results from*
> *Excellence with black on white*

It took a minute before Baker recognized it as a bit of freestyle haiku. It took less than half that for him to understand its message as it related to Cubby, but he didn't assign any more significance to it beyond the possibility that it was a homemade fortune in support of the kid's hockey dreams. More puzzling was a three-digit number neatly printed in pencil crayon on either side of the fortune itself: 641.

Not giving it any further thought, Baker went to return the bookmark to its spot between the pages when he was struck by a strange compulsion to take a picture. (It might have been simply a force of habit, Baker having put his phone camera to considerable use the previous day, spending a full two hours after school taking photos of student artwork he'd accumulated over the years.) So, still in the groove, Baker snapped a couple of pics of the front and back of Cubby's bookmark. If nothing else, it seemed to be a proud moment for the kid. That done, Baker tucked the card into the flap inside the front cover and positioned the book between them on the table. He turned to the first page of the story, pressing it flat, and began to read.

> "My very first hockey stick was handed down to me from my older brother who had grown too tall for it. It didn't matter that the stick was too tall for me... Nevertheless, I loved that stick, having scored a fair number of goals with it..."

As he listened, Cubby shifted his attention from Baker to the book and back again. Otherwise, his gaze never wavered. His hands were busy, though. Baker couldn't help but notice that the boy fiddled with his pencil as it lay flat on the table. It was one of those basic eraser-tipped orange wooden pencils. Cubby had a habit of rolling it back and forth with his index finger, as if he were stick handling it. At other times he pushed the pencil tip around in a circle. But his eyes never strayed from their "target."

> "Then the summer came when I suddenly grew taller. My mother called it a "growth spurt"... That autumn I discovered that my Claude Lambert hockey stick was too short for me... like my older brother, I had outgrown my hockey stick..."

When he had finished, Baker was half expecting Cubby to request a second reading, but the child apparently needed answers to other questions. "Is it true that people from Montreal don't like the Toronto Mighty Pines that much? And do people from Toronto feel the same about the Nationales?"

"Yes. We call that a healthy rivalry."

"When will I have my growth spurt?"

The question came at Baker from out of the blue, and as much as he was enjoying spending time with this kid, he still needed to organize a few things in his classroom before heading home, so he answered in an evasive manner. "That's a question for your parents, Cubby. You should ask your dad or your mom."

Cubby gave him a blank look. "Oh, my mom's dead."

The shock of Cubby's matter-of-fact answer left Baker at a loss for how to respond. With childlike frankness Cubby continued. "She got real sick during the Christmas holidays a couple years ago and died over the March break. It was her brain."

All talk of growth spurts and hockey sticks was replaced with words of sympathy and condolence. "Gee, that's awful, Cubby. I'm sorry to hear that."

The boy shrugged it off. "That's OK."

Baker had a hundred questions for the kid, but feeling that it wasn't his place to ask, he chose couth over curiosity. The potential for an awkward moment between them was negated when Helen, done for the day and ready to leave, came over to see that her nephew had everything neatly put away. While Cubby packed up his things, Baker made sure that *My Hockey Stick* was securely placed under his own arm (unaware that Cubby's bookmark was still tucked behind the inside flap of the front cover).

"I'll tell you what," Helen said, turning to Baker. "This Saturday I'm hosting our ladies' night potluck. How would you like to come over for a nice meal? You can keep my poor husband company. Allen will likely hang out downstairs watching the games on the big screen."

"The games?"

"Yes. At this time of year, Saturdays are a big sports day for Allen. He enjoys his college football, especially the Fightin' Irish."

"He's a Notre Dame fan?"

"For as long as I've known him, and I've known him for thirty-four years."

"What other games will he be watching?"

"The Mighty Pines game. You know, Saturday night hockey—Hockey Night in Canada."

"Right . . . the Pines game, of course." Baker had momentarily forgotten about Saturday's game and Helen's mention of it was a shock to his senses, like he'd been doused with a cooler-sized jug of ice water. It meant he would need to set aside his reservations about watching Pines games in the company of "friends." But sensing that Helen was waiting for an answer, Baker made the conscious decision to just go with the flow. "That sounds ideal—a nice meal *and* sports on a big screen. You can count me in."

Helen gave Baker directions, the time, and the address.

"What about food?" he asked. "Should I bring a contribution to the general meal? A salad? A dessert?"

Helen shook her head. "We've got everything covered. Just your presence will be sufficient." Then added with a wink, "But I'm sure none of the girls would complain if another bottle of wine showed up on the table."

* * * * *

The next time Baker crossed paths with Cubby, it was early spring, a few weeks before Easter, again in the library. Angus had tagged along on this occasion, simply to see for himself if there was any validity to Baker's claim that Helen brewed the best pot of coffee in the school.

Heartened to see the kid again, Baker approached him with an open smile. Cubby had grown thinner since he'd last seen him in November; that, or he had stretched a bit. They shook hands. Cubby looked like he had just woken up, his eyelids droopy and slightly red-rimmed. His handshake was less than robust. A notebook was on the table, opened to an empty page, as well as an illustrated children's Bible. Lying on the table between the books was a wooden eraser-tipped pencil.

Baker gestured to Angus. "Mr. Fletcher, this is Cubby Elyk, Mrs. Nella's nephew. Cubby, this is Mr. Fletcher. Mr. Fletcher works in the Special Education department here at HMV."

Angus exchanged greetings with the boy, then excused himself, making for the librarian's office to fix himself a coffee.

Curious about how Cubby's hockey team was faring at that point in the season, Baker inquired after it briefly, then pointed to the articles on the table.

"What are you working on?"

"Mrs. Lopes gave us each a Bible story to research. She gave me the story of the Praw-diggle Sun."

"The Prodigal Son, huh? I've always liked that parable. It's a good story."

"Do you know it?"

"Oh, yes." He leaned toward Cubby and lowered his voice as if he were sharing a secret. "In fact, it sort of makes me want to cry each time I read it."

"So, it's a sad story?"

"Well, no. It's a happy story, really."

"If it's happy how come it makes you want to cry?"

"I don't know. I guess because it's so beautiful, in the end." Baker reached across the table, took the Bible in his hands, and checked the index. He flipped to the page, then opened the book flat on the table to reveal the story.

Cubby seemed to study the title for a moment, then read it aloud. "The Parable of the Prodigal Son." When his eyes scanned down past the illustration to the print, he sighed and sagged a bit, looking fatigued. Then he brightened as an idea struck him. "Mr. Brooks, could you tell it to me?"

"Now, Cal, I'm sure Mr. Brooks has lots of his own work to do, like marking or lesson planning."

Neither Baker nor Cubby had noticed Helen's presence. She had come over to check on Cubby's progress with the homework.

"That's alright, Helen," Baker assured her. "I'd be happy to help Cubby."

"Are you sure you can spare the time?"

"Yes, of course." He caught a glimpse of Angus behind the glass at the coffee counter, frantically reaching for some paper towels. "You better go on, now. I think Mr. Fletcher needs you."

When Helen left, Baker set about telling the story in his own words. Once again, he found Cubby to be an attentive audience, whose eyes focused at times on Baker and at other times on the book illustration and nowhere else in between. All the while he manipulated that pencil, pushing it smoothly back and forth with a finger, as if he were stickhandling a puck, each finger handling it in turn, from pinky to thumb and back again. If Cubby seemed restless, it was out of an effort to stay engaged and not doze off. Baker tried to help by embedding his name into the narrative, which seemed to snap the boy back into alertness each time he heard it.

"One time there lived a very rich man. This man had two sons. Now, *Cubby*, the dad had strict rules, but he was fair to everyone. The elder son obeyed his father without complaint. The younger son thought his dad's rules were dumb. The day came when he demanded his share of the family wealth and left home to live by his own rules—"

At that point in the story, Cubby held up his hand to stop Baker. "Why did he think his dad's rules were dumb?"

"Well, the family lived on a big, beautiful farm, and the father expected everyone to pitch in and help." Baker tried to think of a sports equivalent. "It's like a hockey player who wants to play on the first line but doesn't want to practise with the team because he thinks practise is dumb. How would you feel about that?"

"I think that player would be dropped from the first line and maybe from the team," Cubby said with conviction. "My dad and Uncle Allen know how important practise is. They say for every one hour of games we play, I should put in six hours of practise—in the driveway or the basement or on the ice. They call it the six-for-one rule."

Baker's mind shot back to the three digits on the back of Cubby's bookmark—641. So that's what that meant! He felt a momentary surge of pride at cleverly making the connection, which was followed by regret because he would have liked to return said bookmark to Cubby, but he realized it was at home between the pages of *The Clarence Cup: A Tradition Like No Other*. (Baker had enjoyed the book so much, he'd purchased his own copy a while back, and at some point had transferred Cubby's bookmark from *My Hockey Stick* over to it.)

He shook off these thoughts and continued with the story.

"Every day the dad would stand on a hilltop, waiting for his son to come home. Eventually, the day came when the son returned, begging his father for forgiveness. To everyone's surprise, the father embraced him, overjoyed at his return, and ordered a great feast to be held for the occasion."

A vision of Rembrandt's masterpiece based on the parable entered Baker's mind as he worked his way to the story's end, causing him to hesitate once or twice to clear the lump in his throat. Cubby caught the quiver in his voice and looked carefully at him. Baker couldn't help himself; there was something about the damn parable that never failed to choke him up. The only other story that affected him so was "The Selfish Giant" by Oscar Wilde.

"Later that evening, the elder son returned from his work in the fields. He was unhappy about seeing his selfish brother return home to a feast of welcome. While the father understood his elder son's resentment, he patiently explained that it was far better to celebrate the return of the brother who was lost and had now returned to the family fold."

When he was done, Baker looked at Cubby, who seemed perplexed in addition to looking generally fatigued. Baker went back to the hockey metaphor. "You see, Cubby, if the dad in the story was the coach of a team, he would let every player play equally, whether they wanted to practise or not. This coach knows that some players take longer to learn what it means to be a part of the team and that it's better to have them learn that lesson *on* the team rather than off it."

"Hmm, if I was a player on that team, I don't think I'd like that."

"And most people would feel the same way. In fact, that's how the older brother in the story felt. He was angry with his father for throwing a party for the selfish younger brother instead of punishing him." Baker saw an opportunity to carry the lesson around to its main point. "But do you remember who was telling the story, Cubby?"

The boy was momentarily caught off guard by the question. "Um, uh . . . Jesus?"

"That's right! Jesus was using the story to describe how much God our Father loves us. You see, God's love is so deep and powerful that it doesn't even make sense to us. It goes beyond our ability to understand it."

The boy seemed to reflect on Baker's last point. "Is that why Mrs. Lopes chose that story?"

"Exactly. And that's also why it's so beautiful . . . and why it makes me cry."

Just then Baker felt a hand on his shoulder. Helen had come to rescue him. "Now, Cal, I think it's time Mr. Brooks left you alone to get started on Mrs. Lopes' assignment."

Cubby picked up the pencil and positioned the open notebook in front of him while Baker and Helen retreated to the librarian's desk, where Angus was flipping through the latest issue of *Sports Illustrated* while working on his coffee.

"How's Cubby been these days?" Baker asked Helen. "He looks tired—like he's coming down with something, maybe."

"Unfortunately, what you just described is what we've seen the last little while. The family is concerned about him, and understandably so. The poor guy sleeps a lot. He can hardly stay upright by this time of the day.

"At first we attributed the fatigue to his heavy schedule and activity level. Then someone suggested that he might be experiencing hormone surges or fluctuations brought on by the effects of his natural physical development. Either way, he's scheduled to undergo some tests in the next couple of weeks."

"That's got to be tough on the family," Baker said. "Does he have any siblings?"

"One. An older sister. They're separated by about nine years, but still very close."

Angus had picked up on some of the dialogue between Baker and Helen, and now all three adults behind the counter were gazing across the room toward the table where the subject of the conversation was seated hunched over his books. Then Angus drained his cup and nudged Baker to indicate it was time to go. "Thanks for the coffee, Helen. Baker was right; that is one mighty fine brew."

"You're welcome to come by any time, Angus," she replied. "Especially now that you know how the carafe pours," she added with a twinkle.

Blushing, Angus smiled, and then turned to replace his magazine on the periodicals shelf while Baker went to say goodbye to Cubby.

Baker's approach seemed to stir the kid from out of his stupor. "Well, Cubby, Mr. Fletcher and I have to get going." He noticed how the boy had managed to get some sentences down on the page of the notebook. "It's good to see you're making progress on the assignment."

"I think so. Thanks for your help, Mr. Brooks."

"No problem. It was my pleasure. And it was good to see you again. You get that work done for Mrs. Lopes. And hey, good luck in the playoffs this year."

"Thank you." Cubby gave Baker a tired smile. "Bye, Mr. Brooks."

Baker returned the smile, thinking the poor kid looked like he could sleep for a week.

That was the last time he ever spoke to Cubby.

* * * * *

Baker was pulled out of his deep reflective state by the sound of Lawrence coming through the door. It took considerable effort to shake the melancholy that came with his memories. He noticed that the librarian was carrying a platter of sandwich wraps and some bagels.

"That's a full tray you've got there," Baker said.

"The ladies in the main office are trying to get rid of some food. There's lots left if you're interested, but you better hurry because it's close to quittin' time for them. What the heck?" Lawrence had discovered the plates of brownies.

"Oh, I was supposed to inform you that Calum and Jorge brought those. I'm assuming you know them?"

"Yeah, they've got the Food Services class last period, and they usually bring stuff they've made down here for me. I share it with anyone who visits the library after school. Here, you better take one of these plates."

"Oh, no thanks. What am I going to do with a whole plate of brownies?"

"And what do you think I'd do with *two* plates of brownies? Take one! Share it with folks in your workroom."

Baker didn't bother to get into the fact that he didn't have a desk in any workroom in the school—he was nicely set up in his art supply room as a personal office space—but he took a plate, anyway, figuring to drop it off in Perreault's Religion workroom. He set his items on the counter for Lawrence to check out. Just then he was reminded of something and took his phone out. "Lawrence, how are you with cell phones? I must be doing something wrong here because I can't get into my voicemail."

Lawrence took the phone, assessed it for a moment, tapped here and swiped there, had Baker input his access code, and left him to listen to his message. It was from Perreault, reminding him that his appointment to meet with her friend Dorcas was still on for that evening.

He thanked Lawrence, took his bag of books and his plate of brownies and went upstairs. His footsteps echoing in the empty corridor leading to the Religion workroom suddenly made Baker feel like he was the last person on earth, let alone in the building. He was quickly disabused of the notion upon opening the workroom door when he was faced with a room fairly buzzing with activity.

Sandra Leung, whose desk was nearest the door, was first to greet him. "Hiya, Baker. How're you do— ohhh, what have you got there?"

"Hi, Sandra. I brought some treats, courtesy of Lawrence in the library and the kids in Food Prep." He found space on an otherwise cluttered table nearby and set the tray down. Sandra hungrily got up out of her seat to check out the goodies and was quickly joined by a couple more likeminded colleagues.

When Baker straightened up and stepped back to give them space, he caught a glimpse of Perreault seated at her desk in the furthest reaches of the room. She was facing away and oblivious to his presence, engaged in a lively conversation with Jonathan Kennedy, a long-time fixture in the Religion department. Jon was a big, bearded bear of a man whose physical profile was only matched by his booming voice, as evidenced by how it was presently carrying through the room. Baker didn't need to strain to overhear their voices.

". . . Yes, people always ask if I am related in some way, and no, I am not. The only thing J.F.K. and I have in common is the initials—except the 'F' in my middle name stands for Farley, not Fitzgerald. But what about you? Any family connection to the guy who wrote 'Walden'?"

"You mean Henry David Thoreau? No, afraid not," Perreault replied. "Although my mother proudly admits that my first name was inspired by her favourite hockey player—"

"Wait . . . are you talking about Julien Perreault? Of the Cleveland Cuyahogas?"

"The one and only."

"Wow. He was on that famous 'French Cuisine' line. I've seen highlights. That guy was downright electrifying in his day. Your mother has great taste in hockey players."

"Yes. I think she was smitten by his talent and flair on the ice—not to mention his flowing hair," she said, dryly.

"Still, that's pretty cool," Jon declared, then appeared to come to a realization. "I must say I have a greater appreciation for your name now . . . I mean, Perreault was always a cool name . . . but now it's even cooler . . ."

Baker secretly had to agree with Jon and then caught himself eavesdropping and figured it was time to make a move. He said goodbye to Sandra and the others, pulled the door open, and took a step out into the hallway where he would have been content to linger a minute longer, head tilted in the direction of the distant conversation still in progress, if not for the door swinging closed behind him.

While contemplating what he had overheard, Baker hustled upstairs to his classroom to grab his workbag and jacket. He then locked the room and descended the flight of stairs one last time for the day, knowing he had to make a quick stop at the main office to unburden the ladies of some bagels and wraps before heading out to his car.

CHAPTER ELEVEN
HOXIXOH

The daily commute to school each morning took Baker twenty-five minutes, rain or shine, whether it was the dead of winter or the middle of summer. Coming home was slower by about three or four minutes, which he attributed to the overall grade change. It was downhill into town, after all; plus, it seemed that he naturally drove faster in the a.m., likely owing to the sense of urgency to get to work on time.

Heading home now, uphill and in no hurry, he was mentally preparing for his scheduled meeting—at precisely 6:36 p.m.—with Dorcas Blanchard, an acquaintance of Perreault's who apparently carried some higher-level standing as a Wiccan. She lived just south of the town of Fergus and insisted on making the trip to Baker's house.

He flipped on the radio for company, which was tuned to CHMV 1090, and was met with the voices of Isaac Dershowitz and Howard Pappas: the hosts of the *Ike 'n' Howard Show*, a sports talk show that aired weekdays from 4:00 to 7:00 p.m. Because of the 1090 frequency, the station was nicknamed *Mullet Radio*, but Baker found the call letters far more intriguing because of how CHMV was almost identical to the HMV of his school. He considered it more than just coincidence, and even a bit bizarre.

As radio personalities, Ike and Howard were tolerable enough, although Ike's attempts at humour too often fell flat. Howard, on the other hand, had a predilection for combativeness, sharing his opinions on topics related to sports and even society and culture in general. When Baker tuned in that evening, Howard was in the middle of a rant about the Mighty Pines.

". . . This whole issue surrounding the Pines' inept play in the defensive zone is a function of the coach."

"C'mon, Howard, you don't think there's plenty of blame to be laid at the feet of the players?"

"Hear me out. I contend that a major problem with this team comes down to a lack of communication. To be effective as a unit, every player on the ice needs to be engaged in a conversation, starting with the goaltender on out. But I'm hearing that's not happening with the Pines. Ask any happily married couple or any effective boss in the workplace, and it's all about communication. Talking. Is it hard? Damn right it is, but then, so is back-checking and playing a two-hundred-foot game. And yet we feel completely justified in making *those* demands on players."

"Yeah, but what about the player who leads by example? There are countless cases of the quiet leader who goes about his business, gives one hundred and ten percent, and gets the job done."

"Please, spare me your fairy tales about effort. I'm sick to death of all this give one hundred and ten percent BS. No one can give one hundred percent, let alone one hundred and ten percent. If a guy can give eighty-nine percent, he's pretty much leaving it all out on the ice. Giving one hundred percent puts you on the brink of death. So, let's cut the crap. Anyway, now that I've got that out of my system, let's get back to the issue of communication. I want to play a clip from December of last year. Kayden Koch is addressing the question of leadership as it pertains to certain players on his team. Listen to this."

After a moment's pause, the coach's unmistakeable voice filled the air space.

"Leadership isn't what you say. It's what you do and how hard you compete. When you look at a guy like Ben Bellamy or a guy like Gianni Valentino, that's what you see. It's not the 'saying anything'; they just do it."

When the clip ended, Ike responded to what he'd just heard. "So, where's the problem? I don't object with anything he said there. In fact, I hear that from coaches all the time."

"The problem, Mr. Dershowitz, is he's preaching an old, outdated message. It's the way losing players play. It's the way losing coaches coach."

"Whoa! You're talking about the only man to coach a Clarence Cup champion and win two Olympic gold medals, along with gold medals in several other international events."

"I'm not referring to the man's resume. My point is that we have a team with flaws, and according to the evidence in that audio clip there, the source of those flaws is the coach."

"OK, let's assume you're right, and the coach is wrong. Tell us, Mr. Pappas, what should he have said in that media scrum?"

"He should have said nobody on his team is allowed to lead by example. Leading by example is an archaic idea; it's not good enough. Instead of preaching 'Leadership isn't what you say; it's what you do,' coaches like Kay Koch should be preaching the idea that it is everyone's responsibility to communicate, provided it's positive and supportive. No one is ever allowed to skate around mutely going about their business."

"But what about the guy who works his tail off day in, day out, but who isn't comfortable going around verbalizing to teammates? What do you say to that guy?"

"I say grow the frick up. It's a big boy's game in a big boy's league. If anyone's not comfortable with it, all the better. Improvement is all about dealing with levels of discomfort. The job is to become comfortable being uncomfortable and then making sure the opponent is even more uncomfortable. If every player on this team was taught that approach, they'd either improve, or they'd be gone. Like I said, it begins and ends with the coach's message."

"There you have it, folks. No less an authority than Howard Pappas is telling you to be comfortable being uncomfortable. Something our homebound commuters can take to heart if they're to survive the mess on the roads this evening. Here's Josh McTavish with an update on the traffic situation."

"That's right, Ike, the trip home is proving to be uncomfortable for commuters this evening due to a number of issues on the roads . . ."

Baker muted the traffic report. Living in the country had its hardships, but traffic was never one of them. He was intrigued by what Howard Pappas had to say about Kayden Koch. He enjoyed listening to Howard because the man typically attacked the usual topics from fresh angles, and it wasn't just for the sake of being different. Howard's arguments carried a legitimacy beyond just seeking to stir the pot. At the moment, however, Baker's mind was, like the road he was driving, veering in another direction. More precisely, he had come to the fork in the road, which either took one north, toward his home, or west, toward the rural town where, another fifteen minutes farther, he would arrive at Helen Nella's sprawling stone-and-timber ranch home, complete with wrap-around deck, cathedral ceilings, and two fireplaces. So, as he drove north toward home to prepare for his meeting with Dorcas, his mind headed west, back in time one year, to the Saturday evening when he met Allen Nella, Helen's husband and Cubby's uncle.

* * * * *

Armed with a bottle of red wine for Helen, Baker had also picked up a sixpack of assorted craft beer for Allen. He wasn't sure if Allen drank beer, but he thought it would be an appropriate gesture either way. The worst that could come of it would be that he'd have to take it home with him.

The Nellas' house was situated on a gravel road about a kilometre off the main paved artery. It was dark and drizzly, so, despite running late, Baker was compelled to drive slowly on the gravel; the road had been recently graded, and he knew from experience that the combination of fresh aggregate and wet weather would produce a quagmire. The Nellas' driveway was generous in size, so although there were six mud-spattered cars parked ahead of his owing to the ladies' dinner party, Baker was able to find space for his own begrimed vehicle.

When Helen opened the door, Baker's senses were not so much accosted as swarmed, as if by a pack of puppies or pre-schoolers. There was an abundance of noisy female conversation combined with delicious aromas and warm lighting. Helen graciously accepted the wine, introduced Baker to her group of guests at large, then escorted him downstairs.

The image of Allen Nella cranking out push-ups was Baker's introduction to the man. Allen popped up off the floor and greeted his wife and their guest.

"Barely two minutes into the game, and it's seven nothing Irish," he said. "I think Florida State's in for a long night." He extended his hand. "Hi, I'm Allen."

Baker shook his host's hand and presented his offering of beer. Allen courteously accepted the gift and put the cans in the fridge by the wet bar, giving Baker a chance to take in the décor. Unacquainted with the rules of decorating a man cave, Baker assumed Allen's basement was the prototypical version of the form. Among several plaque-mounted posters and framed and matted photographs, one item that called out to him was the iconic photo of Joe Zedelko scoring his Clarence Cup-winning overtime goal against Detroit. That picture always intrigued Baker. It wasn't so much Zedelko's heroics that seared the image into his memory as the unflattering position in which Detroit's goaltender Larry McKenzie was captured in that moment for posterity. He seemed completely out of position, falling backwards into his own net and utterly unprepared to make any defensive countermove that might stop the puck. The exclamation point was McKenzie's face, wincing with his eyes reflexively squeezed shut, much like Jersey Joe Walcott on the receiving end of a Rocky Marciano right hook or Lee Harvey Oswald taking a Jack Ruby bullet in the stomach.

Allen brought Baker back to the present by going over some ground rules. "When you came down the stairs, you saw me doing push-ups, and I need to tell you what that's about." He pointed to the football game on television. "The Notre Dame game is on TV tonight, and the hard and fast rule that goes with Notre Dame being on the tube—and I mean *hard and fast*—is that if you're in the room when the Irish score, you drop and do push-ups. That goes for everyone. I'm sorry, but that's the house rule here." He lowered his voice to a whisper. "That's why Helen left so quickly. You won't see her down here when the Irish are playing."

Baker grinned. "No worries, it's all good with me. I'm prepared to do push-ups tonight. Do you think we'll get much of a workout?"

"Back in September they dropped sixty-six points on New Mexico. That was the high water mark of the season. You know, I'm kind of glad I wasn't watching that New Mexico game. By my calculations, I would have had to pump out three hundred and fifty-eight push-ups! I mean, if I was younger, no problem, but at my age, that's some serious devotion to the cause."

"Three hundred and fifty-eight push-ups? From sixty-six points? Wow!"

"Yeah. Since that game they scored fifty-two points twice, against Bowling Green and Navy. So, to answer your original question, we might be in for a bit of a workout. But you look like you can handle it."

Baker thought it wise to mention the hockey game, which was in progress. "What about the Pines? How are they doing? They're in Boston tonight, right?"

"Yes they are. Ugh, those damn Hubs. Toronto carried the play in the first period, created lots of scoring chances for themselves, and wouldn't you know it? They came out of the period down one nothing. I swear they're snake bit."

"At least there's still a lot of game left. Maybe they'll get some bounces. Who's in net? Sanderson?"

"No. Gates."

"Yikes."

"Exactly."

Baker noted the preponderance of numbers on one wall, alternating in colour from green to white, and recognized them as the same numbers that had recently been retired by the Mighty Pines organization. He asked Allen about them.

"Good for you, Baker. Yes, those are indeed the retired Pines numbers."

"It's amazing the power and influence numbers have for hockey players," Baker remarked, "and all athletes, for that matter."

"You name the sport, if numbers are involved, they likely have significance."

"But I don't know if I buy it completely—the power of numbers, that is. Do you?"

"I do indeed," Allen confessed. "I believe in the power of all manner of symbols and representations. That includes numbers and even certain combinations of letters. I'm convinced there's power in the arrangement of words, and in specific patterns even."

"Patterns?"

"Absolutely. Take, for example, a mother who knits a sweater for her child. I believe it's possible for her to imbue it with protective powers if she employs a particular pattern. Isn't that just Feng Shui for clothing after all? Is it magic, or can it be explained away by science? Is the belief enough? Many questions, for sure."

Baker had a growing sense that he was in the company of a man who had much to share—or simply to get off his chest, as if he'd been locked away in his own basement for too long and was only afforded visitor privileges every few months or so. His hunch seemed to be confirmed as Allen continued.

"As a Catholic, I've been taught that transubstantiation is a miracle that turns a mixture of water and wine into the blood of Christ every time an ordained priest presides over the celebration of the Eucharist. Why, then, shouldn't I believe that sitting under a makeshift pyramid suspended from the ceiling can aid an athlete's recovery following strenuous activity?

"I think my parents put some stock in it too. They had fun with the names of their two children. My name is Allen—I'm the elder of the two—and my sister's name is Zoelle. A to Z, get it? As for my full name, well, my folks christened me Allen Jeremiah Nella." He reached over to the bookshelf and took an item off the shelf. "Here's my business card. It refers to me as Allen J. Nella, which is a perfect palindrome. Allen Nella would work just as well, but the introduction of the letter J—while maintaining the palindromic properties—provides, uh—how shall I say? A touch of asymmetry without destroying the underlying balance."

"That's kind of neat, I guess," Baker mused. "But why?"

Allen ignored his question for the moment, attending to the TV to see what Notre Dame would do from the six-yard line.

"Here we go ... back corner ... oh, man, what a catch! Was he in bounds? Yup, touchdown!" Allen dropped and did fourteen push-ups. Baker followed suit. When they finished, Allen turned to his guest. "Baker, what's your full name, if you don't mind my asking?"

"Baker Bailey Brooks."

Allen considered Baker's name while repeating it aloud. "Baker Bailey Brooks ... Baker Bailey Brooks ... I like it! It's got quite a nice bounce to it, don't you think? B, B, B. Like the Better Business Bureau."

"I can't say that I've ever given it much thought."

To further make his point, Allen took the topic in another direction. "Did you happen to notice the licence plate on the vehicle in the driveway?"

"Which one? There were lots of vehicles out there."

"You're right, sorry. Mine's the red Jeep parked in front of the garage."

"I did notice the Jeep, but I can't say I took note of the licence plate."

"Well, my plate is personalized. It consists of seven letters: HOXIXOH. Do you know why?"

Assuming it was a rhetorical question, Baker didn't attempt to come up with an answer, and instead let Allen continue with his explanation.

"One day I did an inventory of the alphabet to see what letters had properties that made them work as 'rotational ambigrams.'"

"Rotational what?"

"Rotational ambigrams. Words or sets of letters that don't lose their meaning when viewed from different directions. So, a capital H, for example looks the same forwards and backwards as well as right side up and upside down. The same can be said for the letters O, X, and I."

"That's cool. And you say no other letters in the alphabet have those properties?"

"That's right. Only H, O, X, and I. What I did with my licence plate was arrange them so the one half was a reflection of the other half. The I is set in the middle, acting as a mirror. The arrangement of the other letters was based on what I thought would work best, aesthetically speaking. You know, if you wanted to do the same thing, I suppose you could go with something like XOHIHOX or OHXIXHO, etcetera."

"Nah, I'd have to take a rain check—because if I was ever set on a personalized plate, my licence plate of choice has already been claimed."

"Is that right? Did you see it somewhere?"

"Yes. It was completely by accident. One day I was locked in traffic along University Avenue after a Jays' game. I was crawling along, heading toward the Gardiner Expressway, when I looked up and the car in front of me has this four-letter licence plate."

"Wait a minute. Your favourite plate is a curse word?"

"No, no, it's nothing like that. This particular plate had four letters: LQQK. So, it appeared to spell out the word 'LOOK,' except it had eyes, you know, with the tails of the Q's working like little eyeballs."

"That sounds clever."

"Sure, but there's more. You see, I'm an art teacher, and I give lessons on the fundamentals of drawing. Now, contrary to popular opinion, drawing has less to do with manual dexterity than developing a practiced eye—being able to observe with care and precision. On top of that, I believe everyone can and *should* learn to draw." (Baker warned himself not to get preachy about a topic he was quite passionate about, but Allen seemed a captive audience, so he continued.) "Not being able to draw is like not being able to read. We don't want our kids to be illiterate, do we? So, why is it alright if they can't draw? It's just another useful way to communicate, after all. And that's where the licence plate comes in."

"Aha," Allen replied. "Learning to draw requires learning to look: L-O-O-K."

"Absolutely. In order to draw well, people need to train their eyes to look carefully and measure things. I also fancy the creative way it's expressed on the plate."

"I hear you."

"Oh, hey. You never did explain what the point of your plate was. What was your motivation for it?"

"Nothing too deep, I guess. There's just something I consider mystically beautiful about it. Oh, that reminds me—there's also the number aspect."

"There's more? This thing is packed with meaning."

"I know. It's great. Let me explain. If you assign a number to each letter, then based on their place in the alphabet, the H becomes an eight, the O is fifteen, and so on. You then end up with eight, fifteen, twenty-four, nine, twenty-four, fifteen, and eight. When you add them all up and reduce it to a single digit, the resulting number is four." Allen looked at Baker as if he'd just divulged the cure for cancer.

"And four is a magic number?"

"Definitely! First off, with all due respect to the Great WOZ, Gabe Wozniak, it's the number of the greatest player ever to lace on a pair of skates in my books. But there's more. The number four denotes stability. 'Four square,' the four cardinal directions, the four elements, the four evangelists, four key ingredients that go into to making the philosopher's stone. In Tarot, four is the emperor, a very masculine symbol. Add up the numbers one, two, three, and four, and you arrive at ten, which is the greatest of numbers: a complete set, a satisfying quantity, the Ten Commandments, the number of digits on both hands, and again in Tarot, The Wheel of Fortune." Allen stopped to catch his breath. "Do I need to continue?"

"Wow, you've done your research."

"I find it fascinating. One year Helen and I were in Prague, in the Czech Republic, and we visited the Charles Bridge, which was built by King Charles the Fourth. Well, it seems that Charles made sure the foundation stone was laid in the year 1357, on the ninth of July, at precisely 5:31 a.m. You see, he recognized the potential significance of the arrangement of odd numbers in that date and time: one, three, five, seven, nine, five, three, one. That number was carved into the wall of the bridge tower." Allen waited to let Baker visualize the order of numbers.

"Hmm, that's actually pretty neat," Baker admitted.

"I agree. There's a whole history of great people in this world who have believed in the mystical and magical properties of numbers. Oh, wait, the Irish have just kicked a field goal. It's seventeen zip. Let's go, buddy."

Seventeen push-ups later, they got up off the floor, and Allen continued to wax philosophical. "Ah, Baker, it's great when your team is winning. You know, I follow sports religiously on TV and the radio, I read about it in the paper and in literary works, and I've attended coaching clinics. Right now my pet project is seeing that my nephew Cubby lacks for nothing as he develops as a hockey player."

"Yes. Helen told me that you—along with his dad—are training Cubby. That sounds exciting. I mean, the prospect of it, sort of like a painter with a blank canvas."

"Certainly. But once you get past the dreaming, you have to face reality. A blank canvas brings with it the burden of having to make lots of tough decisions—finding out what works and what doesn't and then making adjustments along the way. It's exciting, yes, but it can also be quite daunting."

"That sounds like the pressures of being the GM of a big league team. So many decisions and options to consider, and all the while you're under the microscope."

"Absolutely. A GM's job is tough. A team's success involves so many variables."

"You mean, like coaching strategies, team chemistry, player skill levels, and stuff?"

"Of course. Those are the usual measurable variables, but I'm talking about variables that *can't* be quantified: clean living, religious beliefs, a regimen of prayer, the possession of secret knowledge—"

"Whoa, secret knowledge? You mean like the discovery of the Ark of the Covenant or the Holy Grail? Are we talking Indiana Jones here?"

"Not quite Indiana Jones, but I'm willing to believe that an athlete's success can be attributed to virtuous living, prayer, and a bit of arcane knowledge, as much as, if not more than, scientific knowledge."

"C'mon, Allen, big league teams don't spend time or money researching the performance-enhancing effects that clandestine knowledge might have on their athletes."

"I know it sounds illogical and baseless from a scientific standpoint. But then, don't scientists study the effects of placebos? Try telling Achilles that the possession of a powerful secret has no effect. Here's a guy who got through life believing that no man could slay him because he was told about how his mother dipped him in the river Styx when he was an infant. Or tell it to Chief Crazy Horse, whose vision quest revealed to him his invincibility as a warrior. Just two examples of men who performed on the battlefield with supreme confidence and conviction, having this secret knowledge in their pockets."

"I knew about Achilles, but not Crazy Horse."

"Yes. Both men devoted their lives to the art of warfare. Not much different from today's single-sport athletes wouldn't you say? Well, in addition to their dedication and commitment, each man learned along the way that they were special, that they were blessed by the gods, that they were indestructible in battle."

"Sure, but I don't hear any stories about the many warriors who never became legends, their 'secret' knowledge notwithstanding."

"You're right. And no one will ever know. But I'm convinced that if you prepare an athlete, if you train them effectively and feed them properly, provide them with information about their foe, and then on top of that, send them out on the field of battle after imbuing them with special knowledge—maybe by suggesting that their morning smoothie contained a drop of liquid luck, enlightening them to the fact that they wear a cloak of invisibility, or reminding them of the long-forgotten time in their youth when they pulled a figurative sword from a stone, or maybe their mother gave them a bath in the river Styx—well, I might be inclined to bet on that athlete to come out victorious."

"No offence, but that all sounds so crazy," Baker said. "And yet—"

"And yet?"

"And yet it's so damned compelling."

Just then Helen called down to them from the top of the stairs. "Hey boys, is it safe?"

"Huh? What does that mean?" Allen asked.

"It means I'm trying to avoid doing push-ups right now."

"Oh, that. Sure, you're safe," he assured her. "Florida State just scored a touchdown. They're lining up to kick the extra point." He turned to Baker. "We don't do push-ups when the other team scores."

Baker addressed Helen as she descended the stairs to join them. "Boy, you sounded a lot like Laurence Olivier just then."

"Laurence Olivier? How so?"

"Your question on the stairs there, 'Is it safe?' Olivier made that line famous in *The Marathon Man*."

"I can't say I'm familiar with that movie. Is it about distance running or something?"

"Gosh no. How can I describe it? Well, you know how people were afraid to go back in the water after *Jaws* came out? Let's just say that after watching *The Marathon Man*, you'd be afraid to go back to the dentist."

"So, it's a horror movie?"

"More of a suspense—"

"Oh man, look at this!" Allen shouted. "Go . . . go . . . go . . . yesss, he took it all the way! Ha-ha! That's freakin' beautiful!"

"What just happened?" Baker asked.

"The Irish just blocked Florida State's extra point attempt, recovered the ball, and ran it all the way to the end zone." Allen was exultant. Then he realized what it meant for his wife. "Sorry, Helen, but we have to drop, and that includes you."

"I hate you guys. How many? What's the score?"

Baker did the math, "I guess that makes it twenty-four to six?"

"No," Allen said. "Luckily for us, a team that blocks a point-after try and runs it in for a touchdown is awarded only two points."

Helen couldn't hide her sarcasm. "Oh, how *wonderful*. There is a God after all. So . . . how many?"

"Nineteen."

"Good thing I vacuumed the carpet down here this morning."

They all dropped and completed the obligatory push-ups. Baker noticed the relative ease with which Helen pumped out hers, despite being allowed to "cheat" by doing them off her knees. As they got off the carpet, he had to remark on it. "Very impressive, Helen. You know, you might have passed the standards set for all the Pines players on those Cup-winning teams in the fifties and sixties."

"Oh, shoot ... the Pines! Let's see how the game is going," Allen said, changing the channel for a quick update. "By the way, Baker, I should thank you for spending time with Cubby in the library. Helen told me how you were reading with him."

Baker smiled, knowing the truth would paint a less noble picture of himself. "Don't give me too much credit. I needed that book for a lesson the next day. Reading the story was sort of the price I paid for it."

"You don't have to understate it. Cubby spoke about that story for weeks after, along with regularly practising the proper pronunciation of Claude Lambert's name. You were mentioned quite a bit as well."

Baker didn't know what to say, so he directed his attention to the television. It was late in the second period, and the Pines were on the power play, down 3-0 and trying to solve Boston's goaltender.

"I found Cubby to be fairly astute when he spoke about the game," Baker said. "Is he good?"

"Put it this way: have you ever heard of the 'Randall assist'?"

"As in Ricky Randall?" Baker was fully aware of the Randall assist, but he feigned ignorance to let Allen explain it to him.

"Yes. As you know, every goal that's scored has the potential for a primary assist and a secondary assist. A couple of days ago, I heard a reference to something called the 'Randall assist.'"

"Speaking of the Randall assist, did you see that pass?" Baker asked. The timing of the goal couldn't have been more perfect as the Pines' Gianni Valentino scored late in the period, assisted beautifully by Randall. Baker knew that Randall was having a terrific season, earning a reputation as a slick playmaker. He was continually setting up teammates for easy, can't-miss goals. Gianni Valentino would find himself the recipient of many a Randall assist that season.

"Yeah, pretty sweet. And that's the thing about Cubby. He had *four* Randall assists this morning, along with two goals of his own! So, yes, Cubby is good! I mean, sure he's got skill, but more than that, he's got tremendous instinct to make the right play at the right time. That's why he makes a great defenceman, because in high-stress situations he's not prone to mistakes. But offensively he is such a force that it's a shame *not* to play him at centre."

"Sounds like he gets a lot of ice time."

Allen nodded. "He gets a lot of ice time. At weekend tournaments his team might play four or five games, and by Sunday night, the little guy is spent." The horn sounded to end the second period with Boston up 3-1. With the Notre Dame game at half time, Allen saw that the time was ripe to go upstairs and assist with the general process of food consumption. Baker was in no condition to argue, so he followed his host's lead.

The remainder of the evening was a blur of good food, beer, lots of conversation—and push-ups. Notre Dame won, the Pines lost, and Baker came away with a new appreciation for the ubiquity of the arcana of numbers, letters, and words. He remembered looking up the scoring summary of the football game to see how many push-ups he and Allen completed. Discovering that it was 191, he couldn't help but think how Allen would appreciate the numerical palindrome. Allen also seemed to appreciate Baker's company in general that night, whether because Baker seemed to take a genuine interest in his topics of conversation, because Allen liked the male companionship during ladies' night, or because he liked the beer Baker had brought along. Or maybe it was just because Baker never complained about doing nearly 200 push-ups for the sake of a silly superstition.

* * * * *

Pondering over these memories caused Baker to lift his foot off the pedal, to the point that he was soon driving below the posted speed limit. No worries. Another five minutes and he'd be home. He wondered how Cubby was doing and assumed the kid was likely tearing up whatever league he was competing in. It would have been easy just to ask Helen, but she wasn't working at HMV that year. He made a mental note to contact her sooner rather than later. The car in front of him slowed down and came to rest at a four-way stop before proceeding straight ahead. It was then that Baker noticed the licence plate: a personalized one that read HURRY UP. He had to look twice. Was it a sign? Not entirely sure and yet not wanting to be accused of ignoring a potential message from some unseen mystical force, especially right before a meeting with a witch, Baker nudged the accelerator just in case.

CHAPTER TWELVE
SKULL AND PUFFBALLS

Baker had been home for close to an hour and had held off on pouring himself a beer, expecting his visitor to arrive before nightfall. Darkness was hastened when the descending sun was enveloped by a gothic fog that demonstrated genuine contempt for the remaining daylight. Unwilling to wait any longer, Baker reached into the fridge and retrieved the bottle, now deliciously cold in his hand, along with a tulip pint glass. He "snicked" the cap off using his favourite wall-mounted church key then went to the wall next to the bottle opener and tapped the bottle's neck against the Grady Sykes stick shaft for luck before tilting the chilled glass to accept the liquid as it was poured. Just then he heard a car turn into the driveway and make its way down the lane.

"Aw, crap. It figures." He sighed, looking out the window, then shrugged it off and finished pouring.

Soon enough there was a knock at the front door, prompting Baker to hustle out of the kitchen and nimbly negotiate five steps down to the front entry. Arriving at the door, amber ale in hand, he paused to flick the light switch, then engaged the doorknob with a vigorous and well-timed tug, so as to overcome the sticky attraction the recently painted door surface had for the jamb. With his attention on the momentum of the inward swinging door, Baker was a bit startled when he looked up. The visitor in his doorway wasn't quite who he expected. Standing before him was a silhouetted, fedora-topped figure backlit by the glow of the fluorescent porch light overhead. He was surprised to discover how chilly the evening had grown and how the dense Macbethian mist served to make the hour seem later than it was. A shiver of unease engulfed him.

"Father Merrin, I presume?" he asked in an attempt to disguise his trepidation with flippancy. The question seemed to hang in the air with the brume, increasing his sense of creepy uncertainty. Finally, a female voice, self-assured but somewhat bored, responded.

"Unfortunately, no. And neither am I here to perform an *ex-or-cism*." To emphasize the last word, she separated the syllables and pronounced them with phonetic clarity, as if answering a word challenge in a spelling bee.

For some reason Baker was relieved by the fact that, if nothing else, at least this person was acquainted with classic horror movie characters, so he wouldn't need to awkwardly explain his reference. But he was rattled because the woman before him did not match the description that Perreault had left on her phone message. Although garbed in a long dark cloak which would better have suited a count in a forested castle above a Romanian village, her youthfulness was betrayed by unwrinkled feet with painted toenails in the sandals of a 1960s flower child. This person couldn't have been much more than nineteen, while the woman he was expecting was pension eligible. At a loss for words, and remembering the beer in his left hand, which was still behind the door, Baker sheepishly brought it around as if to reveal a secret. "Would you like a drink?" he asked, holding the glass aloft as an invitation to join him.

"Perfect!" she said, which floored him. "You read my mind, which is ironic, because I'm usually the one reading minds." She took the beer and slaked her thirst by quaffing half of it before Baker could fully grasp what was happening.

A scolding voice came from around the corner. "Mary! You're not in a meadow under the Mead Moon with your drinking buddies. Please practise a little restraint—and remember your manners."

"Oh yeah. Um, my apologies. I'm Mary. Here, I'll give this back to you." She handed the half-empty glass back to Baker with the slightest hint of a mischievous smirk, which she covered by wiping her mouth with her sleeve. Just then an older woman entered the scene, thrusting a large wicker basket into one of the girl's hands and what appeared to be a small sheathed knife into the other.

"Here. Take this... and this. Be sure to check the underside for discoloration. If you can't see well enough in this light, bring them back anyway, and we'll take a closer look together. And be gentle. Don't bruise them."

Without another word, Mary—in her fedora, cloak, and Birkenstocks, armed with picnic basket and paring knife—moved toward the tree line with conviction, as if she were embarking for her grandma's house and had walked the trail countless times before. In the meantime, the older woman squared up to Baker and extended a hand.

"Hi, I'm Perreault's friend, Dorcas Blanchard. I'm the witch she told you about. Sorry for my tardiness."

"Hi, Dorcas, I'm Baker Brooks. I really appreciate you doing this. C'mon in."

He stood to one side, allowing her through the doorway. She was refinement personified, wearing a jacket that could have been cut from the cloth of Joseph's coat of many colours, a tweed/wool blend that screamed of the Scottish Highlands and was equal parts brilliant and subdued elegance. Five bluestone buttons perfectly set off her grey-blue skirt, which fell just below her knees to meet her impeccable knee-high highland boots. Everything about her looked well-travelled but well-kept.

SKULL AND PUFFBALLS

"I was expecting you earlier, but I know it can be difficult to find the place—or so I've been told by family and friends."

"Oh, it wasn't that. I know this part of the world well enough. But I had to make a detour and pick up Mary. She needs to get outside, poor thing, and away from her studies for a spell; especially on a night like this."

"Her studies?"

"Mary is my student. You could call her my 'apprentice,' but a term like that, given my 'profession,' conjures images of sorcerers and wizards and whatnot. A friend of mine has basically hired me to homeschool his daughter. It's all been approved by the Ministry." Baker must have looked confused because Dorcas quickly clarified her meaning. "The Ministry of Education, to be clear, *not* the Ministry of Magic."

"So, you're Mary's teacher?"

"My role is to mentor her in the ways of Wicca and even nurture and develop her gifts as a psychic medium." Dorcas then leaned toward Baker in conspiratorial fashion, "But between you and me, I think I'm the one who's going to be learning the most. Mary's gifts are extensive, and they run deep."

Baker was intrigued by that last part. "Run deep?"

"Oh, yes. You see, Mary could go through life having no awareness of her powers, because they're what we call 'latent.' My goal is to introduce her to herself, so to speak, to get her to be comfortable in her own skin and graciously accept her gifts."

"That sounds like a sensitive task."

"With some students it can be, but Mary's a good kid. Heck, my toughest job might be instilling some fashion sense in her. Did you see the hat she's wearing? It's so vulgar. Like a combination of something worn by Harrison Ford and Max von Sydow. Give her a whip and a crucifix, and she's all set."

Baker wondered at the coincidence of her reference to Max von Sydow, given his "Father Merrin" greeting to Mary earlier. He closed the door behind them as Dorcas removed her own head cover to reveal long, thick, jet-black hair braided in a fashion that reminded Baker of black licorice. Suddenly, he felt a craving for fresh Twizzlers. He was slow in averting his gaze. Noticing this, Dorcas felt it appropriate to excuse her hair. "Yes, I'm overdue. I've been meaning to get it cut."

"I was just admiring the colour," Baker said. "It's so black it's almost blue, like Superman's hair in the comics."

"And every follicle is still the original colour that Goddess blessed me with."

"I wish Goddess could bless *me* with keeping my hair colour. I'm already greying at the temples."

"Well, we're all blessed in different ways. For instance, just look around at where you live. You've got a beautiful situation here."

"I can't complain. The place in general is quite nice. But did you say you know this area?"

"Yes, particularly the neighbouring property to the north," she replied, using her thumb to indicate the general direction. "That's one of the reasons I insisted on coming. It's been years since I was here last. I must say it hasn't changed much at all. Who lives next door now, if I may ask?"

"That would be Bert Ohlsen. The place is more like a cottage for him, though. He drops by on weekends to check up on things, cut grass in the summer and such. Bert lives in Port Credit with his wife. He asked me to keep an eye on the place whenever possible."

"That's nice of you."

Baker shrugged it off. "Oh, I don't mind. He's got some decent walking trails and a couple of nice ponds on the property. But tell me, how did you come to know the place?"

"Through one of the previous owners. She was a client slash friend of mine. Passed away—oh gosh, twenty-some years ago. That was the last time I visited."

"A previous owner, huh? I heard some stories about her. Ethel . . . something."

"Ethel Swanson."

"Right. I heard from some of the locals that she was a bit of a recluse. They even suggested she was a witch, on account of her strange behaviour. Crouched in the tall grass by the road, apparently casting spells or placing hexes on motorists that passed by." Baker noticed an odd blank expression on his guest's face. "I hope I didn't say anything offensive. Those are just some things I heard. You know how people like to tell stories."

"Oh, I *do* know how people like to tell stories. And no offense taken. But to be honest, I do consider her to have been a strange bird. Take it from someone who witnessed things firsthand."

"You said she was a client? How so?"

"Back then I was trying my hand at selling real estate. One day I got a call from an Ethel Swanson seeking advice about selling her property. Well, some of the folks in the office felt the need to warn me about her. Still, despite what they said, I drove out to meet her. She took me on a tour of the property, and we ended up spending most of the afternoon talking and sipping tea. Nothing came of the sale at the time, but I found myself drawn toward her, despite her idiosyncrasies. She seemed to like my company, so we became friends. In fact, I can honestly say I am who I am today because of Ethel."

"You mean she's the one who taught you, um, the ways of a witch?"

"Not exactly. Ethel introduced me to a friend of hers: Professor Smythe Ravenstone. It was Professor Ravenstone, along with Ethel, who acquainted me with the theory and practice of modern magic and nature worship. Long story short, it led to my education in Wiccan, pagan, and magical studies, and the formal art of ritual."

SKULL AND PUFFBALLS

"This Professor Ravenstone must have been a character."

"Don't get me started on him; I'll be here all night. But it might interest you to know that he was a big Toronto Mighty Pines fan."

"No kidding. How did you discover he was a Pines fan?"

"I just assumed as much. He often wore this old ratty team jersey—no wizard's robes for ol' Ravenstone, no sir—and he always wore a hat. He had the most beautiful silver hair, and yet he chose to tuck it under a green-and-white baseball cap, the same colours as his Pines jersey."

"Makes sense he'd wear a Pines cap, I suppose."

"Oh, but it wasn't a Mighty Pines cap. It had the logo of a construction firm: Northern Pines Construction."

"You're kidding! That was Nathaniel Sinclair's company back in the day!"

"That's right. The professor said the hat was his dad's when he worked for Colonel Sinclair back in the thirties and forties."

"Wow. Ravenstone's father worked for the man himself."

"That's what he told me. He was proud of that hat. But all this is beside the point. The professor was a valuable source of knowledge for me. Sometimes I'll think about him and find myself missing his company."

"You don't keep in touch with him?"

"Professor Ravenstone never stayed in one place long. I knew him for about a year and a half before he moved on." Her voice turned wistful. "Last I heard he was doing research in Salisbury, England, splitting time between its medieval cathedral and the ancient site of Stonehenge."

"Uh, huh . . . and what happened to Ethel?"

"Ethel? Well, her demise is a bit of a mystery. Although I probably shouldn't use that word; it's got a negative connotation. She basically disappeared."

"What do you mean? You didn't end up selling her property?"

"No, I was already out of the business for a while by the time she sold. I think there was one other person who owned the property before your neighbour purchased it."

"Wow, that's a fascinating story. What a small world." Baker paused, deep in thought. "I'll tell you one thing: I definitely have a new opinion of Ethel Swanson. She sounds like a cool lady."

"Cool is one way to put it. Among her many weirdnesses, the one I remember best was her annoying habit of sneaking up on me and flicking my hat from behind. It always fell over my eyes, and by the time I adjusted it and looked around, she was gone—leaving only a giggle as proof it was her. I could never figure out how she was able to move that fast." Dorcas then adopted a more sober tone. "This will sound like a strange question, but have you ever seen her walking about on the property? Her spirit, I mean?"

Baker was taken aback. "Seriously? Um, no, I've never experienced any such thing. Even though I've been out on the property late at night and in the wee hours of the morning." Dorcas was starting to freak him out. "Why would you ask that?"

"I was just curious, seeing as you live next door. Ethel made a point of leaving me an open invitation to drop by, particularly after she'd passed on. She told me not to be a stranger." She looked at Baker, then shrugged. "I guess I've been a stranger."

Lacking any sort of reply, Baker offered her some refreshment, and she graciously accepted a cup of herbal tea. They settled in the kitchen as Baker made himself busy preparing a pot of peppermint tea. Dorcas looked over into the scantily furnished living room, which was dominated by an arrangement of musical instruments.

"Tell me Baker, what are your general plans for engaging in Wiccan rituals? I don't need specifics; keep those to yourself. But I might be able to give you some ideas that'll help."

Baker attempted to describe his plan. In his mind it sounded rational, but saying it out loud made him feel eight years old again, sharing silly secrets in his neighbour's treehouse. Instead of answering her question outright, he decided to stall. "This is awfully generous of you to offer your expertise."

"Don't thank me yet. You might be disillusioned by my suggestions."

"Well, look at it this way. Presently, I've got zero to go on. Therefore, anything you can provide in the way of guidance can only benefit our efforts."

"*Our* efforts? You mean you're not doing this alone?"

"No. I've got four others willing to help out. Perreault will be in the group, along with Conrad—he's our school chaplain—and Masaccio and Angus, also teachers at our school." He was called away by the whistling of the kettle and then busied himself making preparations for the tea. In the meantime, he poured himself a cup of coffee.

"What school do you teach at?" Dorcas asked.

"Holy Mother of Virtue. Most people just call it HMV. Have you heard of it?"

"Yes. It's a Catholic school, isn't it?"

"That's right." Baker saw an opening to tell Dorcas about the teacher's band. "The four of us will get together and practice after school some days, in the music studio." Then he motioned to the instruments in the next room. "The odd time we'll jam here. We aren't that good, but we have fun." He then added shyly, "We call ourselves 'Bakers' Coven.'"

"Excellent. This is all useful information; it gives us more options." Dorcas moved to pour some tea. "Do you mind if I help myself?"

"Please, go ahead." He got up and went to the refrigerator. "Can I interest you in some wraps and sandwiches? They're leftovers from an after-school meeting, but still fresh."

"Not for me, thanks. Maybe Mary will want something when she gets back."

The mention of Mary made Baker suddenly anxious about her alone outside. "So, what's Mary looking for back there, anyway? It's not exactly the best night to be exploring in the dark."

"I sent her to harvest some puffballs."

"Puffballs? What are they?"

"Mushrooms—edible mushrooms. They're white spheres that look like volleyballs, and they grow on the forest floor at this time of year."

"Hang on. Now that you mention it, I *have* seen one or two in previous years, just off the path toward the back of the property. They're called puffballs, huh? And you say they're edible?"

"As long as they're picked fresh. I remember Ethel harvesting some dandy puffball mushrooms along the tree line between the properties, adjacent to her barn."

"And you're confident Mary will be able to find these puffballs in the dark?"

"Don't worry about Mary. Like I said, she's quite talented, and that includes a considerable comfort level in natural environments. Don't ask me where she acquired it. Fact is, I fully expect Mary to return with some fine specimens, and probably one or two other surprises."

Baker was keen on seeing the puffballs up close. He wasn't too sure about the "other surprises."

"Getting back to the members of your coven, I need to say this right away: The people you are circling with should be competent."

"Competent? How so?"

"They should take this seriously. At least avoid irreverence or obnoxious behaviour. If each member of the Coven is honest in his or her efforts, and if all of you are sincere in your beliefs, then the energy—the magic, if you will—can only be more potent. I might add that having Perreault in your group is a good move. She is a paragon of integrity. So, I'm going to assume your group is committed and in earnest."

Although he had complete faith in his fellow bandmates, Baker could never be sure what criteria a witch might demand of the people who made up a coven—so receiving Dorcas's blessing was a relief.

"I guess I should tell you, uh, our 'rituals' will be in the form of musical jam sessions."

"That's fine. In fact, the making of music and the reciting or chanting of words, like a mantra, are effective ways of communicating your message."

"What about timing?"

"You mean like, time of year, time of month, when should one engage in spell casting, and which days are better than others?"

Baker wasn't sure what he'd meant, so he just went along with it. "Yeah . . . sure."

"Yes, that is something to consider. Here, take this." She reached into her bag and retrieved a copy of *The Old Farmer's Almanac*. "Use this as a reference. You'll find what you need in the calendar pages."

"Find what I need? What exactly am I looking for?"

"Moon phases. The optimal time for planting, creating, embarking on a journey—or conducting coven ceremonies—is during a waxing moon. People typically don't give it much thought, but folks in my business, well, our lives are basically tied to the phases of the moon." She also handed Baker what appeared to be a self-published guidebook.

Baker read its title aloud. *"Coven Craft for Wannabe Witches."*

"The title is still a work in progress. I've written a sort of instruction manual, a guide for novice practitioners of coven craft. Many of the things I'll mention tonight are in the manual. I think you'll find it to be a helpful reference tool."

"Well, thank you for this, Dorcas." Baker sounded ambivalent.

"Trust me, Baker, in my humble opinion, you and your group should feel privileged that I've deemed you worthy of that book. I'm very careful about who I share that information with."

"In that case I do feel privileged." He inspected the front and back covers of the manual, looking for a price, but found none. "I guess I owe you something for it?"

"You needn't fret about that. Miss Thoreau took care of it."

"Wow, Perreault really has my back on this."

"Yes, it would appear that she does."

"So, I need to be sincere and committed, and I should avail myself of *The Old Farmer's Almanac* and its calendar pages. What else—aside from reading the manual, of course?"

"It's all about communication. Your goal is to communicate effectively." Her mention of communication brought to Baker's mind Howard Pappas from his drive home that evening. "You are sending a message. You're conversing with unseen forces and entities. Take some time to consider the setting."

"The setting?"

"Wherever your group meets, it should be evocative. Create an ambiance that is alluring, almost seductive, especially if it's a spirit you're messaging. Think of it as tantalizing your spirits, charming or enticing them. And be accepting and hospitable. Invite them in, and be open to their presence."

Dorcas must have noticed the questioning look on Baker's face. "You'd be surprised how many people enter this activity with fear and mistrust. They suspect the spirit has some diabolical scheme, forgetting that *they* are the ones calling the spirit to come to them."

Baker hadn't considered calling on spirits during their coven ceremonies, but the thought was intriguing. "OK, be hospitable. But what is an alluring ambiance?"

"Simple. Start by filling the place with candles. A candlelit room is a sure-fire way—no pun intended—to create the atmosphere you want."

"Really? Candles?"

"Candles are a staple in all manner of ceremonies. The Catholic Church makes liberal use of candles for its ceremonies, doesn't it? Aren't they often seeking to communicate with unseen entities, like saints and angels?"

"You're right; I guess I always just took it for granted."

"Have you never lit a votive candle and dedicated it for someone, alive or dead? Candles are to ritual ceremonies as butter is to cooking. The use of candles will improve a ceremony the same way butter makes everything taste better."

This talk of butter and cooking reminded Baker that he was still hungry, so he reached for one of the tuna wraps and munched on it as Dorcas went into detail on the efficacy of candles and their flames.

"The first reason is that fire is involved. Fire is one of the four elements, along with earth, air, and water, and is fundamental to earthly existence. It also helps participants in ritual ceremonies feel like they are in a place of solemnity."

Baker mumbled something through his chewing and nodded enthusiastically as Dorcas continued. "Finally, one practical property about a lit candle is that the flame is sensitive to changes in the immediate environment, such as air currents and oxygen content, and those are effective means of communication. Spirits can use candle flames to signal their presence."

Baker finished chewing but didn't catch that last part, as his mind was on something else. "I had originally planned to hold our gatherings right here. But now I'm wondering if it wouldn't be better if I found a more, I dunno . . . 'sacred' place to hold these ceremonies."

"Definitely not. You don't need to be in the parlour of a haunted Victorian mansion or amongst the ruins of a Scottish castle, or even on a sacred hilltop under a full moon." Dorcas paused, sensing uncertainty in his expression. "Look, don't worry, Baker. In fact, I'm getting some positive vibes right here. What would you say, Mary?"

Baker looked up at Dorcas, perplexed that she would call him Mary. Then something registered, and he turned, startled to see Mary standing inside the kitchen door, wicker basket in one hand and a half-eaten apple in the other. She was still munching when Baker remembered his manners and invited her in.

"Hello there, Mary. I didn't hear you come in. Please, have a seat. Let me take that basket."

"Was your hunt a success?" Dorcas asked.

"I was able to gather two decent-sized puffballs. There was one other, but I think it was overripe."

"Let's take a look, shall we?"

Mary handed the basket to Baker while she set her sandals by the door and draped her cloak over a stool, placing her hat on top of it. Baker got his first real look at her and was alarmed by how striking her eyes were. The green was so vivid he automatically assumed she was wearing coloured contacts.

Dorcas took the basket from her host, flipped open one of the two flaps, and gently extracted the larger of the two puffballs. Baker was like a child, eager to see the harvested mushroom, so she held it out for him to examine. It was remarkably white and spherical and if seen from a distance could actually be mistaken for a volleyball. The outer surface was firm and unblemished, save for some random smears of dirt.

"So, you eat this?" he asked. "The whole thing?"

"The whole thing. It's quite good—if you're a fan of mushrooms. Then again, on its own a puffball is fairly bland. It basically takes on the flavour of what you cook it with. But puffballs have a short shelf life—you should eat them soon after harvesting." Dorcas stopped and looked at her host. "I'll tell you what. Why don't you keep this one and try it for yourself? I'll take the other one."

Baker held the specimen up like a crystal ball. "You say it's got a short shelf life? Then I'd better not because knowing me I wouldn't get to it for a few days, and by then it might be beyond its 'best before' date." He placed it in the basket. "How do you prepare it, anyway?"

"I slice it, like bread, but you can cut it into squares. It'll look and cook like tofu or eggplant. You can fry it in butter, maybe with onions. You can grill it. You can even make a sort of French toast with it."

"Sounds delicious. And speaking of food," Baker turned to address Mary, who had moved toward his IKEA love seat, "can I interest you in a wrap or a bagel and cream cheese? Maybe something warm to drink—coffee or tea?"

"Nothing to eat, thanks. I sort of filled up on your apples. I could go for a coffee, though."

Baker went to the cupboard for a mug. "*My* apples? You mean that apple you were eating wasn't one you brought yourself?"

"No. I found several nice ripe ones on an old apple tree back there along the tree line. I hope you don't mind that I helped myself."

"You kidding? I didn't even know those old apple trees produced edible fruit." Something occurred to Baker. "Hey, how were you able to see good apples up in a tree? Isn't it dark out there?"

In answer to his question, Mary simply held up her cell phone.

"Um, you lost me. How does a cell phone help find edible apples? Is there some kind of app or something?"

Dorcas chimed in while Mary stifled a laugh. "I think Mary used her phone like a flashlight, Baker."

"Right . . . right," Baker said, his cheeks pink as he delivered the cup of coffee to Mary. She was standing next to the drum kit, tapping the high hat with the nail of her index finger. "I always forget that cell phones can be used for more than just, um . . . you know, phoning people." Baker went back to his stool at the kitchen counter while Mary casually moved through the room, stopping behind the keyboard.

"By the way, Mary," Dorcas said, "you didn't answer me earlier because we got on the tangent of giant puffballs. Baker and I were discussing optimal locations to contact spirits. I thought that this place would serve well enough. I even suggested there might be some activity as we speak. Do you sense anything?"

The question caught Mary mid-sip. She plunked one of the keys with her free hand. "Hmm? Oh, for sure. This place is humming. It's party central."

"Wait a minute, hold on," Baker said. "You're saying there are spirits present? Right here? Right now?"

"Why not?" Dorcas asked. "It's not that unusual, really."

"Not unusual?"

"Well, it does depend on the circumstances. For instance, here, tonight, you have a unique situation, where there's a lot of optimal energy in one small space."

"Forgive me if I sound naïve, but we *are* talking dead people, aren't we? I mean, wouldn't I need to have had someone close to me pass away . . . a family member, or a close friend?"

"No, that's not always necessary. Mind you, many spirits of the dearly departed do, in fact, reside in or visit the physical spaces inhabited by their loved ones who are still alive. But there's nothing stopping the spirit of a complete stranger from paying a call. It could be the spirit of someone you have admired or someone you deem is most qualified to answer a particular question or request you may have."

"Will they make their presence known?"

"It's possible, if that's your request."

"How will they communicate?"

"It depends. Some forms of communication require more energy than others."

"Some forms? You mean there are different ways that these . . . spirits might communicate with us?"

"Of course. Sometimes you'll have to make an educated guess as to what's being communicated, based on select information."

"Like charades?"

"As a matter of fact, yes. Be alert for signs. For example—and get ready now—" She raised her right hand and pointed across to the entry door. "When Mary came through the door a few minutes ago, I noticed that the pages of your coffee table book flipped." Baker jerked his head toward his copy of *The Clarence Cup: A Tradition Like No Other*, which was open to a random page. "Now, it would be easy to explain that away as the effects of a random breeze associated with the open door," Dorcas continued, "but it's unlikely, not least because there's hardly a breath of wind tonight."

"OK, but why would a spirit communicate by flipping pages?" Baker asked.

"Oh, it's not the flipping of the pages that was the message. I'd bet they were flipped to reveal one page in particular: something meaningful, that maybe only you would understand."

He stared at Dorcas for a moment, then rose and made his way across the room to where Mary was seated, the open book on the table before her. He reached down and spun it around to get a look at it, then froze.

Dorcas noticed Baker's response. "I was right, wasn't I?"

He didn't reply immediately. The book was open to a page that happened to be flagged by Cubby's bookmark. He slid the laminated card to one side to reveal a photo of Toronto captain Cal Ubank on the ice in his Pines uniform, exhausted and sweaty but beaming and basking in championship glory, holding the Clarence Cup.

Searching his mind for a rational explanation, Baker soon abandoned the exercise in order to answer her question. "I'm reluctant to read too much into this, but I'll admit I've been focusing on one player in particular, and wouldn't you know it, the book is open to a photo of that player." Baker looked dubiously at Dorcas. "But that could easily be a simple coincidence, couldn't it?" As Baker walked back to the counter, Mary availed herself of the love seat, setting the coffee down and seeming to take an interest in Cubby's bookmark.

"You're right," Dorcas said, "it could be a simple coincidence, which is why your next step is to make a mental note of it and stay alert for additional signs. It's also nice to know that the messages you're trying to interpret are, in fact, coming from your target spirit. Therefore, it's not asking too much to have them prove their presence."

"No doubt you will show me how that might be achieved?"

Dorcas proceeded to move about the room, pointing out ways in which a spirit might communicate. She explained how a radio could produce moments of static, or events could occur in conjunction with the playing of certain songs. Lamps had been known to flicker or turn on or off for no apparent reason. Strange or unusual deliveries of mail, a specific series of numbers on bills, or cryptic messages through otherwise normal and mundane mailings. Phones brought their own set of combinations and permutations that owners should be alert to. Other messages had been known to reach the intended target while the recipient was walking or driving. In the end, Dorcas spoke of candles again. "As I mentioned earlier, candles are an easy and effective way for spirits to communicate because of their sensitivity to changes in their surroundings."

Eagerly taking in the information, Baker hung on every word the Wiccan uttered. Behind him on the love seat, Mary was scrutinizing the bookmark.

Dorcas turned to Baker with great earnestness, her eyes like lasers. "Magic that is practiced by one person—some call it individual magic—can be effective. But the practice of group magic, where you combine four or five individual wills focused on a single goal—well, now we're talking about results than can flat out inspire awe."

She was freaking Baker out—again. He was envisioning his living room becoming the centre of some cyclonic event, hurricane-force winds blowing out the windows and the roof being torn off.

"Seeing as you are working magic as a group," she continued, "it's vital that every member direct their energy toward a common end. I've got a checklist of four things that should ensure success toward that end."

"Four things? You mean, like, ingredients?"

"Yes. You can think of them as the magical ingredients of a potion cooked up in a cauldron."

"Should I write this down?"

"You don't have to write anything down. Just listen, and it should all make sense. Besides, it's in my manual. Ready?" Dorcas held up an index finger. "The first thing you need is a *need*. Now, that might sound like something borrowed from Dr. Seuss, but it's important to believe that what you're asking for is something you truly need. If everyone in your group shares the same need, well, now you have a combined *will*. It's when people gather in groups that their collective will, and energy, can take a life of its own." Dorcas paused for effect. "And Baker . . . a strong, combined *will* is what produces things like healing and recovery. It can change the course of events, and, in extreme cases, it can even alter the fabric of our physical world, going beyond the physical limitations that humans have come to accept." She stopped to let that sink in. "Pretty incredible, huh?"

Baker just stared at her, enthralled at the apparent gravity of what she was saying. Before he could respond, Dorcas held up two fingers and continued. "The second ingredient is *desire*." Again, she locked eyes with him, but this time Baker was certain he was witnessing a metamorphosis in his visitor, from the older lady he met an hour ago into a young, desirable woman. "You must possess a desire to achieve your goal. Now, a strong desire can be intense and emotional, almost like an obsession." To Baker, Dorcas suddenly looked twenty years younger, and her face, especially her eyes, emitted a lustful sensuality, almost carnal in nature. "To cast a successful spell, you should be impassioned or enflamed by your desire." Baker would remember this part of the lesson for a long time, not least of which because he felt an odd sensation, something close to arousal. "Desire can be expressed through the body by dancing, chanting, singing, pounding drums—even making love. You should be willing to obsess over this. Make it a daily habit to remind yourself how badly you want the thing you need."

For a moment Baker was afraid to move. Then, to his relief, Dorcas was back to the woman he first encountered at his front door, which seemed like years ago. She went on as if nothing happened and held up three fingers. Baker, however, took a few moments to recover, and had to work hard to focus on what was being said. Meanwhile, on the love seat, Mary casually flipped pages with her left hand while her right hand slipped the bookmark into the kangaroo pocket of her hoodie.

"The third item on the checklist is *knowledge*. Knowledge is essential. The best knowledge comes from experience, from doing. Things won't always turn out the way you envisioned, but they *will* turn out. Try to see every experience as an opportunity to learn. Don't hesitate to celebrate your successes, and alternatively, learn from your mistakes and practice patience. Trust that I've given you enough advice to get started."

In unhurried fashion, Dorcas paused to sip her tea before continuing. "And finally, *silence*." She folded her hands together. "This explains why I didn't want too much information from you about your need to engage in coven activity. That is entirely your business, and try to keep it within your small circle of participants. Your coven activity is about manipulating energy to your benefit, and hopefully to the benefit of the world in general. Keeping this energy within an intimate group of like-minded individuals prevents wasteful dispersal. It needs to be focused and conserved. We have a simple but powerful saying: 'Energy shared is energy lost.' Pass that saying on to the others in your group. Be misers when it comes to your needs and desires. Keep the business of the Coven inside the Coven." With exquisite timing, as she finished speaking about silence, Dorcas let it descend upon them.

Reluctant to break it, Baker nevertheless felt compelled to summarize what she had said. "OK, let me review now." He held his fingers up before each point, much like Dorcas had done. "Number one, I *need* a thneed. Number two, *desire*—" Baker hesitated, blushing, "I won't forget that one. Number three, *knowledge*—make use of what I know and learn from experience, and be patient. And finally, number four, *silence*. What happens in Vegas, stays in Vegas." Baker looked at his guest for feedback.

"I've never heard it quite put that way, but, why not? You've got it."

Something still niggled at him, however. He wanted to be able to assure his four colleagues that this witch, this expert in covens and ritual ceremonies, approved of his method.

"I want to make sure I've been clear: the central act during the ritual will be us, the members of our, uh, coven, performing a song, or songs, the lyrics of which essentially call upon the target forces or spirits. Most of all I want our ceremony to be somewhat... 'normal.' One thing I don't want to do is creep anyone out. I want everybody to be comfortable, you know."

"I totally agree," Dorcas assured him. "In my opinion, there's no more effective way of destroying the atmosphere during a coven ritual than engaging in actions that make the participants uncomfortable. So, if your group can lose their inhibitions and be fully invested, because all that you're asking them to do is sustain a rhythmic beat while the leader sings the lyric or recites the verse, then the ritual will be all the more effective."

Baker couldn't help but smile, taking great comfort in knowing how much had been accomplished that night. Emitting a great exhalation of air and still smiling, Baker swivelled around to face Mary, expecting some encouragement from the witch's apprentice, but he was instead met with a semi-reclined figure, eyes closed and hands folded, a teenager put to sleep by the boredom of it all. He turned back to Dorcas. "Is Mary sleeping?" he whispered.

"It would appear so. You are looking at the perfect example of someone with a clear conscience. But if you'll notice how her hands are folded together—" Dorcas' voice rose so Mary could hear her across the room, "—my guess is she's using her fingers like rosary beads. Mary is just praying, am I right?"

Without opening her eyes, Mary answered the question with mock formality. "Lady Blanchard is correct in her assessment, although I did doze off for a minute there, until I heard some stuff about people performing songs." She opened her eyes and looked at Baker. "So, you guys are a band? Hence the instruments?"

"That's right. The rituals are going to take the form of a jam session."

"Do you need a piano player?"

Dorcas spoke before Baker could respond. "Why, are you offering? I thought you'd quit."

"Yeah, but I could be persuaded to take it up again."

The exchange sounded odd to Baker, as if they were discussing the girl's past smoking habit, not her piano playing.

"Too bad, Mary," he said, sorry to let her down. "We already have someone who plays keys."

"Well, if you ever have the need, keep me in mind."

"I certainly will," Baker replied.

"Well then, Mary, what do you say I get you home?" Dorcas said, getting off her stool and stretching. "We've got a busy day tomorrow."

"What's on tap for tomorrow?" Baker asked.

"We're climbing trees and critter spotting."

Not knowing what to make of that, he merely raised his eyebrows. "I could see how that would be both challenging and fun." Then he appeared to look for something. "Can I get you anything for the road? A bottle of water?"

"Oh, no, thank you. If I drink anything more now, I'll be waking up in the middle of the night to go pee. What about you, Mary?"

"My bladder's good. I sleep through the night."

Dorcas rolled her eyes. "I meant do you want anything for the ride?"

"I'm fine, thanks."

As Baker led the way to the front door with Dorcas, Mary lagged a bit under the pretense of collecting her hat, cloak, and sandals, but she surreptitiously removed the bookmark from the pocket of her hoodie and dropped it into her fedora before placing it on her head. Then she collected the picnic basket and hustled to catch up. Meanwhile, Dorcas was expressing her disappointment with the fact that Mary hadn't brought any other surprises back from the forest. "I thought you'd come back with something other than just the puffballs."

"Oh, but I did. I was hoping Baker would find it in the basket for himself."

She held out the picnic basket and lifted the lid for him. Baker reached in and removed the second mushroom, and in doing so exposed the skull of what looked like a forest rodent, completely intact and as clean as a whistle. He gingerly held it up. "You found this in the tree line?"

"It's beautiful, isn't it? You know, some indigenous peoples believe a found skull is a good luck charm, bringing good fortune to its bearer. I thought if you 'found' it in the basket, it would strengthen the luck quotient, so to speak."

Dorcas was impressed. "That's an admirable thought, Mary."

Baker was fascinated by how delicate the skull seemed. "What animal do you figure it's from?"

"My guess would be a red squirrel."

When Baker went to put the skull back into the basket, Mary pulled away and closed the lid.

"It's for you. Consider it my little gift."

"I think you should set that somewhere on display, sort of like your Grady Sykes hockey stick, where it can be of benefit to you," Dorcas advised.

"You picked up on Grady's stick?" Baker asked, surprised.

"Well, it wasn't difficult to spot—and besides, I was sitting across from it most of the visit."

As the two guests prepared to take their leave, Baker turned to Mary. "Thanks for being so patient, Mary. Good luck with your studies. And thank you for the squirrel skull. I'll find a good place to display it."

"No sweat. Thanks for the beer and puffballs—and the apples and coffee."

Dorcas reached for her boots but then turned to address her host. "Baker, it has been a distinct pleasure getting to know you, and thank you for allowing us into your home."

"Good God, Dorcas, don't be silly! You came out of your way to help me." He stopped, his mouth twisting with concern. "I'm just not sure if I feel comfortable knowing I've also invited ghosts into my home."

"Oh, they are gone, dear. This house is decidedly empty of spirits. It's just you and the walls."

"Is that right?" Baker asked, looking to Dorcas and Mary for reassurance.

"Yup. Bar's closed; party's over," Mary replied.

Dorcas was crouched over, busying herself with her boots. "Remember, you can invite spirits into your home and request what you want, but they won't stay longer than is necessary; it requires quite an expenditure of energy." She straightened up, her face flushed from being bent over. Baker noticed that she looked her age again. "Nevertheless, keep your eyes open for any residual signs that they might have left to guide you."

"Huh! Well then, I'm going to have to take your word for it." He stared at the walls and began to regret that his guests had to leave so soon. Then he shook himself and realized it was time for them to say their goodbyes. "Listen, thanks again for being so generous with your knowledge and insight—and for the books. I feel much better about where I want to go with these coven rituals." He opened the front door.

"I'm glad I could be of service. If you need anything else, you know how to get a hold of me. Oh, and after all this talk about best practices for coven ceremonies and stuff, I will leave you with one last thing: if all else fails, be sure to set aside a few minutes once a month, during each new moon, to light a candle and make a wish."

"New Moon—light a candle and make a wish," Baker echoed. "I can handle that."

"Good. Best of luck to you and your coven." She swept a hand in an arc through the air and mumbled something that sounded to Baker like "It is done," then stepped out onto the front porch where she seemed to assess the night air. It had begun to drizzle. She turned back to Baker and with a friendly smile said, "Feel free to keep me informed of the coven's progress whenever you get a chance . . . and tell Perreault I said hi."

Mary stopped and turned to her mentor in alarm, "Oh, shit. I can't believe I forgot to tell you."

"Tell me what?"

"Do you happen to know someone named Ethel? She told me to say hi."

Dorcas stared. "You're kidding. You saw Ethel out there?"

"I didn't 'see' her exactly. It was more like . . . how to describe it . . . she gave me a nudge and then flicked the back of my hat. She said you'd understand."

Dorcas gave Baker a knowing look, winked, and allowed another smile to crease her lips as she turned and followed Mary out toward the car. He remained in the entryway as his visitors climbed into the vehicle, then drove down the laneway and out onto the dark, wet gravel road. Not certain of what he'd gotten himself into, he watched them disappear into the mist, then retreated back into a house that wasn't quite the same as it was two hours ago.

He switched on the TV and tuned it to the Pines-Nationales game, but Baker was less interested in watching hockey than on just having some "company." He couldn't shake the feeling that he was being watched. Heck, not only did he have who knew how many spirit strangers in the house, he also had the ghost of a previous neighbour—a witch at that—prowling around outside. It was too much information—stuff he didn't need to know—and it prompted him to wonder if he'd bitten off more than he could chew with this whole coven thing.

CHAPTER THIRTEEN
MAKE US HAPPY

You can make us happy
Just win the Cup back
You can make us happy
We pray like hell that you do that

Saturday, October 19 – Tuesday, October 22

In Canadian politics, federal Election Day was on the horizon, and party leaders were closing out the final weekend of a forty-day campaign that proved to be generally unkind and at times downright nasty. The Pines, meanwhile, were gearing up for the Boston Hubs, an opponent that brought its own brand of nastiness. Toronto was up to the challenge, however, coming away with an exciting overtime win. Unfortunately, it was followed up two days later with a disappointing loss to Columbus. And so, with ten games in the books in a season that had begun with such high expectations, the Pines' record was a mediocre 5–3–2, for a total of twelve points. While they may have gotten back on track to meet the coach's target of six points per five-game segment, there wasn't a fan within Coney Nation who hadn't expected more from the team just three weeks earlier.

On Tuesday, nearly one month to the day after the autumnal equinox, people in this part of the world heralded the arrival of something called the Sports Equinox, an annual phenomenon that occurs exclusively in North America. The Sports Equinox falls in that small window on the calendar when each of the Big Four major sports leagues are operating and have games scheduled, to the immense delight of every fan on the continent. This year we saw Major League Baseball into its World Series, pitting the Washington Nationals against the Houston Astros. The National Football League was approaching the midway point of its season, with the previous night's Monday Night Football matchup seeing the New England Patriots dismantle the New York Jets 33-0. The National Basketball Association had the Toronto Raptors opening a new season as defending champions at home against the visiting New Orleans Pelicans. (To make it extra special for Raptors' fans, the 2018–2019 NBA Championship banner would be raised to the rafters and the players would collect their championship rings.) As for the Premier Hockey League, its season was nicely underway and in its third week of action. Toronto hockey fans were given the opportunity to watch the Mighty Pines face the Boston Hubs for the second time in three games. (Unfortunately for Coney Nation, Boston came away with a 4-2 win.)

For the Pines, there was much to unpack in the wake of this loss. To begin, the question of player effort was becoming a hotly discussed topic. Was it the responsibility of the players, as well-paid professionals, to motivate themselves to give honest effort, or was it the responsibility of the head coach to inspire his charges? In answer to the second part of the question, with Kayden Koch in his fifth year behind the Pines bench, some wondered whether his message had grown stale in its presentation.

And while the Mighty Pines were struggling to negotiate their way through the PHL landscape of quality teams, Canadians across the land were assessing a slightly changed political landscape the day after the 2019 federal election. The Liberal Party, under the leadership of Justin Trudeau, won themselves another four years in power, but had to settle for a minority government (perhaps Trudeau's message was growing stale for Canadians). The long campaign season was over, and now it was time to govern.

The members of Bakers' Coven decided to meet with Paul Young for a pre-production confab to discuss aspects of the music video, including scheduling, props, costumes, and other details. The enthusiasm with which Paul undertook the task was a bit overwhelming to the others. According to his storyboard sketches, his camera would be everywhere, on every face and instrument, from every angle: over-the-shoulder shots, worm's-eye-view shots, boom shots, zoom shots, handheld shots, and shots on a tripod. They would have costume changes and they would employ different locations. There was apparently no limit to the amount of footage he was willing to collect.

In truth, he was the ideal student for this project, diving headlong into multiple roles, which included recording engineer, sound mixer, producer, director, cinematographer, and editor. Tireless and enthusiastic, open to any and all suggestions, and willing to try anything, it was as if Paul just needed enough material to work with. By his calculations, two days would suffice to get what he required.

"Now, Paul, I assume you're aware that you're eventually going to have to sift through all this footage and edit it into something that makes sense," Baker felt compelled to observe at one point.

"No worries, Mr. Brooks. I'm up to the task. After all, it's my job to tell your story, and in the process, make you sound and look great." Baker figured he did not need to raise the subject again.

On the morning of the first day of shooting, Paul hadn't arrived yet, and the band members were comparing notes on the previous day's meeting.

Mas was impressed with Paul's enthusiasm. "He is super pumped about this. I can't believe he came armed with a rough script and even storyboards."

Perreault felt the same. "Did you see all the stuff he brought in for use as props? He's bringing more today."

"He says he should be able to complete the video by the middle of November," Angus said. "Heck, even December would be good enough for us, wouldn't it? When's the due date, anyway?"

"You know what? I don't think he ever told me what the deadline was," Baker said.

"Well, let's hope for the best," Mas said, ever the optimist. "So far it looks promising."

"He's working like a North Pole elf preparing for Christmas Eve," Perreault observed.

"Is there anything we might be able to do to facilitate the process, so we can minimize the possibility that Paul misses his deadline?" Conrad asked.

"That's a good question," Baker replied. "I mean, look at all the jobs he's taking on. I actually gave it some consideration last night and—"

"And you came up with an elegant solution?" Conrad asked.

"Possibly. How does this sound? We're going to record the music today, right? And Paul mentioned laying down individual tracks, which he would then mix at a later date."

"That's right."

"Well, I thought, what if we all get on the same page and tell him that we'd prefer to do it live, all together? I mean, even if it takes us a few hours, at least it will be done, and he won't have to spend time fiddling with it in the post-production, which will be better for all of us."

Conrad nodded. "That might be one item we can take off his hands. Good thinking, Baker."

When Paul finally arrived, he got right to work setting up the recording gear while the band warmed up. When he announced his readiness, Paul was taken by surprise when each member expressed a desire for him to record them playing the song live together rather than individually. He seemed receptive to their proposal, provided they perform a sort of impromptu audition to allow him to make an informed decision. All were agreed, and after only three false starts, the group was able to convince their young producer that they were up to the task.

That settled, there was nothing left but to get down to the business of recording "Make Us Happy." Fortunately, the acoustics of Janet Sax's music room proved to have aural integrity, which facilitated their efforts and allowed them to lay down a handful of usable tracks. As usual, Conrad brought all of his experience and professionalism to the task of playing lead guitar while Baker's chord progressions supported admirably on rhythm guitar. Mas on bass was like the lead official in a well-refereed hockey game: one never noticed him, but his control of the game was vital and imperceptible. Angus came in on time on the drums, and since the arrangement of Sheryl Crow's hit didn't require the drummer to get things started, he was able to fall in with the pace set by the guitars, making the tempo just right—not too rushed but neither too draggy.

For "Herr Direktor" Paul, getting competent musicianship from the guys was undeniably a bonus, but it was clear from the get-go that the real gift, the centrepiece of his video, thanks to the strength of her vocals and her overall physical presence, was Ms. Thoreau. The song required something of a balancing act from its lead singer, and Perreault delivered with the perfect blend of coquettishness and fair warning, a cross between "let's spend some time together" and "you may want to keep your distance, buddy." From somewhere she found a twang, a southern lilt sprinkled with the faintest echo of a smoker's sexy rasp. Added to that was her timing, which Paul found to be impeccable. She could turn or twist her lips, tilt an eyebrow, and crinkle her nose to get the most out of what a given lyric line expressed. And when it came time to belt out the chorus, all it took was a flick of her head, and with hair sweeping across her face she broke into a smile as broad as the "Happy" suggested in the song. Baker could practically hear a packed house at Nova Tank Arena singing along, turning it into a full-on anthemic plea drawing upon fifty-three years of heartbreak.

To strive for authenticity and achieve the desired emotional impact, Perreault decided to belt it out for real the first few takes, and it was lucky for her larynx that Paul was satisfied with what he was able to get after just five runs through the song. The other takes had Perreault lip-syncing to the final cut of her own voice being played over the speakers.

With the instrumentation and vocals to everyone's satisfaction, it was time for lunch, after which they would move on to film some of the interior scenes. It was around the time when the lunch rubble was being tidied up that Paul subtly pulled Baker aside. "Boy, Mr. Brooks, that Ms. Thoreau—she is one talented lady."

Baker laughed. "You got that right, Paul. And to think that she basically fell into our laps to lead this band to new heights."

MAKE US HAPPY

"And on top of it all, she's 'miss,' right? Man, what angel did you bribe to get that stroke of luck?"

Baker didn't get a chance to answer because Conrad's voice cut into their conversation from across the room. "Hey, you two, let's get this show on the road, shall we?" Baker and Paul wasted no time getting back to their stations, but Baker's eyes lingered on Perreault as he considered the implications of what Paul had asked.

As for Paul, if there was any doubt among the band members about his ability to see the project through to its completion, such doubt certainly didn't apply to his efforts during the process of filming. He seamlessly traded his music producer's cap for that of video director. With his viewfinder ever-present and camera at the ready, Paul recorded it all, documenting every moment. He had the band repeat the song at least a dozen times—probably thirteen—and he treated every take as if it was the first. In his own mind, Paul had resolved not to be the rate-determining step on this project. In fact, he had his own doubts about whether the five teachers-cum-pop-stars could handle the challenge of performing in front of a camera. To get the desired energy out of them, Paul set the playback volume as close to "eleven" as he could get while the guys on their instruments air-played along to the piped-in song, giving them the freedom to jump, dance, and otherwise animate themselves to produce some semblance of stage presence.

The guys also had freedom when it came to choosing their costumes. On lead guitar, Conrad opted to resurrect an old black leather jacket, all buckles and zippers, a remnant from his early days as an aspiring musician when he worshipped at the altar of Mick Jones and the Clash. By pairing it with black jeans and combat boots, he was able to kindle some raunch, enveloping him in an air of menace which he played up by keeping his head down for the most part, only looking up to peer out from under his well-worn Mighty Pines cap. On the other side of the stage was Masaccio on bass, who served as a visual contrast to Conrad by sporting a white Pines away jersey (Mason Andrews version) and topping it off with an old porkpie hat. In the video he is seen adopting a super-wide stance, resulting in his low-slung instrument hanging close to but not quite touching the floor. Behind the drum kit, Angus seized his opportunity to treat the audience to a gun show by pouring himself into a tight-fitting plaid, flannel shirt—sleeveless, of course. (He had actually considered going tarps-off for a breezy moment but ultimately thought better of it, especially since the video was intended for a wider audience beyond, say, fans of hardcore punk.) Whenever he was captured in action, Angus displayed a fair amount of raw muscularity while generally making faces at the camera from underneath a tie-dyed bucket hat. Finally, Baker's choice of outfit saw him pay tribute to one of the country's popular fashion stereotypes: the Canadian tuxedo. He presented himself in a pair of blue jeans and a denim jacket over a white t-shirt emblazoned with a green Mighty Pines pine cone. For Baker, since he didn't have to concentrate on musical precision while on camera, it was a chance to live out his dream of playing an instrument on stage while dancing, spinning, bobbing, and kicking. He even took the opportunity to jump down from the upper level beside the drum kit, performing dry-land versions of a Daffy, a Backscratcher, and a Spread Eagle, which worked quite well on screen when slowed way down.

When it came to the lead vocalist, however, Paul recognized that costume design might warrant a more considered approach. He consulted Ms. Thoreau on her preferences and general taste and then the two of them decided on a look that had her undertake several costume changes throughout his filming of the interior scenes. In the end Perreault's main wardrobe consisted of a flat-toned mini skirt—alternating at times with a green-and-white tartan mini, in keeping with the Mighty Pines colours—and a variety of printed leggings (she opted for patterns that were fun and bright), some with hockey themes whenever possible. For footwear, she employed a couple of elegant leather ankle boots, one a flat-heeled pair, the other sporting a high heel. The mini skirt and heels would provide the requisite sex appeal, as mandated by a song ostensibly meant to get the attention of the Mighty Pines hockey team and entice them into finally winning a damn Clarence Cup. She let down her hair, so it would fall half the time on a casual V-neck T-shirt, the other times on a sleeveless tank sweater. For her makeup she took a toned-down approach, save for the lipstick. She opted for a crimson red after the fashion of Sheryl Crow in the original video for the song.

At one point during a break, Baker found himself alone with Angus. "It's going pretty well, huh?"

Angus nodded. "For sure. This is a blast. I almost feel like a real rock star doing this video."

Baker shared his friend's sentiment about feeling like a rock star, although he didn't come right out and say it. What made the experience truly sweet was seeing how much fun the others were having. He was delighted to see Perreault and Masaccio enjoying themselves, but the real surprise for him was Conrad's commitment to the project. He maintained a youthful energy throughout the process.

"And we haven't even filmed the rooftop scenes yet."

The idea to get footage on the roof of the school had come from a passing comment that Angus had made a couple of weeks earlier. "You know, if we ever do this again, we should consider playing on a rooftop." Angus had been addressing Baker with his remark, but Paul, being within earshot, took the notion and ran with it. (It didn't hurt that, as a student at HMV, he had spent time on the roof of the school taking video of the senior football team during home games.)

Paul had implored Baker to secure permission from the relevant authority, whether that be the principal, the superintendent, the director, or the pope. But Baker didn't waste his time with any of those. Instead, he'd showed up, cap in hand, at the door of Gus—the school custodian. Gus had patiently listened and then generously granted them thirty minutes up on the roof. Paul had also been thrilled to learn that Mr. Baldwin, the computer technology and robotics teacher, had offered to operate his drone and have it circle the school to capture some shots of the band from the sky. It wouldn't be much, but Paul figured even a few seconds' worth would be enough to produce the desired effect.

So, when the time came for the members of Bakers' Coven to simulate a rooftop concert, Mr. Baldwin flew his drone from the parking lot down below, and Gus watched the proceedings on the roof in a fold-up lawn chair, off to the side to avoid getting into any shots, sipping a coffee and puffing on a cigar. (Months later, Paul discovered that Gus *had* made it into the finished video, but one had to look hard and know when to look.)

When their half hour was up, and everybody was packing to head back inside, Baker approached Gus and thanked him again for the opportunity.

"No worries, man," Gus said through a thick cloud of cigar smoke. "Let's just get the fuck outta here before a crowd starts gathering down on the street, wondering when the show's gonna start."

In the end, to capture and record all the material that Paul would need, filming took only one more day than they had planned. He was able to edit the live footage of the band in action while splicing in images from black-and-white Mighty Pines photos along with his film footage of boys and girls engaging in the great Canadian game on ponds and backyard rinks, consisting mostly of shots from three or four locales in town. He also found time to visit the Hockey Hall of Fame to take photos of the Clarence Cup along with its discontinued rings, as well as an assortment of other aspects of PHL history. He ended up visiting Nova Tank Arena, Elysian Square, and the Icemen of the Acropolis, as well as Toronto's Walk of Fame along King and Simcoe Streets.

*****

No one in Bakers' Coven heard any news of the video's progress through November and December, nor did they see the finished video until later in January, roughly the time of the PHL's All-Star weekend. But by then, as is typical in life, there were other things to occupy their time and minds. It wasn't until Baker received an email out of the blue from Paul around mid-January that he was able to view the fruit of their labours. According to Paul's description in the message, the video might not get nominated for an MTV Video Music Award, but it was six and a half minutes of fun—and it got him a good grade. Paul also mentioned that he would stand by for further instructions from the group regarding putting it online.

Unable to wait until he and his bandmates were all together, when classes were done for the day, Baker locked his classroom door, settled in with his earbuds, and pressed "play."

The video opened with a worm's eye view of an empty school corridor. The hallway was soon populated by the walking legs of a handful of people, mostly men, one female, apparently a band of musicians because they were shown carrying guitar cases, drumsticks, and a microphone. The camera followed along as they opened a door labelled "Custodial Room," and then carried on into the room toward a ladder that led up through an exit door and out onto the rooftop. The next cut revealed a low-angle shot of an outdoor rooftop scene, which included a drum kit, amplifiers, and microphone stand, and, in the middle of it all, the Clarence Cup was on display in all its glory—perched on a simple classroom desk. (Paul was able to secure the almost life-size replica from a friend of a friend of a friend—a rental, basically.) The group proceeded to take their positions on a makeshift stage, the drummer at his kit, others plugging into amplifiers, and the vocalist setting her microphone into the stand.

Just before the music began, an impressive drone shot captured the group from above for a few seconds, replaced by close-up shots of each band member in a meditative state, alone with their thoughts. Then with the camera tightly focused on Conrad's hand hovering over the strings of his guitar, he strummed the opening chords that began the song. A lower camera angle from behind Angus showed him joining the guitar with the drumbeat, and when it came time for the vocals to kick in, the audience was treated to a straight-on head-and-shoulders shot of Perreault, ably playing the part of a dyed-in-the-wool Pines fan, making her opening declaration right into the camera lens.

> This is our . . . it's our time this year
> Put on a poncho, slip down the goggles
> We're sprayin' vintage bubbly again

She was dressed to guard against the cold in a cashmere tam and oversized multi-zippered black leather biker jacket, a loan from Baker for the rooftop scene.

> We remember our Hogtown heroes
> Cy Quinn had the touch, and Daly was clutch
> With Jacko standing tall in the net
> Well, OK, they raised the Cup
> It's time to put this drought to a stop

As Perreault leaned into the rousing chorus, imploring the Pines to once again bring joy to their fans, the camera cut to another terrific shot from the drone in the sky, making it seem as if her entreaty was extending out across the rooftops. Paul had discovered that particular shot during the editing process and was stunned to see that

Perreault was actually looking up at the drone cam with her arms upraised at the very moment she sang the first line of the chorus. He was left to ask himself how she was able to find the camera in the sky at that precise moment. It was utterly perfect.

> *You can make us happy*
> *Just win the Cup back*
> *You can make us happy*
> *We pray like hell that you do that*

When he had been trying to decide on the words for the chorus, Baker hadn't initially been sold on the idea of "praying," especially where fans of a secular bent were concerned. And as for all the believers, he had thought they might object to the notion of praying "like hell." He'd consulted with Conrad, who had understood Baker's concerns but had offered no definite opinion either way. To assuage Baker's fears, he'd asked to hear the alternatives. Baker had been ready with a few, but in the end, Conrad suggested leaving the line unaltered.

Drawn back to the video, Baker watched the scene shift to the music room, all the band members having replaced their overcoats and sweaters with more appropriate indoor attire.

> *We've been down, real low down*
> *Stood in the cold rain, feeling our own pain*
> *Well, God knows we've been there before*

> *We dug down, and found the right way*
> *Won the lottery and*
> *Signed Valentino and then*
> *Saw Rick and Addy both cash in*
> *Well, OK, should we get stoned?*
> *We want the Holy Grail to come home*

Earlier in the week Angus had put the question to Baker about his decision to refer to "getting stoned" in the lyrics. He'd suggested it might be a risk, an excuse not to be picked up by some outlet like Mighty Pines Sports and Entertainment because it could project questionable conduct for young and impressionable listeners.

Baker would have none of it. His reasons for employing it included the fact that the reference was in the original song, and he'd never known the song to suffer for it. Also, he'd thought it was faithful to how Toronto fans were searching for any solution to the Cup drought. Finally, he'd just liked the line's edginess and how it fit the verse.

Angus had quickly backed off. "Hey, no problem. Just thought I'd mention it, you know?"

You can make us happy
Just win the Cup back
You can make us happy
We pray like hell that you do that

During the double shot of the chorus, every effort was made to evince a celebration, complete with a room full of green-and-white balloons and white-and-green streamers as the group happily bopped among the balloons and joyfully tangled themselves up in the streamers. The slow-motion footage included individual band members wrestling over the Cup, trying to rescue it from out of the grasp of a pair of white-gloved hands.

You can make us happy
Just win the Cup back
You can make us happy
We pray like hell that you do that

The bridge in the song had been a great opportunity for Paul to introduce his footage of "hometown hockey," which included little kids playing on outdoor rinks and people skating at Nathan Phillips' Square, everything treated to look grainy and dated. He combined that with snippets of original footage of Clarence Cup parades through downtown Toronto as a nostalgic nod to the Pines' vintage years.

At the beginning of the third and final verse, Paul had Perreault singing the lines at the microphone dressed in full Mighty Pines player attire, complete with helmet and visor and gloves. The name on her jersey reflected the Pines of old: instead of highlighting any one of the present team members, she was seen wearing the number five sweater of Jersey Joe Zedelko. The other band members were similarly attired. Then because of Baker's reference to stars and big honchos, Paul included several images from Toronto's Walk of Fame along King Street, showing the names of legendary hockey stars like Jackson Schmeltz, Cal Ubank, Gordie Hicks, and Gabe Wozniak.

You'll be stars, living large right here
Now you're big honchos, play in Toronto
And drinks? Never pay for 'em again
And some day, we'll sing your songs
But just for now can't you right this wrong?

Perreault was terrific at singing into the camera, directing the question of righting wrongs unflinchingly at the people who had the most influence.

You can make us happy
Just win the Cup back

MAKE US HAPPY

You can make us happy
We pray like hell that you do that

It was here that Paul had set up a shot showing Perreault, hockey stick in hand, leaning in close with Conrad on guitar, alongside the iconic image of Gordie Hicks "hooking" the ten-year-old Gabe Wozniak under the chin, and then the album cover photo of Bruce Springsteen leaning on a sax-toting Clarence Clemons.

You can make us happy
Just win the Cup back
You can make us happy
We pray like hell that you do that

Throughout the last repeat of the chorus, the band was seen to be celebrating a championship win, carrying around the Clarence Cup, complete with goggles borrowed from the chemistry lab, dollar store ponchos, and "sham-pagne" spraying everywhere and soaking everything.

In reality, pulling that off had been quite the challenge for Paul. The real guitars and bass had been replaced with imitations that could stand getting soaked. The champagne bottles had been empty magnums filled with fresh Perrier, and the classroom had been emptied of everything that couldn't get wet. Everything else that might have gotten in the line of fire, like desks and chairs, had been left to air dry overnight—all with the permission of Janet Sax, of course.

The final shot of the video had been Baker's idea. The camera scanned slowly across the words "Mighty Pines Capture 11th Cup" from a front-page headline in May of 1962, announcing the Pines as champions. Then the shot dissolved into an extreme close-up of George Daly's name as captain of that '62 squad, etched in silver, the camera pulling out slowly, revealing its position on the present Cup, on the top ring, with the rest of the names of that team entering the screen as the camera continued to pull back. As the zoom-out continued, it showed the whole of the venerable chalice, preserved on its pedestal in the Hockey Hall of Fame, awaiting the next recipient in June. The camera lingered on the iconic image of hockey's holy relic, leaving Toronto fans to dream and hope as the final chords echoed, and the screen faded to black.

CHAPTER FOURTEEN
SAMHAIN

All we want is cause to celebrate
Make City Hall get off its ass
And plan the damn parade

Friday, October 25 – Thursday, October 31

Toronto was already playing its fourth back-to-back of the young season, but to people like Kayden Koch, it was better to face a loaded schedule early in the year, when players were still fresh and the wear and tear of the long season had not yet set in. Others would say that it was difficult to establish a team identity when they were just trying to survive the rigours of one game after another.

Another concern raised by observers had to do with the team's apparent lack of pluck or pushback in the face of certain opponents who did not hesitate to bully them. It was a question that some regarded as a pointed comment on GM Kyle Bulac's disinclination to stock the team with one or two "tough guys." It was clear the Pines had an urgent need for toughness . . . or truculence . . . or sandpaper. The label didn't matter as much as the recognition that winning hockey in the modern age still called for a physical presence on the ice. There was nothing like the ability to strike fear into one's opponent to derive an edge, especially in the later rounds of the playoffs, where teams were separated by only the smallest of margins in terms of skill level. It was a given that the Pines as constituted could match up with any other team based on their speed and skill, but there were those who wondered if they could get far in the playoffs lacking the requisite grit and toughness. And wasn't a deep playoff run the goal for this team?

On Tuesday, with two days off between games, Coach Koch took advantage of the opportunity to schedule a team practice. Practices were something that rarely fit into the grind of fourteen games in twenty-eight days, so it was good to reset a bit and prepare for the Washington Founders—a formidable opponent who was presently leading the division. Unfortunately for the Pines, despite going punch for punch with Washington, they still found a way to lose. The brutal first month of the schedule for Toronto was over. The team finished the fourteen games in October with a tepid 6–5–3 record.

Thursday, October 31 dawned grey and rainy, which under normal circumstances wouldn't be an issue, expect for the fact it was Halloween. There were some locales in Ontario and Quebec that experienced rains of biblical proportions, prompting several towns around Montreal to postpone trick-or-treating.

After having completed the music video for "Make Us Happy," Baker was determined to present the band with something new for their next session—keeping the songs fresh was essential. And so, if the Coven's request with "Make Us Happy" was for the Mighty Pines to "win the Cup back," then his task was to take that same request and express it in an entirely new way. His first approach was to make a plea for the Pines to advance out of the first round, but then he realized that wasn't really much of an accomplishment. (Hell, eight teams were guaranteed to come out of the first round anyway.)

That's when he came up with the idea of playing a game in June as an appropriate standard of achievement. He knew that by surviving to play a game in June, the Pines would take the city and its fans for a memorable playoff ride that would be discussed for decades. He even liked the sound of it. Once that was settled, he needed to find a song that would serve his purposes. Eventually, he decided on Joe Jackson's "Breaking Us In Two," changing the title to "Play A Game In June." Fortunately, he was able to complete the song in a timely fashion, so he and his bandmates were soon able to practice it to the point where they could perform it with a surprising level of proficiency.

Two weeks had passed since Dorcas and Mary's visit with Baker. In the interval, the Pines had played seven games, the result of which was an underwhelming two wins and five losses. It was not surprising then that the members of Bakers' Coven were fairly chomping at the bit to schedule another "band session," which, as it turned out, was set for Friday, November 1: the feast of Samhain.

In preparing for the rapidly approaching session, Baker was eager to apply some of what Dorcas had shared with him during her visit, so he began by opening *The Old Farmer's Almanac*. He perused it somewhat half-heartedly before relegating it to his bookshelf, where it would remain for the rest of the season. Make no mistake; Baker was intrigued by the belief that moon phases could enhance the potency of the magic generated in coven rituals, but he couldn't help but question its practicality in light of their circumstances. Engaging in coven ceremonies according to the lunar cycle would require that each member of Bakers' Coven adjust their personal schedules so they could convene on days that aligned with the moon's optimal phases, not to mention the added complication of trying to synchronize their gatherings with the Pines' schedule during the regular season—a schedule that was built according to the PHL's business model and not the lunar cycle.

Next, he turned to Dorcas's manual, *Coven Craft for Wannabe Witches*. It was a goldmine of information, but for Baker it was *too much* information. Studying the manual was a task best left for the Christmas break, or better yet, the summer holidays. Then he decided it might be best to embrace the KISS principle and just focus on a couple of the ingredients that Dorcas had verbally shared two weeks ago, namely "location" and "candlelight." His main point of attack would be his living room, with the goal being to create an atmosphere, an aesthetic, an "ambiance," as Dorcas had put it. Fortunately, Baker knew a thing or two about design—he was trained in the visual arts, after all—and in his mind, the best way to create ambiance was through lighting.

By the time he was done, he had exceeded his own expectations. The room could have been fashioned by an Aleister Crowley team of interior designers. Albus Dumbledore himself would have felt at home there. Baker saw to it that candles occupied every available horizontal surface. Because three walls of the room boasted windows, there was some ledge space to exploit along with his library coffee table. But that wasn't enough, so he pushed his love seat against a wall, making room for a folding teak patio table, a side table, and two step stools. Then he scrounged up a handful of milk crates, a couple of large storage bins, and a gaudy yellow four-foot fibreglass stepladder (his zeal apparently not extending so far as to employ the seven-foot model, which was hanging on a hook in his garage).

What had once been a bare, clean, open space was now overrun with candles of every colour, shape, and size. Twelve-inch tapered candles, pillar candles of various lengths based on their respective ages and degrees of previous use, snowball candles huddled in the few bare spaces that could be found on a bookshelf, and even a candelabrum—acquired from goodness knows where—taking pride of place on the coffee table. It was surrounded by twenty to thirty votive and tea light candles, like worshipping pilgrims gathered around a sacred monolith. The stepladder was positioned by the drum kit, set back a bit so as not to be a fire hazard. Green and white pillar candles were arranged on each of the four steps in neat rows, like choir boys in a tiered organ loft, waiting for the choirmaster to conduct their angelic voices into heavenly sounds. It resembled a cleverly decorated, Toronto Mighty Pines–themed makeshift Christmas tree that one might see in a small-town hardware store in December.

Baker wracked his brain for additional ideas and harked back to a bright autumn day during his second year at university. His outdoor education instructor had gathered a load of fallen leaves, dumped them unceremoniously at the entrance to his classroom and, in an effort to bring the joy of nature indoors, invited the students to freely kick through them as they came across the threshold. That pleasant memory prompted Baker to likewise empty three shoe boxes heavily loaded with old hockey cards on the floor around the coffee table. His friends would have to negotiate the litter of cards: kick through them, step over them, or even dance around them. He didn't care; it was a free country. He also scattered back issues of the *Hockey News* and *Sports Illustrated* magazines around the room, and finally, as the icing on the cake, he brought back his six inch replica Clarence Cup, perched it on its little pedestal on the kitchen counter facing the candle-ornamented room, placed several pine cones at its base, and then surrounded it with the worshipping figures of four wire-and-plaster hockey player sculptures.

Perfect.

* * * * *

For just the second time that semester, he was out the door with the kids at 2:30, getting home before his bandmates arrived with time to spare. He was busying himself with some final touches to the living room when he recognized Masaccio's voice at the front door.

"Hellooo? Can we come in?"

"Hey, Mas. I'm up here."

Immersed in the task of positioning some tapered candles into the candelabrum on the coffee table, Baker heard a long, drawn out "Oh my gosh!" from Masaccio and then the sound of someone approaching behind him, but he didn't turn immediately. When he did, he was startled to find himself face to face with the broad, pointy-toothed grin of a classically carved jack-o'-lantern, complete with triangle eyes and nose.

He assumed Mas was hiding behind it, until Perreault peeked her pretty face around the side and said, "Boo!" Apparently, she had arrived with him.

"That's one big pumpkin," Baker remarked. "Need some help with it?"

"No thanks. I've got muscles. The room looks spectacular, by the way." She spun away and toted the pumpkin to the kitchen counter. "How about I set it right here? It can gaze out at us as we embark upon this chapter of our Toronto Mighty Pines magic-making, like the figurehead on the prow of a sailing ship."

"Beautiful."

"I'm the king of the world!" Masaccio crowed as he made his way over to the keyboard. Then he stopped at the mess of hockey cards strewn across the floor. "Hey, Baker, you want us to clean this up for you?"

"Don't touch anything. My hockey cards are on the floor intentionally. I'm trying for a certain ambiance."

"If it's meant to mimic a room after a slumber party for a pee-wee boy's hockey team, you've succeeded."

"Holy fuck, Baker!" Angus had arrived and was stationed next to Perreault's pumpkin, scanning the room.

"You like my candles, Angus?"

"No, I was referring to your undersized Clarence Cup on the counter here," he replied, with a smirk of sarcasm. "Of course I like your candles. Whaddaya think?" He made his way toward the drums and then stopped mid-step. "What the hell, Brooks? What's with the mess? Were you drunk when you decorated this table?"

Baker could only slump his shoulders and shake his head while Perreault took it upon herself to brief Angus on the purpose of the hockey cards.

Then Angus noticed the skull on the table. "What's with the carcass?"

"That's a gift," Baker replied, explaining the circumstances behind his acquiring the skull and the beliefs around its powers. "Consider it a good luck charm."

"I could've used it yesterday for the pumpkin decorating contest," Angus said with a tinge of regret.

"What do you mean? What happened?"

For some years now, HMV had a Halloween tradition of inviting all first-period homeroom classes to compete in a pumpkin decorating contest. (It was with the aim of keeping knives and other sharp instruments out of classrooms that pumpkin *carving* had long since been discontinued.) This year Angus had resolved to win the contest outright, and had believed that his brilliant idea would be enough to earn him the victory. It involved taking a microphone stand and setting his pumpkin on it, so it was perched about six feet off the floor. Then he'd filled a dozen balloons with helium, attached six- and seven-foot lengths of string to them, and tied the whole bundle to the base of the stand. He'd labelled it "Balloowe'en."

"I came in third."

"Third place? Congrats. That's excellent. Who won?"

"I think Giacomo's class won this year," Mas informed them.

"How did he decorate his pumpkin?"

Masaccio described how Carlo Giacomo, the school's shop teacher, set up a sheet of Plexiglas to look like a penalty box. Then he set his pumpkin behind it, dressed up as a penalized hockey player, complete with helmet, stick, and gloves. The pumpkin itself was painted with a face that sported a black eye, stitches across the nose, and a broad smile with several teeth blacked out.

"Yeah, it looked great. But the best thing was the entry's name."

"Oh, wait . . . I heard about that. '*Gourdie* Hicks,' right? *Now* I get it."

"Yeah, it was pretty clever. But then so was the second-place entry. Their pumpkin was sitting on a bunch of wooden stakes tied together with twine, like they'd fashioned a raft, you know? But the pumpkin was painted like a volleyball and made to look like Wilson from the movie Castaway."

"Oooh, great idea. But yours was good too, Angus. I mean, 'Ballowe'en' deserves a top-three finish."

"Hmmph, just my luck the competition was so fierce this year."

"Speaking of fierce," Masaccio waved an arm to indicate the candle-strewn living room, "Baker, you went radical decorating this room."

"Blame it on Dorcas. She's the one who recommended candles."

"Uh-uh, you don't get off that easily. Dorcas may have 'recommended' candles, but you took it five steps further. Shit, you outdid the Phantom of the Opera."

Angus laughed "But you forgot one not-so-minor detail."

"And what's that?"

"You're going to have to light them all."

"Not *me* ... *us*." Baker directed their attention to a spot on the kitchen counter where a half-dozen lighters sat. "Everyone can lend a hand. I figure we can wait till just before we commence the ceremony, then we'll spread out and illuminate the room."

"Why wait then?" Conrad said. "Let's get this show on the candlelit road."

"Hell, yeah," Baker exclaimed. He sprang into action and scooped up the lighters and distributed them to the others, whereupon everyone scattered and got to work. "And don't leave anything unlit," Baker ordered.

When the last candle was lit, a hush came over the room as all five stood back, taking it in.

"Wow," Masaccio said, "look at this room."

"Yeah," Angus whispered, awestruck. "Things have suddenly turned serious."

Baker nodded as he surveyed his work. "Dorcas was right."

"It's truly a ceremony now," Perreault said.

"That's good," Conrad said, "because I'd like to begin this ceremony with a prayer—just like we did the first time we got together."

"Shall we huddle up then?" Baker suggested.

"No, that won't be necessary. Everybody just stay where you are and bow your heads."

When Conrad was done with the pre-ceremony prayer, all five took their places. The song for the session required that Masaccio lead the way on the keyboard. "Is it time?" he asked.

"I think so," Baker confirmed.

"OK, then I should warn you—we may want to consider saying one more prayer."

"Oh?"

"For the piano man here," he said, indicating himself.

"C'mon, Billy Joel," Baker said in an attempt to cheer him on. "You can do it."

"Uh-oh . . . I came prepared to play Joe Jackson," Mas joked, holding up his copy of the song sheet.

Perreault, who was standing next to the keyboard, leaned across and squeezed his shoulder in support. "We'd be over the moon with either one." Then she nodded and flashed him a smile that said, *"Let's knock this out of the park."*

That was all Mas needed. He returned the nod, indicating he was ready.

Conrad looked at Angus and Baker. "You guys ready?" They each gave him a thumbs-up, so with candles flickering all around, he took a deep breath and counted them in.

> *Don't you feel like winning something soon?*
> *Don't you feel like bringing home the Clarence Cup in June?*
> *But you can't do the things we ask you*
> *Despite it all we still love you*
> *It would be nice to see you win in June*
>
> *How much longer will you make us wait?*
> *We've not seen a playoff final for some six decades*
> *These words are not meant to hurt you*
> *We didn't say that we were through*
> *We just want to see you win in June*
>
> *Coney Nation hearts all bleed as one for just*
> *The chance to raise a banner soon*
> *We've all the skill just need a little pluck*
> *Though we know it's nice to tilt the ice*
> *It's oh so hard to do*
>
> *If there's one "to-do" before we die*
> *It's to win a Cup before we lose to Father Time*
> *Maybe it's just wishful thinking*
> *Winning's too good to be true*
> *Can't expect our Pines to win in June*

In trying to reduce the complexity of the song, Baker had thought it best if they dispensed with the keyboard solo, having them instead go straight into the chorus for the second time.

> *Coney Nation hearts all bleed as one for just*
> *The chance to raise a banner soon*
> *We've all the skill just need a little pluck*

Though we know it's nice to tilt the ice
It's oh so hard to do

All we want is cause to celebrate
Make City Hall get off its ass and plan the damn parade
But we should drop our expectations
How's about we just ask you
To play a single hockey game in June

Play a goddamn hockey game in June

Play a fucking hockey game in June

The other change Baker had decided on was to have the song end cold, so Perreault would slow to a finish with the word "June" at the end of a third repeat of the final line. All agreed that it worked quite nicely, probably better than the alternative of trying to fade the song out with Mas tinkling the ascending notes on the keyboard.

With nothing left but to close the session by extinguishing the flames, Perreault had a suggestion. "How about we go around blowing out the candles, one at a time, in a kind of meditative fashion, reciting our petitions quietly to ourselves?" She suggested. "Then each extinguished flame can serve as an exclamation point, or an amen."

"Great idea," Conrad said. "OK, folks, let's do this. I really should be going."

"Conrad's right," Angus agreed, turning to Baker and Perreault. "We should be going as well. We don't want to be too late to the party."

Baker actually had some reservations about the Halloween party that Angus had suggested they attend, but he kept them private for the moment and remained silent. He merely joined the others in moving about the room blowing out candles, careful to maintain a level of reverence.

When they were done, the room was darker and smokier. Perreault made sure the final candle to be extinguished was the one in her jack-o'-lantern. Then she stood back and assessed the carved gourd. "This guy is a handful. Would you mind terribly if I just left him here, Baker?"

"No problem. I can set him out on the porch as a defence against evil spirits."

The comment got Angus's attention. "Evil spirits? What's that all about?"

"The glow of a lit jack-o'-lantern serves as a beacon for the spirits of the dearly departed," Perreault explained, "while the scary faces carved in them are meant to keep away any spirits with ill intentions."

"Cool."

"In fact, you can beckon or even tempt benevolent spirits with the food they enjoyed in life," Perreault added.

"Favourite foods? You mean, like, doughnuts for Frank Watson?"

"Actually, come to think of it, doughnuts traditionally have holes in them, right?"

"So?"

"So, stones with natural holes in them are considered good luck charms, especially ones found near water. Wear one, and you're more able to enter the faerie realm and return from it unharmed."

"The faerie realm, huh?" Angus smirked. "Well, I can only speak for myself when I say that's one place I've never thought of entering, nor even care to."

"Oh, I don't know. Don't be so quick to dismiss the faery realm. I'll bet those faeries are plenty hospitable. For all we know, they may be quite the party animals."

"Speaking of parties," Angus said, "we're still meeting at my place, right?"

"You're dead set on going to this Halloween party?" Baker asked in a whiny voice. "I thought maybe I'd pass."

"Aw, don't be such a baby!" Angus said. "It's time you retired the soother and grew a set. You have your costume, right?"

"Uh, yeah, but—"

"But nothing. We're going—you, me, and Perreault. And we're all gonna have a blast."

"By the way," Perreault said, "this party we're going to, it's not a Halloween party, per se. It's a *Samhain* party."

"Is there a difference?"

"For us, not really. But to be clear, the best day for a Halloween party is, well, Halloween. Unfortunately, Halloween was yesterday. Today, however, happens to be November first, All Saints Day for Christians, the Day of the Dead in Mexican cultures."

"Hey, Conrad," Angus called, "did you know this stuff?"

"Of course I did. Now let her finish."

"Sorry. Go ahead, Perreault."

"My point is that today—All Saints Day—is when we remember our dearly departed. This is supposed to be the best time to communicate with them, since the veil between the living and the dead is thinnest. On the Wiccan calendar, it's called Samhain. And so, long story short, we're going to a Samhain party."

"Halloween . . . Samhain . . . either way, we're going to a party," Angus confirmed. "I'll see you two party animals at my place in a couple hours."

*****

No sooner had his friends pulled out of the driveway than Baker got busy putting his costume together. It took him the better part of an hour to get it to a point where he considered it fit for public consumption. He stood back and assessed his outfit in the mirror and determined that it needed something more. All the basics were accounted for: a crisp white shirt, a stylish suit jacket and tie, the superhero glasses were an accurate match, and the hair was perfect, with just the right colour and cut. But it was incomplete. Baker thought a moment, then went to his work desk, pulled open the side drawer to its limit, and fished around under some random notepads to extract a still-wrapped pad of name stickers, the kind people are asked to wear at meetings or gatherings, slapped on just beneath the collarbone.

Baker regarded the package with some deliberation. "Hello . . . My Name Is _____." He tore off the plastic wrap, took a medium-point Sharpie out of his HMV tenth anniversary mug on the desk, carefully executed the cap removal so as to avoid staining his fingers with permanent ink, and in neat block capitals printed the name KYLE BULAC on the first sticker. He held the tag at arm's length, appraising his work, and found it lacking, so he crumpled and discarded it. Seeking to emphasize the youthfulness of the man he was attempting to masquerade as, Baker went back to the work desk in the hopes of finding some crayons, but having none, he settled for his artist's oil pastels. He selected a bright green one and rewrote the name on the next clean sticker, except the block letters weren't so neat this time, as if they were printed by an eight-year-old who needed more practice with the alphabet. He chose to reverse the E in KYLE, and he did the same for the L and the C in BULAC.

Now satisfied, Baker returned to the bathroom where he carefully applied the name tag. *There. That should do it.*

It was then, as he stood there assessing his image in the mirror, that he became cognizant of being alone in the house—and yet, not truly alone. He had felt this way before, having experienced the sensation on and off for the past couple weeks, ever since the visit from Dorcas and Mary. That was when the witch and her apprentice had left him with the notion that his house was a welcoming place for spirits; heck, Mary had gone so far as to describe his place as "party central." And then today, he and his friends had used his house as a base for casting spells, spells intended to harvest positive energy from unseen yet potent mystical forces and channelling that energy toward bringing success to the Toronto Mighty Pines. That had to fall under the category of some pretty serious magic-making, didn't it?

Perreault had explained the significance of Samhain with respect to the proximity of the physical world to the spirit world and how the veil that separated them was at its most attenuated. He stood staring at his reflection, or more precisely, around his reflection, as though the mirror was the veil separating the two worlds. Mirrors were associated with magic, weren't they? Snow White came to mind, as did Alice and her looking glass. He leaned over the sink toward the mirror, entertaining thoughts of easing himself through the glass pane to enter a world where the answers to his questions might be more readily found. Drugs would help, of course. Lewis Carroll alluded to the use of psychoactive substances in his stories, and Snow White bit into a "poisoned" apple, didn't she?

But if truth be told, Baker was not inclined toward the psychedelic trips of a 1960's flower child or the hallucinogen-induced altered states of the avant-garde artist in the early twentieth century. The counterculture of Timothy Leary was not his bag, nor was the surreal world of Salvador Dali. He wasn't about to play a modern-day Alice, slipping through his bathroom looking glass, embarking on some kind of vision quest. No, for Baker it was about the magic of sport and hockey and the Mighty Pines, things that favoured clarity of thought and a level head.

By then he was in a near-hypnotic state, incrementally leaning farther and farther, until . . . *thunk!* Baker's forehead rebounded off the mirror's cold, hard, smooth surface and he was rudely startled back to his senses. Blinking, he straightened up, repositioned his glasses, and rubbed his hairline, then checked the glass of the mirror to make sure he hadn't cracked it.

He shook himself back into action. It was getting late, and he wasn't quite finished with his outfit. One final touch included a paper bullseye he'd acquired from HMV's Phys Ed. department—the ones they used for archery lessons. Pinning it just beneath the shoulder blades of his jacket, he was now the GM with the proverbial target on his back.

Looking at his mirrored reflection, he felt the impulse to take a selfie—for posterity if nothing else. Dressing up in costume was not his strong suit. Even as a kid his imagination hadn't afforded him to go much beyond the typical white-sheeted ghost, so he had to give himself props for throwing together a pretty effective Kyle Bulac outfit. He awkwardly positioned his mobile phone at roughly face height. (It should be noted that although he'd grown up with regular point-and-shoot cameras, Baker had never in his life taken a selfie with a cell phone.)

When he held the device up, it was actually his reflection in the bathroom mirror that the screen displayed, but being in a hurry, Baker had neither the time nor the patience to fiddle with it further. He quickly snapped two shots of his reflected image and then was on his way out of the house to meet up with Angus and Perreault.

CHAPTER FIFTEEN
IT'S IN THE CARDS

Baker felt like he was waiting on the porch longer than was reasonable, to the point that he'd begun to second guess himself about being at the right address. When the door finally opened, it was a relief to see Angus standing there, despite the fact he was only half dressed.

"Look at you. Kyle *fucking* Bulac! Well done, Baker!"

Baker had actually forgotten he was in costume, so he was initially taken aback by his friend's greeting. "Oh, yeah . . . thanks. I wasn't sure I could pull it off, but it works alright, I guess."

"You kidding? It's great. C'mon in."

Baker stepped into a small landing crowded with a garment-laden coat tree and several pairs of shoes, feeling all the more cramped by the addition of a large bunch of colourful helium-filled balloons tied to the newel post of the stairway.

"Nice balloons," Baker said, only half in jest.

"Third place for my efforts, man." Angus gave them a dismissive look. "I don't even know why I brought them home. Should've left them at school."

"The place seems quiet. Aren't your parents home?"

"Nah, they went to a movie. My mom put together a charcuterie board for us. It's in the kitchen. Help yourself. I'm gonna go upstairs and finish putting my outfit together. Perreault should be here any minute, so let her in when she arrives." Full of energy, Angus vaulted up the stairs, taking two at a time. "Beer's in the fridge!"

Baker went down the hall and became aware of music coming out of the living room—"Time Warp" from *The Rocky Horror Picture Show*, as it turned out. *Probably a compilation of popular Halloween tunes,* Baker thought, stifling a cringe. (He would be the first to admit he was a bit of a snob when it came to his taste in Halloween music, turning a deaf ear to much of the typical stuff out there.)

He carried on into the kitchen, which was smallish yet bright and inviting. A breakfast table was pushed against one wall with three chairs spaced around it. A live-edge plank of maple wood was set on it, laden with several cheeses, grapes, apple slices, and an assortment of crackers.

When the doorbell rang Angus called down. "That'll be Perreault. Let her in, will ya, Baker?"

Opening the door, Baker wasn't prepared for the scream that emanated from her when she laid eyes on him. "Baker, you look great! Brilliant!"

He deemed her enthusiasm to be a bit over the top, but considering the source, he was willing to accept it. And besides, it made him feel like the cleverest costume builder in town. That conceit evaporated, however, once his brain processed the image of the figure standing in the doorway before him. More than anything else about Perreault's costume, Baker was struck by the gleeful creativity and fairytale sweetness of it all—and how the heat rushed to his cheeks as she raised her hands in a *tah-dah* motion and then twirled to show off her outfit. She was dressed, for all intents and purposes, as a typical, run-of-the-mill witch. But it was the details that set her apart. On her head was a first-rate leather witch's hat, with wrinkles and folds, a perfect knock-off of the Hogwarts sorting hat. She carried with her a straw broom, the handle taken from some gnarly, century-old ash tree, while the bristles were made of birch twigs, tied and bound with willow. The thing looked as if it had been stolen from some hag's hut deep in a Bavarian Forest, no doubt a neighbour to the Grimm family. On her feet were a pair of black leather witch's shoes, complete with large metal buckles and toes curled enough to rival anything Tim Burton might design.

"Nice outfit. Where'd you get such authentic-looking stuff?"

"Where do you think? From an authentic witch." Perreault gave Baker the same look that Adam probably got from Eve when she held out the apple to him. "Care to guess?"

He worked hard to focus on the question. "Um, don't tell me . . . Dorcas?"

She flashed an irresistible smile and punched him playfully in the arm. "Sure. Pretty smart, huh?" Then she noted the balloons. "I'm guessing those belonged to Angus's third-place pumpkin?"

"Yup." Baker led her through the hallway into the kitchen.

"Eat up, folks, we've got to get—whoa, look at you, you sexy witch." Angus had just entered the room, looking like he'd come off the set of *Game of Thrones*.

"Jaime Lannister!" Perreault gushed.

Angus grinned proudly. "You like?"

"Like? You're the spitting image."

Baker was impressed. "You know, I've heard a few of the ladies at school say how you look like the guy who plays Jaime Lannister . . . what's his name?"

"Nikolaj something-something."

IT'S IN THE CARDS

"Yeah, well, personally, I couldn't see it. But now, dressed like that, you could pass as his freakin' twin."

"Angus, find me a large cue card," Perreault ordered, appraising his outfit. "And two magic markers—a black one and a red one."

Angus dutifully went upstairs, rummaging around before returning with the items Perreault requested. She took the black marker and printed "IOU" in big block letters and, using the red marker, drew a neat circle around it with a diagonal line slashed through it. "Now let's pin this to your chest."

"Ah, yes, a Lannister always pays his debts," Baker observed. "Nice touch, Perreault."

Angus saw that the charcuterie board was untouched. "C'mon, you guys, eat up. I mean it. My mother will be disappointed if she comes home and this plank isn't empty."

The three of them happily indulged in Mrs. Fletcher's appetizer fare. Angus poured each of them a beverage, and for the next thirty minutes they ate, drank, and chatted, and even broke into song at intervals to the Halloween tunes playing in the background. Baker enjoyed himself to the extent that he actually felt a pang of regret at one point, knowing they'd soon be leaving this cozy place for the party.

Eventually, he popped the last of the grapes into his mouth, spurring Angus to acknowledge a job well done. "Thanks, folks. My mom will sleep soundly tonight," then added "Drink up. We'd better be going." Angus led his companions toward the front door. In the entryway Perreault paused, looking up toward the ceiling at the balloons.

"Angus, do you mind if I borrow one of these for the night?"

"Go ahead. You've got lots to choose from."

"I'm eyeing that shiny green Toronto Mighty Pines one there."

Appearing to forget something, Angus scooted back to the kitchen while Perreault teased her selection out of the bunch, then turned to Baker. "Here, give me your hand."

Baker complied, allowing her to tie the string to his left wrist. "I thought we'd accentuate the youthfulness of Kyle Bulac. What do you think?"

"Works for me."

Angus returned with a loaded cooler bag dangling from his shoulder. "OK, now we can go."

The walk from the Fletcher residence to the party was a short one. Angus led them down a street lined with breathtaking century homes, some red brick, others limestone, with leaded windows and fronted by large verandas that looked out onto impeccable green spaces and gardens. He was in good spirits, displaying the effects of short-term ear worm as he alternately hummed then sang snippets of "Ghostbusters," the last Halloween tune that had been playing when they left his place.

It wasn't long before he led them up a narrow, tumbled-stone walkway that perfectly intersected a front lawn covered by a golden-orange blanket of leaves that had dropped from a mature maple dominating the property. They ascended four steps to a verandah that was potlit and tastefully decorated for Halloween. Music and party chatter could be heard coming from within. The front door was magnificent, fashioned from oak with a stained-glass inlay, under which was a heavy black iron lion's-head rapper.

"Get a load of that knocker!" Angus exclaimed as Perreault stepped forward to work it, but before she could, the door swung open, and they were greeted by a young woman in a long, flowing midnight blue dress. She had large, searching brown eyes, framed by long, straight brown hair, but for Angus it was the fact that she was obviously well-endowed that made the strongest impression. True to form, he couldn't resist whispering, to no one in particular, "And speaking of knockers," prompting Baker to cough in an effort to mask the indiscretion—unnecessarily as it turned out because the woman was focused completely on the "witch" standing before her.

"That broom, that hat; I've only ever seen them in one other place. You must be a friend of the inimitable Dorcas Blanchard."

"Impressive! Do you know her too?"

"Yes. I studied under Dorcas for a spell a few years ago—no pun intended."

"Small world. My name's Perreault, by the way."

"Hi, Perreault. I'm Carly—Carly Romanet. She shifted her attention to Angus and Baker. "I see you've brought along a blonde and a brunette. Care to introduce me to your friends?"

"Certainly. The blonde goes by the name of Angus—Angus Fletcher."

Angus stepped forward eagerly, offering his hand. "Hi, Carly."

"Hi." Carly returned the handshake but barely looked at him, focusing her attention instead on where Baker was standing just behind Perreault.

Perreault turned and took Baker's balloon-laden wrist, pulling him forward. "And the brunette's name—"

"Is Kyle, according to his name tag." Carly held her hand out to Baker. "Hello, Kyle."

"Oh, uh, no . . . my name's Baker." He looked down and pointed to the label. "Kyle is the name of the guy I'm dressed up as, you know, as in Kyle Bulac, the GM of the Toronto Mighty Pines?"

"Well, Baker," Carly said, taking his hand in hers, "I'm not really into Toronto's basketball team, but this Kyle Bulac guy must be cute."

Unable to generate a response, clever or otherwise, Baker could only blush. He was rescued when something cold, metallic, and cylindrical was shoved into his other hand—Angus had taken the opportunity to distribute beers from his cooler.

"Thank you, but I shouldn't," Carly replied when Angus offered her one. "I'm working."

"Working?"

"Yes. I'm here to add an air of mysticism to the gathering by providing Tarot readings."

"How much they payin' you?" Angus asked, seeking any excuse to draw her into a conversation.

"Free of charge. I'm more than happy to volunteer my services. And anyway, I could use the practice. This is a great opportunity to hone my skills." She stopped to direct her gaze into the house. "I'd better get back to my station. But promise me that you three will stop by to patronize my services at some point tonight."

"Absolutely. Give us a chance to settle in, and we'll come by," Perreault assured her.

"Great," Carly said. "See you in a bit. You too, Angus . . . and Baker."

* * * * *

As Halloween parties went, this one met all the criteria: a nice venue, not too cramped but still intimate, the hosts doing a good job of ensuring that snack and finger food stations never ran dry, and although it was BYOB, they nevertheless kept a beverage fridge fully stocked with bottles of water. Hell, even the weatherman had bought in. Sure it was cool, but it was also calm, clear, and dry. The party was well attended, and as a bonus, the guests seemed to exude a childlike delight toward dressing up in costume. There was little evidence of the sour cynicism that can cloud such parties, the kind generated by people who considered themselves too cool to dress up. (Baker knew this only too well, being self-aware enough to recognize—and honest enough to admit—there were times that he was guilty of exhibiting such an attitude.)

Eventually, the time came that Perreault suggested they go have their fortunes read by Carly the clairvoyant. Angus jumped at the chance, but Baker wasn't feeling it. Not wanting to spoil the mood, however, he said he had to use the bathroom. And so, while he went to check out the facilities, Perreault and Angus went to find Carly's "reading room."

When he was done in the bathroom, Baker took a self-guided tour to see where else in the house the party may have extended to. His meanderings brought him face to face with some pretty clever costumes, beginning with one hulking dude who came shirtless, sporting louvred glasses and a pair of authentic wrestling boots and tights, using his muscular physique to great advantage as Randy "Macho Man" Savage. On his arm was a woman who'd gussied herself up to play Miss Elizabeth. Then there was the trio of guys who all wore a different cut of white dinner jacket and tie (Baker dubbed them "the triplets"). One mimicked Humphrey Bogart from *Casablanca*, the next Ricardo Montalban from *Fantasy Island*, and the third John Travolta's Tony Manero right off the dance floor from *Saturday Night Fever*. But the best costume, hands down, was the guy who came "dressed" as Jesus of Nazareth, wearing nothing but biblical leather sandals and what could only be described as an oversized linen man-diaper. He was tall and lean and had an air of a stand-up comic about him, like a bearded, long-haired John Mulaney. He even toted around a six-foot cross (Baker figured it to be made from papier mâché or Styrofoam).

Being a practising Catholic and all, Baker wasn't sure if he was permitted to laugh, but the guy was a hoot, using his cross as a leaning post, resting an elbow on it as he engaged in casual conversation, beer in hand, with the same nonchalance (if not precisely in the same way) that Kevin Bowden had leaned on his goalie stick during breaks in the action when he was minding the net and winning a handful of Cups with Montreal in the 1970s.

It came as a pleasant surprise to Baker that his own outfit garnered some praise from other guests at the party. It was a lesson in how impactful the smallest details could be. Case in point, he heard several favourable remarks about his wrist balloon, as well as his infantile-looking name tag and even the target on his back. He also enjoyed having to bob and weave his way around a variety of comments prompted by his dressing as the Pines' GM. Some people suggested remedies for the team's ailments. Others mocked him as being soft in player salary negotiations, much as those same players were soft on the ice. Still others voiced their regret over Xander Galahad's choice to go with Kyle Bulac over a more experienced candidate.

At one point Baker brought the can of beer he was holding up to his lips, mostly out of habit, but then he stopped and assessed the beverage with distaste. It was only his second beer, but it wasn't going down so well. He made do with carrying it around—more as a party prop than anything else. And much as the night saw Baker with little appetite for beer, he likewise had little appetite for flirting, and the last thing he needed was to engage in awkward conversation of that sort with a stranger. Therefore, he thought it best to avoid Carly the soothsayer. He wasn't interested in a Tarot reading anyway. He helped himself to a water from the beverage fridge and found the cold liquid invigorating—or maybe it was just that the musical selection had turned to his liking. He was singing under his breath to the Cranberries' "Zombie" when Perreault's sweet voice cut him off.

"There you are!" she said, tugging at the string of his balloon. "Where've you been hiding?"

"I haven't been hiding," he replied, delighted that she'd found him. "I've been circulating."

"Well, circulate over this way with me. It's almost midnight, and Carly's about to shut it down."

Damn! He thought while trying to act cool about it. "And that matters to me because . . . ?"

"Because you promised her you'd participate in a Tarot reading."

IT'S IN THE CARDS

Baker was certain he'd never made any such promise, but he trusted Perreault all the same.

"What's it like?" he asked.

"What's what like?"

"The Tarot reading."

"You sit at a table across from each other."

"All alone... with her? Isn't that awkward?"

"Baker, it's not a confessional, for heaven's sake! She has set herself up in a little room down the hall. It's actually a small library. It's quaint. You'll see for yourself. I'll even hold your hand if you want."

She led him down the corridor to the last room on the left, which must have been insulated against sound because once they were inside, the music and general party noise was reduced considerably. Three walls were lined floor to ceiling with books on shelves. Carly was chatting with the white-jacketed triplets, but she instantly broke off from them when Baker and Perreault entered the room.

"Baker! I was afraid you'd forgotten about me."

"No, I was just enjoying the party."

Well, I'll try not to disappoint. Please, sit down, I won't keep you long." Then she addressed the triplets. "Thanks again for stopping by, guys. Please help yourselves to one of my cards on your way out."

"Sure, man," said the Mr. Roarke look-alike from Fantasy Island. "But we thought we'd stick around for your next reading." He motioned toward Baker. "If that's cool with him." Baker was a little disappointed that the guy lacked the Corinthian leather voice of Ricardo Montalban.

"What do you think, Baker?" Carly asked. "Would you mind if they stayed?"

"The more the merrier," he replied, although it was plain to see that their real motivation for staying were the two women in the room. It suddenly occurred to him that Angus had disappeared, but the thought instantly vapourized when Carly directed him to take a seat in one of two fancily upholstered wingback chairs set around a circular wooden reading table. Baker sat in the one reserved for the client while she settled herself in the other across the table from him. The part of the room where they were seated was lit by a Victorian tassel-shade floor lamp. He couldn't help but think that it was all a touch too cliché and was half expecting Carly to plop a turban on her head, the kind Crystal Gazers might wear.

At the centre of the table was a small bundle loosely wrapped in satin cloth of the deepest blue. In fact, the cloth could well have been cut from her dress. Beside the bundle was a single candlestick and a box of wooden matches. Carly removed one, struck it, and lit the candle, after which she extinguished the match by waving it dramatically through the air.

The combination of the lit candle and the smoke wafting around not only changed the atmosphere in the room, it also changed Carly's demeanour. Where just a minute before she had been fun and flirty, now she displayed an air of seriousness coupled with intense concentration. She unwrapped the package on the table by gently pulling back four corners of the square cloth until it was flat, revealing a deck of cards.

The cards were well-worn, thick, and a bit oversized. Carly reached out with both hands and encompassed the deck, offering it to Baker. "I want you to shuffle the cards. As you do, think about something in your life—something specific—that you have questions about and seek answers to."

Baker accepted the deck from Carly, took a moment to think, then began shuffling. To his embarrassment, he found his technique, which was usually sure-handed, to be clumsy. The balloon tied to his wrist didn't help. It was comical watching him try to manipulate the cards while a helium balloon bounced just above his head. The triplets, huddled by the doorway, were stifling their chuckles, trying hard not to break the solemnity.

Finally, Perreault came to his aid. "Here, Baker, let me relieve you of that thing. I think we can safely say it has outlived its purpose by now." She loosened the string around his wrist and slipped it over his hand, then let it go, allowing the balloon to rise up to the ten-foot ceiling where it bounced once and then stuck, its string hanging down just out of reach above. Thus unencumbered, Baker could shuffle the cards freely.

"Remember to focus on what you want to learn from this reading," Carly instructed. "Repeat it to yourself as you shuffle—the more specific the better. When you're ready, I'll need you to cut the deck into three piles. Place them on the cloth from left to right, preferably using your left hand."

Baker did precisely as he was told.

"Excellent," Carly said when she saw he was done. "Next, if you would be so kind, select one of the piles. That will be the one from which I will draw the cards."

For the sake of symmetry, he pointed to the middle pile.

"Now then, before I turn over the cards, I will need you to volunteer one general bit of information. That is, what are we focusing on? Ideally, it should be something you are currently putting energy into. For instance, most people seek answers related to love, say, or money."

"Well, to tell you the truth, it's neither of those two."

"Oh? What then? Can you describe it in a word or two?"

"OK, let's see . . . I'll describe it as a special project I'm currently engaged in."

"Perfect. You're engaged in a personal project. With that in mind, I will reveal what the top three cards are. This first one will give us some insight into your past. Here we go." Carly turned over the first card.

It was labelled "The Tower" and was colourfully illustrated—a medieval castle's cylindrical stone tower with windows and crenellations. The top of the castle was being severed from its base by an enormous lightning bolt, and flames were visible within. To complete the disastrous scene, a man and woman were falling from the tower, likely to their deaths. Carly's description of its meaning sounded far from tragic, however.

"The Tower represents a collapse, the end of something you have built. It could be a business venture, or maybe a relationship that for some reason came to an end. But keep in mind that this has occurred in the past. I should add that a collapse may lead to something better in the future. Understanding what happened in the past can put you further along the path toward your goal. We call this 'illumination.'"

Baker's expression was blank, so Carly tried to prompt him further. "Has there been a death within your circle of friends? Or perhaps your family?"

Baker shook his head. "No, nothing like that."

Carly's gaze had grabbed hold of him and was searching, looking for hidden truths that would reveal the meaning in the cards. Baker had seen those eyes somewhere before, in another person's gaze—Dorcas. He recalled her visit two weeks ago and the transformation in her appearance when she spoke to him about having a "desire."

He doubled down on his previous answer. "I'm sorry, but I can't think of any such recent event."

"No worries. That's not unusual," Carly replied. "Let's move on to the second card."

She turned it over, setting the fingers of her left hand along its bottom edge. It was simple enough, with Roman numeral sevens in each of the four corners and seven wooden wands spread out in an arc formation.

"This card speaks to the present time frame of your story. It's the Seven of Wands. I should explain that if this was the *six* of wands, we'd be discussing success and reward, a sense of winning—triumph! But here we have a seventh wand, which represents an obstacle. It seems you will need to get past a hurdle or a challenge facing your project before success can be achieved. The good news is it's an obstacle that can be overcome. Stay true to your purpose, and it will disappear."

Baker's eyes followed Carly's hand as she laid it gently on the pile and left it there. He waited patiently, not bothering to look up at her. "This last card deals with the future," she said, then turned it over. It was labelled as "The Wheel of Fortune."

"We have an eight-spoke wheel surrounded by three animals," she explained. "The first is a monkey, which symbolizes vanity. The second is an ass, for humility. The third is a dragon, for nature's power and unpredictability. Also note that the card is upside down, or as we like to say, 'reversed.'

"Like so many others, you seek success in life, but it's important to be open to the myriad manifestations of success. It may not come in the form you hope for. Such is the meaning of The Wheel of Fortune. Just as God works in mysterious ways, so too does the universe. What matters is how you respond to the outcomes. A good thing is that the reversed Wheel is not negative; it's a symbol of closure. A cycle comes to an end, bringing with it some relief."

Carly stopped speaking, evidently finished with her analysis of the cards, and extended both arms before her upon the table, palms up, echoing Jesus Christ in Leonardo's "Last Supper." For a moment Baker thought she was praying, but then she spoke again.

"Admittedly, my interpretation of what has been revealed in the cards is of a generalized nature. If you seek more insight, this is your chance to ask questions—or provide any added information that may direct us down a path of greater clarity." She looked at Baker, letting the offer hang in the air between them—air that Baker felt had turned uncomfortably thick and warm.

"Um, that's quite alright. I'm good."

"Alright then. To formally end the session, I'll ask you to extinguish the candle."

He leaned toward the flame and snuffed it with a quick puff, then thanked Carly for her time and got up from the table, leaving the clairvoyant with her Tarot deck and wondering if it was obvious to anyone that he had begun to perspire. Unbeknownst to Baker, however, Carly wasn't done with him yet. "Before you go, I would like you to read a card for me."

"What do you mean?"

"Perreault tells me you're an art teacher," she said. Her face, which just a minute earlier had been hooded and business-like, was now open and friendly, showing off her lively eyes and bright smile. "Maybe you could grade the design of this." She reached under the cloth on the table and emerged with one of her calling cards.

Baker accepted the card and made a show of assessing it. In truth, he didn't see much that set it apart from any other run-of-the-mill business card, until he turned it over. What he saw caused him to hesitate, then he slipped it into the back pocket of his trousers, providing a noncommittal type of assessment. "Clean and to the point—it does the job." He looked back at Perreault, seeking any excuse to change the subject, then noticed that the trio in the white suits was no longer in the room and jumped at the opening. "Hey, when did the triplets leave?"

"You mean the guys in white?" Perreault said. "They left after your last card was revealed."

IT'S IN THE CARDS

"I guess we should be going too," Baker said, turning back to Carly one last time and thanking her for sharing her expertise before hustling out of there, abandoning his balloon in the process. Perreault joined him, helping herself to one of Carly's cards on the way out. To their relief, the air in the hallway was palpably cooler.

"There you are!" Angus's voice came to them from the other end of the hall. "You guys want to get going? I told my folks not to wait up, but you know parents. They don't sleep till their babies are home safe."

As they worked their way through the house to the front door, it was evident that the crowd had thinned out. On the verandah, the cool night air engulfed them. It would have had a sobering effect if any of them were inebriated. Still, it seemed to spark a realization in Angus.

"Oops, I left my cooler bag in the kitchen. I'll be right back." As Angus disappeared into the house, Baker and Perreault leisurely drifted down the walkway.

"Hey, I never asked, how did *your* Tarot reading go?" Baker said.

"Oh, pretty positive in general. I just asked for a short reading that covers the next week, like a horoscope."

"What about Angus?"

"About the same. But let's talk about *your* reading. There seems to be some intrigue surrounding it."

Baker shrugged. "To tell you the truth, I found it somewhat banal—didn't see much of it applying to me. Heck, I can't remember half of what she said."

"Well, I can. Would you like me to summarize?"

"Do I have a choice?"

"Um . . . no," Perreault replied. "Let's see now, the focus of the reading was this 'personal project' of yours—which, between you and me, must refer to our coven sessions, right?"

"Well, obviously—"

"Good. Now, the first card—the Past—was about losing something . . . or someone, which you claim means nothing to you."

"Absolutely nothing," he confirmed.

"And that's fine. But I agree with Carly that you should stay alert for any clues that could provide an answer, because it might make more sense in time."

Baker just wrinkled his forehead.

"The second card—the Present—dealt with overcoming an obstacle. I like how she instructed you to persist, to persevere. After all, you and I both know that the odds of achieving the Coven's goal are quite long. Therefore it makes sense that a little backbone, or fortitude, would be helpful."

Again Baker said nothing, content to just listen.

"The third card—the Future—was sort of a reminder that we must learn to accept the outcome. Once again, the odds that our goal is achieved precisely according to plan are pretty long, so . . . however things may turn out, try to make the most of it."

"You really *were* paying attention back there, weren't you?" he said, impressed by her summary.

"I have your back," Perreault replied, throwing an arm across his shoulders and nearly dislodging his glasses in the process.

"I forgot I was still wearing these," he said, removing them and rubbing his eyes. "What a relief."

Perreault looked at him as if to assess the damage. "The bridge of your nose seems to have taken a beating." She reached a hand toward his face, and he responded by standing stock still, permitting her to run a finger along the space between his eyes. Using the gesture as a diversion, she used her other hand to peel the name tag off his chest.

"Hey!" he exclaimed, playing at being shocked.

"What? You don't need it anymore. I thought I'd keep it as a souvenir."

A silly surge of pride coursed through Baker as he watched Perreault take Carly's business card, the one she'd helped herself to a minute earlier, and affix the tag to it like a Band-Aid, wrapping each overlapping end around the back of the card.

"There," she said, with a smile of satisfaction.

Just then Angus's voice reached them from the porch. "Well, that was a fun evening," he declared, tossing the strap of his beer cooler over one shoulder as he jogged the short distance down the walkway to join them. "You guys have a good time? I had a good time."

Both Baker and Perreault concurred that a fine time was had by all.

"How about the music?" Angus asked. "Was it to your satisfaction, Mr. Brooks?"

"Not bad. Sixty/forty I'd say."

"That Carly was somethin' else, huh? You know, I had the sense she was kind of sweet on me."

"Ya think?"

"Well, just now, when I was saying so long, she invited—no, *instructed*—me to take one of her business cards." Angus held it out for Baker to see. "Then she smiled and winked in a sort of suggestive way, ya know?"

"That's terrific," Baker said as he took the card and examined it, thinking, *Better you than me.* He found it identical to the one in his back pocket except that the reverse side was blank. Handing it back to Angus, Baker didn't have the heart to tell his friend that he also came away with one of her cards, except his had included a phone number on the back, accompanied by the words *Call me.*

CHAPTER SIXTEEN

BAD NEWS COMES IN THREES

Saturday, November 2 – Monday, November 11

While Christians the world over observe November 2 as All Souls Day, certain countries in central and South America celebrate it as a continuation of the Day of the Dead. For the Toronto Mighty Pines and the Pittsburgh Pilots, both of whom were entering that night's game sitting on six wins, it was a chance for one of them to get to heaven with win number seven. Sound trite? Maybe, but it was true all the same. In the end, it was the Pines who got there on the strength of an overtime shootout win.

Forty-eight hours later, Donald Trump made headlines by announcing that he was removing the US from the group of countries that had signed on to the 2015 Paris Climate Change Accord. The world's second leading producer of greenhouse gases was officially out!

In Canadian politics, Elizabeth May resigned as leader of the Green Party, citing family priorities. At the same time, a new federal party, going by the name of "Wexit," was established. The party's platform was based on its desire to have the western provinces separate from the rest of the country.

In entertainment news, the Dead Celebrities Income List was released, with Michael Jackson taking the top spot, followed by runner-up Elvis Presley and Peanuts creator Charles Schulz in third place.

As for the Mighty Pines, it proved to be a good week for them, notching two more victories and extending their winning streak to a season high three games, all while Torontonians were navigating their way through the first major snowfall of the year.

Then on Saturday, a day which saw many in the world observing the thirtieth anniversary of the fall of the Berlin Wall, the Pines played host to Philadelphia on the front end of a back-to-back and ultimately lost in a shootout. Although no one knew it at the time, the loss would serve as a harbinger of events that would befall the team over the next ten days. In fact, for GM Kyle Bulac, it was around this time that the matter of replacing his head coach went from a possibility to an inevitability.

When Cheers Are Not Enough

Another inevitability, according to some who regularly tuned in to Hockey Night in Canada's popular *Coach's Corner* segment, was that Don Cherry's penchant for being outspoken would get him into hot water. And so it happened that, during the first intermission on Saturday, Cherry made some pointed remarks on the topic of wearing poppies to honour Canada's war veterans at this time of year and how people generally don't wear them like they used to. He singled out new immigrants living in Toronto and his hometown of Mississauga in particular. The segment ended as cohost Ron McLean mutely nodded and flashed the thumbs-up sign.

In the world of MLS soccer, it was a thumbs-down result for Toronto FC as they fell to the Seattle Sounders 3-1 in the MLS Cup championship match.

It was a busy time for teachers at HMV, as the deadline for midterm report cards was looming, so the decision to cancel transportation services due to inclement weather was a welcome development. The building was essentially devoid of students, affording teachers the opportunity to catch up on other pressing duties. (It should be mentioned that HMV was a school where roughly two-thirds of the student population rode the bus; whenever too much snow or ice kept the buses from running, those kids stayed home, and whenever that happened most of the rest of the student body was happy to follow suit.)

"Oh, baby, who gets the credit for this gift of a snow day?" Angus had just entered the staff room and was bursting to share his delight with Conrad, Perreault, and Masaccio, who were seated at a table by the photocopier.

"No kidding," Masaccio agreed. "What with us playing in the 'Battle of the Bands' tonight, I figured on a late night of marking. But now I can get most of that done right here at school. I might even be able to catch some of the Raptors game."

"Wait a minute, the Raps have a game tonight?" Angus asked. "Didn't they play last night?"

"Yeah. They beat Lebron and the Lakers," Mas reported. "It was beautiful. But they're back at it tonight."

"Oh, right! They play Kawhi and the Clippers." Angus paused to consider the challenge. "That's what I call a tough back-to-back."

"You said it. I guess the only advantage for Toronto is that both LA teams play in the Staples Center, so there's no added burden of travel between games."

"That's got the makings of a brain teaser," Perreault noted. "How's this: if the NBA schedule prevents teams from playing both ends of a back-to-back at home, how is it that the Raptors played both of their games in the same arena?"

Masaccio's face sprouted a quizzical look. "Is it just me or does anyone else get the munchies doing puzzles and brain teasers?"

"I can relate," Perreault said. "Snacking kind of helps me concentrate."

"That reminds me," Mas said, "are we gonna do pizza today?"

"Isn't it a bit early? It's barely ten o'clock."

"Hey, it's never too early for pizza."

"Yeah, something quick and portable," Angus confirmed. "I want to take it back to my classroom so I can nibble while I finish these report card comments. Is Baker coming?"

"He's on his way," Conrad confirmed. "I saw him down the hall locking his door."

"Well, shit, did he get lost?"

"No, not lost. You had it right the first time. He probably made a pit stop."

"God help us."

"God help him."

"And his bladder."

"No, his colon. I told you, you had it right the first time."

"Ugh, let's not go there."

"I agree. In the meantime, let's get out of here. Baker can catch up with us."

"It's pizza or bust, baby."

*****

Baker had not, in fact, made a pit stop at the men's room. After locking his classroom door, he'd headed downstairs to the school's servery to grab a coffee. Walking through the cafeteria, normally a hub of socio-gastronomic activity, he wasn't surprised to see it reduced to a vacant refectory echoing with the sound of two or three conversations. The largest knot of students was a group of four boys playing an impassioned card game. Baker knew them by name as Christian, Jake, Raj, and Anthony. Their chatter included, in intervals, snippets of phrases related to hockey, along with a fair amount of bickering. At the moment, Christian was giving Jake a reprimand.

"Jake, pay attention. It's your turn."

"Oh, sorry . . . OK, uh . . . *stretch pass*."

"*Cycle the puck!*" Anthony declared in turn.

Raj countered with *toe drag* whereupon Christian offered up *top shelf*.

"Aw, I was gonna use that," Jake complained.

"C'mon, Jake. We keep telling you to have some in the bank, just in case."

"I did! Well . . . two, anyway."

"Does that mean you're passing?" Anthony asked.

"No," Jake said. "Give me a second . . . *Start on time.*"

"*Activate the D,*" Anthony responded instantly.

"What's that?" Raj demanded. "I never heard that before."

"Too bad, so sad," Anthony replied. "I heard it last week."

"OK, then, *activate the O,*" Raj said.

"Don't cheat, Raj," Christian scolded. "You just made that up." He broke off when he noticed Baker passing through the cafeteria. "Hey, Mr. Brooks. Wanna play? Pull up a chair."

"Hi, Christian. Hello, guys. Thanks for the offer, but I have to go meet some other teachers for lunch. What are you playing, anyway?"

"It's just a game we made up," Jake said.

"Oh yeah? How do you play?"

"It's simple," Christian explained. "We deal out all the cards, then we go around the table, and when it's your turn, you need to come up with a hockey term. But you have to be quick about it. Right, Jake?"

"I am fast," Jake said, defensively. "It's just that you guys always steal my answers."

"Yeah, whatever," Christian said, then turned back to Baker. "Anyway, if your answer is acceptable, you get to throw a card in the pile. The player who gets rid of their cards first wins. Easy, huh?"

Baker considered the prospect. "Hockey terms, you say?"

"Yes, sir, should we deal you in?"

"Sure, I'll play—but just one hand."

With Baker's answer the boys shifted in their seats as if girding themselves for a challenge.

"Mr. Brooks is gonna win for sure!" Jake declared generally.

"Oh, I don't know, Jake. Don't count on it," Baker assured him as he settled in at the table.

Christian collected the cards and shuffled the deck while Baker shot the breeze with the others. As they conversed Baker couldn't help but notice how methodical Christian was in dealing the cards. Concerned about catching up with his colleagues, he was beginning to regret agreeing to play a hand. Just then Christian voiced a concern.

"Hey, I've got two extra cards!"

"That's correct," Baker confirmed. "There's five of us playing, so everyone should get ten cards with two left over. Why don't we just throw those in the middle to get the discard pile started?"

"Oh, OK," Christian said tentatively, a little uncertain on the math. He placed the extra cards in the centre then addressed the player to his left.

"Anthony, you start. And try to give new answers, not ones we've already used today."

"OK... umm... *five-hole*."

"*Saucer pass*," Raj said.

"*Stacking the pads*," Baker replied, which impressed Jake.

"Good one, Mr. Brooks. You're gonna win."

"Jake, we just got started for Pete's sake," Christian said. "It's your turn."

"Uhh... uhh... *icing!*"

"*Sin bin*," was Christian's response, which seemed to befuddle Jake.

"*Pass!* What's a 'sin bin'?"

"C'mon, Jake, it's another word for the penalty box," Anthony replied. "It's my turn. *Half boards*."

"*One-timer*," Raj said, keeping the game moving.

"OK, how about... *Corsi*?" Baker offered.

This time it was Christian's turn to wonder. "What's a 'korsey' Mr. Brooks?"

"It's a fancy statistic coaches use to measure how well their team keeps the puck in the offensive zone," Baker explained. "I don't really understand how it works, but I hear people mention it all the time."

"Holy cow, Mr. Brooks, you know everything," Jake said, doubly impressed. "See, guys? I told you he was gonna win."

Christian rolled his eyes. "It's your turn again, Jake."

"Oh, boy... um, *breakaway*—"

And so the game continued around the table, taking several more minutes to reach a conclusion. At one point Baker nearly caused Jake to fall out of his seat when he came up with *edge work* as one of his answers. In the end Raj pulled off the win when Baker tried using *video challenge* as an answer and was rejected by the group as it was deemed applicable to other sports as well. Baker congratulated Raj on the win, thanked the group for the game, and then hustled out to meet up with the others. He figured he'd catch them if he jogged.

*****

When Baker finally drew next to his friends a short distance down the slush-covered sidewalk, Conrad was expounding on the controversial things that had been said during *Coach's Corner* on Saturday night.

"... Men like Don Cherry and Donald Trump don't see the errors of their opinions. They engage in debates armed with arguments based on anecdotes. There's very little room for alternative viewpoints and any dissenting opinion is viewed as an attack on their character, which elicits a fight response consisting of personal insults and inane gibes aimed at their opponents—"

He paused in his diatribe long enough to acknowledge Baker's arrival. "Look who finally made it. Nice of you to join us, Baker." Then without missing a beat, he picked up where he left off. "But do I blame men like that for acting in a manner consistent with who they've always been? No! The people I *do* blame are those who should know better, for giving them a forum from which to spout their viewpoints. In the case of Don Cherry, I blame the CBC and now Sportsnet. Hell, I even blame Ron McLean. It's those men and organizations that provide platforms for Cherry to influence generations of hockey fans on topics ranging from how to properly execute a two-on-one to why every Canadian should wear a poppy in November."

"Whatever, man," Angus replied. "I still like the guy. He's entertaining. I kind of agree with the people who tune in to Hockey Night in Canada on Saturday nights just to catch Coach's Corner. Who could ever replace the guy?"

Baker jumped in. "Jesus, Angus, be careful. If you insist on spewing nonsense, I'll have to give you a wedgie."

"What? Why? I'm just repeating what I've heard."

"But why repeat bullshit?" Baker demanded. "I mean, *no one* is irreplaceable. Least of all Grapes. What's wrong with any one of the other talking heads we see on that broadcast from week to week, like Kelly Hrudey or Brian Burke? They're just as capable of providing interesting and informed content." Just then a thought occurred to him. "Wait a minute, they didn't give Ron McLean the boot, did they?"

"No. He didn't say anything objectionable."

"Yeah, he's safe—for now," Conrad added.

Arriving at the pizza place, the group filed in eagerly, welcoming the warmth of the interior as a respite from the cold and damp outside. They greeted the proprietor with a chorus of "hellos" and "how are yous?" then got down to the business of ordering.

"Veggie Delight."

"Make that two."

"Traditional."

"A small meat-lover's pizza, please."

"A *whole* pizza, Angus?"

"C'mon, it's a small pizza. Oh, and I'll have a slice of the Hawaiian too." The others stared in disbelief, causing Angus to raise his hands in self-defence. "What? The wheel is for later. I have a long day of marking ahead, and munching on pizza keeps me going. As fellow teachers, I thought you would understand."

A short while later, they were outside again, heading back to the school, when Perreault, who happened to be flanked by Baker and Conrad on her right and Angus and Masaccio on her left, suddenly stretched both arms wide, effectively halting the entire group in its tracks.

"What time is it?" she asked.

Conrad checked his watch. "Almost eleven."

"Phew. We didn't miss it."

"Miss wha—? Ohhh... The moment of silence," Conrad said, clueing in.

"Shit! I completely forgot," Baker exclaimed. "It's Remembrance Day."

"Can we make it back before eleven?"

Baker directed his gaze down the road toward the high school. "Not unless we can cover that distance in the next minute or so."

"No worries," Perreault replied. "We'll hold our own observance right here."

"What... here?" Angus asked. "On the sidewalk?" They happened to be standing in front of one of the town's unremarkable strip malls, as drab as the overcast sky.

"Over here." She led them a short distance into the parking lot. They drew close in a circle while remnants from the morning's snowfall drifted down upon them, and traffic splashed through the slush just a few feet away. "Nothing really needs to be said. Let's just stand in silence for a minute and reflect."

Together they bowed their heads. And then, a miracle: faint strains of "The Last Post" could be heard coming from somewhere close by, perhaps the fish-and-chips shop two doors down or the convenience store beside it. The exact source wasn't important, because the group's modest observance was served perfectly (although there were one or two moments when the sound of the trumpet was lost on the wind and the rumble of a passing truck).

When the minute of silence had passed, everyone in the circle relaxed, straightening up from their bowed postures, looking at each other, waiting for someone to make the next move. Perreault took the initiative. "Shall we?"

They proceeded to head back to HMV, except for Masaccio, who had something else on his mind. "I'm wondering if this will be my last Remembrance Day for a while." His query came from out of nowhere, causing the group to stop and face him.

"It'll be 'a while' for us all, Mas. You are aware that it only comes once a year, are you not?" Baker joked.

"Yeah, heh, heh." Mas seemed preoccupied. "Does anyone know if Remembrance Day is observed in Italy?"

"Italy? Why would you ask that?"

He took a deep breath, bracing himself as if on the dock at his cottage, preparing to jump into the frigid lake. "Well, folks... sorry I haven't told you until now, but Sal and I have come to a big decision."

Perreault's ears were perked. "Wait, you and Sal have decided to try for another kid?"

"Ha, ha . . . no, I'm afraid that's not the kind of decision I'm talking about. The fact is, we've been given the opportunity to be part of the family business, but it'll require us to move away . . . to Italy."

"What?"

"How?"

"When?"

"Why?"

Masaccio fielded each question adroitly and with efficiency.

"We are moving to Italy . . . on a jet . . . in July . . . to run the family farm."

There was a slight delay as the group took a moment to process his answers.

"What about the girls?" Perreault asked. "What do Lily and Hazel think?"

"Oh, you know, typical eight-year-olds. They're excited about the idea. It's like an adventure for them."

"How do they feel about leaving their friends?"

"I wouldn't worry about Lily and Hazel. They're like best friends. They're thick as thieves. They'll be fine as long as they have each other."

"So, what's this about the family farm? Where is it?" Conrad asked.

"It's in Tuscany, in a town called Poggibonsi."

"Ooh, Tuscany," Perreault said dreamily. "I'll bet the property's beautiful—with vineyards and olive groves."

"Actually, your description isn't that far off. The house is set up on a rise and looks out across a sweeping panorama of the landscape beyond. On clear days you can see the town of San Gimignano, with its fourteen medieval towers."

"Is it a big house?"

"Big enough. It's a 'fattoria'—a farmhouse—built in the eighteenth century."

"With rounded arch doorways and plaster walls and even a fresco painting or two?" Perreault asked.

"It sounds like a movie set for post-war Italian cinema," Baker said.

"Funny you should say that," Mas added. "Sal's aunt insists that she remembers the day, years ago, when Bernardo Bertolucci scouted the property as a potential location for a movie he was preparing to shoot."

"Who?" Angus asked.

"Bernardo Bertolucci. One of the all-time greats of Italian cinema."

The name meant nothing to him, but Angus was impressed all the same. "You mean to say your farm is in some classic Italian movie?"

"No. In the end he chose not to shoot there—something about the light being wrong." Masaccio concluded his story just as the group had arrived at the school's front entrance.

BAD NEWS COMES IN THREES

"Damn, that kinda sucks," Angus said, punctuating his reply by giving the door-activation switch a firm slap.

As they filed in through the opened door, Perreault decided to check on the details of that night's event. "I'm going to the student council office. Hopefully, someone's in there who can tell us what time we're on tonight."

"Good idea," Baker said. "We'll come with you."

Perreault led the way while the guys lagged behind, continuing with the topic of Masaccio's departure.

"Mas, you say you're leaving in July?"

"That's the plan. The first week, right after the school year ends."

"At least you'll still be here for the Pines' playoff run."

"If there *is* a run," Conrad replied, which made him the target of Baker's stink eye.

"Actually, that's my wish," Masaccio admitted. "It's my silent request every time Bakers' Coven gathers for a charm session: that I get to see the Pines win during my final months here in Canada."

"That *would* be quite the parting gift."

Their conversation was interrupted when Perreault came out of the student council office.

"Bad news guys," she announced. "It turns out we won't be playing tonight."

"What? But the kids assured us they'd put us on the bill," Baker replied.

"No, you don't understand." Perreault said. "*Nobody's* playing tonight. They've cancelled the event."

"You're kidding!" Mas exclaimed. "Was it because of the weather?"

"Worse than that. All the facility bookings go through the school board and they double booked the theatre for tonight."

"So of course the student council event loses out, right?" Conrad said, evidently not surprised.

"Unfortunately, yes. They're looking to reschedule it for early February, at the start of next semester."

"What about the gym?" Baker suggested. "Couldn't they hold the Battle of the Bands there?"

Perreault shook her head. "That's booked, too. A local volleyball league runs games every Monday."

"Shit! I was *so* looking forward to finally playing in front of an audience."

"Me too," Perreault said, in an attempt to mollify him.

"And now you're saying we'll have to wait till February?"

"February? No, of course not. You're forgetting the Christmas assembly next month."

Baker said nothing. The Christmas assembly at the end of December was of little consolation.

"Well, that was the second piece of bad news today," Conrad observed.

"Second?" Baker asked, wondering if he'd missing something. "What was the first?"

"Why, Masaccio's announcement, of course."

"Oh... right."

"Beware," Angus said, "bad news comes in threes."

"In threes, huh?" Baker was dubious. "Is that really a thing?"

"Damn right it is," Angus replied with conviction.

"Well, folks, I'm going up to my office," Conrad announced in a tone that implied it was time to move on. "Are we getting together after school?"

The question seemed to catch the others by surprise.

"You know what?" Mas replied after considering his options. "It wouldn't be a bad idea to take advantage of the time we've been afforded by this cancellation. I'd be inclined to just head home at the end of the day."

Masaccio's answer was a brutal shot of reality, but they all seemed to understand that it was probably for the best. In the end they agreed to cut their losses.

"OK, but be forewarned, Mr. Tuscany," Perreault said to Mas, "I've got a million questions that still need answers."

"Hey, you know where to find me," he said in return. "Tomorrow's another day, after all, and I'm not leaving until July."

* * * * *

Baker spent the rest of the afternoon alone in his classroom, hunkered down attending to his stack of marking. Eventually, he found himself turning reflective: sitting motionless at his desk, cogitating on the affairs of his life, which spun around and around in his mind like a carousel of concerns (the news from Masaccio only serving to make the ride bumpier). He directed his gaze across the room to the bank of windows there. The snow had long since stopped but the sky remained a vault of grey, uniform and dull, typical for November. It was always considered a grey sort of month; if not reflected in the weather, then it could be seen in people's moods. The truth of the matter was presented in black and white in the calendar pages of *The Old Farmer's Almanac*: for people living in the northern hemisphere, more than two minutes of sunlight was subtracted with each passing day, so that by the end of the month, more than a full hour of daylight was lost. All of which seemed to be more acutely felt, if not actually perceived, during the thirty long days in November.

At present, however, it wasn't the darkening day but a complaining tummy that was the impetus for Baker to pack up and head out to the car, weighed down with his guitar, marking bag, gym bag, and work bag.

The parking lot had thinned out considerably, but of the few vehicles that remained, his eye was drawn to a red jeep with HOXIXOH on its licence plate. Without hesitating, he turned on his heel and walked toward the entrance to the school, then spun back around to his car to drop off his baggage. Thus unburdened, he hustled once more to the front doors and checked in at the main office.

"Mr. Brooks, you're still here?" the principal's secretary, Klara Scott, called from her desk. "I would've thought you'd left for the day."

"I was on my way, but then I noticed Helen Nella's car outside. Is she here?"

"You just missed her. She went upstairs to pick up a few things from the library."

"Thanks. I'm going to try to catch up with her. I'll see you tomorrow, Klara."

"OK... bye, Baker."

He took the stairs two at a time up to the library but found only Lawrence there.

"You just missed her," Lawrence replied, sounding like Klara. "She'll be back early next week, though."

Rather than turn and leave, Baker headed straight across the room for the library windows that overlooked the parking lot. From that vantage point he saw Helen loading her car with some miscellaneous items. Within a few seconds he was downstairs and out the front doors, jogging to the parking lot.

Helen was seated behind the wheel fiddling with her seatbelt when he caught her attention with a knock on the window. She looked up and, recognizing who it was, smiled broadly and rolled down her window.

"Baker! What a surprise. How've you been?"

"Good. It's great to see you. Boy, we sure miss you around here." He flipped his thumb back toward the second-floor library windows. "Especially Lawrence."

"The sentiment is mutual. I miss this place too."

"How's Allen?"

Helen hesitated, a shadow passing across her face, as if a cloud momentarily blotted out the sun. "Oh... he's fine. I mean, we're all getting older, and we've all got our issues, you know, but we're managing. He's fine."

Baker wasn't sure how to respond, so he tried to keep it light. "Tell him I said hi and that I regret not having the chance to catch an Irish football game and do some push-ups with him."

"I'll be sure to pass the message along."

"Hey, you know who I was thinking of the other day, and then I realized I hadn't seen him in almost a year? Your nephew, Cubby." Baker could see that his mention of the boy touched a nerve. "Is something wrong?"

She turned away slightly, appearing to look down at the steering wheel, but he could see she was fighting back tears.

"Is it Cubby? Is it Calub? Is he OK?" Not getting a response and not knowing what else to say, Baker just stood on the cold pavement outside Helen's car door. Finally, she ran a hand across her eyes and nose before turning to face him, though she seemed to be focused on something in the distance.

"Oh, Baker. It all happened so fast, and there was nothing anyone could do."

"What?" Baker asked as Angus's words about bad news echoed in his head. "What happened?"

She looked up into the face of a man waiting for the other shoe to drop. "Baker . . . Calub's dead. Poor little guy. He passed away in July."

CHAPTER SEVENTEEN
MY KINGDOM FOR A HORSE

Monday, November 11 – Tuesday, November 19

Roughly around the time that Baker was receiving his third piece of bad news for the day on Monday, breaking news of another sort was heating up the airwaves when the president of Sportsnet issued a statement announcing the firing of Don Cherry as a commentator on Hockey Night in Canada. By Tuesday night, Cherry was making an appearance on Fox News channel's *Tucker Carlson Tonight* show, taking the opportunity to tell his side of the story.

The Mighty Pines were back in action on Wednesday, playing their twentieth game and marking the quarter pole of the season. Unfortunately for the team and its fan base, a win eluded them again. It would be more of the same through the weekend with a loss to Boston on Friday followed by a loss to Pittsburgh on Saturday, extending the losing streak to five games.

Two days later, another loss, this time to the Vegas Gladiators, ran the losing skid to six games. For Kayden Koch, only twice before as the Pines' head coach had he lost six games in a row and both those losing spells had occurred during his first season with Toronto—the season of the tank. Back then, six-game losing streaks were considered beneficial to the long-range plans of the franchise, helping to increase the odds of winning the first overall pick in that year's draft lottery. The present squad, however, was expected to compete deep into the playoffs. Instead, they had displayed so many flaws it was more likely to be a struggle for them just to make the post-season. In fact, if the season ended that day, the Toronto Mighty Pines would have found themselves out of the playoffs entirely.

On the afternoon of the day after the Pines' loss to Vegas, a Wednesday, Baker was seated at his desk, alone in his empty classroom, reflecting. More than a week had passed since he got the news of Cubby Elyk's death, and in the meantime the Pines were in free fall. For the moment he put his concerns about the team aside and instead thought back to what Helen had told him nine days earlier. Little of it had registered at the time, and now most of what he remembered was clouded by the shock of discovering that the life of a nine-year-old had been snuffed out so matter-of-factly.

* * * * *

He had been standing in the parking lot beside her vehicle and Helen had suggested they go elsewhere to talk, so he'd climbed into the car and she'd driven them to a nearby coffee shop. When they were seated with their beverages, she had picked up the conversation, offering a sober account of the events leading up to Cubby's death. Baker recalled fragments of it:

"It was quick; a matter of weeks once the initial diagnosis was confirmed. The first signs were persistent fatigue. Alarm bells rang when Cubby began to lose weight. A scan revealed a spot at the base of his skull . . . brainstem . . . rhabdoid tumour . . . treatment . . . operation . . . hospitalization . . ."

When she was done sharing the basic facts, Helen had turned philosophical. "It goes completely against all our norms and expectations for how life and death should work. Children are supposed to outlive their parents. Anything counter to that is a perversion of nature. It's almost too painful to consider . . . and we only have ourselves to blame for it."

"Ourselves? To blame? How do you mean?" Baker had asked, confused.

"I'm not talking about Cal. I'm talking about those of us who are left behind with the memories, the loss, and the pain. Actually, Baker, I'm talking about Allen."

"Allen's struggling to cope?"

Helen nodded slowly. "He is hurting. I wish he could get past it, and yet . . . I can't really blame him."

Baker listened as Helen delivered a brief monologue, spontaneous but fervent. "I guess it's in our DNA. We make our choices, we lay out our plans and set out on careers; we fall in love, have children, build families . . . but all the things that make life worth living can also produce the greatest pain. Life is a complex and potent marinade that relentlessly works away at the human heart to break down and tenderize the fibres . . . despite our best efforts to preserve its toughness."

As Baker looked into his cup, he'd thought of *The Lord of the Rings*. "King Théoden was right."

"Sorry?"

"Oh, it's a reference to something in The Two Towers. King Théoden is standing at his son's gravesite and mournfully remarks about how no parent should have to bury their child."

Helen's thoughts had taken her elsewhere. "When a life as beautiful as Calub's gets cut down—" Then she'd brought herself back to the coffee shop with Baker and nodded in agreement. "Well, all I can say is, Tolkien nailed it." Then, she had appeared to have an idea. "Listen, Baker, why don't you come over? Sit down with Allen and get him out of himself for a spell."

Baker had leaned back in his chair and appraised her. "Gee, I don't know, Helen. I'm not very good at that kind of stuff."

"I'm not asking you to engage in any sort of therapy. Just be a friend and visit. I think it'd be a breath of fresh air for him. Look, I know this is a busy time for you," Helen said. "Midterm marks are coming due, and there are things you still want to cover before Christmas. But consider making a visit—maybe over the holidays."

The holidays! God bless you, Baker thought. Here was Helen, willing to wait five or six weeks. He figured the least he could do was accede to her request. In the interim he assigned himself the task of finding some words of comfort for Allen when they finally did come face to face.

On the drive home that evening, Baker had pondered the mysteries of life and how unpredictable fate could be. It was like a navigation app for your car that insisted on mapping out alternative and circuitous routes to your destination, which was infuriating, until you found out later about the twelve-car pileup on the road you originally planned to take. How could he know that the cancellation of the Battle of the Bands would turn out to be a blessing in disguise? In hindsight it was clear that the news about Cubby would have put him in no frame of mind to perform that night, and afterward he certainly wouldn't have been in any mood to celebrate what would (in all likelihood) have been a solid performance for Bakers' Coven.

*****

Baker shook himself out of his thoughts and got up from the desk to gather the things he'd need for when it came time to meet the others in the music room. Thinking about Bakers' Coven got him to thinking of the Pines, and thinking of the Pines generated an urge, built out of frustration over their crappy play, to check the PHL standings. Looking them up on his laptop wouldn't cut it, though, so he headed down to the school library to pick up a newspaper. He was tired of computer screens and felt the need to handle something concrete, to be able to open a sports page wide, just like in the good old days. Lawrence was there, of course, reshelving some books.

"Hi, Lawrence."

"Afternoon, Mr. Brooks. How's it going?"

"Wonderful. And you?"

"Splendid. Help yourself to a newspaper. There're a few still on the rack."

"You read my mind." Baker thanked him and then removed a paper from the rack, checking to make sure that the sports section was still intact. He passed by the table where he had first met Cubby a year ago and paused. It was now occupied by three students engaged in a debate over the merits of *The Peanut Butter Falcon* versus *The Addams Family*. He must have lingered a little too long because all three looked up at him, as if they were expecting to be told to check the volume of their conversation.

"Sorry, sir, we'll keep it down," one of them said.

"Oh . . . um, that's fine, guys. No worries." Pushing the memory to one side, he gave the kids a friendly smile, bid them a good afternoon, and took his leave.

Out in the hallway, he stopped partway down the corridor and opened the paper's sports section. "Pines Drop Sixth Straight" was the headline that screamed at him. He ignored it, instead turning to the back page where he could find the previous day's results. Leaning back against some lockers, Baker focused on the PHL's Eastern Conference standings. The Washington Founders were leading the league with thirty-six points while the Pines sat in tenth place in the conference, two points out of a playoff spot and only five points clear of last place.

Just then a face popped into Baker's head, but it wasn't Mason Andrews' or Gianni Valentino's, or any other player's, for that matter. No, the face he saw was Sir Ian McKellen's. But not McKellen as Gandalf the Gray. No, it was the actor's portrayal of Richard III out of a movie version of Shakespeare's play. Or was it? Baker wasn't so sure anymore. He could envision a famous English actor standing on the field of battle, pleading in vain, *"A horse, a horse, my kingdom for a horse."* Reflecting on the scene in his mind, Baker concluded that horses must have been pretty important to warriors in battle back then, and so, when the villainous king found himself on the battlefield, horseless and on foot and overmatched, he was willing to trade his entire kingdom for the one thing that would allow him to keep fighting for that very realm.

That image set Baker's mind to constructing a parallel between a king and a coach—or more specifically, a king's *horse* and a coach's *voice*. For a PHL coach, few things were more valuable than their "voice." Baker thought of how a coach's voice was not just the tone and content of what was said but also the reputation of the man behind the voice—and that the man's reputation, more than anything, was built on winning.

When Kayden Koch had accepted Xander Galahad's highest-bid offer five years ago to coach in Toronto, his greatest selling feature had been his voice, which carried with it a veritable booty of winning, including one Clarence Cup ring and two Olympic gold medals, among other laurels. Rare air indeed. And when he'd stood in the Pines' dressing room, before his new team of players for the first time as their new boss, his voice had carried with it one more asset: he was the highest-paid coach in the history of the league, and coincidentally, the highest-earning guy in the room. But four years later, while he was still the highest earner among coaches, in the room among his players he had dropped to fifth place and the weight of his voice had dropped with it. The power of Koch's voice in the room had diminished. His message was no longer reaching its intended target, and the league standings plainly bore this out.

Baker looked at his watch. He was late, and was expected at the music room, but first had to make a quick stop at his classroom to get a picture frame that Conrad had requested for that afternoon's session. He crumpled the newspaper in disgust and slam dunked it into the garbage can. That felt good!

Heading for the art room, he suddenly stopped, sighed, and spun on his heel, walking back to the garbage can. He reached in and recovered his refuse, straightening and refolding it, then placed it in the recycle bin sitting nearby. Only then did he resume his course. As he walked, Baker smiled ruefully to himself, thinking how Kayden Koch was in effect starring in his own version of *Richard III*. How much of a stretch would it be to say here was a man willing to trade . . . what—His past wins? Any future wins? His exorbitant salary?—to have his voice back?

The only person who could say for sure was the coach himself, but it was a moot point because it would ultimately be voices other than Koch's that had the final say on the Pines' direction in 2019–2020.

CHAPTER EIGHTEEN
ANOTHER TIME

A century is what it feels to me
A Cup in '20 would be legendary
Staying loyal never was a crime
I'm always waitin' on another time

"Where the hell is he?" Conrad demanded.

"No idea," Mas replied. "He said he'd be fifteen minutes—twenty minutes ago."

"Why am I not surprised?"

"Hey, I've got an idea," Perreault chimed in. "Why don't we have some fun with this? Let's put our magical powers to use and *will* him through that door. You know, like cloud busting. The three of us should be able to manage that," she added, only half joking.

Mas looked at Conrad then back to Perreault and shrugged. "I guess it's worth a try. We're just sitting here doing nothing anyway. You lead."

"If I'm leading then we're going to have to sing it."

"Sing it?"

"Yeah, like this. We'll sing the line from XTC's 'Senses Working Overtime,' except where they count up"—Perreault sang the line—"*'One, two, three, four, five . . . senses working overtime,'* we'll count down. *Five, four, three, two, one . . .* Then we'll point to the door, and, well, he should appear."

"I must say, you've got this all figured out."

"You're darn right I do," Perreault said, as if she was back at summer camp rallying the kids. "OK now, here we go . . . ready and . . ." She conducted Conrad and Mas through the exercise in sing-song voices, "*Five, four, three, two, one . . .*" Perreault sang the rest of the line herself, changing the words to suit their needs. "*Angus come on through that door!*" They all pointed at the door as if they were armed with magic wands, and held their breath. Three seconds passed before they heard some shuffling outside in the hallway, followed by the handle being worked and the door swinging open.

The three of them made no secret about their chagrin when they saw it wasn't Angus but Baker who entered. "Sorry to disappoint everyone," Baker said, reading their expressions. "Should I leave?"

"Nah, you can stay. We were just expecting Angus coming back from his coffee run," Perreault explained.

"I told him to pick up some muffins too," Mas said.

"Mmm... that sounds good. I'll bet he's just chatting up the girl behind the counter."

"What? At the coffee shop?" Perreault said. "I doubt it. Most of the staff there are either seniors or still in high school!"

"I said 'chatting up,' not 'hitting on,'" Baker clarified. "Oh, by the way, Conrad, here's your picture frame. I hope it serves the purpose."

"Thanks. It's perfect."

Just then the door swung open a second time, and Angus backed into the room, balancing a tray of five hot drinks and a box of muffins. The four of them cheered his entrance and then advanced to offer assistance.

"What took you, Angus?" Baker asked. "We thought you might've been chatting up the server."

Angus looked like he had swallowed a bug. "You kidding? It's just teenagers and old ladies who work there." He was uncertain why his comment produced such mirth in the others.

Baker assessed the tray of drinks. "You know, I'm always amazed at how big the extra-large sizes are. Is that yours, Angus?"

"Hell no. I couldn't drink that much. It's yours."

"Mine? Why would you order me a pail-sized coffee?"

"I don't know. You weren't around when I was taking orders. Maybe an angel whispered in my ear."

"Thanks all the same, Angus, but you should find another angel. This'll keep me up the whole night."

"You don't have to finish it, Baker. I won't be insulted... asshole."

That generated a laugh from Conrad and Mas because, although they knew that Angus was kidding about the asshole part, they also knew that Baker had been raised to clean his plate and not let anything go to waste, *especially* if it happened to be purchased for him.

Conrad took Baker's picture frame and went back to his guitar case, extracting a sheet of letter paper that had a colour portrait printed on it. He didn't waste any time inserting the picture into the frame, then came back to the group and set it upright on a desk as he pointed to the subject of the portrait. "Anybody want to take a guess as to who she is?"

Perreault picked up the framed picture for a closer look. "I'm guessing she's one of any number of saints. Let's see now: She's sitting at an organ. It looks like she's playing it with one hand while the other is holding a small slip of paper, maybe some sheet music. Anyway, she's gazing up to the heavens where two ugly, creepy baby's heads are looking down upon her."

Angus came over to take a look. "Man, they *are* ugly."

Baker took a peek as well. "Oh, those are just a couple of putti."

"A couple of what?" Angus asked. "*Pooh-tee?*"

"Not *pooh*-tee . . . *Put*-tee. You know, like cherubs."

"Aw, who gives a shit about the pooh-tee. Who's the chick?" Angus asked.

"My guess is the patron saint of music or musicians, or something," Mas said.

"Give the man a prize!" Conrad replied. "Next question: who is she?"

No one volunteered an answer, so he revealed it. "That would be Saint Cecilia. Now for a final question: would any of you heathens know when we celebrate the Feast Day of Saint Cecilia?"

"Hmm . . ." Baker mulled. "It wouldn't happen to be today by any chance, would it? November twentieth?"

"Close. It's actually on Friday, November twenty-second."

"So, is she included in our rituals now?" Mas asked.

Conrad was impressed. "Masaccio Clementi, right again! You should be a contestant on Jeopardy."

"Wait," Angus said. "We're going to pray to Saint Cecilia?"

"Even better, we're going to *sing* to Saint Cecilia."

"Cool," Perrault said as she got up to gather her song sheets.

Angus looked at Baker. "I didn't know you wrote something to Saint Cecilia."

"I didn't," Baker replied, turning to Conrad. "So, which song did you borrow from?"

Conrad raised his eyebrows. "Isn't it obvious?"

"Please tell me it's from Simon and Garfunkel!" Perreault called out.

"Bingo!"

"Holy shit, Conrad, I hope you plan to play solo," Baker warned, "Because I'm not prepared for this."

"Don't worry. I've got it all figured out. Everyone is involved."

Before Baker could reply, Perreault jumped in. "Did you put my song sheet somewhere? I set my folder down right here."

"Hmm? Oh, yeah, I may have moved everything to where my stuff is on the desk over there."

ANOTHER TIME

Perreault sifted through the folders and stopped when she saw something that was totally incongruous to the contents of the stack of pages. "What's this? A script for A Christmas Carol?"

"Wait, what? How did that get in there?" Baker walked over and rescued his script from Perreault, appearing flustered.

Conrad watched him with amusement. "What have you got yourself into now?" he asked. "Don't tell me Mr. Esposito has recruited you for the Christmas play."

Baker slumped his shoulders. "Yeah, Vince sucked me in to helping this year."

"Helping in what capacity?" Perreault inquired.

"I'm supposed to assist Iggy Horvat with his lines for his role as Ebenezer Scrooge."

"I know Iggy," Mas said. "I taught him last year. Vince's got him playing Scrooge, eh?"

"Yes. And apparently the poor kid is having all kinds of trouble with his lines. That's where I come in."

"So, how's it going?" Perreault asked, obviously in love with the idea.

"Vince just gave me the script. He wants me to familiarize myself with the lines and then sit down with Iggy after school starting early next week."

"Good for you. I'm sure you'll turn this Iggy kid into a regular Alastair Sim."

"Wow, Perreault, it sounds like you've got more faith in me than . . . me."

"Come on now," she countered. "It's clear you have a way with words, if your song adaptations are any evidence. And I'll bet you love Christmas, which would make you a fan of Dickens' holiday classic. You're a perfect candidate for the job!"

Listening to Perreault, Baker's face got warmer with each sentence. He wasn't used to someone reading him like a book, and the fact that it was Perreault doing it meant she had likely spent at least a smidge of time actually thinking about him. Wanting to hide the blush in his cheeks, Baker mumbled something about needing to learn his lines first, then turned away as if to get his guitar. When he turned back, he'd recovered enough to revisit the topic of Conrad's song.

"Did you at least bring a chord sheet for me? I could use one."

Conrad looked at him with deep compassion and patience. "Bear but a touch of my hand there, and you shall be upheld in more than this!"

Baker stared at him. "Well, if it isn't the ghost of Christmas Past. Maybe *you* should help Iggy with his lines."

"Uh-uh, no way. That's your baby to deliver."

"Then tell me, how do I play 'Cecilia' by ear?"

"You don't have to! I've got the karaoke version cued up on my laptop." Conrad drifted over to where his device was set up. "Shall we begin then?" he said in a Cockney accent. "Come into the parlour. Come into the parlour."

"Get a load of Dickens over here," Baker said. "Seriously, I have to get Vince to recruit you."

"Don't you dare! I'd rather be buried with a stake of holly through my heart . . . or boiled in my own pudding." Conrad replied while he busied himself distributing copies of his altered version of "Cecilia." "Here, I assumed this tune was familiar to everybody, and in the interest of keeping it simple, I figured we'd just sing it together as an added 'charm' in support of our musical efforts today. I call it 'A Prayer to Saint Cecilia.'" He looked around at the others. "I'll play the chords while you guys keep beat with claps or stomps or whatever." He cued up the original version of the song on his laptop and then looked at Perreault. "Ready?"

"Ready . . . hit it."

It took most of the first verse to coordinate the claps and stomps, but soon enough they fell into an engaging rhythm.

> *Cecilia, our patron of art*
> *You're giving us confidence daily*
> *Saint Cecilia, we're down on our knees*
> *We ask you inspire our hearts*
>
> *Cecilia, oh patron of art*
> *You're giving us confidence daily*
> *Saint Cecilia, we're down on our knees*
> *We ask you inspire our hearts*
>
> *Making songs in the afternoon with Cecilia*
> *In the music room (making songs)*
> *So we trust you'll grant us grace*
> *So that me and my friends*
> *Can start rockin' this place*
>
> *Cecilia, oh patron of art*
> *You're giving us confidence daily*
> *Saint Cecilia, we're down on our knees*
> *We ask you inspire our hearts*
>
> *Coney Nation*
> *We love them again*
> *We're asking for your special blessing*
>
> *Coney Nation*
> *We've come here again*
> *To make a request for your blessing*

For Coney Nation
Ask Saint Cecilia

When they were done, Perreault was quick to offer up her praise. "That went well. Good work with the beats, boys."

"Not bad, huh?" Mas concurred. "Considering that for a minute there I was afraid we were banging out Queen's 'We Will Rock You.' Right, Angus?"

Angus had other concerns as he shimmied around on his seat. "Man, I hate this stool. It's not level, I feel like I'm falling forward. I wish I had my other chair—the one at Baker's place."

"Quit complaining," Baker scolded. "It was your idea to jam here at school, remember?"

"That was out of self-preservation," Angus said. "Hell, the rest of you should be thanking me. I'm sparing us from the snake pit." (Angus had sighted a small snake in Baker's basement the last time the Coven had gathered there.)

"C'mon, it was just a baby milk snake. Don't make it sound like a tomb full of asps, Indy."

"It's close enough for me. Spiders and snakes are not my friends."

"It's a good thing you didn't come across any dock spiders at my cottage last summer," Mas said.

"Tell us, Angus, when exactly will you consider it safe to jam at Baker's place again?" Conrad asked.

"Oh, I don't know. You said those things hibernate didn't you, Baker?"

"Yeah. I think I've seen the last of them until probably June."

"OK, the next time we meet it can be at Baker's. Actually, I prefer playing there. I can drink his beer. But didn't you say it's a winter wonderland up at your place now? I mean, what's with all the snow, man? It's like you live in Nunavut compared to the amount we got here in town."

Baker was in no mood to provide a rationale for the wintry weather in his neck of the woods, so he ignored the question and got everyone to settle down in an effort to adopt a tone of reverence. With heads bowed, they listened as Perreault recited Papi Rene's little prayer. This was followed by a few words from Baker, then a few seconds of shuffling and adjusting with their instruments before Conrad gave them the "go" sign. His fingers nimbly worked through the first fifteen notes of the opening to "Otherside," then came Perreault's clear, rich voice.

How long, how long will I bide
And dedicate my time? I don't

I don't believe it's fair
Pinnin' my hope is all I ever . . .

I framed a black-and-white photograph
It showed the Cup and glories of the past
You gotta know how bad we want it back
We're always waitin' on another time

A century is what it feels to me
A Cup in '20 would be legendary
Staying loyal never was a crime
I'm always waitin' on another time
Waitin' on another time
Waitin' on, waitin' on . . .

Mas and Angus were plugging along commendably. *So far, so good*, Baker thought, and he gave a nod to Saint Cecilia. He was also grateful that his responsibility on guitar consisted of some basic chord support while Conrad handled the rest, allowing him to focus on his backup vocals. The beautiful thing was that singing under Perreault, who carried the lead with such conviction, gave someone like Baker—who lacked that self-assurance—an enormous safety net.

How long, how long will I bide
And dedicate my time? I don't
I don't believe it's fair
Pinnin' my hope is all I ever . . .

Pour my life into the Clarence Cup
My patience full but it's never enough
Should I go and sell all my Pines stuff?
I'm always waitin' on another time

Yet again the Pines are in my head
Green and white the colours when I'm bled
Hope's de rigueur but I'm full of dread
That I'll be waitin' on another time
Waitin' on another time
Waitin' on, waitin' on . . .

It had been a couple weeks ago when Baker had heard something in Perreault's voice that gave him an idea for another song devoted to the Mighty Pines. Now he was delighted to see that his hunch about Perreault singing to Anthony Kiedis and the

Chilis was spot on. She fell into it as sublimely as a marshmallow into hot chocolate, or an olive into a martini.

How long, how long will I bide
And dedicate my time? I don't
I don't believe it's fair
Pinnin' my hope is all I ever . . .

You turned me on, sold me on a long ride
Made me doubt, every spring I want to hide
I yell and tell myself it's not the end
I come around, I lose the frown
And then I'm born again

How long, how long will I bide
And dedicate my time? I don't
I don't believe it's fair
Pinnin' my hope is all I ever . . .
How long? I don't, I don't believe it's fair
Pinnin' my hope is all I ever . . .

Although not entirely devoted to the Red Hot Chili Peppers, Baker could not resist the melodious hooks in some of their music, "Otherside" probably being the best example of this for him. On top of that, the clarity of the vocals lent themselves to Perreault's talents and also filled the need to send a strong message to whatever invisible forces might be "listening." Lastly, he always liked a cold finish to a song if it had to be played live, and this one provided that. The others seemed to agree on all counts, evidenced by their reactions.

"Woo hoo!" Mas cheered. "Watch out, Chilis. Bakers' Coven has arrived!"

"That's one we've got to play live—with the original words," Angus added. "Not that there's anything wrong with your words, Baker."

"Are you kidding? Baker's lyrics are great. I especially like how you got 'de rigueur' in there." Mas laughed. "Nicely done."

"I should warn you, however, that if we do play it live, it's probably best we use Baker's words," Conrad warned. "The original is not fit for student consumption in our high school setting."

"That's fine by me. At least the Pines fans'll love it," Angus replied.

It was nearly six o'clock by the time they cleaned up and cleared out of the music room, but while everyone else headed downstairs to the exit and the parking lot, Baker decided to make use of the adrenaline that was still flowing. He went back to his office to put the finishing touches on next week's grade eleven art history test.

When Cheers Are Not Enough

* * * * *

Two hours later, he was settling in behind the wheel of his car. When the radio came on with the ignition it took all of ten seconds for him to realize something big had happened that day. Learning that Galahad had dropped the other shoe and finally dismissed Koch sent a strange thrill through Baker, even though he knew it was never a good thing to celebrate another's misfortune. He listened to the discussion the rest of the way home, paying particular attention to what the experts thought new head coach Boris Duggan—just promoted from the Pines' top farm team—would bring to the table. When he got home, Baker watched a bit of the coverage on TV but soon found himself falling asleep on the couch.

He was tired. The previous night's Pines game in Vegas hadn't started until after 10:00 p.m. local time, so he didn't get to bed much before 1:00 a.m., and in a foul mood to boot. That, coupled with the evening's excitement, exhausted him to a point where he was in a state of near somnambulism. He made the effort to wash and brush, pulled on cotton boxers and an HMV-crested T-shirt (one of many that he'd accumulated over the years at the school), and slid under the covers.

Extinguishing the bedside lamp, he welcomed the all-embracing darkness and closed his eyes—but then he began to rehash the evening's events in his mind, beginning with how well Bakers' Coven had sounded. Maybe Conrad was onto something with his prayer to Saint Cecilia. (Baker had to admit that his own musicianship seemed to be improving anyway.) He remembered thinking at the time how great Perreault sounded, allowing himself to dwell on it now. But then thinking about Perreault's fine singing form got him to thinking about her form in general.

He willed himself to stop, knowing he'd never get to sleep that way, but now he was awake. He rehearsed his lines as Ebenezer Scrooge, thinking that might bring on sleep, but it just made him more alert. Then he entertained fantasies of how the Pines might go on a ridiculous run of winning now that the coaching change was official and Boris Duggan was at the helm. He could hardly wait for tomorrow night's game against Phoenix.

He rolled over to check the time on his clock. Forty-five minutes had passed. *Argh! Time to get serious here.* He was regretting finishing that coffee. Changing positions, he laid his cheek upon his hands, which were placed palm to palm as if in prayer, much like the Albrecht Durer print. He then tried concentrating on the dates that marked Pines Cup victories, not unlike counting sheep: 1937...1938...1942...1945...1949...1951...1954...

Amazingly enough, he was asleep before he got to 1962, the year of Nathaniel Sinclair's ouster: a year which had ultimately compelled the man to curse the entire organization, an entity which had once been his pride and joy, his lifeblood. That was nearly six decades ago. Sinclair's fabled curse had held for fifty-eight years and counting.

CHAPTER NINETEEN
LE ROI EST MORT

Scene: Xander Galahad lounges in his hotel suite at a posh four-star hotel in Pheonix, Arizona. He is joined by newly minted head coach Boris Duggan. They engage in friendly banter as they await the arrival of GM Kyle Bulac. It is overcast and rainy in a part of the country typically known for its sunshine and warmth.

In due time Bulac arrives, pink-cheeked and alert, with an evident bounce in his step. A light film of perspiration on his forehead catches the bit of grey daylight filtering through curtained windows, but none of it registers with Bulac. He has been too busy with events of the past twenty-four hours to concern himself about losing a round of golf to the weather.

Bulac: What a day, what a day. Sorry, Gally. Hey, Duggy.

(Galahad, who is absently flipping through the pages of a magazine, allows the GM and his new coach to exchange pleasantries, then addresses Bulac.)

Galahad: What a day, indeed. I dare say it has been a hectic one. How are you holding up, Kyle?

Bulac: In one sense, a great burden has been lifted off my shoulders . . . only to be replaced by another.

Galahad: *(still turning pages.)* Pray tell, how is it you come to experience these sensations? Perhaps a touch of indigestion? A slight disorder of the stomach?

Bulac: *(casts a curious glance at Galahad before answering.)* No, physically I'm fine, except I could use a good night's sleep. But between having our team wallow in mediocrity for the better part of a year, and then watching us piss away points and drop in the standings, and witnessing a death by a thousand cuts as Kayden, day by day, loses the guys in the room, and finally wrestling with the timing of when to drop the hammer. It's like lugging sacks of concrete . . . before finally sacking the coach.

When Cheers Are Not Enough

Galahad: *(rolls the magazine into a baton and points it at Bulac.)* You, sir, are quite the speaker. I wonder you don't go into Parliament. Nonetheless, it is the lot of all general managers to carry such burdens, fettered by ponderous chains.

Bulac: *(half smiling, as if there's a joke he's missing.)* OK, Gally, what's goin' on? What is that?

(Duggan, who's been listening to the exchange and, like Bulac, is somewhat bemused by Galahad's behaviour, turns to hear the team president's response.)

Galahad: What is what? Oh, this? It's nothing, just a trifle. This week's issue of The Economist. Do not trouble yourself with it.

Bulac: *(waves off the magazine in frustration.)* No, no. Not that. *You.* You sound like a character in a Victorian novel for Chrissake.

Galahad: *(reverts back to his normal speech habits as a slight blush colours his cheeks.)* Oh, that . . . well, I can explain. You see, inside this week's Economist was an obituary for Harold Bloom. Ever heard of him?

Duggan: Wait, isn't that the guy who played Legolas in those *Lord of the Rings* movies? When did he die?

Galahad: No, that was *Orlando* Bloom. He's still alive. *Harold* Bloom is . . . was, a literary critic. So, anyway, I'm reading his obituary, and there's a mention that he had the ability to memorize, word for word, just scads of stuff.

Duggan: Oh? Like what?

Galahad: Like the whole freakin' Bible, for starters. Then Shakespeare's entire body of plays and every novel ever written and every name and number in every phone book in the western hemisphere. I mean, it's just ridiculous. *(Stops to reflect on something.)* Funny thing, though, he couldn't remember his wife's birthday . . . or the date of their anniversary.

Bulac: *(smiling because he thinks he knows where this is going.)* Don't tell me you're trying to memorize something. Is it a book? Not Shakespeare!

Galahad: Right on all counts. It's a book, and it's *not* Shakespeare. Hell, I wasn't about to memorize things in Shakespearean English. That would be like learning a new language.

Bulac: Hang on a minute . . . "touch of indigestion" . . . "ponderous chains" . . . "go into Parliament" . . . *(A light bulb clicks, his eyebrows rising above his generously framed glasses.)* You're not memorizing Charles Dickens' *A Christmas Carol*, are you?

Galahad: Discovered! My good sir, you have found me out.

Bulac: Um, yeah . . . but what made you choose that book?

Galahad: I can't say. Maybe it's the Boy Scout in me—"Be prepared." You never know when you might be asked to play Ebenezer Scrooge in a random production of *A Christmas Carol*.

(Bulac and Duggan exchange looks of disbelief.)

Bulac: How's it going so far?

Galahad: I'm just at the first chapter, you know, the part where Bob Cratchit tries to justify getting the whole of Christmas Day off. *(Under his breath)* The little weasel.

Bulac: Cool! Can you recite the first couple of pages for us?

(Duggan makes a noise with his throat and shifts uncomfortably in his seat.)

Galahad: Shit, what are we doing? We've got real business to attend to here. Sorry, Duggy—can I call you Duggy now that you've finally graduated to the big boys' league?

Duggan: Sure . . . I guess so.

Bulac: *(Walks over to Duggan and delivers a solid slap on the back.)* Yup, you are now the head honcho, the top dog, the alpha male, the king of the castle . . . um—

Galahad: The big cheese, the boss hog—

Bulac: The big enchilada, the top banana, the high man on the totem—

Galahad: The big wheel, the king of the jungle—

Duggan: OK, OK, I get it! *(Silence descends on the room.)* I'd be perfectly happy with just being called the head coach of the Toronto Mighty Pines.

(It is an awkward moment as Galahad straightens his tie while Bulac adjusts his glasses.)

Galahad: Sorry, Shelly. I guess we got a little carried away there. *(He smiles brightly.)* The Toronto Mighty Pines formally welcome you to the show!

When Cheers Are Not Enough

Bulac: OK, now that we've made it official, let's move on to the business at hand. You know, in all the excitement, I forgot... do we have a game tonight? *(He looks at Galahad for confirmation.)*

Galahad: I... uh, I think... wait! Let me check my schedule here... *(reaches for his cell phone.)*

Duggan: Jeeezus, you guys! Yes! There's a game tonight.

Bulac: *(Exchanges a look with Galahad as if to say, "This guy's a little uptight, huh?")* OK, so, you've met with the coaches already. Feel free to tinker with the line combinations and defensive pairings. Reintroduce the importance of puck possession. Hell, with the skill and depth we have up front, why do we need to dump and chase—?

Duggan: Hang on a second, Kyle. Let me write this down. *(He searches his pockets until he finds his notebook and a pencil.)* OK, continue.

Bulac: Where was I? Oh, yeah, bring the puck in to the offensive zone under control. Puck possession. It should be a frickin' mantra around here by now.

Duggan: *(feverishly writing in his notebook.)* You got it, boss.

Bulac: And activate the D and allow them to jump in on the rush or pinch when appropriate. As for the netminders, rather than playing them according to some archaic formula, utilize them in ways that will maximize their strengths. The point is, let these guys play. Let's just get back to having fun.

Galahad: Can I add something here?

(Both Bulac and Duggan look over at Galahad, nodding assent.)

Galahad: *(Before he begins, he turns to Bulac and whispers some private advice.)* By the way, Kyle, you really ought to consider that Parliament thing. *(Then turning to squarely face both men and clearing his throat, he proceeds with his original point.)* While I recognize the virtue of patience, there is nonetheless a definite urgency to win, and I don't mean just in the short term. Here we sit, the brains of a team that is presently in tenth place and out of the playoffs, so yes, we need to win hockey games... *now*! I also believe there's a common hunger in this room which needs to be transferred to our players, every last fucking one of them. *(He gets up out of his chair, and his voice rises with him, quivering with growing passion, like a minister at the pulpit.)* Our message must be clear to one and all, from the youngest rookies to the longest-serving veterans, regardless of skill level, whether they're big-money earners or on entry-level contracts, and regardless of the number of Twitter followers they have. It's up to the three of us to communicate that our only goal is to take the name that is on the front of the sweater and put it on the Clarence Cup—more than once, if possible.

Bulac: *(Inspired by the passion of Galahad's speech, he claps his hands, firmly and with resolve.)* Now look who's quite the speaker. It's a wonder *you* don't go into Parliament.

Galahad: Aw, maybe I'm just showing my age. But these opportunities are so rare, and it's maddening to see them wasted by players who lack that awareness due to their immaturity. George Bernard Shaw was right. Youth *is* wasted on the young.

Duggan: I thought that was Oscar Wilde.

Bulac: No, I'm pretty sure that was Groucho Marx.

Galahad: Whoever, Marx, Wilde or Shaw, it certainly applies to this team, and as I said, it's our job to see that these guys get wiser, and fast.

Duggan: No problem, Gally ... can I call you Gally?

(Galahad shrugs in noncommittal fashion, but before he can answer, Bulac interjects.)

Bulac: Listen, guys, I think this would be a good time to share something with you two.

Duggan: *(poised with his notebook and pencil.)* Should I write this down?

Bulac: No. Let's keep this just between us, okay?

Duggan: Absolutely. Whatever you say will stay within these four walls.

(Bulac looks toward Galahad for confirmation. He replies by doing some weird stuff with his hands, almost as if he were making the sign of the cross, then finishes with his palms together as if in prayer. Bulac takes the funny hand signals as consent.)

Bulac: You'll understand why I was reluctant to share this with you earlier. *(He hesitates, then begins to blush.)* I think I might be getting advice from otherworldly beings ... uh, spirits ... from the past.

(Duggan's eyes are saucers while Galahad's face brightens.)

Galahad: Cool! Sort of like the spirits that visited Scrooge?

Bulac: Sure, I guess so, but Scrooge didn't know the three spirits who called on him, except, of course, for Jacob Marley. On the other hand, I can tell you that my guys are Mighty Pines players from years gone by.

Galahad: Holy fuck. You mean *Toronto* Mighty Pines players?

Bulac: Exactly. Toronto Mighty Pines players from the forties, fifties, and sixties. But not just any players. The greats, the legends. The ones at Elysian Square.

Galahad: Holy double-fuck! The Icemen of the Acropolis?

(Bulac nods in a slow, profound fashion. Silence descends as the impact of his words settles over them.)

Galahad: So . . . what did they tell you?

Bulac: It was pretty clear. Their message was focused around pulling the trigger on this coaching change.

Galahad: No shit! Well then, how did they communicate? Tell us, did they speak to you in the middle of the night, like, in your dreams?

Bulac: They didn't "speak" to me, really. They left messages, or signs . . . yeah, that's it. I got discreet signs. Three of 'em, to be precise.

Galahad: When, exactly? *(He shifts in his chair to face Bulac, leaning forward.)*

Bulac: It was just before the Philadelphia game a few weeks ago. I was busy that week, doing a bunch of errands, putting a lot of miles on the car. The first sign came when I filled up on gas one day. The pump stopped at forty-six dollars and sixty-nine cents. In other words, four, six, six, nine.

Galahad: *(calls to Duggan over his shoulder.)* Write that down, Duggy.

Bulac: I didn't think much of it at the time. My next stop was the grocery store to pick up a few items on the way home, and the total for the groceries was exactly the same as the cost of the gasoline, forty-six dollars and sixty-nine cents. Just a crazy coincidence, right?

Galahad: You gettin' this, Boris?

Bulac: Finally, when I got home, I saw some mail waiting for me; the hydro bill. So I opened it, and, well, guess how much my bill was this month?

Duggan: I'd say forty-six dollars and sixty-nine cents, but then I wouldn't believe you, because unless you're on some alternative fuel source, a typical monthly hydro bill comes out to considerably more than that.

Bulac: No, you're right. It was more than that. It was one hundred and forty-six dollars and sixty-nine cents.

Duggan: That's pretty weird. What do you think it means? What significance would the numbers one, four, six, six, nine hold?

Bulac: I don't believe the number one matters in this case. I took the numbers four, six, six, and nine, and tried to keep it simple. So, I made a list of possibilities: a phone number, a lottery number, a lock combination, a password, a birth date or some other significant date, a licence plate number . . . stuff like that.

Galahad: Jeez, this is like something right out of *National Treasure.*

Duggan: Yeah, except with ghosts.

Bulac: Then I concentrated on the likelihood that it was a date—a birth date or a death date or the date of some momentous event—and eliminated the rest. I determined that the last two numbers indicated the year, 1969. If you arrange it as day/month/year, then June 4, 1969, is the date. But if it's month/day/year, the date becomes April 6, 1969. I couldn't come up with anything I considered significant on June fourth, but do you want to guess what happened on April 6, 1969?

(No one answers for a time. Duggan looks up at the ceiling with a creased brow and pursed lips while Galahad studies the floor. Bulac detects an odour of wood smoke.)

Galahad: I'm drawing a blank.

Duggan: Oh, wait! Was that the day they discovered the body of Joe Zedelko?

Bulac: No. But you're right about it being a key date in Pines history.

Galahad: Can you give us a clue?

Bulac: OK, think "head coach."

Duggan: *(fairly jumps out of his chair.)* Hey! That's the day Lefty Monaghan was fired!

Bulac: *(snaps his fingers and points at Duggan.)* My guess exactly. It's the only thing I figured it could be. The great Lefty Monaghan came to the end of his time in Toronto on that day in 1969.

Galahad: Wait a sec . . . you're saying they used the dismissal of Lefty Monaghan a half century ago to say the time is right to fire Koch?

Bulac: Maybe it's a lesson, a way to encourage us to learn from the past. Out with the old, in with the new, so to speak.

(All three pause to consider Bulac's suggestion.)

Bulac: What do you think, Boris? You think I'm a few pucks shy of a bucket?

Duggan: Well, the way I see it, your spirits got me this job, so who am I to argue?

Bulac: Good point. After all, you're the guy directly benefitting from this.

Galahad: Yes, but I'd like to think we're all benefitting here: management, the players, the coaches . . . hell, the entire freakin' organization benefits.

Duggan: Let's not forget our legion of faithful and long-suffering fans.

Bulac: Ah, yes, Coney Nation. I'm amazed they've hung on this long; that we haven't at least seen an exodus from the portion of fans who are on the fringes.

Galahad: *(sounding preoccupied.)* Then they had better do it, and decrease the surplus population.

Bulac: Huh? What!?

Galahad: *(coming out of his trance.)* Oh, don't mind me. I was just reciting a line. Listen, guys, this can be a dirty business. No one takes pleasure in giving someone the sack. But on the flip side, someone is getting promoted to the vacant post. To many people it's like the dawning of a new era. Come to think of it, it's a lot like when a monarch dies and is replaced by the next in line. Isn't there some sort of decree—a traditional proclamation—that goes with that?

Duggan: Le roi est mort, vive le roi.

Galahad: No, I don't think that's right. But impressive all the same! What language is that? Sounds German . . . or Belgian or something.

Duggan: That would be French.

Galahad: French, eh? Well, whatever the language, I was thinking more like "The king is dead, long live the king."

Duggan: It means the same thing.

Galahad: It does? Oh. *(He adopts a troubled expression.)* But what if we were tardy in acting? What if it's too late for a coaching change?

Bulac: It's never too late, Xander. Ebenezer Scrooge taught us that, remember? He was an old dog who thought himself way past learning any new tricks in the ways of living amongst his fellow men, but the spirits convinced him otherwise. I'm certain the same can be said for our situation. It's never too late.

Galahad: I just hope unseating the old monarch and replacing him with a new king will be enough. Do you think it's enough?

Bulac: It's something, anyway. Again, Scrooge said it well: "If the deeds be altered, the ends may also change." The way I see it, this succession of "kings" is the first step in altering the deeds, and I'm confident the dominoes will fall in a favourable fashion.

Duggan: Jeez, Kyle, you sound like a frickin' *Christmas Carol* scholar.

(Bulac smiles as the rouge returns to his baby-smooth cheeks. Galahad reaches under the table and comes up with a bottle of Napoleon brandy and three snifters.)

Galahad: I thought it'd be appropriate to have a little something for the occasion.

Bulac: Well, it's not exactly a Christmas bowl of smoking bishop, but I guess it'll do.

Galahad: *(pours three generous hits then invites his colleagues to raise their glasses.)* You know, I've got mixed emotions. I'm excited for Duggan, but I can't help but feel bad for Kay. The king is dead—and I was the guy with the axe.

Bulac: Be that as it may, the deed is done. The only thing left now is to announce it throughout the realm. *(Raises his glass high toward Duggan.)* "The king is dead, long live the king!"

Galahad: *(joins Bulac and Duggan in tipping back his brandy, then catches sight of something across the room, which produces a coughing fit.)* Holy shit! What the hell is that up there?

(Bulac and Duggan, momentarily startled by the terror in Galahad's voice, follow his gaze toward the ceiling behind them.)

When Cheers Are Not Enough

Duggan: You mean the spider web up in the corner there?

Galahad: No! I mean the spider *in* the web.

(Duggan gets out of his seat and approaches the offending arachnid for a better look.)

Galahad: What are you doing? Get back here. Don't disturb it.

Duggan: Don't worry, Xander, it's all good. Oh my, he is handsome, isn't he?

Bulac: Uh, Boris, maybe just get rid of it. Gally hates the things. *(Bulac takes Galahad's magazine and passes it to Duggan.)*

Galahad: Hey, I'm not finished reading that!

Duggan: Trust me, Xander, I won't ruin your Economist. *(Duggan opens the magazine and coaxes the spider onto the page, then goes to the bathroom with it. The sound of a toilet lid being lifted followed by a satisfying flush sets Galahad at ease.)*

Galahad: Thanks, Duggy. Spiders belong in the jungle—or attics and basements—but certainly not in a place like this. This is a suite in a four-star hotel for Chrissake.

Duggan: *(comes back into the room, giving Galahad his magazine.)* Well, this *is* Arizona.

(The group shares a chuckle, and Galahad pours another toast. The mood is light, with the promise of a brighter future.)

Galahad: *(holds up his glass.)* Kyle, since you're the Dickens scholar here, I'll allow you to grace us with one final quote as we toast to close this meeting.

(Bulac looks at his colleagues and smiles with a twinkle in his eye. Galahad and Duggan seem to know where this is going.)

Bulac: Gentlemen, may the spirits strive within us as we embark on this path toward nothing less than the Clarence Cup, and so, as Tiny Tim observed, God bless us—

Galahad: God bless us—

Duggan: God bless us—

All three in unison: Every one!

(*Each man downs his drink, then Galahad gathers the snifters and goes to the bathroom to rinse them in the sink. Bulac and Duggan sit back and savour the burn of the alcohol until their reverie is interrupted by a commotion and muffled noise coming from the bathroom.*)

Duggan: Oh, shoot, I forgot to warn Xander. I couldn't bring myself to kill the spider, so I just left it in the sink.

Galahad: Duggan, come in here, goddamn you! I thought you flushed this thing!

Bulac: (*Quietly to Duggan.*) Oops ... It's probably best if we just leave.

(*Bulac and Duggan get up out of their chairs and tiptoe for the door while in the bathroom Galahad stands frozen in front of the mirror, staring down at the spider in the sink.*)

Galahad: (*calls to Duggan and Bulac, who have long since left the room.*) Hey, you guys, what am I supposed to do with this thing? (*Then to himself*) Oh, let me retire to Bedlam ... !

(*Realizing no help is coming, Galahad resigns himself to the task of removing the spider. He gingerly reaches out to turn the faucet handles but over cranks them, causing water to gush violently, as if it were an open street hydrant, splashing beyond the edges of the basin. The accompanying noise of the rushing water is almost deafening, but the decibel level increases when the bathtub faucet abruptly turns on full force, while the toilet, with its oversize tank, begins to flush like a whirlpool in the Niagara gorge beneath the falls. With the spider long since forgotten, Galahad struggles to stay upright as the water, its level in the room having risen to his knees, jostles him about. He stumbles and splashes face first into what is now a surging river, carrying him right through his hotel suite and out into the corridor ...*)

The vivid image of Xander Galahad being swept through the halls like Paul Newman in *The Drowning Pool* was interrupted when Baker's eyes opened wide in alarm. He remained motionless in his bed, the din of rushing water in his dream now replaced by the quiet of the darkened room and reality. When he did venture to move, his first instinct was to slide one of his hands, which still happened to be supporting his cheek on the pillow, cautiously below the covers to his boxer shorts. Relieved to discover that the cotton fabric was still dry, he breathed again, slipped out from under the comforter, and made his way to the bathroom. *That was close*, Baker thought. *Damn Angus and his extra-large coffee. And what's with these dreams? They're beginning to feel way too real.*

When he was done in the bathroom, he went back to his bed, thinking of what Dorcas and Mary had said about the presence of spirits in his house on the night of their visit. Overcome by the disconcerting feeling of being watched, he curled into a fetal position in an attempt to make himself smaller, then sank deeper under the covers, pulling them all the way up to his chin, and waited for sleep—hopefully, a dreamless one—to overtake him.

CHAPTER TWENTY
THE SEASON OF GIVING

I wish each day had one more hour
God knows I need the time
To find the best words for this song
And get these lines to rhyme

Wednesday, November 20 – Sunday, December 1

"The coach is dead, long live the coach." Admittedly, that was not exactly how it was worded in the Pines' press release Wednesday, but it could have been translated as such. "Today, we made the decision to relieve Kayden Koch of his coaching duties and named Boris Duggan our new head coach," were the actual words in President Xander Galahad's statement. The man who hired Koch fired Koch.

Of course there were those who had, for some time now, seen the writing on the wall for a coaching change. Twenty-three games into the season, the Pines were floundering in tenth place in the Eastern Conference, reflected by a 9–10–4 record and in the throes of a six-game losing streak. In addition, with just eight days until US Thanksgiving, they were approaching a point on the calendar regarded by PHL organizations as a key benchmark: any team not among the top eight in the conference by the time Turkey Day rolled around had the odds strongly stacked against them making the playoffs.

Koch was in the fourth year of a seven-year contract, and while his tenure in Toronto had featured a sparkling regular season record, it was post-season failure that proved to be his bane: he never managed to coach the team past the first round of the playoffs. Ever since the evolution of the PHL away from the 4H style of hockey (i.e., hooking, holding, hitting, and hacking), some teams sought to build a winning product based on speed, skill, and puck possession. Such was the vision of GM Kyle Bulac. Kayden Koch, however, was old-school and made no bones about how he had always found the Pines' roster wanting when it came to grit and toughness. (In fact, it was rumoured that Koch's most embarrassing moment in Toronto came not on the heels of any particular playoff loss but the day a local newspaper columnist wrote a piece that suggested a more appropriate name for the team would be the "Frighty" Pines.) His detractors notwithstanding, the coach revelled in the spotlight of the Toronto sports media, feeding into the perception that he was the man in charge, if three-plus years of Koch decisions, Koch strategies, Koch quotes, Koch opinions, and Koch wisdom and philosophy, were any indication. With Koch's dismissal, however, Kyle Bulac was free of all that; it was really and truly his team now. All personnel decisions would be based on a consideration of circumstances according to the big picture as *he* painted it.

According to Bulac, the prospect of making a move turned serious a week ago, following the team's 3-2 shootout loss at home to Philadelphia. That loss was the one to begin the present losing streak and turned out to be the straw that broke the camel's back—or at least stirred the hemlock cocktail that had Koch's name on it. Perhaps more intriguing was the date of that Philly game: November 9, 2019. Arranged according to day/month/year, it becomes a neat and tidy palindrome: 9–11–19, or 91119.

Now, for anyone not inclined to believe in the power of numerology, 91119 means nothing. But for all those who might be open to their potential significance, the numbers raised some interesting questions. Was it possible that the date had some mystical import? Could it be the spirits whispered something to Bulac on that November night, or possibly foisted themselves and their ideas into Xander Galahad's designs for his team? If so, did the team President or the GM listen?

Whatever the impetus for Wednesday's coaching change, its impact had the desired effect as the Pines notched a victory over Phoenix the very next evening to snap the streak. With their tenth win of the season in the books, the team celebrated Boris Duggan's first win in his first PHL game, then travelled from the arid desert of Phoenix to the Mile High City of Denver for a Saturday evening tilt against the Mountaineers, where they proceeded to make it two wins in a row. They then followed it up with a decisive victory in Cleveland, as Eddie Sanderson stood tall in the net and earned the shutout against the overmatched Cuyahogas.

Next up on the schedule were two games against a middling Buffalo squad in home-and-home, back-to-back fashion, on Friday and Saturday. Unfortuntely, while Coney Nation could be forgiven for planning to mark Black Friday—America's busiest consumer spending day—by celebrating a fourth straight win, the Buffalo Border-Brats had other ideas, coming away with a 6-4 victory to end Toronto's modest win streak. The next night Toronto exacted some revenge by squeaking out a 2-1 overtime victory.

Meanwhile, for folks in and around the GTA, November went out like a lamb, owing to a thaw that effectively eliminated all traces of the snow that had fallen mid-month. What melted was quickly replaced, however, as December came in like a lion, with some nasty weather forecast for Sunday and into Monday morning. The dump of snow

THE SEASON OF GIVING

wreaked havoc on the new work week as over five hundred accidents were reported on local roads in a twenty-four-hour span.

Any chagrin Baker may have felt watching the Pines' disappointing loss to Buffalo on TV Friday night was mollified by the anticipation of a new month on the calendar. Indeed, not even the Border-Brats could put a damper on his weekend as he bid adieu to November and extended greetings to December, one of his favourite months of the year. A case in point was how he could afford to smile ruefully in appreciation of the commentator's remarks during the broadcast of the game, some of which were coloured by the fact it was Black Friday and that most of the Ontario visitors that night were likely *not* in town for the game so much as for cross-border shopping. For instance, there was this zinger in the second period following a third straight Buffalo goal: "Boy, the red light behind Pines' backup goalie Timothy Gates is shining like all the festive beacons in all the malls across Western New York, beckoning shoppers to part with their hard-earned cash." And in the third period, a glaring brain-fart by Mason Andrews leading to the Brats' game-winning goal inspired this one: "I must say, with all their eye-popping giveaways tonight, the boys in green have been doing an admirable job in resembling the local retail outlets that are offering Black Friday discounted prices and blowout savings on all major brands and labels."

Under normal circumstances such remarks would sting, but Baker managed to compartmentalize them, along with Toronto's loss, and put everything into healthy perspective. After all, December heralded the season of giving, with the promise of its own special warmth and wonder, synonymous with magic and mystery. He'd actually hoped to up the enchantment factor this year, anticipating the time later in the month when he could observe the winter solstice and celebrate the coming of Yule. He pictured an alchemical feast for the senses: the touch of a thick woollen sweater under the chin, the taste of mulled wine on the tongue, the sound of a crackling fire in the hearth, the room imbued with the season by the flicker and glow of firelight, and finally, two stoves working in harmony to kindle the nose with the melding of wood smoke and Christmas baking.

His mood as the week progressed, therefore, was light (notwithstanding that the Pines continued to stumble on the ice, losing in back-to-back fashion against Philadelphia and Denver) as he set himself the task of adapting the lyrics of not one, not two, but three songs. This time, however, the songs were not aimed at Mighty Pines' success. Rather, Baker's intent was to have the band perform them at the annual HMV

Christmas assembly. It was scheduled for the last day of school before the holidays, and for this reason the songs would require a festive, seasonal theme. Under normal circumstances he'd need two or three weeks to complete the task—but as proof of how much the Christmas season inspired him, he completed three songs by the end of the week and was actually making progress on two more. Thus, when Friday rolled around, Baker was ready to share the results of his creative efforts with the rest of the band. It was in the morning, just after first-period class, that he dialled Perreault on the classroom phone to see about getting together after school. When she agreed to meet in the staff room at 3:30 p.m., Baker's heart rate ticked up a notch and (to his surprise) stayed that way for the rest of the day.

When classes ended at 2:30 there was still an hour to burn, so he set off for the staff room with a pile of grade nine life drawings that needed marking. Upon arriving he was greeted by a scene of raucous activity. Masaccio was there, with a half-dozen other teachers from his work room. It looked as if they were celebrating someone's birthday.

"Baker!" Mas called across to him. "Care to join us?"

"What's going on?"

"It's Manny's birthday." Manuel Pacheco taught business and entrepreneurship. "Have a slice of cake."

Baker took a helping of cake, congratulated Manny on his "achievement," chatted with Mas and the others, and then withdrew to a corner of the room. Along the way he said "hi" to Janet Sax, who was at the photocopier, standing in a perfect contrapposto as she waited for the machine to print off a class set of song sheets.

"Wow, Janet, that's a perfect imitation of a Greek sculpture—weight on one leg, torso twisted, hip popped."

She looked at him blandly. "Blows your mind to discover that all those classic works were just idealized images of Greek women—wasting away in front of ancient photocopiers."

Baker laughed. "I guess some things about mundane office work never change—even after twenty-four centuries." He sat facing the celebrants and spread the artwork in front of him on the table, taking up most of the rest of the available surface.

When she was done at the photocopier, Janet came over to Baker's table for a visit. Meanwhile, across the room the decibel level ratcheted up when someone produced a large, colourfully wrapped and ribboned box and presented it with much fanfare to the birthday boy. Manny made a show of resenting all the fuss and went so far as to avoid handling the present for several minutes, resulting in repeated calls for him to get on with revealing its contents.

Richie de Kaizer, who taught in the automotive arts, was growing impatient.

"C'mon, Manny, the suspension is killing me."

THE SEASON OF GIVING

The malapropism elicited a round of laughter, whereupon Richie turned pink-cheeked. "Hey, my literature ain't ace," he said, which triggered even more good-natured teasing.

Manny opened the gift at a glacial pace, meticulously removing bits of tape and tenderly peeling back the wrapping paper, stopping to respond every time someone delivered a friendly jibe. Eventually, he revealed a green-and-white bundle of fabric which turned out to be a Mighty Pines number fourteen Ricky Randall jersey wrapped around a bottle of wine. Although school rules prohibited Manny from opening the bottle, nothing stopped him from proudly donning the sweater, which prompted a variety of comments from those assembled.

"It makes you look years younger."

"But not a penny richer."

"Yeah, you might have Randall's number on your back, but it'd be nicer to have his *numbers* on your paycheque."

"Miss Thoreau! Come join us!" Richie's voice boomed across the room when Perreault came through the door. "Have some birthday cake."

"Thanks. It looks delicious. You're sure there's enough?"

"There's lots."

"OK, then. Give me the biggest slice you've got." She did a perfunctory scan of those present and made her conclusion. "Happy Birthday, Manuel."

"How did you know?" Manny asked, evidently forgetting that he was standing with a bottle in one hand, wrapping paper in the other, and was proudly wearing the shiny new Pines jersey with its oversized label still dangling from his neck.

"My mother had a saying: 'You never look or feel younger than when celebrating your own birthday with friends and family.' And nobody in this room looks younger than you do right now."

Manny broke into a smile so broad that it was a good thing he wasn't going anywhere soon, because he would have struggled to fit through the door.

"Oh, my gosh, we didn't sing 'Happy Birthday,'" someone observed. "We have to sing 'Happy Birthday!'"

Someone produced a couple of candles and stuck them in what was left of the cake, then lit them as they chorused through the ubiquitous tune. When the final line was sung, rising above the rest was Perreault, casually tossing in some impeccable harmonies. Whereas Baker, Mas, and even Janet had long since been aware of Perreault's gifts, the others in the room were caught off guard.

"Wow, Perreault. You ought to quit your day job."

"I've been telling her that for months now," Janet said. "Her talents are wasted teaching religion."

"I'd bet she could do some serious damage working with your kids in the musical, Janet."

"Way ahead of you. I recruited Perreault the same day I first heard her in action."

All this complimentary talk was too much for Perreault, so she gave Baker a look that said, "Let's get out of here." To her relief, he picked up on it immediately, hastily gathering up his drawings and graciously making an excuse for the two of them to take their leave.

"Thanks for picking up on my signals," Perreault said to him once they were down the hall and out of earshot. "I hope I didn't take you away from your work. You seemed to be settled in quite nicely."

"That's OK. I wasn't getting much done anyway, what with all the activity in there."

"I've never been good at handling effusive praise," she confided.

"I'd say you were quite graceful in there. But then I'm sure you've had lots of practice."

Perreault shot him a look of exhaustion, as if to say, *Not you, too!*

"Sorry... a slip of the tongue."

As Baker led the way to the art room, Perreault noticed him struggling with his armful of drawings, owing to the awkward way he'd gathered his things in their haste to leave the staff room. Anticipating the likelihood that his classroom would be locked, she extracted his school keys by pulling the lanyard dangling from his pants pocket. Her touch was so deft that he barely noticed.

"Which colour?" she asked, referring to several colour-coded key rings.

"What? Oh, uh... the red one."

She unlocked the door to the darkened room and blindly reached along the wall to where she knew a panel of light switches would be. Once illuminated, Baker's classroom offered a visual cornucopia, the walls festooned with laminated posters, prints, and cuttings from books, magazines, and newspapers.

"Ahh, your room is so interesting. So visually stimulating."

Baker laughed in self-deprecation. "I figure it gives the kids something else to turn to when they get tired of looking at me; at least their eyes can wander to things that have some cultural significance."

"C'mon, Baker, give yourself more credit," Perreault said. "Have you ever considered how many students might actually look forward to coming to art class just so they can watch Mr. Brooks for seventy-five minutes each day?"

Because it took all of his will just to keep from blushing, Baker failed to generate a reply, let alone a clever one. Perreault spared them an awkward moment by bringing the conversation back around to the original purpose for their meeting. "So, Leonard Cohen, what's the plan? What do you have for me?"

"Oh... right. Just some songs for the Christmas assembly that I'd like you to see."

"*Some* songs?"

"Actually, I've prepared five songs."

"Five songs? What the hell, Baker?"

"Of course, we don't have to perform all five—"

"No one's gonna want to *hear* us perform five songs. And besides, the Christmas assembly has its time constraints."

"I know, I know. It's just . . . well, it's so easy to generate lyrics for Christmas songs, especially when we're in the thick of the season."

"The thick of the season? It's barely the first week of December!"

"Listen, once Remembrance Day is done, I'm in Christmas mode. What can I say? It leaves me feeling warm and fuzzy. And why should I have to wait until Christmas to feel warm and fuzzy?"

Perreault could only smile at him and shake her head. "Five songs, huh? Do you happen to have them with you?"

"I've got three here. The other two are still works in progress."

"OK. Who did you cover?"

"The first song is based on 'Wish List' by Pearl Jam."

"'Wish List'—yes, of course, I know it. Show me."

"Um, alright—." Baker shuffled through his song sheets until he found what he wanted. "I call it 'A Christmas Wish List.'" He shifted his laptop into position, typed in the song, and when Perreault was ready, he played it, volume turned up. She followed along with his lyrics sheet, allowing the words on the page to replace the ones Eddie Vedder sang.

> *I wish the noise at Christmas time would cease and peace prevail*
> *I wish that every student could achieve and never fail*
> *I wish that kindness and compassion were gifts on Santa's sleigh*
> *To have the bullies of the world see the error of their ways*
> *I wish the answers to our problems were apps on my iPhone*
> *For seven billion hands upraised have questions of their own*
>
> *I wish that people's differences were ironed out for good*
> *Then we could live in harmony like a tight-knit neighbourhood*
> *I wish that all the needy folk could stand on their own two feet*
> *So that the food banks in our towns were rendered obsolete*
>
> *I wish each day had one more hour, God knows I need the time*
> *To find the best words for this song and get these lines to rhyme*
> *But I know the ups and downs of life, we face them every week*
> *So I wish less darkness at the troughs and more sunshine at the peaks*

Baker looked at Perreault with anticipation.

"This is awesome!" she declared.

"Whew, that's a relief. I can't wait to hear you sing it."

His remark gave her pause. "Listen, Baker, I've been meaning to apologize."

"Apologize? For what?"

"Well, I'm aware that before I was recruited into the band, you were the lead vocalist, but ever since we played 'Five Years,' the job has been assigned to me. I hope you don't think I was staging a coup or anything."

Baker vehemently shook his head. "No need to apologize, especially since your presence has literally transformed this band. Personally, I'm just glad I can contribute with backing vocals."

Perreault happily took him at his word and expressed her gratitude before moving the meeting forward. "So, what's next?"

Baker reached into his pile of pages for the next song. "This one is adapted from 'Open Arms' by Elbow."

"Isn't that the song they played at the opening ceremonies for the London Olympics?"

"That's right! But mine's based on the Nativity story. It's called 'Everyone Sing.'"

The song played and Perreault followed along, after which it was evident that she was sold. "Let me just say, that would be quite the inspirational Christmas anthem to end the set with. If done right, that would make the hair on the back of people's necks stand up. And it will be a hit with the Catholics in the audience, who crave traditional Nativity-type themes in their Christmas music."

"The Catholics in the audience? Hmm . . . I never considered that," Baker admitted.

"You teach at a *Catholic school,* silly man. What about the other three songs?"

"Actually, all three are borrowed from songs by the Weakerthans, but two of them aren't quite ready yet."

"Oh well. What I've heard so far is good, really good. We've got to try them."

"That's what I was hoping. Is Monday doable?"

"No, I mean right now. Let me give Angus a call."

Giving Baker no time to think it over, she had her phone out, and a couple of taps later she was waiting for Angus to pick up. Baker's stomach dropped with the realization that she must have had him on speed dial—and likely called him regularly.

"Hey, Fletch, it's me . . . Yeah, I know . . . No, I'm with Baker in his classroom . . . Shut up . . . No, he's got three songs ready for the Christmas assembly . . . My thoughts exactly . . . The music room . . . Yup . . . OK, great. See you there."

From Baker's end of the conversation, it sure sounded like Angus and Perreault had developed a rapport that went beyond friendly. Did he sense a flirty intimacy in the exchange? Could it be that they—?

"Let's go, Leonardo." Perreault's voice had interrupted his thoughts.

"Who . . . ? Leonardo?"

"Yeah. While I was on the phone, I noticed the Vitruvian Man on the wall there, and it occurred to me that you're our Renaissance man. You know, like Leonardo da Vinci."

Baker could only laugh. "That's a bit of a stretch, don't you think?"

"Not really. You're our lyricist, our guitarist, our backup vocalist, who can sing lead whenever necessary, and you're the school's visual arts teacher. Heck, you even dance pretty well. I'd say that merits the title of Renaissance man."

He looked at her sideways. "How would you know if I can dance?"

"I saw you during the video shoot. You were showing off some nice moves there."

"I can say the same about you, you know."

"OK, OK. I guess we're a Renaissance pair then. Happy? Now grab your guitar. We're going to the music room."

He did as he was told and followed her down the hall with his guitar and gym bag in hand.

When they arrived, Angus seemed vexed. "What the fuck happened this week?" he demanded.

Baker remained calm. "I can only assume you are referring to the Pines?"

"Four games and nothing to show for it but an overtime win against Buffalo."

"A tough week for sure. Two back-to-backs in a row, with three regulation losses."

"I think we should play a song," Angus said, energetically, "for the team, you know."

"What? Right now?"

"Sure. We have to do something."

"Angus is right," Perreault said. "This losing has got to stop."

"But it's just the three of us," Baker objected.

"We can manage," she assured him. "My bones tell me the Pines need a little love. The best way to express that is by saying it—two hundred times!"

"So, it's 'Go Green' then?" Angus asked.

Perreault confirmed it with a nod. "Let me find a tambourine. There's got to be one in here somewhere."

"I just happen to have a box of candles with me," Baker said, diving into his gym bag. He soon busied himself prepping the room with some mood lighting.

Despite forty percent of Bakers' Coven being MIA, the ceremony, which consisted of Perreault's short prayer and one song, went remarkably well. Then the trio devoted the next hour to acquainting themselves with Baker's Christmas songs, after which they discussed next steps for getting everyone together for a practice session.

"I'll set something up for next week," Baker offered. "The sooner the better, dontcha think?"

"Angus and I are good almost any day," Perreault replied. "Let's see what the other two have to say."

"I'll call Mas first. I haven't been able to get a hold of Conrad all week," Baker said, reaching for his cell phone while Angus and Perreault huddled together to discuss the songs. A couple minutes later, they were interrupted by the sound of Baker's voice, which rose considerably as he spoke into his phone, in apparent anger.

"Holy shit, man, is he in or not?" Baker didn't want to sound petulant, but things weren't going according to plan, and now he felt a level of desperation setting in. "We can't seem to get hold of the guy either. We've texted him, sent emails, called and left messages . . ."

"I hear you, but try to understand," Mas replied. "This is a busy time for him as school chaplain. He's got the Advent mass to prepare for as well as organizing the grade ten retreats. I'm pretty sure next week should be better for him, when things quiet down a bit."

Baker wasn't in the mood for excuses. Hell, they were *all* busy at that time of year. Going halfway was only ever good if one aspired to mediocrity. He'd be damned if he would stand by and watch as Bakers' Coven took its place among the undistinguished masses, like the lunatics in the asylum from the final scene in *Amadeus*, seeking absolution from maestro Salieri, their self-proclaimed Patron Saint of Mediocrity.

In disgust, Baker mimicked F. Murray Abraham, raising a hand and blessing his fellow losers with a sign of the cross. "Mediocrities of the world, I absolve you . . . fuck!" Perreault and Angus exchanged quizzical looks.

"Let me contact him," Mas said, trying to assuage him. "In the meantime, email me your songs."

"Email?" Baker replied as if he'd never heard the term before.

"Jesus, Baker! Is Perreault there? Get her to do it if you can't."

"Oh, yeah . . . OK."

Fifteen minutes later, Baker's phone sounded. It was Masaccio calling back.

"I've got good news and bad news."

"Hit me."

"The good news is I got a hold of Conrad. The bad news is he won't be able to join us till Monday."

"Monday would be perfect."

"Um . . . That would be Monday the sixteenth."

"Wait . . . you're kidding, right?" Baker closed his eyes, praying for strength. "Jee-zuss!"

"On a happier note, I went over the songs you—er, Perreault—sent me. I think they're terrific."

"Well, I guess *that's* a good thing."

THE SEASON OF GIVING

"In fact, why don't the four of us meet next week and work on them together so that, at the very least, we'll have our parts down by the time Conrad joins us?"

Baker began to give serious consideration to the notion that he was being tested in some way, that this was all part of some grand scheme. The one thing he could be certain of was that in this, the season of giving, the thing he needed now more than ever was also the very thing that was most being asked of him: patience.

CHAPTER TWENTY-ONE
OPENING STATEMENTS

Monday, December 9 – Tuesday, December 17

New Zealand's White Island experienced a volcanic eruption early Monday morning, inflicting damage and taking five lives. Meanwhile in central Italy, a 4.5-level earthquake was recorded, impacting the region of Tuscany, just north of Florence. (When Masaccio Clemente heard the news, he wondered aloud to his wife, Sal, about the family's move to such a vulnerable area and how real the danger might be for them. Sal's response was to remind her husband how the coast of Southern California was a high-risk area for earthquakes, located as it was in the heart of the San Andreas Fault, yet it remained a desirable destination for people.)

On Wednesday, *Time* magazine announced sixteen-year-old Greta Thunberg of Sweden as its Person of the Year for 2019. Back in August 2018, she had skipped school to demonstrate against her government's climate inaction and triggered a movement. Now she was being hailed by Margaret Atwood as a modern-day Joan of Arc.

Two days later, across the pond, Friday the 13th was filled with nothing but good omens for Boris Johnson—who became Britain's next prime minister, scoring a landslide win in the UK general election on his promise to "get Brexit done."

Volcanic eruptions, earthquakes, climate change, and landslides aside, no such disasters befell the Mighty Pines as they concluded their annual three-game Western Canadian road trip on Saturday, coming away with two regulation wins. Then, on Tuesday, Toronto added a home victory over Buffalo for good measure. Tuesday's win was a bit unexpected, because it was not unusual for teams returning from long road trips through several time zones to come out flat in their first game back.

Speaking of flat, some of the air was taken out of US President Donald Trump's tires earlier that same day when the Democrat-led House of Representatives passed a resolution to impeach him on charges of abuse of power and obstruction of Congress.

OPENING STATEMENTS

The first two words out of Baker's mouth when he rolled out of bed and peered through the blinds of his bedroom window were "Holy fuck." It was Friday, December 20, the morning of the last day of school for the 2019 calendar year. After having woken up to news from his bedside clock radio that the overnight snowfall had necessitated school bus cancellations—a "snow day" in other words—he wanted to see the damage for himself. Indeed, not only did the weather resemble Christmas in the way it covered the landscape with a blanket of white, it also did so for how it had snuck up on him. Then, as jarring as a sour note sung at the climax of "O Holy Night," he was hit by a sudden realization: no school buses meant no students, which made it likely that the Christmas assembly would be cancelled, which prompted his next two words: "Aw, *fuck*."

But since cancelling the assembly wasn't his call to make, he would just have to wait until he got to school for the official word. One thing Baker did know for certain: there would be no regular classes that day, making his morning routine less of a stress despite any delays the snowy roads might present for his commute.

With the usual morning urgency now reduced, he allowed himself the luxury of ensuring that he was equipped with all the necessities for the day, which included his shoulder bag of marking (his usual ball and chain) along with his regular school bag, a duffel bag with extra clothes (whether for working out or changing into something more comfortable at day's end when Bakers' Coven met), his guitar case, and his lunch-bag. During the drive to school, he realized there'd be time to stop by the cafeteria and grab a coffee, so upon arriving he detoured upstairs to drop his stuff off in the classroom, then scooted back down to the caf. The ladies in the servery were pushing fresh Christmas gingerbread muffins two-for-one, not wanting them to go to waste (seeing as the regular traffic of students had dropped to nearly nothing). Baker asked for two, so, of course, they gave him four.

Exiting the servery, he was having trouble managing four muffins and a large, scalding coffee. Having neglected to dress his cup with a protective sleeve, he was lucky to make it as far as the first table in the dining hall, managing to set down the hot beverage just as the muffins popped out of his arms and rolled onto the tabletop. *Oh well, better than the floor,* he thought. In his distress Baker barely noticed the quartet of students seated at an adjacent table.

"Hey, Mr. Brooks."

When Cheers Are Not Enough

Baker turned his head toward the voice. "Oh, hi Christian. Hi Jake...Anthony...Raj." All four boys returned the greeting. Christian was shuffling a deck of cards with what Baker observed to be newfound dexterity and confidence, and he mentioned as much.

"Thanks, sir," Christian replied, clearly proud that the teacher had noticed. "I've been practising at home. Shall I deal you in? One game?"

"Why not?" Baker needed two trips to bring his muffins and coffee over to the boys' table. "What's the topic du jour?"

"Huh?"

"What's the theme for today's game? Hockey? The Pines?"

"Nope."

"What then? The Raptors?"

Christian shook his head. "It's the last day of school. Today's theme is Christmas!"

"Ah, yes. So...Christmas characters? Or maybe Christmas carols?"

"No. It was Jake's idea to do Christmas *movies*," he explained.

"Yeah, it was my idea," Jake confirmed.

"Christmas movies?" Anthony asked, sounding distressed at the news. "Well, I lose, because I only know, like, three Christmas movies."

"C'mon, Tony, everybody knows a few Christmas movies," Christian said.

"Speak for yourself. My parents let me watch maybe one a year."

"What, you're not allowed to watch TV at home?" Jake asked.

"Sure, but mostly educational stuff and reality cop shows—my dad loves those."

"Don't worry. You don't need to have seen the movies. Just name them."

"I'll give it a try, but don't blame me if I can't go more than a couple rounds."

Privately hoping the game would end quickly, Baker nevertheless enjoyed watching Christian deal the cards. Once underway, the game proceeded rather smoothly as the boys responded with movie titles that included familiar favourites like *The Polar Express, The Santa Clause, Home Alone, Home Alone II, White Christmas, How the Grinch Stole Christmas, Home Alone III,* and the like. Even Anthony managed to hang in remarkably well. The speed bump in each round of play, however, turned out to be none other than Baker. Despite his best efforts to avoid inciting lengthy discussions around films like *Die Hard*, his answers were nevertheless met with general skepticism, as though he was pulling them out of thin air and trying to cheat. For instance, when he offered up *Love, Actually,* Jake was compelled to question it.

"Whoa...what? Is that even a Christmas movie?"

"I never heard of that one," Raj added.

"Trust me, it's a Christmas movie," said Baker. "It's a romantic comedy."

His answer was grudgingly accepted, if for no other reason than to keep the game moving. When his turn came around again, Baker answered with *A Child's Christmas in Wales*, this time causing Anthony to pipe up. "What's that?"

"Yeah, who ever heard of A Child's Christmas with Whales," Jake wondered.

"A Child's Christmas *in Wales*," Baker corrected. "You know, the country in Great Britain? It's based on a story by Dylan Thomas..."

There was silence at the table for a moment or two until Christian moved things forward. "Let's keep going. It's your turn, Anthony."

Baker was certain his next answer would pass the group's muster, but again he was proven wrong.

"An American Christmas Carol."

Four teenage jaws dropped in unison.

"C'mon, Mr. Brooks," Christian said. "Now I know you're making these up."

"I'm not! Honest. It's like the original Christmas Carol, except it takes place in New England. Ebenezer Scrooge is played by Henry Winkler ... you know, the Fonz?"

He might just as well have been pleading his case to four empty chairs.

The final straw was Baker's use of *Black Christmas* as an answer. Jake, Raj, Anthony, and Christian stared back at him.

"What the heck is Black Christmas?" Jake demanded.

"It's an old Canadian slasher film—"

"—that takes place at Christmastime. Yeah, we get it, sir," Christian replied, whereupon he tossed his remaining cards into the pile. The other boys followed suit, conceding Baker the win.

Recognizing the culture gap was too wide to breach, Baker prepared to take his leave. "Sorry, guys. I guess you picked the wrong theme to invite me to play." With coffee in hand, he got up from the table. "Thanks for the game. I should get going. Help yourself to the muff—" Four hands snapped up four muffins before he could complete the sentence.

Thank-yous and Christmas wishes were exchanged all around, after which Baker headed upstairs to his classroom. The card game had set him back a good twenty minutes, so he quickly fired up his computer. When he opened his email, he read the following message from Perreault:

Leonardo,

Bad news: Xmas Assembly X'd, but the Coven still performing. Today—3 p.m.—music room. Be there.

Luv, PT

Baker looked up from his computer screen to consider what he'd just read, directing his gaze across the room through the bank of windows that revealed the blowing snow outside. So, it was official. The Christmas assembly was cancelled. Up to that point he had still entertained the notion that they might get the chance to play before a live audience, which made Perreault's message more of a letdown than it should have been. At the same time, her email was intriguing, loaded as it was with plenty of other things to ponder. He went through each point in his mind.

1) "Leonardo:" A reference to the time she complimented him as a Renaissance man two weeks earlier in this very room.
2) "Bad news:" It was nice to know she shared his disappointment.
3) "The Coven is still playing after school." That was good news. It meant he wouldn't need to chase people down.
4) "Be there." A command—almost as if his absence would be a definite loss.
5) She signed off with "Luv." Was that usual for her? Did she throw "Luv" around regularly, like the British did, or could it mean something more?

He reread the email and decided to lie low. The message was received, so there was no need to reply. Reaching across his desk, he pulled a stack of tests out of his school bag and settled in to do some marking. After taking a sip of his coffee, now tepid, he regretted not keeping one of the muffins for himself.

By midday he'd had enough of schoolwork, so he went back to his school bag and exchanged the tests for a bright yellow folder. Since September he had been keeping a record of the Coven's activities and comparing them with the game-by-game results of the Pines, not unlike a growing boy who, upon discovering spinach and vitamins, habitually marked his height on the door frame. He spent the next little while reviewing his notes, enthused by the Pines' recent progress yet still trying to maintain some objectivity. He resolved to introduce the topic when Bakers' Coven met that afternoon, a thought that prompted him to take out his guitar and strum through the Christmas songs. By 2:30 he decided to gather his things and head over to the music room.

While still down the hall, Baker was met with the sound of someone on the drums. When he entered, he discovered that Angus was already working up a sweat on the kit.

"Hey, Baker, you're early."

"I could say the same of you." He looked around the room. "How'd you get in?"

"Custodian Gus."

"Ahh." Baker busied himself tuning his guitar. "So, what are you working on?"

"Your Christmas tunes. Maybe you can give me a hand."

"Sure. Where do you want to start?"

"Let's do the 'Empty Greetings' song."

Angus put his sticks down while Baker finished tuning, then posed a question. "By the way, did you read the email I sent you this morning?"

"You sent me an email?"

"Just a short one. Mostly about the cancelled assembly and us getting together today."

Shit. It was only Angus, Baker thought, then kicked himself for not cluing in right away. "That was you?"

"Yeah. I was in Perreault's work room this morning when she instructed me to contact everyone. Her computer email was open, so I fired off three messages."

"I gotta admit I was a bit confused by how it was signed off: 'Luv, PT'?"

"Sorry about that. It just popped into my head, probably because my mum uses it a lot."

"What about 'Leonardo'? Where did that come from?"

"Don't ask me. Perreault threw that one in. I thought you'd know."

Baker pretended to pass it off like it was some obscure joke, then he and Angus got down to work on the songs.

A half hour later Perreault, Masaccio, and Conrad arrived. Conrad entered the room lugging a cardboard box, the contents of which emitted a clinking sound as he set it down just inside the door. Perreault did the same with a shopping bag she was carrying.

"Well, folks, we made it," Conrad announced. "I can't believe I got here in one piece."

"What do you mean?" Baker asked. "Did something happen on your way up?"

"No! I mean we made it to Friday."

Masaccio's mind was elsewhere as he stood at the window, looking out over the parking lot. "I can't believe how dark it is already."

"It's the darkest time of the year," Conrad said. "The eve of the winter solstice. As of tomorrow, the sun begins to make its return."

Conrad's mention of the solstice was a rude reminder for Baker that he'd let it slip his mind. The only consolation was that he hadn't missed it entirely.

"The solstice is tomorrow?" Perreault asked. "What time does it arrive, officially?"

"11:19 p.m.," Masaccio replied after consulting his phone.

"Perfect!" Angus said. "I can celebrate a Pines' win and then celebrate the return of ol' Sol."

"Actually, they're playing tonight *and* tomorrow," Baker said. "It's a back-to-back."

"Another one? Wow, they really cram in the games."

"They must be at the midpoint of the season by now," Conrad mused.

"Not yet," Baker replied. "After tonight's game, they've got six more. New Year's Eve in Minnesota will officially mark the end of the first half."

"That means New Year's Day is the fulcrum of the Pines' schedule," Conrad observed. "That's some pretty nice symmetry, I'd say."

"Hey, isn't that when the Toronto sports media share their mid-season Pines evaluations?" Mas asked.

Baker looked up at the mention of Pines' evaluations. There it was, the opening he was waiting for. "Listen everybody, I'm kind of curious . . . if the media guys and the experts were to evaluate Bakers' Coven thus far, I wonder what grade they'd give us."

"Ha, that's easy!" Angus said. "How about a D-minus?"

"Really? That's a little harsh, don't you think?"

"Not if you're grading our impact on the Pines' success. Face it, they were a sub-five-hundred team who had to fire their coach two months into the season. Sure, they've picked it up a bit since, but so far it's been a crappy year."

"I might have said the same thing," Baker admitted, "until I took a closer look." With that he extracted a sheet of paper from his yellow folder.

"Doing some homework, were you?" Conrad observed.

"Yeah, I cross-referenced our Coven sessions with Pines' game results, you know, across corresponding time frames. Believe or not, the results have been pretty positive. Let's not be so quick to give up on our rituals."

"Who said anything about giving up?" Angus said. "My point is maybe we should go *bigger*."

"Bigger?"

"Sure. Like, hold more sessions, increase the frequency of them. Maybe even take it outside."

"Outside?"

"Yeah, you know, pick a night when the moon is full—build a bonfire . . ."

"Easy there, Grindelwald, douse the flames for now," Conrad said, bringing the conversation back down to earth. "How about we hear what the man has to say?" He turned to Baker. "So, you evaluated our performance? What grade did you come up with?"

"Yeah, Professor Brooks, share your research," Angus prompted.

In truth, Baker felt less like a professor delivering a grade than a lawyer presenting evidence before the bench. The opportunity to share his findings—or make his argument—had arrived. He regarded his four seated colleagues as an inquisitorial tribunal, gravely prepared to bring down a binding sentence. He wondered if this would prove to be a pivotal moment in the Coven's brief lifespan. It might all come down to how he presented his case to the four esteemed members of the jury seated before him. Now he found himself wishing he had prepared some formal opening statements.

The floor was his. Baker smoothed out the page and cleared his throat.

"Keep in mind that I don't have any firm grades here. Actually, I'd call it more of a progress report. I wanted to see how we were trending."

"Very well, councillor. Proceed with your argument," Conrad instructed.

Baker smiled to himself at being compared to a lawyer, then he began. "OK, so, you might remember that we launched this thing in September at my place, prior to the start of the season."

"Oh yeah. That was when Perreault came up with 'Bakers' Coven' for our band name," Angus recalled.

"Exactly. Then a week later the Pines won their season opener against Ottawa. The very next day we held our second session, right here in the music room, which happened to be followed by a second Pines win."

Angus was impressed. "Woo hoo! Look at us, batting a thousand."

"Yes, but unfortunately we didn't gather again for about a month after that."

"Not formally, no," Perreault said. "We were busy producing the music video."

"Right. And the Pines' inconsistent results reflected as much." Baker took a moment to refer to his notes. "Let's see . . . three losses, two wins, a loss, a win, two losses, a win, and two more losses. A record of four, six, and two over that span. Certainly not what you'd see in a Cup contender."

"Maybe we shouldn't have gotten so hung up on making the video," Angus said.

"That was a lot of work, though, all on behalf of the team," Mas declared. "It's got to count for something, doesn't it?"

"I agree," Baker said. "The effort that went into our video sessions was greater than any one of our rituals. But here's something to consider." He paused to make sure his next point was delivered with clarity. "The time we spent working on the video coincided with the time when the Pines were experiencing strife and mired in a general malaise."

"Are you implying that anything we did at that time would have been in vain?"

"I'm saying that the coaching change was something already in the works. Therefore, we were either working against the forces of change—which was probably not the best thing to do—or aiding and abetting the eventual decision to fire the coach."

"Fire the coach? That's *negative* spell casting," Conrad observed. "We made a pledge *not* to engage in that."

"You're right. But let's leave that question unanswered for now," Baker said, continuing with his summation. "The next time we gathered was the day after Halloween—the Samhain session at my place."

"Ooh, yeah, the room with more candles than the Phantom's lair," Perreault recalled.

"Yup. And after that, the Pines won three straight."

"Holy shit, is that right?" The news was like a revelation for Angus. "Why didn't we realize it at the time?"

"Wait, I'm not done yet," Baker went on. "Next came the misery of a six-game losing streak, and it wasn't until we gathered again here in the music room—the same day Xander Galahad announced the coaching change—that they managed to win again, three straight to be precise." He consulted his notes again. "Then a loss, a win, and two more losses before Perreault, Angus, and I got together informally two weeks ago. That resulted in two wins, then a loss. Our most recent session, last Friday with Mas, produced two more wins." Baker looked up from his notes with a shrug. "And that brings us to our present gathering here tonight."

The others sat and waited, anticipating something more from him.

"So, what do you think? Am I grasping at straws or is there any validity to this?"

"It would be easy to dismiss your findings as entirely circumstantial," Conrad replied. He sounded like a stern courtroom judge before shifting gears to adopt a defiant, rascally tone. "But then, who gives a shit? We don't have to validate what we're doing to anyone but ourselves."

"Like you said at the start," Perreault replied, "it's better if we believe our rituals actually have an impact."

"No shit, man," Angus said. "After hearing your progress report, I'm convinced—Bakers' Coven magic produces Pines wins."

This declaration touched off an energetic debate about what it all could mean and where it all could lead, until the discussion swung around to the plan for that evening's session. Through it all, Baker kept silent, content to watch and listen as though he was the proud patriarch at an annual clan gathering, presiding over the festivities while everyone enjoyed the blessings of health, happiness, and prosperity. He reflected on how it was only a few months ago that he was contemplating whether it'd be wise to even suggest spell casting as an activity, and now here they were, enthusiastically discussing which of his songs to perform in the ceremony like it was a customary thing. He was jolted out of his musings when Conrad looked at the clock on the wall and saw the time.

"Hey, gang, I'm having a blast here, but I have two hours before home time. Shall we play some music?"

CHAPTER TWENTY-TWO
EMPTY GREETINGS

*Now the stores are full of shoppers
And I'm checking out the deals
Mama's at home preparing for our Christmas meal*

"Let's rock this joint!" Angus exclaimed, once it had been established that they would close out the evening with two songs to charm the Pines.

"'Another Time' gets my vote," Perreault said.

"OK, but I have a special request," Mas cut in. "Last night I was tinkling on the piano and happened to reacquaint myself with 'Play A Game In June.' I'd love to perform that one with you."

"Count me in," she replied enthusiastically, then appeared to survey the room. "But we need to set the mood." She turned to Baker, "Did you happen to bring candles?"

Baker stared back at her, immobile, as if waiting for the synapses to fire. "Ho—lee—crap," was all he could say. Those three syllables encapsulated the shittiness of the day because he'd left the candles at home. He pictured himself standing in the kitchen that morning, prevaricating over a box of pillar candles on his counter, followed by what he thought at the time was an expedient executive decision to *not* bring them along. Now he saw it as a nothing more than a misguided choice made in haste.

Looking to make the best of things, he went over to the tiny room where the instruments were stored, flicked the light switch, and left the door open a crack. "Although it lacks the atmosphere of candlelight, we'll have to settle for a bit of indirect light from offstage," he said. Then he turned off the main bank of overhead fluorescents, leaving only the light from the instrument room to filter in.

Conrad had come prepared with a few words to open the service, after which Bakers' Coven delivered a performance that was so inspired it could have carried the Pines through their next few games every bit as effectively as a weeks' worth of motivational locker-room speeches from the head coach.

Following the ceremony the room was crackling with energy. Seeing that they had time to spare, Perreault suggested they carry on and perform a couple of the Christmas songs they had been deprived of playing earlier that day.

"Great idea," Masaccio said. "We've got five to choose from."

"Can we do 'Breadlines'?" Angus pleaded.

Conrad acceded on one condition. "After that we need to play 'Empty Greetings.'"

"Seriously?" Baker asked.

"What, you've got objections?"

"Of course not, but a few days ago you said it deserves the right kind of audience, remember?"

"That's right. We'll be playing for the people that truly appreciate the genius of it: ourselves."

Baker couldn't help but smile. It was the second time in a week that a comment from Conrad had carried high praise for his efforts. It made him recall the after-school session they conducted this past Monday, when the four of them had played for their lead guitarist, seeking feedback on which three songs should make the final cut for their Christmas set. Because his opinion meant a lot, it felt a bit like they were auditioning in front of the old pro. Thinking back now, Baker had never before seen the man respond quite like he had that afternoon in the music room.

* * * * *

Conrad was first in the room on Monday and once everyone else had arrived he wasted no time catching up on the Coven's progress in his absence.

"Masaccio tells me you guys got together for some spell casting last week."

"It was pretty informal, but yeah, we did," Baker replied. "And the week before as well, but it was just myself, Angus, and Perreault."

"We felt horrible without you," Perreault admitted, sounding penitent. "It was just an impromptu mini session, really. We almost weren't going to go through with it."

"Good God! Please don't ever think that you need to wait for me," Conrad instructed. "What'd you play anyway?"

"On Friday we played 'Go Green,' and the week before? Umm . . . what did we play?"

"The 'Happy' song," Angus replied from across the room.

"And now I understand that you have some Christmas songs for Friday's assembly?"

"We have five to choose from," Baker explained, handing Conrad the lyrics to each song. "But is there enough time for you to learn them?"

Conrad was magnanimous, as if he understood how significant these songs were for Baker. "I'll be ready; don't you worry. Now, let's hear the first one on your list."

EMPTY GREETINGS

"We're in luck with this one because it's already in our repertoire. It's The Weakerthans' 'This is a Fire Door Never Leave Open.'"

Conrad pointed to his song sheet. "Is this the one? 'Breadlines and Christmas Dreams'?"

"Yes. I turned it into a comment on how Christmas is a time for food drives and replenishing food banks for those less fortunate in our communities, but deep down there's this acknowledgement that we could do more, and so we're left facing uncomfortable choices."

"Wow, you got all that in there?"

"Uh-huh."

"OK, then. Let's hear it."

"Alright, but don't be too critical. I'm playing *your* part here."

"No pressure, Mr. Brooks. I'll just sit back and listen."

Baker made a visual check with Angus and Mas, both of whom were poised and ready on drums and bass, respectively. As usual, Perreault sang lead, and since no backing vocals were required, Baker just needed to worry about his responsibilities on guitar, which, as it happened, required that he kick off the song with a simple six-bar chord intro that led into the vocals.

> *Breadlines snake toward the counter of the dining room*
> *Half-illuminated faces turn to hide their fear*
> *You bring in cans of food to ease their hunger once a yearly*
> *I bring out change to match donations, got to play this Christmas game*
> *Our greetings sound the same*
> *Full of all our feelings for greater change*
> *That all those bread lines shorten sometime*
>
> *You say "Deck the Halls" then also send best wishes out to*
> *Those less fortunate for whom we'll maybe stop to pray*
> *Somewhere sympathy is more than just a cursive greeting*
> *Somewhere someone says we're sorry*
> *Someone's making plans to pay*
> *But tell me it's OK*
> *Tell me anything or show me there's a pull*
> *Unassailable*
> *That will lead them clear of the dark and cold*
> *With benevolence that they've never known*
> *Or they knew when they were young and can't remember*
> *Where a small plea seeks generosity*

> *Though my conscience knows what my silence brings*
> *I still hesitate (as mixed emotions take me)*
> *To bring our dreams together*
>
> *I still hear bells at night when the wind is right*
> *I remember Christmas dreams, lick my lips and sing*
> *Songs that never end with a sour chord*
> *With my memories of the Christmas lore*
> *Or the fireplace that we kept stockings over*
> *And I love this time with the darkened skies*
> *But the faces, hands that I can't walk by*
> *Oh why can't I forget these people*
> *Who've nothing we call home?*
>
> *Breadlines snake toward the counter of the dining room*
> *Half-illuminated faces turn to hide their fear*

Perreault delivered the last two lines haltingly, with respectful detachment, as if watching the scene from the wings, while only Mas continued to play, plucking at his base like a heartbeat, and then he too stopped when the final word was spoken. After a brief pause the four of them looked out at Conrad in silence. He stared back, nodding solemnly.

"Powerful stuff." He stood up to emphasize his point. "That was great. Everything about it works for me. And Angus, nice job. It sounds like you're having fun back there."

"Thanks, Conrad. That's always been one of my favourites."

"OK then, what's next?"

Baker introduced the next song, which he titled "Empty Greetings," after The Weakerthans' "Tournament of Hearts."

Unfortunately, they started in rough fashion. The first take saw Angus miss his cue from the get-go. On their second attempt, they got as far as the end of the first verse, but then Perreault tripped over the six syllables of "my favourite Santa." On the third try, Baker came in late, and everything broke down from there.

"Jesus, Baker! Get your head out of your ass!" Conrad said.

"Sorry, sorry!"

From that point on, Conrad took it upon himself to conduct. "Let's try it again. Everybody ready now? Angus? Baker? OK. One and two and three and *four*."

This time they began on cue. Conrad listened and followed along with his copy of the lyrics.

> *Now the stores are full of shoppers*
> *And I'm checking out the deals*

EMPTY GREETINGS

Mama's at home preparing for our Christmas meal
So I pull out my last fifty, and I buy that pink bathrobe
Maybe get a double-double for the snowy road
And I wave to my favourite Santa, with his yellow beard and all
But I'm sure I'll see more like him at other malls

I approach a diorama
Holy Family and three Wise Men
Figures of shepherds wandering in Bethlehem
And I'm kneeling at the stable
As the church bells peal their call
Dance down the street to Jingle Bells and Deck the Halls

And the snow squeaks with the question
Wonders why I'm not at home
Where she waits beside a silent telephone
Ladles gravy onto turkey all alone
Have to stop myself from buying
Up this table full of merchandise to yell
Why?

As he sat listening to his friends perform, an odd expression blossomed across Conrad's face. When Perreault built up to the chorus and rang out the word "Why," he rose out of his seat, not unlike King George II must have done the first time he heard the "Hallelujah Chorus" from Handel's *Messiah*. The other four cast inquiring glances his way but managed to play through the distraction.

Why can't I ever shop for what I want to say?
Why is it not enough to afford to pay?
When I buy for Christmas Day
I'm always going halfway

Enough! No, better get the yellow sweater
Enough! No, get her boots with better leather
Enough! No, longer hours in December
Enough! No, tell her that we'll get together

Enough! No, never better winter weather
Enough! No, stellar Peller for her cellar
Enough! No, laser printer, paper shredder
Enough! No, better send these Christmas letters

When Cheers Are Not Enough

Now my parcels they all glimmer
And I smile sheepishly
Mama's staring, glaring disapprovingly
From her frown I sense that all she wants is me
And I know she's always waiting
For the Christmas I can't give her
But tell me—

Why, why should I never shop for what I want to say?
Try as I might I'm never gonna see the day
When I take the time this year
To gift my time and love
No need for cash to pay
But I'm always going halfway

Enough! No, better get a redder sweater
Enough! No, line up at the Auto Teller
Enough! No, better sales are on at Zellers
Enough!

When the song ended in abrupt fashion with the final "Enough," Conrad was still standing, looking at the words on the sheet in his hands.

"Wow. I've got tears in my eyes," he said, looking up at Baker. "That's brilliant stuff, sir. Well done! Well done, indeed."

Baker was taken aback by such effusive praise, especially considering the source. "Now I'm confused. Are you referring to my playing? I was the worst one of the lot. I must've made half a dozen mistakes."

"No, you idiot. You know I'd never compliment you on your guitar playing. It's your lyrics." Then he looked at Perreault. "I mean, it helps that you express them so perfectly, of course."

"Thanks, Conrad."

"What, in particular, do you like about the words?" Baker asked.

"The song gets right to the heart of a first-world Christmas," Conrad explained. Then he commenced to wax lyrical, delivering something resembling a soliloquy, but instead of Hamlet contemplating the skull of Yorick, it was Conrad addressing his page of lyrics. "The perennial battle between choosing to spend *money* on loved ones and choosing to spend *time* with them. Often we can't do both, so we feel guilty if we fail at either. But it's not until we stop and gather with family that we understand where the true value lies. Christmas charity begins at home, and that manifests itself as time. Take it from a guy who's lost his mother. When I sing along with these words, I get a lump in my throat. Yes, they're cute and quirky, but I'm drawn to them. They get to the heart of a sensitive topic in an oddball, irreverent way."

Everyone contemplated his words in silence until Angus burst the Shakespearean bubble.

"I gotta ask: what's the Zellers reference?"

"You don't know about Zellers stores?"

"Only vaguely. But my point is, they don't exist anymore, do they?"

"Right. They went tits up about five years ago," Conrad confirmed.

"So, why include them in the song?"

"Because it rhymed," Baker replied. "Besides, it's got a nostalgic ring to it, dontcha think?"

"So, I guess that's one we'll do for the Christmas assembly then?" Mas said.

He was greeted with enthusiastic declarations of approval from Angus and Perreault, but these were rudely broken off.

"Hell no!" Conrad replied.

The others fell quiet and looked at each other quizzically.

"Wait a minute. Didn't you say you liked it?"

"I love it. But we can't do it."

"Why the hell not?"

"Don't you see? It's too good for the type of audience you'll get at the Christmas assembly. Most of the message will be lost on them. We may as well just play it with the original words, but then it won't be Christmasy.

"But who gives a shit if the audience gets it?" Angus objected. "It's a good tune, and we'll have fun playing it." His point was endorsed by everyone but Conrad.

"No, it deserves a better moment, a better audience. Trust me, you'll come away from the experience disappointed, and I wouldn't want to see that happen with material like this. Be patient with this one please. Let's hear the next option."

*****

Baker was nudged out of his ruminations on Monday's session and back to the present when Perreault made an observation.

"Hold on . . . we forgot Saint Cecilia," she said. "Let's sing to her, even if it's a little belated."

Following the musical tribute to Saint Cecilia, the Coven proceeded to bring off the Christmas songs with such flair and proficiency—Conrad's contributions playing a big part in it—that they could only ponder what might have been had the assembly proceeded as scheduled.

Recognizing that their time together was coming to a close, Perreault sprang up from her chair. "Time for Christmas presents!" she declared, then fairly skipped to the door to retrieve her grocery bag. Conrad took the cue and followed her to get his box as well—albeit not with the same childlike enthusiasm.

"Here you go, guys," she said. "Merry Christmas!" She revealed four colourful gift bags, each of which contained a homemade tree ornament wrapped in tissue paper along with a Christmas card, which contained a Sugar Watson's gift card. "They're copper-wire figurines shaped to look like you guys on your instruments. I just put wings on them to turn them into little rock 'n' rolling Christmas angels."

"I didn't know we were doing a gift exchange," Baker complained.

"Yeah, me neither," Angus echoed.

"It's nothing, really. My mother and I make Christmas ornaments every year. Consider them tokens of my gratitude."

"*Your* gratitude? *We're* the ones who are grateful."

"OK, then. Let's accept that we're all equally grateful for each other. But I can't imagine any rookie teacher having as much fun as I've had this year."

Angus was thrilled with his ornament. "Hey, that's me, wailin' on the skins."

"These are wonderful, Perreault," Baker said. "You could start your own little cottage industry."

Conrad, meanwhile, gruffly presented a bottle of wine to each member of the Coven.

"What the hell, Conrad?" Baker exclaimed. "What's with the wine gifts?"

"What can I say? I won third prize in the staff wine draw yesterday. Took home fifteen bottles."

"Wow! Congratulations!"

"It's very kind of you to think of us, Conrad," Perreault said.

"Oh, I deserve no credit. It was all Winnie's idea. Before I left the house this morning, this box was waiting for me by the door. You're all lucky my lovely wife thinks of you more than I do. Merry Christmas, assholes."

"Jokes aside, Mas, I just realized this will be your last Christmas in Canada," Perreault observed. "Doing anything special?"

"You know, I haven't given it much thought. Sal makes sure that the family enjoys a typical Martha Stewart/Trish Romance kind of Christmas."

"Sounds pretty fancy. What about you, Baker? What are you doing for Christmas?"

"I'll visit my mother and my sister for a couple days."

"Nice!"

"What would really be nice is if we could establish our next Coven sessions before we leave."

"Hang on," Conrad interjected, "didn't we decide to meet up over the last weekend of the holiday?"

"That's right, we did." Baker said. "But I was thinking maybe we could gather a couple times over the holidays—you know, in addition to the last weekend."

"Sorry, Baker, next week is shot for me," Perreault said. "I'm going to Montreal with my folks on Tuesday, and we won't be back till Friday."

"Moi aussi," Mas said. "Next week is all family, all the time."

"I think it's safe to say next week is out," Conrad said. "Heck, even the Pines will get three days off."

"OK then, how about the weekend?"

"Sorry, I can't." It was Conrad again. "We're out of town all weekend and won't be back till Monday. But nothing is stopping you four from gathering without me."

"Nah, I don't think so. I'd prefer if we all were involved. What about Tuesday?"

"Tuesday is New Year's Eve," Perreault observed.

"If we got together during the week," Mas said, "then I wouldn't be inclined to do it again on the weekend."

It seemed that every suggestion that Baker offered was shot down. Then Conrad finally put the issue to bed. "Why don't we just meet over the weekend, as we originally planned?"

When it was clear that Conrad's proposal would receive general consent among the others, Baker's initial dismay was palpable, but he recovered quickly, having trained himself to deal with such disappointment through previous experience. Thereafter they commenced to gathering up their Christmas gift detritus and music paraphernalia before exchanging final holiday wishes. Baker slowly made his way up to his classroom to collect his things, determined to put a happy face on an otherwise mediocre end to the week. He felt a level of shame for having overlooked the arrival of the winter solstice and the celebration of Yule, and felt cheated by being denied another chance to play for an audience—this time by the weatherman. He also felt tired. It would be a relief to forget about school for a couple of weeks and get his life back in some semblance of order. But then he realized that Tuesday was Christmas Eve, and, not having done a stitch of shopping, he knew that at some point in the next three days he'd have to merge onto the Christmas freeway, which was gridlocked with holiday buyers. He hoped he wasn't setting himself up to catch a cold.

On the bright side, the band was in good spirits, and that evening's session had proved particularly satisfying. He could also look forward to feasting on some Mighty Pines hockey over the holidays. The team was rolling, and the next handful of games were all winnable, increasing Baker's desire to see the Pines scoop up points in bunches.

And what the hell? Maybe, just maybe, he'd strike up the courage to arrange something with Perreault over the break.

Feeling re-energized, he prepared to head home, arranging his bags and guitar case in a way that would require just one trip out to the car. Pushing out of his little office, he made sure the door locked behind him, then fairly floated down the three sets of stairs to the front atrium, singing The Weakerthans' "Tournament of Hearts" and not caring if anyone heard him.

Hopping off the last step, he reached the landing and grabbed the nearest door handle, swung it open, and caught sight of two people at the far end of the atrium ahead of him. It was Perreault and Angus on their way out of the school, sharing a laugh, almost giddy. Angus was leaning in close, saying something to her. She cracked up in response and playfully pushed back, throwing him off balance, but then she reached out and grabbed his elbow to steady him and put an arm around his shoulders. Baker, who was headed in the same direction, froze in place and held his breath, partly from the shock and disappointment of what he'd witnessed and partly to avoid being discovered. More than anything at that moment, he needed to make himself invisible.

Giving them a head start so as not to intrude on their intimate chumminess, he watched Perreault put her hip into the push bar of one of the doors, holding it open for Angus as he continued on through. Just then she happened to look back across the atrium, locking eyes with Baker. Reflexively, he dropped his gaze, as if he'd been studying the floor the whole time, and turned left toward the other end of the school. Taking one last furtive look, he saw her smile and wave but pretended not to notice as he vanished down the hall.

For her part, Perreault was certain Baker had seen her, so she was perplexed by the evident snub. She focused on the spot where he had just disappeared. "And a Merry Christmas to you too," she muttered. Then she turned and continued through the door to catch up with Angus.

"What'd you say?" Angus asked.

"Oh, nothing. I was just offering Christmas greetings to any spirits that might still be in the school."

"A Christmas greeting to an empty school?" He laughed. "Well, that's weird."

* * * * *

The next morning saw Baker absentmindedly putzing around in his kitchen. More than anything, he wished he hadn't witnessed Perreault and Angus leaving the school together because now the image was haunting him. (Going home and watching the Pines invade Madison Square Garden and beat the New York Empires hadn't done much to soften the blow.) For the past few weeks, he had been concocting scenarios that had him engaging Perreault in conversation that was irresistibly witty and charming. It was all perfectly planned—in his mind, anyway. He had simply been waiting for the right moment. And yet he realized that in waiting he may have missed his window of opportunity, which brought to mind all the cliched idioms; coming late to the party, or how he had been beaten to the punch, or how he could put his plans to bed because that train had left the station.

He sorely needed to get out of the house and clear his head, find something to distract him. Standing there in the kitchen, he stared at a wall calendar and began counting the days before the return to school, when he saw Carly Romanet's business card tucked into the lower corner of the calendar frame. He reached out and removed it for closer inspection.

Baker turned over the business card and considered the number she had scribbled on the back, then set it down, walked across the room to his phone, and dialled. By the third ring, the other end picked up.

"Hello."

"Hi . . . Helen? It's Baker. I hope I'm not calling at a bad time . . ."

CHAPTER TWENTY-THREE
ON THE NICE LIST

Saturday, December 21

Saturday's game against Detroit gave the hometown fans at Nova Tank Arena a chance to cheer on another winning effort from their heroes, who made it four wins straight and six out of seven. The team was definitely rolling now and Coney Nation was, for the first time this season, being treated to a stretch of Pines hockey that was meeting all the expectations that had been placed upon a squad with so much talent up and down the lineup.

In the Eastern Time Zone, the winter solstice arrived at 11:19 p.m. on this, the longest night of the year, leading into the first day of winter and the Wiccan season of Yule. Over in Salisbury, England, nature worshippers of all stripes gathered to greet the sun which cast its rays across the ancient rocks of Stonehenge at 8:04 a.m. on Sunday, December 22. (We can only assume that Dorcas Blanchard's friend, Professor Ravenstone, was in attendance, celebrating with them.)

It was nearly 10:00 am Sunday morning when the klezmer ringtone of Angus's cell phone sounded. It was on the verge of playing itself out before he picked up.

"Y'ello."

"Hi, Angus."

"Baker! What's up, my man?"

"Not much since I saw you two days ago. Did you catch the Pines last night?"

"Damn right. That was a solid win. Four in a row, baby!"

"The snipers came through and the goaltending held."

"I suppose, but most of the credit should go to Bakers' Coven," Angus crowed. "Thanks to us the Pines are rolling."

"Things are looking good, that's for sure. I just wish we could meet this week to hold a session."

"You know I'd be there. But since it's not happening, we'll have to make do with cheering them on through the TV screen."

"That's actually why I called," Baker said. "Are you free tomorrow? I thought you might like to come by and watch them make it five in a row over some pizza and wings—and beer, of course."

"But I thought you weren't a fan of 'watch' parties."

"I know, I know. But it's just the two of us, and I won't feel awkward if things go bad cuz I know you can handle my mood swings."

"True enough. Alright, buddy. I'll be there just before seven."

"No, no, not seven. It's an afternoon affair: the Coney Family Classic. You know, lots of families and kids in attendance—a two o'clock matinee."

"Oh man, I had no idea. I can't, Baker. Not if it's in the afternoon. Perreault and I are doing our own matinee."

Baker's throat thickened. "Who? Perreault?"

"Yeah. We're going to a movie."

It took every ounce of Baker's will to prevent the sound of dejection from creeping into his voice. He had to be careful how to respond to Angus's news. Sounding disappointed would not do (although he was decidedly that), nor did he want to come across sounding delighted. The only response he could generate was a noncommittal "That's sounds nice. What movie are you going to see?"

What Angus said in reply didn't really matter, of course, because none of the conversation from that point on registered with Baker. He was sure of one thing, though: the news had effectively thrown the equivalent of a wet tree-skirt over his Christmas plans. He'd be cheering the Pines all by himself tomorrow, which wasn't the end of the world, but it was also likely that the only female companionship he could look forward to during the holiday would be in the form of his mother and his sister.

* * * * *

Two hours later, Baker was pulling into the driveway at the Nella residence. He had called Helen the previous night to see if she and Allen were amenable to a visit some time over the holiday. (Somehow, Carly Romanet's business card had called to mind the fact that he hadn't touched base with Helen since he had last spoken to her on Remembrance Day.) He'd apologized for allowing so many weeks to pass before contacting her, but Helen wouldn't hear of it, expressing instead how his call was a welcome surprise and asking if he would be available to come over for brunch on Sunday, at noon. For Baker, the timing of the visit couldn't have been more perfect, forcing him to get out of the house and take his mind off Perreault and Angus and the thought of what might have been if not for his frigging inaction.

Standing on the Nella's wrap-around porch, Baker could see they'd enjoyed decorating for the festive season (he attributed it more to Helen than Allen). The entire length of the wood railing was draped in garland made from fresh cedar sprigs. Two large floor lanterns were set on either side of the front door, which was adorned with a large wreath of thick greenery, pinecones, red berries, and a hand-tied red ribbon. Helen greeted him at the door, wearing a holiday-themed apron upon which she was patting her hands. She gave him a warm hug, invited him inside, found a place for his coat and shoes, and then led the way to the kitchen. On the way they passed the living room, which was dominated by a majestic nine-foot balsam fir decked out in a style that reminded Baker of Christmas in Bavaria. A few potted Norfolk pines were placed strategically in nooks and corners, under which faux Christmas parcels could be found, wrapped in brown paper and tied with colourful ribbon.

"It's just the two of us this weekend," Helen said, referring to herself and Allen. "Marinelle went up to Kingston to visit with our daughter, Eleanor, who's in her third year at Queens."

"Marinelle? You mean Cubby's sister?"

"Yes. She's been living with us for the past little while, since the start of the school year."

"Living with you?"

The question hung there for a moment before Helen explained. "After Cal died, well, Marinelle took it pretty hard. Her coping strategy was to sow some wild oats. Unfortunately, it involved some recreational drug use, going out with friends till all hours, sleeping over at people's houses—people you can only hope are friends. Anyway, David was afraid she could get hurt."

"David? You mean Marinelle's father?"

"Yes. He thought it might be good for her to come live with us for a bit—as a change of scenery, you know? That was back in September."

"Where is he now?"

"His job took him out to BC, to Victoria. He's an architect. His firm secured a contract to design some municipal buildings."

"So now she's living here, with you and Allen?"

"Yes. Just until David returns."

Baker surveyed the room. "Where's Allen now?"

"Good question. He mentioned something about a headlight on the Jeep, so he might be in the garage."

Their discourse was interrupted when the oven timer beeped, signalling that the dish within required attending to. It was then that Baker sensed his chatter might be serving as nothing more than a distraction for Helen, so he offered to help in come capacity.

"You can start by going into the fridge and helping yourself to a beverage," she directed.

"That's not exactly what I meant."

"I've got things under control here," Helen assured him as she extracted a tray of roasted vegetables from the oven and transferred them into a serving dish. "But if it'll ease your conscience, you can slice the baguette that's on the bread board there. While you're doing that, I'll go find Allen."

* * * * *

Not surprisingly, lunch was delicious. The conversation, however, was awkward in that it was primarily a two-person affair, restricted to the input of Helen and Baker while Allen hardly said a word. Helen was spot on with her description of Allen. He was withdrawn, reticent. Although he was there in body, in spirit he was somewhere else. Almost six months had passed since Cubby's death, but Allen was still putting up barriers. Helen had thought a visit from Baker might set in motion the process of bringing down those walls and that perhaps they could rediscover some of the chemistry that existed between them the last time he had visited.

When they had finished eating, Allen helped clear the table and then made for the basement. Not certain what his next move should be, Baker looked at Helen, who nodded for him to follow Allen downstairs. She remained in the kitchen, busying herself with putting things away, so the boys could have some time together.

Baker descended the steps into the basement with a light bounce. Allen was already settled on the couch, locked into the TV, which was tuned to an NBA game. Electing to engage Allen in a bit of companionable discourse, Baker tried revisiting some of the topics they had discussed the last time he was there, beginning with Notre Dame Football.

"Boy, it's a good thing the Fightin' Irish aren't playing today." He patted his stomach. "I'm so stuffed I'd puke if I had to do push-ups now."

Allen barely looked at him, emitting a kind of grunt.

"I was seriously considering a personalized licence plate," Baker said, moving on to the next topic. "I figured if LQQK was taken, I could go with a variation on that theme. Something like GOT2LQQK or HAVALQQK."

Then he brought up historic European landmarks. "You know, it's funny. No sooner did you tell me about Prague and the Charles Bridge than I kept hearing good things about the Czech Republic as a must-see tourist destination."

In every case he got grunts and one-word answers in response. In the end he tried plain-spoken directness. "Look, Helen tells me something's been bothering you since Cubby passed away. She's concerned."

Allen finally directed his attention away from the TV and toward Baker. "What, isn't a guy allowed to mourn the death of a loved one anymore?"

Although it was a bit of an attack, Baker was good with any reply from Allen. "Yes, of course. But she's worried about how hard this has hit you."

"Listen, nobody needs to lecture me about the stages of grief and which one I should be at."

"That's fine. But she's wondering if it's not something more. Getting it off your chest could present a solution—you never know. I think you'll find I have an incredibly open mind."

"Look, Baker, I consider you a friend, and I trust you, but there are some things I won't share even with my wife and family. I'm sorry, but you'll just have to figure it out on your own . . . or not. To be honest, I really don't care."

It was clear that Baker had broached a toxic subject. Allen's defence mechanism was to turn on a personal fog machine and disappear into the mist.

Some instinct told Baker not to quit, however. Allen had provided a clue, after all, saying "he'd have to figure it out on his own." That meant Baker just needed to dispel the offending vapours to attain some clarity. At the same time, he sensed Allen's resolve in the matter and did not want to come across as disrespectful. He was willing to pursue the matter only if there was a possibility it would help Allen reconcile himself with Cubby's death.

"OK then. I'll figure it out on my own," Baker said. "I'm sure I can manage that. But point me in some direction because I don't want to waste my time or yours. I think I can safely say the sanctity of your secret will remain intact."

"My secret?"

"Well, that's just my word for it. Look, I'm not going to pretend I know what I'm doing. Fact is, I'm here as a friend."

Allen looked at Baker for what seemed like an eternity, then turned. "Do you know what he said?"

"What who said?"

"Cubby. It was the last time he spoke to me. He was in his hospital bed. He would be dead in a couple of days." Allen was standing by the fireplace mantle, focused on a picture of his nephew. In the photo, Cubby was in his hockey gear, leaning over his stick, eyes hungry, challenging the camera, as if he were ready to win a fifty-fifty puck battle. Allen shook his head. "He could hardly keep his eyes open. I leaned over the bed, so he wouldn't feel the need to turn his head. He could barely focus, but he looked at me . . . and he said, 'I'm sorry, Uncle Allen. I'm sorry I couldn't finish the season. I'll try to get better. I promise.' He apologized. Can you believe it? Cubby . . . felt he needed to apologize . . . to me! Then he promised he'd try to get better. I'm still not sure if he was referring to beating the cancer or improving his hockey skills."

There was a long moment of silence before Allen turned away from the photograph to face Baker. "Have you visited Cubby . . . at his gravesite I mean?"

Baker wondered if the question was meant to kindle some guilt in him. "No. I can't say that I have. But what's that got to do with this particular business?"

"You should go see him."

"Sure, OK. Where is he resting?"

"A local cemetery called Heaven's Gate. Heard of it?"

"I think so. It's in the north end of town, isn't it?"

"That's right."

"I guess you must go fairly regularly."

"Actually, no—not since the funeral. I figure if I need to say anything to Cubby—" Allen paused and turned, making a gesture as if he were proudly showing the room to Baker. "I'll do it from right here. Don't get me wrong; his resting place is beautiful. Lots of mature trees, very peaceful. But my fondest memories come from the time we spent together in this very room. Talking, working out, watching hockey and football games on TV—" The memories elicited the faintest of smiles from Allen, but then it disappeared, replaced by a sober mien. "Go visit his gravesite, Baker. If you're looking for answers, it's the best clue I can offer right now."

Monday, December 23

Monday's tilt in Toronto against the Quebec Citadelles would be the final game before a four-day Christmas break for the Pines. It was a matinee, with the early start time being part of a Mighty Pines promotion called the Coney Family Classic. As might be expected, with the Pines on a roll and having won six of their last seven games, Nova Tank Arena was packed with a sizeable contingent of festively-charged parents and children. The early minutes of the game were scripted perfectly as the Pines went up 3-0. It seemed at the time that the quality of Toronto's young stars would be on full display.

Then Quebec proceeded to score the next five goals.

It was a good thing for the Pines that there were three periods in a hockey game. They rallied to dominate the next two frames, outscoring the Citadelles five to one and earning them a thrilling 8-6 win. For Toronto fans it was a perfect pre-Christmas gift.

For the coaches, however—well, as Boris Duggan and his staff could attest, there was nothing like a fourteen goal game to test one's nerves.

Whatever the final goal count, the Mighty Pines had won their fifth straight game, and Coney Nation families could go home and snuggle in their beds while visions of sugar plums and Clarence Cups danced in their heads. Yes, for hometown fans at Nova Tank Arena, the days leading up to Christmas did not lack for excitement: full of emotional shifts, anxious moments, absolute horror, and ultimate joy, not unlike witnessing Santa transfer one's name from the nice list to the naughty list and back again. For now, the Mighty Pines seemed to be enjoying membership on the nice list. Christmas was a day away, and Boxing Day would bring a new moon. Celestially speaking, things were looking up for the boys in green and white.

CHAPTER TWENTY-FOUR
MATCHMAKING

No sooner had the final horn sounded on the Coney Family Classic game than Masaccio and his twin daughters, Lily and Hazel, were out in the driveway, geared up to play some serious ball hockey, still feeling the high of the comeback win they had just witnessed on television. They were joined a short while later by Mas's wife, Sal, who positioned herself behind the net where her husband was playing goal in order to discuss an issue that had come up.

"Sylvia just called me. There may have to be a change of plans."

"Don't tell me," Mas groaned. "She broke up with Anthony again?"

"Is she that predictable?"

"What is it, the fourth time now?"

"I've lost count. Regardless, this impacts our New Year's Eve plans."

"Are you implying that we might be able to enjoy ourselves now?"

"C'mon, Mas, don't be cruel."

"It's also true." With the quickness of a ninja, Mas flicked an elbow at a shot taken by Hazel, redirecting the ball out to the front lawn and in the process thwarting what the girls thought was a sure goal.

"The point is, I don't think Sylvia is keen on attending the dinner dance without a date."

"Meaning if we find a substitute for Anthony, she would go? What am I, a matchmaker now?" Mas proceeded to belt out the song from *Fiddler on the Roof*, demonstrating his best Topol baritone. "Matchmaker, matchmaker make me a match..."

Sal had to speak up to be heard over her husband's voice. "Not necessarily. But if you have any ideas, we're all ears."

Mas stopped singing. "We?"

"Me and Sylvia. I'm just trying to help out my lovelorn cousin."

Lily wound up and fired a slap shot at the net, but Mas coolly snatched the ball out of the air with his glove, going so far as to talk a bit of friendly smack to his daughters. Lily and Hazel returned it in kind as he rolled the tennis ball back out to them. They retreated down the driveway a bit, passing the ball back and forth, then regrouped for another attack on the net. Mas, feeling sprightly and quick, paraded a bit in goal, playfully goading the twins and showing off for Sal. Ever the consummate multitasker, he continued the conversation with his wife as the girls closed in. "So you're saying Sylvia would be OK with me setting her up?"

"Let's say we're keeping all our options open."

"There's that 'we' again."

Hazel tried to go forehand, backhand, five-hole, but her dad shut the door in time and flicked the tennis ball back out to Lily, wagging a gloved finger at both of them.

"We were wondering if you could think of anyone from HMV who's single, eligible, and good-looking."

Mas stood up and half-turned toward Sal, "Is that all?" Then he took a shot flush on the ear. "Ow! What the heck was that?"

"Sorry, Daddy, I was trying to go top shelf," Hazel replied.

"Not top shelf," Lily corrected. "Top cheese. You were going top cheese."

"Yeah, I was trying to go top cheese, like Mason Andrews. Besides, you should keep your eye on the ball. That's what you always tell us."

"It's a good thing I'm wearing my Mighty Pines toque. By the way, how much do I owe you two?"

Lily was the bookkeeper. "We've got six goals so far. That's three dollars each."

"Six goals? Really? I think you miscounted. I don't remember letting in six goals."

"I deflected the first goal between your pads," Hazel said. "Then I batted a rebound out of the air, remember?"

"She's right," Lily said. "And I scored the next four, two on really wicked slap shots, then a deke five-hole, then a backhander over your glove hand. Remember? You were all stretched out on the ground, and I flicked it up and over." Both girls giggled as Lily did a little dance, re-enacting the goal. "That's six."

"You tell him, girls," Sal said. "Don't get cheated."

Mas turned and winked at Sal, then motioned for the girls to back up to the end of the driveway before passing the ball out to them. "Young, eligible, and good-looking, huh?" he said, resuming their conversation. "The first person who comes to mind is Angus."

"I didn't say young, I said *single*. Keep in mind that we're talking Sylvia here. What is Angus, anyway, twenty something? She can be fussy about the age of her men. Personally, if it were my choice, I'd be happy to go to the dance with Angus, but I already have a date."

"Yup. You're the lucky lady who gets to spend New Year's with the best goalkeeper on the block. As for Sylvia, what's up with her, anyway?"

MATCHMAKING

"Simple. Sylvia is thirty-one. She's got something against going out with guys younger than her."

"I'm going to need some time to think about this," Mas said, then turned to the girls. "Hey, you two, I'm getting cold standing here."

Hazel and Lily were huddled at the end of the driveway, devising a way to score on their father. They came to an agreement on a plan of action, then separated and passed the ball back and forth, stealthily making their way toward the goal. Lily moved forward with the ball, made a drop pass to Hazel, then ran headlong at her father, shouting incoherently and jumping in his line of sight, attempting to screen him. Hazel wound up and stepped in, putting everything she had into her slap shot, which found the net just inside the post, low on the glove side. The girls celebrated like it was the Cup-clinching goal in game seven of the finals, while Mas reached into the net for the ball. "So, that's how it's going to be, huh? Well, I'm cold and I'm hungry. What do you say one more goal, and we call it a game?"

"Let's do a shootout," Lily replied. "Hazel and I each get three shots, and Mommy can be the referee."

"Sounds good to me. Lily, you get the first shot, then we'll alternate."

Lily went to the end of the driveway as Sal walked out from behind the net to place the ball at a point midway to the goal. Then, on a signal from her mother, Lily gathered the ball and stick-handled in, weaving back and forth just like Ricky Randall. Mas overreacted to a deke, unable to stack the pads enough to prevent a goal. Lily, Hazel, and Sal went nuts. When the bedlam subsided, Hazel stood at the end of the driveway, looking mildly disinterested as she waited her turn. On her mother's cue, she rocketed forward and wound up like Mason Andrews, catching even Mas by surprise as the ball whistled between his legs before he could react. The ensuing pandemonium allowed Mas to adjust his equipment and gather himself as he waited for the cheering to settle.

It was then that the solution to his wife's problem occurred to him. It was so obvious, he wondered why he hadn't thought of it before. Baker and Sylvia: what a perfect match! Problem solved. He would unveil his genius idea to Sal later.

With renewed confidence, Mas stopped each of the four remaining shots, high-fived everyone on a game well played, promised to pay Lily and Hazel each $4.50 after dinner, and then helped the girls put the equipment away.

* * * * *

When the family was done eating, and Lily and Hazel were paid up and busy elsewhere in the house, Mas told Sal of his brilliant plan.

"Some friend you are," Sal replied. "How could you even consider putting Baker in that position?"

Masaccio's face dropped like New Year's balloons from the ceiling at midnight, which is to say slowly but steadily. "It's not such a bad idea. Baker and Sylvia are somewhat acquainted. She flirted with him at our first Communion gathering last spring."

"You're right, now that I remember," Sal said, but she was still skeptical. "I guess I know Sylvia better than you, or that knowledge makes me more hesitant about throwing Baker into the fire."

"Fire? That's how you'd describe her? Heck, it's just one evening."

"I know, I know. Let's not do anything just yet. Wait till after Christmas. Then if we can't come up with another option, you can give Baker a call."

Masaccio sighed. "Honestly, Sal, that's probably the best idea you're going to get from me."

She simply stared at him, her eyes searching her husband's. Then, nodding slowly, she seemed to reach a decision. "OK—call Baker."

* * * * *

Like the rest of the western world, Masaccio used the end of the year to create some personal resolutions. But unlike everybody else, he was all about *Christmas* resolutions. For him, resolutions of the New Year's variety were too secular, too shallow, whereas a promise made in earnest during Christmas carried much more meaning. This year Mas made his resolution on Boxing Day—or St. Stephen's Day, if you prefer—which involved a return to a regimen of jogging, if for no other reason than to keep up with his girls. But for all his good intentions, it had only served to land him flat on his back on the couch. He had twisted his ankle. The irony of the thing was that he hadn't even been running at the time. He'd just completed a twenty-minute jog and was walking to cool down on the roadway outside his house when he stepped up onto the curb and came up short, landing awkwardly, half on and half off, and cleanly rolled his right ankle.

Sal was in the kitchen preparing a fresh pot of coffee when she heard Mas in the front hall returning from his workout. "How was the run?"

"The run? The *run* was fine."

Detecting something funny in the way he responded, she pressed "start" on the coffee maker, then stepped into the hallway to meet him halfway.

"Uh-oh. What happened?"

"Ah, nothing. I just rolled my ankle stepping onto the sidewalk."

Sal sprang into action. "OK—go lie down in the living room and elevate it. I'll get an ice pack."

When she returned, she found Masaccio on the couch in front of the TV, remote in hand, his right foot resting awkwardly on a couple of pillows. Before applying the cold pack, she gently rolled back the cuff of his sweat pants to assess the damage. After taking

MATCHMAKING

one look at the swelling and discoloration, she was piling her pain-wracked husband into the car for a drive to Emerg. Four hours later he came out in a walking boot, his Christmas resolution on hold for at least a month and his attendance at the following Tuesday's New Year's Eve dance in question.

* * * * *

"Wait a minute. Are we talking about the same person here?"

Baker was confused about his date for the New Year's Eve dance. He had stopped by the Clementi residence to see how Masaccio was progressing with his recovery, and when Mas assured him that he was a go for the event three days hence, the next topic of discussion was Sylvia. There turned out to be a distinct gap between Baker's recollection of Sylvia and Masaccio's description of her.

"I swear," Mas insisted, "she has got herself looking mighty fetching, if I may say so. Keep in mind that the last time you saw her was in April, when we had the family over for Lily and Hazel's first Holy Communion."

"Yeah. The Sylvia I remember was more—"

"Yes?"

"Well, I don't want to be unkind, but the word that comes to mind is . . . 'saggy.'"

"Saggy? Yes, I suppose saggy would be a good description of Sylvia that day. In her defence, the scuttlebutt was that she'd broken up with Anthony that same weekend—which apparently was *his* idea at the time. This time, however, it's Sylvia who's looking for a bit of space."

"When did you see her last?"

"Two days ago, on Christmas. The last time before that was early July, just after school ended. She sure has changed in half a year. I hardly recognized her. Apparently, she's been eating better and working out regularly." Masaccio's voice dropped. "And just between you and me, Baker, I think she's had a procedure."

"A procedure? What for?"

"Her boobs, of course! I doubt that shedding a few pounds and taking some Zumba classes would produce *that* much of a difference."

"Maybe she was wearing a different bra—you know, one with more support."

"Sure, maybe. What do I know?"

"Did you ask Sal? She might have the inside scoop."

"Nah, that would be awkward—me asking about her cousin's breasts, you know. Trust me, though, you won't be disappointed . . . not if looks matter, anyway."

Baker shook his head. "I've never been on a blind date before."

"I wouldn't call it a blind date. More like semi-blind—or better yet—an astigmatic date." Mas could see that his attempt at lightening the mood wasn't working, so he took a practical angle. "Look, you're doing us a big favour. I'll make it simple for you: Sal and I will pick Sylvia up at her apartment and meet you at the hall. No fuss, no muss." Then his tone turned fatherly. "Just promise you won't be late. Sylvia can be a little sensitive about these things. If there's the slightest hint that she's been stood up—well, it could foul up the whole evening."

The sound of a reprimand even before a blunder had been committed seemed to give Baker focus. "C'mon, Mas, you can count on me. I won't be late. Oh, by the way, would you know if this party is going to involve hats and noisemakers and stuff?"

"Gee, Baker, I would expect so. It's tradition—New Year's Eve and party favours go hand in hand. What's the matter, not into noisemakers?"

"Noisemakers are fine. It's the goofy hats I could do without."

"True, the hats are stupid. But who cares? It's all in good fun."

"I feel like such a clown, with a shiny paper dunce cap on my head, and the only way it stays on is by pulling an elastic string under your chin!"

Mas had to laugh at Baker's description. "At least it's only once a year."

"I can give you four hours—a couple of beers, some dancing, and when midnight strikes, hang around long enough to share a New Year's kiss and have a sip of champagne—then politely take my leave."

"Perfect. And who knows? Maybe you two will hit it off and—"

"Stop it! You sound like my mother."

CHAPTER TWENTY-FIVE
BUTTERFLIES, BATS, AND PARTY HATS

Friday, December 27 – Tuesday, December 31

With the end of the twenty-teens just days away, the American press released the results of a poll that ranked the top five athletes of the past decade. Swimmer Michael Phelps came in at number five, with Argentine soccer superstar Lionel Messi fourth and Jamaican sprinter Usain Bolt at number three. NFL Quarterback Tom Brady came in at number two, while the top spot was reserved for none other than LeBron James, someone who was never shy about declaring himself the greatest basketball player on the planet.

On Saturday the fans at Nova Tank Arena were abuzz with high expectations for their boys in green who were riding a six-game winning streak as they prepared to face New York. The Empires scored first, however, and their goaltender was a nightmare all night, forcing the Pines to chase the game. In the end Toronto had to settle for a 3-2 overtime loss.

The next part of the schedule had them spending New Year's on the road, beginning with a stop in Minnesota. It was only natural to expect that if a hockey team had to spend the feast of Saint Sylvester—better known as New Year's Eve—in the city of Saint Paul, it made sense that they at least came away with a win. The Pines did not disappoint, ringing in 2020 with a 4-1 win, their ninth in the past eleven games. Coney Nation was confident that this victory was just the first in what would likely be another extended winning streak.

The unmistakeable sound of Bobby Jenkins doing play-by-play on Pines Radio filled the car as Baker was en route to the New Year's Eve dance. Having left the house early to give himself plenty of time, he drove stress-free and let his mind drift, ultimately settling on thoughts of the Pines, the Coven, his date Sylvia, and the evening ahead.

The second period in Minnesota was winding down and Toronto was up 3-1. Baker pulled into the parking lot, found himself a spot, and turned off the radio—it was always easier to tear himself away from a game in progress when the Pines were winning. If they could hold the lead for another twenty minutes, they'd improve to nine wins in their last eleven games, a nice way to end 2019. Now, however, it was Baker's time to close out the year in style.

Heeding Masaccio's warning about not being late, Baker made sure he was a good ten minutes early. Still, Mas, Sal, and Sylvia were already seated at the table when he arrived. Sharing the table with them was another couple, acquaintances of Sal and Mas and fellow church parishioners.

Baker's arrival precipitated a fair bit of commotion, what with the introductions and all the attendant chatter, but he was deaf to most of it, his attention drawn instead to the vision that was Sylvia. (Masaccio had been right; she looked absolutely stunning.) Distributed around the table was a colourful array of party favours; shiny, bright, and festive. There were all manner of noisemakers, including horns, party blowers, clappers, kazoos, maracas, and even a cowbell. Each place setting included a New Year's cracker. And, of course, there were the hats: top hats, bowlers, leprechaun caps, and conical caps—or dunce caps, according to Baker (except these dunce caps were decked out in finery, including fuzzy pink trim and a matching pink pom-pom). Strangely enough, Baker found himself stuck with the most clownish dunce cap, a circumstance of such improbable and suspicious coincidence that he mentioned it to Masaccio at the first opportunity.

"It's wonderful to see I drew the short straw where hats are concerned."

"What? You don't like your cap?" Mas tried to sound surprised and disappointed, but he failed miserably.

"Asshole," was Baker's deadpan response.

Soon thereafter, Baker took orders from everyone around the table for a bar run, and Sylvia volunteered to help out. Masaccio nudged Sal and tilted his head toward them as they left the table together. It was plain to see that the two of them made a damn good-looking couple.

For his part, Masaccio had pledged not to drink, wanting to avoid the toxic combination of alcohol and painkillers (his ankle had been throbbing all day inside the walking boot). So, instead of nursing a beer, he settled for nibbling on a plate of fruit and baked treats that Sal had assembled for him from the dessert table. Sal, on the other hand, was plainly feeling good, enjoying the music and bopping in her seat to the beat. Seeing this, Baker made a mental note to invite her to dance at some point, especially with Mas's availability being severely limited by his lower-body injury.

Then, with timing that could only be described as impeccable, Dead or Alive's "Brand New Lover" was mixed into the previous tune. Sal yelped in delight, jumped out of her seat, and yanked Baker onto the dance floor. Of course, Sylvia, who was no stranger to the song herself, would have preferred to be dancing, but she felt enough compassion for her cousin that she resigned herself to sitting the song out—but just this one. Seated next to Mas, she started up a conversation about his ankle. But then one dance turned into two, and while Mas was content to carry on sampling the items on his plate, Sylvia stared daggers at Baker and Sal.

Back out on the floor, when the beat of the second tune began to evolve and mix into a third, Sal decided two was enough. "That was fun," she said, "but I'd better rescue Mas from Sylvia. Besides, I know my cousin well enough not to push this into three songs."

And she was proven right because on their way back to the table, as Sal was saying something further to Baker, forcing him to lean in close to better hear, he felt a surprisingly firm grip on his arm and was spun around by Sylvia as she led him back out onto the floor.

* * * * *

When the time came for Sal and Sylvia to powder their noses, the boys were left alone at the table. Mas couldn't resist making a comment to Baker, one buddy to another.

"Boy, Sylvia's looking mighty fine tonight."

Baker was taken off guard by how his friend sounded a lot like a high school senior at prom night. Then he responded by returning the compliment in a way he assumed would be both polite and sincere.

"I could say the same for Sal."

"Whoa, easy there, big fella. Watch what you're saying about my wife."

"What the hell, Mas? How come you can comment on my date, but I can't comment on yours?"

"Because Sal is my wife, the mother of my children. She's not in the business of sending that kind of message. But Sylvia absolutely is, and tonight she's hitting it out of the park."

"I'd bet Sal would appreciate knowing she's an attractive woman—to men other than just her husband. Which brings me to another topic: I hope you're not planning on sitting out the entire evening. You should get yourself on the dance floor."

"What, in my walking boot? C'mon, Baker, I'd look like a friggin' wanker out there."

"On the contrary, I think you'd look like a party animal. Hell, people might consider you a hero for not letting a bum ankle prevent you from twistin' on New Year's Eve. And besides, who gives a shit what other folks think? It's what Sal thinks that matters, and I'm pretty sure she'd love you for making the effort."

Sure enough, Baker's suggestion that Masaccio would be considered more chivalrous than ridiculous for joining the fray on the dance floor decked out in a walking boot was bang on. At one point, a knot of girls came and encircled the couple, producing a cross between a protective gauntlet and a ring of honour.

When the song ended, the ring of eligible women opened at one end, allowing Sal and Mas to retreat back to their table, hand in hand, to a chorus of appreciative whoops and applause. It was then that Mas, still clutching Sal's hand, raised his own, hopped up off his good foot and nimbly kicked his heels, then touched back down and, not missing a beat, limped off the floor.

* * * * *

"Mmm . . . Thompson seedless grapes . . . my favourite," Baker said, appraising the plate of fruit Sylvia had brought back with her from the dessert table.

"Well then, allow me," she replied, pulling a grape off the main stem and holding it out, inviting him to partake. Like a toga-clad centurion accepting offerings from a servant girl in a bathhouse in ancient Rome, he leaned forward and met her halfway as she placed the grape in his accepting mouth. Then she took another one off the plate and this time held it nearer to herself, forcing Baker to lean in close until they brushed cheeks. The third grape she held up for display, then slowly and deliberately brought it back to her mouth and placed it between her perfectly white incisors.

Baker feigned a look of concern, made a show of glancing around and over his shoulder, then leaned in close. "Wouldn't Anthony have something to say about this?"

With heavy-lidded eyes that never left Baker's, Sylvia ate the grape. "Fuck Anthony."

Knowing that his next reply might jeopardize the entire evening, Baker threw caution to the wind (a primary assist could have gone to the three beers he'd consumed since arriving). "I'd rather leave Anthony out of that equation for tonight."

Sylvia's smile made her look as enticing as the apple on the tree of knowledge. "Oh, it would drive Anthony crazy if he knew what my plans were for tonight."

Midway through Sylvia's sentence, music came blasting out of the speakers, drowning out the final words, but Baker was sure he'd caught her meaning, nonetheless. The volume of the music made saying anything further pointless, so Sylvia jumped up and grabbed Baker by the hand. "Let's dance!" And dance is what they did for most of the rest of the night, which was fine with him.

One thing that was decidedly *not* fine with Baker was that whenever anyone felt the moment was ripe for a photograph—of which there were several such moments throughout the evening—Sylvia would insist they all put on their party hats. Baker, of course, was resistant to wearing his, which only served to make her all the more insistent. She even went so far as to have his hat at the ready and place it on his head whenever the time came to pose for another picture. It got to the point that he began to suspect it was her attempt at some lame joke that only she found funny. In a strange way it was during these moments that Sylvia seemed to be all the more drawn to him. In the end he was left with no option but to grin and bear it (and avoid being anywhere in the vicinity when a phone camera came out).

At around eleven o'clock, Baker had decided to substitute mineral water for beer. By midnight, between the water, the dancing, and the passage of time, he was as sober as a documentary on Mother Theresa. In fact, the only thing he was high on anymore was Sylvia.

Shortly after the house rang in the New Year, Baker informed Masaccio that Sylvia would be leaving with him.

"Well, duh! Thanks for the newsflash, Captain Obvious."

Ten minutes later, Mas and Sal bid everyone goodnight and a Happy New Year.

It wasn't long thereafter that Sylvia made a sexy show of stifling a yawn and suggesting it was time for the two of them to follow suit and take their leave.

"I'll get our coats," Baker said.

On their way out to the parking lot, Baker hoped that Sylvia wasn't expecting his car to be some badge of sexually charged manhood. For Baker it was enough that earlier in the day he'd acted on the urge to tidy up the interior of his white 2017 Chevy Cruze. Now, as he took a few quick steps ahead of Sylvia to open the passenger door for her, he was glad of it. As he reached for the door handle, a flash of something silver and fuzzy pink in her coat pocket caught his eye.

"What are you doing with that?"

"What, this?" She produced the offending party favour as proudly as if it were an endearing and sentimental Christmas craft from her childhood. "I wanted a souvenir—a keepsake—to remember the night."

"Really? My silly party hat is what you chose for a keepsake?"

"Listen mister," Sylvia replied, leaning in close, "this hat was a game changer. Without it you'd be no different than any other good-looking guy here tonight. But the moment you put this thing on, you were the cutest one in the room. It was as if your fairy godmother waved her magic wand, and poof! You were transformed."

It was Sylvia's performance in delivering this last line that revealed her genius for beguiling her quarry. In making the reference to Baker's fairy godmother, she adopted a bit of a slur, playing at being inebriated, and then she mimed a wand wave, resulting in the most convenient little stumble. Reflexively, Baker shifted to catch her, such that at the word "poof," she was in his arms. They were nose to nose and eyeball to eyeball when she finished with "you were transformed." Baker could feel the warmth radiating off Sylvia as she closed the tiny gap between their lips and drew him into a long, luxurious kiss. He willingly took it as a promise of things to come.

It was a memorable evening to be sure, but it didn't come without its own collateral damage in that the result of the Pines' game (a 4-1 win for the good guys) was something Baker never actually discovered for himself. Under normal circumstances, following such victories, he could look forward to sleeping like a baby, content in the knowledge that another two points were in the bank, much like collecting a paycheque for an honest day's work and a job well done. Presently, however, sleep had dropped down significantly on his list of priorities. For that matter, so had Andrews, Randall, Valentino, et al.

When American mathematician Edward Lorenz first introduced his theory of the Butterfly Effect in the 1960s, he was applying it to the notion that tiny changes in the atmosphere could have huge impacts on weather. One had to wonder if, at some point toward the end of 2019—perhaps even in the span of days when the Pines were winning eleven of thirteen games between December 7 and January 4—a pathogenic version of this same Butterfly Effect wasn't occurring half a world away. On a global scale, this development was increasingly gaining traction across major news and media platforms, but its growing significance did not yet warrant the attention of the general populace.

Not that anyone could be certain, but the series of events that would soon impact almost every human on the planet probably began innocently in a Chinese forest. It was there that one small, insignificant bat, minding its own business, did its usual business high up in the trees. That bat's poop likely landed on some random pieces of fruit down below. The fruit was then consumed by a rodent-like mammal called a palm civet. Along with others of his brethren, that civet was slaughtered for meat and put on display for sale by a vendor at the Huanan wet market in Wuhan, China. It is typically in such markets that animals, both dead and alive, come into contact with the multitude of locals and visitors who frequent the crowded stalls. These are normal events under most circumstances, except when the original bat happened to have been the host for a new and highly infectious coronavirus.

CHAPTER TWENTY-SIX
SIREN'S SONG

Thursday, January 2

While the Pines were no longer top of mind for Baker, their relevance within the PHL was increasing based on their recent string of successes. Since Boris Duggan took over as head coach, the team had elevated itself in such a way as to be considered among the league's best. In the category of individual player accomplishments, Mason Andrews and Eddie Sanderson were both announced as selections to participate in the All-Star festivities later that month.

That night's contest in Winnipeg was the Pines' forty-second game on the schedule, making it the mathematical start of the second half of their season. And while it wasn't a thing of beauty, Toronto was content to come out of Manitoba with the *W*.

"Did you hear us? We sounded great! Who the hell needs Baker?"

No sooner were the words out of his mouth than Angus knew he was out of line. "Just kidding!"

Perreault was appalled. "Oh, Angus, it would kill Baker if he knew somebody said that. He would positively perish."

"Perreault's right," Masaccio said. "And besides, who would write the words to the songs we play?"

"You've got a point," Angus admitted. "And I'll admit he's pretty good at it too."

"Damn straight!" Masaccio said. "When it comes right down to it, he's the spirit of our band. Without him we wouldn't be meeting like this. All this coven stuff was his baby, remember?" Then he adopted a remorseful tone. "His head's not right, that's all. Sal warned me it wouldn't work, and she was right. I'm sorry I ever suggested we pair those two up."

"That was your idea?" Angus asked. "Why didn't you ask *me*? What am I, chopped beef?"

"I think the term you want is chopped liver," Masaccio corrected. "And no, you're not chopped beef, but you *are* chopped veal."

"Huh? What does that mean?"

"It means you're too young for her, Angus. Sylvia never dates guys who are even remotely younger than her. Come to think of it, I *did* put your name out there, even before Baker's, but Sal wouldn't entertain the idea. She knows Sylvia too well."

Perreault brought them back to the subject of Baker's absence. "Conrad, you were the last to speak with him. What exactly did he say to you?"

"Our conversation was quite short and to the point. He said: 'The Pines are on a roll. We can afford to back off a bit, don't you think?'"

"And I said: 'What I think—and the others would agree—is that now is the time. We should keep a good thing going.'"

"Then he said: 'Well, you'll have to hold it without me because I promised Sylvia I'd spend the weekend with her in Collingwood.' And I said: 'You're going to leave us hanging?' And he said: 'Save the guilt trip for somebody else.' And that was pretty much the end of our conversation."

Conrad's rehashing of his conversation with Baker was met with silence, until Masaccio broke it.

"Did he forget we had scheduled this session two weeks ago?"

"Oh, he didn't forget about our session," Conrad replied. "Of that you can be sure."

"That's hard to believe," Perreault said. "He wanted so badly to have us gather over the holidays. And he seemed so disappointed when it wasn't going to happen." Then something occurred to her. "Would you know if he's working on a new song?"

Conrad chuckled. "He's definitely working on a song, but it's not about the Toronto Mighty Pines. In fact, he's been lured away from the Pines by the song of the siren."

"What does that mean?" Angus asked.

"You know, in ancient Greek mythology, the sirens were mermaids-slash-witches who lured sailors with their singing."

Angus imagined the scene. "Mmm . . . sounds enticing."

"Yeah, well, any man who gave in to the enticement would be dashed upon the rocks."

"So, you're saying he's being lured by the siren song of Sylvia?"

"For a time, yes." Conrad replied. "But I think that's passed. If you ask me, Baker has scratched the itch. They've both served each other's purposes, you might say."

"Do you know when she was born?" Perreault inquired, looking to Mas for the answer.

He was momentarily caught off guard. "Who, Sylvia? Um . . . no. Why do you ask?"

"I'm just wondering about her zodiac sign. You have no idea when her birthday is?"

"No," Mas confirmed. Then a light went on. "Wait a minute. What am I saying? Of course I know. Sylvia was born on October thirtieth—Devil's Night. I remember Sal and Sylvia would joke about how appropriate it was, given her devilish nature, and how ironic that her family name is Innocenti."

"That makes her a Scorpio. And when was Baker born?"

"I think I remember him being a spring baby," Conrad said. "In fact, didn't he tell us his birthday was ten days after Ricky Randall's?"

Mas quickly looked up the information. "Randall was born on June ninth, which puts Baker's birthday at June nineteenth."

"A Gemini, huh?" Perreault said, considering the possibilities. "Ooh, that could be trouble."

"How so?"

"Simple. Scorpios and Geminis don't always pair well. Kind of like oil and water."

"Or like a snowball in July," Angus suggested. "Or salt in a wound."

"Or the Pines in the first round of the playoffs," Conrad offered.

"So, according to your horoscope rules, should we add Sylvia Innocenti and Baker Brooks to that list?"

"Tough to say. Maybe it's just another life lesson."

"How's that?"

"Things don't always conform to rules. Astrology and horoscopes are no different. What does she do, by the way?"

"She's a technician at a beauty salon," Mas replied. He scrolled through the photos on his cell phone. "Here are some pictures I took of them at the New Year's Eve dance." The group crowded around him to have a gander.

"Man, Baker gets no argument from me," Angus said. "That chick is smokin'." Realizing they were in mixed company, he turned to address Perreault. "I mean, you're pretty hot yourself, Perreault, just, you know, in a different way . . . like, when I look at Sylvia, I see a girl who . . . uh—"

"OK, Angus. I think we all get your point," Mas said. "But Sal tells me that Anthony is trying to work his way back into Sylvia's life. She says he's on the warpath."

"What? He's not threatening to go after Baker, is he?" Perreault asked.

"Who, Anthony? God no! He's actually a bit of a softie if you ask me, so maybe warpath is the wrong term. Perhaps *bridal* path would be more accurate. I think he's considering long-term commitment."

"Sounds to me like it'll just be a matter of time before our man Baker is back in the fold," Conrad said. "In the meantime, the Pines are rolling."

"And so are we," Angus replied. "Let's do another song."

When Cheers Are Not Enough

It had been two weeks since the solstice, and the Pines' record in the first fortnight of winter was 5–0–1, earning them eleven out of a possible twelve points. All told, since Boris Duggan had taken over, Toronto had won fifteen of twenty games, making him the first coach in the history of the franchise to accomplish that feat. Sweetening the pot was a Boston loss to Edmonton earlier in the day, moving the Pines to within six points of first place in the division. More and more, the idea of Toronto overtaking the Hubs for first place was a possibility in people's minds: something that would have been unthinkable back in November.

CHAPTER TWENTY-SEVEN
HOUSTON, WE HAVE A PROBLEM

Monday, January 6 – Tuesday, January 14

The eternal search to find compelling narratives any time two teams squared off at this point in the PHL season, forty-three games into the eighty-two-game schedule, was a fact of life for any media hound.

With Edmonton in town, the main storyline was the matchup between Drillers' captain C.J. Starr, arguably the game's best player, and Mason Andrews, Toronto's top young talent. And while both players' performances provided much for reporters to discuss—Starr scored two goals and set up two others while Andrews notched a goal and an assist—the Mighty Pines found themselves on the short end of a 6-4 final score, putting a rude halt to their ten-game point streak.

Despite the tough loss to Edmonton, the Pines were enjoying a fruitful run of fourteen games, having earned twenty-three out of a possible twenty-eight points. Naturally, the expectation was for more success, especially since Toronto's opponent two days hence would be the Winnipeg Whiteouts, the same team they had manhandled just six days ago. Come Wednesday, however, all the optimism in the building couldn't keep Winnipeg from exacting their revenge for last week's loss as they dropped the Pines 4-2.

The schedule afforded the Pines three days off to travel to Florida for a Sunday night tilt against the Everblades. As it happened, seventy-two hours between games didn't do anything to help the team, as the Pines took it on the chin 7-3, making it three losses in a row. On the bright side, they were heading back to Toronto for a nice little three-game home stand. And Tuesday's game proved once again how one should never underestimate the value of home cooking as Toronto rediscovered its scoring touch, potting seven goals on the way to a decisive 7-4 defeat of New Jersey to end its three-game losing streak.

When Cheers Are Not Enough

On the topic of ending things . . .

One thing Baker was discovering, slowly but surely, was that Sylvia was beginning to wear on him. The *bomb*shell was morphing into an *empty* shell. He first noticed it as early as the New Year's Eve dinner dance. She exhibited her interest through physical contact, and given her overall attractiveness, any red-blooded man would find that pleasing, even arousing. The problem for Baker was that it never ceased, such that it soon became disconcerting, then plain suffocating. Eventually, it reached the point that Baker sought respite from her hands. She was exhausting. Between the late nights, the daytime activities, and the incessant demands on his attention, Baker's energy was sapped. Under normal circumstances he'd like to think he could play the stoic and suffer in silence, trusting the maxim "what doesn't kill you makes you stronger." Then again, Friedrich Nietzsche had never met Sylvia Innocenti.

Baker had always fancied himself a generous person where his patience was concerned, so it came as a surprise when he perceived in himself a faint but growing irritation with her. It began innocently enough when she picked up on Baker's affinity for dropping movie quotes, and soon she began doing the same, randomly inserting popular lines into their conversation. The problem was that she had an incredible talent for misquoting or unwittingly combining quotes, which drove Baker to distraction. Like the time she impersonated Humphrey Bogart and came out with "Frankly, my dear, this could be the start of a beautiful friendship." And then Monday evening she walked into the room as the Pines-Oilers game was winding down, took one look at the score, and with a Texas twang remarked, "Houston, we've got ourselves a problem here." The worst of the lot, something he considered her chef-d'oeuvre, happened when they were sharing an impassioned moment, and she caressed his ear with her lips and whispered, "Call me by my name, and I'll call you by yours." That was too much for him. How could she get it wrong? It was in the frickin' title of the movie! *Call Me by Your Name.*

Then there were the times Sylvia would drop what she considered profound sayings but to Baker sounded like nothing more than infantile gibberish. One day, when he was lamenting another Pines loss, complaining about how this was hardly the way it was planned, Sylvia adopted the tone of the wise old owl and said, "This altar is zoom!"

Baker directed a blank look her way. "I'm sorry?"

"This altar is zoom! It's something my grandfather said when things didn't go according to plan."

"This altar is zoom? Seriously?"

"Yes. It's Latin or something. Look, don't get all angry and stuff just because your blessed Pines lost . . . again."

After this exchange they both stewed for the rest of the evening, Sylvia because she felt belittled and Baker because ... well, because thanks to another Toronto loss, he was sour to begin with, and her silly maxims just irritated him further.

The relationship had hit a low point; that much was plain to see. How could it have come to this? He fully blamed himself for his recent choices and for letting his friends down as well. On top of which, he had allowed the fortunes of his team to take a backseat to his personal life. The Pines had reverted to mediocrity while his hopes and dreams of making something good happen were slipping away with each passing day. There was no option: his relationship with Sylvia needed to be terminated, but initiating the breakup was something he had little experience with and dreaded doing.

On Saturday they went out for a meal, and the tension between them was palpable. When dinner was done and they were back in the car ready to head home, Baker turned to her and asked for some basic technical help with his mobile phone. Sylvia obliged, flipping through his photos in the process. She lingered over his selfie pics, the ones of him in his Kyle Bulac outfit on Samhain last November. Before she could delete what to her were no more than silly, childish photos, Baker took a moment to examine the offending pictures and noticed something that instantly propelled him into action. Begging her indulgence, he drove to Heaven's Gate cemetery on the edge of town and parked the car in a small lot outside the entrance. It had begun to drizzle.

"Here we are," Baker said, hoping that Sylvia wouldn't feel too creeped out being led to a strange cemetery on a dark, misty night. "Could you reach into the glove box and grab the flashlight that's in there, please?"

She looked at Baker as if he'd asked her to get him a shovel. "You're kidding, right?"

"No. There's a little flashlight in the compartment."

She just sighed, the sarcasm lost on him, and indicated his phone. "There's a flashlight built into your device, you know."

He picked up his phone as if for the first time. "Oh yeah. I forgot about that." He stared at his phone but didn't move.

"Do you need me to show you how to turn it on?"

"I can manage." He pulled his hood up, got out of the car, and headed into the drizzle and the darkness. Guided by the light of his phone, Baker proceeded through the entrance arch to walk among the burial plots and monuments, leaving Sylvia waiting in the car.

With the aid of his phone light, he went straight to the tombstone he was seeking and read it carefully from top to bottom. He squatted for a closer inspection of the bottom portion of the monument, and then he saw it. Was that the clue that Allen Nella hinted at? He straightened up to dwell on the evidence, wondering if he had just discovered the man's secret. If so, the path forward would certainly be clearer. Crouching down again, Baker took a few pictures, which he would study at his next opportunity. When he got back up he took one final look at the tombstone of Calub Merlin Elyk and spontaneously mumbled a prayer, which included the words "rest" and "peace," then turned to leave, taking his cue from the rain as it began to fall harder.

As Baker walked among the tombstones, a quiver of anxiety stirred in him. When he saw his car's headlights, he realized it wasn't about being alone in a cemetery on a dark and stormy night, but rather the possibility that Sylvia might have driven off rather than wait for him to return from his silly adventure in the rain. As he headed back to the car, a sense of purpose had shown up at his front door, ready to move back into his life. But to make room for it, he would need to draft an eviction notice for Sylvia.

For Baker, the Pines' win on Tuesday over New Jersey had brought to mind Sylvia's proclivity for misquoting popular lines—specifically her reference to Apollo 13 astronaut Jim Lovell's oft-used line. Although her delivery may have been flubbed, it was not altogether inappropriate where the Toronto Mighty Pines were concerned. Perhaps there was a lesson to be learned from how the crew of Apollo 13 and their support team back at Mission Control worked together to solve a series of life-threatening problems to bring the three astronauts and their ship safely back to Earth. Clearly now was the time for Boris Duggan and his staff to use all the resources at their disposal to guide this Pines ship and her crew back to safer shores.

CHAPTER TWENTY-EIGHT
MR. ONE-EIGHTY

There was no doubt about it; Baker's classroom sink was clogged. The annoying discovery prompted him to reflect on how the Pines would be better off if they could learn to clog the neutral zone as thoroughly. His only recourse was to attack the drain with the plunger.

Witnessing what his plunger coaxed back up the drain was always an adventure for Baker: chunks of hardened acrylic paint, caps from empty paint bottles, Popsicle sticks, pencils, and even paintbrushes—short ones, long ones, it didn't matter. And yet the cause was no mystery to him. When the students rinsed their palettes and brushes during cleanup, some would leave their tools in the sink as the water ran, and then random items would somehow drain with the rest of the detritus that came from making art in a high school classroom.

The art excrement always came up black and smelling of sewage, so he removed his sweater, rolled up his sleeves, and donned vinyl gloves, scooping it out by hand. It didn't take long, after which he let the water gush from the tap, hot and hard, for a good five minutes, as per the instructions of the plumber who had once needed to be called in some years ago.

Turning his attention back to the sink, Baker saw that the water was draining cleanly and so turned the tap off. He took a final look around his classroom, making sure nothing was left undone for tomorrow's first period, then retrieved his sweater. Carrying it in one fist, he went downstairs to the chaplain's office to discuss the playlist with Conrad—if one could call it a playlist. Bakers' Coven was on the bill for that evening's Battle of the Bands event and had settled on a shortlist of five songs, from which they would perform three to fill the fifteen minutes allotted to each band. Baker had bigger plans, though, which he had shared with his bandmates a week earlier.

"I think it'd be a good idea to have a fourth song ready, you know, in case we do an encore."

This generated a laugh from the others. "No one's going to be playing any encores," Conrad said, then relented after one look at Baker. "But if it puts you at ease, we'll be ready with another—just in case."

Bakers' Coven had made great strides since the school year began, and Baker would not be dissuaded from going into this event with heightened expectations. In his mind the time had come for them to be heard, starting with their band name. There was only one teachers' band, and for high school students there was nothing like watching teachers let their hair down after hours. It made them more human, and who knew? Maybe they were good. Despite all that, Baker thought it was time to change the status quo, so he would see to it, for tonight's event anyway, that it was Bakers' Coven and not "the teachers' band," who would open the second half of the programme, right after intermission.

He had scheduled for them to meet in the music room at 6:30, and so with time to burn, he decided to drop in on Conrad. Baker enjoyed visiting the chaplain in his office to engage in friendly, insightful banter. Fondly known among the staff as Mr. One-Eighty, Conrad Wiederschoen had a reputation for arguing opposing viewpoints and forcing people to reassess their long-held opinions on issues as wide-ranging as the justification for the colonization of Mars to the virtue of screening episodes of *The Gilmore Girls* in order to teach lessons of morality and ethics in Religion class.

Humming an Orville Peck tune and feeling good about the prospects for that night's performance, Baker whisked in through the open door and came face to face with his friend who, with jacket on and guitar case in hand, strangely appeared to be headed out.

"Hi, Conrad. I just came by to confirm the set. Are you leaving?" It was a little after four, and some quick mental math told Baker that if Conrad was going home before they all met at 6:30, he'd be hard pressed to do it in little more than two hours.

"Yeah, I'm leaving." He said it in a funny way, as if it was something final. Baker ignored it and continued with his original point.

"That's fine. I'll walk you out. I just wanted to double check the songs for tonight."

Saying nothing, Conrad eased his way through the office door, forcing Baker to back up into the hallway. He led the way toward the stairwell doors while Baker fell in step and continued rambling on about the rationale behind his song selection.

"So, I figured it'd be best to stick with the material we're most comfortable with. I mean, you and Perreault always handle everything with aplomb, but I was thinking more Mas, Angus, and me. Well, mostly Angus and me."

He stopped short when Conrad paused by the elevator doors and pressed the "down" button.

"Oh. We're taking the elevator?"

MR. ONE-EIGHTY

Conrad turned to face him directly. Perhaps it was the lighting in that part of the hallway, but Conrad was looking worn down. Evidently, there was much more on his mind than the songs for that night's set.

"Have you ever heard of Nikos Kazantzakis?"

"Nikos? Uh, no. I don't think so."

"How about The Last Temptation of Christ?"

"Sure. The Martin Scorsese movie, with Willem Dafoe. I've seen it."

"Well, I haven't. It's actually the book I'm referring to. Nikos Kazantzakis wrote it."

Baker had no inkling where this was going. "Okaaay . . ."

"It's a powerful book, and it has had a strong influence on my personal relationship with Jesus Christ." Conrad paused as the elevator doors opened, and the two of them stepped in, then he continued. "You see, Baker, I was always a good Catholic kid, having grown up in a good Catholic family. Nothing extraordinary, mind you. But it wasn't until I read the words of Nikos Kazantzakis that I began to see Jesus in another light: a light that revealed his humanness." He paused again, apparently in no hurry, deliberately reaching for the elevator panel and pressing the "Main Floor" button.

When the doors slid shut, Baker was overwhelmed by the feeling that he had entered a confessional. Almost by force of habit, he played out the rite of disclosure in his mind. *Father forgive me for I have sinned. I have forsaken both the Coven and the Pines for the sake of carnal pleasures. While my friends were playing the two-hundred-foot game, I was cherry picking, looking to score with Sylvia in order to pad my personal stats . . .* He was guilty as charged and ready to do some sort of penance. He also had a sneaking suspicion that Conrad was setting him up for precisely that.

"I saw Jesus as a man, like me, rather than as Almighty God on Earth. And like me, he was taught to worship God the Father and respect his parents and elders and to count his blessings and appreciate the simple pleasures in life. He was someone who grew up learning and taking cues from the people in his community and, like them, craved a comfortable existence, a good job, a wife and a family in a nice house—"

"Wait a minute, you got all this from that book?"

"Oh yes, and more. You see, Jesus also made his share of mistakes, and searched for answers to questions. He felt fatigue and cold and hunger, experienced loneliness and moments of fear and uncertainty, and like many of us, he didn't always live up to his parents' expectations. He, too, dealt with the vagaries of inhabiting a physical body—the male of the species, prone to hormone fluctuations and corporeal desires. The human stuff, you know? Reading that book helped me see Jesus as someone I could relate to, as a big brother in whose footsteps I could strive to follow."

The elevator settled on the main floor, the doors slid open, but neither of them moved. Baker wasn't sure what Conrad was getting at, so he just stood and waited, even as the doors slid back shut.

"All that being said, there is one thing—in my opinion—that separates Jesus from me and the rest of humanity. Care to guess what that might be?"

"Well, I suppose it's that he is God."

"Close. It is that he *knows* what God knows. He *knows* that there is a God, first and foremost, and that there is a heaven, and what its nature is. You see, he knew the answers to the big questions that the rest of us are just expected to accept on faith."

Conrad looked around and suddenly seemed to recognize that it might appear odd for two men to be conversing in a closed, stationary elevator, so he pressed the button to open the doors and motioned for Baker to lead them out. Then he continued with his point. "And I believe that such knowledge made his existence on earth difficult. You might say it just served to add more misery to his life."

"Misery? Was Jesus' life on earth so miserable—other than his arrest and execution, of course?"

"I wouldn't want his life. Would you want his life? It wasn't exactly filled with warmth and contentment." They had arrived at the front doors of the school, and as he turned up his collar, Conrad pointed to the sweater in Baker's hand. "Speaking of warmth, you may want to put that on." Baker did as instructed, then followed Conrad out to the parking lot. They felt the cold instantly.

"The point is, Jesus knew what he was in for. He knew what was coming, and yet he still obediently and unswervingly carried out the grand plan, right to the end. You see, when it comes to the human condition, I believe that it's *not* knowing how things will turn out that allows us to get through life's hardships."

"Sure, but despite that, aren't we constantly searching for more knowledge, knowledge that will help us more accurately predict the future?"

"Absolutely. It's in our nature." Having arrived at his car, Conrad reached into a pocket and fished out his keys. He placed his guitar and carry bag in the backseat, then opened the driver's door and got in behind the wheel, all the while elaborating on his point. "We gather facts to make calculated decisions because it sucks not having the answers. But there are so many other times, in the midst of our suffering, that all we can do is hope and pray that it will soon come to an end, without ever knowing when it actually will. And sometimes the misery goes on longer than desired." He turned on the ignition, rolled down the window, and shut the door, never taking his eyes off Baker. "Good, bad, or indifferent, it's precisely because we *don't* know the outcome that in an absurd way helps us get through the tough times. Just look at how we survived the world wars or times of plague—" Conrad broke off, searching for a timely example, then his mouth curved impishly. "Imagine being a part of Coney Nation celebrating a Cup win in 1962 and knowing you wouldn't see another one for over five decades, let alone a finals appearance. How ironic that our blissful ignorance is in itself a blessing."

Between the sub-zero temperature and Conrad's labyrinthine homily, Baker was getting fidgety. An involuntary shiver ran through him as he listened, waiting for his friend to get to the point.

"All that being said, I'm desperately searching for answers right now. My ignorance—my not knowing—is causing me nothing but misery. All this Coven activity on behalf of the Toronto Mighty Pines has made me rethink some things. I don't know if I'm doing the right thing here, so I don't know how much further I can go with it. I mean, as Catholics, we're allowed to ask a saint—Saint Cecilia, for instance—to intercede for us, right? Our church leaders don't object to that. Then why not call upon the spirit of Cal Ubank, a man who, although he may not have martyred himself for Christ, still lived an upstanding, noble, and selfless existence?"

Certain that Conrad's question was rhetorical, Baker said nothing. In the end all he managed to do, through numbed lips, was stupidly ask, "So . . . will you make it for 6:30 in the music room?"

Conrad smiled sadly. "Unfortunately, no. I'm going home, Baker, and you should go inside. You're freezing out here."

Baker began to panic. "But we can't play the set without you. I mean, shit . . . we'll have to cancel."

"Don't you dare cancel. You get up there and play those songs. Trust me, you'll do fine."

"How can you say that? You're the one who's always telling me how shitty I play!"

Conrad's demeanour turned compassionate. "That's only so you don't get complacent—so you'll keep working and improving. You're good, Baker. You can do this. You don't need me for tonight."

"Aw, that just sounds like a lot of bullshit. This wouldn't be about me cancelling last week, would it?"

"And the week before that?" (Conrad couldn't resist the jab.) "No, Baker, it's not about that. Although I must admit, I'd much rather be succumbing to the pressures of a shapely Italian siren than struggling with my inner demons over the propriety of engaging in coven-like rituals."

"So if it's not about me skipping out on the last couple of band sessions, what is it?"

"Trust me, this has nothing to do with anybody in the band. I just need some distance. I'm asking you to cut me some slack here."

"What happened to you never passing up an opportunity to play, huh? You said that yourself at the Misty River."

"I can't believe you're taking me to task for a frivolous comment I made last summer when we were celebrating our first gig, high on beer and wings."

"Well, I thought the comment was completely sincere."

Conrad shook his head slowly, as if regretting a mistake. "At least I'll come away from this experience having learned an important lesson." He looked up at Baker. "Care to guess what it is?"

"I don't know. Always stay true to your word?"

"Never say never."

Baker just stared, dumbstruck by what he perceived as Conrad's complete and unyielding self-regard. Only pride prevented him from begging the man to reconsider his actions.

"Don't look at me like that," Conrad pleaded. "Have fun tonight. I would ask you to wish the others luck on my behalf, but by the look on your face, I doubt that's going to happen. Listen, we'll talk tomorrow, alright? Now get back inside. Oh . . . and be sure to break a leg."

Baker stepped aside as Conrad slowly reversed out of the parking space, then put the car in drive and manoeuvred through the laneway, onto the road, and into traffic. He was left standing there in the frigid parking lot, feeling like the Grinch, with his Grinch feet ice cold in the snow. It occurred to him that he had been standing in roughly the same spot when he'd been told of Cubby's death last November. If it weren't so sad it would have been funny, a source of juicy material for some sick comedy writer.

Had the conditions, climatically speaking, been more benign, Baker probably would have ventured around the block, taking the long walk in solitude that he so desperately needed. But with hypothermia setting in, he just headed back to the shelter of the school. Once inside he walked stiffly upstairs to the staff room, figuring that was where he'd find Perreault at that time of day. *Boy, when she hears this news, she'll have a conniption*, he thought. *Maybe we'll have to cancel. Yeah, that's probably what she'll say. It's the right thing to do, after all. We can't be expected to perform with half our band missing.*

Once he'd convinced himself that this was essentially the only route for the Coven and that Perreault would completely agree, a wave of relief swept over Baker. His would now serve as the voice of reason, providing words of comfort and reassurance for the others. Admittedly, the present situation threw all their plans into the shitter, but this was a time for perspective, not panic. He worked his key in the staff room door and found Perreault alone, singing something under her breath as she stood by the microwave reheating her coffee.

"Well, bad news about tonight," Baker began, dispensing with a preamble or a greeting.

"What? Is it cancelled . . . again?"

MR. ONE-EIGHTY

"I wish. That would have been *good* news compared to this."

"What is it then?"

"Conrad is out for tonight. He went home."

"What happened? Is he not feeling well? Did something happen at home?"

"No, nothing like that. He told me he just can't do it tonight. Can you believe it?"

"So, he's OK?"

"Yes, he's fine. But he went home—without any warning. He basically told me on his way out the door. I mean, what if I hadn't run into him on his way out? When would he have told us?"

"Aww, Baker, there must be a good reason. We'll manage. Cut him some slack."

Damn, there was that request again. "Cut him some slack? We'll manage?" Baker's voice rose with incredulity. "Perreault, you sound like Conrad, for Chrissake. It's not like he forgot his guitar at home. Hell, if that was the case, he could use mine. No, he's not playing, period. How're we supposed to manage? He just left us in a frickin' lurch."

While Baker vented, Perreault removed her mug from the microwave, not noticing that it had overheated in the process and bubbled over. Hot mug in hand, the burning sensation registered just as she turned toward Baker. "Ow, ow, ow!"

To her credit, rather than drop it outright, she withstood the pain long enough to lower it to knee level before releasing it. The mug still smashed on the floor, but she managed to contain the damage, even though some of it splashed on Baker's pants.

In his agitated state, he jumped back. "What the hell?" he exclaimed, looking at Perreault as if she were clumsy *and* daft.

"Ouch, that hurt." Shaking out her hand, Perreault assessed the damage, then apologized to Baker and immediately set to cleaning up the mess.

"I can't play these songs by myself," Baker said, continuing his tirade. "What are we gonna do? We're gonna sound like shit."

"Don't overreact. We're going to sound fine," she said, pulling a mop's worth of paper towels from the dispenser above the sink. "We're still a four-piece band: guitar, bass, drums, and vocals. That's all we need."

"What's wrong with you, Perreault? Don't you get it? I'm the one playing guitar! I'm not prepared for this!"

"Confidence, Mr. Brooks. All is not lost. You just take that guitar of yours and make it talk."

While Perreault was trying to downplay Conrad's absence, Baker just heard annoying insouciance. He was in no mood for cheap faux support. He wasn't one of her grade nine students, after all. He was fully aware of the situation, and it didn't bode well, so he got back at her by dredging up some history.

"I find that funny, coming from someone who, as I recall, wasn't inclined to play bass when we needed her to, and then dropped it the first chance she had—as if it was an over-nuked beverage."

Normally, Perreault would laugh off such a retort from Baker. But this felt different, as if he'd revealed a side that she had neither seen nor expected. It was delivered in a tone meant to be harsh, and it hinted at something that he had harboured for months. How many other resentments might he be concealing? Surely he didn't hold that one time with Angus against her, did he? She realized it was the kind of thing that could impact a friendship—or break up a band.

Doing her best to maintain a smile, she invited him to help her clean up, but Baker would have none of it, deliberately stepping over the spill and heading for the door, tossing back an excuse dripping with as much sarcasm as her paper towels did with spilled coffee. "Sorry, but a guy's got to practise if he's going to make his guitar talk." And with that he left the room, leaving Perreault to deal with the mess alone.

With plenty of time to kill, he spent the interval hiding in his office, staring at his guitar but not playing a note. In his mind Baker chewed on the reasons, like some cerebral cud, for why he was justified in being so angry. Anyone could see—if they were paying attention—that the night's set would be a disaster. It'd be like a bad dream, only worse for the reality of it. And all the blame would lay at his feet and no one else's, not Perreault with her fuckin' amazing voice and stage presence, nor Mas with his steady bass support, nor Angus with his rudimentary drumming skills. Nothing could change the fact that the lead guitarist was so obviously not ready for prime time. Conrad was such an asshole for doing this on such short notice. Hell, even a couple days' warning might have helped.

Soon hunger set in, so he nibbled on some nuts and an apple left over from his lunch. He pulled some tests out of his marking bag, but he couldn't concentrate for any length of time. How could they let him down like that? First abandoned by Conrad and then patronized by Perreault. Compounding the situation was his petulant reaction to Perreault's response. He hated himself for it. He recognized it as shameful, but he could think of no remedy for it, so he just sat in his room, stewing. What a fuckin' idiot he was.

* * * * *

Eventually, like Wiarton Willie, Baker emerged from his den. With guitar in hand, he went down the hall to the music room where Perreault was sitting with Masaccio, discussing Conrad's situation. Baker greeted them in a subdued fashion. He wouldn't have blamed Perreault if she was cold to him, but once again he was way off the mark, and her warm greeting proved to him that she was genuinely above that sort of thing—and that perhaps, back in the staff room, she had sincerely believed he was fully capable of filling in for Conrad. By the time Angus joined them, Baker was resigned to the fact that the only thing left was to reorient himself. He tried valiantly to flip his mental state and adopt a positive approach to the challenge ahead.

With any fantasies of playing three tunes and an encore having long since vanished, the consensus was that they'd perform two songs, opening with "Fireworks" and finishing with "If It Makes You Happy," (or the 'Happy' song, as Angus had taken to calling it). Then, with about ten minutes before it was time for them to head to the theatre, Perreault asked Baker for his master key and left the room. She returned in short order with Conrad's framed picture of Saint Cecilia, setting it on the teacher's desk at the front of the classroom.

"OK, guys, gather 'round. I think it would be completely appropriate at this time to sing our Saint Cecilia song." With that, they sang their prayer to the patron saint of musicians. Then they went downstairs to the theatre, arriving backstage just as the crowd broke for a short intermission.

When the second half of the show commenced, they were introduced as "The Teachers' Band"—not that Baker much cared anymore, nor did he even notice. They got through two songs remarkably well, garnering a fairly decent response from all those assembled when they were through. Of course, it didn't hurt that Perreault was in top form, living the music in her low-rise skinny jeans, zip-up suede ankle boots, and white unzipped hoodie over a black T-shirt. She was literally owning the stage, to the delight of the smallish but enthusiastic crowd,

In choosing "Fireworks" for their opening tune, the band had guaranteed themselves a bit of audience participation simply because it contained an f-bomb, so when Perreault sang the line as, "You said you didn't give a *frick* about hockey," no one could hear it because the kids in the seats drowned her out with the real thing. When the vocals gave way to guitar, she threw the microphone over her shoulder and strutted around like Gord Downie himself.

Perreault's presence on stage could at times be catlike and sultry, at other times playful and bouncy. She had a hypnotic effect on the crowd, which only intensified during the 'Happy' song. Naturally, the line about getting stoned was a hit, but when she sang about being "real low down," she got real low down, and when she sang about putting on a poncho, she flipped the hoodie up over her head, triggering quite an audience response. After that, it didn't take much to get them to join her in the chorus. And since they lacked a true lead guitar, Perreault filled in by humming the parts so effectively that the guitar wasn't even missed. Truthfully, no one in the audience would have minded had the band chosen to play an encore.

*****

Once they were back upstairs in the music room rehashing the experience and packing things up, Angus declared that it had, in fact, been a pretty good performance. "Heck, the kids were even singing along with Perreault during the 'Happy' song."

"Yeah, that went pretty well," Mas agreed. "What say we go out for a modest celebration—one drink?"

"Nah, you guys go on," Baker said. "I should dig into some work I've been putting off for way too long."

"C'mon, man, another day isn't going to matter, is it? This was a moment we've waited for since last August. It won't be the same without you."

"No, really. I'm just going to head home. Thanks anyway."

Baker knew Mas was right about the moment, but why did it have to unfold so contrary to the way he'd envisioned it? He drove home feeling miserable. His sour mood was only aggravated by listening to the update on the Pines game, which had Toronto trailing Calgary 1-0 at the second intermission.

As any sports fan would attest, when your team is playing, it's always best to give your undivided attention to the game in progress. Anything less introduces the potential for bad karma. Baker believed this, even though the rational part of him knew it was bullshit. As a result he felt conflicted whenever his professional obligations at school prevented him from watching a game, such as during the twice-yearly parent-teacher interviews, or an academic awards ceremony, or an event like the Battle of the Bands. It was at those times that he functioned best by putting the game out of his mind completely. Now his brain was humming, the thought processes working overtime, but it had nothing to do with the Pines game.

He was wrestling with a problem of his own making (was there another kind?), and found the solution to be frustratingly elusive. Later on, when he finally climbed into bed, he could swear he was undergoing a veritable mind-body split, with his mind acting like a drum filled with bouncing lottery balls while his body took the form of a long-legged blonde turning the crank. Each tumbling sphere represented a possible scheme for how he might apologize to Perreault; how he might express his regret over his childish actions or at least make it up to her somehow, or present her with some collegial proposal.

Then his frontal lobe calved an idea with such force it pulled him out of bed. He slipped on sweatpants and a hoodie, grabbed his warmest pair of socks, and left the bedroom to root through a collection of watercolour paper in the basement, eventually opting for the thicker 200-lb variety. From that he cut a rectangle that could be folded in half and fit into an envelope borrowed from a stash of unused Christmas cards. He set about composing the words that might elicit a smile on the woman's face as well as compel her to respond.

MR. ONE-EIGHTY

Violets are blue
Roses are red
Can you ever forgive
An old stoopid-head?

—B.

The words went inside the fold, while he added a little guitar doodle for the outside of the card. Then he mixed up a few drops of paint and applied a splash both inside and out. That done, he left the card to dry and cleaned up before turning in. Baker didn't get back to bed until nearly 2:00 a.m., wondering if four hours' sleep would keep him from being a complete zombie in front of his students the next day. For the moment, though, he was feeling better about his prospects where his personal life was concerned, despite the attendant risk. The ball would be in her court (he was playing tennis now, having finished with the draft lottery), and she could choose to drop her racquet and refuse to play entirely, or she could smash the goddamned ball a mile over the fence in anger. Or maybe, just maybe, she could return the serve, teeing it up ever so sweetly for him to begin a nice long rally . . .

He stared at the dark ceiling for a long time, fiercely hoping that Perreault would lean toward the third option.

CHAPTER TWENTY-NINE
HALLELUJAH

Friday, January 17 – Monday, January 20

The topic of cheating made sports headlines when revelations of a cheating scandal in Major League Baseball came to light. MLB's subsequent investigation into the Houston Astros' sign stealing during the 2017 World Series resulted in the commissioner's office announcing that the Astros organization would be fined $5 million in addition to losing future draft picks. The Astros subsequently dismissed Manager A. J. Hinch and General Manager Jeff Luhnow.

On Saturday the Pines hosted Chicago in what was the final game before their league-mandated eight-day lay-off, which included the PHL's All-Star weekend. Unfortunately, Toronto's skaters appeared disinterested (perhaps preoccupied with the thought of catching their flights out of town for the week-long break) and fell 6-2 to the Millionaires. Head coach Boris Duggan expressed frustration with his charges following the loss, citing a general lack of discipline and consistency. But who could he look to for help? There were thirty-three games left in the season for the team to find a solution to the myriad problems facing it.

On Sunday, in the middle of the January holiday weekend in the US, a thirty-five-year-old man, coughing and feverish, walked into a medical clinic in Snohomish County, Washington. The individual would eventually be designated as the first detected case of COVID-19 on American soil.

January 20 was holiday Monday in the US—Martin Luther King Jr. Day. It was also known as "Blue Monday," thanks to one Cliff Arnall, a self-described psychologist, life coach, and happiness consultant, who had, in 2005, calculated January 24 (generally the third Monday in January) to be the most depressing day of the year. He based this on four main factors: 1) Post-Christmas bills, 2) abandonment of New Year's resolutions, 3) low sunlight levels, and 4) cold weather. Arnall then generated a mathematical formula in an attempt to offer a more scientific explanation for the cause of this apparently widespread malaise.

HALLELUJAH

Whether the Blue Monday phenomenon was real or not was a matter of opinion. There were those who felt best when they embraced the blues, either by listening to sad music, or avoiding happy greetings, or opting to just stay home and not leave the house. Other people made an effort to resist the blues. They watched upbeat movies or enjoyed "blue" foods like blueberry pie, blueberry yogurt, or blueberry wine.

For members of Coney Nation, Blue Monday had come at a bad time. As every athlete and sports fan knew, the best way to get over the blues that stemmed from a loss was to lace 'em up and get right back out and play the next game. Unfortunately, the Pines found themselves coming off Saturday's ugly defeat having no games to look forward to until a week Monday in Nashville.

With the school day done, Baker wandered down to the library and seated himself at a carrel. He was perusing the front section of a Toronto newspaper when a headline caught his eye. Struck by the flash of an idea and feeling compelled to act on it without delay, he walked over to the nearest recycle bin and lowered into a semi-squat. He was rummaging through the detritus for something clean and useable when he heard a voice from above.

"Lose something?"

Baker looked up and came face to face with Lawrence Wynn.

"Oh, hi, Lawrence. I'm just scrounging for some scrap paper."

"My dear man, there's no need to go through the recycle bin." Lawrence pointed back toward the checkout desk where a twelve-inch vertical post was wrapped in carpeting, and beside it sat a shallow box containing a stack of paper. "You can use my scratch post for that kind of thing."

"Your what?"

"Scratch post," he repeated, a gleam of pride in his eye. "It's a hit with the kids." Lawrence fully expected Baker to be able to appreciate how attractive such a thing might be for the patrons, seeing as those patrons consisted of teenagers negotiating a world that made never-ending demands on their attention spans.

Still crouched over the blue bin, Baker looked across toward Lawrence's "scratch post," furtively dropped the piece of paper in his hand, then stood up and followed the librarian to the checkout counter. He made a tactile show of massaging the fibres of the carpet and testing the box that contained the paper for sturdiness.

"This is first-rate. Did you construct it?"

"I designed it and gathered the materials. My father put it together."

"Well, tell your father he's a true craftsman."

"Thanks, Baker. He'll appreciate the feedback. But don't let me take up anymore of your time. Help yourself to all the paper you need."

Baker thanked Lawrence, took a couple sheets of "scratch" paper, and then retreated to the nearest table with his newspaper. Once seated, he turned to the section that contained the Blue Monday article he'd come across earlier and folded it just so, arranging it by his left elbow. Baker cared not a whit about the fact that Cliff Arnall was likely a fraud and that his formula was meaningless because that wasn't the point. This wasn't about devising an equation that objectively measured the most depressing day of the year. This was about using math to determine another kind of formula—a winning formula. He needed to identify a select number of variables that could be slotted into a workable equation, kind of like using WAR to determine a player's value to his team. *"It's about getting things down to one number,"* was the line delivered by Jonah Hill in *Moneyball*. In that spirit, Baker wondered if his formula could produce a number that revealed the probability of the Pines winning the Clarence Cup in any given year. After a few false starts, he came up with the following variables.

T = time (years) since the team last won a playoff round
D = depth of their most recent playoff run
P = present position in the standings
$G^{E\&T}$ = goaltending strength (E&T=Eddie and Timmy)
UFA = years remaining until the Big Four contracts expire
C = available cap space
DNA = team makeup and chemistry

Try as he might, however, Baker repeatedly failed in his attempt to formulate an equation that generated a range of numbers which could be used as a scale to indicate the probability of Pines playoff success in a given year. At an impasse, he eventually resigned himself to the fact that this was beyond his expertise—something perhaps more suited to left-brain types like those in the math department.

Baker put the Blue Monday formula aside and instead wrote two words at the top of the page: "Pines Poetry." He began with general thoughts about the team as a whole and then moved on to consider key individuals like Mason Andrews, Ricky Randall, and Addy Brouwer. To his surprise and delight, it was easy; the lines seemed to write themselves.

*****

The next day saw Baker in a different mood, seeking to spend his lunch break socializing with the guys in the staff room. He found Conrad, Angus, and Masaccio seated at their usual table, joined by Jackie Klein. Sitting down with them, he noticed there was no mention made of the musical activities—or lack thereof—of Bakers' Coven. Predictably, the conversation turned to the topic of Baker's love life, specifically his recent misadventures with Sylvia.

Masaccio wasted no time. "So . . . are they real?"

Baker looked at him stonily. "You, my friend, are a sick man."

"C'mon, we're not altar boys here. Answer the question."

Baker had no interest in divulging his bedroom affairs, especially as Jackie was seated with them.

"Sorry, Mas, but you're gonna have to find someone else to answer that question."

Masaccio made a show of looking disappointed, as if he'd been sorely let down by his friend.

Conrad was less crude but just as insistent. "Never mind what Masaccio wants to know. Fact is, you and Sylvia parted ways quite speedily. What happened?"

"Let's just say she's high maintenance. There were times that I had to be careful with what I said or how I said things. She's really a wonderful girl—with a few minor quirks. That's all."

"Throw us a bone, man. Give us an example of one of her quirks—and it can't be a hypothetical. It has to be concrete; something you actually said that spoiled her day."

While Baker took a moment to think, the others leaned forward in their seats.

Not wanting to "kiss and tell," he nevertheless chose to relate the time when Sylvia had challenged him to name a favourite body part of hers. Assuring Sylvia of how difficult a task it was to choose from among her many "gifts," he'd admitted that, if pressed, he would go with her legs as his favourite. Evidently flattered, she'd cozied up and asked him to explain why. Baker had happily confided that his reason probably had something to do with the fascination he'd had with his grade five teacher's legs—

They had consisted of a combination of arcs and curves that were a revelation for a young boy, producing a dizzy giddiness that easily rivalled the high that summiting mountaineers must experience as they gaze, like gods, on a horizon so distant that the curvature of the earth is on full display. In Baker's case, the curves he had admired were the ones that swept down Mrs. Lema's calves to her elegant pumps, which had supported world-class ankles.

Once, years later, when he had been a university student studying for an upcoming art history exam, it had been the memory of Mrs. Lema that got him through a comparative analysis of major artists and their respective styles. Which of the great artists in history, he'd wondered, would have best portrayed those legs for posterity? Picasso would have made them disproportioned and ugly; de Kooning's expression of them would have been sweetly mocking and altogether too savage; Renoir's representation, though wonderfully joyful, would have been overly pink and fleshy. Michelangelo? Too manly and muscular. In the end, Baker had been able to think of no artistic genius more capable of doing justice to Mrs. Lema's legs than Raphael. No doubt the master would have divinely frescoed her image on the walls of the Vatican's Stanza della Segnatura, right next to his other masterpiece, "The School of Athens." Baker, leaning over his study notes, had chuckled at the thought of how all the popes and cardinals through the centuries would have stolen glances at Mrs. Lema—and then had to hustle off to confession.

"Once again, I miscalculated," Baker explained to his rapt audience. "I thought my story about Mrs. Lema would come across as quaint and sentimental. Rather than be touched or amused by it, Sylvia was insulted to have any part of her body be compared to that of an elementary school teacher's."

"So, you had a crush on Mrs. Lema, your fifth-grade religion teacher?"

"I had a crush on her *legs*," Baker corrected. "Don't get me wrong. I liked her, and she was a cool teacher, but my obsession was with her legs."

Mas smiled, his eyes twinkling in sweet comprehension. "Yeah, for me it was Shirley Jones. I don't remember how old I was, but she was definitely my first love."

A sudden recognition prompted Conrad to chime in. "*The Partridge Family*! I remember that show. It starred David Cassidy, and the family rode around in a school bus that was painted in bright colours and psychedelic patterns. You had a crush on Mrs. Partridge?"

"No. I had a crush on Marian the librarian from The Music Man." Mas smiled at the memory. "She was single, young, pretty, wholesome—all the ingredients to steal a young boy's heart and drive his fantasies."

In the midst of the boyhood reminiscences, the staff room door opened and Perreault walked in. For Baker, it was as if a beam of sunshine had just brightened the room, lending a warm, friendly glow to the mundane, everyday drabness of the place. She was sporting a fresh new hairstyle that accentuated her elegant Nefertiti neck, running into collarbones covered by a cute, classy, short-sleeved blouse, which ran down over shapely breasts and across her toned tummy to tuck into a red pencil skirt, with a thin black belt resting on her slightly curved hips. The skirt was cut just above her knees, with a three-inch slit over her left leg. Perreault's healthy, active lifestyle was revealed in the form of her legs, enhanced further by pumps.

True to form, Perreault was completely oblivious to the effect she had on those in the room, particularly those with XY chromosomes. Appearing to be in a bit of a hurry, she went about her business, checking her mailbox, reading something in a file folder, and turning to head back out the door.

Baker felt a flood of disappointment when he realized she wasn't coming in to chat; maybe she'd been assigned an on-call and had to cover someone's class.

"Hey, Perreault," he said, "you're looking fancy. Got a job interview or something?" He was hoping to sound casual and friendly, with just the right amount of platonic indifference. Jackie, however, read him like a book and followed his gaze toward her.

Perreault turned in the doorway, stepping sideways to let someone through. She looked across to focus on who exactly was addressing her, then spotted the group at the table. "'Afternoon, guys . . . uh, thanks." She blushed just enough to reveal that the comment mattered. "Sorry, I can't hang around right now, but I'll see ya later." She smiled and gave the cutest little wave and then was gone, click-clicking down the hall in shoes that Baker was sure he'd never seen her wear before.

"Wow. Perreault's looking pretty swanky today, eh Baker?" Jackie said.

"Yeah, even more attractive than Marian the librarian, I'd say," Masaccio added.

"What?" Baker pretended he hadn't noticed. "Oh, yeah . . . heh, heh."

Like two proud parents, Jackie and Mas quietly exchanged knowing looks.

*****

"I'll see ya later" was the last thing Perreault had said to them that afternoon, and Baker had put it on a loop in his head and let it play repeatedly the rest of the day, hoping that doing so would increase the likelihood of it actually materializing. (The two of them hadn't spoken face to face since the previous Thursday in the staff room before the Battle of the Bands, and we all remember how *that* conversation had gone.) When that didn't pan out, he headed for the one place in the school that promised some quiet inspiration—and it wasn't the chapel. It was getting on five o'clock, and standing just outside the library, it was evident to Baker that Lawrence had long since left for the day. (The likelihood that Perreault was gone as well was far more disheartening.) Seeing as the room was completely dark, he didn't bother to try the door. It was Gus the custodian who came to his rescue.

"Did you want to get in, Mr. Brooks? Here, allow me."

Gus worked his master key in the lock and swung the door open. Baker thanked him and stepped through, moving trancelike toward his personal shelf of children's books. It wasn't long before he spotted it, the red-white-and blue spine of *My Hockey Stick* among the dozens of other book spines, all in a row. With a tilt and a pull, it was in his hand, and he walked to the same table that he first sat at with Cubby. Just then his phone alerted him to an incoming message. He retrieved it but ignored the message, instead unwinding the earbuds that were wrapped around it, inserting them into his ears, and effectively shutting himself off from the rest of the world as he lost himself in his playlist and Felix Cote's story.

Baker wasn't aware of how long he sat there. He had been slowly flipping through the pages, attending to the illustrations more than the words, and seeing Cubby in the faces of all the hockey-loving boys throughout the book. He let his eyes close as through his earbuds the ethereal voice of k.d. lang sang of beauty and moonlight and broken thrones and baffled kings. The meditation on music and memories magically lifted Baker out of his funk, and he felt peace for the first time in weeks.

He pictured the faces of Cubby, Allen and Helen, and black-and-white images of Cal Ubank, Beezer Sharpe, and Joe Zedelko. Then his mind turned to Sylvia and how their days together had started sweetly but ended sour and toxic, followed by warm memories of a romance during his university years, further followed by images of the people who filled up the better part of his days now, including his teaching colleagues, and his students, and those who comprised his small group of friends: Mas and Sal, Conrad, Angus, and, of course, Perreault. These thoughts were replaced by an image of his candlelit living room during one of the Coven's sessions, except that the candles were scented, and the air was filled with the smell of apples and cinnamon—

The unexpected touch did not startle him, maybe owing to his state of mind, or the tenderness of the hand on his shoulder, or (more likely) a combination of the two. He calmly opened his eyes and was greeted with the face of the one person he'd truly longed to see at that moment: Perreault. She was a vision, plain and simple. He tugged on the wires of his earbuds to release them.

"Whatcha doin'?" That was pure Perreault, a charming, childlike inquisitiveness that belied her kind, mature rationality, and Baker realized he loved her for it.

"Not much. Just enjoying this book—and listening to music. I think my phone is set to repeat because k.d. lang's version of 'Hallelujah' has played about six times now."

"You can easily adjust that, you know."

"Oh, I know." Baker's too-quick attempt to seem like he was comfortable with all things IT was comically transparent. Perreault raised a dubious eyebrow, so he confessed. "OK, maybe I'm not so sure after all."

"Well, I texted you earlier. Luckily, I ran into Gus, who told me you were here. Sorry I kind of brushed everyone off earlier, but it's been a crazy day."

"No problem. You know, at lunch the guys were wondering where you were all day—saying how your absence deprived them of their daily dose of vitamin D."

Perreault blushed at the compliment. "Don't talk about lunch. I haven't had a chance to eat all day. I thought maybe you'd want to join me and grab some dinner."

He wasn't prepared for the invitation. "Thanks all the same, but I think I'm just going to head home."

HALLELUJAH

In response, Perreault spun her DeMellier shoulder bag so it was in her lap, allowing her to reach into a front pocket and extract a card that looked surprisingly familiar to Baker.

"But I've got this voucher I'd like to redeem," she countered brightly.

A thrill shot through him when he recognized his homemade card in her hand. "Voucher?" he wondered.

"Well, my absolution comes at a cost, so I am considering this as your offer to buy me a burger," she announced cheerily, after which her expression became one of mock concern. "All the same, I thought you were a little hard on yourself."

Baker tried to recall the exact words he used for the inside of the card. "Umm... you thought 'stoopid-head' was a bit harsh?"

"Actually, I was referring to your describing yourself as 'old,'" she replied with a prankish smile. Baker had to laugh, then coolly acquiesced. "Oh, alright then. I guess I'd better pony up."

Walking on clouds, he went to return the book to the shelf, then stopped and looked at her. "Perreault, do you have a favourite song?"

"A favourite song, eh? That's a million-dollar question, right up there with travel destinations or movies." She gave it some consideration. "Now if you're referring to 'Hallelujah,' I'll admit it's a good one, but it's not my favourite. No, I think my favourite song is Pink Floyd's 'Wish You Were Here.'"

"Really? I would've guessed something by Janice Joplin or Joni Mitchell."

"Oh, I like singing their tunes, but few songs speak my language like 'Wish You Were Here.' It's a little secret I don't typically share with people."

"Well, I'm flattered, then—that you'd share that with me, I mean."

"Now that you know mine, what's yours?"

"That's a tough one for me. At this point in my life, I don't think I have a favourite."

"OK then, last time you had a favourite song, what was it?"

Baker exhaled. "Hoo boy. D'you have time for a story?" Taking Perreault's encouraging smile as a yes, he proceeded to tell it. "Back in university I fell into my first serious relationship, and those first few weeks, well, it was all giddiness and light—" He broke off, catching himself. "God, listen to me."

"Not at all. It sounds delightful. Keep going."

"Well, during those early days, when we were getting to know each other, she revealed to me that one of her favourite bands was the Psychedelic Furs... you know, with heartthrob Richard Butler as the frontman and all that. Naturally, they would often be playing in the background when were together, so when I hear them today, all these years later, I'm still flooded by the warmth and sweetness of that time in my life..." His voice trailed off, never having shared that story with anyone before now.

"The Psychedelic Furs, huh? Any one song in particular."

"Yes, as a matter of fact. 'The Ghost in You.' I heard it the other day while driving home from school. That's one song that makes me reminisce. It makes me feel young again."

"C'mon, Baker, you make it sound like you're someone's grandfather," she teased. "Richard Butler, eh?" She paused as if trying to recall the words to the song, then softly sang a bit. "Angels fall like rain . . . and love, love, love . . . is all of heaven away . . ."

Baker was relieved to discover he had been right to confide in her; she completely empathized with how deeply he treasured those memories. Before things could get awkward, she broke the silence and brought them both back to the present.

"That's a lovely story. Thanks for sharing it with me. But my stomach's still growling, so if you don't mind, I'd like to get something to eat."

Baker reshelved the book and followed her out of the library. Perreault suggested he drive, so she could reset his phone. "And maybe I'll add another version of 'Hallelujah' to your playlist. Have you heard Rufus Wainwright's cover? I've always considered it the best of the lot."

He hadn't delved very deeply into Rufus Wainwright's catalogue, but he began to think that anything that earned Perreault's recommendation would be fine with him. He gave her his phone and got out his car keys.

As they walked shoulder to shoulder, Perreault commenced to working through the options on Baker's phone. "Right, the first thing I'm going to do—with your permission, of course," she nudged Baker off stride by playfully leaning into him, "is include my number in your list of favourites."

CHAPTER THIRTY
DIVINE INTERVENTION

I don't know if I'm gonna live long enough to tell the tale
About the day I saw my Pines finally claim Doc Gawain's Grail
And so I'm counting on some Divine intervention

Tuesday, January 21 – Wednesday, January 29

Coney Nation woke up Tuesday to news that the Florida Everblades had moved ahead of Toronto into third place in the division when they had defeated Minnesota the night before. Mighty Pines fans could be forgiven if they were shocked at the speed of change in the hockey landscape. To think that just two weeks earlier there had been talk of the possibility of the Pines overtaking Boston for first place, and now, six games later, they found themselves out of a playoff spot.

In other news, Catholic teachers across Ontario held a province-wide one-day strike, hitting the pavement outside their respective schools to protest the Conservative government's cuts to education and the ongoing impasse at the bargaining table.

Saturday was the 25th of January on the calendar—Robbie Burns Day—which in 2020 happened to coincide with the observance of the Lunar New Year and the Year of the Rat. It was also at this time that Canada's first confirmed case of COVID-19, a Toronto man in his fifties, was placed in isolation at Toronto's Sunnybrook Hospital.

On Sunday the sports world took a vicious hit with news that basketball legend Kobe Bryant had perished when his helicopter crashed in Calabasas, California, just northwest of Los Angeles. Bryant, forty-one, had been travelling with his thirteen-year-old daughter, Gianna, to her basketball game. Seven others were on board, including the pilot. All nine passengers died. Tributes poured in throughout the day as the tragic news spread. All NBA games went ahead as scheduled, albeit under a cloud of heaviness. Bryant was honoured at the start of the Raptors-Spurs game when the Raptors, on their first possession, let the twenty-four-second clock run down, as the fans in attendance graciously stood and cheered. San Antonio did the same when they took their first possession. (Kobe's number for the last ten years of his twenty-year career was twenty-four.)

The start of the work week saw the expanding impact of the coronavirus continue to dominate the news cycle. There were two presumptive cases in Toronto, a man and his wife who had flown in from China the week before. Attempts were being made to contact all the passengers on the same flight who were sitting within three rows of the couple.

It had been a long week for members of Coney Nation, who had to suffer through seven days without Mighty Pines hockey, but Monday mercifully saw the team back on the ice in Nashville to play the Honky-Tonks. The week off seemed to agree with the Pines as they took the game to the 'Tonks, recording a 5-2 win. Toronto then moved on to the state of Texas for a midweek game in Dallas against the Stetsons. Again, the Pines displayed some offensive punch for another five-goal night to win 5-3.

Earlier that day in Edinburg, Texas, Canada's women's national soccer team had played an Olympic qualifier against Saint Kitts and Nevis. With 820 spectators in attendance, Christine Sinclair made international soccer history when she scored her 185th goal in international competition, thereby surpassing American Abby Wambach for first place among all international players, male or female. In comparison, among the all-time great male soccer players, Iranian Ali Daei topped the list with 109 goals scored, followed by Portugal's Christiano Ronaldo with 99.

Having spent the better part of the day finishing off a set of exams and recording the marks, Baker desperately needed to get up out of his seat and do something—anything—else. Jumping out of his classroom window was one option, but fortunately his gaze happened to carry across the room to where a clutch of miniature clay gargoyles made by his grade eleven students was sitting on a drying rack, waiting to be baked in the kiln. Happy for the excuse to engage in any sort of physical activity, he immediately set about preparing the kiln to accept a class-load of sculptures.

While gathering the gargoyles, Baker stopped at the sink and cranked the faucet open to give the plumbing a thorough flush. The sound of water swirling down the drain caused him to marvel at the way random events sometimes occurred in freaky congruence. For instance, he was in the process of loading the clay gargoyles into the kiln for firing, and the gurgle emanating from the sink was a perfect onomatopoeia from which the name of the sculptures he was handling had derived. In fact, it was during one of his lessons about cathedral building in the Middle Ages that he mentioned how authentic stone gargoyles had originally been downspouts placed along the eaves of

French Gothic cathedrals. Their function had been to take water from the roof and direct it down and away from the structure. The artisans had transformed the stone into creatures with leering faces and gaping mouths, meant to strike fear into the faithful as they approached the building to attend mass.

As was his wont, Baker thought about how this knowledge might be applied in a way that would serve to help the Toronto Mighty Pines. For instance, would there be any benefit to setting gargoyles up in the rafters to survey the ice surface and aim hexes at members of visiting teams? On the other hand, they could serve as talismans or charms that produced positive energy, not unlike Whitey Kilpatrick's use of pyramid power for his Pines' playoff run in 1976. Baker knew that the Rogers Center (formerly the SkyDome) had gargantuan gargoyles of a sort, fashioned to look like caricatures of the fans in the stands—albeit without the downspout properties of authentic ones. Maybe that's what the Pines could use: strategically placed gargoyles on the roof of Nova Tank Arena, looking down upon Elysian Square, where nine bronze statues of Pines legends were assembled.

As these thoughts pinballed within his cranium, Baker leaned over the edge of the kiln, reaching down into its bowels to set two gargoyles on a large round pedestal. That done, he pulled his head out of the kiln and paused, continuing to stare inside while another image played in his mind. He envisioned himself a bedraggled pilgrim in France some six hundred years ago, having completed a gruelling overland journey that began in a rural peasant village and culminated in one of the great cities in the realm. At the hub of that medieval metropolis stood a towering cathedral of carved granite and coloured glass. As a peasant-cum-pilgrim, he stood next to the massive base of a stone buttress, gazing in awe at a sky pierced by a towering, tapered spire. Suddenly, he was struck by a flash of insight, as if a bolt of lightning deflected off the spire and landed at his feet, bringing him back to the present with a thought so lucid it caused him to literally straighten up. A pilgrimage—that's it! An act of true devotion where the faithful entered the presence of a holy relic to obtain God's blessing. He would engage in his own little pilgrimage, complete with petitions and prayers and—

"Hey ... nice gargoyles."

Conrad's voice interrupted Baker's thoughts, and just as quickly as his brilliant idea struck, it vanished in the maze and tangle of cerebral synapses. It would not be retrieved again for another two weeks.

"Seems like a good crop this year."

Baker looked at Conrad, then at the gargoyles in the kiln, then back at Conrad while nodding in agreement. "You know something? You're right. It *is* a good crop."

Conrad grinned, pleased with himself. But Baker's gargoyles weren't the reason for his stopping by. "It's good to see you. It's been, what, two weeks? How did your semester finish up? Got all your marking done?"

They spent the next few minutes catching up, trading shop talk and basically discussing the weather. Then Conrad revealed the main reason for his visit. "I wanted to get your take on the Battle of the Bands gig. How do you think it went?"

Up until that point Baker hadn't been directly asked by anyone for his impression of the performance. And now that he was faced with having to offer an opinion, it was difficult to clearly recall the moment on stage, as if he'd discarded it like something that didn't warrant inclusion in the scrapbook of his mind.

"I guess it went pretty well. I mean, Perreault was a star, of course, that much could be expected. And Mas and Angus were clutch when it mattered."

"What about you? How was your experience?"

"I'd describe it as a necessary evil. Just trying to minimize the damage, you know?"

"If it makes any difference, the others were unanimous in considering the performance a success."

"As far as I'm concerned, it's in the past."

"OK, then, how about we talk about the present: You ready for today?" (That day was the first time all five members of Bakers' Coven would play together since the Friday session before Christmas.)

"Well, I haven't got anything prepared as far as music goes, if that's what you mean. What I do have is more in the way of spoken-word stuff—a bit of poetry, you might say."

"Terrific. It sounds like we're all set then."

"Ya think?"

"Absolutely. We're coming back off a break. It's a new start—a new semester with new courses, new classes, new kids. And I've taken the liberty of putting a little something together—with Perreault—for this session."

"You mean you two have a song prepared?"

"I hope you don't mind."

"Of course not. In fact, it's a huge relief to hear that you have something. Now I feel there's a point to us getting together today."

"Good, because it's been one hell of a month, for you and me both. We can shake off the rust and get back to it. The Coven's back." Conrad put an exclamation point on it with a firm slap on the back. "But I'll let you carry on with your gargoyles." He stepped out of the kiln room, then stopped and turned to face Baker. "See you in an hour?" Only when Baker gave his assurance that he'd be there did Conrad take his leave.

An hour—Shit. Suddenly, Baker was pressed for time. But at least he could shrug the last bit of remorse off his shoulders, now that he had Conrad's blessing. The best part about having an hour was that with each passing minute, he was one minute closer to the time he'd see Perreault.

Thinking of Perreault reminded him that Valentine's Day was on the horizon. He looked at the gargoyle in his hand and saw it in a new light; considered it actually kind of cute. If someone were to manufacture it out of fur and stuffing, it would have made a great cuddly toy. He smiled at the thought and was suddenly seized by another idea, an inspiration.

* * * * *

Sixty minutes later Baker was in the music room chatting with his bandmates. He was inclined to take a backseat for this session, but not in the way he had before Christmas, as a proud patriarch. No, this time it was simply the most suitable way to behave given his indiscretions and all the self-serving choices he'd made since New Year's Day. Although he would have loved to host a session in his living room, he felt it wasn't his place to suggest such a thing. He was unworthy of leading a group that he'd abandoned.

Of course, no one else saw it quite that way. None of them demanded any kind of penance from him for his recent absences. It was business as usual as far as they were concerned.

Conrad reached into his guitar case and pulled out a typewritten note. "I was hoping you folks would indulge me as I read this short prayer before we begin in earnest."

"Look at you!" Angus gushed. "A prayer *and* a song."

"Let's just say I wanted to make sure the Guy Upstairs understands what we're trying to accomplish here."

Baker was thrilled to see that Conrad was back in earnest. "OK, everybody, bring it in. Let's begin with a prayer." He motioned everyone to gather in a loose circle. Thus assembled, they all naturally bowed their heads. That was Conrad's cue.

> *Our Father in Heaven*
> *We humbly ask that you pardon our frailties and indulge our whimsies*
> *We gather here, loath to burden you with this trivial request*
> *As our petition pales compared to the urgent needs of the wider world*
> *Therefore, we turn to the forces of the unseen world*
> *(A world that falls within the realms of the universe you created)*
> *We place this petition on behalf of the Toronto Mighty Pines*
> *Who seek the ultimate reward: the Clarence Cup*
> *An achievement which will return the city to its rightful place*
> *In the pantheon of hockey greatness*
> *And so we call upon the spirits of earth, air, fire, and water*
> *We call upon the spirits of Pines legends past*
> *We call upon the spirits of those who have gone before us*

> *And shared similar hopes and dreams*
> *Hear us now*
> *Amen*

The other four repeated the "amen," and a few seconds of silence passed before Baker realized it was his turn.

"Oh, I guess it's me." He reached into his pocket for a folded sheet of crumpled paper.

"Hang on," Conrad said, hustling over to arm himself with his guitar. "I'm just going to pluck the strings as you read, you know, as accompaniment."

When he saw that Conrad was ready, Baker fixed his eyes on the first line, cleared his throat, and began.

> *Here I stand, a member of Coney Nation*
> *With a voice in my head I cannot ignore*
> *That persists in putting paid to my doubts*
> *That Pines supremacy can be restored*
> *And if tradition is our guide*
> *A banner will be raised in October*
> *And the fans in this town may find peace*
> *With the losing finally over*
> *Our heroes will get their rings*
> *And proudly hold them up*
> *But the ring that matters most*
> *Is the one encircling the Cup*
> *A silver-plated ring whose polished surface*
> *Is due to be marred and dented*
> *With the names of every person*
> *Who directly contributed*
> *To ending what at the time*
> *According to all reports*
> *Was the longest championship drought*
> *In North American pro sport*

Baker paused at this point but dared not look up lest he ruin the moment. Conrad's accompaniment beautifully set off what was being read, such that Baker had to concentrate to stay focused.

> *Like an artist on skates, Mason Andrews displays creative brilliance*
> *Not since Glenn Gould sat down to record the Goldberg Variations*
> *Has so much virtuosity been seen in a pair of hands around these parts*
> *At twenty-two, Andrews is the same age as Gould was*

DIVINE INTERVENTION

When he first tackled Bach's masterpiece for posterity
And just as Gould was re-interpreting the work of a genius
Andrews is putting his stamp on the standards of goal scoring as a Pine

Ricky Randall, I dedicate these next four lines to you:
With the quintessential bluff
You shrugged off the doubters that an overall lack of size engenders
Sleight of frame you may seem, your sleight of hand proves lethal to opposing teams
Don't sleep on those sleepy eyes; they see teammates where scoring opportunities lie
If a disarming smile is any indication, Randall's signals winning to Coney Nation

This year Addy Brouwer should prosper on the ice
Having replaced the business of winning contract negotiations
With the business of winning hockey games
Number eighty-eight plays with speed and finesse
And like a smoothly swinging saloon door
he is exceedingly adept at zone entries and exits
Addy is a sight to behold in many respects
If hair and looks counted, he would cause opposing goaltenders to swoon in their nets
Much the way his admiring fans swoon in their seats

Baker's initial plan with his Pines poetry was to have a verse composed for each of the core four. Partway through the third stanza, however, he suddenly remembered that he hadn't quite finished the task. He had written absolutely nothing about Gianni Valentino. This was confirmed when he turned the page over and saw that it was blank, save for the initials G. V. at the top of it. Baker had no choice but to sputter to a stop.

"Um, that's all I have for now—"

Caught off guard, the others just looked at him. Conrad ceased playing in an awkward fashion.

Perreault came to his rescue. "Oh . . . well, that was terrific, Baker. Well done." She began to clap her appreciation, joined by Masaccio.

"What? What about Gianni Hockey?" Angus asked. "You said you had something for all four."

Goddam you, Angus, Baker thought. *Why must you insist on being such a toddler sometimes?* Then for the second time that afternoon, his thoughts were interrupted by Conrad's voice, counting aloud to lead his bandmates into the song, but it was only his guitar that came in on the opening beat, working through the catchy intro, followed thereafter by Perreault's angelic voice.

I don't know if I'm gonna live
Long enough to tell the tale
About the day I saw my Pines
Finally claim Doc Gawain's Grail
And so, I'm counting on some
Divine intervention

On days that I pray to my God
I ask that he will grant for me
The wish I made when just a boy
To see my Pines make history
It's all depending on his
Divine intervention . . . Alright

We're all counting on his
Divine intervention

'Cuz he loves us
He will hear us
And then see us
Through this crisis
Ahhh . . .
Oh yeah 'cuz he loves us
I look around
And I see Coney Nation
They're all counting on his
Divine intervention

The performance was first-rate—which went without saying. What stood out for Baker, however, was the manner in which Conrad had stepped up to the plate for the session. There was no doubt that today was his show, his baby. He had evidently taken some time to search his soul and had come back determined to put in the request to the Big Man. For Conrad, there was no point in prevaricating. Ask and ye shall receive. Divine intervention.

And yet Baker was aware that asking the Almighty to intercede still required a significant leap of faith, because one never knew what God had in store. (Humans could be such unsubtle creatures at times, unable—or unwilling—to fathom the depths of the Lord's plans. Heaven knew Baker had been guilty of that many times over.) In the end it was important to remember that what one asked for was not necessarily what one received.

He could only pray it didn't involve many more Cup-less years for the Mighty Pines.

CHAPTER THIRTY-ONE
A MOST UNUSUAL DRAFT

Saturday, February 1 – Wednesday, February 5

It had been fully two weeks since the Pines played in front of their fans at Nova Tank Arena, and on Saturday they gave the Toronto faithful something to cheer about with an overtime win against Ottawa. They had come out of the All-Star break with guns blazing, earning three straight wins. Was it due to the intervention of a beneficent deity or the influence of some pretty lines of poetry? No one could know for sure, but any bit of help would be appreciated as the team was now entering the busiest four weeks of the season, which coincided with a time on the calendar commonly known to players and coaches alike as the dog days of winter.

In fact, the month of February had the Pines facing a schedule of fifteen games in twenty-nine days (this being a leap year). There were still twenty-four games until the playoffs, and players were bone-weary and travel sapped. It was a matter of managing the persistent aches and pains and the ever-present fatigue. (Rare was the player who was one hundred percent healthy at this point in the season.) Every coach in the league knew this was the time of the year he truly earned his salary, inventing ways to keep his charges fresh and motivated. This was precisely the challenge facing Boris Duggan and his staff, knowing they would need to navigate these dog days with care if they were to assure themselves of a playoff spot.

Sunday was February 2, Groundhog Day, and the early morning long-range weather forecast was of the glass-two-thirds-full sort: Two of the three most famous rodent Nostradamuses predicted an early spring. Both Wiarton Willie and Pennsylvania's Punxsutawney Phil came out of their burrows and saw fit to linger awhile. Out in Halifax, however, Shubenacadie Sam was driven back into the security of his den by his shadow. For those who liked to believe in weather forecasting based on things like red skies in the morning and groundhogs at dawn, it appeared that Old Man Winter would be vacating the premises early this year—according to Willie and Phil at any rate.

Meanwhile, down in sunny Florida, people's minds were on football predictions rather than groundhog predictions as the city of Miami hosted Super Bowl LIV. The

Kansas City Chiefs came back from a ten-point deficit in the fourth quarter to claim the Lombardi Trophy by a score of 31-20 over the San Francisco Forty-Niners. Voters for game MVP settled on Chiefs' quarterback Patrick Mahomes.

On Monday, the Mighty Pines' three-game winning streak was brought to an abrupt halt with a disappointing 5-3 home defeat to Florida, Toronto's closest pursuer in the standings. The loss dropped the team into a tie with the Everblades for third place in the division. Two days later the Pines were in New York and looking to get back on the winning track, only to take it on the chin for the second straight game.

Perreault had called a meeting of the Coven for the end of the day and was now addressing the guys as she sat on the edge of the teacher's desk in her classroom, next to a bright yellow file folder and a large, luxurious, vintage hat box (something from out of the 1920s).

"Thanks for setting aside the time to be here," she said. "I have every intention of keeping this short and sweet, so I'll get right to it. As much as I love performing our musical spells, something occurred to me during our session last week, particularly when Baker was reading his Pines poetry."

Baker raised his hand. "Just a point of clarification: will it take us in another direction? If so, I would vote in favour because, to be honest, I don't see what we're presently doing as being all that effective."

"I might have just the thing, then," Perreault offered. "I went back through the songs that you wrote and discovered they were consistent in bemoaning five decades of losing, followed by a request for an overall increase in team success. But that request was directed toward the 'gods of hockey,' so to speak. It got me thinking about how we might do ourselves a favour by targeting the players themselves."

"But 'Five Years' *did* target key players," Baker said. "As did my Pines poetry."

"Yes they did, and I propose we do more of the same—the operative word being 'more,' as in making mention of the entire team."

"You might have something there," Conrad said. "The players are the ones who impact the game directly, after all."

"That's right. And it was one line in Baker's Pines poetry that stood out for me." She opened the yellow file folder and fished out a piece of paper. It was Baker's original poem sheet.

"'Ricky Randall, I dedicate these next four lines to you.'"

That was all. She set it back on the desk and looked at the others. "That one line triggered something in my mind, but I couldn't put my finger on it until later. Turns out I was reminded of a song by the Nails: '88 Lines about 44 Women.' You guys know it?"

"Oh, good tune," Angus said while the others nodded their assent.

"The original song dedicates two lines to each woman, as the title implies," Perreault explained. "But for our purposes, two lines for each player on the team would leave us short on content, so I did some simple math and came up with something I think we can work with: eighty-eight lines for twenty-two Pines."

"Wait," Mas said. "You wrote a new song about twenty-two Pines players?"

"God no!" She looked pointedly at Baker. "And I have no intention of throwing this entirely in your direction either—although I don't doubt you'd be up to the task. But on such short notice, I figure we can all pitch in and get this done in a timely fashion. Everybody will have a hand in this one."

Conrad nodded sternly, like a military bobblehead. "Great thinking, Perreault. Let's not leave everything up to Baker all the time."

"So, how're we going to divvy this up, boss?" Baker inquired.

Perreault went to the yellow folder again and took out a smaller manila envelope. She held it aloft and jiggled it as if it contained assorted enticements. "I've got twenty-two slips of paper in this envelope." Then she directed their attention to the mystery box, opened the lid, and pulled out the most magnificent top hat.

"Whoa, that's a fucking awesome lid," Angus exclaimed.

"Isn't it? It's my Papi Rene's. Must be close to a hundred years old. I thought we could have some fun and do this in style."

"You ain't fooling around. That's one stylish topper. It looks like it should be on display in the Smithsonian—or Buckingham Palace."

"Like I said, I've got twenty-two slips of paper here with the names of twenty-two Pines on the present roster." She opened the envelope, turned it upside down over the top hat, and shook it so that a cluster of white squares tumbled down into it. "Now we just pass the hat around until we've each picked out four names."

"Wait a minute," Angus said. "That leaves some extra names, doesn't it?"

"True, the work can't be divided evenly, but—"

"I'd be happy to take the other two," Baker cut in.

"Excellent. Our resident songwriter will deal with the leftover names."

"Um... you want to do this right now?" Masaccio asked.

"If no one objects, yes, I thought we might choose names now. Unless, of course, you have someplace you need to be. It shouldn't take too long."

No one voiced any objections, so it fell to Perreault to lead them through the process.

When Cheers Are Not Enough

"Why don't we have some fun and do this like a playoff pool? We'll hold four rounds of selecting names out of the hat. Then Baker gets the two that are leftover at the end." Since Conrad was seated closest to Perreault, she walked over to him with the hat. "Let's not waste any time. Conrad, you get first pick."

He rubbed his hands together. "I'm just taking one, right?"

"Yes, we each pick one at a time."

"Can I reveal my pick?"

"Sure, I don't see why not."

Masaccio injected some pageantry into the proceedings by announcing the opening pick using his best commissioner's voice. "With the first pick of the 2020 Bakers' Coven Mighty Pines entry draft, Conrad Wiederschoen selects..."

Right on cue, Conrad pulled a slip of paper and read the name. "Kalle Makinen!"

"Hey-hey, K-Mak," Angus cheered. "How perfect that our German selects a speedy German."

Baker couldn't believe his ears. "Angus, you idiot, Makinen's Finnish."

"Finished? That's your opinion. He's only twenty-three years old. He's just entering his prime."

"No, no, I meant he's from Finland, not Germany."

"Finland, Germany, Russia—wherever he's from, I think he's gonna be a force. Right now, though, he's gotta get his butt in gear."

Perreault knew if she let them carry on like this every time a name was pulled, they'd be there till midnight. "OK, Angus, seeing as you're next in line, pick a player."

Mas did his thing again. "With the second overall pick, Angus Fletcher selects..."

Angus rummaged in the hat before withdrawing a slip of paper and snuck a peek at the name, then thrust it into his pants pocket.

"Who'd you pick?" Mas asked.

"I'm not telling. I'm going to keep it a secret until we're all done. You'll have to wait until the end of the draft."

Perreault rolled her eyes. "OK then, Mas, your turn."

"Let's see... Masaccio Clementi selects..." he reached into the hat, extracted a slip, and triumphantly announced the name. "Gianni Vaaa-len-tiii-nooo!"

The room erupted in whoops and cheers.

"El Capitan goes to Mas!"

"Gianni Hockey."

In the midst of the hoopla, Perreault held the hat out to Baker, using a booming announcer's tone to cut through the noise. "With the fourth overall pick in the draft, Baker Brooks selects..."

"Alex Cazwell!"

"Beautiful," Perreault said. Then she held the hat up high and reached in herself. "And to complete the first round of the inaugural Bakers' Coven Mighty Pines entry draft, Perreault Thoreau chooses . . ." She fished out one of the squares, glanced at the name, hesitated, looked at the other four breathless faces, and inhaled for suspense before adopting her best Bobby Jenkins play-by-play voice. "May-son Aaan-drews!"

The room exploded. One might have thought big number thirty-four had just scored the winning goal in game seven of the Clarence Cup final. Gus the custodian, carrying out his after-school chores down the hall, heard the commotion and popped his head into the room to see what all the fuss was about.

"What's going on? Somebody win the lottery?"

"Sorry, Gus. We're just having some fun. We'll try to keep it down."

"Aw, that's OK. Make as much noise as you want. There's no one left in the school anyway."

And so it went through three more rounds. Despite Perreault's best intentions to make it a quick process, the other four seemed in no hurry to finish, enjoying themselves and savouring the experience of selecting players out of a vintage felted beaver fur top hat.

When the draft was finally done and twenty-two slips of paper had been selected, Perreault kept everyone focused on the task at hand, cueing the original Nails' song up on her laptop so they could listen to it together. True to form, Angus couldn't resist several choice comments regarding some of the descriptions of the forty-four women, specifically the lines referring to Carla, Joan, Karen, and Tanya Turkish.

"I didn't think we'd need ground rules, but for Angus's sake: keep it to hockey," Perreault advised.

"OK, I got it," Angus joked. "No details about kinky sex."

When they were through listening to the song, the magnitude of the task suddenly dawned on Angus. Writing verses about four different hockey players seemed light years beyond his level of expertise. He asked for some direction on getting started and was hit with a range of suggestions from the others.

"Well, you can start with the player's name," Baker offered.

"First or last?"

"Either. It doesn't really matter as long as we know who you're referring to."

"Then what?"

"Any detail that is specific to the guy. His number, his position, his nationality . . . what else?"

"What line he plays on," Perreault added. "You can key in on certain skills, like speed, puck handling ability, a hard shot."

"Even personal details," Conrad said. "Like how Mason Andrews is from the Louisiana Bayou and Gianni Valentino was born and raised in Toronto's Little Italy."

"Anything else?"

"It's important to have the words follow the rhythm of each line," Baker directed.

"The rhythm?"

"Yeah, you know, the beat. You're a drummer, aren't you?"

"And stick to the rhyme scheme," Perreault said. "It goes like this: A – B – C – B."

"What?" Angus asked, growing more frazzled. "A – B – C – B? What's that mean?"

"Basically, you need to make sure the second and fourth lines rhyme."

"Geez," Angus moaned, "I didn't know it would be this complicated."

"How about if we do one together?" Baker offered.

"That'd be helpful."

"But first you have to reveal your picks."

"Sure. I told you guys you'd find out when we were done." Angus reached into his pocket and produced four slips of paper, dropping them on the desk. Baker opened them one by one, announcing each player in turn.

"Anders Lundin, Addy Brouwer, Reg Harmon, and Sergei Nikitin." Baker stopped to consider the names. "OK, let's take Anders Lundin. Perreault, can I write some ideas on your envelope?" She passed him the envelope. "What's Lundin's number. Mas, can you Google Lundin's—"

"Thirty-eight."

"Thank you. Now then, let's say I begin with his name and the fact that he's a rookie. How old is he?"

"He's nineteen," Angus said. "That much I know. Also that he's undersized for a defenceman."

"Excellent." Baker took another minute to scratch out some words on the back of the envelope. "OK, how's this?" Baker read his verse.

> *Anders Lundin is a rookie*
> *He wears number thirty-eight*
> *At nineteen he's just a kid, but*
> *With more size he should be great*

"Holy shit, that's amazing," Angus marvelled. "You just came up with that on the spot?"

"Don't be too impressed. It's not very good. It's just a sample of how this can work."

"Just a sample? It works for me. I'm gonna use it. Thanks, man. Now I've only got three more to do."

A MOST UNUSUAL DRAFT

Perreault proposed they meet the following Friday for the actual session. "Send me your finished verses sometime during the day on Friday. And since we don't need instruments, we can just meet back here in this room. Oh, and a couple of props would be useful. Baker, I'm going to need you to bring five pillar candles, one for each of us."

"Five pillar candles, got it."

"And we each need to bring a Mighty Pines jersey to wear during the ceremony. Is that OK?"

"Uh... what if we don't own a Mighty Pines jersey?" Baker asked.

"What do you mean?"

"Well, I don't own a jersey."

"But that's impossible," Angus said, stunned. "How can you be a freakazoid Pines fan and not own a jersey?"

"I don't like wearing hockey jerseys. I never have. I think they look goofy."

The others looked at Baker with incomprehension.

"I have eyes," Baker continued. "But I should qualify what I just said. Hockey jerseys *do* have a cute sexiness to them when worn by the ladies. As for guys, well, they just make us look like out-of-shape, middle-aged, wannabe hockey players. Me? I don't care to look like that, thank you very much."

"Enlighten us further on the sex appeal of women who wear hockey jerseys," Perreault demanded, half-teasing, but Baker answered in all earnestness.

"Well, I find it has the same sexy quality as when a chick wears a man's oversized pyjama top to bed."

Angus laughed. "Yeah, but it also helps that she's buck naked underneath that pyjama top."

"Good news for you, Perreault," Mas announced. "*You* get a thumbs-up to wear a jersey because it'll make you cute and sexy, but the rest of us will just look like overweight, over-the-hill losers."

Perreault stuck to her guns. "Sorry Baker, but regardless of any fashion faux pas, I need us all to wear a Pines jersey. Does anyone have an extra they could loan this guy for fifteen minutes next week?"

"Yeah, I've got, like, three of them," Angus replied. "Go figure, Baker. You'll even have some choice to select the one that's least distasteful."

"That's it then," Perreault concluded. "We have a week to complete the verses for our respective players. We'll meet back here next Friday."

Masaccio and Angus were the first to leave, while Conrad hung back, assisting Perreault and Baker with tidying up. Before long, Masaccio came rushing back into the room.

"Shit! I forgot that next Friday is Valentine's Day. I've got a reservation for dinner with Sal and the girls."

"How wonderful," Perreault exclaimed.

"No, it's not." Baker countered. "That means we'll have to reschedule our Coven session."

"We won't have to reschedule if we can make it quick," Mas said.

"How long can you stay?"

"If I left, say, by 3:30, I'd be good."

"Seeing as we're not going to do the full-on band session with instruments and stuff, and as long as we start by 2:45—?" Perreault looked at Baker and Conrad for confirmation.

"Sure, that'll work just fine," Conrad said. "Besides, it wouldn't hurt if we all went home a little earlier that day. It's the Friday of the Family Day long weekend, after all."

"That's great," Mas said, relieved. "Thanks. I'll be sure to tell Angus. Have a nice weekend."

"See ya," Perreault replied, and then turned to face Conrad and Baker. "Can either of you think of anything else? No? OK then, I'm heading home. I'll see you two on Monday. Good luck to the Pines this weekend!"

Conrad jumped forward and swung the door open for Perreault as she swept through.

CHAPTER THIRTY-TWO
88 LINES ABOUT 22 PINES

Andrews has a wicked shot
He could really fill the net
In him we have a franchise player
Fifty goals is a sure bet

Friday, February 7 – Friday, February 14

Coming off the previous night's win at home against the Hamilton RIMshots, Toronto was in Quebec City on Saturday to face the Citadelles. The visit happened to coincide with Quebec's Winter Carnival, a ten-day event that had been running since 1894 and was promoted as a way to ward off the winter doldrums and cabin fever. There were no such winter doldrums for Timmy Gates, however, as Toronto's backup goaltender was called upon to start both ends of a back-to-back for the first time in his career. Alas, the Pines struggled to dent the score sheet against the Citadelles and were ultimately shut out 2-0.

On Sunday the ninety-second Academy Awards, billed annually as Hollywood's biggest night, resulted in some surprises as voters ignored the higher-profile American-made movies and selected the South Korean film *Parasite* as its big winner. Less surprising was the Best Actress award going to Rene Zellweger for her portrayal of Judy Garland in *Judy* and Joaquin Phoenix winning Best Actor for his leading role in *Joker*.

While many of the 3,400 attendees crowding the Dolby Theatre would not hesitate in voicing concern for social justice and environmental issues, just such a cause was playing itself out in British Columbia. A dispute between the hereditary chiefs of the Wet'suwet'en territory and the provincial government over the Coastal GasLink natural gas pipeline heated up when RCMP officers arrested protesters taking a stand against the $6 billion project. Demonstrations spread to other parts of the country as people expressed solidarity with the protesters.

When Cheers Are Not Enough

On Monday, the Toronto Raptors beat the Minnesota Timberwolves to stretch their winning streak to fifteen games. With the accomplishment, the Raptors claimed the record for most consecutive wins by a Canadian-based professional sports franchise, eclipsing the fourteen-game win streak set by the Calgary Stampeders of the CFL in 2016.

Two days later, a streak of another kind was celebrated when the Guinness World Records formally recognized 112-year-old Chitetsu Watanabe of Japan to be the oldest man alive. Meanwhile, China's reported tally of cases of the coronavirus exceeded 1,000.

In a similar vein, health was the priority for the Mighty Pines, what with the busy PHL schedule affording very little time for rest and recovery. It was a constant battle for players to maintain their health and now there were signs that something of a viral nature was sweeping through Toronto's locker room. The team was looking to gain some traction in order to climb up in the standings, but for all their efforts this week the Pines were just managing to tread water, as evidenced by an overtime win over Phoenix on Tuesday being negated by a regulation loss to Dallas on Thursday. It was a good thing that Friday—Valentine's Day—would be a rare day off before the busy Family Day holiday weekend, with the team scheduled to play a back-to-back beginning in Ottawa on Saturday and finishing in Buffalo on Sunday.

When Baker arrived at Perreault's classroom on Friday after school, Masaccio and Conrad were already there, so he offered a general greeting toward all three but avoided making eye contact with Perreault. Mas and Conrad were oblivious to it, but Perreault sensed it immediately. Rather than be troubled by this behaviour, she found it amusing, mainly because she had her own idea about the reason behind it. She decided to watch and wait. In the meantime, Angus arrived out of breath, clutching two dog-eared sheets of paper.

"Sorry guys. Am I late?"

"You're not late, but I didn't get your song verses," Perreault scolded. "I hope that's them in your hand."

"Yeah, I've got them here." He slapped them down on Baker's desk. "It took me most of the week to figure these out."

Baker perused the top page, which contained three stanzas. The first one was devoted to Anders Lundin, but it hadn't changed since he'd composed it on the spot a little over a week ago.

"I see you kept the Lundin verse?"

"Yeah. I told you, it's terrific. I even used it to help me with the others."

Baker soon discovered what Angus meant. By some freak coincidence, Lundin, Addy Brouwer and Reg Harmon had the number eight common to their jersey numbers, which allowed Angus to conveniently apply it to the second line of each verse, which in turn allowed him to end every fourth line by rhyming the number "eight" with the word "great."

Baker read the three stanzas on the page aloud. When he finished, Conrad and Mas were stifling laughter while Perreault had to look away from them lest she begin giggling in kind.

Angus was beaming. But then his expression turned serious. "Sorry about the next one, though. I've got to admit I only did that one fifteen minutes ago, at the end of class."

Baker cringed inside but maintained his composure and read the only verse that was printed on the second sheet of paper.

> *Nikitin has a favourite food*
> *Popeye's spinach? Sergei's soup!*
> *This Russian comes with speed and skill*
> *He'll fit right in with this group*

"Well now, that's a good one. I like it," he said in evident shock and amazement.

"Thanks," Angus said, relieved. Then something dawned on him. "But does that mean you don't like the others?"

"Of course not," Perreault said, jumping in. "The others are wonderful. But your reference to spinach and soup in the Nikitin verse is brilliant. I guess you work well under pressure." Then she looked up at the clock above the door. "Oops, we'd better get a move on here."

While Baker set up the candles, Perreault took Angus's verses, quickly typed them up, arranged them with the others so that the song was complete, and then went down the hall to her work room to print the requisite copies. When she returned with the song sheets, the other four were seated in a semicircle around her desk, like grade ones on the first day of school, attired in their Pines sweaters and waiting for their teacher to arrive.

She distributed the pages. "It's nice to see that you guys are ready. Just one final thing, though. Take your jerseys off and turn them inside out." The others realized Perreault had already turned her sweater inside out and slipped it back on.

Baker laughed. "If I didn't look goofy before, I know I will now."

"I suppose you're going to tell us there's some sort of magic in doing this?" Mas asked.

"Yes. Having our Pines jerseys turned this way will strengthen the spell, like rally caps in baseball. Besides, wearing clothing inside out protects against faerie mischief."

Baker did a double take. "Did you say, 'faerie mischief'?"

"Uh-huh. Consider it as hedging our bets. You know, covering all the bases."

Conrad flipped his jersey back over his head so that it was inside out, then slipped it back on. The oversized tag that contained the brand name, jersey size, textile composition, and washing instructions—all in two languages—was flapping under his chin.

"Aha! Now I get it," Baker said. "Any faeries with mischief on their minds will be overcome by fits of laughter when they see us."

Perreault looked around at everyone and smiled in satisfaction. "That's better. Now we can begin."

She had the instrumental version of the song cued up on her laptop. The others sat in a tight circle around her desk, each with a lit green pillar candle set before him. Baker opened the ceremony by reading a short prayer he had composed, after which Perreault recited her grandfather's verselet. Then she tapped the "play" arrow on her laptop. The beat of the song began and continued through four repeats before the words came in.

Perreault had arranged it so that her own stanzas would come first, allowing her to begin the tune.

> *Andrews has a wicked shot*
> *He could really fill the net*
> *In him we have a franchise player*
> *Fifty goals is a sure bet*
>
> *Sanderson's between the pipes*
> *With him back there naught can go wrong*
> *His health is sometimes a concern*
> *Load management will keep him strong*

The song was constructed such that after every two players, the vocals would pause for an instrumental bridge while some voices hummed the simple melody (the humming to be performed by the five bandmates in unison). When that was done, Perreault completed her part.

> *Randall has magician's hands*
> *A potent weapon for the team*
> *At even strength, on power plays*
> *And even killing penalties*
>
> *Scanlon is a rookie winger*
> *Who displays the longest strides*
> *We're hoping his deceptive speed*
> *Will catch opponents by surprise*

88 LINES ABOUT 22 PINES

Then it was Masaccio's turn to recite his verses, beginning with:

> *Valentino is a local boy*
> *A true professional is he*
> *When the Pines needed a leader*
> *They chose him to wear the "C"*

Next up after Mas was Conrad with his four stanzas, the last of which was arguably the best of the lot, with its clever reference to ex-Pine Sean Whitney (who was guilty of ill-advised hits that earned him multi-game suspensions in each of the last two year's playoffs). Toronto had bowed out to the Washington Founders both times, and many attributed those disappointing first-round losses to Whitney's actions. Apparently it had been enough incentive for Kyle Bulac to trade him to Buffalo this past summer, straight up, for winger Alex Cazwell.

> *Cazwell takes the place of Whitney*
> *In a trade with Buff-a-lo*
> *And rest assured come playoff time*
> *He won't be running Founders foes*
>
> *Uh-uh. Not Cazwell*

Angus took over when Conrad was done, beginning with his verse about Sergei Nikitin. The next two were essentially knock-offs of the one about Anders Lundin that Baker improvised last week, with Angus rhyming the words "eight" and "great" in each instance.

> *Brouwer has the softest hands*
> *He wears number eighty-eight*
> *With speed and skill around the net*
> *A few more goals would sure be great*

The final six verses were Baker's to recite. The song ended with this one dedicated to the team's most physically imposing player, who was also a master at the faceoff dot.

> *Patrick Dane's the Pines' big dog*
> *Winning face-offs with a twist*
> *At six-five, two thirty-nine*
> *We chose him to end this list*
>
> *88 lines about 22 Pines*

The consensus within the group was that the first time through the song was plainly a mess. Everyone struggled with the rhythm (the words had to be delivered at a pace that was deceptively quick), some more than others. At other times certain individuals

(Angus!) simply broke out in uncontrollable laughter. Next to Perreault, Conrad proved to be the most proficient and professional of the lot.

Because there was still time before Masaccio had to depart, they decided to perform a second take. Despite a few minor miscues, it was, in Baker's words, "better than the first by a factor of light years."

When they had finished, it was time for Mas to fly, so multiple wishes of happy Valentine's Day and happy Family Day were exchanged all around, as were best wishes for the Pines on their impending back-to-back over the weekend. When the room finally cleared, Perreault and Baker were left to tidy up some odds and ends. She tried to engage him in small talk, but he seemed bent on maintaining a reticence that to her was almost laughable.

"For a while there, I wasn't sure we'd get through all twenty-two verses," she began.

"Heh, yeah ... reciting those lines was tougher than I expected."

"I was relieved Angus was able to come through for us."

"Me too. He actually did a nice job with that Nikitin verse. What a surprise, eh?"

Perreault couldn't wait any longer. "Speaking of surprises—" She walked to the nearest cupboard to retrieve a small but colourful gift bag. "Imagine mine this morning when I found this on my desk." She held it up, then set it down and extracted what was inside, revealing a plush toy rodent. "Isn't he cute?" She pointed it at Baker and gave it a playful shake. "At first, I thought it might be a Valentine's Day present, but then I read the card that came with it. Thank you for the belated Chinese New Year's gift." She stood in front of him, placed her hands on his shoulders, and kissed him. "It's very thoughtful of you."

Baker's cheeks were almost as pink as the tissue paper that was showing out of the top of the gift bag. He smiled shyly. "Aw, you know, I saw it and couldn't resist. How many girls can say they got a stuffed rat for Valentine's—er, Chinese New Year? I thought it was appropriate since it's the Year of the Rat, you know."

"The card also informs me that we're going out to dinner tomorrow night."

He had almost forgotten. "Oh ... yeah, well ... I was hoping ... only if you're free, of course ..."

"Baker, you're wonderful." She gave him a warm hug. "I'd love to have dinner with you. Thank you."

Perreault set the stuffed animal on display beside the gift bag and took the greeting card out. Her hockey jersey was draped over a chair, so Baker took it and held it up, apparently assessing the Mighty Pines pinecone crest.

"So ... what's the rule with stuffed animals?" he asked.

"Rule?"

"Yes, like, do you give them a name?"

"Oh, for sure. I've already named this little guy. It's Robespierre."

He began to fold the sweater. "Robespierre? How unique—and appropriate. It's so French Revolutionary—and ratty."

"It's a good one, huh?" she said, admiring the front of the card.

Baker placed the folded garment on the desk beside Robespierre. "You know, I was a bit disappointed that none of the guys acknowledged that I was right."

"About what?"

"About women looking sexy in hockey jerseys," he said with a semi-straight face. "Seeing you in this sweater was slam-dunk proof of it."

To her knowledge this was the first time Baker had ventured to comment on her physical attractiveness. She was ready with a response: "I guess we should move on to proving the second part of your theory then."

The hint went over his head. "Huh? You lost me. What second part?"

"The part about women in men's pyjama tops."

Latching on to the innuendo, he found himself trying to suppress another blush. "But, remember what Angus said last week—"

"About how it helps to be naked underneath? I remember. You *do* own pyjamas, don't you?"

"Just one pair—a hundred percent cotton and covered with cute woodland creatures, like beavers and bears and such."

"You mean you don't have elegant silk sleepwear, with lapels and cuffs and velvet piping?"

"You should know by now that I'm no Hugh Hefner."

"Pity. But I'm sure we can make do with forest critters and cotton."

"Hmm . . . This sounds like it could be fun."

"I agree," Perreault said impishly before adopting a scholarly tone. "All in the interest of research, of course."

"Oh, of course."

CHAPTER THIRTY-THREE
REVELATIONS

"Energy shared is energy lost" was how Dorcas justified the need to keep Coven business within the Coven. It was the basis for her "rule of silence," and to this point in time Baker had taken her rule to another level—not even divulging his own personal "desire" to his bandmates. But now the circumstances had changed, what with the Pines finding themselves in a life-and-death struggle just to make the playoffs, and deep down he knew that the benefits of enlisting a trusted second opinion outweighed the possibility that sharing his personal and private desire would weaken the magic. He had an idea—a risky one at that—and he needed to bounce it off someone he could trust. Perreault was that someone.

As it happened, she was seated directly across from him.

It was the day after the "88 Lines about 22 Pines" session. He felt fortunate to have been able to secure reservations at a stylish restaurant that was part of a hotel and spa retreat setting about twenty minutes north of where he lived. They were seated at a cozy candlelit table for two in a corner of the room, beside a large window that looked out on a picturesque mill pond, windswept and frozen.

A perusal of the wine menu had Perreault suggesting a Sonoma County Pinot Noir. Baker was amenable to it, although he could just as easily have gone with any one of the options on the beer list. The wine arrived promptly, and after the smiling and effervescent waiter filled their glasses, Perreault raised her glass toward Baker. "Here's to friends and family, the Coven and the Pines, and a year that promises wonderful things."

"Boy, that's a mouthful, but I'm in," Baker said. "Here's to all of that. Whatever happens, it should be an interesting ride."

They drank together, then set down their glasses, Baker's gaze drifting to the scene outside, where he caught sight of someone walking a dog on a trail along the pond's far shoreline.

Before the silence turned awkward, Perreault looked at him and smiled, as if recalling something. "Do you remember the first time we spoke?"

REVELATIONS

The question seemed to shake him back to the interior of the restaurant. "Huh? Oh ... you bet, like it was yesterday. I held the staff room door for you, and on your way out you assured me that Ricky Randall would get signed before the season started."

Perreault beamed and nodded in agreement. "I remember the first time I saw you. You came into that staff room like a laser, looking neither right nor left, bee-lining for the table where the guys were sitting. You whisked right past—didn't even notice me."

He half smiled at the realization of how he must have looked that day. "Conrad had made mention of a new teacher named Perreault, but in my defense, none of us—not even Conrad, knew if you were male or female. The first time I found out was when you joined in as we sang 'Fireworks' that afternoon." They shared a chuckle at the memory, after which he looked down at his place setting, fidgeting with the cutlery.

Baker was clearly distracted, but Perreault made no mention of it. There was no way she could know that he was at that moment engaged in an internal tug-of-war, trying to decide when it was most appropriate to broach an important topic and make his proposal. Waiting until they got through the entrée was a painful prospect, what with his growing anxiety likely resulting in some nasty indigestion. So, he took a deep breath and braced himself for the dive, which was when the waiter glided over to gauge their interest in an appetizer or two. They decided to share some stuffed mushrooms and a plate of fried calamari, with a small loaf of toasted artisan bread.

That done, it was time for Baker to speak. "Perreault, I would like to use you as a sounding board for an idea that's been rattling around in my brain for some time."

"Of course. I'd be happy to help. What's up?"

"It's only because I know that you'll understand. I mean, if someone took what I'm about to say out of context, it might sound like a conspiracy theory, like some crazy, convoluted plot from a deluded mind. But because you're in the Coven and can appreciate what we're trying to do with our gatherings and songs and stuff—I mean, I wouldn't share this with anyone outside the Coven, except maybe someone like Dorcas." Baker paused because he heard himself rambling. The ridiculous sound of his voice, in combination with the expression on Perreault's face—one of infinite patience and understanding—made him gather himself and start from the beginning.

As a preamble he revealed the details around his time spent with Cubby and of the two meetings they had in the school library. Then he described his first visit to the Nellas', meeting Allen, and learning about his nephew's hockey prowess. Then came the difficult task of relating how Helen had broken the news of Cubby's death in the school parking lot on Remembrance Day. Finally, he brought up his visit with Allen again in January and how he had come away with many puzzling questions.

"It seems that Allen has a secret—something he hasn't even shared with his wife. Of course, I wasn't about to get it out of him, but he did send me off with a clue."

He walked Perreault through the details of how that clue led to his visiting Cubby's grave a few weeks earlier (he thought it best not to mention Sylvia). Reaching for his phone, he scrolled to the photo he took that night in the cemetery. "Here, this is a picture of Cubby's tombstone. Take a look at it."

Perreault looked at the photo and slowly shook her head, "My goodness, how sad—born January 25, 2008. He would have just turned twelve."

"Yes, there are few things sadder in life than a child's tombstone." Baker let the thought sink in for a moment before getting back to his original point. "I wanted to draw your attention to—"

"Oh my gawd!"

"What?"

"Sorry to interrupt, but my brain just flashed back to the Samhain party and your Tarot reading. Remember?" She gave Baker time to think back to his session with Carly. "Your first card—the Tower—referred to a loss in your life. What are the chances that Cubby's death is what that card meant?"

"Holy shhh—." He took a moment to consider the ramifications before continuing. "But what would it matter—if you're right, I mean? What's the upshot of it all?"

"Probably just that it proves the relevancy of the reading and gives it greater merit."

"Maybe, but I'm not really prepared to think about that now. Can we get back to the tombstone?"

"Of course." They both took a drink to reset themselves.

"Now where was I?"

"You were drawing my attention to something."

"Right. Look at the picture on the screen, but focus on the name."

She saw Cubby's name printed as "Calub Elyk" across the upper portion of the monument. "OK, what about it?"

"Notice how it's on the stone twice."

There was another version of it toward the bottom of the stone, etched into what looked like a short, flat cylinder.

"It's the second version of Cubby's name, the one on the hockey puck, that's of interest to me," he explained.

REVELATIONS

She considered the image, shifting his phone this way and that. "Hmm... maybe it's not a hockey puck," Perreault observed. "Maybe it's supposed to be a ring."

"You know, I thought that too," Baker held his left hand out, indicating the third finger. "But then the ring thing didn't make a lot of sense for me."

"Oh, no, I didn't mean a finger ring, I meant a hoop ring, like the ones that encircle the Clarence Cup."

Baker stopped studying his hand and looked at Perreault. A sudden comprehension jolted him as thoroughly as if he'd taken a whiff of Ricky Randall's pre-game smelling salts. Her interpretation was nothing short of an epiphany. Of course, that had to be it! Cubby's name was on one of the five rings that formed the body of the Clarence Cup. In other words, according to the tombstone, Cubby's name was etched on the Clarence Cup!

"Perreault, you are brilliant! Thank you, thank you, thank you."

"You're welcome," she replied, somewhat startled. "Now tell me what I did to earn such gratitude."

"Because of you everything else makes perfect sense. Now it all fits." He took a moment to catch his breath. The time had come to verbalize his hypothesis. "I've got a theory I'd like to share, but it's pretty extreme. There's just one more piece of evidence you should see first." He reached across the table for his phone and then took the napkin out from under his wine glass. Extracting a pen from his pocket, he copied the name from the photo of the tombstone. Then he scrolled to the selfies he took in his bathroom when he was dressed as Kyle Bulac for the Samhain party back in November. "Take a look at this, but don't laugh. It was a mistake—an accidental selfie taken of my reflection in the mirror."

Perreault's face lit up when she saw the image of Baker dressed as Kyle Bulac. "Look at you, all dressed up for Halloween."

"No, no, it's not me I want you to look at. Here, give me that back." There was a hint of frustration in his voice as he took the phone and zoomed in on something in the photo. "There. It's my name tag. Check it out."

She looked at the screen again.

She raised a Spockian eyebrow. "Well, this certainly is fascinating." The tone in her voice indicated she was more amused than convinced. "And you believe the similarity in the names is more than a crazy coincidence?"

"Coincidence? First of all, the names aren't just similar, they're *identical*."

"And because of this photo, you've made the connection that has allowed you to . . . what? Guess at what Allen's secret might be?"

"Ahh, now that's the tricky part because, as I've said, Allen refuses to reveal anything at all about that. I practically had to coerce him into divulging the clue that sent me to Cubby's tombstone, which still would have left me empty-handed, if not for that fluke photo of my reflection in the mirror. As it is, I've got to believe the similarity in names goes beyond mere coincidence."

"Are you suggesting that Cubby's parents named their kid—in some sort of reverse acronym fashion—after Kyle Bulac?" She shook her head as if to dismiss the idea. "The notion is too far-fetched. Not to mention that, chronologically speaking, it doesn't make any sense."

"I totally agree," Baker said. "That would have been twelve years ago, after all. I doubt they even knew who Kyle Bulac was when they chose to name their newborn son. No, "Calub Merlin" is actually a riff on Cal Ubank."

"You mean the Pines captain from their dynastic years? He's a legend in the history of the franchise."

"Exactly. You see, Calub is a contraction—or rather, a combination?—of the first half of Calvert and Ubank, respectively. C-A-L plus U-B becomes CALUB. Simply put, the kid was named after a favourite PHL player." Baker leaned back in his chair, smiling at Perreault. "Apparently, that's a common practice—regardless of the kid's gender." He pointed an accusatory finger at her. "And sitting directly across from me is exhibit A—the case of a baby girl named after Julien *Perreault*."

"What can I say, councillor?" she replied, playing along. "Guilty as charged."

"But there's more—" Baker was cut off again, however, this time by the waiter returning with their appetizers. He also took their main course orders. Perreault went with a chestnut-mousse-stuffed capon dish while he chose the pan-roasted Ontario beef tenderloin. They paused to serve themselves a helping of food, but Baker didn't eat right away. Instead, he took a sip of wine and turned to gaze at the idyllic winter scene outside the window. Perreault, meanwhile, was savouring a mushroom when she looked up and noticed Baker wasn't eating and had gone silent again. "You were saying there was more?" she prompted.

"Oh, right." He shifted in his seat to face Perreault, then picked up the story. "Soon it came time for the real work to begin, and now we see the story playing itself out."

"The story?"

REVELATIONS

"Yes. The story of the stereotypical Canadian youth donning skates and venturing out onto the frozen pond with a stick and a puck. In this case, the kid's dad and uncle introduced him to the game, nurturing him in meticulous fashion through his developmental years. Soon they saw their efforts paying dividends as the kid showed himself to be a damn good player. He had loads of skill and excellent instincts. Eventually, at some point along the way, they began to talk up the possibility of Cubby getting his name etched on the Clarence Cup."

Perreault frowned. "Wouldn't that have been a little premature? I mean, talk about setting a kid up for disappointment."

He shrugged it off. "It was harmless enough, you know, all in fun. And Cubby liked to join in on the fantasy. I guess they figured it wouldn't hurt to dream a bit." Baker shifted in his seat and held his hands at shoulder height, index fingers pointed up as if to refocus her attention. "But here's where the story gets interesting. Still with me?"

"Oh, I'm not going anywhere."

"Alright. The time comes when the family goes out to celebrate the kid's ninth birthday at a Chinese restaurant. When dinner's over, everyone opens their fortune cookie, including Cubby. But Cubby, being the birthday boy, is delivered a *special* fortune cookie, different from all the others at the table." Baker reached for his phone. "Give me a second, and I'll show you." He scrolled through the photos. When he found the picture of Cubby's homemade bookmark with the original fortune laminated onto it, he handed the phone across to Perreault. "See what I mean? It's significantly larger, it's on authentic rice paper, and most importantly, the message reads like no ordinary, run-of-the-mill, mass-produced-for-North American-consumption type of fortune." He paused for effect. "I call it the Haiku Prophecy."

Perreault looked up from the screen. "Wait . . . you gave his fortune cookie fortune a name?"

Baker blushed like an embarrassed ten-year-old. "Yeah, when I discovered that it's a kind of freestyle haiku. Instead of the usual five-seven-five formula, this one has a five-three-seven rhythm to it."

She stifled a smile and proceeded to examine it.

> *Your name in silver*
> *Results from*
> *Excellence with black on white*

"So, the way I figure it," Baker said, continuing with his theory, "what was once just a pipe dream, an idea that was fun to kick around, became something more, something that is now fated to happen. It's as if the gods of hockey, or whatever, have preordained it."

"Gods of hockey? Preordained?"

"Yes. But then things changed dramatically with Cubby's sudden illness—and, sadly—untimely death. The family had hitched their wagon of hopes and dreams to Cubby's rising star, only to see it brutally snatched away." Baker paused, eyes blazing with zeal as he tapped the table in front of him. "And this is where the Pines' young general manager enters the story.

"Somehow, someone, at some time, recognized that Cubby's name, Calub Elyk, which is the name etched into the ring at the bottom of his tombstone, is unique—in the sense that, when you spell it backwards, amazingly enough, 'Calub Elyk' becomes 'Kyle Bulac.'"

"This discovery—this name connection," Perreault observed, "must have been fairly recent because the real Kyle Bulac hasn't been in the Pines front office for long."

"That's right. It would have been within the past five years or so. After all, Bulac wasn't in any position to get his name on the Cup anyway. That is, at least until he became the team's GM. And that, according to my theory, is what this is all about—getting Kyle Bulac's name on the Clarence Cup. If that happens, then this name association thing suddenly serves as a pretty convenient consolation prize."

"Consolation prize?"

"Yes. Remember how it all started, as some silly fantasy, you know, Cubby getting his name on the Cup and stuff. And then it became a sort of prophecy written on a Chinese fortune cookie. But then it all unravelled with Cubby's death—" Baker broke off, apparently uncomfortable with revisiting the tragic loss. Instead, he skipped to the main point. "You see, if fate, in all its cruelty, deemed that Cubby Elyk would never get his own name on the Clarence Cup, then David Elyk and Allen Nella would spit back in its face and make it so Cubby's name got there another way."

"Just out of curiosity, who do you think was the one to discover the name connection?"

"I mean, I can't be a hundred percent sure because I've never met Cubby's dad, but after having spent an evening with his uncle Allen last year, and hearing him expound on his belief in the power of numerology and semiotics and such, well—I'd peg Allen as the likely candidate."

"Hmm... can we go back to Cubby's fortune for a moment—the 'Haiku Prophecy'?" Perreault paused in response to the broad smile that blossomed on Baker's face. "What's so funny?"

"Oh, nothing's funny," he replied. "It's just that, well, hearing someone say it out loud—the Haiku Prophecy—it's got a nice ring to it."

"It does have a catchy hook. But getting back to my point, I'm not convinced by your interpretation of what the message means. It's so vague; it has the potential for any number of things, I wouldn't know where to begin."

"That's true—in a vacuum—but within the context of Cubby and his family, I think it's pretty clear how they would read it. And anyway, discovering the true meaning of

REVELATIONS

the fortune probably doesn't matter. Remember, we're here to help Allen. Therefore, we need to find out what *he* thinks it means—how *he* interprets the message. It becomes a debate over what's more powerful in this case: the actual truth or Allen's perception of the truth."

"But couldn't we just ask him?"

"Based on my conversation with him, I'm thinking he'd sooner throw me out of the house than divulge an answer. But now I understand the reason for Helen's concern. Her husband is overcome with self-blame. He's guilt-ridden, and I think he believes that getting Kyle Bulac's name on the Clarence Cup will redeem him in a way and resolve this issue."

"You're convinced that will heal what ails him?"

"Yes! If Kyle Bulac gets his name on the Cup, then Cubby gets his name on the Cup, and the Haiku Prophecy is fulfilled, and Allen can sleep peacefully knowing that his promise to Cubby has been kept."

"Then as stupid as it may sound," Perreault said, "the easy solution to all of this is to just have the Pines win the Cup."

"You're right; it does sound dumb. Too simplistic, because it's not a simple thing to ask. I mean, it's been fifty-seven years, for Chrissake. Who's to say we are not going to have to wait another fifty-seven years before they win? A drought of that magnitude seems incredible, but it's not unprecedented in sport. The Boston Red Sox went something like eighty-five years between championships, and the Chicago Cubs went over a hundred years between titles.

"All of which brings us to the real problem: the fact that Kyle Bulac's tenure as Pines' GM is uncertain. It's the business of pro sports—a constant merry-go-round of players and coaches and GMs and presidents. And that puts us on a tight timeline. We can't wait another fifty-seven years. We need something more immediate. This seems to be the window of opportunity—as small as it is—if Cubby is going to get his name on the Clarence Cup. The sooner Toronto wins, the better."

He paused to take a breath, feeling good about the way things had gone to that point. There was just one more tiny detail. "All that being said, I believe there's a better way."

"Don't tell me . . . you have a plan."

Baker fiddled with the stem of his wine glass before answering. "What if we arranged a way to have Cubby tell us his feelings from beyond the grave?"

Perreault leaned forward in her chair. "You mean get in touch with Cubby's spirit?"

"Yes. We just need to talk to the kid, right?"

"So you're suggesting a séance?"

"That's exactly what I'm suggesting," Baker said, amazed and delighted at Perreault's perspicacity.

"My immediate response is that it'll never happen."

His expression went from glad to glum. "You don't like the idea?"

"Oh no, It's not me. It's Allen."

"Allen Nella?"

"You just finished telling me how Allen resists even talking about this. You really believe he'll participate in a séance?"

Baker had to admit to the weakness in his plan. "Geez, you might be right." His shoulders drooped, but just for a moment. "But why *wouldn't* Allen want to take part? It would be an opportunity to clear the air, you know, in case Cubby had questions, or in case he harboured some resentment over having been given an empty promise . . . or worse yet, in case he shouldered some of the guilt—the off chance that Cubby blamed himself for the failure to get his name on the Cup."

Baker turned and looked through the window into the darkness beyond as he formulated a plan. "I really should strategize this. Let's see . . . I'll talk to Helen and get her take on my idea. No! I'll discuss this with Dorcas first, see what she thinks, and when and where we might hold this mystical meeting. Only after I get her approval will I go and visit Helen."

"Sounds like a plan," Perreault said, wanting to sound supportive. "And now that your focus is on this séance, am I to assume that our Coven will be taking a bit of a respite from its usual activities?"

"On the contrary, I see this as a way of doubling down on our efforts."

"So, in your mind this séance can also apply to what we're doing within the Coven?"

"Look, we all want the same end result: the Pines winning the Cup. The way I see it, though, we'll be demonstrating that there's more at stake. It gets back to our personal wants—our deepest desires. We all have our own reasons for wanting to see them succeed. Allen's cause is just another example of that. Fact is, there are a number of ancillary benefits to the Pines winning it all. And each of these activities—like our coven gatherings and séances—hopefully contributes to it."

"I must admit, a séance sounds intriguing. I wish I could be there to experience it."

"Of course you'll be there," he assured her. "Your attendance is vital."

"And why is that?"

"Because I'm hoping to perform a song as part of the séance."

"A song?"

"Yes . . . to help us make contact with Cubby."

"I'm assuming you have an idea for this song?"

"Not yet, but I'll figure something out."

"And you figure the two of us can pull this off?"

"I was thinking more like four. You, me, Angus—"

"And either Masaccio or Conrad?"

"Not exactly. I was leaning toward ... Mary."

"Mary? You mean Dorcas's apprentice?"

"Uh-huh. You'll handle the vocals, of course, Angus on drums, me on guitar, and Mary will play piano."

"Well, OK. Now all we need is to get approval from the key parties and the time and place."

"Like I said, I'll talk to Dorcas and Helen. Leave that to me."

Perreault helped herself to more squid. "This is quite tasty. You should have some before I eat it all."

Baker took the hint and set to cleaning his plate, suddenly feeling famished.

Perreault had a sip of wine and leaned back in her seat. "This has been quite an education. So many revelations and so unexpected. I feel like Saint John on the island of Patmos."

"Who? What?" Baker said, through a mouthful of bread.

"Saint John the Apostle. He wrote the Book of Revelation. He was exiled to the Greek island of Patmos, which is where he received his visions."

"How the heck do you know this stuff?"

"Don't give me too much credit. It's just something I picked up this year prepping for my religion classes."

"So, why was he exiled?"

"As a punishment for his preaching."

Baker took a moment to imagine St. John's situation. "You know, I'm sure it was miserable for him, but I have to admit that being exiled on a Greek island doesn't sound so bad—although it might get boring."

"I guess it depends on the company. I can think of ways to pass the time—some spicier than others."

Baker shot her a look of mock astonishment. "Oh? And what might they be?"

Her countenance turned sly. "We can discuss those after dinner—at your place—over a nightcap." She twisted in her seat to indicate her designer shoulder bag hanging on the back of the chair. "I packed my pyjamas."

"You've got pyjamas in that little purse?"

"Uh-huh." Her reply came with a seductive wink. "A T-shirt folds up quite compactly."

Baker was prevented from responding because just then the food arrived. The remainder of the meal was filled with epicurean delights and engaging conviviality as the two, exhibiting the obvious effects of being struck by Cupid's arrow, discussed things other than séances, spirits, covens—and the Pines.

CHAPTER THIRTY-FOUR

PRAYERS

Baker was in a quandary. While his evening with Perreault had been so perfect it could have been lifted from the pages of a romance novel, he was also in a serious relationship with the Pines and, therefore, struggling to balance his love life with his efforts to charm the team to a Cup. Granted, he was in no position to complain, seeing as this year he'd had the good fortune to enjoy some female companionship on what are arguably the two most favoured and marketable windows for romance on the calendar: New Year's Eve and Saint Valentine's Day. But on both occasions he was so immersed in the magic of the moment that the result of the Pines game on each of those nights was relegated to an afterthought, or worse, lost to oblivion—as if the game had never been on the schedule. Luckily, an entire nation of Pines fans *was* paying attention, and in the case of Saturday's game in Ottawa, they were rewarded for their efforts.

Saturday, February 15 – Tuesday, February 18

With the flu bug making its way through the team, Boris Duggan cancelled practice on Friday to give his charges some needed rest and recovery. By all appearances the day off helped as the Pines went into Ottawa and fended off the spunky Federals to come away with a 4-2 decision, Toronto's first regulation win in the month of February. The team then travelled to Buffalo where, despite playing their fourth game in six days, were expected to dominate the Border-Brats.

But as Perreault's grandfather, ninety-three-year-old Papi Rene, often said to anyone within earshot: "The other guys are trying hard too, you know." On this night Buffalo played the role of "the other guys" perfectly, outskating and outscoring the Pines to the tune of 5-2. It was just one more lesson in how this team managed to find new ways to stumble into a steamy pile of horse shit and then look up to find that another game had gotten away from them.

PRAYERS

With no recourse but to lick their wounds and wipe the manure off their collective skates, Duggan and his troops had two days to prepare for a two-game home-and-home series against the red-hot Pittsburgh Pilots, beginning on Tuesday.

All the eager anticipation Baker may have had for Tuesday's matchup was effectively doused by the midway point of the game. Having seen enough when the Pilots scored their fifth goal to go up 5-0, he fired up his laptop to draft an email that was intended for his Coven bandmates. To say he was in a tizzy would be understating his emotional disposition, which was why the message never actually reached its intended targets—he had neglected to follow through on clicking "send." The undelivered email was intended to inform his friends that he was planning to take Thursday, the day after tomorrow, off from school. His plan was to dedicate the day to an act of devotion, one that would take him into Toronto, specifically Elysian Square outside Nova Tank Arena. He shut down the computer and began mentally prepping for his solo pilgrimage. He knew in his heart it was the right thing to do. In fact, he should have acted weeks earlier, but at least now he was resolute.

*****

By the close of business the next day—hump day—overcast skies were causing the early evening February light to fade prematurely as Baker threw his school bag into the back seat of his car, a pang of hunger serving as a reminder that he hadn't stopped to eat during the day. He shut the back door with a thunk, the sound coinciding with a shout from someone some distance behind him. He turned to see Angus in shorts and a T-shirt running out to the parking lot to catch up with him.

Baker assumed his friend was between sets of a workout. "Hi, Angus, what are you doing out here? You're going to catch your death—and lose your pump."

With what breath he had left, Angus responded with a flurry of information. "I wanted to see you before you left 'cause I knew I wasn't gonna see you tomorrow, but it's been such a crazy day, and when I started my workout, I forgot, then between sets on the bench press I looked out the window and saw you heading to your car, so I just ran outside and—well, here I am."

"No rest for the wicked, eh? What do you need?"

"I need you to come back inside so I can get my prayers."

"Prayers?"

"Yeah. You asked us to write up some prayers for you to take to the Icemen tomorrow. I don't want anyone to think I'm not doing my part. I must be the last one."

"Are you kidding? You're the only one."

"Shut up! You telling me you got nothing from the others? What about Perreault? I was sure she'd put something together."

"If she did, I haven't seen it. Where are we going, by the way? To your work room?"

"Yeah. Sorry, man." Angus began to jog toward the doors.

"No problem. And no need to rush. We can be civilized about this."

"Sure, but I'm frickin' freezing!" Angus replied over his shoulder.

Once inside, he led them past a stairwell, offering greetings to Nancy, the evening custodian, who was sweeping the area of salt and grit tracked in by hundreds of shoes during the school day. They continued on through the gymnasium corridor, where the boys' basketball team could be heard practising, preparing for the following day's semi-final playoff game, then past the weight room and around another corner before arriving at Angus's work room.

Pulling a lanyard of keys from his shorts pocket, Angus found the one he needed, worked the lock, and swung the door open. The L-shaped work room was a cramped space with desks, chairs, desktop computers, books, binders, paper, and personal clutter, including everything from coffee mugs to organizers for office supplies. Baker offered greetings to Anne van de Voort and Brett Doyle, two fellow staff members still busy at their desks, while Angus went ahead to his workspace, which was so covered with miscellany that the faux wood desktop was nowhere to be seen. Perched precariously atop some open binders were several file folders of student assignments, attendance tracking sheets, a well-thumbed copy of that year's *Pines Annual*, a back issue of *Drummer Magazine*, and a special-edition Blu-ray version of the movie *Whiplash*. Somehow there was also space for a large-ish cooler bag, an old takeout coffee cup half filled with sunflower seed shells, a bag of barbeque Spitz, two empty Gatorade bottles, and three bottles of water.

Baker picked up the DVD. "Great movie," he said.

"I haven't seen it. Janet loaned it to me."

"I must have watched it five or six times by now. Did Janet tell you anything about it?"

"She referred to a line in the movie about the 'wrong tempo' or something."

"'Not my tempo!' Yes, that's a good scene."

"She also said it's a good lesson in perseverance and dedication. And something about a car crash?"

"Right. Yet another good scene."

Angus extended his hand, which held a small, shiny gold-coloured metal container.

"What's this?"

PRAYERS

"My prayers. I went to see Conrad after school for something sort of sacred that could hold five small slips of paper, and he gave me this. He called it a pyx."

"It looks like a container for Eucharist wafers, like, for people who can't make it to mass on their own. What'd you say he called it?"

"A pyx. He's got more if we need them. A silver one, a wooden one, one made out of pewter, and one that's looks like some kind of shell."

"So, there are five slips of paper in here?"

"Yeah. You can open it if you want, but don't read them. They're, um, personal, you know."

"No problem, but how will I be able to tell whose is whose?"

"What do you mean?"

"Well, which prayer goes with which legend? Or are they identical and interchangeable?"

"No. They're all different. I wrote individualized prayers for each guy."

"So then how will I tell them apart without opening them?"

"I labelled them." Angus took the container and extracted some of the slips to show Baker. "Each one is folded, and on the outside I wrote the player's initial and number, like Whitey Kilpatrick is W4, Sugar Watson is S7, and so on."

"I guess that's easy enough. This is excellent, Angus, thanks."

"Well, thanks for making this, uh, what'd you call it—pilgrimage?"

When Angus uttered the word "pilgrimage," both Anne and Brett, seated nearby, lifted their heads.

"Hey, Brooks, you taking the day off tomorrow?" Brett asked.

"Yeah, I'm taking my personal day. I've got some things I want to do in Toronto."

"Taking sort of a long weekend, huh?" Anne said, referring to the fact that the next day was a Thursday, and schools everywhere would be closed on Friday owing to the province-wide one-day strike, which meant Baker wouldn't see his students again until Monday. "The weather should be alright, other than the cold, I mean."

"I guess I'll just have to bundle up." Baker pocketed the pyx and replaced the *Whiplash* DVD on top of Angus's mountain of stuff. "But I'd better be pushing off now. Maybe we'll see you guys Friday on the picket line."

"Yup. See you Friday, Baker," Anne said.

"Have a good night, Baker," Brett added, then turned to Angus. "Are you leaving us too?"

"I have to get back to the weight room and finish my workout."

"Taking your frustrations out on the pulldown bar?" Anne inquired.

"Don't worry, Anne. I'll be sure and dedicate my next set to you."

"Atta boy, Angus. Think of me when you're pulling on that bar."

Baker found that last comment surprisingly suggestive, compelling him to shoot a look at Anne over his shoulder as he opened the door, but she had already turned away to focus on some paperwork on her desk. He led Angus out into the hallway, who then expressed his disappointment in Conrad, Masaccio, and Perreault. "I can't believe the others didn't prepare anything for you, Baker."

"Don't be too quick to blame them. It could be that I simply fucked up sending them the reminder email. I tell you, man, I'm still not completely comfortable with that stuff."

"Well, I got my email."

"I didn't send you an email. I spoke to you in person this morning, remember?"

"Oh yeah. I guess you're right. Hey, that reminds me. Conrad *does* know about your plans because I told him when I saw him this afternoon to borrow the pyx. You're sure he didn't leave you any prayers or anything?"

"Positive. It was probably short notice for him."

"Maybe." Angus changed the subject as they made their way downstairs. "So, did you see that mess of a game last night in Pittsburgh?"

"Unfortunately, yes."

"You know, I've been rehashing Toronto's tough losses—some close and heartbreaking, others embarrassing blowouts—and it seems all the league's big guns have had terrific games against the Pines this year. They all just seem to be feasting on us; like they're schooling us into submission."

He looked to Baker for an opinion, but his friend seemed to be brooding, lost in thought, his mind elsewhere. Then, like a shock wave, Baker erupted. "Fuck, man! They can't put anything together that resembles consistency. In fact, that's their identity: inconsistency. How do they expect to win anything with that as their distinguishing trait?"

Angus knew that nothing else needed to be said, because however dismal it may have sounded, Baker's assessment was spot on. As an alternative to gloom, Angus went with hope. "Maybe your pilgrimage and our prayers will make an impact." Something then appeared to dawn on him. "You really owe it to yourself to attend a live Pines game, considering all the work you've put in to try and help them win."

"I told you, there's no way; it'd be too stressful. I'd just be miserable if they lost."

"Naaah. We'll go together. You and me, man; I'll show you a good time in Toronto."

For Baker, it was wasted effort to argue what was a moot point anyway—Angus wasn't getting tickets to a Pines game anytime soon.

"Speaking of good times in Toronto," Angus continued, "you'll be there tomorrow morning. How are you getting there? Are you driving?"

"No. I'm taking the train. I just want to sit back and enjoy the scenery."

"Gosh, last time I was on the train was in June for the Raptors' victory parade."

"That's right. I remember now. You took the day off and attended that crazy scene." Baker smiled enviously at his friend. "Memories of the madness, huh?"

"All I can say is if two million showed up for the Raptors, they'll get double that when the Pines win."

"*When* they win?"

"Fuckin' right, man. And we're gonna help make it happen. You, me, the rest of the Coven—" Angus trailed off as he walked with his friend toward the stairwell and the exit doors. He did not care to go outside again, having cooled off from his last set, which had been a good ten minutes ago. He was actually getting chilled standing in the entry nook.

"You go and salvage what you can of your workout," Baker said. "I'll see you Friday and tell you how my visit to the Acropolis went. In the meantime, we'll keep our chins up." He straightened to his full height and spoke in Lincoln-esque—or Churchillian—fashion. "We shall remain undaunted and resolute in our convictions . . . Now fuck off! I'll see you on Friday."

"Undaunted and resolute," Angus replied, mimicking him. "OK! See ya Friday."

The two men went their separate ways, Baker into a blast of cold air and the gloaming of the February evening, Angus to the weight room to recommence his workout.

Angus had decided to pick up where he'd left off, but couldn't recall exactly where that was. He took a seat on the bench at the lat pulldown machine and stared at the floor, thinking of Baker and the next day's pilgrimage. Then he thought back to the day last June when he'd taken the train into Toronto to witness the Raptors' championship parade. It had been an experience of a lifetime, something the city hadn't felt since the Blue Jays in 1992 and 1993—or so he'd been told. He recalled relating his adventures of that day to his parents later that same evening, over a celebratory drink.

He'd first noticed it in the morning—there was something in the air that indicated the day was different; something about the people boarding the train. They'd had a festive look about them: almost to a man (and woman and child), they'd been wearing Raptors jerseys. The red-and-white "North" jerseys, the black-and-gold "City Edition" jerseys, the blue Toronto Huskies jerseys, and lots of throwback purple-and-white "Dino" jerseys. Some people had come equipped with posters, others had carried flags . . .

"Ooh . . . did you take your flag, dear?" his mother had asked.

"No, Mom. I left it here, on my wall."

"Oh, Angus. You should have taken your flag."

Three stops later the train had been standing room only with Raptors fans of all ages. By the time they pulled into Union Station they were packed shoulder to shoulder. When the doors opened they had flowed in one direction out of the train cars, spilling out and then joining together along the platform, like blood cells in plasma. They moved as one toward the stairs, then into the station, then through the station and up and out onto the street.

Popping out of Union Station onto the intersection at Front and York, Angus was struck by the atmosphere. It was euphoric—no more Monday blahs. There had been pedestrians everywhere, mostly in Raptors colours. The original schedule had set the parade beginning at 10:00 a.m. and ending at 12:30. But of course, it had been considerably delayed. Angus met up with a couple of friends outside the Hockey Hall of Fame and got out to the parade route shortly after eleven.

"*We were in the bright sun, crammed among thousands, standing there, waiting.*" he'd told his parents. "*It was pretty intense, what with the heat and the confined space and the inability to move...*"

The press of the crowd had been almost choking, to the degree that Angus was forced to focus on his breathing at times in order to stay calm. At one point, among the people around him, there'd been a mother with her little kid—a young boy. The poor thing had been so small, engulfed by the mass of humanity. Angus had tried to hold back the people around him with his arms outstretched so the kid wouldn't get hurt. But that had been futile, so he'd just picked him up and held him at shoulder level, above the crowd, before handing him over to his mom.

Shortly thereafter he'd lost contact with his friends—they'd gone off to find a washroom and never found their way back to where he'd been waiting with their cooler. People had been climbing lampposts, and others had clambered onto the overhanging roof of a nearby restaurant, despite being told repeatedly by security staff to get down. (By the end of the day, the roof had been standing room only.) The windows of the office buildings that looked down on the street had filled with more and more people as the parade had crawled north along University Avenue.

"*Of course, at street level, we had no idea how much longer the wait would be,*" he explained. "*We tried to figure out where the parade was by the reactions of the people in the windows. So, there I was, waiting, and wondering: should I stay or should I go? And every time I told myself it was time to go, I was more convinced that I had to stick it out.*"

The double-decker buses that had been carrying the players didn't reach Angus's location until around three o'clock. When the parade had finally arrived, there they had been; Kyle Lowry embracing the Larry O'Brien trophy, Kawhi Leonard smiling and looking relaxed, and Marc Gasol giving his teammates a lesson in how the big boys drink after winning a championship. Angus had even had a few drops of beer land on him when Fred VanVleet had sprayed the crowd.

The parade had taken about twenty minutes to pass, and not because of its length. The street had been so jammed that the parade vehicles could only proceed about fifty metres, then stand for five or six minutes, then move another fifty or so metres, then stand for five minutes, and so on, all the way to city hall and Nathan Phillips Square. The crowd had stood for three and a half hours in the blazing sun, crammed among countless other bodies, unable to move, all for twenty minutes of seeing their conquering heroes. And when the last vehicle had passed, which had sported a live band keeping the masses entertained, there had been nothing left but for everyone to disperse.

And so, Angus allowed himself to be slowly carried along, like a member of the herd, amongst all the moving, sweaty, tired bodies. He happened to fall in behind two young women walking side by side, obviously exhausted from the long day, but still flush with excitement. It was then that Angus experienced one of the best moments of that crazy, wonderful day. One of the girls, all smiles and bubbles, had turned to her friend and gleefully exclaimed, *"That was so worth it, wasn't it?"*

Angus hadn't moved from his perch on the weight bench, still smiling at the memories of that day—memories that didn't include the incident that had occurred just outside Nathan Phillips Square. He hadn't heard the details about that—the packed crowd scared by the sound of gunshots, leaving people injured—until watching the news on TV with his parents that night.

He remembered the day fondly, mostly because he'd felt a real kinship with the people all around him that afternoon, and with the team, and with the entire city. For Angus, that love had been delivered gift-wrapped beautifully with a bow. In that package were five words; the exchange between the two girls in the crowd immediately following the parade: *"That was so worth it!"*

Let the Toronto Mighty Pines win, Angus thought. *So we can hold a parade. We can gather and celebrate together. Let the fans of this city get a reason to show their love, and it'll last a lifetime.*

CHAPTER THIRTY-FIVE
THE PILGRIMAGE

I would read, and then reread
The great hockey stories, of legends and glories
And even some tragedy

Thursday, February 20

The day and a half leading up to the rematch with Pittsburgh was angst-filled as Coney Nation could only stew over the prospect of their team missing the playoffs. The ink-stained wretches and video vultures that were the Toronto sports media had gathered at a table that was set to examine a team whose work ethic and dedication had been thrown into the blender of public discourse. News hounds were collecting quotes like coins and comic books.

Ben Bellamy was mined for this one: "This team needs to rekindle that passion for the game, then display it on the ice with urgency and a willingness to compete for each other."

Boris Duggan answered a question about what the process might be for his team to establish a sense of winning identity: "We are at the point where the only thing left is to look in the mirror and make some tough decisions."

Ricky Randall offered up this bit of insight: "We all know we have the skill but we don't have the work ethic every single night and every single guy buying in. Skill only takes you so far."

The situation with the standings was a fluid one, as would be expected going into the final quarter of the season. With twenty-one games remaining, Toronto found itself in tenth place in the conference and out of a playoff spot.

THE PILGRIMAGE

Not being in any particular hurry, Baker waited a good ninety minutes past rush hour before heading out of the house to embark on his day of devotion, driving to the GO station to board a train that would take him to Toronto's Union Station. Pulling into the lot, however, he discovered it to be full. So, with nowhere to park, he was forced to scour the surrounding neighbourhood. He found a spot a couple of blocks away and had to hustle not to miss his train. He jogged on the hard, dry concrete sidewalk, which was fine, considering it was cold—not quite as cold as the previous week, however, when the mercury had contracted to -26°C and he'd prayed his car would start for the morning commute to school. Today it was a little more civilized. Still, he was bundled up and glad he had brought his toque. Although not the least bit fashionable, the hat spared his ear cartilage from the inevitable ache when exposed. (Just wearing the toque made his ears ache as well, but it was the lesser of two evils.)

He proceeded through the full parking lot, down the stairs, and through the underground tunnel—where damp, grimy concrete walls added to the chill—then back up the stairs to the platform. He was careful to stay well back of the yellow line as his train arrived, because even now, as a full-grown adult, he had a grudging respect for these machines with their noise and power. Staring down the track, he felt as J. M. W. Turner must have felt 160 years earlier when he had been inspired to paint "Rain, Steam and Speed:" the menacing form of the train engine angling into view, about to burst through the plane of the canvas, all roiling mist and clatter and hiss.

Boarding his chosen car and settling into a window seat in the upper compartment, Baker was glad to see he had the place pretty much to himself. As the train eased out of the station, the thought of Turner's ghostly steam engine brought to mind his own hockey legends, and Baker pictured the men whose spirits he would call upon that day, to recruit their aid to help him achieve his goals, goals that, if met, would for himself, for Allen Nella, for Cubby, for the Coven, for the Toronto Mighty Pines, for Coney Nation, for the country—

Stop! Don't be an idiot and get too far ahead of yourself. Keep it simple. Remember what Dorcas advised.

Views from his window seat revealed the backyards of private residences, parking lots, storage sheds, mounds of rubble, fences and walls—some covered in graffiti, others ugly, broken, and crumbling. It was a world of concrete, aged and spotted, which on some days mirrored the sky, although that day's long-awaited sun came equipped with a backdrop of Carolina blue and nonthreatening, apathetic clouds. The trees were brown, grey, and dead. If not dead, dormant; but then, who could tell at this time of year? Hence the orange *X*'s painted on the trunks of those slated for removal, identifying them for the inevitable cull. Some construction sites along the way included the crews in their fluorescent hazard coats, labouring in the cold all day, counting the minutes to break time, to lunch time, to punch time, to dinner time, to game time, day by day, month by month, season by season, middle-class incomes spent on Mattamy homes and Japanese cars and Rogers cable—and beer. Life was good. Coney Nation helped drive the economy.

Baker's eyes glazed over as he stared at the indifferent upholstery, coloured Go Train green. The voice of the train's "customer service ambassador"—Chris, by name—announced each stop along the way, and always a safety reminder to "stand clear of the doors; the doors are now closing." Thirty minutes later they were two stops from Union Station, with Lake Ontario visible in the distance—a level band of grey blended with mercury, silver, and lead—or perhaps with the metallic sheen of a gargantuan skate blade of the gods, freshly sharpened. The horizontal lake was intersected by the vertical lines of exhaust stacks spewing steam, along with streetlamps, hydro poles, fence posts, and the perfectly plumb edges of countless buildings.

In due course, the train arrived at Baker's destination, coasting to a stop. Chris came over the intercom to thank the riders for their patronage and reminded them how to manoeuvre and negotiate the platforms in order to ensure the safety of everyone on board as well as to expedite any potential evacuation. Exiting the train, Baker followed the crowd down into the station. He was inclined to stay indoors as long as possible, so he followed the underground network—called the PATH—to Nova Tank Arena. He wasn't certain of which direction to take, but he was confident the combination of overhead signs and his nose would ultimately get him there. And it did. In the ground-level concourse, he stopped in front of a concrete pillar commemorating Bon Jovi's induction into the Rock & Roll Hall of Fame. The pillar was adjacent to a large wall illustration comprised of a quilt-like patchwork of individual squares of Toronto Mighty Pines players. He weaved through a light lunchtime crowd toward the exit doors that opened onto the north quadrant of Elysian Square.

Once outside, the bright sunshine did little to beat back the cold as he walked past four vans parked at the big bend in Athena Lane (now called Raptors Way). He looked down at the pavers below his feet and took note of the few stones shaped like Mighty Pines pinecones interspersed here and there. The cold was insistent, so Baker began to move about the Square, which was devoid of pedestrians. He migrated toward an area called the Acropolis: a raised plateau of concrete upon which sat the monument, comprising nine bronze statues dubbed "The Icemen." It was fairly awe-inspiring, standing alone in the cold before the slightly-larger-than-life figures; the greatest of hockey legends who played for the greatest of hockey franchises. It was a sensation that took him back to the day he'd stood looking up at Michelangelo's magnificent David in the Uffizi Gallery in Florence. Then it dawned on Baker that this arrangement of nine

THE PILGRIMAGE

statues was actually more comparable to the grouping of six bronze figures that made up August Rodin's great masterpiece "The Burghers of Calais."

Shaking himself out of his trance, Baker unzipped the breast pocket of his winter shell and removed Angus's shiny metal pyx. Holding it in his gloved hand, he positioned himself at a central point in front of the monument, taking a few minutes to do some reconnaissance—a roll call, of sorts—as his gaze moved left to right across the group of assembled legends. First up was Captain Jan Pieter, then Whitey Kilpatrick and Cyril Quinn, nicknamed simply "Q." The next four players were positioned behind a thirty-foot granite wall that served as the team bench, beginning with Beasley Sharpe and Cal Ubank, placed side by side and acting as a sort of fulcrum to the monument as a whole. Next came the figure of "The Chairman," George Daly, the last Pines captain to hoist the Cup, followed by fan favourite Wayne Brody. Brody's likeness was the one statue among the nine not in a standing pose; instead, he was straddling the wall, as if in mid-leap over the boards to take a shift. Finally, at the far right of the monument, Frank "Sugar" Watson stood next to goaltending legend Jackson Schmeltz, the two appearing to be deep in conversation.

"Yup, they're all still here," Baker joked to himself.

He looked closely at the faces of the individual players and concluded that the likenesses of the figures meant to represent Whitey Kilpatrick and Cyril Quinn lacked a convincing resemblance. He was then drawn toward the statue of Cal Ubank, who was standing in a gentle contrapposto, his gloved right hand at shoulder height, holding his hockey stick vertically, like a staff, the blade balanced on the toe of his right skate boot, facing inwards toward the player. *And so, here he is,* Baker thought, *Cubby's namesake, Calvert Merlin Ubank. Will he come? Will any of them come? Will they even hear my prayers?*

In the end, it didn't really matter, because just being here—just engaging in this mini pilgrimage—made Baker feel like he was accomplishing something positive.

It was then that he heard voices. He looked around to see a knot of young business types in expensive suits, heads down and shivering, evidently using the Square as a shortcut to some other office building, too benumbed to take any notice of him. Not wanting to waste his window of opportunity, Baker figured he better commence with the ceremony.

According to Dorcas's instruction manual, it was strongly recommended that practitioners of ceremonial rituals employ things like chanting, singing, or drumming, none of which interested Baker as far as that day's visit was concerned. But one thing in the manual that did have potential was the idea of incorporating some form of movement, like swaying, rocking, stepping, and dancing. The dance could be as simple as stepping one foot in front of the other, which could then lead one to move in a circle, a figure eight, or a serpentine pattern. Baker settled for moving in a circle. But there was more

When Cheers Are Not Enough

because apparently the direction mattered. In her manual, Dorcas used the terms "ayenward" and "widdershins." Baker knew that "widdershins" meant counter-clockwise. Therefore, he assumed "ayenward" was its opposite, or clockwise. The clockwise direction—also referred to as sunwise—was recommended because it followed the movement of the sun and moon across the vault of the sky, left to right. Baker decided that would suit his purposes just fine.

The one key detail in Baker's pilgrimage required that he target a select group of players, in particular those whose spirits could be addressed or summoned: in other words, those who were deceased. Of the nine Icemen, five had passed away. This group of five dear departed Mighty Pines legends consisted of Whitey Kilpatrick, Beezer Sharpe, Cal Ubank, Sugar Watson, and Jacko Schmeltz. Baker's plan was to walk around the entirety of the monument, executing a total of five laps or circuits, each devoted to one individual. In the midst of each loop he would stop at the appointed player to insert a prayer slip, in the same way pilgrims insert prayers into cracks in the Wailing Wall at the Temple Mount in Jerusalem. Baker also hoped not to draw attention to himself, especially since this was meant to be a private, intimate ceremony, and so he wondered about the chances of carrying out his little ritual in plain sight without being discovered.

On the plus side, there were a few things working in his favour, not least of which was the time of year. Elysian Square was deserted in February, with the cold serving to keep people indoors. It was also the middle of a work/school day. So, who knew? Maybe he could get through this undetected.

Baker needed to make one final adjustment to the ceremony, something he'd been considering since yesterday after Angus gave him his prayer slips. It centred on the person of "Jersey" Joe Zedelko. For some reason Zedelko's image kept intruding on Baker's thoughts and it wasn't long before he cottoned to the notion that Jersey Joe would be a perfect fit for his plans. Just as there was strength in numbers, so too was there power in a name—Allen Nella would surely agree. Therefore, what he needed was a catchy name for his select group of legends, something that packed a punch. The notion of "packing a punch" brought to mind a six-pack. *A Six-pack of Icemen*. It was catchy enough and Jersey Joe was just the candidate to fill out the group of six players—Baker's six-pack of legends. If there was one complication, however, it was that Zedelko wasn't included among the group of nine Icemen immortalized in bronze on the Acropolis. Baker quickly decided that he would dispense with a prayer slip for him and have to settle for creating a picture of the man in his mind as he made his requests during the actual ceremony. (Of course, Angus's prayer slips didn't include Jersey Joe's name either, but Baker was sure his friend would understand.)

Then the realization hit him that up until that point he hadn't actually opened Angus's pyx, which held his prayers. He turned it around in his gloved hands and found a tiny push-button mechanism. To work it he had to remove his gloves and shove them under his armpit, then depress the button to release the lid. Instantly, the wind caught two of the paper slips, scattering them onto the pavement. Baker snapped the lid shut before any more could escape and quickly moved to collect the tiny squares of paper before the wind blew them God-knew-where. He managed to pounce on one, but in the process he dropped his gloves while the other prayer slip was blown skimming along the pavement. Before it got too far, Baker unceremoniously stomped on it with his right boot. He bent down to reach under his toe, incrementally lifting the ball and arch of his foot, and pulled the paper out. The prayer slip was open and staring up at Baker who, resisting the urge to read what Angus had set down out of respect for his friend's privacy, quickly folded it twice and tucked it back into the pyx. With the prayer slips successfully rescued, he went back and gathered his gloves.

The inauspicious start to his prayer ceremony forced Baker to reset and organize himself. It occurred to him that it might be proper to introduce himself to the Icemen, followed by a mention of his intentions. Having never before addressed a monument to hockey legends, he wasn't quite certain how to proceed, so he decided just to stand tall before his audience, to get their attention, like a conductor might stand before the orchestra prior to counting them in. Then he began "Hel—" only to have his voice crack and a frail squeak issue forth, so Baker stopped, cleared his throat and began again.

"Um, hello gentlemen. My name is Baker Brooks and I'm here on behalf of the Pines, er, the Toronto Mighty Pines, that is—not that they have sent me or anything—I've come on my own accord. But, uh, considering you are all legends and champions of old and have held the Cup and stuff, I thought that maybe you could inspire the team—the players and the coaches—to find a way to actually get it done this year and, you know, to win the Clarence Cup and bring it back to this city of ours—"

Baker paused, if for no other reason than to let his message sink in, then concluded with "Well, that's basically it—so, uh, thanks for listening—"

He broke off and moved to a corner of the square out of the wind where he gingerly opened the pyx and found the folded slip of paper upon which Angus had scrawled C10. Baker was aghast at Fletcher's brutal penmanship. The C and the 1 were combined to look more like a "cent" symbol next to a zero. He combined Angus's prayer with his own tiny, folded slip of paper and looked around again, making certain he was alone in the square. He felt a little like an MI6 operative out of a John le Carré novel, but rather than the spy who came in from the cold, he was the guy who went out into it.

His first stop would be Cal Ubank, the captain of the Pines' first dynasty in the 1930s and '40s. Walking back to the spot that faced the Mighty Pines pinecone insignia (which was front and centre on the granite wall of the team bench), Baker spun ninety degrees to the left and took roughly seven paces until he was eyeball to knuckle with

Jan Pieter's gloved right hand. It was clutching a hockey stick mid-shaft, blade up to the sky. With his own right hand, Baker gripped the bronze stick shaft as well, a little below Pieter's glove, about waist high, and used it as a pivot point, turning the corner around back to the right. He made sure to do it in a respectful manner—not too exuberant—with a special effort not to mimic the iconic image of a rain-drenched Gene Kelly gleefully singing and swinging around a sidewalk lamppost.

He progressed behind the players, first passing the broad backs of Whitey Kilpatrick, Cyril Quinn, and Beezer Sharpe. He felt like a short-of-stature coach in street shoes, trying to peer around and through a line of athletic bodies, all standing atop a platform of skate blades that made them taller while at the same time wrapped in padded protective equipment that made them broader.

The next figure was Ubank. Attempting to look inconspicuous, he tucked the prayer slips into a gap he found in the player's gloved right hand. At the same time, he mumbled an informal request. "Cal, if it's not too much trouble, could you help us out, please?" Tapping the great captain's forearm once, Baker continued on his way, past George Daly then Wayne Brody. Stepping out from behind the bench past Frank Watson and Jackson Schmeltz, Baker stopped to contemplate the two legends, as if he were the sculptor assessing his work. Both had friendly, avuncular faces. Their physical gestures suggested they were both heading in the same direction, each urging the other to proceed. "You first," one might have been saying, while the other replied, "No, no. After you." Or maybe they were just chatting, captured in mid-sentence, comparing notes on the finer points of defending against many of the game's greatest scorers.

Baker was standing directly in the players' line of sight, their eyes fixed upon a spot in such a way that he could position himself within their focal point (like the time when he'd stood facing a Rembrandt self-portrait at the National Gallery in Washington DC, feeling privileged to engage in a private moment with the great master). Finally, he turned and moved off to the left a few paces to complete the first circuit. One down, four to go.

It was then that he realized he hadn't included Jersey Joe Zedelko into his calculation of trips around the monument. He felt it only fitting to devote a circuit to Jersey Joe, and while he was at it, why not extend a personal invitation to his spirit? (Just evoking a mental picture of the man wouldn't really cut it, after all.) Now it was a question of what form such an invitation might take. The game plan for today was to communicate through "prayers," but under normal circumstances, i.e., their Coven sessions, he'd have written a song for the occa—

The solution came to Baker in a flash and was so exquisite in its simplicity and economy he had to laugh. O Wretched Bliss had already done the work for him with their song "Back Panel Vignette." It was perfect. He knew the song well enough, so now all he needed to do was sing it—to himself, under his breath. *What the hay, now is as good a time as ever,* he thought. He hummed the intro before diving into the lyrics.

> *As a kid, my whole world was hockey*
> *Wake up at dawn, put my gear on*
> *And carve up the backyard rink*
> *And when done, exhausted and hungry*
> *I'd pour me a bowl, of breakfast cereal*
> *Fruity Flakes delicious in milk*
> *Well, OK, the box was cool*
> *An education better than school*
>
> *The back panel vignette*
> *Is where I got all my facts*
> *The back panel vignette*
> *For me that's where it was at*

Now that his devotional ceremony was nicely underway, and seeing that he had the Icemen all to himself, Baker felt he could relax and enjoy the experience. It didn't hurt that the tune he was singing was a personal favourite. O Wretched Bliss had certainly hit upon the formula for success with their hockey song, having constructed it on the foundation of a compelling story—a chapter out of Canadian sports folklore—and marrying it to a catchy tune with an irresistible hook. The song suited his vocal range perfectly, and so, as he leaned into the wind, he also leaned into the second verse, feeling emboldened to up the volume several notches, especially since there was no one near enough to hear him, and the words would be swept up in the breeze, anyway.

> *I would read, and then reread*
> *The great hockey stories, of legends and glories*
> *And even some tragedy*
> *Like when Jersey Joe Zedelko*
> *Who in '49, won the Cup for the Pines*
> *And then that summer disappeared*
> *On Red Lake, canoeing alone*
> *That story haunted me in my home*
>
> *The back panel vignette*
> *Is where I got all my facts*
> *The back panel vignette*
> *I'm guessing you never knew that*

When Cheers Are Not Enough

The back panel vignette
Is where I got all my facts
The back panel vignette
For me that's where it was at

He held the final note for an extra two beats, then paused to catch his breath before smoothly executing a third circuit, this one devoted to Beezer Sharpe. When he came around to Jackson Schmeltz toward the end of his fourth trip, the wind gusts caused Baker to decide against tucking the prayers into the goalie's bare left hand, opting instead for the security of the goal pad straps at the back of his legs. "Jacko, if it's not too much bother, could you help us out, please?"

The fifth trip around the Icemen to call upon Whitey Kilpatrick was uneventful, but it was during the sixth pass that Baker discovered he had company. It turned out to be more like an audience: a woman and two boys, one a teen, about the same height as the woman, who was likely their mother, and a younger boy of about nine or ten. The fact that it was a school day made Baker wonder about the boys' presence there, but he didn't dwell on it for long. Maybe the mom was giving her kids a long weekend, since tomorrow was anticipated to be a day off for students across the province owing to the planned teachers' strike action.

Trying to look natural, he sidled up to Frank Watson, looking up at the defenseman's face, feigning interest in his jawline, buying time, waiting for the opportune moment to reach across and insert two pieces of paper into the laces of his left hockey glove. He heard the excited voices of the boys, with Wayne Brody's name being thrown around, as well as Jan Pieter's. Baker surmised the kids would be unfamiliar with any of the Pines legends who played prior to the 1970s. Damn, was it his paranoia, or did the trio seem to be as interested in his movements as in the sculptures? He felt stymied, unable to move forward or backward lest it upset the rhythm of his orbit. The wind found his exposed neck, and the cold bit his nose and gloved fingers. He also sensed a photograph coming and wanted to be able to do the polite thing and get the hell out of the shot. He nearly settled for just saying a quick prayer and walking away, the papers still in his hand, but his personal sense of propriety in the ritual prevented that. A thought bubble floated overhead that said *fuck it,* and he inserted the papers in the laces, quickly and quietly mumbling the words, "Sugar, give us a hand, please," then moved on in his sunwise direction.

As he popped out from behind the figure of Schmeltz, Baker was sure he overheard the younger boy ask his mother why that man was sticking stuff in the players' hands. The kid made no attempt to be discreet about his curiosity, scooting from player to player and excitedly calling out his discoveries of which ones held similar crumples of paper, as if he were engaged in an Easter egg hunt. Baker was relieved to see that at least he didn't go so far as to remove any of the prayer slips.

"Hi!" The kid had stepped forward to address "that man" directly.

"Hi there," Baker replied.

"Is it OK if I look at the statues?"

"Absolutely. That's why they're here, so people can look at them."

"Are those hockey cards or something?"

If much of the day's events had been planned and contrived, the smile that blossomed on Baker's face just then was not one of them. "No, they're not hockey cards. I guess you could call them homemade mini greeting cards."

"Whatcha doin' with them?"

Baker wasn't prepared to answer such a question. How could he possibly explain his motives? He tried to change the subject instead. "Do you play hockey?"

"No, I play basketball."

"Good for you. I guess you're a Raptors fan then?"

"Sure, the Raptors are OK, but I'm a fan of the GOAT."

Baker was amazed that the kid would know about M. J. "Of course, Michael Jordan *was* the greatest."

"Who? Michael Jordan? No! I like LeBron James."

A second smile, this one wry, creased Baker's face. Kids these days; they sorely needed a lesson in sports history. In another place, in another time, he might have spent his energy expounding on the merits of Michael Jordan over LeBron James, but not that day.

"So, you're a Lakers fan?"

"Yeah, LeBron's my favourite, but I also like Anthony Davis—'the Brow'—and Danny Green's probably gonna get another ring this year."

Well, the kid was nothing if not confident, Baker thought. He would also swear that it was Cubby's voice he was hearing. Even some of the kid's mannerisms reminded him of Cubby.

These reflections merely served to jolt Baker back into action. He needed to complete his "mission." Besides, it was official now; he was cold. He hadn't been outside in the square that long—maybe forty-five minutes—but the wind was whipping up, and the pavement was making his legs stiff and achy. Elysian Square would definitely be more fun in May or June. Apparently, the mom was getting cold too, directing her son to pose with his brother for a few pictures, so they could wrap up their visit and head back inside. Baker stood off to the side, out of the frame as a half-dozen pictures were taken. Then he volunteered to snap a few with the mom in the picture. When they were done, they thanked Baker for his services.

Then the kid gestured toward the statues of the Icemen. "I hope the players like their greeting cards."

"Oh... thanks, Cubby."

Baker couldn't believe himself. His brain had to be going numb. He had actually just called the kid *Cubby*. Thankfully, it was ignored, as if the final word had been lost in the wind. And now Baker found himself standing on the spot where he had begun his ceremonial march around the monument. He paused to take a breath and reflect on his completed task. *There... all done.*

Then he was struck right between the eyes by the realization that he didn't know what to do next. He hadn't mentally rehearsed that part of the ceremony. How should he wrap up his pilgrimage? Leaving his prayer slips where they were, tucked within the nooks and crannies of the sculptures, was out of the question. He needed to retrieve them. But how? For starters, the "closing ceremony" would need to be carried out with appropriate reverence. But should he walk around in the same direction? And then wouldn't that be an extra lap, thus possibly weakening the magic? Maybe he should walk around once in the opposite direction. No. A circuit in the widdershins direction would definitely negate the power of the charm. He tried to remember the Old Testament story that described how the Israelites marched around the walls of Jericho. Was it one time each day for seven days, or once each day for six days then seven times on the seventh day? *Damn! Conrad would know for sure—maybe even Perreault; she teaches religion.*

Knowing if he stood here any longer the stiffness in his legs would prevent him from executing his prayer retrieval with any degree of gracefulness, he began to shift left, in the a clockwise direction, but stopped again when it occurred to him that something needed to be done with the prayer slips themselves. In his fantasy world, he would retrieve the slips, return to that spot, crumple everything into a tight ball, then set fire to the prayers, cupping them in his hands as the flames consumed the words and the wind lifted the ashes, dispersing them into the air. Unfortunately, he wasn't a hardened guerrilla soldier, so it would be a real trick burning paper in his bare hands without burning his bare hands as well (not to mention the tiny detail that he didn't have matches or a lighter with him).

Having lost track of time, Baker decided that no amount of ruminating would result in any one option being better than another, especially given his ignorance in the matter, so he just let instinct take over. He counted down from six, one count for each spirit in his select circle of Icemen, and then took a quarter turn left to go collect up the prayers. (In the end he settled for stuffing the slips of paper into his pants pockets.) As he shuffled along, he could swear the cracking of his joints was audible throughout Elysian Square. Then he felt the urge to quietly call Cubby, as if it was the right thing to do, so he repeated the name in a whisper with every step he took. "Cubby, Cubby, Cubby, Cubby, Cubby, Cubby, Cubby, Cubby." He stopped beside Whitey Kilpatrick to collect his prayers. Taking another four steps, he reached Beezer Sharpe and relieved him of his prayers, then four baby steps to the far side of Cal Ubank. It was there that Baker was struck by the most vivid mental images of Cubby, taking him back to when they were seated together in the library at HMV. He could hear his voice as if they were together at that moment. And then, because his mind was elsewhere, and the cold had made his movements crude and stiff, when he extracted the prayer slips from the glove of Cal Ubank, his thumb got wedged in the gap, almost as if the bronze figure had closed his hand around the digit to get his attention. *Ow!* (Later, on the train during his return trip, Baker would look down at his tender thumb, having to accept that he'd be feeling the lingering effects right through the weekend.)

* * * * *

The westbound afternoon train was jam-packed with the rush hour crowd heading home. Baker gave up his seat for a woman who was standing in the aisle, one hand grasping an overhead rail while the other held the hand of a little girl, roughly four years old. The girl was adorable, not only because of how she was transfixed by the passing scenery but also by how she used her free hand to keep her balance by absent-mindedly grabbing the nearest thing, which happened to be a seated gentleman, previously dozing but startled into wakefulness by having the shoulder of his suit jacket in the clutches of a tiny fist. In surrendering his seat, Baker was amused by the notion that he was providing assistance to three people: the mother, her child (now seated in her mother's lap), and the gentleman, who devoted several minutes to smoothing the wrinkled fabric of his jacket.

Forty minutes later, as the train finally approached its terminus, Baker took a moment to reflect on the day. He concluded that it had felt, if not mystical, then at least worthwhile, making the outcome of that night's Pines' rematch with the Pilots all the more intriguing. As he stepped off the train onto the asphalt platform, it dawned on him to give Perreault a ring when he got home, out of courtesy, in case she was wondering about the reason for his unannounced absence from school that day. Thinking about school reminded him that he would be participating in a protest the next day rather than teaching. He had to be in the HMV parking lot by 8:30 for his morning shift on the picket line. He'd see the rest of the Coven there and fill them in on his latest adventures. It was forecast to be cold, but at least they wouldn't lack for things to talk about.

CHAPTER THIRTY-SIX

A SIX-PACK OF LEGENDS

The spirit of Cal Ubank hovered before the five bronze representations of Mighty Pines legends on the Acropolis. His attention, however, was not on the sculptures so much as on Baker Brooks, a pilgrim to Elysian Square who appeared to be progressing through a devotional ceremony. So intent was Ubank on tracking the man's movements around the bronze figures that he did not sense the presence of Beasley "Beezer" Sharpe, which was saying something because Sharpe's proximity to Ubank had them practically arm in arm.

"What do you think, Cal?" Sharpe asked. "Will this pilgrimage and the prayers be enough to bring out the others?"

The question roused Ubank. "Good afternoon, Beasley. I'm thrilled to see that you responded to the call by this Baker fellow here. And in answer to your question, take a gander over there." He pointed to two figures at the far right of the monument. "As reliable as my grandpa's pocket watch. If it isn't Jackson and Joseph."

The spirits of Jackson Schmeltz and "Jersey" Joe Zedelko had materialized, side by side. Ubank and Sharpe approached them, but before anything could be said they were interrupted by the sound of a boisterous voice in a low register. The spirit of Frank "Sugar" Watson, as brash as ever, arrived on the scene, accompanied by Whitey Kilpatrick.

"Have no fear, gentlemen, we have arrived," Watson announced, throwing a heavily muscled arm across Kilpatrick's shoulders. "Sugar Watson and Eight-Finger Kilpatrick at your service."

A paragon of patience, even in the afterlife, Kilpatrick turned to Watson and sighed. "Aw, Frank, who in the heavens above, or down upon this green earth, put it in your head to call me "eight-finger" Kilpatrick?"

"Sorry, Whitey, but you've only got yourself to blame. Anybody who goes and wins eight Clarence Cup rings deserves to have a handle like "eight-finger" preceding his name. But tell me, why have we been summoned to the Acropolis this time?"

"I don't rightly know. Let's see what the boys have to say."

A SIX-PACK OF LEGENDS

The six spirits acknowledged each other's presence as if they were all back in the locker room at Mighty Pines Coliseum, having just arrived on the first day of training camp.

Ubank brought the group to the main order of business. "By hum, fellas, what do you say we read the mail?" He extracted himself from them and moved toward his own bronze likeness to see what was written on Baker's prayer slip.

"Right behind you, Cal," Jackson Schmeltz said, agreeably. Sugar Watson, meanwhile, was in the mood to poke fun at anyone in the group.

"Jacko, you really think the fans are gonna turn to you to do favours for them? You could barely stop a black rubber disc from denting the twine."

"Tell me, Sugar, how many 'Tenders you win in your career?" Schmeltz countered.

"Not a one, but I should've at least *shared* a 'Tender Trophy, considering all the shots I blocked playing defence in front of you for eleven years."

"Poor Frank," Beezer Sharpe chuckled. "Shoulda, coulda, woulda."

"Gentlemen, if I may interrupt," Ubank said, positioned next to his own statue and holding two small pieces of paper. "I think we need to focus on why we've been called here today."

"Tell us, Cap'n Cal, what are our orders?" Schmeltz inquired. "What's the game plan?"

"It appears we've been asked to intercede."

"Intercede? Like, lend a hand?"

"Yes. The Pines need our help—again."

"It sounds like another kick at the Cup," Sharpe added.

"Count me in, Beezer," Whitey Kilpatrick called, then added with a smile, "You know what they say—the fifty-eighth time is the charm."

Watson issued a derisive laugh. "Another kick at the Cup? What this team needs is a kick in the ass. It's time they got serious."

"It's enough to see how serious our host is," Sharpe replied with optimism. "Hell, look at him doing laps around the monument. It's like an act of devotion."

"Why do you figure he calls on us for help?" Joe Zedelko wondered aloud.

"I think it's because of our connection to the legacy of the Toronto Mighty Pines, Joseph," Ubank explained. "We're a part of the great history of this franchise—a franchise that celebrated eleven Clarence Cup victories in its first thirty years of existence."

"But now, unfortunately, it is a team that has yet to claim even a single title in its last fifty-seven," Sharpe added soberly. "And every year that the Pines fail in the playoffs is another puncture wound in the belly of Toronto fans," he proclaimed. "Coney Nation has sustained fifty-seven cuts to the flesh—and counting."

"Brilliantly stated, Beasley! You're quite the wordsmith," Ubank cheered. "But it has just occurred to me that while five of us here have never experienced a Cup win since our passing, Joseph, on the other hand, has seen several." He turned to Zekelko. "Tell us, Joseph, how many championships *have* you witnessed?"

Zedelko was ready with an answer. "Four Cups, Cal. At first I figured I'd hang around at least until the canoe was discovered. But that took a lot longer than I—or anybody—expected. By the time that happened, the Pines were on their way toward winning four Cups in seven years, and let me tell you, it was a fun ride. And then somewhere along the way I told myself that if I could witness five wins—you know, to match my sweater number—I'd be satisfied . . . Well, I'm still here."

He suddenly noticed that Whitey Kilpatrick was positioned in front of his own statue, inspecting it a little too closely. "Hey, take a gander at Whitey over there. He looks like Nursis, fallin' in love with his own reflection."

"I think you mean Narcissus, Joe," Sharpe corrected.

"Yeah, that's what I said, Narsissisis," Zedelko replied.

"You keep workin' on it Joe," Watson laughed, then turned to address Kilpatrick. "Hey, Whitey, Joe's right. You're getting' mighty close there. Someone might think you're gonna plant a wet one on your own mug."

"Son of a lumberjack! I don't even recognize myself," Kilpatrick complained. "All the rest of you fellas look identifiable."

"Don't be too hard on the sculptor, Whitey," Watson said with apparent sympathy. "I'm sure he was just trying to make a handsome guy out of you. That's why you can't recognize yourself. Your statue is too good-looking!"

"Aw, Frank, you don't have to tell me what I already know."

Zedelko was also studying the life-size figures, but for a different reason. "Identical look-alikes or not, I admit I'm a tad jealous that you guys are represented here in all your bronze glory. Heck, I gotta believe I deserve to be standing here too. Wouldn't you agree, Cal?"

"I wouldn't agitate too much over it, Joseph. It's just something Mr. Galahad and his selection committee decided upon," Ubank said, putting it in perspective. "I'm sure they would've loved to have you represented—and several others as well, no doubt—but they had limits imposed upon them. And who knows, your time may come."

"Hell, Joe, you're one to complain," Schmeltz added. "Least ways you got a fancy song written about you. In fact, I don't know which is more of an honour: being remembered in a song or as a statue? Either way, you got one, and we got another."

"Jacko makes a good point, Joe," Sharpe said. "I mean, folks affiliated with the Pines are kind of obliged to erect monuments, but 'Back Panel Vignette' is a tribute song created by fellas outside the hockey community because it's, well, just damn good Canadiana."

"You know something, I never really looked at it that way," Zedelko admitted. "Thanks a bunch, Beezer."

"Your welcome, Joe. But my real point is, it's all fine and dandy to have statues dedicated in our memory, to have our jerseys raised to the rafters, and to have our numbers retired. Individual achievements are nice, but our greatest achievement was winning the Clarence Cup—together, as a team."

"Sure as sugar," Ubank concurred. "So then how do we get the present team to play at the level needed to claim the Cup?"

"Maybe we need to think outside the box," Schmeltz suggested.

"You got something in mind, Jacko?" Sharpe asked.

"What about a good luck charm?"

"Hmm, interesting. Has that ever been done before?"

"Sure it has. And it's worked, sort of. Ask Whitey; he came up with the idea. Ain't that right, Whitey?"

Kilpatrick was way ahead of him. "If you're referring to pyramid power, first of all, it wasn't a good luck charm. Second, it wasn't my idea. My wife, Annie, came up with it. She was looking for some way to ease the pain of her chronic headaches."

"Hold on, your wife used pyramids as a cure for her headaches?" Zedelko asked.

"Yessir. Annie placed a little pyramid by her pillow, and, wouldn't you know, it worked. Her headaches disappeared! Then Annie suggested it might be good for my boys to undergo some pyramid therapy as well."

"Now, remind me, Whitey," Sharpe said. "You tried this during the playoffs, didn't you?"

"That's correct, Beezer. I was coaching the Pines back in '76 and we were up against the Pittsburgh Pilots. My boys were in tough—we'd lost the first two games in Pitt—and I was looking for answers. We needed more energy to match Pittsburgh's physical game. And we all know what Colonel Sinclair liked to say—"

Right on cue, each of the five spirits listening knew the drill and chimed in as one:

"You gotta expect to take a punch if you want to win in the crunch."

"That's perfect, fellas!" Kilpatrick enthused. "So, I took Annie's advice and got me some of those little pyramids. And then a few hours before the game I went out to our bench, and when no one was watching, I placed them underneath it."

"You mean you did it quiet like?" Sharpe asked. "With no hoopla or fanfare?"

"Yup. Just like our fella Baker out here. Look at him, discreetly going about his business with the prayer cards, drawing as little attention to himself as possible."

"And it worked?"

"Dang if our guys didn't come out spitting and snarling, giving as good as they got and better. Lo and behold, we won the next two games."

"And you believe the pyramids made all the difference?"

"Just as the perfect combination of sun and rain leads to a bountiful harvest, those pyramids seemed to do the trick—although nobody can know for certain."

"Did you eventually share your secret with anyone else?" Sharpe wondered.

"You're darn tootin'. I shared it with the players. I explained how pyramid power emits mysterious energy that can sharpen dull razor blades and help plants grow and stuff. That's when someone came up with the idea of suspending a large plastic pyramid in the centre of our dressing room. The boys put their sticks under it, and they'd even stand under it themselves for a prescribed amount of time. The players sure bought into it, as if we possessed a secret formula or magical elixir that no one else had—they're always looking for some advantage."

"That's for sure," Zedelko said. "One time, I never washed my uniform for three weeks."

"Come to think of it, George Daly made sure to put his socks and skates on left-foot-first every time," Watson added. "And Max Moore always taped his sticks a special way. Nowadays, the boys just grow playoff beards."

"Forgive me, Whitey, but didn't your team ended up losing that series and getting bounced from the playoffs?" Sharpe inquired.

"That's right, Beezer. Regardless of the magic, some teams are just better than others. Still, it was quite an experience. And to think, all I tried to do was harness the energy people call pyramid power; something that's still considered a mystery."

"Gosh, Whitey, it sounds like you're describing all of us here," Cal Ubank observed, having been quietly taking in Kilpatrick's story.

"How so, Cal?"

"Don't you see? As spirits we're a mystery to humans. Most folks don't even believe we exist. It's like we're make believe. But, by golly, we *do* exist! And we have abilities that humans don't."

"Cap'n Cal's right," Watson said. "Look at us, the six of us here. We're spirits who can do things humans can't. Ain't there some way we can take advantage of that?"

"And do what?" Kilpatrick asked.

"Maybe we can fog up a visor," Watson suggested, always looking for hands-on solutions. "Or ripple the air and distort a goalie's vision at a key moment. If nothing else, I can kick a keester or two."

"Sounds good! Let's do it," Kilpatrick exclaimed. "There's six of us to share the load, after all."

"Unfortunately, we can't," Ubank countered. "It wouldn't be right."

"How on earth could anything that helps the Pines win not be right?" Kilpatrick challenged.

"For one, it's dangerous. Things can backfire, making the situation worse."

"Holy unforeseen consequences, I never thought of that."

"But the simplest answer is: we weren't asked to."

"Hmm, I s'pose," Kilpatrick said grudgingly, then turned and wandered away, downcast, back to the spot in front of his bronze self. In due course, Joe Zedelko quietly migrated over to join him. Beezer Sharpe, meanwhile, continued the discussion with Ubank.

"We were, however, asked to help in some way," Beezer noted. "But I have no ideas for how we might intervene—short of holding the player's sticks for them, which is out of the question."

"Darn it!" Ubank spat, which got everyone's attention because it was so uncharacteristic of the man. "Sorry, fellas. Sometimes I put too much vinegar in my parlance. But it drives me to distraction."

"What does, Cal?" Sharpe asked.

"The fact that it's easier to impact earthly events in a negative way than in a positive one."

"You know what they say: it's always harder to build a wall than to tear it down."

"What's that got to do with hockey, Beezer?" Watson challenged.

"Plenty, Frank. For instance, it would be easier for me to nudge the stick of an opposition forward on a breakaway, or push him off stride, than to help Ben Bellamy aim better, so his point shots at least hit the goddamn net."

"Hang on a minute. When were we ever even capable of that?" Watson asked.

"That's just it; we aren't. Not to that degree, anyway. But you would be surprised how a little whisper can make an impact. Our influence can be subtle, yet significant."

"It's a lot like that old Bavarian fable," Jackson Schmeltz suggested, "Where the North Wind and the Sun make a bet to see which of the two is stronger."

"I'm not sure I'm familiar with that one," Watson said. "How does it go?"

"One day the Sun and the North Wind observed a traveller walking along the road. The North Wind challenged the Sun to see which of them could make the man remove his coat. The North Wind went first and blew and blew, but the man just buttoned up his coat, bent into the wind, and continued on his way. When it was the Sun's turn, it simply rose high in the sky, heating up the day, and caused the traveller to unbutton his coat and then remove it entirely."

"Interesting," Ubank said. "But are you sure that's a Bavarian fable?"

"Of course. My Oma taught me that one."

"I don't know, Jacko, it sounds very ancient Chinese to me," Watson said, ever the instigator.

"Dad gum, Franky. Why must you always contradict what I say? I swear, if I had a doughnut for every time we argued over something, I'd be able to open up my own shop—call it Jacko's Doughnuts."

"That'd never happen," Watson laughed. "You'd eat all the doughnuts before you could sell them!"

Like an on-ice official, Sharpe stepped between the two combatants. "Fellas, you can quit arguing because you're both wrong. Turns out Jacko's story is an Aesop's fable."

"See, Jacko? I told you it wasn't Bavarian. It's Scandinavian."

"What in blazes are you on about, Frank? Aesop was a Greek storyteller."

Ubank sensed the group needed to refocus. "Alright, gents, I think we should get back to the original point of the discussion."

"What was the original point?" Sharpe wondered.

"We were pondering a course of action that might help these young Pines play winning hockey—but I dare say it has left us completely flummoxed." As he spoke, Ubank kept an eye on Baker, who had just finished taking photos of a family of three.

At the same time, Schmeltz noticed that Kilpatrick and Zedelko were hovering in close proximity to Baker. He called over. "Hey, Joe, you and Whitey have been huddled up for some time now. Why all the secrecy?"

"What's that?" Zedelko replied, somewhat startled. "Secrets? No secrets." He jabbed a thumb in Baker's direction. "We wanted to get a closer look at our host here, admiring the way he's carrying out his ritual." He paused to appraise him. "You know, I'm actually growing fond of this Baker kid. He seems like a throwback—someone who would have been more comfortable back in the day when we were playing in the PHL."

"That's true," Watson put in. "Just look at him—out here, alone, in the cold. Here's a guy who stepped away from the computer and left the office to deliver his prayers in person. Heck, I'd even wager he took the train into town—Uh-oh . . . what just happened?"

"What do you mean?" Sharpe said.

"He's not doing anything. He's not moving."

"Hmm . . . you're right. It looks as if he's stuck."

"What . . . to the ground?" Zedelko asked.

"No, not literally stuck, but uncertain, undecided, as if he's not sure what to do next," Sharpe explained.

"I could give him a tiny push," Zedelko suggested. He was standing beside Baker, perpendicular to his right shoulder.

"You better leave him be, Joseph," Ubank advised. "Let him figure it out for himself." No sooner did he say the words than Baker seemed to arrive at a decision and continued on his way.

"Oops ... There he goes," Zedelko observed.

Sharpe looked around at the others. "Well boys, I'm gonna say that's the horn to signal the end of this gathering."

"I'm with you, Beezer," Schmeltz said. "Seems our time here has run its course."

"Hang on there, fellas," Kilpatrick called and then turned to Ubank and Sharpe. "So, what did we decide? What's the plan?"

"Well, with all the uncertainty, I'd vote for playing it safe for now," Ubank answered. "Let's lie low, at least through the weekend."

"OK, everybody, we're going to take a 'wait and see' approach for the time being," Sharpe echoed.

"We can always discuss things further the next time we're called together again," Ubank added.

"If there is a next time," Watson cracked. "It seems you boys just want to deny me the opportunity to kick some butt."

"C'mon, Frank, just take a look at our friend Baker there. I'm plenty certain he'll be calling on us again before long," Sharpe replied.

"OK, then, till we meet again," Watson said, accepting the decision.

"Right behind you, Sugar," Schmeltz said, joining him.

Sharpe then called over his shoulder to Kilpatrick and Zedelko. "Hey you two, we're all done here!" But then turned to discover they'd already left. "Humph, they're gone, without as much as a fare-thee-well." He pivoted back to Ubank, who was still studying Baker. "I'm pretty sure he's done, Cal. I wouldn't be expecting much more activity here. Do you mind if I skedaddle?"

"Of course, Beasley," Ubank replied. "I'll be leaving shortly myself. We'll meet up again next time."

He gave Sharpe a little wave before returning to scrutinizing Baker, who appeared to be speaking to himself. Straining to hear, Ubank could make out a single word, repeated with every step he took. Was it a name? Yes, definitely a name: "Cubby." But who was Cubby? Perhaps it hinted at the imminent arrival of another spirit.

Seeing that Baker's next stop was his own statue, Ubank whisked over and wrapped himself around the bronze figure, mimicking the pose. When Baker reached into the gloved hand to remove the paper slips he'd place there earlier, Ubank couldn't resist a bit of fun and gave his fingers a little squeeze.

In short order, he detected something materializing behind one of the television vans parked nearby and so he broke off from studying Baker's movements and approached the vehicle. It is there that he came face to face with a youthful spirit, a boy of about nine.

"Hello, there, young fella. Welcome to Elysian Square and the Acropolis. My name is Cal Ubank."

Cubby's eyes widened when he heard the name. "Hi, it's nice—I mean, it's an honour to meet you, sir."

"You must be Cubby."

"That's right! Um... but Cubby is my nickname. My real name is Cal, like yours. My mom and dad always told me I was named after you."

Cubby's words worked like a time machine for Ubank, conveying him back to a day ten years earlier, when he'd been summoned to bear witness to the christening of an infant boy—his own namesake, as it turned out. It was a cruel twist of fate, he reflected, that the next time he'd come face to face with that same boy it was as one spirit to another.

CHAPTER THIRTY-SEVEN
A WALK IN THE SNOW

It was three and a half decades ago, on a cold February night in Ottawa following a winter storm, that Pierre Elliot Trudeau went for his famous walk in the snow. The next day he announced his retirement as prime minister of Canada and from public office in general.

Thirty-six years later, the province of Ontario saw a half million people take a collective walk in the snow, although the circumstances were different in terms of the time of day, the weather, and the politics. On that bright and sunny but bitterly cold Friday morning in late February, every schoolteacher in Ontario was out on the sidewalk, but not to ponder their retirement (though many may have gone so far as to consider their options). No, they were participating in a one-day province-wide strike to protest Premier Doug Ford's proposed cuts to education: specifically, the government's unwillingness to come to an agreement where collective bargaining was concerned. As a result of the job action, schools were closed to two million school-age children for the day, and teachers gathered in front of schools, school boards, MPP offices, and even on the lawn at Queen's Park. They carried signs and flags as they marched in picket lines that stretched several kilometres in some cases.

Every member of Bakers' Coven had signed up for the three-hour morning shift, an 8:30 start on the sidewalk in front of HMV. Before departing from home, Baker checked the thermometer outside his kitchen window and found the mercury had contracted to read -16°C—and that was without taking into account the wind chill. During his commute, the force of the wind became more apparent as he entered town, leaving all the flags tightly stretched horizontally. Sunglasses were the fashion of the day, with the sky a piercing blue and the morning sun low on the horizon, aimed directly into eastbound commuters' retinas.

Baker was halfway across the school's parking lot, heading for the sign-in table near the front doors, when he was diverted by Conrad's voice. "Hey, Brooks, get over here!"

He stopped and turned toward the command. Huddled next to one wall of the building was a small knot of his colleagues, holding picket signs and protecting themselves from the wind.

"We missed you yesterday," someone said, standing arm in arm with Perreault to keep warm, their face covered in a balaclava, sunglasses, and the fur-lined hood of an oversized parka.

"Mas, is that you? Congratulations, man."

"What for?"

"You've succeeded in covering every last inch of exposed flesh. You could pass for the Invisible Man."

"What can I say? It's minus twenty-four with the wind chill."

"Speaking of invisible men," Conrad said, "I heard you spent the day in the Big Smoke."

Baker gave Angus an accusatory glare. "Oh yeah? Did Fletcher here fill you in?"

"Sorry, Baker," Angus said. "I couldn't wait to tell them about your pilgrimage, especially after watching the game last night. I mean, holy shit, mission accomplished, eh?"

"Yeah, that was a solid win."

"Why didn't you tell us?" Mas asked. "At least give us a heads-up to prepare some prayers of our own."

"I know, I know. It was a last-minute thing, more or less. And I actually *did* compose an email requesting your contributions, but I guess I fucked up in the process of hitting 'send.'"

Conrad never ceased to be amazed by Baker's ineptitude when it came to computers. "You seriously need to petition Saint Jude for help—and maybe light a candle while you're at it."

"And Saint Jude is the patron saint of—?"

"Lost causes. Because that's what you are, a lost cause—with technology, anyway."

"So, you made the journey to Mecca to commune with the spirits," Mas said. "How was it?"

"Oh, it's a long story."

"That's OK. We've got three hours," Perreault said, then flicked a mittened thumb toward the attendance table. "You should go sign in first, though."

"Hey, I didn't know we had to sign in!" Angus exclaimed.

"You'd better—if you want to collect your fifty bucks," Conrad advised.

"Oh, right," Baker said, pulling Angus along with him. "We get paid for today. I completely forgot."

A WALK IN THE SNOW

"And don't forget to grab some signs for yourselves," Perreault added.

After checking in, they went to select a couple of picket signs. Angus, however, saw something that made him want to go bigger. "Hey, that guy's got a flag. Can I get a flag?"

"I don't see why not—if there are any available."

When they rejoined their friends, Baker was bearing a picket sign that read "CUTS HURT KIDS," and Angus had his flag, which bore the name of the union's local branch affiliate. He couldn't have been prouder if he'd been the country's standard-bearer at the Olympic Games.

It wasn't long before the school's union rep called everyone to assemble near the sign-in table. He thanked everyone present for their attendance and reiterated that their ultimate goal was to send a strong, unified message to the government and the Ministry. The teachers were also reminded to be friendly and professional out there. Then, with some final words of inspiration, they were sent off to commence the march.

Angus wasted no time mining Baker for details regarding the previous day's adventure. "I'm curious, what does someone do on a pilgrimage? Like, did you bow to each statue? Genuflect? Get down on your knees?"

"No, no. I just sort of did a slow walk around the grouping of nine statues. During each lap I stopped at a different player and left two prayer slips—one of yours and one of mine."

"But how did you know there'd be someplace to hold the prayers?"

"I didn't. I just assumed there *would* be. As it turned out, there were lots of places to wedge a piece of paper, mostly around their hands and fingers."

"And what did you do with the prayers afterward? Did you leave them there with the statues?"

"No, of course not. When I was done, I retrieved them."

"Can I get mine back then? I'd like to file them away as a keepsake."

"Uh, sorry, Angus. I don't have them. I burned 'em all."

"Really? When?"

"Last night, at home, before the game."

"So, you had, like, a second ceremony in your living room?"

"Nah, it wasn't like that, really. I just basically 'tidied up,' sort of like a priest does after Communion."

"How many Icemen did you say there are?" Conrad asked.

"Nine. But I focused on five."

"Which five?"

"The deceased ones."

"Was Elysian Square busy? Like, did anybody see you?" Angus inquired.

"It was mostly empty. But I *was* being watched by one little kid." Baker smiled at the memory. "He just walked right up to me and asked what I was doing."

"No shit! That must've been awkward."

"Not really. He was cool. He was just curious. His mother was there in the background, but she was too busy trying to keep warm."

"It was cold, huh?"

"Oh, yeah. It was cold—but not like today. This is *stupid* cold."

"OK, now, time for the million-dollar question," Masaccio said.

"What's that?"

"Did you sense a spiritual presence? Did any of the Icemen show up? Did they answer your call?"

"Um . . . no, I can't say that I felt anything like that." There was a murmur of disappointment from the others, compelling Baker to expand on his answer. "But I *can* say the experience was a positive one. It was very meditative—spiritual and inviting—a sense of comradeship with the sculptures, the players, you know? I felt like I was actually accomplishing something."

"Still," Mas persisted, "it's a shame that out of five spirits, not one of them made its presence felt."

"Actually, I reached out to six players."

"Six? But I thought you said five. I only made five prayer slips," Angus protested, sounding as if he'd been cheated.

"That's right. I did, originally. But at the last minute I added one more."

"Who did you add?"

"Jersey Joe Zedelko."

"Hey, I know about Joe Zedelko—O Wretched Bliss and their song about how he died and all that. Did you go around singing 'Back Panel Vignette'?"

"Believe it or not, that's exactly what I did," Baker admitted.

"So, let me get this straight," Masaccio said. "You had six in your little group of spirits?"

"Yes. And you'll never guess what I call them."

"Being an art teacher, it would be cool if you added one more, then you could call them the Group of Seven," Perreault suggested.

"Hey!" Angus exclaimed. "You could call them the Magnificent Seven—No! Better yet, the Silver Seven. That would be perfect, because they're metal sculptures, you know."

"That *would* be perfect, except the statues are made of bronze, not silver—and anyway, there are only *six* players in my group, not seven."

"So then, what did you name this group of six?" Perreault asked.

A WALK IN THE SNOW

Baker hesitated in responding because it suddenly sounded childish, but he swallowed and revealed it nonetheless. "I call them the Six-pack."

"Six-pack," Angus repeated. "That's a cool name, I guess." Then he shifted the topic. "And this pilgrimage stuff sounds cool, too. If you ever do another one, take me with you. Results don't lie. That was one hell of a win last night."

The discussion continued along that line for the better part of an hour. It included an assessment of the previous night's game; a trivia challenge, with the category of the players in Baker's Six-pack as its focus; and Conrad waxing pedagogical on the topic of the religious history of pilgrimages. If nothing else, it served to pass the time in the sub-zero temperature.

At one point during the three-hour walk in the snow, Perreault and Baker found themselves alone, separated from the others, giving her the opportunity to thank him for his phone call the previous night.

"All day I was wondering what might have happened," she said. "It's so unlike you to miss school."

"Sorry about that. I wanted to keep it quiet. I was afraid that announcing it to everyone, well, there was the potential for it to turn into a big deal, you know? It was just something I preferred to talk about *after* it was done."

"How did Angus know?"

"I ran into him outside the main office Wednesday morning. That's when I happened to make mention of my plans." Baker chuckled. "I've got to say, I was surprised that he came through with his prayers."

"I think we all would have if we'd known. But then I get the feeling you were glad not to be burdened with a mitt-full of prayers and slips of paper and whatnot."

"Yes, I had enough trouble yesterday with two sets of prayers, never mind five. At one point I thought I was going to lose them in the wind."

"I've got to admit, up until you called, I had begun to suspect that you had taken the day off to visit Dorcas about Cubby's séance. By the way, have you gotten in touch with her yet?" Although it wasn't her intent, Perreault's question served as a punch in Baker's gut, adding to his frustration over his habitual procrastination.

"Nope, I haven't called her. I'll do it this afternoon, as soon as I get home from this shift—I promise."

"Do you have her number?"

"As a matter of fact, I don't think I do."

"No problem. I can give it to you."

Baker stopped walking, set down his sign, and checked his pockets, beginning with the various outer and inner compartments of his winter coat, then the pockets of his sweater and then his pants.

"Did you not bring your phone with you?" Perreault asked, watching him.

"No, I have that right here." He patted his breast pocket. "I was just looking for something to write with."

Perreault gave an exasperated sigh, pulled off a mitten, and held out her bare hand. "Your phone, please."

"Oh, shit, I did it again, didn't I?" He reached into his coat and extracted his phone. As he did, something popped out with it and fell to the snowy ground. Perreault thought it was a tin of lip balm, but when he picked it up, she saw that it was something more precious. "What's that expensive looking thing?"

"I forgot I had this. It's called a pyx. It holds Communion wafers. Angus gave it to me as a container for his prayer slips. I should give it back to him."

"Where did he get to, anyway?"

"He's behind us—six o'clock," Baker said in military fashion.

Perreault turned to look. "Oh, I see him back there. Who's he walking with?"

Baker searched the group for a familiar face, although the assorted hats, hoods, and scarves were working against him. "I don't recognize any of them. My guess is they're teachers from the elementary panel."

Perreault smiled like a proud mother. "Look at him with that flag, flirting with a half-dozen ladies."

"I would think it'd be a bit risky to flirt with anyone who is bundled up to the point where they resemble the Michelin Man, so you can't tell if they're young or old, pretty or plain, fit or flabby."

"Apparently, Angus is willing to take that risk. Maybe we shouldn't interrupt him."

"Wait, what was I thinking?" Baker whacked his forehead with the base of his hand. "Angus isn't the person I need. Jeez, am I a dummy or what? Uh . . . don't answer that."

"Why? You don't trust me to say, 'No'?" Perreault joked. "Who's the person you need, anyway?"

"The guy who would have said, 'Yes.'"

"Oh, you mean Conrad."

"Who else?" Baker scanned the sidewalk ahead of them. "He's up there, walking with Mas. C'mon, let's catch up with them."

Baker broke into a jog to manoeuvre around a knot of fellow protesters. Perreault gave a whoop and a wave when a random driver tooted his car horn in support of the protesters as he cruised past. The two of them came up to Conrad from behind and bumped him on either side in childlike fashion.

"Ahhh . . . the young 'uns," he said, in a congenial manner. "What's up? Having fun yet?"

"I've got something of yours," Baker replied, holding out the pyx. "Thanks for this, but I think I can return it now."

"You sure?"

"Pretty sure. I have no more use for it."

"Why don't you keep it for now? It'll come in handy when you go on your next pilgrimage."

"My *next* one?"

"My bet is you haven't made your last devotional visit to Elysian Square and the Acropolis—based on yesterday's success."

"You know, Conrad, there are times when I'm not sure if I should take you seriously."

"Well, my friend, in this instance you can trust that I'm in earnest. Do us all a favour and just hang on to that thing. You can return it to me at a later date."

"OK, but when do you figure that might be?"

"Considering that the goal is to see the Pines win, how about sometime in June?"

Baker's reply was interrupted when someone boisterously hugged him from behind and thrust a cell phone in his face. He managed to maintain his balance as Angus jumped up and piggy-backed him, loudly announcing how he had secured two ducats for tomorrow night's game against the Washington Founders. "You, my friend, are going to your very first Mighty Pines game. What do you think of that, eh?"

In order to comprehend exactly what Angus was shouting in his ear, Baker's first response was to pull the device away from his nose so he could focus on the screen. When the news finally registered, he was struck by a dizzying spectrum of emotions, causing his second response to be surprisingly reserved.

"Aw, gee thanks, Angus, but you might want to invite someone else. You know how I feel about watching Pines games in the company of others."

Angus jumped down off his friend's back and spun him around so they could face each other squarely. "Baker, this is not just the company of others, it is about being among 18,000 strong at Nova Tank Arena! Besides, we'll have a blast—don't be such a killjoy."

"Killjoy? Now there's a word I don't hear much anymore," Perreault laughed. "Angus, have you been watching episodes of Downton Abbey again?"

"What? Oh . . . I guess it's my mom's influence; blame her." He then turned back to Baker. "Seriously, man, you and I are going. I'm not taking no for an answer."

Baker stood there in silence, evidently weighing his options.

"Oh, for heaven's sake, Baker, go to a game already," Perreault urged. "Heck, this could be a sign of better things to come for the team. You never know, your very presence could help them win."

"Perreault, you might have something there," Conrad said. "Maybe our man Baker here is the lucky charm for the boys in green."

Yet again, Baker sensed a degree of fun in Conrad's voice. He looked at each of his friends in turn as they stood there in the cold, awaiting his answer, but his reply just served to buy him some time.

"Let's keep walking; I'm freezing."

CHAPTER THIRTY-EIGHT

MARY

With the morning shift in the books and his picketing obligations met, Baker got in the car, cranked the cabin heat, and headed straight home. It took a few minutes for the circulation in his extremities to return, and with it came a general sense of euphoria.

There were several reasons for his good spirits. First, the reviews of his pilgrimage were entirely positive. Second, so was the result of the Pines game the previous night (whether there was a direct correlation between the two, however, was anybody's guess). A third reason was that Baker had a good feeling about the Pines. They had obviously figured things out and were likely due for an extended spell of winning, starting with the following night's game against Washington—a game which he had ultimately agreed to attend in person with Angus. Lastly, it was the weekend; it had finally arrived, and he could put a bow on what had been a crazy week. There was just one more task to see through, which was to get in touch with Dorcas Blanchard, something he'd been putting off for several days.

True to his word, the minute he got home and inside the front door—actually locking it behind him as a defence against the cold—Baker got out his phone and tapped on the contact number for Dorcas, which Perreault had added to his list. He tried to rehearse the conversation in his mind, but, having never before asked someone to preside over a séance, he had no idea how the call would go. If nothing else, Baker wanted to ensure his intentions were clearly expressed in order to increase the likelihood that Dorcas would consider his plan legitimate. The last thing he wanted was to come across as a fair-weather dabbler in the methods of the occult.

"Hello?" The voice at the other end of the line was unmistakeable.

"Hello, Dorcas? It's Baker . . . Baker Brooks."

After a pause Dorcas responded heartily. "Well, knock me over with a feather. How are you, Baker?"

The next few minutes were spent catching up, most of which consisted of Baker fielding questions about the Coven's activities.

"Actually, the reason I called has nothing to do with our coven activity. It so happens that I'm in the market for a psychic medium. You see, Dorcas, I would like to make contact with someone who passed away recently."

"It sounds to me like you're planning a party."

"A party? I'm not sure I understand."

"My apologies. It's a term I use. You're looking to converse with a spirit by means of a spirit council?"

"Well, I was looking to hold a . . . a séance, and I was hoping you would preside over the proceedings."

"I'd be happy to help, but it will depend on the circumstances. I'll need some details from you first. By the way, we don't use the term 'séance' anymore. We prefer calling it a 'spirit council' or even a 'family council.'"

"A family council? Um . . . OK." *So far so good,* Baker thought. *She hasn't hung up on me.* "What details do you need from me?"

"First off, might I inquire as to who the guest of honour will be?"

"A young boy of ten. He died almost a year ago."

"Does he have a name?"

"Of course, sorry. His name is—was—Cal. I mean, Calub was his given name, but he mostly went by Cubby—Cubby Elyk."

Baker's answer resulted in a protracted silence on the other end, causing him to think they'd been cut off. "You say the boy's name is Cubby Elyk?"

"Yes."

Dorcas made some vague remarks about *"stars in Camelot"* and *"an abracadabra moment,"* but Baker wasn't sure if they were meant for him to hear. Her next question, however, was delivered clearly. "Who will be attending this event?"

"Perreault, for one."

"Perreault Thoreau? She knew Cubby?"

"No, but I need her to sing vocals."

"Vocals?"

"I should explain. I'm planning for us to perform a song—the same way our band performs songs during our coven ceremonies, except that this song will be devoted to Cubby." Baker didn't want to sound pushy, so he made it seem like a request. "What do you think? Will that work?"

"Well, it's something I've never seen done before, but I can't imagine how it would hurt."

"Good! I might also need our drummer, Angus. But more importantly, I thought it would be beneficial to have Cubby's aunt and uncle attend. I figure they would also serve as a strong familial attraction for the boy."

MARY

"Excellent point. But I have to ask, why do you feel the need to conduct this council? What do you hope to achieve by making contact with Cubby Elyk?"

"It's Cubby's uncle, Allen Nella."

"This is his idea?"

"Oh, no, it's all mine." Not wanting to come off sounding like a proud schoolboy, Baker caught himself and cleared his throat. "The goal is to help Allen move along the process of mourning. Long story short, he seems to be stuck at 'regret,' and his wife, Helen, has asked if I could assist in some way. Allen was close to Cubby, and I believe he feels that Cubby's death left certain things unresolved between them. I'm hoping this sé—uh, family council, can bring some closure where that's concerned. I just want to do everything I can to optimize the chances that Cubby will answer our call. Does that make sense? I mean, can you understand where I'm coming from?"

"Trust me, Baker, I *over*stand where you're coming from. Everything you've said checks all the boxes. About the Nellas, though: are they on board with your idea?"

"Actually, they don't know about my plan. I thought I'd get your opinion first."

"If you can get the Nellas' approval, I would suggest we hold it at their house. After all, Cubby spent time there, so it's a place of familiarity for him, right?"

"That would be perfect."

Baker and Dorcas then engaged in a discussion about what a typical family council might entail, what he could anticipate as a result of it, and what was and was not appropriate for such a gathering. This was followed by Dorcas suggesting a date for the event.

"Let's try for two weeks tomorrow, on the seventh, a Saturday. That'll be our last opportunity for a while, because two days later, Mary and I will be boarding a plane for England."

"England! Very nice. Visiting friends? Family?"

"Yes, I'm going to spend some time with my old friend, Smythe Ravenstone. I may have mentioned him."

"Oh yeah, the guy who had a connection to Nate Sinclair and stuff. He was your mentor, right?"

"Correct. He's still working on his project in Salisbury. I'm taking Mary along with me. I think meeting the professor will serve to further cultivate her education." She paused for a moment. "Baker, I want to thank you for considering my services for this event. To be honest, I'm looking forward to it."

Baker exhaled audibly. "Boy, you don't know how relieved I am to hear that. I mean, if you declined, my only other option would have been Mary."

"As it happens, I expect Mary to be there."

"That's great!" Baker was pleased but also confused. "Out of curiosity, why do you *expect* Mary to be there?" Dorcas didn't reply right away, as if the answer was obvious, so Baker didn't wait for one. "Oh, I see, you need her to assist you. So, she's really that good, eh?"

"It's simpler than that, Baker. She lives there."

"Hold it. Mary lives with Helen and Allen Nella? What a coincidence!"

"Not really. Helen and Allen are her aunt and uncle."

Baker didn't respond to Dorcas's last statement, but he did find it noteworthy that the Nellas had a full house of young women, which included their own daughter Eleanor, and two nieces in Mary and Marinelle. The thought of Marinelle served as a reminder of another key detail he needed to touch on.

"Oh, and one more thing. It'd be ideal if Cubby's sister, Marinelle, could be there. She also lives with Helen and Allen. Apparently, she and Cubby were really close. I've never actually met her, but I thought her presence at the council would be a strong attraction for the little guy."

"I agree completely. But did I hear you right? Did you say you've never met her?"

"Who, Marinelle? No, never."

"Oh, but you *have* met her."

"Uh . . . no, I'm certain I haven't."

"You do know Mary, right?"

"Of course."

"Well then you've met Cubby's sister."

"That can't be. Cubby had only one sister, and her name was Marinelle."

Dorcas tried to be gentle as she spelled it out for him. "Baker, David Elyk hired me for my services last September. Since then I have also come to know Helen and Allen Nella quite well. Mary has been struggling with Cubby's death, and I imagine the shortening of her name from Marinelle to Mary has something to do with that. Although I never met Cubby, I am fairly well acquainted with the members of his family. Although it might be a shock to your system, the fact remains—Mary *is* Cubby's sister."

CHAPTER THIRTY-NINE
THE HORROR

Saturday, February 22

A mere forty-eight hours after Thursday's decisive win, hockey fans across Canada and select parts of the US, namely those in the District of Columbia, witnessed Mighty Pines history. Old-timers would be hard pressed to remember an on-ice event in the franchise's eighty-seven-year existence that was more embarrassing. Two days after one of their best games of the year, this assembly of players seemed to have left their pride in the locker room. Contrary to the notion of valiantly representing the team crest on their chests, the Pines might as well have worn their sweaters inside out that night, given the amount of respect they showed for the front of them.

For Baker and Angus, who were among the 18,467 fans in attendance Saturday night, the hours leading up to puck drop offered no portent of the bizarre events that would transpire. Apart from being delayed by the usual game day snarl of eastbound traffic into the city, nothing truly foreboding occurred. In fact, they still managed to enter the queue at Gate One of Nova Tank Arena with a full fifteen minutes to spare.

"Where are our seats, anyway?" Baker wondered aloud, his voice betraying a level of excitement.

Angus's reply came with a sort of smug chuckle. "You'll see soon enough—just stick with me."

"By the way, thanks for driving. I hate driving in the city. We'd still be looking for parking if it was me doing the driving."

"No sweat, man," Angus said, throwing a fatherly arm across Baker's shoulders. "What'd I tell you? Leave everything to me. It's gonna be a night to remember."

The line at the gate moved steadily and soon they came to the head of it, at which point Angus presented two tickets for the attendant to scan before proceeding through the turnstile. The attendant called after him jovially, "Enjoy the game. Go, Pines!" But Angus didn't acknowledge him, apparently not having heard. Seeing this, Baker took it upon himself to exchange pleasantries with the man while simultaneously reaching a hand out to advance the turnstile bar, but suddenly pulled back, hit with the thought, queasy as it was, about all the palms that had already made contact with it—sweaty, sticky, grimy, greasy—and applied his hip instead. It all lasted less than a count of five steamboats, yet when he looked up to reconnect with Angus, his friend was nowhere to be seen.

Baker stepped forward so as to allow others behind him to pass and then executed a full pirouette in slow motion, scanning the crowd in every direction, but ultimately came up empty. Not knowing where else to turn, he decided his best option was to remain in place and wait, so he moved to one side and stood next to a concrete pillar situated in no-man's land, apart from the crowd, proximate to a washroom entrance on one side and a concession stand on the other.

He didn't have to wait for long. "There you are. Where the fuck'd you go? Never mind." Angus shoved a large tub of popcorn and a frosty tallboy into Baker's chest. "Here, take this . . . and this, and stay close. Let's go find our seats; I don't want to miss the opening faceoff."

Being of the same mind, Baker wasn't about to argue. He was feeling the fervour of time and place—the thrill of finally being in the house that Colonel Sinclair built, about to watch, live and in person, his very first Mighty Pines game. And yet, owing to the team's habit of finding new ways to disappoint, a little bird in his head insisted on chirping at him, like a chickadee of doubt. It warned of pending misfortune with a Shakespearean lilt, no less, saying: *"Your guard keep fortified lest grief betide."*

There was no time to dwell on it, however, because Angus was leading the way with purpose, making it a challenge for Baker to keep up as he balanced his popcorn in one hand and cold beer in another. It was a situation which took him all the way back to when he was a primary school kid on a field trip, obediently following the teacher with the other classmates, except back then his one hand was clutching a rope and the other a cookie.

Not wanting to lose Angus a second time, Baker zeroed in on the back of his head where the shock of blonde hair met the collar of his black puffer jacket, until his eye was drawn to an odd flap of orange fabric hanging from Angus's pocket. Between the hair and the fabric, Baker kept dutifully in tow and soon found himself navigating the concrete steps of the lower bowl section. He read the aisle numbers as they descended, expecting Angus to stop at any moment, but they just kept moving headlong down toward ice level until there were no more steps to descend, at which point Angus stopped and turned to Baker.

"Whadda ya think? Pretty nice, eh?" he said, tapping on the Plexiglas as they stood beside the visitor's bench.

"Yeah, this is cool," Baker replied, gazing out at the activity on the ice. He was awed by the size and speed of the players as they warmed up, Washington in red, white, and blue at the far end of the rink while the Pines skated circles in the near end, wearing Kelly green and white. He then looked back up the way they came. "Um . . . where are our seats?"

"You're looking at them," Angus replied, indicating two empty seats leading into the first row next to where they happened to be standing.

Baker needed a moment to digest the news. "Angus, these are frickin' amazing!"

"No shit, huh? And I plan to take full advantage of them."

It seemed a weird response to Baker but he was too busy settling into his seat to dwell on it. Angus lifted his beer and invited Baker to join him in clinking cans. "Cheers, my friend. Here's to a memorable game—guaran-*fuckin'*-teed." In the process of taking a pull on his beer, Angus noticed two young children seated directly behind him along with the accompanying adult, who shot him a look of disdain. Angus could only offer a weak smile and a weaker apology, "Oh, shit—sorry," before turning around to face front, leaving the adult frowning and the kids giggling.

Careful not to laugh too loudly, Baker shifted his focus elsewhere and got busy removing his jacket by first setting his beer and popcorn on the floor between his feet. Then, not wanting to bump the gentleman to his left with an errant elbow, he contorted himself in trying to get an arm out of its sleeve, leaning over into Angus's space for an instant, but it was at that precise moment that Angus thrust two fingers in his mouth and blew, producing a piercing whistle that carried across the rink. Unfortunately, Baker's right ear caught most of it, causing him to reflexively duck downward out of the way—and bonk his nose on Angus's knee in the process. Of course Angus was oblivious to what had just happened, so Baker suffered in silence, shaking it off by finding solace in the salty, buttery goodness of his popcorn, which in turn caused his fingers to acquire a greasy shine, prompting him to extend a hand toward Angus, palm up. "Please tell me you loaded up on napkins."

Angus was way ahead of him and reaching into his jacket pocket. To Baker's surprise, however, he extracted not napkins but a large rectangle of fabric coloured green, white, and orange. Baker instantly made the connection between the dangling piece of orange cloth he'd eyeballed earlier and what he now recognized as the tricolour flag of Ireland. (He vaguely recalled Angus once making mention of how he had some Irish blood in him. Apparently he was intending to celebrate his roots here at the game.)

Baker was left to lick his fingers and watch in semi-amazement as Angus stood up, shook the flag out, and waved it jubilantly overhead, whooping and cheering as if the

Irish had just landed on the moon, or won the World Cup of soccer. When Angus sat down again he seemed overcome by spasms of indecision over what to do—he had no intention of disrespecting the flag and was especially careful not to have it touch the ground—but he had to do *something*. He continued to wave it around a few more times, then wrapped it across his shoulders like a cape before ultimately pulling it over his head and tying it under his chin as though it were a headscarf or a babushka. It's a good bet he'd have worn it like that all game if not for feeling compelled to remove it during the playing of the national anthems. In the end he settled on draping it over a section of Plexiglas that extended back from the visitor's bench in front of him, a convenience that allowed him to take in the action while gorging on popcorn and beer.

The first five minutes of the game saw the Pines playing like a team possessed, hemming the Founders in their own end, winning puck battles, and basically using the goalie as target practice—tallying no less than a dozen shots on net. (The Founders had assigned the starting goaltending duties to nine-year veteran Zac Middleton—he'd actually had a cup of coffee with the Pines' organization early in his career.) Middleton proved up to the challenge, however, keeping Toronto off the scoreboard and allowing Washington to weather the storm, after which the game settled into a balanced, back-and-forth affair with neither team able to break the ice.

Then, midway through the period, Middleton was involved in a tangle of players in the goal crease and came out of the ensuing pileup gimpy. Forced to exit the game, he was replaced by backup Paul Kratz. To the delight of the capacity crowd, Toronto eventually opened the scoring in the dying seconds of the period, taking a 1-0 lead into the first intermission.

For Baker, all the reports about Pines fans at Nova Tank Arena being uncommonly subdued were proven to be mostly accurate. To be fair, whenever the game turned in favour of the home team, the fans did prove capable of fomenting a degree of raucousness, but alas could not sustain it for any appreciable length of time. Credit to Angus for trying damn hard to make up for it. Presently his seat was vacant but when he returned it was with two more beers and a couple of hot dogs.

THE HORROR

"What the hell happened?" Angus asked as he handed a hot dog and a beer across to Baker.

"Wow, thanks, Angus," Baker laughed, graciously accepting the offering of beverage and food before pausing a moment to assess the latter. "How'd you know what I like on my hot dog?"

"I didn't. Besides, what's there to know? I just pretended both were for me and loaded them with the works. Now tell me what happened. When I left we were up a goal and now it's tied."

Baker described how the Pines were assessed a penalty for too many men on the ice, which led to a quick Washington power play goal. At the moment the Founders were tilting the ice and only Eddie Sanderson's wizardry in the net for Toronto was keeping the game tied. "If they're not careful, this could quickly turn ugly for the Pines," Baker said.

"Don't worry; things can change fast. A penalty here, a power play there—" Angus broke off to take a hungry-man bite of his dog, causing the rest of the sentence to be lost in a garble of mastication. But before he could swallow the Founders scored to go up 2-1.

"Fuuu-aaarrrgghh!" was the response from Angus, who made the mid-curse adjustment for the sake of three sensitive pairs of ears sitting behind him.

"Here, hold this, please," he said to Baker, entrusting him with his hot dog.

With both hands now occupied, Baker watched as Angus half-turned in his seat to reach into his jacket pocket and pulled out, of all things, a bobblehead doll wearing the red, white, and blue of the Washington Founders. On its back was a large number "40", identifying it as Igor Zlatkin. Zlatkin was the Founders' captain and leading goal scorer who hailed from Kazan, Russia, hard on the banks of the Volga River. During his rookie season he was asked what significance the number forty had for him. His reply in a thick Russian accent was simply, "Goals—every year I score forty goals—minimum." That was fourteen years ago and since then he had routinely led the team in goals each year, and was consistently in the mix for the PHL goal scoring crown.

Angus balanced the doll on the ledge in front of him and for a second time half-turned in his seat to rummage in a pocket of his jacket, revealing a bandage this time. He peeled back the wrapping and applied it delicately across the Zlatkin doll's forehead and eyes, where it served more as a blindfold than as a bandana. Then he firmly laid the doll face down on the ledge in front of him. Whenever it happened that the real-life Zlatkin shifted along the team bench toward them, Angus snapped the blindfolded bobblehead off the ledge and held it out at arm's length, in the same way a priest might wield a crucifix to ward off evil. "The power of the Pines compels you!" he would scream, or "Back, Igor, back!" or at other times "Get behind me, Zlatkin." It got to the point that

When Cheers Are Not Enough

Angus's histrionics were garnering the attention of patrons seated one and even two rows back. Not surprisingly, however, nary a soul on the visitor's bench, be it player, coach, or support staff, took any notice whatsoever. Still, Angus persisted in trying to be a nuisance behind the Founders' bench.

All the goodwill and positivity within the fan base courtesy of the Pines' 1-0 lead vanished early in the second period when Toronto allowed three consecutive Washington goals in a span of five minutes. And it was at this point that, with the Founders up 3-1, the game shifted into another dimension, perhaps the Twilight Zone. The weird stuff happened when, with Washington controlling the play in Toronto's end, a cross-ice pass was deflected at the blue line and the puck slid all the way into the Founders' zone. While Kratz came far out of his net to play the loose puck, Pines' 6'2" 215 lb winger Eddie "Moose" Mortenson came barrelling down in hot pursuit. The two collided at the top of the right faceoff circle, sending bodies and equipment flying, with Kratz resembling Charlie Brown getting hit by a line drive on the pitcher's mound.

Naturally, the Founders took exception to Mortenson flattening their goaltender, and players from both sides scrummed along the boards while Kratz lay prone on the ice. After a few minutes, he was able to get to his skates. Doubled over in obvious discomfort, Kratz made his way to the locker room, escorted by medical staff. The game clock had stopped with 6:36 remaining in the second period.

Washington was now out of goaltenders so it fell to Toronto as the home team to provide the Founders with an emergency backup netminder. Enter Myles Pullman. A native of Huntsville, Ontario, the forty-year-old Pullman had been with the Pines' organization for the past five years, working in the office of the Assistant General Manager, crunching numbers in the interest of salary cap analysis. A career junior level goalie and having never played a game in the PHL, Pullman would sometimes serve as a spare goaltender for the team at practices.

After a delay of about fifteen minutes, Pullman came out of the visitor's dressing room in a Founders sweater, wearing number 80 (credit to the equipment manager to get his name stitched on the back of the jersey). His mask bore the logo of his Junior B team and he was wearing green Mighty Pines-issue pants (he managed to secure a pair of red Founders pants for the third period). Washington head coach Mike Reynolds could not hide his disbelief at the sudden turn of events, and was caught on camera smiling ruefully and shaking his head as he watched his new third string goalie glide gingerly across the ice to take his position in net.

THE HORROR

Once it was evident that the game would be delayed for a few minutes for the goalie change, Angus disappeared up the steps to the concourse. Ten minutes later he was back with what seemed to Baker like a family size platter of steak fries.

"They haven't started yet? At least I didn't miss anything."

"That's a lot of French fries," Baker remarked. "I didn't know they offered serving sizes so big."

"Well, they're for both of us. Can you hold this?" Angus said, more as a command than a question, passing the carton of food to Baker and adding, "Go nuts, by the way. Help yourself."

Baker watched as Angus used his free hands to empty his pockets of salt packets—*lots* of salt packets. Rather than ask about it, Baker just dug into the fries and was pleasantly surprised by how hot and delicious they were.

"Who's the guy in net?" Angus asked, helping himself to some fries.

"His name's Myles Pullman."

"Who the fuck is Myles Pullman?" He said, sounding characteristically unamused while looking across the rink toward the player in the Washington goal who at present was fielding practice shots from his new teammates.

Baker glanced sideways at his friend. "Is that your attempt at Colonel Nathan Jessup?"

"Pretty good, huh?"

"Not bad, I guess," Baker replied, helping himself to more fries. Angus did likewise, resulting in a moment of silence as both men chewed and stared vacantly out at the ice. Angus washed his fries down with a sip of beer then turned to Baker. "Seriously though, who the fuck is Myles Pullman?"

"Oh . . . he's the Pines' EBUG."

"What's an e-bug?"

"It stands for 'emergency backup goaltender.' Every home team has one, just in case the visiting team runs out of goalies. This guy basically came out of the stands to fill in as the Founders' goalie."

"Hmm, he doesn't look too steady on his skates . . . This should be good."

When Cheers Are Not Enough

As a result of his over-zealous pursuit of the puck, Toronto's Eddie Mortenson was assessed a charging penalty for his troubles, and when the game finally resumed, Washington was able to take advantage of the power play to go up 4-1. The score didn't tell the whole story, however, because despite trailing by three goals, it may have occurred to the Pines that they were actually in the driver's seat now. In fact, the next two shots that Pullman faced hit the twine behind him, and just like that Toronto had come to within a goal.

The crowd noise in the arena had risen considerably and the chant of "Go, Pines, go" seemed to resonate from deep within the bowels of the building, rising up to the highest rafters. Toronto nearly tied the game on a close play in the waning moments of the second period but the Founders were saved by the horn. The building was now abuzz with anticipation for the barrage of goals to come. The Pines just needed to carry the momentum through the intermission into the final frame and the win was assured. After all, overcoming a one-goal deficit against a forty-year-old practice goalie should be child's play for the team's snipers. Some even dared to suggest that the game might well result in a blowout.

Hoping to beat the rush to the concourse between periods, Baker was halfway up the steps of the aisle by the time the horn to end the period finished sounding. It was actually a relief to distance himself from Angus for a spell; the guy had been whistling and hollering tirelessly for the last half of the period. (In fact, Baker was pretty sure the Washington players on the visitor's bench seemed to feel his presence behind them, and more than that, he would be willing to swear that the source, the very epicentre, of the "Go, Pines, go" chant that had shaken the building late in the second period was none other than Angus Fletcher himself.)

When he came out of the men's room, Baker took a leisurely stroll along the busy concourse to the other side of the arena and back again, returning to his seat just as the teams were returning to their benches. He was surprised to find Angus seated and subdued but assumed he was saving himself for the third period. Baker skooched past his friend and as he did he caught a whiff of something delicious. It hit all the right olfactory notes and he pictured a scrumptious homemade meal in an Italian household.

"Holy, Angus, did you get more food while I was gone?"

"Who, me? Nah."

"Why does it smell like pizza—or garlic bread?"

THE HORROR

Angus gave an evasive shrug, as if he had better things to attend to. Instead of pursuing it, Baker helped himself to some more fries, and it was then that he noticed a pile of salt—not unlike a snowdrift—on the ledge in front of Angus. Lying face down in it was the Zlatkin bobblehead.

"Whoa, what happened? What's with the salt?"

"Don't worry about the salty mess," Angus assured him. "I'll make sure everything's cleaned up before we leave. I'm a no-trace camper. You just drink up, your beer's getting warm."

"Oh, Angus, I really shouldn't. You know me; two's my limit. I'm a cheap date."

"Well then, give it here. We can't let it go to waste."

"Are you sure?" Not that he was counting beers, but Baker was pretty certain it would be Angus's fourth.

"Don't worry about me," Angus assured him. "I'm fine."

Perhaps it was a function of the bizarre circumstances that took the Pines out of their usual mindset. Maybe waiting in the dressing room between periods, knowing that they would soon be teeing off on a replacement goalie barely able to stand on his skates—a rarity in the PHL—had a deleterious effect. Maybe it was the pressure to score four, five, or even six more goals. Whatever the reason, something definitely short circuited the motor functions of the boys in green and white. How else could one explain what transpired in the third period?

It proved to be nothing if not a chamber of horrors for the Mighty Pines, who looked ungainly and out of rhythm. While the Founders scored two goals before the period was four minutes old, Toronto could only generate a handful of shots on Myles Pullman. It was clear that the Washington skaters were not about to let their emergency goaltender face much from their opponents. To a man, the Founders stood up to every attempt on goal that Toronto could muster, protecting Pullman over the final twenty minutes.

Understandably, the final frame was a tough watch for Pines fans; the very definition of frustrating. When it became apparent that Washington was not likely to surrender its lead, and any hope of a Toronto comeback was small, the fans found other things to cheer for—namely the Founder's emergency replacement goaltender. It seemed that everyone in attendance at Nova Tank Arena had taken to rooting for the local guy who was living out a dream before their eyes. Every time Pullman touched the puck or made a save, he was roundly cheered. At one point, with the Pines trailing 6-3, Duggan called a timeout to forcefully address his charges at the bench, but it was plain that several of the players were only half-heartedly attending to their coach's exhortations, displaying defeatist body language and very little eye contact.

The sound of the final horn to end the game was accompanied by a mixture of boos and Bronx cheers directed at the hometown side. To some ears the final horn translated as a peal of mercy, signalling the curtain-drop on a shameful game, while for others it was no different than the loser horn commonly heard on popular TV game shows. Then there were those for whom this 6-3 loss signalled the death knell on the season—or worse still, this era—of Mighty Pines hockey.

On the ice, Pullman was mobbed by his Washington "teammates," while over at the Pines' bench Boris Duggan stormed off, making a beeline for the dressing room—perhaps trying to distance himself from a game that would go down in Mighty Pines lore as "The Myles Pullman Game," or the Pullman fiasco, or mess, or horror—or any other noun one chose to insert. Duggan certainly recognized that his group would have to wear the stench of this embarrassment for some time; indeed, they might never completely live down the ignominy of being involved in a game that saw the storied franchise lose to its very own forty-year-old assistant financial analyst.

Much of the crowd had dispersed, as if the crime scene had been sanitized and there was nothing more to see. Baker and Angus were still seated, however, staring out at the ice surface, seemingly mesmerized by the leisurely yet purposeful movements of the Zamboni.

Although completely spent, Angus understood that despite the party having gone sideways, the time had come to clean up. Slowly, almost lovingly, he swept up the salt from the ledge in front of him, using the empty French fries carton to catch every granule. Then he took the Zlatkin doll and tenderly peeled the bandage from its face, carefully returning it to the security of his jacket pocket. With great ceremony, he "lowered" his flag and proceeded to impeccably fold it, the way a Boy Scout might. He took one final look at the "campsite" to satisfy himself that he'd left it better than when he arrived. Then, almost as a final act of repentance, he reached into another pocket, pulled out his car keys, and held them out to Baker. "Would you mind? I probably shouldn't drive."

Baker shot him a sour look. "Ya think?"

* * * * *

THE HORROR

Naturally, Baker's mood was foul by the time he and Angus were on the road and headed for home. It wasn't until they were finally on the highway that Baker, no longer able to contain himself, gave voice to the question that had been hanging in the air between them since the game ended. "So, what the fuck was it all night long with the flag and the bobblehead and the salt and shit?" he demanded, venomously.

Realizing the time had come to answer for his actions, Angus preceded his reply with a long sigh. "I was trying to help the *Flounders* live up to their name."

"What the hell does that mean?"

"I guess it means that the success of your pilgrimage the other day inspired me to the point where I felt I needed to do my part for the Pines."

"But how does celebrating your roots with the Irish flag accomplish anything?"

"The flag had nothing to do with me being a proud Irishman. I brought it because the colours green, white and orange are complementary to red, white and blue. They are *anti*-Washington colours. Get it? I'd think as an art teacher, you of all people would understand."

"Humph. You don't need to be an art teacher to know that the complementary colours of red, white and blue are green, *black* and orange."

"I know, I know—but I figured two out of three ain't bad."

Baker rolled his eyes. "Anything you say, Meatloaf. Now, explain the bobblehead."

"It was supposed to be like a talisman that represented the entire team. I used it like a voodoo doll, blindfolding it and plopping it face down, to reverse the juju, you know—I didn't think sticking pins in it would be appropriate."

"Oh, how big of you," a sardonic Baker replied. "I'm afraid to ask, but . . . why the salt?"

"Salt has long been believed to ward off evil; going back centuries. Same for the garlic spray."

Baker could hardly believe his ears. "Garlic spray? Is that what the smell was? Garlic spray? Really?"

"It's just something I had lying around the house. I bought it last year as a prop for Hallowe'en."

"Well, for your information, I'm pretty sure garlic works only on vampires and not evil in general." He paused for a beat, then continued as if speaking to himself. "Unbelievable. If it wasn't so stupid it would almost be—" Baker didn't finish the sentence because he was slapped in the face with a frightening thought. Angus had engaged in negative spell casting, and the Coven had clearly pledged to refrain from that sort of thing. It was entirely possible, therefore, that any benefit having accrued from his pilgrimage on Thursday had been undone by Angus's black magic machinations. It sounded crazy, and yet . . . you screw around with this stuff, you get reckless, and the good gets erased faster than you can say "Myles Pullman." It might explain the shit show that was tonight's game.

His expression turned ominous, then he slowly shook his head and, like a parent expressing not anger but deep disappointment in their progeny's disastrous life choices, gravely said, "Good God, Angus . . . what have you done?"

The rest of the trip passed in silence.

Feeling existential, Baker took a personal inventory as he drove. Physically, he was a mess; stomach bloated, ears ringing, and temples throbbing—what he wouldn't give for a Tylenol. As for his emotional state, well, all the figurative language that came to mind about surviving tough times—stiff upper lip, chin up, darkest before the dawn, nowhere to go but up—offered no consolation. Even random thoughts of Perreault, normally a balm for his soul, failed to produce the usual uptick. Perhaps the only blessing was that tomorrow wasn't a workday, otherwise he'd have to call in sick.

Typically, in moments like these, when a brutal loss dropped Baker into a pit of despair, he would turn to a line from Joseph Conrad's *Heart of Darkness*: "The mind of man is capable of anything because everything is in it, all the past as well as all the future." Under normal circumstances, when he found the mental wherewithal to recall it, the quote was a source of inspiration that gave him strength. At present, however, Baker was so disheartened that he referenced the line more as a source for sarcasm than encouragement, because from a fan's perspective it would require nothing less than tapping into the vast potential and power of the human mind to envision this Pines team as capable of winning a single playoff series, let alone advancing to a Cup final. In fact, Baker thought of another line from Conrad's novel that was more fitting for what he'd just witnessed, and it consisted of only four words. He pictured the shaved head of Marlon Brando as Colonel Kurtz, dying in the shadows in the culminating scene of *Apocalypse Now*, staring up at nothing and whispering with his final breath, "The horror . . . the horror."

CHAPTER FORTY

PRAY THAT THEY HEAR

His spirit would do wonders, we'd love to have him near
So we sing him this song, and pray that he hears

It had been nearly twenty-four hours since Toronto's embarrassing loss, and Baker was still trying to make sense of what had transpired. If the Pittsburgh game on Thursday had been one of the most complete team efforts of the year for the Pines, what could explain the debacle two days later? And while the answer to that question continued to be frustratingly elusive, what really stung Baker was the apparent ineffectiveness of his pilgrimage. Something had gone amiss. So, what now?

He leaned on his kitchen counter, staring down at the patterns in the floor tiles as fatigue settled in upon him. The following day was Monday, and he knew that if he felt this way now, he was in for a long week. The clock on the microwave read 8:58. Though it was still early, his best option might be to just turn in and sleep on it. And yet one thought festered in his mind. Was he being tested? It was a question that invaded his headspace anytime life threw a nasty curve at him. In this instance, Baker wondered if it was an opportunity to prove himself—or more to the point, to prove his loyalty to the spirits of Pines gone by. If he remained firm in his resolve to stand by the Icemen, he could continue to attempt to communicate with them. Maybe this time, however, it might best serve his purposes if the message was conveyed in a conventional manner—no prayers or pilgrimages, just a song with individual verses dedicated to each member of the Six-pack. It wouldn't hurt to massage their egos as well. (As spirits, surely they still had egos, didn't they?) Therefore, getting the Coven back into the "studio" was his best course of action, and for that he needed a song.

This called for a pot of tea. Baker took the empty kettle from the stovetop and brought it to the sink, all the while searching his cranial bank for song ideas that might fit the bill. He needed a song that had verses dedicated to a group of individuals—six, to be exact.

When Cheers Are Not Enough

It was when he held the kettle under the running tap that the idea struck him. *Holy shit! Of course!* Mike Scott and the Waterboys had a tune called "And a Bang on the Ear." It was perfect. The original version contained six verses, each one dedicated to a different woman—romances from Scott's past. It perfectly matched the number of spirits in Baker's group.

The microwave clock flashed 9:06. Was it an omen? The notion of going to bed vanished along with his sense of weariness. He did the math: six verses at roughly thirty minutes a verse. If he started now he'd be done by midnight and still get six hours sleep. No problem.

In need of a writing utensil, he went to his kitchen wall calendar, which was set in a wooden frame with a small ledge upon which he kept a ballpoint pen. In reaching for it, Baker's eye caught the box on the calendar page devoted to that day's date, and tucked in a corner above the bold number "23" was a tiny circle coloured black—the new moon. Baker had never really made note of the little moon symbols on his calendar before, even after Dorcas had suggested he make it a habit to observe the phases of the lunar cycle. But now it seemed to be perfectly timed, even fortuitous—especially considering the abomination he had witnessed yesterday. The moment was right to light a candle and make a wish.

He had his pick of candles to be sure, and choosing a hefty white pillar candle sitting on a milk crate in the far corner of the "music" room, he brought it to the kitchen counter, lit it, and, bowing his head, made a private, heartfelt wish. He observed a few seconds of silence, then left the candle to burn while he got to work.

The song's title came to him instantly. He neatly printed the words "Pray That They Hear" at the top of a note pad. That was the easy part.

Unfortunately, it was typical of Baker to drastically underestimate the hours that the rest of the task would require. By the time he'd finished his new version of the song, there were faint streaks of light on the eastern horizon. He had worked through the night. With the opportunity for sleep having come and gone, Baker could only hustle to wash up and get ready for the school day.

An hour later he was striding through the halls at HMV on his way to the place he felt certain he'd find the others. Entering the staff room, his hunch was proven correct when he saw all four of them seated together at a table. He could barely contain himself as he approached.

"Good news! I'm planning a coven session for Tuesday after school."

Perreault, Angus, Masaccio, and Conrad looked up at him blankly, needing a moment to take in what they'd just heard.

"To be clear," Conrad replied, "by 'Tuesday,' you mean tomorrow." He had long since stopped being surprised by Baker's short-notice demands.

"Um, yes. I wrote a new song for us this morning."

"What do you mean 'this morning'?" Angus said. "Did you wake up at, like, three?"

"Well, you can't really wake up if you never went to sleep."

"You did an all-nighter?"

"What can I say? I was inspired." Baker took a folder out of his work bag. "I've got copies for everybody."

"Holy shit, Baker." Angus looked at his friend as though he were appraising his value in order to make a bid on him at auction. "You'd be a dangerous man if you didn't have to sleep."

"Don't I know it. Although I expect to crash pretty hard later today." He distributed copies to everyone like a dealer at a card table, then chose to address the elephant in the room. "Were you guys rehashing Saturday's wreck of a Pines game?"

"Nope, not a chance," Perreault replied. "Mas forbade us from mentioning it."

"I promised myself I wouldn't talk about it," Masaccio explained. "It's too painful, and it's too soon. I need some time. There's nothing to be said, anyway. As one game, it's a throwaway. We can revisit it at some later date—like maybe after the Pines win the Cup. Then the embarrassment will be something we can all laugh about."

As Mas spoke, Conrad was examining his copy of Baker's handiwork with a confused expression. "What's this?" he asked. "This looks like some poetry or something. Where's the song?"

"What?" Baker looked at the page in Conrad's hand and realized his mistake. "Oh, wrong thing. Just ignore that." He went to his folder again and produced another sheet of paper. "*This* is the song."

Conrad took Baker's lyrics and quickly assessed them. "So, you're having another go at your Six-pack of Icemen? Except this time we're all gathering at your place?"

"Yeah. I didn't think it would be practical to ask you four to join me on a pilgrimage. Mind you, it would have been less hassle for me. I wouldn't have had to come up with a new song."

"OK, but what's this?" Conrad asked, holding up the page of poetry.

"Oh... well, I thought I'd add some spoken-word stuff to the ceremony."

Mouth agape, Conrad leaned forward in his chair and held the sheet of poetry toward Baker. "You wrote *this* last night? *And* the song?" He looked around at the others. "That settles it. I'm in for tomorrow's session. I mean, how can we deny the man his wish, especially after how much work he put into this?"

"I'm in," Angus said.

"Me too," Perreault added.

All four turned and looked toward the one member who hadn't responded. "Jesus, you guys," Masaccio said. "You can put away the needles and thread."

"Needles and thread?" Baker asked.

"This 'guilting bee' of yours. You all look like you're in the process of sewing a 'guilt quilt.' Well, there's no need. I'm in too."

"A guilt quilt?" Perreault inquired.

"Yeah. It's something Sal says whenever someone tries to play the guilt card."

"Don't sweat it, Mas," Baker assured him. "There'll be no bedding at this session, just the usual candles. And don't forget to bring your bass."

"That much you can count on me for," Mas assured him.

"Good. But the bass is for me. You'll be tickling the ivories."

"You've got me playing keys? And I have one day to prepare?"

"It should be pretty straight forward," Baker said. "All you need to do is echo the melody of the vocal line and then fill in other parts with some basic chords."

"You make it sound so easy. How could I possibly decline?"

"On the bright side, we should be done with these sessions by mid-June—if all goes as planned."

* * * * *

A day later the members of Bakers' Coven had assembled at the home of its eponymous leader. Perreault, Angus, Conrad, and Masaccio announced their arrival at Baker's front door with a clatter of foot stomps, each of them attempting to shed the snow they had picked up on the short walk from the driveway. They were loaded down with two guitar cases, two party platters of vegetables and fruit, and one large box of Sugar Watson's doughnuts. Perreault knocked three times and politely waited for an answer, only to have Conrad scoff at her unwillingness to enter the house uninvited.

"I never feel right about just letting myself into someone's home," Perreault explained.

"Oh, yeah?" Conrad retorted. "Well, I never feel right about standing in the cold with my hands full, waiting for Baker to answer the door. Besides, you know he's probably busy in there, so we'd be doing him a favour by taking the initiative." With that he stepped around her, opened the door, and led them in, at which point Baker's voice called down from the kitchen, "Let yourselves in. I'm just getting organized."

Conrad flashed a smug smile at Perreault. "See? I told you so."

The four of them then proceeded to dance around the tight space of the front hall, arranging wet boots and shoes and removing winter coats and scarves and hanging them on the few available hooks of Baker's coat tree. From there they herded into the kitchen, where Baker was busy with some last-minute preparations. They entered the room like a whirlwind, delivering their combination of foodstuffs, musical instruments, and random questions and comments.

"You sure do have a lot of snow up here," Masaccio observed.

"And apparently no time to shovel it," Conrad added.

"Sorry, but that's, like, the twenty-third item on my to-do list, and presently I'm at number four."

Perreault looked across into Baker's front-room-cum-music-studio/sacred-space. "Hey, you brought the candles back!"

"To be honest, I never put them away," he confessed.

"It's just as well," Perreault said. "We can light them for today's session."

Baker hastily cleared space on the counter for the food items, careful not to disrupt his miniature Clarence Cup shrine. "Thanks for bringing this stuff, you guys. And doughnuts too!"

"They were my idea," Conrad said proudly. "Care to know why I brought them?"

"You mean it wasn't just about fattening us up?" Perreault asked.

"Of course, there's always that," he agreed. "But today, my reasons go deeper, and I have two of them. The first is based on utility, the second on sentiment."

"By all means then," Baker said, "enlighten us."

"I thought the doughnuts might prove useful today in that they could improve our chances of success. For example, we're going to be calling on these hockey legends, and Sugar Watson happens to be among them, right?"

"Absolutely. Eighteen years of loyal service and four Cups."

"Let's offer up a carrot to entice him, then. And it comes packaged as a box of his own brand of doughnuts."

"Ah ... good thinking. Now I can't wait to hear your second reason."

"Yes, the sentimental reason. Today is Shrove Tuesday, better known in the secular world as Pancake Tuesday. Well, eating doughnuts is a way to honour the memory of my dear mother and her wonderful tradition of annually deep frying a big batch of doughnuts for the family."

"Your mother made doughnuts on Pancake Tuesday?"

"*Re*ligiously."

"Sounds delicious—greasy too."

"Right on both counts."

Baker announced that he would put on some coffee, but Perreault waved him away. "I'll take care of it. You guys can commence with lighting the room."

"Oh, shit!" Baker exclaimed, realizing there was still work to do. "Here you go, guys. Grab a clicker and hit the candles."

As Conrad came forward for his lighter, he noticed Angus eyeballing the open box of doughnuts.

"Don't be shy. Help yourself. I made sure to include a couple of chocolate dipped just for you."

"Um . . . no thanks."

"Shut up!" Conrad said with incomprehension.

"No, really. I'm good."

"Something to drink then?" Baker offered. "Let me get you a beer." He swung the fridge door open and reached for a bottle, but Angus gently pushed the door shut.

"Not right now." Then he laid a hand on Baker's shoulder and guided him out of the room toward the front hall. "I wanted to ask you about your coat tree," he said in a loud voice. "My mum and dad were looking for something just like that."

Actually quite proud of his coat tree, Baker began to explain how he had found it in an obscure antique shop on the way to Collingwood, but then he stopped short when it was clear that Angus was really seeking some place to have a quiet word.

"What's up?" Baker whispered.

"I'm ashamed to admit it, but I'm a little anxious about our session here today."

"What do you mean? You were so pumped about it yesterday."

"I know, I know, but I didn't fully comprehend that we'd be inviting spirits into your home."

Baker put on a happy face in an effort to assuage his unsettled friend. "They're not just any spirits. They're spirits of the greatest Clarence Cup-winning Pines."

"Whatever, man. Spirits are spirits. In the end, they're the ghosts of dead guys."

Baker turned serious. "True enough. I can't argue with you there." Then he brightened again. "But they're not evil. We are calling on them to help us—and help the Pines."

"Still, I'm not sure if I can do this."

"Wait—you *did* go over the song, didn't you? I mean, you *are* ready to play?"

"Oh, I can play the song. I just don't know if I can play it while my skin's crawling. I mean, what if they took offense to my efforts to curse Washington on Saturday? Maybe they're still pissed about it."

"Gee, Angus, I'm no expert, but I really don't think the spirits of old Pines legends care all that much." Of course, Baker had no clue about what the Icemen thought, or if they thought anything at all, but he was searching for words that might mollify his friend. In the end he appealed to his sense of being a team player. "Look, all I can ask is that you give it the ol' college try. We need you and we're all here with you."

Angus just stared and said nothing, seeming to consider his predicament. Then he nodded, gave Baker the feeblest of smiles, and slowly made his way back to the others. Following him, Baker watched as Angus walked through the kitchen past the food trays and doughnuts and manoeuvred his way around Conrad and Mas, who were busily lighting candles, to his seat at the drums, apparently resigned to his fate.

With the coffee machine happily gurgling fresh, hot java into the pot, Perreault attended to Baker, looking at him like a concerned mother. "So, did you manage to get some sleep last night?"

"I did. I was unconscious for about ten hours."

"Good for you," she replied, tousling his hair playfully. "There's nothing like a good night's sleep to keep you healthy and productive."

"On the contrary," Masaccio chirped, having just finished lighting his share of the candles. "After seeing how prolific he is when he works through the night, it's a good thing for us that he slept. Otherwise, he might have written a three-act opera."

"Indeed," Conrad added, "We might have seen all these candles replaced with an eighty-piece orchestra."

For Baker, being the brunt of the mockery was great fun, but he also knew they were pressed for time. "Alright, cut the bullshit. How about we run through the song?"

"Baker's right," Mas agreed. "Let's rock 'n' roll. I told Sal I'd be home by five."

The Coven's warm-up routine, which included Conrad's prayer, Perreault's verselet, and the song to St. Cecilia, happened so fast that Baker felt woefully unprepared for what was supposed to come next. It had nothing to do with his knowledge of the song or his ability to handle the bass line. It had more to do with the fact that, for the first time during their coven sessions, he had misgivings about the prudence of their actions.

Perhaps it was the words that were about to be sung.

Perhaps it was the warning bell Angus had privately sounded a few minutes ago.

Perhaps it was a general fear of failure.

Perhaps it was fear of the unknown and the fact they were now truly dealing with forces beyond their control.

Today they would be dealing with actual entities. In which case what was the chance that things could backfire? But then Dorcas surely would have warned him off if the risks so outweighed the rewards? Shit. Why was he thinking about this stuff now? Why hadn't he considered these things before? His heart took a sudden leap within his chest. Was this a point of no return, or was he just being overly dramatic?

There was little time to dwell on it, though, because Conrad was ploughing into the song with the opening guitar chords, followed by Perreault's vocals.

> *Beezer was the best Pine to ever wear the "C"*
> *The last one to be voted the league's MVP*
> *As an all-round leader he was a man without peer*
> *So we sing him this song, and pray that he hears*
>
> *Cal Ubank was the captain, but the "C" it stood for "class"*
> *For his honesty and effort you never had to ask*

He won a seat in office and was Father of the Year
So we sing him this song, and pray that he hears

Kilpatrick was a winner, on that you can rely
Four Cups with Chicago, then four more with the Pines
He played several positions in a twenty-year career
So we sing him this song, and pray that he hears

Frank Watson roamed the blue line, a fearsome Pine was he
More than just the doughnuts; played four decades in the league
Won four Cups with Toronto, to him the team was dear
So we sing him this song, and pray that he hears

Next up is Jackson Schmeltz, the most beloved Pine alive
Called the ageless wonder, he quit at forty-five
His spirit would be welcome, we'd love to have him near
So we sing him this song, and pray that he hears

And lastly there's the hero of "Back Panel Vignette"
Jersey Joe Zedelko, with him this song we'll wrap
He helped the Pines to four Cups in a five-year career
So we sing him this song, and pray that he hears

As Perreault was completing the sixth and final verse, Baker was visited with a moment of panic when he realized they had never actually rehearsed an ending to the song. Considering that their performance to that point had been quite praiseworthy, the last thing he wanted was for it to end on a sloppy note. His fears were immediately allayed when Perreault, apparently sensing the same thing, stepped up to guide them home. Employing a combination of expressive hand signals and direct eye contact, she conducted them through some repeats of "Pray that they hear" before navigating her crew into the safe harbour of a smoothly executed cold finish.

"Nicely done, everyone, very nice."

"Don't take this the wrong way, Baker," Conrad said, unable to resist, "but I'm pretty sure that Jackson Schmeltz retired at age forty-six."

"I know. But I needed it to rhyme, and besides, I was pretty tired when I wrote it."

"All is forgiven. I'm sure if the spirit of Jacko Schmeltz is here right now, he's not holding it against you."

"Yeah, well, that's the part I can't be sure of—whether the spirits heard our call, and if so, did they respond?" Baker set the bass down and stood up with his sheet of poetry. "Shall we move on to the next order of business?" He looked around at the others in formal fashion, giving them a chance to adopt the requisite tone of respect.

PRAY THAT THEY HEAR

To Pines legends one and all, heed our beck and hear our call
Hear us now, oh legends of an age, when Depression struck and War was waged
You men whose wondrous deeds brought glory to our fair city
You captains of dynasties from the thirties to the sixties
Each one a true champion in days that were halcyon
You fought for and won the ultimate prize
Upon which your names are now incised
And evermore became heroes in our eyes

Baker stopped reading and looked around at the others like a preacher from his pulpit. "As I call out the spirit of each player, please respond with the words 'Hear us now.'"

Spirit of Cal Ubank...Hear us now
Spirit of Beasley Sharpe...Hear us now
Spirit of Joe Zedelko...Hear us now
Spirit of Jackson Schmeltz...Hear us now
Spirit of Frank Watson... Hear us now
Spirit of Whitey Kilpatrick...Hear us now

We make this request to act at our behest

Our young Pines need strength so put wind in their sails
And help them to pay close attention to detail

Instill within them, oh you leaders of men
The way to embrace a true winner's traits

Serve as their inner voice, they need only make a choice
To seek not personal laurels, or gold-filled amphoras

So be gentle, be kind, but firmly remind
That winning it all, takes guts and resolve

Claiming the Cup is a long row to hoe
It takes four full rounds to defeat every foe

Competing at this level, on a razor's edge they stand
The finest of lines separate champions from also rans

Whisper in their ears, and allay their fears
For this may well be their best opportunity

We gather and pray, and ask that they may
Find another gear, to get it done this year

So with this request our rite may now close
Upon this team a Cup do bestow
And thereby end our Nation's woes
Amen to that ... and go, Pines, go!

As Baker ended his prayer with the iconic cheer, he was greeted by spontaneous whoops and applause.

"Thank you," he said. "Thank you. I guess that brings an end to our session."

"That was great," Masaccio said. "I loved everything about it, but I think you could end it better if you changed that last part to 'the Hubs suck and the Nats blow, Amen to that ... and go, Pines, go!'"

Baker had to laugh. "Your version has more sandpaper behind it. That's for sure."

"Whichever version, my vote is for using those last four lines as a regular finish to our Coven ceremonies," Conrad said. "All five of us can join in on the last line."

"I like that idea," Perreault said, "and it'll make us sound more like fans in the stands than churchgoers in pews."

It was then that Angus, who had been unusually quiet and reflective, stood up and placed his hands firmly on his hips. The others stopped to watch as he took a deep breath and exhaled, then did it again.

"What's up, Angus?" Baker asked. He had been wondering when and how his friend's anxiety might manifest itself. "You look a little pale."

"I don't know. I suddenly feel funny."

"Well, we're done with the ceremony. Why don't you get yourself something to eat? Can I get you a beer?"

Angus didn't answer, but he shifted his gaze from one end of the room to another and across the ceiling. Then he jerked his head in another direction, over his shoulder, and up again to the ceiling.

"This is freaky, man," he said, sounding overwhelmed.

"What is it?" Perreault asked.

"I don't know how to describe it—um—you know how some people have the ability to identify musical notes when they hear them, just out of the blue?"

"Yes," she replied. "It's called perfect pitch."

"Perfect pitch—well, don't laugh, but I might have perfect pitch for sensing the presence of spirits."

"That's called clairvoyance," Conrad said, "or clair-sentience, or something."

"It feels like there's a dozen people in the room." Angus looked around at the others. "Can't you feel them?"

"No," Baker said, trying to keep things light, "but it sounds like our ceremony was a success."

"I guess so, but man, do I ever feel claustrophobic."

"Can you see them? Can you hear them?" Masaccio asked. "Have they said anything?"

"No. I can sense people moving around, though, and it's definitely warmer."

"Well, I feel the warmth too," Masaccio confided, "but I blame that on the candles."

Angus wasn't listening, seemingly lost in his own world. "Do you guys need me for anything right now? Because I'd like to step outside." He paused to scan the room, as if to confirm something. "Yeah, I'll be on the deck."

"Sure, but maybe you want to take a plate with you? Something to munch—"

Angus was out the door before Baker could finish the sentence.

It was ten minutes later, after Conrad and Masaccio had taken their leave, that Perreault wondered aloud to Baker if Angus had been on the deck long enough. The candles had been extinguished and the supposed spirits that had made him feel so squirrelly had likely moved on. And besides, it was cold outside. The two of them stood at the window, watching Angus bounce on his toes and pump out some modified push-ups on the handrail.

"Look at him," Perreault said. "Is he working out?"

"It looks like he's trying to stay warm, if you ask me."

"At least he's making good use of his time." Perreault observed him for a spell from the warm side of the door, then sighed, "Ah, hell, let's rescue him." She turned the knob and opened the door.

Baker stepped out with her and addressed Angus. "Hey, Rocky, I think it's safe for you to come back inside now."

"OK, just let me finish here," Angus said without breaking rhythm. "Forty-seven, forty-eight, forty-nine . . . fifty!" Having completed the set, Angus straightened up and shook out his arms in a satisfied manner. "Yeah, that's better—lots better." Then he looked at Baker and Perreault as if feeling the cold for the first time. "It's frickin' freezing out here. Let's go inside."

Baker swung the door open and stood aside. "So, leaving a crowded room of spirits and coming out on the deck really put you at ease, huh?"

"Damn straight. I felt better the moment I set foot out here." Angus stepped back into the house with confidence, as if the conditions that had caused his earlier anxieties had never existed. "I guess Conrad and Mas left?"

Baker confirmed their departure, then went straight to the counter where the plates were stacked and handed one to Angus. "It's time to pull your weight around here. Someone's got to eat this food."

Angus obliged with gusto. He loaded the plate with a selection of everything that was available from both party platters. Then he fell upon the Sugar's box of doughnuts, coming away with a chocolate dipped and an apple fritter.

"Here, let me get you another plate for those," Perreault offered.

"What? Nah, don't bother," he replied, unceremoniously plopping them on top, effectively crowning his multi-coloured assemblage of vegetables and fruit with the two doughnuts.

Perreault looked on with distaste, but was glad her friend was in better spirits.

"I'm suddenly feeling hungry again," Angus said, stating the obvious. Then he headed to the fridge. "Mind if I grab a beer?"

"Go nuts," Baker said.

Angus found a bottle, opened it, tapped it on the Grady Sykes stick, took a long, satisfied pull, then settled himself on a stool at the kitchen counter. "That was the weirdest session we've had all year. I'll be happy not to have to do that again too soon."

Perreault looked at Baker with concern. "Don't tell me—he doesn't know?"

Baker winced as Angus jerked up his head. "Huh? Know what?"

"Oh, nothing," Baker replied, trying to sound blasé. "It's just that, well, I'm planning on hosting a séance—a family council— in the near future, and you should be prepared to attend."

"A séance? You mean, like talking to the ghost of someone's dead relative?"

"Exactly! You're familiar with it?"

"No, not really. But then why would I need to attend one?" he asked, taking a man-sized bite of his fritter.

"Because we are going to perform a song—me, you, and Perreault—for the, uh, dead relative."

"Jeez-us!" Angus replied through a jawful of fritter. Then he chewed and swallowed. "When is it happening?"

"I'm hoping to confirm it for next weekend," Baker replied.

"On the Saturday, March seventh," Perreault added, as she stood there beside Baker, both aiming dumb, semi-apologetic smiles at Angus.

Looking incredulous, Angus slowly set his half-eaten fritter back down. "Ay-yay-yay," was the only response he could generate.

CHAPTER FORTY-ONE
PINES WHISPERERS

Around about the time that Perreault finished singing the first verse of "Pray that they Hear," the spirit of Beezer Sharpe arrived in the room. He "stood," invisible and unacknowledged by the members of Bakers' Coven, just to the left of Angus, who was concentrating hard not to lose the rhythm of the song. Beezer listened with interest as Perreault sang the second verse, this time about a man who had held a seat in political office and was once named Father of the Year. Soon there were two spirits in the candlelit room, as Sharpe was joined by Cal Ubank.

As one verse followed another, so too did another Pines legend arrive. There was Jackson Schmeltz, standing face to face with Masaccio, followed by Whitey Kilpatrick next to Baker's wall-mounted bottle opener. (Had he come equipped with a beer, he could have put it to use—although a bottle of ginger ale would be more suited to the teetotaling Kilpatrick.) Finally, Jersey Joe Zedelko appeared, finding himself a seat on one of the stools directly across from Perreault.

Cal Ubank surveyed the room, which was now quite congested. "Is everybody here? Have we got six?"

The other spirits looked around, taking inventory, all except for Joe Zedelko, whose attention remained fixed on the band's vocalist. Ironically, it was Jersey Joe who answered first.

"Frank's not here!"

"Right you are, Joseph," Ubank said. "I wonder what could be delaying—"

"Don't get your knickers in a knot, boys! I'm here," Frank Watson announced, having just arrived.

"Dear, dear Frank, you should know that knickers ain't fashionable anymore," Jackson Schmeltz quipped, "but I guess being late still is."

"Listen, Jacko, if I wanted advice on what's fashionable, I certainly wouldn't come to you."

"My goodness, aren't you in a mood," Schmeltz observed. "If I didn't know any better, I'd say you came out of the dressing room with your skates on the wrong feet."

Beezer Sharpe stepped forward to mediate. "All the same, Franky, it's good to see that you could attend our little gathering. But what delayed you? Was it perhaps another doughnut shop grand opening?"

"Bullseye!" Watson replied.

"And where was this one?"

The question stumped him. "Oh, gosh... Thorncliff... Thornhill... Thornbury...? Ah, hell, I can't remember. It was Thorn-something."

"Quite the ceremony, was it?" Sharpe asked.

"It was nice enough," Watson said as he looked around, taking in the surroundings. "But not as nice as this place. I'm really enjoying this candlelit room."

"Take a gander at Joe over there," Schmeltz interjected, pointing a stubby finger across the room. "It appears he's enjoying the candles too."

Five spirits looked over to where Zedelko had shifted his attention from Perreault to a nearby grouping of pillar candles, apparently testing their heat by waving his hand back and forth through the flames. It was Cal Ubank who moved to focus the group on the task at hand.

"Well gents, it appears we've been called together once more by that Baker fellow."

"And it looks like he's enlisted the help of some friends," Watson noted.

"Pretty ones, too," Zedelko added, having finished with the candles and returned to regarding Perreault.

"What intrigues me," Ubank said, "is *how* we've been summoned by this 'Bakers' Coven.' Their song has a separate verse dedicated to each of us—sung beautifully, I might add, by that young lady there—"

"You mean Perreault?" Zedelko volunteered.

"Yes, Perreault. It seems this group has a mighty high opinion of us in general."

"I'm curious—what did she sing about me?" Watson asked. "I arrived too late to hear it."

Captain Cal was ready with an answer. "Well, Francis, in a word, she said you were 'fearsome'—a 'fearsome Pine.'" Then he looked up and raised his voice for the benefit of the other spirits. "And in case the rest of you missed what she said, I can summarize." He proceeded to go around the room. "Whitey, you were described as 'a winner,' while Jackson was the 'most beloved,' and Joseph, you were nothing less than 'a hero.'"

"You hear that, fellas? She called me a hero," Zedelko repeated with pride.

"That's right, Joseph," Ubank said. "But I'm afraid I missed her description of Beasley."

Beezer Sharpe turned the question back on his friend. "First tell everyone what she said about you, Cal."

Ubank waved him off. "Just something about what the 'C' on my jersey stood for."

"Don't be so modest," Sharpe said, then turned to the others. "She said it stood for 'class.' As for me, well, I was 'without peer.'"

"You know, I kinda like this Bakers' Coven," Zedelko said brightly.

"They sure were generous with their praise," Watson noted. "D'you think maybe they meant to stroke our egos?"

"You might be on to something there, Frank," Schmeltz replied, pointing over to the doughnuts on the counter. "After all, they even brought a box of Sugar Watson's finest." The observation occasioned the popular pastry's eponymous originator to beam with unalloyed pride.

"Even so," Ubank cautioned, "I can't help thinking it only serves to inflate our heads unnecessarily. In fact, it's beginning to feel a little crowded in here. Shall we go outside?"

"Hold on, Cal," Kilpatrick said. "There seems to be more to this request."

The six spirits remained in place and listened as Baker read the words he had composed in the wee hours of the morning the day before. When he finished, they adjourned to the deck outside to deliberate their task.

"Well, that certainly settles the question of why we've been called here," Sharpe said, conclusively. "Our assignment couldn't be plainer: 'Help them' . . . 'inspire them' . . . 'remind them.'"

"It's like they want us to inspire this new crop of Mighty Pines players by serving as 'inner voices,'" Zedelko elaborated. "We should 'whisper' to them and remind them of the things that are important to winning."

The spark of an idea caused Jackson Schmeltz to raise both eyebrows along with a stubby finger. "So, they're requesting that we Pines "Icemen" transform ourselves into—Pines whisperers."

"Pines whisperers," Watson echoed as he considered Jackson's point. "I like the sound of that."

"It makes us exclusive members of a newly minted club, that's for certain," Ubank declared.

"Based on Saturday's debacle of a game, it's a fair bet that no amount of whispering by us would have made any difference," Sharpe suggested.

"By golly, it was a mess," Schmeltz concurred.

"There was a frightening lack of cohesion out there," Sharpe said. "It was like watching five strangers from off the street playing together for the first time."

"It all looked so random at times," Ubank added. "I couldn't tell if they were skaters manoeuvring around the rink or snooker balls ricocheting on a billiard table after the opening break."

Schmeltz shook his head ominously, struck with an unsettling thought: "It's almost as if we cursed them."

"Cursed them?" Sharpe repeated, alarmed. "How could that be?"

"I dunno," Schmeltz shrugged. "Maybe just by meeting like this we tapped into something negative."

Sharpe wasn't buying it. "That's not possible, Jacko. We made the decision *not* to do anything, didn't we?"

"We did," Ubank confirmed, "which is why I think we need to stick to the original plan and just write Saturday's game off as one of those troughs every team goes through over the course of a long season."

Watson did a sharp double take as Cal's comment seemed to snap him out of a trance. "A trough? Ha! That's generous," he countered. "I'd describe Saturday's game more as a pit—a deep, dark, dank, stinky pit."

"Gall dang!" said Schmeltz in alarm.

"Gee willikers!" said Kilpatrick.

"Good gosh!" said Schmeltz and Kilpatrick together.

"Jesus, fellas, you sound like my grandma," Watson grumbled. "It's time to get serious here."

"Now, Francis, blasphemy doesn't serve to help matters," Ubank said in a fatherly tone.

"Sorry, Cal," he replied, duly chastened. "But the more I think about it, the more I'm convinced they just need a good ass kicking."

"Who . . . us?" said Schmeltz and Kilpatrick together again.

"Not you, the team!" Watson clarified firmly.

Watson's evident frustration caused Sharpe to look at him with suspicion. "Now that you mention it, Frank—*you* weren't kicking, er, putting boots to behinds at the game Saturday night, were you?"

"C'mon, Beezer, you don't think I'd be daft enough to get physical with the boys, do you? Nah, not me," Watson assured him. "Besides, I was at another grand opening right about the time all the shit went down at Nova Tank Arena."

Just then the door opened and Angus came out onto the deck, stretching his arms overhead and taking in great lungfuls of air. The spirits observed him in silence as he unknowingly walked directly through their circle and toward the railing. They looked around at one another for a bit before Zedelko shared a thought.

"Getting back to this Whispering Pines idea—"

"It's 'Pines Whisperers,' Joe," Sharpe corrected.

"Okay, okay. But let's say we *did* serve as Pines Whisperers, how would we even know if they heard us? I mean, just speaking for myself, I never heard any spirits whispering to me when I played. How 'bout you fellas?"

"You make a good point, Joe," Ubank said. "But keep in mind, back in the day when we played, there were no spirits of Pines Icemen to do any whispering." Then he turned to the others. "In fact, if you think about it, ol' Joe here would've been the first."

"Who you calling 'ol' Joe'? I'm the youngest one here," Zedelko replied, slightly offended.

"In regular earth time, yes," Ubank explained. "But based on spirit time, you're the oldest of the six of us. I guess that's the paradox of this spirit world. The point is that you, Joe Zedelko, are among the first legends of the Mighty Pines franchise."

It took a moment for the realization to settle upon Zedelko. Then, with a fresh awareness of his place in the pantheon of Pines legends, he said, "Well, ain't that an unexpected feather in my cap," and puffed himself up, standing taller and adopting something of a newfound swagger.

Watson assessed Zedelko and with a sly smile quietly remarked to the others, "Looks like Joe's got a serious dose of 'big dick pride.'"

(It should be noted that Sugar Watson's observation was a reference to the oft-told story—now more of an urban legend among pickup hockey players—about the meek young man who, being uncommonly well-endowed but naïve to his natural gifts, was made aware by his locker-room buddies that he has won the genetic lottery for cock size. Armed with this knowledge, the young man went on his way, walking taller and prouder.)

Kilpatrick swung the conversation back to the issue at hand. "So then, how should we proceed as the founding members of this new club of Pines whisperers?"

"Simple," Sharpe proclaimed, "we just stick to the game plan."

"The plan?" Schmeltz and Kilpatrick replied, again in unison.

"Beasley's right," Ubank said. "Always stick to the plan. If six of us make a commitment to the plan, the final score should end up in our favour."

"To be honest, Cal, I'm not sure what plan we are committing to," Watson said, earnestly.

Ubank's reply was halting. "Hmm ... There appears to be some confusion regarding the plan ... Let me try to explain. The plan is ... well, the plan is what the plan always was. The plan hasn't changed."

"Jeepers Cal, you sound just like Jean Chretien," Kilpatrick chuckled, "back when he was trying to explain his idea of a 'proof.'" It was a reference to the time both he and Ubank held seats in political office.

"Jean Chretien?" Ubank said, feigning mild disgust. "Might I remind you, Mr. Kilpatrick, that I served as a *Conservative* member of provincial Parliament. So while I don't mind being called out for failing to elucidate my ideas, I'd rather not be lumped in with your federal Liberals."

When Cheers Are Not Enough

"Let the record show that the point made by the honourable member for Kingston has been duly noted," Kilpatrick announced, clearly enjoying the partisan repartee.

Zedelko, meanwhile, had lost the thread. "Jesus, fellas, I have no idea what you're talking about anymore. Can someone just explain to me what the plan is?"

"I think it's plain to see, Joe—there is no plan," Watson said, recognizing the truth of the matter.

"On the contrary, the plan couldn't be simpler," Sharpe countered.

"Well, then quit hogging the puck, and pass it around," Watson demanded. "Share it with us!"

"Alright then, here's the plan—" Sharpe allowed for a pregnant pause to precede his answer. "We continue to do *nothing*."

"Nothing?" Zedelko asked.

"Nothing—for the time being," Sharpe confirmed. "We stand down and watch."

"Watch?" Kilpatrick asked.

"Uh-huh," He confirmed again. "Leave well enough alone, as it were."

"Well enough?" Schmeltz asked.

"Cripes, boys, is there an echo out here? Yes! Leave well enough alone."

"Jumpin' catfish, Beezer. You call what we've been watching from this team for over half a century 'well enough'?" Zedelko replied, reasonably.

"Of course not, but—"

As everyone considered the question raised by Jersey Joe, the only movement on the deck came from Angus who, feeling the cold settle in, started bouncing on the spot, like a boxer in his corner waiting for the bell to begin the round. The six legends migrated to the part of the deck where Angus was stationed. He was now leaning on the rail and looking out over the snow-covered yard beyond, then slowly and deliberately began performing modified push-ups against the top of the railing.

It was Ubank who tried to impart a spin of optimism. "Honestly, fellows, there's no need to sound the trumpet of doom just yet. I have complete faith that the kids will figure it out," he said. "You'll see, they will find a way through this rough patch."

Beezer Sharpe, meanwhile, was directing his gaze back through the window as if checking on the activity within. "Well, boys, I guess that settles it, because it appears the folks inside are done—and so is our time here. Let's conclude our business, shall we?" He gestured for everyone to huddle up. "Now then, are the six of us in accord? Are we agreed on a plan that has us taking an arm's length approach where the team is concerned?"

There were assorted murmurs of assent among the other five.

"And what if we are summoned again?" Watson asked.

Ubank had an answer for him. "If and when it happens that Bakers' Coven calls upon us again, we can revisit our 'hands off' approach if necessary. Leastways it will give us another opportunity to come together. Truth be told, I'm quite enjoying these gatherings."

"You can count me in," Watson said. "But I'd prefer to do more than just sit on my hands."

"Atta boy, Frank!" Zedelko cheered. "It's been forty-six years since you patrolled the blue line, and nothing's changed—still trying to make your presence felt."

"You know me. I have always been a loud and proud supporter of the green and white."

"Oh, I have my doubts," Jackson Schmeltz said in mock seriousness. "I was certain you'd switched over to brown and red some years ago."

"What the blazes are you on about, Jacko? Brown and red?" Watson demanded. Then, recognizing Schmeltz's allusion to the colours of his doughnut franchise, he aimed a friendly fist at him. "Always putting your two cents in, eh? How's about I colour you black and blue?"

Schmeltz just laughed off the threat. "Ha! Flesh and bone turn black and blue, Frank, but in case you haven't noticed, we lost ours years ago."

And so, having been given their marching orders and not being of flesh and bone—as Jacko Schmeltz had observed—the six spirits wished each other well, vaporized, and were gone. Angus was left alone on the deck, counting out his push-ups, blissfully unaware that he had stood among some of the greatest Mighty Pines players ever to have laced 'em up. "Thirty-one, thirty-two, thirty-three . . ."

CHAPTER FORTY-TWO
BREAKING THE LENTEN FAST

Tuesday, February 25 (Shrove Tuesday) – Wednesday, February 26 (Ash Wednesday)

Moving on from the humiliation of losing to a team with a forty-year-old financial analyst in net, the Pines escaped the February blahs of Hogtown in true snowbird fashion and travelled to the Sunshine State for two games, starting with a Mardi Gras affair in Tampa. Toronto came away with a 4-3 win, keeping them two points ahead of the Florida Everblades.

With a win in the books and considering it was "Fat Tuesday," the Pines could celebrate by filling up on some post-game pancakes. The next day was Ash Wednesday and the beginning of the Lenten season. The time had come to get lean and mean.

Baker had called Helen after school, asking if she'd mind him stopping by on the way home to discuss an urgent matter regarding Cubby. (He didn't mention the spirit council over the phone, preferring to do that face to face.) It came as no surprise to Baker that Helen was completely amenable to the visit. But it wasn't Helen who worried him; it was Allen. The man had been so cold and distant when Baker last visited over the Christmas holidays.

By sheer force of habit, and in true Baker fashion, he shouldered his school bag as he climbed out of his car—and then, for whatever reason (maybe because he was there on business regarding Cubby), he brought *My Hockey Stick* along with him as well. Ever the consummate host, Helen helped him with his assorted winter outerwear. Baker lightened his load by setting the book down against the wall in a small nook behind a deacon's bench in the entryway and placed his school bag in front of it. Then he followed Helen into the kitchen, which was full of delicious smells.

As an Ash Wednesday observance, he had been planning to refrain from eating solid food (the act fell within one of the three pillars of lent: prayer, fasting, and almsgiving), beginning Tuesday after dinner and extending until Thursday morning. But when Helen invited him to share a modest meal, and not wanting to be the author of an awkward situation, Baker politely accepted the invitation (not to mention his mouth was watering, and he was feeling a touch lightheaded, so it was probably for the best that he joined her for a bowl of the butternut squash soup that she'd made that afternoon).

She explained how Allen would be back shortly, having stepped out to pick up some artisanal bread to have with the soup. "But I honestly don't know how long he'll be. He always finds a reason to stop at the hardware store when he's running errands."

Baker sat across from her at the kitchen table, and as the conversation progressed he found that he was quite comfortable asking details about the family and Cubby's relationship with Mary. Helen's motherly, Type B personality made it easy for him to broach what might otherwise be considered a sensitive topic. She spoke quite candidly, beginning with her feelings about having Mary reside with them.

"With my daughter Eleanor gone to university, Allen and I are empty-nesters, so we were more than happy to have Marinelle—er, Mary—move in with us."

Baker confided that he found Mary to be quite the enigma. "Try as I might, I can't get a read on her."

"Mary is a wonderful girl," Helen said. "She always looked after Cal like—well, I don't want to say like a son. That would be extreme, but definitely a cherished younger brother. That was true when Angela, their mother, was alive, but especially so since her death. Mary was always there to support Cal, even in his training, right along with Allen and David. They called it 'the plan.'"

"That sounds almost cryptic. What was the 'plan'?"

She met Baker's question with a Sphinx-like expression.

"C'mon, Helen, how far out can 'the plan' be?"

After another moment's hesitation, she replied with dispassion. "The plan was to get Cal's name on the Clarence Cup."

Helen's answer was not news to Baker, just a clear confirmation of what he had deduced.

"You knew?" she asked. "Did Allen tell you?"

"Oh, no. Not directly. He wouldn't do that. Let's just say I put two and two together. But I assumed it was just a casual thing—more of a fun fantasy than a concrete goal. By your description, however, it sounds like it was a serious consideration."

"You're right. It started out as a bit of fun, but circumstances conspired to have it evolve into something actually worth aiming for."

"I must say, it sounds like an ambitious goal."

"Of course it's an overly ambitious—even ridiculous—goal. But Allen and David just assumed that Cal would eventually put it all in perspective as he matured and recognize the underlying point of it. It was a little boy's dream that inspired Cal to the core."

Baker sensed that now was the time. The compass of the conversation was pointing in the optimal direction, steering them nicely toward the topic of Cubby's spirit council. Allen's absence was also proving to be perfectly timed, so without further delay, Baker dove in and presented Helen with a coherent and compelling argument to not only attend the event for her nephew but also to host it.

"Hearing myself say it out loud, it's a little embarrassing to ask you to do this on such short notice."

"Next weekend you say?" Helen replied as she considered his proposal. "On the Saturday?"

"Yes."

"And Dorcas thinks it's a good idea?"

"Yes."

"And she'll preside over the gathering?"

"Yes—but she advised that Mary be present."

"Well, I'd think that would be a given." Then she seemed to arrive at a decision. "If I had to think about it, I might have second thoughts and renege, so maybe the short notice is a good thing."

"I wouldn't blame you for having qualms. A spirit council sounds pretty intense, especially to those of us who have never experienced one."

"Oh, but this wouldn't be my first. Dorcas had me attend one last fall. She thought it would be good for me to witness firsthand what Mary would be participating in."

The information was a relief to Baker. "And what about Allen? What did he think?"

"Allen wasn't there. In fact, I don't know if he's ever experienced a spirit council. Knowing Allen, it'll likely take some time to win him over to the idea. It's a process. A couple of days should do it."

"Dorcas recommended we bring an item—something Cubby was fond of in life, something that might attract his spirit to us," Baker said, eager to move the conversation forward. "She gave it a term, but I can't—"

"A conduit."

"That's it. A conduit. I was thinking *My Hockey Stick*. I thought I could do a reading."

"Oh, Baker, that would be perfect. Cal loved that story."

Baker beamed. Helen was sure making this easy. But then he had a sobering thought. "What would Cubby's father think of this? Would he approve?"

"Leave David to me. We speak to each other about once a week. In fact, I'll give him a call tonight. We're three hours ahead of them, after all."

Baker's hunger pains having been soothed with the soup, his instinct now told him it was probably best to leave before Allen returned from his errands—so he graciously thanked Helen for the meal and the company, then awkwardly wished her luck with her husband and her brother, saying he'd reconnect with her early in the week. He donned his shoes, coat, hat, and gloves, then shouldered his bag and beat a somewhat hasty retreat down the driveway to his car.

"Do you have everything?" Helen called to him from the porch.

"I think so."

On the drive home, Baker couldn't shake the feeling that he'd forgotten something, but dismissed it as just a symptom of having a lot on his mind.

Thursday, February 27 – Friday, March 6

The Mighty Pines closed out February with two solid regulation wins. The first week of March had them jetting off to California for three games against the also-rans of the West. Back in the GTA, the first day of the new month—rabbit, rabbit, rabbit!—looked more like a lamb as Southern Ontario experienced above-zero temperatures with no significant precipitation expected. It was a welcome spell of weather considering the previous week's blast of snow and wind.

Just as the weather was a daily topic of conversation, so too was progress of the coronavirus, with increased case numbers of COVID-19 being reported in Iran, South Korea and Italy. Meanwhile, International Olympic Committee President Thomas Bach reassured all athletes and their respective national Olympic committees that the IOC had no plans to postpone the 2020 Tokyo Olympics (scheduled to begin on July 24) in light of the health risks surrounding COVID-19. He urged the athletes to "Go ahead full steam with regard to their training and their preparations."

For the Pines, California proved to be anything but full steam ahead, especially where scoring goals was concerned. The first game on Tuesday in San Jose was a 5-2 loss, after which the team travelled down the Pacific coast to Los Angeles for a game which saw neither team able to register a goal in sixty minutes of regulation time. The Royals would ultimately win 1-0 in a shootout. The very next night in Anaheim, Toronto suffered its third straight loss, managing to go "0-for-California" and having to settle for a single point against three teams that were not only out of the playoffs but actually the three bottom feeders in the PHL's Western Conference standings. For the Pines, what was expected to be a trip fit for California dreamin' turned out to be a west coast nightmare.

CHAPTER FORTY-THREE
THE BOY WITH HIS NAME ON THE CUP

Fifty-plus years and no Cup is a long time
This pattern of losing has been such a tough grind
I want to cry

Midway into the forty-five-minute drive to Baker's house, Perreault was regretting the late-afternoon cup of coffee with her mother and wishing she'd used the bathroom before leaving home. Exacerbating the situation was the uncommonly heavy traffic, which slowed her transit time considerably. It seemed everyone and their dog was out on the road that Saturday afternoon. When she finally arrived, Perreault found herself getting no response to her raps at the front door. As she stood idly on the porch, the urge to relieve her bladder was growing more insistent by the minute, made worse by the thought of how Conrad would be giving her all kinds of grief for politely standing there on the verge of peeing her pants.

After about the fourth series of knocks, she detected a faint voice telling her to let herself in.

She opened the door. "Hi, Baker. It's me, Perreault."

"Yeah, I know. C'mon in. I'll be right with you!" he replied from somewhere in the basement.

"OK. I just need to use the facilities."

She quickly removed her coat and hung it on the coat tree. She paused to reach into one of the pockets, removing a school-issue plastic recorder in its cheap vinyl sleeve, then hustled up the stairs and down the hallway to the bathroom.

Several minutes later, Baker came upstairs looking somewhat dishevelled and positively frustrated. "I can't figure it out. I could've sworn the book was on my shelf."

"Was this something you intended to bring to the spirit council?" Perreault was back in the kitchen, nibbling on some assorted nuts from a tray on the counter.

"Yeah, but I can't find the damn thing. I'm sure I brought it home with me a couple weeks ago."

"What book was it?"

The question shook Baker out of his funk, or more precisely, it was the person asking the question that transformed him. Unfailingly, Perreault's mere presence brought blue-sky clarity to Baker's life, even when his mood was coloured overcast grey. "It was an illustrated version of *My Hockey Stick* by Felix Cote. Hello, by the way."

"Hi there." She smiled and held up a cashew. "Want a nut?"

He wrapped his arms around her waist. "If you're referring to yourself, then yes, please." They shared a warm embrace and a smooch. "How was the drive? Can I get you anything? Coffee, tea . . . beer?"

"No thanks. I'm all coffee'd out, actually, and I'm not really in the mood for a beer. And the drive was slower than usual today, but scenic as always." She picked up her recorder. "I'm all set with my weapon. When should we expect Angus?"

"I'm hoping any minute now." Baker had suggested the three of them travel together to Helen's place for that evening's event. "What did you bring for tonight?"

"You mean besides my instrument? Just something small. I never knew the young fella, remember?"

"Right." Baker returned to a state of preoccupation.

Recognizing this, Perreault tried to help. "What if you can't find it? You must be able to substitute something for *My Hockey Stick*."

"What? Oh, well, yeah, my next option was Cubby's bookmark. I kept it here in this book, but I can't find that either." Baker went over to his library table and retrieved *The Clarence Cup: A Tradition Like No Other*, dramatically flipping through the pages as a demonstration. "I must have gone through this thing a hundred times, and I'll be damned if it's here."

"You might have to settle for just bringing that book," Perreault suggested as she walked over to the table, her eye having been caught by a softcover manual that was revealed when Baker picked up his book. "And if you don't mind, I'm going to take this." She held up Dorcas's *Coven Craft for Wannabe Witches*.

Baker frowned. "You're taking that to the spirit council?"

"No, no. I'm just going to study it in my spare time, if that's OK with you."

"Sure, sure," he replied, too preoccupied to care. The possibility of having to settle for his third choice made Baker look like a kid who'd found coal in his Christmas stocking.

Perreault knew how important this evening was for Baker. "You're sure it's not in the car, under the seat, or in a corner of the trunk?"

"What, *My Hockey Stick* or the bookmark?"

"Either."

He stared at her, considering the question. "I'll be right back." Then with renewed purpose, he left the room for the garage.

Looking to occupy herself, Perreault perused the coven manual, then took up her recorder and practised the few lines of melody she'd be playing for that day's event. She stopped when she spied an electric pencil sharpener in a corner on the counter by the coffee maker. Beside it was a box of pencils. She opened the box and tipped it sideways, allowing two virgin HB pencils to spill out. Then Perreault put the idle pencil sharpener to use. The machine emitted a surprisingly loud and high-pitched sound, but it also produced a flawless, ready-to-use writing tool. Just the sight of the pristinely-sharpened pencil gave her an odd yet delightful satisfaction. This was fun.

Perreault had sharpened half the box by the time Baker re-entered the kitchen. His check of the car produced nothing.

"You know, Baker, this is a beautiful little machine you have here. I'd invest in one myself, but I don't ever use old-school eraser-tipped wooden pencils like this."

Baker's expression went from pain to delight, as if he'd found a forgotten Sugar Watson's gift card among the junk in the car console. Perreault wasn't sure how to read Baker's changing expressions, so she just waited, watching with trust as he approached her, took her face in his hands, and planted a kiss on her cherry-flavoured Burt's Bees-balmed lips. "My dear, you are a genius!"

"I seem to remember being called that before in this room."

"You're right. It was when you came up with the name Bakers' Coven for our band, remember?"

"Sure, but why am I a genius this time? By the way, what were you planning with this box of pencils?"

"My rubber tree was looking dry, so I thought I'd put mulch around its base. Then I got the idea to use those pencils, whittle them down to the nub in the sharpener, and then use the shavings that they produced as mulch. Pretty clever, huh?" He gave her a schoolboy smile.

"It's an interesting idea for sure. Whether or not it works is something to be determined, though." Then she returned his smile. "So, now that we know why *you* are a genius, tell me how I fit into that category."

"You're a genius because you showed me how this particular box of pencils can be put to better use. And now I no longer need to find *My Hockey Stick*." Baker saw by Perreault's expression that his answer was unsatisfactory. "I'll explain later, but right now I'm going to give Angus a call to see where he's at. You finish sharpening the rest of those pencils, please."

Perreault did as she was told while Baker gave Angus a ring.

* * * * *

When Angus arrived, Baker and Perreault met him at the front door. "Shall we?" Baker asked.

"Hold on," Angus replied. "Do I have time for a beer? I've had this weird craving all day, and this might be my only chance."

Baker looked at Perreault for approval. "Sure, if you're quick about it," she said.

Angus led them back to the kitchen, stuck his head in the ice box, came out with an obscure Irish ale, and tapped the Sykes stick before downing half of it. "Aaahhh, that hits the spot."

Baker took a sheet of paper from his folder. "Here's your copy of the song."

"Thanks." Angus directed his attention to the page but then looked back at Baker with a flash of anger. "Fuckin' Pines. I can't figure them out. They close out February with three wins and score thirteen goals in the process. Then on their California trip, against the three shittiest teams in the West, they score three measly goals, losing all three games." He paused to take another swig from his bottle, which seemed to spark an idea. "Hey, do you think there's a chance this séance-thing we're holding tonight can help the Pines?"

A heavy sigh prefaced Baker's answer. "Angus, I just don't know anymore. I mean, our coven sessions are a blast—I have no regrets. But as to their usefulness—?"

"What about the witch lady?"

"Dorcas?"

"Yeah, Dorcas. She'll be attending, right?"

"Uh, huh. And her student, Mary."

"Two witches. This should be good."

"Mary's not a witch—at least not yet. She's more like Dorcas's ward, or protégé."

"The sorcerer and her apprentice. Isn't that a Disney movie?"

"Not quite. *The Sorcerer's Apprentice* is one of the chapters in Fantasia. But get back to your point. Why did you ask about Dorcas?"

"Do you think she'd mind if I got her opinion?"

"On what?"

"Our coven rituals. You know, if we could be adding something or whatever?"

"Go ahead and ask her. I think she'd be willing to share some advice."

"Fantastic! I'm gonna get advice from a real witch. How cool is that?"

"If we're just hanging out here, waiting for Angus to drink up, why don't we run through the song?" Perrault suggested.

Baker, who was standing in the doorway, guitar in hand, went over and found a place by the drums. Angus took the cue, collected his sticks, and sat on his stool. Perreault pulled up one of the kitchen chairs, recorder at the ready, and counted them in.

When Cheers Are Not Enough

*****

An hour later Baker, Perreault and Angus were walking up the driveway of the Nella residence. No sooner did they step onto the porch than Helen opened the front door and greeted them. "What have we here? A trio of wandering minstrels. Come in, come in."

She led them into the front hall from where Baker could see Dorcas in the background in conversation with Allen. Once Helen completed the introductions, she led Angus to an area in her living room where he could set up his drum kit. He didn't waste any time and was on one knee working a wing nut when a voice from over his shoulder posed a question.

"Is it true what they say about drummers?"

"What's that?" Angus asked, without turning.

"That they're the hardest partiers in the band?"

"Guilty as charged. But then, with my band, the bar for partying isn't all that high—" He swivelled around to face his questioner and was stunned into silence by a pair of trance-inducing green eyes. While there was no way to measure the magic of the moment, the truth is that if Mary Elyk had lived to practise witchcraft for another hundred years, no charm, spell, or incantation of hers would prove as pure, potent, or powerful as the one she unwittingly cast upon Angus Fletcher at that moment.

Seeing that Angus could only mutely stare, Dorcas swooped in to the rescue. "Angus Fletcher, this is Mary Elyk. Mary . . . Angus."

He was momentarily baffled. "Mary?" Then it dawned on him that *this* was the Mary described by Baker. "Oh, Mary. Uh, hi, my name's Angus."

"Yes, and I'm Mary." She took his hand in greeting (he would remember the firmness of her grip for a long time afterward). "You were describing a low bar for partying with your band?"

Sensing that her presence was now redundant, Dorcas ducked away, leaving them to their conversation. Meanwhile, across the room, Helen approached Baker and slid her arm in his, pulling him to one side.

"About Allen—"

"Right, I was meaning to thank you for persuading him to take part today."

"Well, you're welcome, but I should warn you, his presence might be all we get from him. When the time comes for us to address Cal, Allen was firm in his refusal to participate."

"Really? What did he say?"

"How did he put it? 'I'm not going to talk to the walls,' or words to that effect. He said he'd have to be convinced Cal was in the room before he spoke. And of that he was dubious."

"I can understand his reluctance. But he just being here and supporting us is a bonus."

Just then Dorcas stepped forward and invited everyone to assemble in the dining room at a large, distressed oak table with six chairs spaced around it. An industrial-style overhead lamp hung down from the ceiling, but it was kept dark, even thought it was late afternoon, and the daylight coming through the windows was quickly fading. The room was lit with an array of pillar candles, ever-present for such gatherings. To any neighbourhood passersby, the glow through the windows might have produced a sense of equal parts warmth during a power outage and ongoing sinister activities within.

Dorcas called attention to the fact that some of the participants came to the table equipped with a keepsake or token of attraction for Cubby, making it their first order of business. "If anyone has a conduit that might connect us more closely to Cubby, now is a good time to bring it forward," she instructed.

Perreault was the first to produce her token, which elicited an emphatic "Hey!" from Baker the moment he recognized it. "That's my Kyle Bulac name tag!"

"Very good," Perreault said. "I told you I was bringing something small."

Helen was next. She reached down to the floor by her chair and came up with a book, which Baker instantly recognized as *My Hockey Stick*, prompting a second "Hey!" from him. "I was looking all over for that. Did I leave it here the other day?"

"Yes you did," Helen said. "I'm sorry for not calling you about it, but I knew you'd be here today." Baker was just happy that the mystery of the missing book had been solved.

"Mary, you also have something for your brother?" Dorcas asked.

"Yup, and like the first two items, Baker was the source for this one, but it's actually something that was mine originally. It's something I made for Cubby a couple years ago."

For a third time, Baker cried "Hey!" as Mary placed Cubby's bookmark on the table.

Now everything made sense for Baker. He already knew that Cubby's sister had made the bookmark, but now that he knew that Mary was his sister—well, it explained her interest in the item on that misty October night when she and Dorcas had visited him. In addition, her natural talent as a psychic medium pointed to the likelihood that the spirit responsible for turning the page of his book that night wasn't Cal Ubank at all, but rather her brother, Cubby. In other words, the pages of the book hadn't been turned to reveal the picture of the Pines captain, but to unveil the bookmark that happened to be tucked into that same page.

Baker was prevented from dwelling on it further when he noticed that everyone was waiting on him to produce his token of remembrance. He duly produced his box of HB pencils, and Helen instantly recognized the genius of it. Mary also made the connection, and actually had to stop herself from saying *"Hey!"* Perhaps more importantly, she realized that Baker might have known her brother better than she'd given him credit for. Oddly enough it was Angus who next discerned the link between Cubby and the pencils, recalling how the kid twirled his pencil on the table when Baker first introduced them to each other that day in the school library.

Tipping the box to release a handful of pencils, Baker set one in front of him like a piece of silverware, then proceeded to circumnavigate the table, placing a pencil in front of each person seated there. Once he was done, Dorcas went over the ground rules.

"First, I want to thank everyone for devoting their Saturday evening to participating in this event. And I would be remiss if I didn't take this opportunity to thank our gracious hosts, Allen, Helen, and Mary, for making their home available to us and putting on this delicious spread." Perreault, Baker, and Angus took a moment to echo the sentiment, then Dorcas continued. "Before we begin in earnest I'd like to run through the agenda.

"We are brought together by a common bond—our love for a dear family member and cherished friend. Cubby passed away nine months ago. He was Mary's little brother and nephew to Helen and Allen. Baker knew him for a short time as well. As for Perreault, Angus, and I, the three of us never had the pleasure of knowing Cubby, but we are present to support the process of making contact with him." Baker watched Dorcas with interest. She seemed to direct her comments to the air above the table, as if to instruct any other invisible forces that might be listening. "Let me assure you that a spirit council is not an occasion for engaging in acts of malevolence. There is no sinister intent. Any such entity is not welcome here. No one here seeks to lay blame or openly grieve. The messages we bring are positive and welcoming in nature."

No one spoke and no one moved as Dorcas continued. "We gather with pure hearts and focused minds to invite Cubby into this room and for him to dwell among us if he is able. In life, this setting, this room, was a place Cubby was familiar with and happy in. In closing, everyone present will have an opportunity to reach out to Cubby if they desire, but right now, I would like to ask Mary to deliver a message to her brother." Dorcas gave her apprentice a slight nod, indicating that the floor was hers.

Mary shifted in her chair, then sat up straight and closed her eyes. "Hey, Calub . . . Hey, Cubby. It's me, your sister Marinelle. C'mon, little man, come in now." She appeared to wait for an answer before continuing. "We haven't heard from you in such a long time. How was your workout? I'll bet you're getting stronger. You must have grown out of your skates by now."

Mary smiled at the thought, then perked up as if she had something exciting to share. "Hey, Cubby, we're having a party for you. Yeah, a bunch of us are here at Aunty Helen and Uncle Allen's, having a little party just for you, and we were hoping you would come in and visit. Aunty Helen baked cookies and other treats." Mary chuckled. "There will be no food left if you don't come in soon. And guess what? I'll be playing the piano today. I know, I stopped playing for a while. It just wasn't as much fun without you around to hear me. But I'll be playing today. I wouldn't want you to miss it. C'mon in, little man, we've got a special song planned for you. Then Mr. Brooks will read *My Hockey Stick*. I know you liked that story. I did too." She finished her invitation by adopting the tone of a big sister assuring her younger sibling that everything would be fine. "Come in now, Cubby. C'mon in, my little bear Cub."

With eyes still closed, Mary raised her chin and turned her head slightly, as though she were straining to hear or sniffing the air. Baker was watching her so intently that he was slightly startled when Dorcas spoke again.

"Our next order of business is a song. Baker, Perreault, Mary, and Angus have prepared something for Cubby. It should be noted that music can be an effective means of transmitting messages, and since our goal is to communicate with him, we are indeed fortunate that this ceremony includes a live musical performance."

Taking their cue, Perreault, Angus, and Mary got up and went to their instruments while Baker, who had brought along extra copies of the lyrics, distributed them to Dorcas, Helen, and Allen. "Just in case you want to know exactly what is being said in the song." Then he took his place with his guitar over by the others.

Perreault made a final check to see that everything was ready, then counted them in. Mary sounded her chords, and the rest followed as smoothly as Baker could have hoped.

> *Fifty-plus years and no Cup is a long time*
> *This pattern of losing has been such a tough grind I want to cry*
> *Day upon day of this wondering gets me down*
> *Nobody knows if the Pines can bring glory to this old town*
>
> *We're gathered together as friends and as family*
> *And calling on Calub to join us here now as our dear Cubby*
> *A hovering spirit of you is a sure way*
> *To show that you answered the call*
> *If you're here in this place, just let us know*

Perreault looked over at Mary. She definitely knew her way around the piano, not only playing the chords with confidence but filling in here and there with playful trills.

> *We guaranteed much but delivered on little*
> *It's hard to adjust when you're lost in the middle*
> *Of fantasy land; it all seemed so grand*
> *Promises made and promises broken*
> *We'd like to atone for preaching the notion; you need to trust*
> *That inspired play*

When Cheers Are Not Enough

> *And a timely bit of luck*
> *Puts your name on the Clarence Cup*

Helen and Dorcas were clapping along with Perreault, which was a good thing because this was the point in the song where she had to break off and put the recorder to her lips to perform the playful melody. She had been anxious about getting her part right, and once she got through it, Perreault was relieved to return to singing and clapping. In the meantime, she made two observations: 1) Mary on the piano was actually carrying the tune in an infectious sort of way and 2) even Allen was buying in, keeping the beat in his own quiet manner, tapping the table with his hand.

> *And now we can speak of a way for achieving*
> *The honour of having your name in silver and made to last*
>
> *No need to suffer or carry a burden*
> *A man whose name magically now can be found in a looking glass*
> *A Pines torch he does bear*
> *For the team is his as well*
>
> *There is a location for you on the Cup*
> *And it may come about if the Mighty Pines do their victorious most*
>
> *The GM and you share a name through a mirror*
> *From this side it's his from the other it's yours and sure as this tune is sung*
> *The boy who we loved a lot*
> *Has his name on the Clarence Cup*

The song ended with Mary's piano leading them to a cold finish. After the audience of three expressed their appreciation for the performance, everyone returned to the table and settled back into their seats.

It was now Baker's turn to speak to Cubby, but he would begin by reading aloud from *My Hockey Stick*. He welcomed the chance to warm up, as it were, putting himself at ease by calling to mind the first day they had met. Helen passed the book to Baker, who opened it to the first page, pressed it flat, and began.

"I remember my very first hockey stick; it was handed down to me from my older brother who had grown too tall for it . . ."

As he read, Baker kept his head down, his eyes glued to each page, instead of looking up at intervals as if he were speaking to his audience from a podium. The message, after all, was intended for Cubby's spirit rather than the earthly folk gathered around the table.

"We all taped our sticks like Claude Lambert. We all skated hunched over, like Claude Lambert. And when we scored, we celebrated like Claude Lambert."

By the midpoint of the story, Baker began to wonder whether any of it was actually working. Cubby wasn't responding. He would have expected the young fella to have made an appearance by then. Baker's instincts told him to deliver the lines with more force and volume, so as to be heard in the spirit world. In the end, however, he elected not to force the issue and chose instead to read as if Cubby were in the room as his corporeal self. It was in this fashion that Baker managed to finish the story.

"I still have my Claude Lambert hockey stick . . . I keep it safe in my garage . . . ready to be handed down to my own child one day."

Having gotten to the end of the story, Baker gently closed the book and looked across at Dorcas, who was directing an effervescent smile back at him.

"That was delightful!" She said. "Thank you, Baker. And thanks to Felix Cote for such a charming story. Now, I believe you have a message for Cubby?"

Baker nodded, knowing it was time for him to communicate directly to the boy. All day long he had been uncertain about how to address Cubby, but hearing Mary speak to her brother earlier gave Baker all the assurance he needed that it was OK to keep things informal.

"Hey, Cubby, it's Baker here . . . Mr. Brooks. Um . . . I just wanted to tell you how I wish I'd been able to see you play hockey. Your Aunt Helen and Uncle Allen and your sister Mary—er, Marinelle—have all told me how skilled and smart you were on the ice. But more than that, I wish I'd gotten to know you better, just as a friend, you know? I really mean that. I enjoyed spending those times with you in the library, talking and reading together and eating cookies—" Baker had to stop himself from choking up. The candle flames flickered to the point that they nearly blew out, although there was no discernible breeze felt by anyone around the table.

Then Baker's pencil moved.

Ever so slightly, almost imperceptibly, like the creeping of a sundial's shadow, it rolled to the right. It came to rest two centimetres from its starting point, then rolled to the left, back to where it began, and sat there, motionless. Baker wondered if anyone else had detected what he now began to doubt that he'd seen.

He continued speaking. "I wanted to let you know that a few of us here have been calling out to some of the Toronto Mighty Pines spirits, asking if they could inspire the players to finish this season as champs, kind of like the Raptors did last year. Anyway, besides Toronto winning the Cup, it would mean your name would be on it too. That sounds like a really cool thing, and I hope you agree." He was about to look around at the others when the pencil moved again, this time with increased energy, right then left, moving with purpose, as if it came equipped with a wind-up mechanism that Baker had engaged before letting it unwind. Once, twice, three times. It rolled to the right a fourth time, then stopped for a spell, only to begin rotating in place, counter clockwise.

It rotated a full turn, then a half turn more, stopping with the sharpened tip pointing directly at Baker. That was all the evidence he needed that Cubby was not only present in the room but clearly communicating with them.

Unfortunately, all the paranormal activity, welcome though it was, caused Baker to lose his train of thought, preventing him from finding the words to close out his message with any sense of polished finality.

It was Helen who stepped up in timely fashion, clearing her throat before addressing the spirit of her young nephew. "My dear Calub, you make me so proud. And I know you made Uncle Allen proud, and Marinelle too. It brought me so much pleasure to bring you to school with me and introduce you to the teachers and staff. You know, I actually learned a lot from helping you with your homework." She was cut off by a movement on the table in front of her. It was the pencil Baker had placed there—it was slowly rotating in place, much like Baker's pencil had a minute earlier. Helen watched, then continued, opting to keep things light and short. "Thanks for making all my baking worthwhile, Calub. Stay as long as you want; you are always welcome here. We miss you. Take care, my boy."

Helen's pencil gradually slowed and then came to a stop. Everyone around the table seemed to hold their breath. It was Dorcas who opened her mouth to speak, only to have another voice break the silence.

"May I say something?" Allen asked, apparently having had a change of heart.

"Yes, of course," Dorcas replied. "The floor is yours."

He had nothing of a formal nature prepared and instead let the words come from his heart. "Hi, Cubby . . . it's me, Uncle Allen . . . You know, I often think of the times we spent together, talking about how your career might unfold. We shared our dreams. Those were some of the sweetest moments. But no one can predict how things will turn out."

It was when he mentioned dreams and sweet moments that Allen detected the movement in his pencil. He continued to speak but as he did he eased himself up off his elbows, never taking his eyes off it, as if staring down a venomous snake. Then he set his hands on the table in karate-chop fashion, shoulder width apart, like he was trying to be helpful by providing end boards lest the pencil stray too far as it magically rolled and spun.

As Allen spoke, Dorcas watched Mary intently, knowing she was like an antenna, picking up on the energy that would be felt when a spirit joined the party and set out to communicate. Dorcas also knew that with Mary this could sometimes be infuriatingly difficult because the girl's apathy with respect to her talents resulted in her often choosing to ignore the signals. But not that day. By all appearances Mary seemed relaxed, almost bored, but to Dorcas the girl was wired up and alert. She watched as Mary's eyes went from one end of the table to the other, as if she were following the movement of someone invisible to all others but plainly detectable to her. It seemed her gaze stopped at her uncle, who was still speaking, trying to find his words, but Mary's eyes were actually fixed at a spot next to him.

"I did the best I could, Cubby. I mean, your dad and I . . . we only wanted . . . the last thing we wanted was for you to think you owed us something. You are a true champ. If anyone deserves to have their name in silver in among the names of their heroes, it's you, Cubby. And that's how we remember you, as a dear member of this family. You made us all so happy. Stay safe, little man. I hope you've found some friends."

As Allen ended his invocation, Dorcas kept her eyes on Mary, whose gaze was still fixed on a spot next to her uncle's shoulder. There was the smallest change in her chin and bottom lip, then she swallowed. The candle flame was reflected in her eyes as she blinked once, releasing a tear. Dorcas stared at the tiny bead of emotion, which settled, glistening, on the curve of Mary's cheek—the most she had seen in the girl since first coming to know her.

Dorcas shook herself back to the moment and saw that Mary's eyes were dry again. The girl shifted her attention to the bookmark in front of her, then seemed to realize her cheek was wet and brought a hand up to wipe it. Dorcas took that as a sign that Cubby was no longer present and that the séance was ended. Just then Mary's eyes swept up and across the table, catching Dorcas's stare. Feeling intrusive and a bit embarrassed, Dorcas blinked and looked away, but then quickly looked back, expecting the girl's usual scolding gaze anytime she acted too much the mother. Instead, Mary directed the warmest smile at her, as if to say, *"I know we're kindred spirits, you and I, and I'm grateful for it."*

Not wanting to make too much of a beautiful moment, and never one to get too emotional herself, Dorcas simply smiled back. Then remembering this was supposed to be a celebration, she reverted to party mode the best way she knew how. "Perreault, be a dear and pass the wine, please."

If there was any residue of spiritual tension in the room, it was effectively lifted when Dorcas made her wine order. The social habits of humans are such that, given the choice, engaging in conversation with the living is preferable to chatting with the dead. It was no different for the seven living souls who had gathered in the hopes of communicating with one of their own from the spirit world. Having succeeded—to the complete and utter satisfaction of each person present—it was time to reconvene and celebrate life among the living. Angus, Baker, and Allen each seemed to have the same idea, rising from their chairs and leading the way to the kitchen where a generous spread of food called to them. Once everyone had loaded their respective plates, they split off into ever-rotating knots of people. The rest of the evening saw Baker circulating and engaging in several discussions, as the following snippets of conversation would attest.

* * * * *

With wine in hand, Dorcas approached Baker. "Congratulations, young man. That's as successful a spirit council as I've ever experienced. And the pencils were a stroke of brilliance."

"Thanks, Dorcas. But the credit should go to you and Mary."

"Now, now, this is not a time for false modesty. You were able to bring together just the right sort of audience, and the programme you planned was simple enough yet entirely to the point. Let me tell you from experience, those things are not always easy for people to balance out."

"Hey, did I mention that I recently engaged in a personal pilgrimage?"

"Really? A pilgrimage? When? And where to?"

"It was about two weeks ago. No place exotic. I went on a little meditative retreat into downtown Toronto."

"Ah, yes. Instead of heading for the hills in search of peace and solitude, you chose to confront the noise and activity head on—right in the belly of the beast, as it were."

"Well, that's not quite how I'd put it. You see, my destination was Elysian Square. I went to, um . . . worship? At the Acropolis."

"Seeking to commune with spirits of great hockey heroes of the past?"

"Exactly," Baker replied, amazed at her freakish ability to discern people's motivations. "I'd ask how you knew that, but I figure a person who deals with this stuff regularly can read someone's intentions like, uh . . . a spread of Tarot cards."

"Oh, speaking of Tarot—" Dorcas reached deep into a pocket of her skirt. "Do you remember Carly Romanet? I ran into her this week and mentioned your event this evening. She asked me to give this to you."

Baker recognized the business card immediately. He resisted the instinct to back off and instead thanked Dorcas and accepted the card. He tucked it into his back pocket, thinking that, for the moment, it was probably best not to dwell on it—let alone inspect it to see what information he might find written on the back.

* * * * *

Allen was the next person to approach Baker. "I'd like to express my gratitude for your efforts to make this evening happen. To be honest, I wasn't keen on attending, but Helen insisted, and I can't say no to her." His expression then transformed into one of childlike innocence. "Your reading of *My Hockey Stick* added a nice element to the proceedings."

"Thanks, Allen. I hope you understand that I was just trying to help in some way."

"I'm aware of that now, Baker, and I appreciate it. I'll admit it's been tough for me, these past months since Cubby's death. Up until now I could never be sure, but after this evening's events, I believe Cubby is in good company. I'm confident this is a chapter I can close." Allen lowered his voice. "I've been meaning to ask you, though—" He took Baker's arm just above the elbow and led him three or four steps away from the others, making it the second time Baker had been pulled aside by someone that evening. "My clue—the one I gave you around Christmas—did it help? Did you go to Cubby's gravesite like I said?"

"Yes, I did."

"And?"

"Well, I just have one question: Who first discovered the uncanny association between the names of Kyle Bulac and Cubby?"

Allen shrugged his shoulders in a way that suggested the discovery was something that couldn't be helped. "I have to take credit for that."

"Which makes perfect sense," Baker said, nodding, "owing to your fascination with numerology and signs and symbols and stuff." He paused. "Can I ask one more thing?"

"Shoot."

"When did you make the discovery?"

Allen seemed to make a mental check before answering. "Shortly after Cubby's death. We were making decisions about the design of the tombstone." His voice rose a notch. "You'd have to understand my frame of mind at the time. You see, after Cubby died, I was searching for answers—"

Baker saw that Allen was growing agitated trying to express himself, so he put a hand on the man's shoulder. "That's OK, Allen. You don't have to explain. I think I understand."

"By the way, this song—these words," Allen indicated the song sheet in his hand, "would you mind if I printed this and had it framed for posterity? I'd like to display it on my wall downstairs."

"Would I mind? Allen, it would be an honour for me."

"Good. I have just the place for it: next to the photo of Cubby on the mantelpiece."

"Nice. But I'd expect an invite to come over and see it in person, of course. I'll bring the beer."

"Deal. But you've been here enough to know the only thing you'd really need to bring is your appetite."

* * * * *

When Cheers Are Not Enough

Allen's mention of his appetite prompted Baker to get himself some more food. In the kitchen, he closed the circle on a group that included Helen, Mary, Angus, and Perreault. The topic of conversation came around to the song performed earlier.

"So, Baker," Helen said, "If I understand correctly, you altered the words to an existing song?"

"Right. The original title is 'The Boy with the Arab Strap.'"

Helen appeared to consider the title for a moment. "Would anyone care to fill me in on the meaning of that? I won't pretend to know anything about 'Arab straps.'"

Silence descended on them, each waiting on the next one to answer Helen's question in a graceful way.

Perreault was the first to find her words. "An Arab strap is like a ring that goes on a guy's, um—"

Helen held up her left hand and indicated her wedding band. "You mean, like a friendship ring or a wedding ring?"

Not one to dance around the truth, Mary set her straight. "Aunt Helen, an Arab strap is a sex toy that serves to extend the duration of a male erection during intercourse."

Baker, Perreault, and Angus held their breath, waiting for Helen's response.

"Oh, of course. Thank you for making that plain, Marinelle."

In attempting to stifle a laugh, Angus's gaze drifted to the various items on the kitchen counter, causing him to make an observation. "One thing's for sure, you'll never look at a napkin ring in the same way."

Helen turned her attention to the cluttered countertop, seeming to take inventory, then returned her attention to the group. "Would anyone like some tea?"

* * * * *

A short time later, Baker happened to be standing with Perreault and Angus. Maybe it was the delicious food, or maybe it was the cold beer, but a wave of euphoria swept over him. "Man, I feel good. I feel good about the coming month. There are thirteen games left on the sked for the Pines. They have two games this week and then Montreal on the weekend.

"You know something, why don't we get the Coven together Saturday at my place? We can jam and then watch the Nationales game. Gosh, it would be the first time we all caught a game together. Let's kick off the March break in style."

"Wait—are you talking about a *watch party?*" Angus asked. "You?"

"Sure, what the hell? We'll have a super jam—a coven fest where we play all the oldies. From 'Go Green' and 'Five Years' to 'Play A Game In June' and 'Another Time.' What else?"

"There's 'Divine Intervention' and '88 Lines,'" Perreault offered. "And the only other one is 'Pray That They Hear.'"

"Don't forget 'Make Us Happy.'" Angus added.

"That's right. How could I forget? How many is that?"

"It think that's eight songs," Angus said. "Eight is a good number, isn't it? Infinity and balance and stuff? How perfect is that?"

"Actually, a 'perfect' number would be nine songs," Baker pointed out. "The number nine represents achievement and the culmination of a task. And back in the good old days, it was considered the best hockey number to wear. Hey, I know—I'll come up with a new one for us this week. Then we'll have nine."

"C'mon, Baker," Perreault objected, "do you really have the time for it?"

"No! Of course I don't have the time," he replied with a devil-may-care laugh. "But that never stopped me before. Besides, it will kick off what I feel is going to be an interesting final few weeks leading up to the playoffs."

Angus was infected by Baker's enthusiasm over the promise of the coming games. "Strap in, folks. It's gonna be great."

* * * * *

"Have a gander at those two over there." Dorcas directed Perreault's attention toward Angus and Mary, the latter sitting at the drums, sticks in hand, taking instruction from the former.

"Yes, they seem to be getting along famously."

"Correct me if I'm wrong, but it would seem that a young, eligible, socially active fellow like Angus would have occasion to test the waters at his workplace."

Perreault glanced over her shoulder, then moved closer, ready to share something in a lowered voice, but Dorcas cut her off. "I don't think you need to worry about being overheard. Those two are in their own little world." Then she raised her voice to be heard over the din of the drums. "Hey, you two, keep it down! We're trying to have an adult conversation here."

"Sorry," Angus replied from across the room, although his apology did little to reduce the sound emanating from Mary on the skins.

Perreault leaned in, nevertheless. "I must confess: Angus did pursue me for a time before Christmas."

"Didn't work out?"

"For one thing, the age difference proved to be an obstacle."

Dorcas made like she couldn't believe her ears. "You're not *that* much older, are you?"

"Not that much, but I guess I'm just into older men." Perreault smiled and looked directly at Baker. "Isn't that right, Mr. Brooks?"

"Huh? Oh, yeah, sure." Baker agreed despite not fully catching all that was said because he was watching Mary and Angus with fascination. A half second later, though, the echo of Perreault's comment suddenly registered. "Hey!"

Dorcas had to laugh, having heard him utter the same word in exclamation for the fourth time that evening. She adopted a Spanish accent and borrowed a line from *The Princess Bride*. "You keep saying that word. I don't think it means what you think it means."

He identified the movie moment at once. "Very impressive, Dorcas! You do a terrific Inigo Montoya."

* * * * *

At the close of what turned out to be a successful and productive evening, Baker and Perreault had said their goodbyes and were making their way down the driveway while Angus and Mary were walking ahead of them, shoulder to shoulder, saying their own goodbyes. Abruptly, Baker remembered something. "Hey, do you know if Angus ever got a chance to speak with Dorcas?"

Perreault laughed. "Wishful thinking, I'm afraid. Don't you know? Romance trumps research every time."

Baker nudged Perreault, flicking his head at the two sweethearts. "There they go, looking just like Humphrey Bogart and Claude Rains from that final shot in Casablanca."

For the third time that evening, someone took his arm and steered him in another direction. On this occasion it happened to be Perreault.

"My dear Baker, put the stone down," she said with a smile. "I think you're aiming from a glass house. Those two could just as easily be the pair of us."

CHAPTER FORTY-FOUR
MAN PLANS; GOD LAUGHS

Monday, March 9 – Wednesday, March 11

Utah Jazz centre Rudy Gobert made health headlines at a post-game media event on Monday, when he felt compelled to make a point about what he considered a general overreaction to the coronavirus. When he got up from the podium, Gobert proceeded to lay his hands on every object in sight, going so far as to lean over and touch all of the reporters' microphones and recorders. At that time, the infectious nature of the coronavirus was still very much a mystery to the North American populace; the prevailing belief was that the virus would only infect those who had either travelled overseas or spent time in Italy or China.

Coming off a three-day break, the Pines played host to the Chicago Millionaires on Tuesday. In a tight checking game, Toronto treated the crowd at Nova Tank Arena to a 2-1 homecoming victory. The win was big—not just because it kept the team ahead of the Florida Everblades in the standings but also because it strengthened the belief that the Pines could play a shutdown game when necessary. With seventy games in the books, Toronto sought to establish some winning consistency and momentum through the final stretch of a dozen games heading into the playoffs.

Alas, those games would never be played.

The next evening, in downtown Oklahoma City, the NBA's Thunder were preparing to play host to the Utah Jazz at Chesapeake Energy Arena. With players from both teams about to take the floor, the scene turned surreal. OKC's head medical doctor ran out from the locker room and informed game officials that two Jazz players, centre Rudy Gobert and guard Emmanuel Mudiay, had likely contracted the coronavirus. Thunder officials subsequently made the decision to postpone the game. The fans in attendance were sent home while players and team staff remained in the arena.

When the NBA learned Gobert was a presumptive positive, it had no option but to suspend the season. The effects of the decision were swift and widespread—like expanding concentric circles of radiation following a nuclear explosion—and were felt by the North American sports world on a scale greater than anyone could have imagined. Within forty-eight hours of the events in Oklahoma City, the big business world of sports and entertainment—with its attendant bright lights, swelling crowd noise, fast-paced action, and constant stream of money—had been shut down. COVID-19 had brought the industry to its knees.

For Baker, the shutdown was fascinating and frightening all at once. But in his mind the one saving grace was that the postponements and pauses, necessary evils though they were, would in all likelihood be short-term and lifted in a matter of weeks—a month, at most.

His laissez-faire attitude toward the coronavirus stemmed largely from the fact that things at his workplace were business as usual. He was still expected to greet the kids at his door in the morning as they showed up for class. But seeing as it was the Friday before March break, a good percentage of families in the community typically kept their kids at home, apparently looking to get a head start on the week-long school holiday.

As expected, when he arrived at school, Baker found it to be devoid of students and minus the daily morning activity. He dropped his stuff off upstairs and then headed down to the cafeteria to get himself a coffee and something to snack on. Finding the treat fare to be minimal owing to the scarcity of student traffic, he settled for a large dark roast and then exited the servery. There, seated at a table and true to form, were the four students—as reliable as a Yellowstone Park geyser, dealing cards and enjoying each other's company. Baker fiddled with his coffee lid as he approached the group. The first to greet him, as usual, was Christian.

"Hey, Mr. Brooks. Wanna play a hand?"

"That depends. What's today's theme, the March break? Or maybe vacations?"

"Nah. Today's theme is COVID-19."

"Really? Wow, I'm impressed."

"Yeah, we figured we'd give it a try. So, should I deal you in?"

There were easily a hundred things Baker would have preferred to be doing at that moment, but given the day's theme, he figured the guys would have a limited bank of responses, making for a quick game, so he agreed to sit in for a hand and pulled up a chair. As soon as Christian finished dealing the cards and gave final instructions, Baker discovered how wrong he was.

"OK, so the theme is COVID-19, but since this is a brand new topic for us, let's loosen the rules a bit and give a pass to 'weaker' answers," Christian said. "And for this game we'll change it up. You only discard when you can't answer or the answer you give is not accepted by the group, so the last player holding any cards is the winner."

Anthony sat to the dealer's left and so was given the honour of starting.

"*Vaccine.*"

"*Pandemic,*" was Raj's response.

Baker followed with *quarantine* while Christian came up with *Wuhan.* Jake completed the first round with *testing.*

Anthony wasted no time in blurting out *contagious,* which caught Raj unprepared.

"Umm . . . uh, *China?*"

"That works for me," said Baker. "My turn. *Rudy Gobert.*"

"Good one, Mr. Brooks!" Christian exclaimed.

"Yeah. I never even thought about the NBA," Raj admitted.

"It's my turn," Christian said. "*Lockdown.*"

"Aww, thanks a lot, Christian. That was my answer," Jake complained, then struggled to generate another one. "Umm . . . give me a second . . . uhh . . ."

"You gonna pass, Jake?" Christian prodded.

"Hang on . . . OK, uh, *flu!*"

"Ooh, that was close," Anthony said. "My turn? Umm . . . *infection.*"

Raj went with *catchy* while Baker threw down *coronavirus.*

Bats was Christian's contribution, which was greeted with resistance from Anthony.

"Bats? Bats don't count for this game."

"Yeah they do."

"I don't think so."

"Uh-huh."

"Nuh-uh."

"OK, guys, bats is acceptable," Baker said, intervening. "Whose turn is it?"

"Mine," Jake said. ". . . um, *doctor.*"

Baker sat through answers like *nurse* and *hospital* before he went with *isolate*. When he heard *fever, temperature, thermometer,* and *sick* being accepted as legit answers and feared that the boys' responses might only get weaker with each passing round, Baker tried to coax up their quality. His use of *contact tracing,* however, didn't quite have the desired effect; as evidenced by answers like *chest, sore throat, lungs,* and *headache.*

For his next contribution, Baker went with *Center for Disease Control,* but got only questioning stares from the others, as if he were the one trying to get away with soft answers.

The next round of offerings were delivered in snappy fashion and included *sniffles, sneeze, cough,* and *fever.* It was then that Baker began to suspect some of the answers were being repeated. He resorted to making a show of slowing down his responses when it came his turn, in an attempt to indicate that perhaps more thought needed to go into everyone's answers. He dramatically closed his eyes and wrinkled his brow before offering *social distancing*. It didn't work. Baker had to sit through several rounds of answers which included *hand washing, soap, water, germs, death,* and *life*, with each answer delivered in lightning-quick fashion.

Seeing that none of the players were being forced to discard, Baker feared he could be trapped in a game with no end in sight. He began racking his brain for any legit-sounding excuse to get the hell out of there when, with exquisite timing, a voice came over the PA system. "Mr. Brooks, report to the main office. Mr. Brooks to the main office, please."

Baker couldn't believe his ears—or his luck—and he did not hesitate in playing up the need to answer the page immediately. "Ahh, sorry guys, but duty calls. I have to answer that." He collapsed the fanned cards in his hand into a tidy pile and set them face down on the table, then got up and bumped knuckles with each student. "I wish you all a nice March break—however long it turns out to be. And hopefully when we get back, we can talk about how the Pines are getting ready for the playoffs."

"I sure hope so," Christian said. "See ya, Mr. Brooks."

"See you, boys. Stay safe."

Making sure not to look back, Baker exited the cafeteria and headed toward the main office at the far end of the atrium, which was empty and cavernous that day. The reason for his being summoned was a mystery until the answer revealed itself in the figures of Perreault and Conrad stepping out of the office. They were both grinning broadly at him.

"Hope you don't mind us taking the liberty of having you paged," Perreault said.

"We thought you'd appreciate being rescued," Conrad added.

Baker glanced over a shoulder and kept his voice down. "Actually, your timing was perfect."

Perreault beamed. "In the words of Indiana Jones' friend Sallah, 'Better than the United States Marines, eh?'"

Baker was thrilled at her movie reference. "Holy shit, Perreault, you are freaking me out right now."

Listening to the exchange between the two movie geeks, Conrad rolled his eyes. "Jee-zuss, what a pair you two are. You're really made for each other." Seeing how they both blushed at his remark and averted their eyes, he realized there was too much truth in what he said and promptly changed the subject. "Listen, let's get out of here. I'm going upstairs to the staff room."

"But we just came from there," Perreault countered.

"I know, but I left something on the table. I just hope Angus hasn't recycled it already."

"You two go ahead, then," she said. "I'm going up to my work room to organize myself. I have to figure out what I should take home for this extended holiday."

"OK," Baker replied. "By the way, Mas wanted me to drop by his place after school. I'll call you from there. Maybe we can meet up later."

"Sounds like a plan." Then she turned to address Conrad, who was already halfway up the staircase. "Oh, and Conrad, if I don't see you before you leave today, have a marvellous March break."

Conrad turned to look at her. At that time he—and almost everyone else—assumed it would be just a couple of weeks before they were back at school, and yet he was seized by some compulsion. Returning to the bottom of the stairs, he gave Perreault a smile and a warm hug. "Thanks, sweetie. Same to you."

Then he and Baker continued on their way. Two minutes later they were entering the staff room.

"There he is," a voice called from across the room. "Hello, Mr. Brooks."

"Morning, Mr. Fletcher," Baker replied. Conrad moved past him with purpose toward the table where Angus was seated, scanning it with an anxious eye.

"Angus, I left a couple of pieces of paper on the table—"

"Oh, did you need those? I recycled them. They should be on top of the pile in the box there."

Conrad smiled and shook his head as he went to the blue bin to retrieve his items. "Thanks for keeping them safe," he deadpanned.

"Hey, no problem," Angus replied, oblivious to the intended sarcasm. Then he raised his arms and clasped his hands behind his head in smug fashion, leaning way back in his chair.

"At the risk of sounding like Lou Gehrig, I consider myself the luckiest man on the face of the earth."

"Really? Why?"

"Why not? Didn't you hear? We've been gifted a sweet spring vacay!"

"Oh, I heard alright. I just don't consider it as much of a gift as you do."

Angus straightened up, bringing his hands down with force onto the armrests. "What, you too?"

"What do you mean 'me too'?"

"I mean you sound just like Perreault. She wasn't keen on it either. I tell ya, you two are like peas in a pod. You're quite a match. You think the same way."

Baker had to will himself to keep from blushing. He found a convenient diversion in the form of Conrad returning from the recycle bin.

"So, you found your papers?"

"I did," Conrad said, holding up two pages as if they were exhibits "A" and "B" in a court case.

"Are you working on a sermon or something?" Angus inquired.

"Jesus, Fletcher, I'm not a priest."

"Well, you're the closest thing to one in this school."

Conrad sighed. "Sure, whatever."

"What is it then?" Angus persisted. "Some prayers for our next Coven session?"

"If you must know, it's something for Winnie. Just the lyrics to a song I'm working on."

"Aww, that's so sweet."

"Yeah, I positively drip syrup and honey."

"What about you, Baker?" Angus inquired. "You working on any new songs for the Coven?"

"Nah, I figured I'd give the Six-pack some time off. Give the spirits a holiday, you know?"

"That's shitty news," Angus replied, but then he perked up again. "Oh, hey, speaking of spirits, did you tell Conrad about Saturday night?"

"The séance was a success, then?" Conrad asked.

Baker was not inclined to share details about Saturday's spirit council, feeling it was somehow inappropriate to engage in idle chatter about something as profound as a visit by the spirit of a dead ten-year-old. Therefore, he kept his answer fairly vague. "It was good. I think the family came away satisfied."

Angus couldn't believe his ears. "What're you talking about? It was fucking awesome, man."

Baker just smiled, knowing that his friend's experience that evening was likely sweetened by the presence of one Mary Elyk. To his credit, Conrad did not pursue the topic any further.

Angus brought the conversation back around to Baker's plans for the Coven. "So, you're really considering taking a hiatus from making magic?"

"Yeah, I was leaning that way. What do you think, Conrad?"

"I think we might not have a choice in the matter. Besides, is there any point, given that the season has been put on hold? It might be best just to pause along with the league."

"I have to agree with Conrad, Angus. I mean, under normal circumstances, I doubt we'd be gathering during the off-season, you know, over the summer months. Isn't this sort of the same thing?"

Angus knew they were right, but he still needed a minute to absorb the news that Bakers' Coven would be shutting it down for the duration of the pause.

"You figure we'll get together when the PHL decides to start up again?"

"I would think so—I *hope* so."

"OK," Angus said, satisfied with Baker's answer. "In the meantime, I'll keep honing my skills."

"Skills?"

"Yeah, you know, the drums, man. I'm gettin' pretty good."

"Sounds great," Baker said, pleasantly surprised. "Move over, Buddy Rich."

"To be honest, all the credit goes to Mary. She's been cracking the whip this week—um, but not in a dominatrix kind of way—"

"Thanks for clarifying that. But I thought she was in England with Dorcas."

"That was the plan, but then Dorcas reconsidered. I guess she thought it would be better if Mary stayed home."

"Lucky you."

"Yeah, as it turns out, she may have been right, given how serious this coronavirus stuff is."

"It certainly has thrown a wrench into our world," Baker said.

Angus concurred. "It sure wasn't in the plans."

"Once again we are dealt a cruel lesson," Conrad intoned soberly as he made his way to the door. "The best-laid plans aren't worth the sticky-note they're written on." Then his expression brightened. "Have a good break, guys. Keep in touch." And with a wave he was out the door.

"See ya in the funny papers," Angus replied.

Not long after, Baker also took his leave, heading upstairs to his classroom, where he spent the remainder of the day ruminating on Conrad's words. He'd had such big plans for the season, but few, if any of them, had materialized. This realization only served to cast an unwelcome pall over his afternoon, most of which was spent taking inventory of everything he'd need to bring home for the extended March break. But with two visits to make—first with Masaccio, then Perreault—home was still several hours away.

* * * * *

"What's the matter, Baker? You seem a little bummed out." Masaccio passed a cold beer across to his visitor. It should have been the best beer of the week, but Baker was too preoccupied to notice. His countenance suggested someone troubled and careworn. He settled into a corner of the couch while Mas deposited himself into a cushy chair across from him, waiting patiently for his friend to formulate an answer to his question.

"I don't know. It's just—" Baker broke off, pensive, his gaze landing on a framed A. J. Casson print on the wall. Struggling for a response, he instead posed a question of his own. "Mas, do you ever get the feeling, like, just when you think you've got it all figured out, just when things seem to be working out for you—"

"Absolutely," Masaccio replied before Baker could finish. "Just when you think you've got it all under control, you hit a raccoon on your way to school and you're suddenly shelling out for costly repairs to the car's front end, or you get into an argument with your wife over something stupid, or your twelve-year-old dog needs costly surgery to remove an intestinal blockage—"

"Exactly!" Baker exclaimed, awed at how precisely Mas had divined his meaning. "Believe it or not, I feel that way about the Pines this year." Masaccio nodded and took a sip of his beer as Baker continued. "It's been an entire season—seventy games' worth, anyway—of this team spinning its wheels."

"Oh, I completely agree," Mas replied. "The year has been one long laundry list of issues."

"Tell me, Mas, because I'm not paying enough attention. Do other teams go through this much crap?"

"By and large, yes," he replied, more as succour than as cold fact. "I guess it's the nature of the beast for teams in professional sports. But with the Pines it feels as if *more* bad stuff happens over a longer period of time—like decades. I think we're discovering a hard and uncomfortable truth about this team: there's more to winning than just an abundance of talent."

"A hundred percent!" Baker said, feeling inspired. "Skill will only take you so far. You need leadership and experience, along with that undefinable quality called team chemistry—" He lost himself in the thought of what such a team might look like, especially in Pines colours.

"It sure is complicated," Masaccio said. "Winning a championship takes a shitload of luck and circumstances converging just so, and for PHL teams that stuff has to extend through four rounds of playoffs."

Baker scoffed. "Ha! In all its history, this franchise has never experienced four rounds of playoffs. And now, with their inability to go beyond the first round, I find that each year I'm girding myself for disappointment, wondering what events will transpire to derail the Pines' Cup train this year."

"You are describing all of Coney Nation," Mas said. "Because Toronto fans have suffered so much, we tend to be careful about how much we're willing to believe. Nobody wants to fall for another false promise."

"The scary thing is, I find myself dreading the day the Pines actually *do* win the Cup."

"You're afraid it won't live up to the hype? That it will turn out to be something *less* than the life-affirming experience you expect it should be?"

"Uh-huh." Baker nodded, yet again impressed at how astute his friend could be.

"I don't think you need to worry yourself with thoughts of a possible letdown—especially if you take the attitude of those who fervently believe it will never happen anyway."

"Gee, thanks," Baker replied dryly. "That makes me feel so much better."

"OK, bad joke," Mas said, then adopted a tone of sentimentality. "Remember last August, at the Misty River Bar and Grill?"

"The Misty River? Sure, I remember." Baker smiled. "We played a pretty good set that night."

"We did. But I was referring more to our meeting after the set, when you proposed we transform our band into a coven."

"Oh, *that*." It seemed like a lifetime ago. Baker had almost forgotten how pumped he'd been about the prospects for the season. Baker's voice carried a tinge of regret. "Man, back then I had such aspirations."

"Of course you did. That's only natural."

"No, you don't get it. My vision for the Pines was more than just seeing them struggle for a playoff spot."

"What, you expected them to go eighty-two and oh?" Mas said in jest.

"Of course not, but certainly better than a team on pace for a win total in the low forties. Hell, I expected them to finish first in the division, even the conference. Call me crazy, but I actually saw them as having a shot at winning the league's regular season title."

"Wow, you *did* have high aspirations. But don't kill yourself over it. In fact, you had us all pumped about engaging in coven gatherings and musical rituals and stuff."

"I was just glad you guys didn't laugh me out of the pub when I suggested we try magic."

"Look, we're all dreamers to a degree—me, Conrad, Angus—so, no, we weren't about to laugh you out of the pub. But the clincher for us may have been the music more than the magic. Your plan gave us a reason to get together and jam regularly. It forced us to commit to the band."

"How ironic, then, that we never even performed in front of an audience this school year."

"That's not true. We played in the Battle of the Bands in January. Remember?"

"Oh, shoot, you're right." Baker had repressed the memory of that evening. "Then again, Conrad wasn't there. The band was incomplete."

"Aww, Baker, don't let yourself get in such a funk over some things not turning out according to plan that it blinds you to all the good stuff that happened. And you can't deny that a lot of good things came our way this year."

"Oh, yeah? Well, I'd love to hear them."

"OK. Let's begin with our band. We were able to accomplish things that I never would have predicted back in August."

"Hmm . . . I suppose," Baker said grudgingly. "It certainly didn't hurt that Perreault showed up when she did."

"True, Perreault was a key addition, but we all contributed. Everyone grabbed an oar and pulled."

"Sure, I guess so."

"And speaking of Perreault, she was one of two romantic relationships you were involved in. I mean, as dissimilar as Perreault and Sylvia are, a lot of eligible men would consider you one lucky dog. Oh, and, newsflash—Anthony finally got off his ass and popped the question. That's right, he and Sylvia are engaged to be married. So you see? All things work out in the end."

Baker smiled at Masaccio's Pollyanna take on things. "Good for them. I'm sure they'll be very happy together."

"Don't overlook the fact that you also met Dorcas and Mary, two key additions to your personal orbit of friends and acquaintances."

Baker had to concede the point.

"And you took on the challenge of trying to find a solution to the Pines' Cup drought—which compelled you to attempt a variety of methods for coven rituals and spirit summoning. Hell, you even organized a séance."

"They're called spirit councils."

"Still, in my opinion, the year was quite a memorable one. And it's not over yet."

Baker didn't reply, waiting for the punchline.

"Imagine how silly you'll feel if and when the Pines go deep in the playoffs this year." Mas shook his head in wonder. "I tell you, man, there's simply no accounting for the curves life can throw at you."

"This altar is zoom!" a voice said from the kitchen.

Baker whipped his head around and saw it was Masaccio's wife, Sal, who had just entered the room, carrying a tray of melted cheese-topped nachos.

"What did you just say?" Baker inquired.

"This altar is zoom."

"Oh—my—gawd!" he replied, enunciating each syllable. "Sylvia said that to me once, but it didn't make any sense at the time."

Sal nodded as she set the tray on the coffee table, then straightened up to explain. "My grandfather often dropped that one on us when we were growing up. It was usually in response to someone complaining about things not going to plan. Without fail he'd pronounce 'Dis aliter visum.' And because Sylvia and I were just dumb kids at the time, the Latin went over our heads, so we corrupted it and turned it into 'This altar is zoom.'"

MAN PLANS; GOD LAUGHS

Listening to Sal's story, Baker now understood what Sylvia had been talking about back in January. He suddenly pictured the two cousins as little girls, playing together and poking fun at their grandfather's wisdom, marching through the house proclaiming "This altar is zoom!" at the top of their lungs.

"So, the original is Dis all-ter viz—"

"Dis aliter visum," she repeated. "It translates as 'Man proposes, and God disposes.' A simpler way to say it is 'Man plans; God laughs.'"

"That's incredible. It describes this season to a T."

They were suddenly interrupted by the sound of fun in the form of energized kids and a bouncing ball. Lily and Hazel had come upstairs from the basement, red-cheeked from exertion and looking for something to snack on.

"Buongiorno," Lily said with Italian gusto.

"Buongiorno," Hazel echoed as she twirled a soccer ball on her index finger.

"Hello, Lily. Hi, Hazel," Baker replied.

"Zio Baker, how are you?" Lily inquired. "Come stai?"

Baker hesitated, searching for a response in Italian. "Um, I am well...uh...splendido."

"Ahh...bene."

Hazel, who was always working on her game, held the ball out with two hands, then lifted a bent knee to hip level and let the ball drop and bounce off it a few times. Sal immediately reminded her of the house rules.

"Hold the ball, Hazel. Keep it on your hip in this part of the house, remember?"

"Oops, my bad. Scusami, Mama," she said, hugging the sphere to her chest with crossed arms like a goalie securing the ball after a big save.

"Are you girls hungry?" Sal asked. "Hai fame?"

"Si, si," Lily replied.

"We are molto appetito," Hazel said, eyeing the tray of munchies on the coffee table.

"Good because there's plenty in the kitchen for you both."

"Bene, molto bene. Grazie, Mama," Lily said.

"Let's go, Lily," Hazel said. "Andiamo! Mangia!"

The hungry twins took their "palla" and headed for the kitchen, cheering on their soon-to-be-adopted nation's pride.

"Azzure!"

"Azzure!"

"Forza!"

Sal watched with parental pride as her daughters exited the room, then turned back to Baker.

"As you can see, Lily and Hazel have bought in. They're ready for our move to Italy and looking to make the culture their own."

When Cheers Are Not Enough

"It kind of reminds me of the lead character in the movie Breaking Away," said Baker.

"I don't think I've seen that one." Sal looked to her husband for help. "Have you, Mas?"

"Breaking Away? God, no. But don't worry, my dear, Baker's the king of obscure movie references."

"You should watch it with the girls sometime," Baker said. "I highly recommend it as good family viewing. It's cute, it's funny—"

"I know, I know. You laughed, you cried—"

"Another beer?" Sal asked, as out of nowhere she was poised to crack open a tallboy and pour. Baker covered his beer glass with his hand.

"No thanks, Sal. I'd love to, but I'm going over to Perreault's from here, and I should give myself a buffer of time before getting behind the wheel."

"Fair enough, but that shouldn't stop you from eating. Don't be shy—mangia, mangia," she said with motherly admonishment and some pointed hand gestures.

Baker was happy to do as he was told. Over the next forty-five minutes he, Sal, and Mas enjoyed sampling the tray of eats on the coffee table as well as a veritable buffet of topics for conversation, including their March break plans, the Raptors' season, life in Tuscany, school gossip updates, and, of course, COVID-19—anything other than the Toronto Mighty Pines.

As the time came for him to take his leave, the conversation swung like a compass needle around to his next port of call: a visit with Perreault.

"I've never met the girl," Sal said, "but based on everything Mas tells me, she's quite the catch."

"She's like a good cigar and a brandy after the perfect meal," Baker said, waxing lyrical. "At other times she's a fusion of the excitement of Christmas morning and the anticipation of summer holidays on the last day of school."

"You two are a perfect match," Masaccio said.

"I'm happy for you, Baker," Sal added.

When it came time to see their visitor off at the door, Sal and Mas were joined by their daughters.

"Bye, bye, Baker."

"Ciao, ciao!"

"Arrivederci!"

Baker opened his car door and settled in behind the wheel, feeling good about the world again. As it turned out, taking the opportunity to visit Masaccio and Sal when he had was a good call because, as fate would have it, he wouldn't be speaking with his friends face to face for some time.

Of course, none of that was on his mind as he pulled out of the Clementi family driveway and made his way to the Thoreau residence. He was more intrigued by the fact that, strangely enough and yet again, some things—and not necessarily bad things—happened in threes. This time it was how three of his friends, on separate occasions, had made a pointed remark about how he and Perreault were a good match. On top of it all, Sal had said how she was happy for him, and that meant a lot. Dis aliter visum? One thing was certain: if this particular turn of events had God laughing, well then, Baker was more than happy to laugh along with him.

CHAPTER FORTY-FIVE

THE END OF THE WORLD AS WE KNOW IT

It was during the winter of 1918, as World War I was entering its final stages, when we last saw a health crisis so widespread as to merit the designation "global pandemic." With the outbreak of the Spanish flu, fully one third of the world's population—a half billion people—became infected, and 50 million lives were lost. It took over two years and four waves of infection before the virus was brought under control. By then the Spanish flu had claimed 55,000 Canadian lives (one in six people contracted it) and an estimated 675,000 in the US (one in four Americans were infected). It ranked as the deadliest flu epidemic in recorded history.

Fast forward one hundred years and the winter of 2020 was winding down, with the month of March coming in like a lion—but in this case the well-worn idiom could rightfully be applied to more than the weather, because roaring out of the Chinese jungle was a new strain of coronavirus that was spreading globally with disturbing speed.

While it would be an untruth to say that Baker was completely ignorant of the coronavirus, it would also be an untruth to say it was foremost in his mind. As we have seen, ever since the start of the school year, Baker had been devoting his cerebral efforts to the enigma that was the 2019–2020 Toronto Mighty Pines. Like assembling a monochromatic jigsaw puzzle, finding the pieces that fit was a near-impossible task, requiring more time and patience than he'd been prepared to give. By the end of February, he'd about had it with the Pines' inability to break free of their "one step forward, two steps back" tendencies. And yet, despite his frustration, Baker had been ever the optimist, always alert to see blue sky between the clouds. In fact, at that time the team had appeared to be setting itself up for a nice little run as it headed out to California for a three-game road trip against a trio of lower echelon teams in the PHL's Western Conference.

THE END OF THE WORLD AS WE KNOW IT

It was then, during the middle of the first week in March, that Baker's perspective on current events took a broader turn. While the Pines were still in California, Baker was in his classroom, standing front and centre, addressing his fourth-period grade nines on the topic of how art movements and styles throughout history were often products of impactful or even tumultuous events. He began with an example from the eighteenth century.

"It was about three hundred years ago that archaeologists digging in southern Italy discovered the lost cities of Pompeii and Herculaneum."

A hand in the third row shot up. "Hold on, sir. What do you mean 'lost'?" Oddly enough it was Travis Caldwell, someone more apt to dwell on things like skateboarding tricks or the sex appeal of Ariana Grande than Baker's preamble to an art history lesson. "Did somebody bury them? Kinda like a secret treasure?"

"Close, Travis. Your description of Pompeii and Herculaneum as being buried like treasure is a good one. However, they weren't so much buried by some*body* as by some*thing*."

"Huh?"

"Well, there's this volcano in Italy. You may have heard of it—"

"Vesuvius!" Angela DeSantis called from her seat in the back row.

"That's right, Angie. Mount Vesuvius violently erupted about two thousand years ago, not long after the time of Christ."

"Wait, what?" Noah Mancini had been jolted out of his semi-slumber. "Did you say Jesus was killed when Mount Ve-*true*-vius exploded? I thought he died on the cross."

"It's called Mount Ve-*soo*-vius," Angie corrected, "and Jesus *did* die on the cross. Pay attention, Noah."

Noah turned and made a face at Angie while Baker smiled patiently. He took a minute to clear up any misconceptions, knowing full well that if one student was confused, others probably were as well. When he was satisfied that no one would go home that day thinking Christ's Passion played out under an Italian volcano, he continued with his original point.

"It was a natural disaster on a grand and tragic scale. Both cities were buried and destroyed. Amazingly, as the centuries passed, they were eventually forgotten. That's why it was such a big deal when they were rediscovered in the seventeen hundreds." As he spoke Baker made his way to a wall on the far side of the room. Among the two dozen or so laminated reproductions affixed there was Jacques-Louis David's "Oath of the Horatii."

"My point is that the excavations of Pompeii and Herculaneum led to a new form of artistic expression that turned out to be quite popular." With a flourish of his hands, he presented David's masterpiece. "It was called the neoclassical style."

As another example, Baker cited the terrorist attacks of 9/11. "That tragic event profoundly influenced the issues and themes that contemporary art and culture focused on throughout the first decade of the twenty-first century."

Almost as an afterthought, he went on to urge his students to be alert to such moments in their own lifetimes, whenever they might arise. It was then that Francesca Luciani's hand went up. Francesca was fourteen going on forty—in an intellectual sense—and as brilliantly insightful and creative as she was humble and polite.

"Sir, I was just wondering, um . . . well, lately there's been a lot of stuff in the news about this coronavirus. Is it possible that we're heading toward a moment in time similar to what you're describing? You know, one that will hugely impact art and culture and society and such?"

The question gave Baker pause. He had to concur, commending Francesca for her insight. It was then that he addressed the class as a whole and suggested they may want to pay close attention to current events as they developed in the coming weeks and months.

Later that day as he was driving home from school, Baker tuned his radio to the CBC, hoping to catch some of the news at the top of the hour, when he was struck by the preponderance of stories dealing with the coronavirus. It caused him to reflect on Francesca's comment in class. *Damn if she wasn't right!*

The realization prompted him to go out that same weekend and purchase a fancy bookstore journal, the kind covered in faux cracked leather. He decided to take his own advice and resolved to make regular entries for posterity, keeping a record of history in the making, as it were. Who knew? Maybe he would revisit his notes at a later date, possibly even embedding them in some future lessons.

But while Baker's intent was to record headline news stories as they related to the coronavirus, his actual entries revealed a certain favouritism toward the world of sports. And for good reason. When the COVID-19 pandemic shook the world, all the various sports leagues and organizations, big and small, fell like dominoes, their vulnerabilities suddenly exposed.

Perhaps it would be best at this time if we opened Baker's journal to see how events played out according to the entries written there.

THE END OF THE WORLD AS WE KNOW IT

Monday, March 9

- US President Donald Trump tweeted on the topic of the coronavirus in an effort to play down its severity, blaming the fake news media and the Democratic Party for inflaming the situation.
- Trading on the New York Stock Exchange is halted after a 2,000-point drop in the Dow.

Wednesday, March 11

- With the global number of confirmed COVID-19 cases surpassing 100,000, the director-general of the World Health Organization officially declared a pandemic.
- Air Canada cancelled all flights to Italy. (While Canada's COVID-19 case count was at 100, there were 10,000 cases reported in Italy.)
- Donald Trump announced borders closed to international visitors. Several state governors across the US declared states of emergency.
- In the wake of Rudy Gobert's testing positive prior to the tip-off of the Utah @ OKC game and the game's subsequent postponement, Commissioner Adam Silver announced the NBA would suspend its season.

Thursday, March 12

- Sophie Gregoire Trudeau tested positive, becoming Canada's 158th reported case. Prime Minister Justin Trudeau entered self-isolation.
- Members of the Toronto Raptors self-isolated for two weeks.
- PHL morning skates and meetings were cancelled while PHL officials were told to pack up and go home.
- The NCAA announced the cancellation of all Division I men's and women's basketball tournaments as well as all NCAA winter and spring championships.
- PHL Commissioner Barry Stetson announced the league would suspend its season.
- Major League Baseball decided to delay the start of its season by two weeks.
- Formula 1 cancelled its season-opening Australian Grand Prix.
- Resisting the trend to pause or cancel events, UFC president Dana White announced they would continue holding events over the next month. White had received counsel from President Trump and Vice-President Mike Pence.

Friday, March 13

- In the interest of containing the spread of COVID-19, Ontario Premier Doug Ford announced that Ontario schools would have their March break extended by two weeks.
- European soccer's Premier League, Champions League, and Europa League games were all cancelled.
- Augusta National chairman Fred Ridley announced the 2020 Masters would be postponed to a later date.
- The 124th running of the Boston Marathon was postponed to September 14.
- NASCAR postponed its scheduled events.
- The London Marathon was postponed to October 4th.
- MLS soccer suspended its season for 30 days.
- The XFL suspended its season.
- The PGA Tour cancelled the Players Championship after the first round as well as all other tournaments up until the Masters.

Saturday, March 14

- The International Ice Hockey Federation cancelled this year's Women's World Hockey Championships.

Monday, March 16

- The latest three-country comparison of COVID-19 case counts:

    Canada = 425 cases   US = 4,000 cases   Italy = 25,000 cases

- The PGA tour announced that tournaments would continue but without galleries.
- Donald Trump announced that the US border with Canada was closed to "non-essential traffic."
- The World Figure Skating Championships in Montreal were cancelled.

Tuesday, March 17

- The PHL announced its first positive test: an unidentified Ottawa player was showing mild symptoms in isolation.
- The NBA's Brooklyn Nets had four players test positive, including Kevin Durant.
- The Kentucky Derby announced the postponement of the most exciting two minutes in sport.

- Ontario Premier Doug Ford declared a state of emergency. All restaurants and bars were ordered closed except for drive-thru and takeout.

Saturday, March 21

- New York State was declared the epicentre of COVID-19 in the US.
- In open letters to the IOC, the heads of US Track and Field and US Swimming requested that the Tokyo Games be postponed. Canada's swimming governing body agreed.

Sunday, March 22

- Canada's Olympic organization announced it will not send athletes to the games scheduled for July, making it the first nation to pull out of Tokyo 2020.
- Australia sent notice to its athletes to prepare for Tokyo 2021.

Monday, March 23

- The City of Toronto called its own state of emergency.
- Doug Ford admitted that an April 6 return for kids to school was unrealistic.

Tuesday, March 24

- The International Olympic Committee officially postponed the Tokyo 2020 Olympic Games for one year.

Thursday, March 26

- The Indy 500, annually held on Memorial Day weekend, was postponed to a later date.

Friday, March 27

- UK Prime Minister Boris Johnson tested positive for COVID-19, becoming the first leader of a major nation to contract the virus.
- The PGA postponed this year's US Open at Winged Foot in Mamaroneck, New York.
- Canada exceeded the 4,000 mark in confirmed cases of COVID-19.

Wednesday, April 1

- The biggest celebration of arts and culture on the planet, the Edinburgh Fringe Festival, normally held in August, was cancelled.

- The City of Toronto closed down all public venues.
- Stock markets tumbled in response to news out of the US that upward of 240,000 people would likely die due to COVID-19.

Sunday, April 5

- In an attempt to buoy and reassure her subjects, Queen Elizabeth II delivered a national address. It was only the fifth such address made by her in sixty-eight years as monarch.

Monday, April 6

- On what would have been day one of Masters Week, Augusta National confirmed this year's event would take place in November.
- This year's British Open Golf Championship, slated for July 16–19, was cancelled.

Saturday, April 18 – Sunday, April 19

- In what was the deadliest mass killing in Canadian history, 51-year-old Gabriel Wortman engaged in a 13-hour crime spree across 16 locations in Nova Scotia. Twenty-two people died, and 3 others were injured before Wortman was shot and killed by RCMP officers at a truck stop in the town of Enfield.

Monday, May 11

- The American Hockey League cancelled the Calder Cup playoffs.

Tuesday, May 12

- The Canadian National Exhibition called off its event for 2020, the first such cancellation in its 142-year history (except for once during WWII).

Monday, May 25 (Memorial Day in the US)

- George Floyd, a 46-year-old black man, was killed during an arrest after a Minneapolis police officer, Derek Chauvin, knelt on his neck for 8 minutes and 46 seconds. Chauvin was charged with third-degree murder and manslaughter. The other three officers assisting in the arrest were not initially charged. Nine days of protests for racial justice ensued, beginning in Minneapolis and extending to New York, Los Angeles, Philadelphia, and Washington, DC. Protests extended to cities across Canada as well as England and Australia.

THE END OF THE WORLD AS WE KNOW IT

Thursday, May 28

- Commissioner Barry Stetson declared the 2019–2020 PHL season officially ended. The statement went on to reveal the league's plan that would ultimately see the awarding of the Clarence Cup, all the while ensuring the health and safety of the players, on-ice officials, team staff and associated individuals involved.

Baker's journal entries ended with Barry Stetson's announcement. The news from the commissioner served as a relief of sorts because it meant there would be closure to the season. And the decision to conduct the Clarence Cup playoffs during the month of August in empty arenas, as distasteful as it was to some, would require the trophy's metalsmith to punch one team's name under the year 2019–2020, followed by the names of its players, coaches, and support staff—certainly preferable to the alternative of filling the next empty space on the Cup's silver ring with three blunt words: "Season not completed."

By the end of May, Baker's journal became more of a scratch pad for new song ideas. From those pages, however, one thing was perfectly clear: for all those fans who relied on a steady diet of games as a distraction from their quotidian lives, a new reality was suddenly imposed upon them. The wide world of sports had been completely shut down (except for the UFC; Dana White was not about to suspend his show over a silly pandemic). To borrow the words of Howard Cosell, "If the world of human affairs is a department store, then sports is the toy department, and although customers don't always buy the toys, they *do* come in and look." Now, however, the toy department was closed. Our fields of play were swathed in caution tape, both figuratively and literally. There would be no thrilling victories or agonizing defeats—not even a mundane sister-kisser (social distancing rules being what they were). Our daily diet of sports television was reduced to reruns of last year's most memorable games.

When it came to general news items, COVID-19 was the top story; the only story. Coverage of the pandemic was wall to wall. (Indeed, in Canada it took the horror of a one-man murderous rampage in Nova Scotia to nudge the coronavirus off the front page.) The world had changed in the blink of an eye, and information came at us from all angles. Society was riding a steep learning curve, and within a week we were experts on something that a month before none of us gave a thought to, save for the off chance we experienced a severe cold or were among those who bared their arms for the annual flu shot. Daily case counts became the norm, as did the growing death toll.

But as May gave way to June, people increasingly grew weary of the protracted shutdown (the very thought of a second or even a third wave was inconceivable) and began to anticipate the coming of the summer months, hoping that warmer weather would bring a return to some form of normalcy. In the meantime, there were many who sought coping mechanisms, some finding solace within the sphere of pop culture—specifically pop music. For many of them, R.E.M.'s 1987 stream-of-consciousness rant "It's the End of the World as We Know It (And I Feel Fine)" seemed to resonate and serve as an anthem of sorts. The quirky little tune experienced a huge revival in popularity during the early weeks of the pandemic. It didn't matter that its content bore little if any resemblance to the present situation. The lyrics, as sung in hyper-kinetic fashion by vocalist Michael Stipe and backed by bassist Mike Mills, made mention of earthquakes and hurricanes and even the Rapture and the Furies but nothing of plagues or viral pandemics. On the other hand, there was one eerily familiar reference to how there were always those in society who, despite being presented with solutions and alternatives in tough times, still chose to decline.

CHAPTER FORTY-SIX
THE ZOOM MEETING

Home sweet home is where we have to stay
Sad to say we'll see sidewalks empty
For the Clarence Cup parade

Baker fidgeted with his seat and situated himself in such a way as to compose an optimal backdrop for the Coven's first ever Zoom session. It was the last Sunday in June, fully one week since the sun had merged with the Tropic of Cancer, officially plunging the northern hemisphere into the summer season—complete with all the potential and promise that the heat of the middle months brings.

Conrad and Masaccio arrived first, their smiling faces filling two of the four boxes on Baker's laptop monitor, followed a minute later by Perreault. Top of mind for all those attending was the pandemic, of course. In fact, if conversation was a heliocentric universe, then COVID-19 would, as a topic, be the sun, with all other subjects acting as celestial bodies that revolved around it—the Toronto Mighty Pines included.

"Boy, it's such a relief to say adios to this school year," Masaccio began.

"I'll be glad not to have to go through that again," Perreault replied.

"Don't hold your breath," Conrad warned. "I wouldn't be surprised if we're not right back here come September."

"We've got two months," Perreault countered. "You don't think that'll be enough to flatten the curve?"

"I'm no expert, but history clearly shows this is something that takes a year, more likely two, before it's under control."

"I don't want to believe you," Masaccio said as he shook his head gravely. "I *can't* believe you."

"Look, if you're in a hurry to see this thing gone, you might be setting yourself up for disappointment," Conrad advised.

Baker jumped in. "If the coming school year is anything that even remotely resembles what we just lived through to close out this semester, my first instinct is to sit it out."

He jerked a thumb at Masaccio's face in the corner of his screen. "Maybe I'll go work for you, Mas, on your farm in Italy."

"Just give me the word, Baker," Masaccio replied invitingly. "I can't promise you a wage that would match a teacher's salary, but I'm sure we could arrange some lodging for you."

"Thanks, Mas," Baker laughed, "these smooth hands of mine could use some callouses—" Baker was interrupted when Angus popped up on everyone's screen, dishevelled and out of breath.

"Hey, everybody! Sorry I'm late. I was out doing a favour for the lady next door."

"You look like you've been moving furniture," Perreault observed.

"Nah, I was just out walking her dog," Angus replied. "It's pretty hot this morning."

"How kind of you, doing your neighbour a good turn like that," Masaccio said.

"No big deal. I think this pandemic has spooked her. She's convinced she's immuno-compromised."

"I'm sorry for your neighbour," Conrad said. "What's her condition?"

"How should I know? The upshot is I take her dog out twice a day for a walk and a crap."

"I can think of worse things," Perreault said. "What kind of dog is it?"

"The breed? Oh, I don't know. It's tiny—a lap dog."

"At least the cleanup is minimal with the crap part."

"Hell no! Just the opposite," Angus declared. "This thing shits like an elephant. Small dog, big dumps. I always take two poop bags with me, just in case one doesn't provide enough of a shield between my hand and the poo logs."

Masaccio wrinkled his nose. "OK, I think we've heard enough—what's the dog's name?"

"Priscilla," he answered, evoking smirks and smiles from the others. "Yeah, I know. Trust me, I make sure not to call her by name in public."

"You could just call her Pris for short," Baker suggested.

"What kind of name is Pris?"

"It's a good name. It's the name of Darryl Hannah's character in Blade Runner."

"Never seen it," Angus said flatly. "Anyway, I just call her 'Rat' because that's what she looks like. Besides, it's the year of the rat, isn't it?"

"Ohhh, poor little Priscilla," Perreault said in sympathy. "You're going to give her a complex."

"Nah, she loves me. She thinks I'm her new boyfriend. But enough about that. What'd I miss?"

"We were just discussing how this pandemic has impacted our everyday lives," Conrad explained. "Challenging times and all that, you know?"

"Bah, I've had it with these 'challenging' times," Angus spat. "I tell ya, if I had a nickel for every time someone described our present situation as 'challenging', I'd have, um... about a million nickels."

"Which may sound like a lot," Conrad said, "but by my quick math it would only amount to about half of Masaccio's yearly salary. Ain't that right, Mr. Sunshine List?"

"Without a calculator I can neither confirm nor deny your claim," Mas replied smugly.

"Hey, speaking of challenges," Angus said, "is it just me or has anyone else had trouble with masks?"

"Trouble?" Conrad asked. "How so?"

"I just can't get the hang of them. Whenever I put them on, they end up inside out or upside down, and I can't wear them for long before my ears start to ache. And that's not including the times I've dropped them on the ground or they've blown away in the wind or I've accidentally pulled the straps off—"

"I might have a solution for your aching ears," Perreault offered. "My mother has a simple formula for measuring your face that guarantees a perfect fit. I can get her to make some for you." Angus appeared to hesitate, considering the pros and cons, to which Perreault replied: "What have you got to lose? She's made a few for Baker."

"Hey, that's right," Baker confirmed, then reached off screen and returned with a neat stack of cloth masks. "Get a load of these babies." He held two up, displaying them proudly.

"Most excellent. Hey, is that a Toronto Mighty Pines design?"

"Sure is," Baker replied proudly. "Pretty sweet, huh?"

"Pretty sweet," Angus agreed. "I just hope this year's playoffs turn out as sweet for them."

"There's that word again," Masaccio said sarcastically. "It seems 'hope' is all we've got with this team."

"My hope is there are no more setbacks this year," Baker said.

"A big setback was the pause in the schedule," Angus observed. "I would have liked to see them play those last twelve games. I think they were ready to put it all together, just in time for a lengthy playoff run."

"Oh, I seriously doubt that," Conrad countered.

"Of course you would," Angus smirked, "you're Mr. One-eighty. I think the Pines were on the verge of returning to the form they showed when they were almost unbeatable. You know, when they won, like, twenty straight back in December and January."

"Easy there, Angus," Conrad warned, "your memory might be failing you. Their hottest spell was right after Kayden Koch was fired. They won fifteen of Boris Duggan's first twenty games. In fact, the Pines' longest win streak this year was six games."

"But I remember them having some good stretches this year," Perreault suggested. "Especially during December."

"You're right," Conrad agreed. "There was a window where they were easily the hottest team in the league. But if you exclude December, the year was pretty much a roller coaster ride. Shall I summarize it for you?"

"Put your seatbelts on, folks," Baker announced. "Conrad's going to take us for a ride."

"Don't worry, I'll be succinct," he assured them. "Ready? During October they were hamsters in a cage, putting in time on the exercise wheel but getting nowhere. In November the coach was fired—say no more. December was profitable; they raked in the points. January: mediocre. February was up and down, every proud moment negated by embarrassment. Finally, a solid win over Chicago was capped by the pandemic shutdown."

"Whoo, that's an impressive summation of the season," Perreault

"Thanks, but my point is it might be a stretch to suppose that the last dozen games of the year would've played out much differently than the first seventy."

"True. It seems the Pines this year would have needed ninety games—or even a hundred—to figure things out."

"Speaking of ninety, Perreault, how's your grandfather doing in this pandemic?" Masaccio inquired. "How's Rene?"

"Oh, um, well, if I can speak for my papi, I'd have to say he's good."

"Spirits high?" Mas asked.

"I'll admit he's always had a cheery disposition, an optimistic worldview. The pandemic has done nothing to change that. When he visits we mask up and practise physical distancing. Pretty simple."

"What about hand sanitizer?" Conrad inquired. "You use that much?"

"Sure. But then my dad's a GP. He's always preached the value of conscientious hand washing."

"In our home, Winnie has completely bought into hand sanitizer. Every room has at least one bottle prominently displayed. Just the other day I discovered an enormous refill jug on the floor in the linen closet. I mean, you'd almost need a hand cart to move it around; it's that big."

"Under normal circumstances that would be funny," Perreault said, "but it's just another example of how much our everyday lives have changed."

"No kidding," Masaccio said. "But what I find really sad is how we have to resort to meeting like this: a group of talking heads on our screens."

THE ZOOM MEETING

"Hey! Speaking of talking heads," Baker called, "I've been meaning to ask: how much effort did you guys actually put into prepping your rooms and your backdrops for these Zoom meetings?"

"Well, Baker, why don't you start us off?" Masaccio suggested.

"Me? I didn't do anything to the room. But I'll admit I spent some time framing the shot."

"Of course you did," Conrad quipped.

"Conrad, I must say I'm a little disappointed," Angus said critically. "I thought you'd at least have a crucifix on the wall or a picture of a religious icon, you know, a classic Mother Mary with baby Jesus."

"Apologies, folks, bare bones is all you'll get from me," Conrad replied.

"Ah, yes. Like a Dark Ages monk in his humble monastery cell," Baker said. "But how about you, Mas? I noticed you've got quite the shelf of books behind you there."

"You like? I built it myself."

"That's some outstanding craftsmanship," Perreault enthused. "But if I had to vote, Angus wins hands down. Did you notice the room he's in? It looks like something right out of Masterpiece Theatre. All it lacks is a crackling fire and a decanter of brandy."

"The brandy I've got, but I'm afraid a fireplace didn't come with the room," Angus admitted. "All the credit goes to my dad. He let me set up in his study once online learning became official."

"Perreault, yours isn't too shabby," Mas noted. "It looks like you've taken up residence in an art gallery."

"If that means you like my pictures, I'm flattered."

"If you guys like Perreault's room then you're in luck because it's time that we commence with our little ceremony, and that means we get to watch her perform the song for this session."

"Cool. I was wondering if there was a Coven song for us today."

"Yessir, Baker and I prepared a new one."

"So . . . who did you borrow from this time, Baker?"

"I 'borrowed' from Sylvan Esso. I turned 'PARAD (w/m) E' into something I call 'A COVID Parade.'"

"And it's about the Pines, as usual?"

"Sort of. Let's just say it reflects our challenging times—sorry, Angus, here's another nickel for you. It deals with what winning the Cup might look like during a pandemic. Specifically, how it would impact a Clarence Cup parade. I should admit it was convenient to be able to use the Raptors' championship parade as a standard for how it might look."

"Sounds good. Let's hear it."

"OK. I emailed everybody the words."

"Look at you, Mr. Technology," Conrad raved. "A few months ago you couldn't hit 'send,' and now you're emailing people and hosting a Zoom meeting and collaborating with Perreault to pull off a live musical performance."

"Yeah, well, this freakin' pandemic has dragged me kicking and screaming into the world of virtual classrooms and remote learning and stuff. It was pretty painful, believe me."

A timeout on the floor gave everyone a chance to retrieve their song lyrics and for Baker and Perreault to engage in other assorted preparatory tasks.

"It looks like we're set here," Baker informed the others. "Are we going to say a prayer?"

"Absolutely. Allow me," Conrad offered.

Everyone fell into the routine of bowing their heads while Conrad said some words, followed by Perreault, who recited her little prayer.

"You know, I almost started singing the 'Song to Saint Cecilia,'" Perreault admitted. "I guess she'll just have to wait until Bakers' Coven physically gathers again in person."

"I'm sure she'll understand," Conrad assured.

"Alright then, gentlemen," Baker said, "if there's nothing more, I give you Perreault Thoreau singing 'A COVID Parade.'"

A karaoke version of the song began, with some funky electro-pop beats serving as an introduction before Perreault came in, singing Baker's words.

Pretty city wonders why
Day by day they're stuck inside
Mhm, eh eh, mhm
Pity, pity, bright sunshine
Say goodbye to summertime
Mhm, eh eh, mhm

Home sweet home is where we have to stay
Sad to say we'll see sidewalks empty
At the Clarence Cup parade
I go left, someone's there
I go right, back up a step
I go left, don't get too close
I go right, six feet of space
COVID, COVID, COVID, COVID
Dominates the news all day

THE ZOOM MEETING

P-A-R-A-D (virtual) E
Yeah there's no point left in asking when we'll finally be free
How dare you risk infecting my family
P-A-R-A-D (virtual) E

Disinfect and sanitize
Wash your hands on every side
Mhm, eh eh, mhm
Isolation's such a crime
Wash my hands on every side
Mhm, eh eh, mhm

How we long to see a playoff game
Plan to see the sidewalks all empty
For the Clarence Cup parade
I go left, someone's there
I go right, back up a step
I go left, six feet now
I go right, don't get too near
COVID, COVID, COVID, COVID
Is all the news I ever hear

P-A-R-A-D (virtual) E
Yeah, there's no point left in asking when we'll finally be free
How dare you risk infecting my friends and me
P-A-R-A-D virtually
P-A-R-A-D virtually
Yeah, don't even bother asking when we'll finally be free
How dare you risk infecting my family
P-A-R-A-D virtually

As the synth beats faded out and the song came to a close, Perreault's four bandmates expressed their appreciation and voiced their accolades. In the midst of the applause and cheers, some additional voices could be heard in the audience.

"I think I hear some females in the virtual crowd out there," Perreault said.

"Hi Perreault. It's me, Sal Clemente—and Lily and Hazel. Hope you don't mind that we eavesdropped on your performance. It sounded great!"

The heads of the twins squeezed into the screen on either side of Masaccio and Sal. "Hi there!" Lily and Hazel each gave a quick wave and then disappeared from the screen, but their voices could still be heard in perfect harmony, singing the refrain from Sylvan Esso's original version of the song. "P-A-R-A-D-(w/m)-E—"

"Sorry for interrupting," Sal said. "I just wanted to toss a small bouquet out to you, Perreault. That was well done. But I'll let you folks get back to your meeting."

"Thanks for the compliment, Sal. And you're not interrupting. I think we were done here anyway. Baker? That's it, isn't it?"

"Yeah, I've got nothing more," Baker confirmed. "It's actually a good thing you joined us, Sal. Now we can all say goodbye and bon voyage."

"That's right!" Perreault agreed. "You must be excited."

"Of course, I'm thrilled with the prospect. It will be an exciting change in our lives," Sal admitted. "But I'm also saying goodbye to my Canadian home. It's bittersweet." Just then a clamour could be heard emanating from somewhere off screen. The twins called to their mother from another room.

"Oops, I should get back to the kitchen," Sal said. "The girls and I are baking." She blew kisses and formed a heart with her hands. "Take care, everyone. Mas and I will be sure to 'Zoom' in on you before the summer is out. Go, Pines, go! Love you. Bye, bye. Ciao, bello!" She took her leave from the meeting amid a bevy of heartfelt "Goodbyes," "Ciaos," and "Bon Voyages."

"Listen, gang, I should get going too," Masaccio said, reluctantly. But don't worry, I won't leave for Tuscany without saying goodbye."

"You better not," Perreault warned. "Otherwise, I'll have to come over there and put you in a headlock."

"I don't know, that doesn't sound so bad," Mas laughed. "But honestly, I feel horrible abandoning the Coven." Looking reflective, he sighed heavily. "Life goes on, however. New adventures await across the pond."

"It's too bad you won't be around to experience the glory of a Pines' Cup win," Angus said.

"The Toronto Mighty Pines will be forever in my heart, if not foremost in my mind," Mas declared. "Dis aliter visum, eh Baker? Man plans and God laughs, and we muddle through." He paused for a moment of reflection then roused himself to sign off. "But I'd better get going. You folks take care. I'll keep in touch." And Mas departed, amid a chorus of "Goodbyes" and "Arrivedercis."

"Boy, it sounds like Mas is in for a busy summer," Angus said.

"It sure does," Perreault agreed. "What about you? Any big plans?"

"Nothing. I'm taking it a week at a time. The Nellas invited me over on the weekend for a swim. Mary and I will probably just hang out and relax by the pool."

"How is Mary doing these days?" Baker asked.

"That girl is amazing. She picks things up so fast. You should see her on the drums these days."

"Fantastic. Tell her we said hi."

THE ZOOM MEETING

"Will do. But right now I'm gonna go rustle up some eggs, I'm starving. It was great catching up—you too, Conrad."

With the departure of Angus, only Conrad and Perreault still remained on Baker's screen.

"And what's Conrad up to today? Any plans?"

"As a matter of fact, Winnie and I are going to do some exploring in the Niagara wine region."

"That sounds lovely. Can I come?"

"Sure. You can be our designated driver."

"Oh . . . in that case, I'll pass."

"Atta girl. You'd just get bored hanging out with us two geezers anyway."

When Conrad signed off, Baker and Perreault stayed on the line for another forty-five minutes, catching up, reluctant to leave each other's company.

"I should commend you on running a first-rate Zoom meeting," Perreault said. "That went quite well."

"Thanks, I appreciate it." He laughed at a thought. "Next thing you know, I'll be writing instruction manuals on the subject."

"Speaking of instruction manuals, I've been going through Dorcas's *Coven Craft for Wannabe Witches*. You know, our coven ceremonies may need more oomph. It might be time for us to consider engaging in something more serious—something that has been practiced by believers across the millennia."

Baker's expression hinted at an acknowledgement, a grudging acceptance, that their coven activities would inevitably lead them to consider this next option.

"So, you're talking about—sacrifices?"

"What? No, silly—dancing."

"Riiight . . . The power of dance."

"Exactly. You know, there's actually a lot of truth to the old joke: Why do some religious communities forbid couples from having sex standing up?"

"Because it leads to dancing?"

"Hey, it's not called the dance of life for nothing. But why don't we get together in person to discuss it at greater length?"

"Great idea. Are you coming over this evening?"

"It'll have to be tomorrow. We're expecting Rene for dinner tonight."

"Tomorrow it is," Baker confirmed. "And don't forget to bring that grimoire."

"Grimoire?"

"Yeah, the book Dorcas wrote."

"Actually, if I may correct you, what Dorcas wrote is more of a condensed manual for beginners. A grimoire contains spells, recipes, and observations that have been handed down across the generations."

"Listen to you," Baker said, thoroughly impressed. "Anything else?"

"Yes. A grimoire looks different—um, remember in *Raiders of the Lost Ark,* an early scene shows Indy with this big book with buckles that he opens to reveal a picture of the Ark of the Covenant? Kind of like that."

Baker's face on her computer screen betrayed awe.

"You do have a gift for movie minutiae. And on the topic of gifts, I wanted to thank you for the masks. Your mother made some cool ones, and they really are comfortable. I didn't experience that annoying ache around the ears."

"There you go; my mom's formula works."

"And they smell so fresh and fragrant," Baker said. He'd grown quite familiar with the fragrance as it was something Perreault carried around with her regularly. He wasn't about to admit it aloud, but that was another reason he liked Mrs. Thoreau's masks. Just putting one on brought back pleasant reminders of her daughter.

"Again, just another of my mother's habits," Perreault explained. "She keeps a small baggie of homemade potpourri in all the clothes drawers, especially the underwear and sock drawers. That will fade when they're washed."

"That's too bad," Baker said, then he held up another item. "What's this, though?"

"That's a sleep mask—for covering your eyes. You mentioned how you can never sleep in because the morning light streams into your bedroom. The mask should help. Try it tonight."

"OK, I'll give it a try. But then you better not call me in the morning—at least not before ten."

"Deal."

* * * * *

That night Baker tucked himself in and found he couldn't get Perreault out of his mind—the forced absence was taking its toll. Unable to stop himself, he got up and retrieved one of Mrs. Thoreau's COVID masks from his drawer. He felt silly putting it on but ultimately convinced himself it was within the bounds of acceptable behaviour. A sudden chill from the A/C caused him to shiver, so he wasted no time getting back in bed and nestling under the covers. He made some minor adjustments to his face mask, then reached over and clicked off his bedside lamp and slid the sleep mask down over his eyes. His world became one of darkness and silence and the fragrance of apples and cinnamon. He inhaled slowly but deeply, rehashing the day's events in his mind. A couple of full-body twitches later, he had entered the realm of sleep and dreams.

CHAPTER FORTY-SEVEN

MASKS AND METAPHORS

Scene: Xander Galahad, Kyle Bulac, and Boris Duggan have agreed to discreetly meet in an indistinct office space at an undisclosed location. They are seated around a large wooden table, taking appropriate precautions and observing the necessary physical distancing rules. Since it is still early times in the pandemic, and the efficacy of wearing face masks to prevent transmission of COVID-19 is as yet unclear, it is understandable that neither member of the Pines' triumvirate is thus protected. Dominating the scene, however, is a ridiculously oversized bottle of hand sanitizer, placed smack in the centre of the table. Our three protagonists settle themselves at one end of said table.

Galahad: Hey, guys. Thanks for agreeing to meet like this. It sure is great to be able to talk face to face.

Bulac: *(Having taken a large dollop of sanitizer, he is rubbing his hands vigorously.)* It's refreshing to get out of the house and come to work. *(He opens a laptop that is sitting on the table and logs in.)*

Duggan: Isn't this crazy? Who could have predicted how quickly events can transpire to change the landscape of our day-to-day lives.

Bulac: *(takes a moment to regard his two colleagues more closely.)* So, what are we doing here today? What's this meeting about, boss?

Galahad: Simple. I thought it'd be good to see you two in person regarding how the season went—and in particular, how it ended. Duggy, let's start with you.

Duggan: *(laughs sarcastically.)* I felt cheated. I would have preferred playing out the last twelve games.

Bulac: I'll bet there's not a coach in the league who wouldn't say the same thing—the ones with playoff aspirations, anyway.

When Cheers Are Not Enough

Duggan: That's what was so frustrating. It would have allowed us to finish third and earn our way into the playoffs, you know? In honourable fashion.

Galahad: All told, I'd say our season was trending in the right direction when the league shut down.

Duggan: Yeah, I suppose.

Galahad: No, really. We were looking good. The numbers will bear me out. Kyle, what was our record just before Duggy took over last November?

Bulac: *(refers to the screen on his laptop and taps a few keys.)* It was bad. We were exactly forty games under .500.

(Duggan double takes and stares at Bulac, his eyebrows raised.)

Galahad: See that, Duggy? When you stepped in as head coach, we were forty games under .500. By the end of the season, you took the team to new heights, finishing... Kyle?

Bulac: *(refers to the screen again.)* 120 games over .500.

(Duggan, who has been growing impatient with this charade, jerks his head to scowl at Bulac, but Galahad just continues, ecstatic over the numbers that Bulac is quoting.)

Galahad: You hear that? 120 games over .500! Now, just imagine if you'd had the team from the start of the season.

Duggan: You can spin the numbers any way you want. It's in the past. Now we need to prepare for the playoffs—whatever those will look like.

Bualc: Humph. Let's hope there even *is* a Clarence Cup playoffs this year.

(Galahad senses the mood in the room dropping, so he tries to change the subject.)

Galahad: What about you, Kyle? How've things been?

Duggan: Yeah, Kyle. Have you had any more spirit signs or visitations?

Bulac: Now that you mention it, yes, I have had a recent episode. One afternoon a couple days ago, I was in the kitchen pouring myself a drink. My dog Pris was looking at me like she was gonna explode. So, I grabbed some poop bags and latex gloves—I really hate dealing with dog poo, you know—and out we went for a short walk. We didn't get far before Pris stopped to do her business. I got a poop bag out and cleaned up the droppings—I only gagged once, by the way. Then I looked down at Pris, and, to my shock and awe, my Boston terrier was no longer a Boston terrier. Goddamn if she hadn't turned into a rat!

Galahad: Was it well behaved? Like, did it heel nicely, or was it pulling and tugging?

Duggan: *(interjects.)* Pulling and tugging? Jesus, Gally. What difference does it make?

Galahad: I was just curious, is all. *(Turns back to Bulac.)* So—?

Bulac: Oh, um, I guess it was pulling a bit. It was sort of leading me forward, through a dirty alleyway, filled with overturned garbage cans and broken refuse bags. The air was damp and thick, and there was this foul stench. It was all pretty disgusting. I mean, I had to put a bandana over my mouth and nose, and, luckily, I had some latex gloves. No sooner did the rat and I make it through the alleyway, than it transformed into this huge, wrinkly circus elephant.

(Galahad and Duggan stare at Bulac, their mouths hanging open. Galahad recovers first.)

Galahad: Let me get this straight. You're telling us there was an elephant on the end of your leash?

Bulac: Exactly.

Duggan: What happened then?

Bulac: Well, not long after, the elephant sort of squatted and did this *huge* dump on the sidewalk. There's not a poop bag on Earth big enough for what that elephant produced. And then it turned back into Pris, my Boston terrier. Then everything sort of ended there. I found myself on my front porch with the dog, and the walk was over. I suppose it all must mean something. I just can't put a finger on what it could be.

Galahad: It seems pretty obvious to me.

Bulac: Tell me then. I'm all ears.

(Galahad slides back his chair, gets up, and then walks to the far end of the table and faces his colleagues, like a detective preparing for the moment of the big reveal—although he has to stand on his toes to see past the bottle of hand sanitizer.)

Galahad: To you it is cloaked in fog, but to me, it's like chalk dust revealing an incriminating fingerprint. The clues in your story point to one thing—Shit!

Bulac: What's wrong?

Galahad: Huh? Nothing's wrong. Why would something be wrong?

Bulac: You said "shit." Why'd you say "shit?"

Galahad: Because that's the answer. The point of the events in your story lead to "Shit."

Bulac: Seriously? "Shit" is the lesson I should take away from that experience?

Galahad: Isn't it obvious? You just gotta get through the shit in life! Ain't that right, Duggy?

Duggan: I dunno, Gally. I think there's more to it than that. *(Rising from his seat, he walks to the far end of the table and, standing on his tiptoes, begins to expound on his interpretation of the events.)* Let's begin with Priscilla. A Boston terrier implores you, Kyle Bulac, GM of the Toronto Mighty Pines, to take her out, so she can relieve herself. Then you are obliged to clean up the mess. Doesn't that tell you anything?

Bulac: I'm not sure, but continue.

Duggan: Then a rat takes you through an alley of filth. Consider the rat for a moment. The rat is the Chinese symbol for the year 2020, and rats carried the black plague. The way I see it, the rat, representing the year 2020 as well as the coronavirus, leads you through an environment that forces you to put on personal protective equipment in order to safely get through it.

Bulac: Yeah, I can see it. The episode with the rat is a metaphor for this crazy year we're experiencing. That's good, Boris, really good. But what about the elephant?

Duggan: The point of the elephant is not so much the fact that it produces the largest turds on Earth *(as he says this he looks sideways at Galahad)* but that elephants never forget. Maybe it's telling us to remember and heed the lessons of the past, especially when it comes to the history of the Toronto Mighty Pines. I think the message is not to underestimate the power of our Pines heritage, especially when it comes to winning.

(Galahad, who was looking dubious throughout Duggan's speech, doesn't get the chance to offer up his opinion as all three men are startled into silence by a knock at the door.)

Galahad: Kyle, you expecting anyone?

Bulac: No, not me.

Galahad: Well, answer it and get rid of 'em . . . fast.

MASKS AND METAPHORS

Bulac: *(approaches the door and opens it a crack.)* Yes? Can I help you?

(Galahad and Duggan can only detect a mumbled response from the visitor in the hallway, which seems to come in the form of a question because it prompts Bulac to look back at his two colleagues in the room before replying.)

Bulac: Well, no ... actually.

(Bulac's answer is followed by more mumbling.)

Bulac: Really? Uh ... OK. Um, thanks.

(Galahad and Duggan watch as Bulac accepts a small silver platter that holds what looks like some neatly folded, colourful fabric. Before closing the door, Bulac turns back to the visitor.)

Bulac: Oh, hey—be sure to thank Commissioner Stetson for me.

(There is another mumbled response before the visitor retreats down the hallway. Bulac watches him for a moment, then closes the door and returns to the desk with the platter.)

Galahad: What was all that about?

Bulac: Apparently, the league offices are taking it upon themselves to give us reminders to stay safe when we meet in person. Hence, the delivery of three protective face masks—on a silver platter, no less. *(He places the silver platter on the table for all to see.)*

Duggan: Oh, my, look how fancy—

Bulac: Yeah, and it appears that each mask is different. *(He takes the masks and arranges them on the table.)* Here, Sandy, pick one out for yourself.

Galahad: OK, but right now I'm focused more on that platter. *(He reaches across the table to pick it up, admiring its craftsmanship.)* I dare say this thing was fashioned out of flattened Clarence Cup rings. I held the Cup three times in my career, I should know. But this metal is clean. It's still fresh and not engraved with any names. *(He examines it more closely.)* Except for one name I see here. *(He points out the name as he hands the platter to Bulac.)*

Bulac: Geez, that's my name! What the—?

Duggan: Let me see.

(Bulac passes the tray to Duggan and looks over to Galahad for an explanation.)

When Cheers Are Not Enough

Duggan: *(inspects the engraving.)* It's your name, alright. But they misspelled it or something.

Galahad: *(takes the platter back from Duggan.)* No, it's spelled properly, but the letters are printed backwards. Wait... this is the wrong side. It's the embossed side that would normally be on the inside of the Cup and hidden from view. *(He turns the platter over and inspects the underside of the etched name, then reads it aloud.)* CALUB...ELYK. *(He looks up at the others.)* Anybody ever heard of Calub Elyk?

Bulac: I'll do some searches and see what comes up. *(Taking back the platter from Galahad, he looks at the etched name from both sides of the metal plating.)* Funny how it's my name spelled backwards, though.

Galahad: Hey, isn't there a word for that?

Bulac: Whatever it's called, we should probably get these masks on before there's another knock at the door. Here, pick one out for yourself.

Galahad: *(looks distastefully at the selection of masks.)* How did they send us three PHL masks and not manage to get a single one in our colours?

Duggan: Who delivered these, anyway, Kyle? Did you recognize him?

Bulac: I can't be certain because he kept turning away. But it was clear that he'd been sent by Commissioner Stetson who wanted to know if we were wearing masks during our meeting here.

Galahad: I must admit you dealt with him in pretty slick fashion. You deserve a prize or something. I'd give you the silver platter, but I— *(He turns to the platter on the table but stops when he sees that it has been replaced by another object—a large book.)* Hey, where'd the tray go? *(He pulls the chair aside, then bends down to look under the table.)* What the—?

Duggan: Call me crazy, but I'd say your silver platter has been replaced by—or transformed into—some sort of book or manual.

(The three of them converge on the book. It is large, thick and heavy, more of a tome than a manual.)

Bulac: *(leans in close over the book to read the title.)* Coven Craft for Wannabe Witches. *(He looks up in total incomprehension.)* Anybody want to explain this?

Galahad: *(still looking at the cover of the book and ignoring the question.)* There's more. Looks like some fine print under the title. What's it say?

Duggan: *(squints as he tries to make it out.)* "In case of emergency, turn to page 1,962."

(Duggan notices a silk ribbon protruding from the top of the book. He moves to open the manual to its marked page, then feels a firm grip on his arm. It's Galahad.)

Galahad: Wait! We'd better not open it.

Duggan: Why not? You know something we don't?

Galahad: No, but the idea of witches and covens gives me the creeps.

Duggan: You serious? Don't you want to see what's inside? I have to believe this book is here for a reason. Maybe it's an answer to our problems in the playoffs.

Galahad: Yes, but the fine print on the cover says, "In case of emergency." I don't think our present playoff problems qualify as an emergency.

Bulac: I know some people who would beg to differ.

(Nothing more is said by either man. Duggan is positioned in front of the book with Galahad close at one shoulder and Bulac at the other, any concerns over physical distancing long since forgotten. Fully aware that the next move is his to make, the coach of the Toronto Mighty Pines stares at the cover, carefully considering his options. The smell and feel of the aged leather jacket, the gilt-edged onion skin pages, the title embossed in gold, all combine to serve as a seduction for Duggan. A moment passes, then another. Somewhere in the room a clock is ticking.)

Duggan: Ah, what the hell. *(He opens the book.)*

(The contents of page 1,962 are never revealed because, without warning, the lights go out. The office is plunged into darkness, as if they've all dropped the gloves against tough guy Wayne Brody and been knocked senseless with a vicious haymaker flush to the jaw. The three men crumple to the floor, reaching for their masks, straining to breathe, clawing at the offending pieces of fabric in the blackened room with no hope of rescue—)

Unable to see, unable to breathe, unable to cry out, Baker found himself struggling in the darkness. Feeling like he'd been blindfolded, gagged, and tossed in a sack, he panicked, thrashing violently and ripping the sleep mask, face mask, and heavy comforter off himself. He sat up and was abruptly thrust into wakefulness, the cool night air bringing blessed relief as it bathed his sweaty face and entered his lungs. His gasping subsided into steady panting until, along with his heart rate, it slowed down to the point where he could think clearly.

"It was just another nightmare, you idiot," he thought. Straightening the covers and fluffing the pillow, he settled back into bed in the hopes of falling asleep. But try as he might, the awful vision of Pines management struggling in vain against, and ultimately being overcome by, some nefarious enemy's master plan was not soon forgotten. Along with that, distinct voices from the nightmare still echoed in his head, preventing any semblance of restful slumber. The voices included one that spoke about Toronto's playoff woes as not being an emergency just yet, countered by another that represented all those who begged to differ, and last but certainly not least was the voice ridiculously insisting that any lessons to be learned for the Toronto Mighty Pines could be found in nothing other than a big pile of shit.

CHAPTER FORTY-EIGHT
A NATION OF CHARLIE BROWNS

The dream had rattled Baker because it was all too weird—and all too real. Thankfully, most of it had faded from memory. Try as he might to convince himself—and others—that the pandemic was having no tangible effect on him, there were moments, particularly when he was alone in the house, feeling isolated, and even a little abandoned, when Baker's mood turned grey. He attributed it to the combination of a crappy end to the school year, a crappy end to the PHL season, and no end in sight to the crappy pandemic.

Strange, then, that rather than find solace in the company of his friends and bandmates in Bakers' Coven, he opted to back away from engaging in any further coven activity. He had decided to mothball the whole enterprise and allow the Coven to quietly fade into the sunset—for this season anyway. It was a tough call to make, and he arrived at it mentally bruised and bloodied. Ultimately, his decision came down to the fact that the PHL was heading into its most critical and stress-filled time of the year: the Clarence Cup playoffs. That was the clincher, and Baker had his nighttime vision to thank for it.

The playoffs were a different animal altogether, and not something to be trifled with. The heightened sense of urgency during the PHL's "second season" was in sharp contrast to the regular season, where a head coach had the luxury of eighty-two games to experiment with the team roster in order to discover what worked and what didn't. Likewise, Baker felt secure in testing the waters of magic during the regular season. It allowed him to try different approaches to song spells and tuneful incantations, safe in the knowledge that he could afford a misstep or two along the way. A playoff series was another matter entirely and he was not about to fiddle with something as sacrosanct as that, especially on behalf of a team as hard up for a series win as the Pines.

It was for these reasons that Baker chose to revert to his old self as a run-of-the-mill fan, one who followed the game on TV and did nothing more than watch and hope and pray, from opening puck drop to final horn. But while some fans regarded the playoffs as a time to fly car flags and wave foam fingers (donning team jerseys and caps went without saying), for Baker it was enough to engage in small personal rituals, like sitting in a designated spot on the couch for luck, or taking his eyes off the screen only during intermissions to fetch himself a beer or a snack, but that would be the extent of it—at least until the Pines got past the first round.

The press release issued by the PHL in the middle of July revealed details of the plan that would determine a Clarence Cup winner for the 2019–2020 season. It consisted of an altered and expanded playoff format that involved a total of twenty-four teams, twelve from each conference. The Western Conference qualifiers would play at a hub site in Edmonton while the Eastern Conference teams would play their games in Toronto at Nova Tank Arena. Once things were whittled down to four surviving teams, everything would shift over to Edmonton for the conference finals and the Clarence Cup final. All games would commence on the weekend of August 1.

While there were many additional details to consider regarding hubs and bubbles and health protocols, for members of Coney Nation, the only thing that mattered was that Toronto would be going up against the Cleveland Cuyahogas in their best-of-five qualifying round at Nova Tank Arena. The Toronto-Cleveland series was an eighth-place versus a ninth-place matchup involving two teams whose regular season records were almost identical. And thanks to the four-month pause leading up to July's "restart" training camp, both Toronto and Cleveland would benefit by having their full complement of players healthy and ready to go. Most prognosticators gave the Pines a slight edge and predicted them to win in five.

* * * * *

Sunday, August 2 – Sunday, August 9

One hundred and forty-four days had passed between Toronto's last game prior to the pandemic pause on March 10 and their first game of the Clarence Cup playoffs on August 2. (It should be remembered that the term "playoffs" was being loosely applied in this case, since this best-of-five series was not, in fact, a true playoff round. The PHL was calling it a "play-*in*" round. The first round of the Clarence Cup playoffs proper would commence upon the completion of this preliminary round.)

One question on everyone's mind was what playoff games would feel like as the teams prepared to go toe-to-toe in empty arenas with the crowd noise being artificially piped in. Ultimately, it was the action on the ice that would carry the day. And so, following the singing of the national anthems—the vocalist did the honours in remote fashion from the living room of her home—and with 19,267 empty seats surrounding them, the Cuyahogas and the Mighty Pines lined up for the opening faceoff.

The first period saw both teams resembling defensive-minded boxers in the early rounds of a fight, doing a lot of bobbing and weaving at the expense of actually throwing punches. It wasn't until early in the second period that the Cuyahogas landed the first blow and scored to go up 1-0. The score remained unchanged until late in the third period when Cleveland added an empty-net goal to make the final 2-0. Just like that, Toronto found itself down a game in a short series, needing to win three of the next four games, and all the supposed advantages the pandemic pause might have offered appeared not to matter a whit.

Two days later the Mighty Pines found their footing, along with enough scoring punch to come away with a 3-1 win to tie the series at a game apiece. Coney Nation could breathe easier—for now.

* * * * *

Not much needs to be said about game three other than that Toronto coughed up a two-goal lead in painful fashion late in the third period and ultimately lost in the early minutes of overtime, gifting the Cuyahogas a 4-3 win. The stunned Mighty Pines—suddenly on the brink of elimination—would have to shake off the tough loss and regroup quickly, because the playoff schedule had the teams playing games three and four on back-to-back nights. The boys in green and white would get the chance to exact their revenge in less than twenty-four hours. Failing that, the season would be over.

Which was precisely how game four played out—as the end to the Mighty Pines' season—at least for the first fifty-six minutes. Cleveland was enjoying a 3-0 lead late in the third period, having dominated Toronto in every way to that point, when, with just over four minutes remaining and with nothing but pride left to play for, the Pines emptied the net for the extra attacker. For despondent Toronto fans, it appeared once again to be a case of too little, too late.

And then the impossible happened—impossible, incredible, inconceivable. Hollywood could not have scripted it any better. (After all, how much disbelief could a screenwriter expect one fan base to suspend?) Hockey history will show that Toronto scored three goals with just over four minutes to play to tie the game. Each of the goals was scored with Eddie Sanderson on the bench and the net empty for an extra attacker. Under normal circumstances, i.e., no pandemic, the roar of the hometown crowd would have been beyond deafening, but owing to the empty arena, when the third and tying goal hit the back of the Cuyahoga's net, the six Pines on the ice could be heard to emit a collective "Yeah!" sounding much like a group of excited schoolboys responding to news that afternoon classes had been cancelled. All the while the headmaster himself,

When Cheers Are Not Enough

Xander Galahad, was watching from the executive box high above, eyes bright and unbelieving, revealing what his PPE face mask concealed: a smile that could light up the city. His team had come all the way back to tie the game with seconds to spare.

Of course, overtime still loomed, and the win was not assured, but the Pines' miraculous comeback had given them a fighter's chance to extend the series. Many wondered how the respective teams would respond in the first minutes of overtime following the crazy finish to the third period. Of one thing we could be sure: the referees would pocket their whistles for all but the most egregious infraction.

As it happened, it took fifteen minutes of overtime before just such an infraction occurred. When defenseman Ben Bellamy was unceremoniously cross-checked into the boards by an over-zealous Cleveland forechecker, the Pines found themselves on the power play. Eighteen seconds later, Mason Andrews one-timed a pass from Ricky Randall into the back of the net, capping off a most improbable comeback win to ensure that there would be a game five. The golf clubs could remain in storage for another day.

On the heels of a two day roller coaster ride that rivalled anything on offer at Canada's Wonderland, it was understandable if members of Coney Nation were finally ready to buy the notion that this collection of Mighty Pines was destined for something special. Surely a comeback of this magnitude was a harbinger of greater things to come. Although few dared to speak it aloud, the big question was difficult to ignore: was this a team of destiny that could really and truly put an end to the city's Cup drought?

* * * * *

A warning to members of Coney Nation who suffer from triskaidekaphobia, the following bit of numeric trivia may require reader discretion: keeping in mind that the number thirteen has historically been tied to malevolent forces and inauspicious events, perhaps it was fitting that precisely 313 days since the start of this most remarkable 2019–2020 PHL season, the Toronto Mighty Pines meekly and ignominiously bowed out of it, losing 4-0 to the Cleveland Cuyahogas in game five and failing to advance beyond the qualifying round of the playoffs. It was the fulfillment of all Pines fan's worst fears. Any dreams of getting to a Clarence Cup final and snapping the fifty-seven-year drought were dashed with the loss.

Post-playoff angst, which was typically an April phenomenon in the GTA, had struck yet again, except this time it was the middle of August. In falling for another false promise, Toronto fans found themselves wearing labels like "dupes," "suckers," and "chumps." Coney Nation? It might be more fitting to refer to this fan base as "Peanuts Nation," as in Charlie Brown and the Peanuts gang.

The reference makes perfect sense when we are reminded that a well-known tradition in the lore of the popular comic strip had Lucy teeing up a football for Charlie

Brown to kick, and each and every time pulling it away at the last moment. Again and again, poor old gullible Charlie Brown approached the ball, swung his leg through, and tumbled, helmet over cleats, in humiliating fashion. It left us wondering how Lucy got away with it, year after year, but the answer was simple: Charlie Brown was completely driven by his need to believe that this was the time he would finally succeed. He was willfully blind to the reality that Lucy would never let him have the satisfaction of kicking that ball.

In this fashion, Coney Nation was a membership of Charlie Browns, a fan club of like-minded suckers who, as the years of defeat piled up, wanted so badly for their team to win that the slightest hint of success had them sprinting toward that ball, only to end up on their backsides. Perhaps Lucy's baby brother Linus summed it up best when, on another occasion but in a similar circumstance, he regarded his friend and declared: "Of all the Charlie Browns in the world, you're the Charlie Browniest."

Linus could just as easily have been describing the whole of Coney Nation.

Baker wept, then slept.

The morning after the game five loss, he awoke feeling remarkably refreshed, and, despite the lingering taste of defeat in his mouth and a severe case of bed head, his eyes were clear. Having forgotten that he'd pre-set the coffee maker, he was pleasantly surprised when the aroma of freshly perked dark roast greeted him as he made his way to the kitchen. Pouring himself a large mug, Baker took it outside to enjoy on the deck. Marvelling at how good he felt physically, it wasn't until he drained his cup that he realized he couldn't remember dreaming last night. It was as if the Pines being eliminated effectively released him from the burden of deciphering yet another nighttime vision. He revelled in a newfound sense of freedom that would not be polluted by the smog of another playoff disappointment—something that annually manifested itself as a state of melancholy, lasting for about twenty-four hours.

It was then that he would relive the momentous occasion six years earlier when he had been seized by some compulsion to commit to this team as a fan. In viewing that moment through an objective lens, he knew it originated with the hiring of Xander Galahad as team president, a move which ultimately led to acquiring the services of Kayden Koch and Kyle Bulac. It appeared that the Pines had finally turned a corner that would return the franchise to relevancy.

The funny thing was, Baker could be prone to flights of fancy, causing him to remember that moment six years ago in more dramatic fashion, as though some higher power were to blame for his transformation into a hardcore Pines fan. He envisioned himself standing at a crossroads, windswept and desolate, and he was naked as a newborn—cold, shivering, and alone. He was approached by a stranger with a helpful, friendly demeanour who happened to be attired in the most glorious of Pines jerseys. They stood face to face until the stranger, in one sweeping motion, raised both arms and pulled the jersey overhead. When his arms came back down, it was Baker who found himself bedecked in the green and white. It was that quick and easy, a ceremonial sweater transfer that served as a kind of knighthood or initiation into a brotherhood. Baker consummated the pact when he was handed a handsomely feathered quill pen, dipped it into a well of his own blood, and signed the contract that bound him to the team.

To this day he puzzled at the identity of the stranger at the crossroads, and always settled on the presumption that it was a person of no consequence. But then once a year, in the hours after the Pines' final loss, he would recognize that face as belonging to none other than the devil himself.

Standing on his deck now, coffee in hand, the August morning sun already heating up the day, Baker reflected on his present status as a member of Coney Nation. When he had decided to step back and separate himself a bit from the team earlier that month, it might have been in the effort to pre-emptively avoid having to face the devil yet again. His summertime decision, however, had ultimately sowed the seeds of guilt, and now he saw himself as something of a prodigal son. He had left the family that was Coney Nation and gone away to a foreign land—not so much to live a life of wasteful extravagance, in the manner of the Bible story, but rather to find something that was lacking in his life as a fan of the Toronto Mighty Pines. Dedicating his heart and soul to the team was not reaping the desired benefits—not on his timeline anyway. Then again, his conscience told him this wasn't the time for demanding instant gratification. (Winning championships was hard, after all, and the last time he checked, the PHL still held to the tradition that only one team's name would be added to the Clarence Cup each year.)

No, this was the time for stoicism. He knew that being a true and loyal supporter of a team, regardless of the sport, was more often than not a marginal investment where the payoff was never assured. (Unfortunately, lifelong Pines fans had been waiting over a half century to see a payoff of any kind.) Therefore, for a fan like him to survive and maintain a healthy balance of passion and perspective, it was essential that he view the journey as being greater than the destination.

As it happened, that year's journey had taken Baker along a route he'd never travelled before. It had even led him into the teeth of a few storms, yet he'd managed to limp into port intact and come away with some valuable lessons. He resolved that the experience would not deter him from weighing anchor yet again and setting off into more uncharted waters, to forge ahead into a new season, with a clean slate, a tabula rasa.

Thus resolved, he went back inside for a second cup of coffee and found that he couldn't shake the sense that there was something else on the agenda for that day, something beyond the grasp of his mental recall. Absentmindedly, he opened a magazine and was flipping through the pages when it hit him: the PHL draft lottery! The team order of selection would be revealed that day, and Pines fans actually had a rooting interest in it because, through a quirk of this year's altered playoff format, each of the eight teams eliminated in the qualifying round were automatically entered into the draft lottery. The previous night's loss, therefore, meant that the Toronto Mighty Pines would be included as one of the eight.

It made Baker think of how fate never ceased to deal some crazy cards in life. Could it be that getting ousted from the play-in round was all a part of the master plan? It was enough to make one begin fantasizing about how exciting the next season might be with this year's number one pick in a Mighty Pines uniform. He began counting down the minutes to the announcement.

* * * * *

"And the first selection in the 2020 PHL draft belongs to ... the New York Empires."

Commissioner Stetson's announcement elicited a wry smile from Baker—of course, New York. He thought back to the 1985 NBA draft and how conspiracy theorists held that a "frozen envelope" allowed the New York Knicks to nab the much-coveted Patrick Ewing with the first overall pick. Was it possible that the Empires had benefited in a similar fashion, except this time with the help of a "loaded" ping-pong ball?

Baker swore at the TV before turning it off, paraphrasing Masai Ujiri: "Fuck New York." But then he stopped to reconsider his sentiment. Deep down he knew this year's Pines failure did not come without its irony, its painful lessons. And so, at the same time that he cursed New York (and for that matter, Boston, Montreal, Pittsburgh, Washington, and all the rest), something within him said, *God bless them. Bless them for trying and caring and competing, because their efforts will make Toronto's winning the Clarence Cup—whenever that happens—all the sweeter.* So, crude though it was, "Fuck 'em ... and God bless 'em too!"

Then he caught himself thinking something so infantile his cheeks blossomed crimson. The words *wait till next year!* had scrolled across his brain like a neon news ticker. He couldn't help himself, despite knowing too well that those four words encapsulated defeat more than anything else. They were the default response for every pouty fan who'd witnessed the premature end to their team's season. "Wait till next year" was not something one typically heard from fans of championship teams.

With impeccable timing, the words dissolved seamlessly into a technicolour shot of the bronze figures that made up The Icemen at Elysian Square. That image was all the incentive Baker needed to begin formulating a plan of action for next season, one which involved continuing to invoke the influence of the spirits of legends past.

Baker began to consider song possibilities, with new ideas blossoming and coming to life in his primordial soup of an imagination. For instance, Guns N' Roses' "Sweet Child O' Mine" had promise, with the title being changed to "Sweet Mighty Pines." Then, for all those fans who considered the regular season to be meaningless, Elvis Costello's "What's so Funny 'Bout Peace, Love, and Understanding?" could be modified to read "What's so Funny 'bout Pines Losses in the Standings?" And who knew? Maybe he'd try tackling something on the scale of an epic ballad, a la Gordon Lightfoot.

As for the Coven, surely Perreault, Angus, and Conrad would sign up for another season. Of course, with Masaccio gone they'd need to find a bass/keys player. He actually gave thought to the possibility of recruiting Mary Elyk. She was certainly an accomplished piano player. As for her connectivity to the spirit world, well, the signal strength was excellent.

The notion of signal strength set him to thinking of open skies at night under the stars. Yes, the Coven could take their sessions outdoors. He pictured them gathered outside under a full moon, and then realized that would necessitate a fire pit—and he was just the guy to build it. He had the space, the raw materials, and the privacy. And now he had an excuse to get it done. He sprang into action.

But instead of heading out to the backyard to dig up his lawn (that could wait till tomorrow), he headed downstairs to dig up his music sheets, shuffling through the pages of his song files for something he'd been working on during the weeks leading up to the restart, when there were no real PHL games to look forward to. Back then his thoughts had frequently steered him toward one song in particular. With that song now in his hands—a rock classic that had originally been written and performed by a true American icon—he was roused to begin setting down new words to the tune. But first things first: he reached for his phone and dialled Mary Elyk.

"Hi, Mary. It's Baker." He dispensed with the niceties and got right to the point, knowing that Mary was of the same mind regarding phone etiquette. "I have a favour to ask, and it involves your musical talents—"

CHAPTER FORTY-NINE
WONDER ROAD

Put your money aside fellas, you know just what this beer's for
We don't care what you're drinkin'
You'll never need to pay in a pub anymore

So much had changed in a year, and yet through it all what remained unchanged, to Baker's increasing dismay, was the gap—a chasm, really—between the Pines and the Clarence Cup, as evidenced by their most recent failure. With his grief in its early stages, the best medicine was to keep busy with another song project. Luckily, the hard part was done. Earlier in the summer, he had adapted the lyrics to Bruce Springsteen's "Thunder Road," the acoustic version, slowed down and wistful, accompanied by solo piano, and he retitled it "Wonder Road." He would sing this one himself, as a form of therapy if nothing else. He'd need someone on keys, though, and that's where Mary's participation came in, and it began with a phone call.

* * * * *

A week later, as he was making final preparations before his guests arrived, Baker was marvelling to himself how it had been nearly six months since he'd last played host to a physical gathering of this sort. Now, with summer's end nigh, and the approaching Labour Day weekend signalling the return to school, here he was welcoming his friends into his home.

Perreault was the first to arrive, looking as radiant as ever and bearing a box of freshly baked items she had picked up en route. "Sweets for my sweetie," she said, proudly displaying them. Baker took the package and set it to one side, then engaged her in an embrace that was so sweet it would've measured up to any hug you'd expect from the cuddliest bear in the forest.

"Well, it's nice to see you too," she said, then wrinkled her nose. "What's that? I'm catching a whiff of raw onions and minty freshness."

Baker's cheeks reddened. "Oh, um, that's chives—and Halls."

"Chives?"

"Yeah. I cut a bunch of wild chives that were growing in the yard. I've been munching on them all morning. They're supposed to give your voice a richer quality."

"That's interesting. I'd never heard that before. And the Halls? Did you catch a cold or, heaven forbid—"

"No, no. I just needed something to cut the onion smell, and an old bag of throat lozenges was all I had."

"Well then, you may want to take a few more—or have one of these breakfast Danishes and then a lozenge." She followed Baker into the kitchen. "Wild chives, huh? I'll have to tell my mom about that. Which reminds me, my dad asked me to inform you that he'd like to get an early start tomorrow."

"Right—the backyard deck." Baker tried to hide the fact it had slipped his mind completely. "No problem. How's eight o'clock sound?"

"Perfect."

"What about you? Will you be up and about at that hour?"

"With bells on. I'll be there to lend a hand. Besides, I wouldn't want to miss seeing you looking all hunky in work boots and a leather tool belt," she added, with a wink.

Not long after, Conrad made his entrance bearing gifts of a different sort. "Here you go, Mr. Brooks, Happy New Year," he said, setting a loaded LCBO bag on the counter. "Just a little something for a post-ceremony celebration." Then he set to pouring himself a cup of coffee to accompany the lemon-blueberry scone he'd selected from Perreault's box of breakfast pastries.

As the three of them waited for Angus and Mary to arrive, Baker reminisced aloud about the observation Masaccio had made back in March; how it had been quite a year for discoveries where the band was concerned—first Perreault, and now Mary.

Then, as if on cue, Angus and Mary arrived. Baker's first instinct was to welcome Mary into his home and give her a quick tour, but then he remembered her visit with Dorcas the previous fall and how she had exhibited a strange familiarity with the place—as if she'd been there before, perhaps in another lifetime. So, he moved on to the next priority, which was to introduce the girl to Conrad.

"Ahh, yes," Conrad said, extending a hand. "It's a pleasure to finally make the acquaintance of the oft-mentioned Mary Elyk."

Mary raised her eyebrows in surprise. "Oft-mentioned?"

"Indeed. Angus can't stop talking about you. He holds you in high regard; you are an inspiration." Then he leaned in and dropped his voice. "Between you and me, I think he's found his muse."

Mary was clearly unprepared for such a disclosure. She shot Angus a look that seemed to say, *did you really place me on that pedestal?* It was coupled with an expression that alternated between pride and embarrassment. To her credit, she returned a like-minded compliment to Conrad. "You know, I've heard *your* name dropped often enough. It sounds like you've achieved nothing less than legend status around here."

Conrad had to chuckle. "Look at us, a muse and a legend. Quite the mutual admiration society, I'd say." Then he stood taller and raised his voice to ensure that he was heard by everyone in the room. "I'm very much looking forward to your performance, and would like to thank you in advance for rescuing us from having to listen to Baker on guitar. It's not enough that he'll be singing. We also have to live through this onion smell."

Baker could only smile and shake his head, having grown accustomed to hearing Conrad talk trash about him. "It's chives that you're smelling, and I've long since accepted that I will never meet your standards."

"Hey, I didn't set the bar," Conrad said, then gestured at Perreault. "You're filling some formidable shoes."

"Now, Conrad, be kind," Perreault said, coming to her man's defence. "Baker, don't you listen to him. I'm sure your take on Springsteen will be better than anything I could do."

"I can promise you one thing," Baker said, "the effort will be sincere and heartfelt. But don't expect the Boss's New Jersey drawl."

"New Jersey? I always considered it more of a Texas twang," Conrad replied.

"I think they're interchangeable—depending on his mood and the song."

"Which one does he employ to sing the blues?" Perreault asked. "You know, a real lamentation song?"

"You mean like after the Pines get eliminated?" Angus remarked with a snort of derision.

"You had to bring it up, eh?" Conrad said. "I hope we're all fully recovered from our annual playoff disappointment."

"I wouldn't describe how I feel as being 'fully recovered,'" Baker admitted. "The bruises take a long time to heal. There will definitely be some scarring."

"Don't say I didn't warn you. It was a year ago, almost to the day, remember?"

"I remember perfectly. The night the Misty River Replacements performed their one and only live show."

Conrad and Angus recounted the events of that night for Perreault while Baker and Mary busied themselves with their own preparations, after which everyone was brought to order. "I think Mary and I are ready here," Baker announced, prompting Perreault to jump up, find a lighter, and go about lighting some of the candles in the room.

When Cheers Are Not Enough

When she was done, Baker spoke again. "You know, seeing as we never really declared this to be a proper meeting of the Coven, shall we just dispense with the formalities and move straight to the song?"

"Hang on," Conrad said. "You and Mary have prepared something for the Mighty Pines and their fans. It would behoove us to make the most of our coven family being together here by injecting a bit of ritual formality. Besides, it wouldn't be anything out of the ordinary—just routine, as they say."

"But we don't have any set rules in place," Baker said. "I'm not sure how Mary would feel about it." (Baker's problem was that, deep down, he was shy about holding a Coven session while an "expert" was present to witness it, and Mary Elyk certainly fell into that category.)

"Hey, whatever floats your boat," Mary replied. "I'm open to pretty much any type of ceremony, so long as your heart's in it. Conrad makes a good point, though. It's always prudent to take advantage of an assembly of people, even if it's just a handful."

It didn't take long. Conrad recited his prayer, and Perreault followed up with hers, and just like that, it was Baker's turn. He nodded to Mary, who was stationed at the keyboard. She took the cue, closed her eyes, and inhaled. If Baker had any doubts that Mary could handle her assigned task, they were immediately put to rest. She completed the song's intro in masterly fashion and then eased into the opening bar. Baker held his page of lyrics at the ready, although it really just served as a prop, a safety net of sorts—by then he'd read through his own words a hundred times and had sung them either in his head or aloud just as many. Then he closed his eyes and proceeded to share his fondest dreams for his favourite team.

> *A sea of fans, the city's crest waves*
> *Televisions are broadcasting coast to coast, what an awesome parade*
> *Joy flowin' like sparkling Royal Pommery*
> *On the street we're all driving slowly*
> *Won't honk my horn again*
> *Just pinch me and tell me how we won again*
>
> *Put your money aside fellas*
> *You know just what this beer's for*
> *We don't care what you're drinkin'*
> *You'll never need to pay in a pub anymore*
> *Show us how to skate, make magic on the ice*
> *Create a beauty and play it all night*
> *Oh, and that's a sight to see*

WONDER ROAD

Foes can cry 'neath their covers and wallow in shame
Explain away their errors, throw tantrums all in vain
Waste their summers praying for fame
While our saviours ride in these streets
Well we've got our heroes, that's understood
In Nova Tank Arena numbers hang, life is pretty good
It's our chance to make it last somehow
So what else can we do now?
Except rally the people to meet at Nathan Phillips Square
The town's busting open, this new fame will take you anywhere
With a dynastic chance for us right here
We're craving more rings for next year
What the heck, here's to winning crowns back-to-back

So go and make your brand
Discover how Toronto feels when it's the promised land
Oh, go Pines, go down the road, give us a show, on Wonder Road
Flying so high we can nearly touch the sun
Life is great now the hardware has been won
Oh, crowds will flow down the road, it's bright, like gold, Wonder Road

Well you got this far when you learned that it's more than talk
And the carpet's red if you're ready to take that long walk
Along Lakeshore and up York Street
Across Front on to University
And though it's only your words for which the media are pokin'
Speak tonight for this town, together we're unbroken

There's regret in the eyes of all the fans who went away
They'll want to witness firsthand the historical scale of our Clarence Cup parade
They dreamed of a return to glory
This Nation no longer yearns to be free
And as the echoes fade from this song
You hear the faithful cheerin' on
As for the critics who scorned, they're gone
On the wind

They'll never again
See a town full of losers
'Cause we've proven we know how to win

When he was done with the vocals, Baker allowed himself the luxury of sitting back and listening to Mary carry on to the finish in inspired fashion. Shifting his focus to the audience, he noticed that Perreault and Angus were smiling, while Conrad's expression indicated a clear respect for a good performance; content in the knowledge that he wasn't being cheated for his money. When Mary closed out the tune, Conrad was the first to his feet. For Baker, the sound of his three friends applauding may just as well have been a stadium of thirty thousand. It was a moment to cherish, worthy of sharing with the grandkids.

"We're back, baby!" Angus cheered.

"Yes, we are," Conrad said, making for his liquor store purchase. "Now fetch me some wine glasses from the hutch."

"What have you got there?"

"A Tuscan Chianti—my tiny tribute to Masaccio Clemente. If he can't be here in person, we'll drink to him in spirit. By the way, I touched base with Mas the other day. He says hi and sends his love."

The news elicited a burst of excitement and a flurry of questions from Perreault, Angus, and Baker. Conrad did his best to sum up the conversation as he opened the bottle and poured. "He admitted that life is definitely different in Tuscany. He is very busy but in a different way. More importantly, he hopes everyone's keeping healthy. He misses us all, and he misses our Coven gatherings. He's also happy to hear that Mary has ably replaced him on keys."

They collected their glasses and held them up high in a toast to Masaccio and, in an unspoken way, a return to the good old days, before lockdowns and masks and social distancing.

To say Baker felt a level of warmth and contentment would be sorely understating it; this was nothing less than life-affirming. Like Angus said, they were back. They had persevered, they had survived, and now they were ready to resume life as it had been in the year 2020 BC (Before COVID). Baker's mental catalogue of movie moments drummed up an image of Steve McQueen in the closing scene from *Papillon*, having just escaped from Devil's Island and clinging to his raft of coconuts in the open sea, screaming in absolute defiance, *"Hey, you bastards, I'm still here!"*

While Baker would have loved to re-enact the scene for his guests, culminating in that most apropos line, what he actually said was something entirely different: "You know, next season, I wish we could just skip to the playoffs."

Watching the other three original members of Bakers' Coven respond with simultaneous double takes—as if they were perfectly choreographed—was almost funny.

"Well, the regular season games are meaningless, right?" he reasoned. "Especially for the Pines. Nothing matters until the playoffs."

Conrad looked like Socrates about to enlighten a pupil. "My dear boy, when did you acquire such contempt? You've got to stop listening to the naysayers. Always remember that the joy is in the doing. No one knows what will come to pass, so take pleasure in the moment. And besides, why go through life encumbered by cynicism? Doubt and cynicism are for people who fear to dream, who live for nothing more than to say, 'I told you so.'" He held up three fingers. "I have three words for those people: enjoy it now."

Baker smiled. "Is that something from your personal book of wisdom?"

"I wish. It's borrowed from one of the foremost experts in how to get the most out of our day-to-day lives."

"Who's that? Eckhart Tolle?"

"Tony Robbins?"

"Oprah?"

"No, no, and *no!*" Conrad said, in response to the answers offered up by Baker, Perreault, and Angus, respectively. "I'm referring to King Solomon."

"Ah, yes, the Book of Ecclesiastes," Perreault said.

"Yes. You'll find the meaning of life and the best way for us to live it in Ecclesiastes, and it was King Solomon who elegantly spelled it out for us." There was a shift in Conrad's demeanour, as though he were the old monarch himself, full of infinite wisdom and patience. Then he recited the following lines from memory.

> *Generations come and go, but it makes no difference.*
> *The sun rises and sets and hurries around to rise again.*
> *The wind blows south and north, here and there, getting nowhere.*
> *The rivers run into the sea but the sea is never full.*
> *Everything is unutterably weary and tiresome.*
> *No matter how much we see, we are never satisfied.*
> *No matter how much we hear, we are not content.*
> *So I saw that there is nothing better for men than that they should be happy in their work,*
> *For that is what they are here for,*
> *And no one can bring them back to life to enjoy what will be in the future,*
> *So let them enjoy it now.*

He let the words sink in a moment, then repeated the last three. "Enjoy it now—it's the best advice I can give to all the doubters."

"So, I guess we're in for the long haul?" Baker asked.

His question was answered with unanimous affirmation.

"Besides," Conrad said, "the regular season will benefit us. We're just beginning to figure things out."

"And it'll just get better," Angus said.

"Better? How so?"

"Maybe next season we can actually hold a Bakers' Coven watch party."

"And we can make a pilgrimage to Nova Tank Arena together as a group," Conrad said.

"And build a big fire pit in your backyard for us to dance around under the waxing moon," Angus added.

Baker's laugh was not meant to convey derision but rather astonishment at the irony—because unbeknownst to his friends, the fire pit was ready and waiting. (He had followed through that week and devoted a couple of days labouring in the heat, lugging rocks and gathering fist-size stones from along his tree line, all the while picturing himself as one of the villagers in Shirley Jackson's *The Lottery*.)

"And next season will be better because we have a psychic medium for our new pianist, someone who knows all about magic rituals and coven ceremonies and such," Perreault noted. "By the way, Mary, that was an inspired performance. Baker chose well when he recruited you."

Mary, however, was unconvinced. "Hmm . . . I'll say it was adequate. It served the purpose."

"You are your own worst critic, you know that?" Angus said.

"Let's say it wasn't wretched," she admitted grudgingly. "I'll be better next time."

Baker picked up on the "next time" and considered it a positive sign.

Mary had wandered from the keyboard to Baker's bar hutch and was examining the rodent skull displayed there, the same one she had discovered along his tree line last October. Then she gently set the skull down and spoke over her shoulder.

"If you guys don't mind, I'd like to revisit something that you said a few minutes ago, about things turning out better next season."

She turned away from the hutch to address the group more formally. "I feel I should warn you. I know you're all teachers and you know this stuff better than me, but I'm talking about how improvement doesn't happen in a linear fashion. Well, the same applies to the results you get when engaging in ritualistic magic or coven ceremonies. Dorcas taught me that, and boy, was she ever right."

"You mean, you have trouble with this stuff too?" Perreault asked.

"You kidding? Most of it is trial and error. The effort to recruit the forces of nature or call upon otherworldly spirits doesn't always produce the desired results. Take my little brother, Cal. Gosh knows how many times I've called on him and gotten no response. Yet the rare success, the odd time that Cubby answers my call, just makes me come back for more." Mary seemed to indulge in the thought of a nice moment, then returned to the present. "So, as long as you don't get discouraged when things go sideways, I say go for it. Sing your songs and weave your spells. Make your wishes and recite your prayers.

Continue to call on your spirit friends, this six-pack of Pines legends that Angus told me about: Cal Ubank and Beezer Sharpe, Jackson Schmeltz and Jersey Joe Zedelko, and Whitey Kilpatrick and Sugar Watson—"

Mary's mention of the players was met with four pairs of raised eyebrows, causing her to chuckle and explain. "Yeah, I know them all. I'm actually pretty well-versed in Mighty Pines history; I was introduced to all the stories as a kid."

She then returned to her original point. "Listen, I'll be happy to help whenever possible, that much you can count on. However you should be aware that, even with my participation, most days you'll get a busy signal." Her face suddenly blossomed into a smile, her green eyes lively and bright. "But the times that they do answer, well, it's like hitting the sweetest drive off the tee. It makes you forget about all the shanks."

*****

The summons had come from a powerful source, as evidenced by the negligible time lapse between the call and the arrival, like when thunder immediately follows a nearby lightning strike. The spirit of Cubby Elyk now hovered undetected behind Mary, at a respectful distance, as if coming too near would distract his sister while she was in the midst of motivating the troops. The boy was soon flanked by six more spirits, three on each side, in the form of the Icemen, the Mighty Pines legends whose names Mary had just rhymed off.

Cal Ubank wasted no time in greeting Cubby, draping a fatherly arm around the boy's shoulders and introducing him to the others. They instantly accepted him into the group, as though he'd always been a member. It was a typical gathering of hockey players, involving much friendly banter and the usual jocularity and exchanging of jibes—a hearty congregation which, though not quite rowdy or unruly, was decidedly lively all the same.

Inevitably the conversation turned to this year's Mighty Pines squad and the disappointment of another lost season, and worse still, a wasted opportunity—the team unable to take advantage of the benefit of having every game through the first three rounds of the playoffs on its home ice at Nova Tank Arena.

One spirit among them who seemed not to feel the gloom was Ubank. His demeanour was exceptionally effervescent, something Jersey Joe Zedelko did not hesitate in drawing attention to.

"Cal, you seem to be in especially good spirits, pardon the pun. Why so gregarious?"

"Indeed, Joseph, I am as merry as a schoolboy. As it happens, I have some promising news to report."

"Oh? Good news about the Mighty Pines?"

"Correct. And more to the point, it's about Colonel Sinclair's curse."

"This should be good. Spill the beans already and let us in on the news."

"I have made something of a discovery. But first, catch me up on something: Is everyone familiar with the story behind the curse?"

The five senior spirits made like a collection of bobblehead dolls, nodding together in the affirmative.

"Alright then. My news involves the two conditions—hold on a second," Ubank pointed an accusatory finger at Whitey Kilpatrick and Frank Watson, both still nodding. "How is it that you two know about Sinclair's curse?"

Whitey and Frank responded in mute fashion, each man pointing an incriminating finger at Zedelko.

Jersey Joe shrugged and managed a weak smile. "Sorry, Cal, I figured you wouldn't mind if I told the fellas."

"Not a problem, Joseph. Now, as I was saying, my good news has to do with the Colonel's curse, specifically, the conditions by which it can be broken. As you may recall, the first condition—"

Jackson Schmeltz shot a hand up to the sky like an excited schoolboy. "Oh, I know, I know. One stipulation was that the Clarence Cup playoffs would have to be held in the summertime."

"That's right," Ubank said, exhibiting both surprise and delight. "And do you recall the second?"

"Um . . . uh . . ." Schmeltz appeared stumped, having brought his raised hand down to rub his chin.

"Allow me, Jacko," Kilpatrick said. "I believe it had something to do with the Cup final being played entirely in Canada."

"Bingo!" Ubank's eyes were ablaze as he employed a slow and distinct cadence in uttering the next sentence. "And as fate would have it that is precisely what transpired in this year's PHL playoffs."

The others exchanged looks of incomprehension and confusion until Frank Watson spoke.

"Um, that's really amazing, Cal, but are you sure?" he asked. "I don't really see it."

"Yes, Francis. Incredible as it seems, the circumstances of this pandemic have served to meet the conditions Mr. Sinclair placed upon his curse. Think about it. The season was paused and ultimately cut short, and then re-started in August with the playoffs. That fulfills the condition about holding the playoffs in summertime. Then there was the league's precautionary move to establish Toronto and Edmonton as hub sites for those playoffs, thereby ensuring that all the games would be played out in Canada, a circumstance which fulfills the stipulation about having an all-Canadian final."

Ubank paused, allowing each man to process the information.

Zedelko was first to respond. "Ho-lee fu—" but he wasn't allowed to finish, muzzled by Beezer Sharpe (who gestured toward young Cal, reminding Jersey Joe that they were in mixed company).

Sharpe, for his part, wasn't convinced. "But Cal, the circumstances you describe are not what old man Sinclair had in mind. Does it really count if it's not quite what he meant?"

"I understand what you're saying, Beasley, but the way I see it, regardless of what Mr. Sinclair meant, the fact remains the parameters of his conditions have been met. Therefore, the Colonel's curse, whether real or imagined—or simply unacknowledged—has finally been lifted from the shoulders of the Toronto Mighty Pines franchise."

"So, you're saying Toronto should win it all next year!" Frank Watson pronounced.

Ubank smiled patiently. "Unfortunately, Francis, I cannot make such guarantees, but I will say that perhaps it is a sign of how the unseen forces of nature are finally on the side of the Mighty Pines and working in the organization's favour."

Through it all, Cubby Elyk watched and listened, dividing his attention between the six hockey legends and the five members of Bakers' Coven—each party, respectively, discussing the Pines' prospects for the coming season. And while it was true that he didn't mind so much not having his name on the Clarence Cup—regardless of whether it was inscribed into the metal so as to be visible on the surface in the plain light of day, or an embossed version, decipherable only from inside the trophy, hidden in the dark, secret and safe—Cubby sensed that the Mighty Pines' journey towards re-claiming said Cup would not lack for excitement, and being a part of it would make for an interesting ride. He decided that it was something he would gladly sign up for any day of the week (and twice on Saturdays).

* * * * *

The four original members of Bakers' Coven digested what Mary Elyk had to say and appeared satisfied, having received the affirmation they'd been seeking.

"It's settled then," Perreault declared. "We won't wait for the playoffs. Every Pines game is worthy of our efforts. Baker, you go ahead and keep writing your songs, and we will keep playing them." Her eyes gleamed with the light of promise. "As for the rest, well, between the efforts of the Mighty Pines on the ice and Bakers' Coven off it, we'll just have to let the ice chips fall where they may."

"And who knows," Conrad added, "maybe fortune finally smiles upon us, those chips fall just so, all the stars align, and the puck bounces our way, and we get to witness the words in 'Wonder Road' actually coming to pass—like some kind of crazy and beautiful hockey prophecy."

Baker could never be sure of Conrad's sincerity, especially when it came to the Pines' chances of success. "A prophecy, huh? Any words in particular?"

Conrad was ready with a reply, delivered in complete earnestness. "For me it's all summed up in the last three lines of the song."

Everyone's eyes shifted downward to the bottom of their song sheets as he read the words aloud.

> *They'll never again*
> *See a town full of losers*
> *'Cause we've proven we know how to win*

Then he added some words that Baker recognized as more of his own, written for a previous Coven session back in February when they had attempted to summon the Icemen.

> *So with this request our rite may now close,*
> *Upon this team a Cup do bestow,*
> *And thereby end our nation's woes—*

Baker came in with Perreault and Angus to join Conrad in delivering the final line.

> *Amen to that . . . and go, Pines, go!*

They withheld their cheers this time and instead sat in silence, nodding and smiling, reflecting on the words—all except Mary. The newest member of Bakers' Coven had evidently detected something as the candle flames flickered, producing a change in the light. Baker instinctively looked over at her, a question in his eyes, because for him there was a definite sense that the room was more crowded. It was then that Mary finally joined the others in nodding and smiling, but to Baker her smile and nod confirmed something else completely, something he had suspected: that the number of occupants in the room had just increased by seven.

Seven spirits, each of them hockey players and fans of the Mighty Pines, and two of them named Cal.

ACKNOWLEDGEMENTS

Like a hockey season, the writing of this book has been a marathon, not a sprint—a five year marathon to be exact. In all that time, however, I have never felt the urge to quit on my dream of seeing this story become a published novel. Credit must be given to those who helped in keeping that dream alive. Although it is a short list of people, their contributions have been numerous, without which this project might never have crossed the finish line.

First on the list is John Merlini, a friend and colleague from my teaching days who kindly agreed to spend time with the manuscript when it was in its infancy. (At 700 pages it was a big infant.) Nevertheless John did yeoman's work and provided feedback which was brutally honest and invaluable. I took his comments and spent much of the next year cleaning and tightening things up before—either out of desperation or audacity—I asked him to read it again. And he did! In the end, although the finished product bears little resemblance to what John had toiled with, his voice still resonates throughout these pages.

High fives are owed to Mike DePelsmaeker, Daniel Pocrnick, and Andre Manbodh, who took the time one day prior to their after-school pick-up game, to participate in an impromptu photo shoot and serve as models for the three hockey legends that appear on the cover of this book. It is because of them—along with the technical assistance of Stefanie-Rose Fontana—that the Icemen now have physical form.

Much love goes out to Sue File, Scott VandeValk, and Dan Rupcic. All three are poster children for the best the teaching profession has to offer, but more importantly, they are friends so treasured that I consider them family. Their contributions mattered more than they know.

If I could, I would launch a huge thank-you blimp and float it over the workspaces of the editors, designers, coordinators, and consultants at Friesen Press who laboured on this project. Although nameless and faceless to me, their efforts and professionalism toward making this book the best it could be is much appreciated.

Kayla Lang, my Publishing Specialist at Friesen Press, was simply a gift from above. At every step of the process she was a wondrous mix of guidance, patience, and understanding. Kayla's gentle reminders kept me on my timeline and she met my every comment, query, and complaint with grace and good humour.

Finally, my deepest gratitude goes to my family:

My son Ben, mister reliable, was there for me whenever I needed a sounding board to bounce ideas off of, or to discuss the odd plot problem, or to get an opinion on the merits of employing this or that cultural reference (because getting the perspective of a Gen Z-er is always useful)—or to simply unwind by re-hashing the previous night's Raptors' game. He is gifted with a fine blend of wisdom and calm. Ben Ray: our family's very own Zen master.

My daughter Lucy was a pioneer on this project. She was the first person I turned to for an assessment of some of my earliest chapters. Her critiques were, in typical Lucy fashion, an elegant combination of a keen eye, insightful honesty, and kind-heartedness. Later she would don her artist's hat to provide invaluable support during the process of designing and constructing the book's cover. Lucy Ray: so beautiful and so talented.

Above all it was my dear wife Christine who gave me the space—in both the physical and the creative sense—to labour on this book in my own way. While it soon became clear that by taking on this project I had introduced an unexpected wrinkle into our new life as a recently-retired couple, Christine nevertheless soldiered on in silence. As one year led to another, however, I wouldn't have blamed her had she quoted at me Pope Julius II's exasperated refrain to Michelangelo during his painting of the Sistine ceiling: "When will you make it end?" (Especially since Michelangelo took only *four* years to finish.) Alas, the words never passed her lips. In fact, in the spirit of full disclosure, it was Christine's own special qualities of love and compassion, strength and resilience, and generosity and humour, that I attempted to inject into the main characters of this story. I have her to thank for modeling those qualities for me each and every day.

ABOUT THE AUTHOR

Slavko Ray enjoyed twenty-eight years teaching and coaching at high schools in Oakville and Georgetown, Ontario. Now retired, he lives in Erin with his family and does his share of cheering when he tunes into Leafs, Jays, and Raptors games on a trusty old AM/FM pocket radio.

When Cheers Are Not Enough is his first novel.

Printed in Canada